EX
LIBRIS

Romance Treasury

THE ROMANCE TREASURY ASSOCIATION

NEW YORK·TORONTO·LONDON

These stories were originally published as follows:

FOLLOW A STRANGER
Copyright © 1973 by Charlotte Lamb
First published by Mills & Boon Limited in 1973

MAN IN CHARGE
Copyright © 1973 by Lilian Peake
First published by Mills & Boon Limited in 1973

THE BRIDE OF ROMANO
Copyright © 1973 by Rebecca Stratton
First published by Mills & Boon Limited in 1973

ROMANCE TREASURY is published by
The Romance Treasury Association, Stratford, Ontario, Canada

Editorial Board: A. W. Boon, Judith Burgess, Ruth Palmour and
Janet Humphreys
Dust Jacket Art by Bill Biddle
Story Illustrations by Bill Biddle
Book Design by Charles Kadin
Printed by Kingsport Press Limited, Kingsport, Tennessee

ISBN 0-919860-26-5

Printed in U.S.A.   A027

CONTENTS

FOLLOW A STRANGER

Follow a Stranger

Charlotte Lamb

Kate knew it was useless to argue. Yet how could she make Marc Lillitos see that his sister needed freedom of choice, not an arranged marriage?

"You chose the man you wanted to marry," Marc said accusingly, "and see what a mess you've made of your life! Can you deny that Peter Hardy is selfish and indifferent to you? All he thinks about is his work. Peter doesn't love you, Kate, and I don't believe you love him!"

Try as she might, Kate couldn't deny it. Nor could she any longer deny her love for Marc.

But she must keep him from finding out her true feelings!

CHAPTER ONE

There had been a frost overnight, leaving the grass white and sparkling in the early morning sunshine. When Kate looked out of her window, pearly mist obscured her view; shivering, she dressed quickly, hoping that it was not going to be another gray day. But at nine o'clock, when she left the house, the wind had blown the mist away, and the sky was a bright, clear blue.

The change lifted her spirits. She walked along slowly, her dreamy eyes fixed on the tops of elm trees that showed above Cheddall's walls, swaying slowly against the heavenly blue of the sky. The black branches were thickened by crows' nests, and as she watched, some of the ungainly black birds rose up, cawing.

The sound reminded her of summer. She shivered, clutching her coat closer. Despite the sunshine it was still a chilly January morning.

Still dreaming, she stepped into the road, and was dragged back to earth by the blare of a car horn. She leaped back to the sidewalk and looked around, heart pounding.

A sleek black car had pulled up, brakes screeching dramatically. The driver got out and walked around to her. "What the devil do you think you're doing, walking in front of my car like that?"

Kate had the impression of looking up a long way to his dark, angry face. "I'm sorry," she stammered. "It was my fault, I know. But—" her nerves shaken by his harsh tones "—there's no need to shout at me like that."

"You must expect people to lose their temper if you try to commit suicide under their cars," he retorted. "Are you hurt?"

"No, thank you," she said in the same angry tone he had used for the question.

"You needn't sound so aggrieved," he snapped, staring at her, "I'm the one with a grievance, I think."

"I've said I'm sorry. What more do you want?"

"You really sound sorry," he said sarcastically.

Her hair bristled on the back of her neck. "I was very sorry at first, but your attitude would put anyone off."

"Women!" he grunted. "How very logical! Well, if you're not hurt, good morning."

She watched him stride back to his car and felt like childishly stamping her foot. Male superiority triumphs again, she thought, as he drove past without a second glance. Men like that would make the mildest female join Women's Lib!

She glanced at her watch and was horrified at the time. She would be late if she did not hurry, and her first lesson was at nine-fifteen. She crossed the road, looking both ways, and ran the rest of the way to the school.

The summons to Miss Carter's study came while Kate was listening to a first-former attempting to play the piano. Both pupil and teacher sighed with relief at the interruption. Kate grinned as she followed the reluctant pianist out of the music room. If only parents knew what resentments they bred in their children when they forced them to take up music against their inclination!

It was true, of course, that sometimes they developed an interest at a later stage and were then grateful for their early grounding. But somehow, she did not think that this would apply to the girl scuttling eagerly in front of her. Lucy Salmon had fingers like sausages and was almost totally tone-deaf. Her musical father was doomed to disappointment.

She paused at a pale yellow door and knocked softly.

"Come in," Miss Carter commanded, and when Kate entered, smiled at her across the pleasant, sunny room.

"Ah, my dear. I'm sorry to disturb you during a lesson, but I'm leaving shortly to have lunch with the mayor, and I wanted to discuss something with you. Sit down."

The headmistress of Cheddall Public School for Girls was as pleasant as her room. Sensible, sandy-haired and blue-eyed, she had an enviable calm that Kate had never seen ruffled. Her appointment last year, at the early age of 40, had surprised no one. She had been acting as deputy for the previous five years with great success and was popular with parents and girls alike.

Some of the staff had disapproved of the changes she had made; others had heartily supported her. But there were few people who disliked her.

Kate sat back, wondering what she had done wrong. A summons to the headmistress was usually a sign of the wrath to come, but she could not remember having fallen from grace lately, so she smiled and waited patiently.

Being a very modest girl, she was unaware that when she smiled two dimples appeared in her cheeks, or that her eyes had a warmth in their depths that usually produced a responsive smile from the people she was with, but she was relieved to see Miss Carter smile back.

Leaning forward with her square hands flat on her desk, the headmistress said, "We expect a new pupil tomorrow, Kate." She paused, as if searching for the right words. "Rather a special case." Then she paused again, as if anticipating questions.

Kate nodded. If a girl was allowed to join the school in the middle of a term it must, indeed, be a special case, but since the head clearly wanted some reply, she said politely, "Yes, Miss Carter?"

The head laughed. "I'll be frank. . . . I feel rather

doubtful about accepting this girl." She shook her head and stared at the window in silence for a moment. "She's hardly the sort of girl we normally have here." She paused again and began to sketch an odd little doodle, then without looking up, added, "Her brother is Marc Lillitos."

Kate blinked. Who was he? Clearly she was expected to know the name, but although she searched her memory, she could not remember having heard it before.

Miss Carter looked up, her eyes curious. "You do not know the name?"

"No," Kate admitted.

"He's a shipping magnate, a very wealthy man. He came to me today and asked me to accept his sister Pallas—"

"Pallas!" Kate interrupted, without thinking.

Miss Carter smiled. "Pallas Athene, the Greek goddess of wisdom, but I'm afraid the name does not fit this girl. She has been expelled from three excellent schools already."

"Goodness!" exclaimed Kate.

"Quite. As you know, we don't take problem children here at Cheddall, so I hesitated. But her brother assures me that, despite the evidence, she is a talented and clever girl, and he convinced me that she deserves a final chance. After a long discussion, I agreed, but on my own conditions." She paused again, frowning. "That's where you come in, Kate."

Kate nodded. "Yes?"

"I gathered that she is rebelling against the discipline of school. She wants to go to a music college, where she feels she'll have more freedom."

"She's musical?" Kate said, seeing how this affected herself.

"Very, it appears. She plays the violin and sings. But her family wants her to have a sound education before she specializes. I sensed vague disapproval of a music career, but nothing was said on that subject."

"If they're rich, I wouldn't have thought it would matter," said Kate.

"They probably fear she will make the wrong friends. I suspect they give her very little freedom at home. A strict background, strict schools. . . . You can see the pattern."

Kate grimaced. "Only too clearly. What do you want me to do, Miss Carter?"

She smiled. "Make friends with her."

"Of course," Kate agreed. "But as I live away from the school, it may not be easy."

"On the contrary, it's an advantage. It gives you a less claustrophobic attitude toward the school. It might be an idea to take her to your home, let her have a taste of ordinary home life. Boarding schools tend to narrow one's horizons. I realize it's asking a great deal, Kate. You would prefer to get away from school when you're off duty. But I feel sorry for the girl."

"So do I," said Kate.

"Well, you won't let her suspect that, will you? I would prefer the relationship to develop quite naturally. Pity would only make matters worse. The poor-little-rich-girl theme is poisonous."

Kate laughed. "I understand. I think I can handle it."

"Good." Miss Carter smiled at her. "Thank you, Kate."

Kate Caulfield was 24, slightly built, with long, straight blond hair, unusually vivid blue eyes and the strong, flexible fingers of a pianist.

She had trained in London, and had had dreams of

being a concert pianist. However, she was a practical girl beneath her dreamy exterior; she soon realized that she did not have the necessary ability.

When she left college she accepted the position of music teacher at Cheddall Public School, which was only a few minutes' walk from her home.

After Miss Carter became the headmistress, the school had been reorganized along more modern lines. There was less severity, more freedom; and the girls seemed to thrive upon the new régime. Kate was very happy there, especially as it left her with plenty of free time for her fiancé, Peter Hardy.

Peter ran the local museum and, in his spare time, was an ardent archeologist. Kate had known him all her life.

Her father had died five years earlier, leaving his wife to bring up the four children. Kate's salary was the only family income for the time being. Her younger brother, Sam, was studying art at the local art school, and her twin brothers, Harry and John, were only 11.

That evening she told her mother about Pallas Lillitos while they did the supper dishes.

Sitting astride a chair, Sam listened idly, eating a bag of peanuts.

"She sounds terrible," he remarked, "spoiled and conceited."

"Didn't you have enough supper?" Kate countered. "You eat as if you never expected to see another meal!"

He grinned, wrinkling his freckled nose at her. Sam had red hair, big ears and an inexhaustible passion for food. His blue eyes were the only reminder that they were brother and sister.

"You're just jealous because I don't have to diet to keep my figure."

She threw the tea towel at him. "How true, you abominable boy!"

Mrs. Caulfield smiled, her gaze resting on Kate's trim waist. "You don't need to diet either, Kate."

With a sigh, Kate put her hand on her waist. "I do if I want to wear my new dress for the spring dance at the tennis club. I need to lose an inch off my waist, or the dress will burst at the seams."

"You should have bought a larger size," said her mother.

"They only had it in one size, and it was too gorgeous to resist."

"It cost a fortune, too," Sam said. "Which reminds me—lend me a quid, Kate. I want to take Karen to the pictures."

Kate groaned, but produced the money. "I thought girls went dutch these days."

"Not Karen," he said proudly. "Half the male population of Greyford is trying to date her. I wouldn't dare suggest we go dutch."

When he had vanished to change into even sloppier jeans, his mother laughed. "Karen isn't a girl—she's a prize. Sam is delighted to be dating her."

"I can't think why," said Kate. "She's the most boring girl I ever met."

"But she looks like a beauty queen," said Mrs. Caulfield with amusement, "and all the other boys are crazy about her."

The doorbell rang and Kate jumped up. "That will be Peter—I'll go."

She opened the door and a tall, bearded young man wandered in, smiling vaguely at her. "Hi!"

She sighed and reached up to kiss him. "Hello, darling. Have an interesting day?"

He looked almost lively. "Yes. . . . Guess what was brought in? Another urn fragment from the Roman fort at Lower Greyford. And it fits perfectly! The urn is really taking shape now. Another few pieces and I'll have a complete second-century urn."

"How fascinating, darling. Like a jigsaw puzzle," she said, pushing him into the sitting room.

Peter Hardy was a few years older than Kate but looked less, because his features were less mature. Sam had once said that Peter looked like a Viking, talked like a professor and hardly knew one girl from another. Blond, gray-eyed and pleasant, he was too passionately involved with his work to be aware of much else.

Kate, who had fallen in love with him years ago and had only managed to make him notice her by being continually underfoot, often wondered if he remembered that they were engaged to be married. Certainly he never suggested a wedding date. But she curled up beside him on the sofa and let him talk of Roman urns while her mind wandered to more romantic ideas.

A few days later Miss Carter came into the music room and introduced her to Pallas Lillitos.

Kate was taken aback to find her new pupil far more adult than she had expected. She was wearing a plain black skirt and white blouse, the usual sixth-form version of the school uniform. But she managed to invest it with a Parisian chic that, combined with her sleek black hair and flawless complexion, made her look nearer 20 than 16.

Miss Carter left them alone together after a moment or two, and Kate looked thoughtfully at the new girl.

"Perhaps you'd better show me what you can do," she suggested. "Shall we start with the violin?"

Pallas shrugged indifferently. Taking out her violin, she played a dazzling piece of Paganini, her face remote and austere beneath her black cap of hair.

Kate smiled at her when she had finished. She knew

very well that Pallas had chosen that particular piece in order to startle her by her technical brilliance, and, she had to admit, it was very clever. But something had been lacking. She could not quite put her finger on what it was, so she said nothing and asked Pallas to sing for her.

The girl looked a little annoyed. Sullenly she chose a song. Kate played the introduction on the piano, and Pallas sang.

Kate's fingers almost halted in amazement as the clear, sweet notes spilled out. She looked around and saw a dreamy expression stealing over the girl's face.

Afterward, she closed the piano lid with a gesture of finality. "You don't need me to tell you that you have a very lovely voice," she said, smiling at Pallas. "I shall arrange for our specialist violin teacher to come in and teach you. Your voice is really almost beyond me. You need serious training."

"When I am 18 Marc will let me go to a music college," said the girl. "But he has no intention of letting me take up a professional career, so what does it matter?"

Kate leaned back and stared at her. "Why won't he let you become a musician?"

"He wants me to marry," said Pallas, "as I'm sure you know!" And her eyes bit contemptuously at Kate.

"How should I know? I've never met him. Why shouldn't you marry and still have a career?"

Pallas shrugged without answering.

Kate waited, then changed the subject. "I'm sure Miss Carter could arrange to have someone really good come in and teach you singing. Madame Liovitch lives 20 miles away—she might accept you as a pupil."

Frowning, Pallas looked at Kate. "No," she said at last, "I want you to teach me."

"Me?" Kate was absurdly touched. "My dear girl, I'm

not fit to shine Madame Liovitch's shoes. I really think you could teach me rather than the other way around."

Pallas smiled with sudden and surprising charm. "I'll take the risk."

"Why?" Kate asked curiously.

Pallas flushed. "I . . . I like you. You seem honest."

The friendship between them grew quickly. Because she lived out, Kate had no real friends on the staff, and Pallas found the other girls far too schoolgirlish for her. She asked Kate about her family, and was very amused by descriptions of Sam, Harry and John.

"Sam's a nut case," Kate explained.

"What's that?" asked Pallas. When it was translated, she went off into peals of laughter.

Kate invited her to visit her family and was touched by the eagerness of the girl's acceptance. She wondered what the autocratic Marc Lillitos would think if he knew that Miss Carter was encouraging his sheltered little sister to visit an ordinary family. He sounded like a tyrannical *paterfamilias*, a type she had thought was extinct years ago.

When Pallas appeared at the Caulfield home she was wearing a chic gray dress, pretty gray shoes, which looked handmade and very expensive, and a very smart hat on her black hair.

Sam, lounging on the carpet with his head on a cushion, gazed at her as though at a very rare and peculiar animal. Kate introduced her to the assembled family and invited her to sit down on the sofa. There was a difficult silence.

Then the twins, rarely at a loss for long, politely offered her one of their awful jokes; they were pleased, if surprised, when she laughed. Thus encouraged, they told a succession of them. Pallas, conscious of Sam's unrelenting stare, laughed at each with as much enjoyment.

Mrs. Caulfield disappeared into the kitchen, and the twins, drawn by the sound of cakes being taken out of the oven, drifted after her.

"Have you any younger brothers?" Sam asked pointedly.

Pallas looked around, as though amazed to find him present. "No, but I have an older brother," she said. "I did have two, but one died three years ago."

"I'm sorry," said Kate.

Pallas said honestly, "I did not know him very well. He lived in the United States. His wife still does."

Mrs. Caulfield called Kate who, excusing herself, left the two young people alone.

Pallas sat up very straight, her hands in her lap, like a little girl at a grown-ups' tea party. Sam lay back, staring at the ceiling. She furtively inspected him from his red sweater to his purple, fringed velvet trousers, then back, with widened eyes, to the brown red curls that fell to his shoulders in wild abandon.

He turned his head lazily and stared back until her eyes fell and she flushed.

"What's with the gear?" he asked obscurely.

"I'm sorry?" She jumped and looked bewildered.

"The clothes," he translated. "Why are you wearing that stuff?"

In a flash of temper she retorted, "I look no stranger than you do. I couldn't make up my mind whether you were a girl or a boy."

He laughed and leaped up in one supple movement. Bending over her, he kissed her mouth before she was aware of his intention.

She gasped, backing away.

"Give you three guesses," he offered wickedly.

Bright pink, she said angrily, "Don't ever do that again!"

"Go on," teased Sam, "you know you loved it! I bet that was the first time you were ever kissed!"

She bit her lip in fury. Brought up in an atmosphere of luxurious reverence, she was not accustomed to boys like Sam. She was as sheltered as a novice from a convent school. Sam baffled, alarmed and fascinated her.

Throughout the following weeks she became a fixture in the Caulfield home. She and Kate shopped together, and Pallas bought a number of new clothes, with an eye to surprising Sam. Jeans, bright sweaters, miniskirts and flared trousers were added to her wardrobe week by week. The neat, Paris-made suits and dresses were pushed aside. She flowered out into vivid colors, wild designs and heavy, esoteric jewelry.

Sam whistled admiringly when she arrived one day in an emerald green dress made of silky clinging material, which ended way above her knees, revealing long brown legs. She looked much younger, much prettier, more alive.

"You're quite a doll," he complimented her, and Kate, seeing her blush scarlet, suddenly wondered if she was wise in allowing their friendship to develop. The girl's family would undoubtedly disapprove. Yet she did not have the heart to cut Pallas out of her family. The girl was so clearly happy. The sullen look she had always worn at first was never seen now. Her schoolwork had improved enormously since Sam made a few pointed remarks about the dignity of labor. Sam worked very hard himself and had no time for those who shirked.

Pallas had never enjoyed the casual, cheerful atmosphere of an ordinary home before, and Kate suspected that if it was taken away from her now, the girl would be twice as unhappy.

Her interest in Sam was unfortunate, but Kate knew her brother too well to fear any romantic entanglement. He was level-headed, kind, ambitious. The glamor girls of his world amused him, but he would not let himself get involved seriously while he was still at art school, especially knowing that his mother and brothers would need his economic support later.

She was convinced that she was right some weeks later when she watched Sam and Pallas dancing to a record. Pallas was tense, nervous, clumsy as she tried to follow him.

"You're too uptight," he complained. "You dance as if you had a poker stuck up your back."

Pallas went bright red. "You beast!" she shouted, pushing at his chest.

Sam laughed and grabbed her by the shoulders.

"Stop the fireworks! Try it again, and put some give into it this time!"

Pallas did better this time, and Sam grinned at her, "You're getting it! That was better!"

She beamed at him, her black hair loose and swinging. She was a totally different girl from the one who had first visited them. Today she wore bright yellow jeans, an orange sweater with Mickey Mouse appliquéd on the front, and an Egyptian enameled pendant.

They danced again, not touching each other, gyrating like strange birds performing a ritual mating ceremony.

Kate watched, grinning. The veneer of maturity had been stripped away from Pallas, leaving her a normal teenager.

When the music ended this time, Sam hugged Pallas in a friendly way. "Great, kid! You can really move!"

And she, flushed and excited, threw her arms around him. "Oh, Sam, do you think so?"

Kate heard the door open and glanced around casually, expecting to see her mother. But a tall man stood in the doorway, his gaze fixed icily on the two in the middle of the room, who were too absorbed in each other to have noticed him.

Kate recognized him. It was the man under whose car she had almost committed suicide.

Then Pallas glanced over Sam's shoulder, froze, and dropped her arms as if they had suddenly developed paralysis.

Sam turned and stared curiously at the intruder, who stared back, his thick black brows meeting over his nose.

"Well, Pallas?" he asked coolly. "Aren't you going to introduce me to your . . . friends?" The hesitation was deliberate and insulting.

A flash of intuition told Kate who this man was before Pallas spoke, and she got up nervously.

He looked around, gray eyes hard, and studied her. Forcing herself to remain calm, she looked back and saw a man of 30 or so, very self-assured, his features arrogantly good-looking, his clothes discreetly well cut. He was as dark as Pallas, his black hair thick and straight, his skin very tanned.

Pallas came forward awkwardly, as pale now as she had been red, and falteringly introduced Kate.

Kate held out her hand, making herself smile, but Marc Lillitos took it with a firm grip, unsmilingly.

Then he looked at Sam. Pallas mumbled Sam's name. Kate was very proud of her brother as he came forward, suddenly dignified, and shook hands. He did not allow the older man to stare him down, but met his eyes directly and frankly.

There was a brief silence, then Marc Lillitos said coldly, "Wait for me in the car, Pallas. I want to have a word with Miss Caulfield."

She stumbled out of the room with the old sullen uncertainty back in force. Kate felt a surge of anger against this man.

Sam took Kate's elbow. "Shall I stay, Sis?"

She was grateful for his offer of support but shook her head. "No, thank you."

Sam met her eyes, grimaced and left the room.

Marc Lillitos looked at her, very slowly and carefully, as though inspecting a loathsome slug found in his lettuce.

"I was surprised when I was informed that my sister was at your house," he began coolly. "I was horrified when I came in here and saw her, looking like some hippie, apparently kissing your brother. Have you any explanation of why you have encouraged her to behave in this disgusting way, or must I draw my own conclusions?"

Kate went scarlet. "Is it disgusting to dress like other teenagers, to learn to dance, to enjoy herself?" She found it hard to find words to express what she wanted to say, under the steely and contemptuous gaze of this man.

"You would like me to believe, I suppose, that her money had nothing to do with it?" he asked coldly.

"Of course it didn't! I was sorry for her!"

His lips twitched mirthlessly. "Sorry for her? Envied her, you mean. Let me make some facts clear. Pallas is my ward. Her money is tied up in a trust. If she marries without my consent she gets not a penny of that money. Do you understand?"

A tidal wave of rage swept over her as she listened. She drew a deep breath and let loose a flood of angry words.

"If you are implying that my brother might try to marry her for her money then let me tell you a few facts about him. He's proud, hard-working and kind-hearted, and far too busy trying to date much sexier girls to be aware of Pallas as anything other than a kid sister. Like me, he was sorry for her, as he would be for any girl who wears straight, old-fashioned clothes, has no fun and feels it would be better to be dead. You've stifled Pallas all her life. You buy her safe, dull, expensive clothes that she hates and that make her look ridiculous to her own generation. You shut her away in safe, dull, expensive schools rather than let her find out what life is really like. I suppose you'll take her away from Cheddall now, and put her in another tidy little box where she'll suffocate."

Her blue eyes shot flames at him. "Well, Mr. Lillitos, sir, your money doesn't interest us." She curtsied exaggeratedly. "Nothing about you interests us, Mr. Lillitos, sir. But next time you look at Pallas remember she's an ordinary teenager of 16, not a nun, and think what you're doing to her!" She walked to the door and held it open, glaring at Sam, who grinned at her before vanishing down the hall. "Goodbye, Mr. Lillitos. It may sound trite, but your money is just a millstone round your sister's neck. So give her a chance to find out what sort of human being she really is, and stop trying to force her into an iron mold marked Lillitos."

He stared in total silence as she spat out the last words and walked out of the room.

CHAPTER TWO

When he had gone she sat down on a chair, her legs giving way beneath her, and tried to stop herself trembling. Now that her blind rage had faded, she was ashamed of herself. He would certainly take Pallas away from Cheddall after her outburst, and all the good they had accomplished would be undone.

The thought of Pallas made her mouth go down at the corners. Poor girl. No wonder she had lacked self-confidence, always being reminded by big brother that men were only interested in her money, never in herself. It would sap anyone's self-respect.

Sam came in grinning and hugged her. "You were fantastic! I was proud of you! He came out of here like a jet-propelled rocket. I bet no one ever told him a home truth before in all his sheltered life!"

"Oh, Sam," she wailed, "but what have I done to Pallas? If only I hadn't lost my temper!"

Sam's face fell. "I'd forgotten that. You think he'll take her away from the school?"

"I'd gamble my year's salary on it!"

She did not sleep very well that night. She lay, taut and anxious, mentally rehearsing an apology to Marc Lillitos but each time choking as she opened her mouth and saw, in her mind's eye, that arrogant dark face. After all, he had insulted Sam! And she was not really sorry for anything she had said. It had all been true. She just regretted having said it so forcefully.

She thumped her pillow irritably. What a pity he had come at that particular moment. She was certain neither Pallas nor Sam were emotionally involved with each

other. It was just friendship. But to a man like Marc
Lillitos a friendly hug looked like moral depravity.

She arrived at Cheddall very early next day, anticipating a summons to Miss Carter's study. The head
would quite rightly feel she had behaved very stupidly in
her response to the situation. She could have been more
tactful. The trouble was, thought Kate wryly, that
although she had blond hair, she had inherited her
redheaded father's blazing temper. As a child she had
often had lectures from him on the subject, no less stern
because he fully understood her problem.

"I have a temper too, Kate," he used to say, "but one
must learn to control *it*, rather than let *it* control you."

It was odd that Sam, who had his father's hair, had
been bypassed by the family temper. He was a very good-
natured boy.

She waited all morning in suspense, but no summons
came. Her discreet inquiries in the staffroom told her that
Pallas was still at the school, and no one seemed aware of
any trouble concerning her.

Had Miss Carter persuaded her brother to leave her at
school? Or had he changed his mind last night after all?
Puzzled, anxious and uneasy, Kate waited all day, but
when she left that afternoon she had still heard nothing.

As she turned out of the drive she heard a voice calling
her name, and looked around in surprise.

The sleek black car was drawn up at the curb and Marc
Lillitos was leaning out of the window.

"I want to talk to you," he said brusquely. "Get in."

Despite all her good intentions, she stiffened resentfully. Who did he think he was? His tone was as arrogant
as ever. "I'm sorry," she said coldly, "I'm in a hurry."

His gray eyes were sardonic. "Then it will be quicker to

go by car," he pointed out, opening the passenger door for her.

"I prefer to walk," she said, turning away.

The door slammed and suddenly he was beside her, gripping her elbow painfully. "Don't be ridiculous! I want to talk to you."

"Are you kidnapping me?" she asked, her eyes flashing. "Let go of my arm . . . you're hurting me! How dare you? Just being a millionaire doesn't give you the right to order me around."

He stared down at her, eyes amused. "What a little spitfire you are, aren't you?" he murmured. "Come, must I go down on my knees to you before you will consent to get into the car? Be reasonable, Miss Caulfield. Let me drive you home so that we can talk quietly without causing a scene."

She looked around and saw several passersby halting, watching them curiously. Very pink and feeling very silly, she gave up the unequal struggle and allowed him to help her into the car. He climbed in and silently started the engine. Purring smoothly, the car moved away up the road.

"I wanted to apologize to you," he said quietly, staring at the road ahead.

She looked sideways at him. The long, arrogant profile was turned toward her, the droop of the eyelids hiding any expression in the hard eyes.

As she did not reply, he shot her another of his amused looks, one eyebrow quirked. "I see you want your pound of flesh before you will relent. Well, that is your privilege. Miss Caulfield, I unreservedly apologize. I was quite wrong in my accusations. I am very sorry for any hurt or offence I caused you or your brother."

She was too dumbfounded to speak yet, and he turned his head again, smiling at her. At the charm of that smile she felt a peculiar leap of her heart.

"Why have you changed your mind?" she asked huskily.

"I had a long talk with Miss Carter, who explained to me how much she had to do with my sister's visits to your home, and, by the way, reinforced your comments about Pallas, although more politely, I must add."

She flushed. "I . . . I'm sorry I was so rude. I lost my temper."

"So I observed," he said blandly. "But I am grateful to you for your kindness to my sister. You were very perceptive. I should have realized what was wrong myself. The trouble is, my mother has been in delicate health for a long time, and I have been too busy to take much notice of Pallas. But I had a long talk with her last night, after I had seen Miss Carter, and I hope I shall do better in the future."

"You intend to leave her at Cheddall, then?" she asked.

"Yes, I do. I cannot pretend to approve of the peculiar clothes she now wears, or her new hairstyle. She looks just like any untidy, longhaired student in Greece. But I did appreciate what you said about letting her become a normal adolescent, and I am prepared to put up with all this for a while." His smile was derisive. "I presume it will not last too long? I cannot guarantee a long-term indulgence."

She smiled back. "Oh, I think you can be sure that she'll grow out of it . . . eventually."

His eyes mocked her. "That last word was intended to frighten me, I think?"

Kate laughed. "Perhaps a little."

"You think I need to be frightened?"

"Don't we all need it, at some time or another? Pallas, at the moment, needs to be part of the scene."

He raised an inquiring eyebrow. "Translate that, please. I am not *au fait* with current slang."

"She needs to feel like every other person of her age ... to be accepted, to merge with her background. At school, of course, she will wear the school uniform, and she accepts that as normal. Out of school she wants to dress like the other kids, and that's normal too. It's all a question of convention, although you may not think so at first sight. Long hair, jeans and bright colors *are* the teenage uniform."

"So that what I took for a gesture of rebellion is, in fact, sheeplike following of fashion?"

"Precisely," Kate said, smiling. She looked around and realized that they had been parked outside her home for some time. "I must go now. Goodbye, Mr. Lillitos."

"Wait!" He reached across and held on to the door handle, his face close to hers. She could see faint specks of yellow around the black centers of his eyes. "I have something else I wish to discuss with you, Miss Caulfield ... another matter concerning Pallas. Will you dine with me tonight?"

"I'm sorry," she said politely, "I have another engagement."

He released the door and she opened it and got out.

He leaned forward, smiling with that surprising charm. "I am sure you can break your appointment just this once. I leave for Greece tomorrow and will not have another chance to talk to you."

"Well, I ..." she began, intending to refuse firmly.

"Good," he broke in, before she had finished. "I'll pick you up at seven-thirty."

The door slammed shut and before she could speak again, the car had drawn silently away.

Kate stared after it, clenching her fists like a child. "Well!" she exploded. "He's the most insufferable high-handed man I ever met!"

She had had a date with Peter that night. They had intended to see a local amateur production of *Carmen*. When she phoned him to explain he was irritatingly complacent.

"That's all right. I wasn't that eager myself. I want to finish reading Howard Carter's book on the discovery of Tutankhamen's tomb anyway. Make sure this guy buys you a decent meal. Oh, by the way, I think I've persuaded Colonel Feather to leave his collection of flints to the museum. Isn't that wonderful?"

She agreed flatly that it was, and hung up. Her mother looked up as she drifted into the kitchen.

"You look upset, dear. Did Peter object to you dining with Mr. Lillitos?"

"Far from it," Kate sighed. "He seemed quite pleased to have a free night to read archeology."

Mrs. Caulfield smiled but watched her with concern. She often wondered if Peter were the right man for Kate. They were more like brother and sister than lovers. Peter was nice enough but rather too wrapped up in his work, and Kate was an impulsive, warmhearted girl. It would be a tragedy if she married a man who could never respond to her. Sometimes Mrs. Caulfield had a nightmare in which Kate was buried alive, under dusty tomes, and Peter worked on, deaf to her cries for help. She shook herself mentally and began to whip up a cream dessert. The twins would be back from school soon, ravenous and noisy.

"What are you going to wear?" she asked Kate, beating the mixture lightly.

"Goodness knows. I haven't got a dress even remotely suitable for dinner with a millionaire."

"Your pink one is pretty," her mother suggested.

Kate laughed at her. "My pink one, Mother, is the only formal dress I possess, as you know perfectly well!" She shrugged her shoulders. "But so what? I'm not trying to compete with the glamor girls he usually takes out, am I? It doesn't matter what he thinks of my dress."

Sam put his head around the door and grinned. "There was a false ring to that remark. What are you talking about?"

Kate stuck out her tongue but told him.

Sam whistled. "You must have penetrated that thick hide of his after all! It's your big blue eyes and Goldilocks hair, Sis."

Kate was annoyed to feel herself blushing. "Don't be silly," she told him severely, and went upstairs to have a bath.

She took her time getting ready and it was almost seven when she looked at herself in the mirror for the last time. Her dress was very simple, a high-waisted pink crêpe, with a scooped neckline and long, wide sleeves which floated as she moved her arms. With her blond hair in a smooth chignon, a matching pink lipstick and her favorite false eyelashes, she decided she looked passable.

If only she did not look so maddeningly young! She suddenly longed for a glittering sophistication. She would have liked to sweep downstairs and see his eyes open in stunned admiration.

Then she made a face at herself. What silly nonsense! They were ships passing in the night. What did it matter what he thought of her?

She touched behind her ears with some scent, tucked back a wandering hair and then heard his voice below. He was early! Kate felt her heart flip over peculiarly, as it had once before that day, and ordered herself to be calm and collected.

As she approached the sitting room she heard him refuse the drink her mother was offering. She opened the door quietly. He turned to look at her, his expression inscrutable.

"Ah, there you are," he said calmly. "I am afraid I am rather early."

"It doesn't matter," she stammered, conscious of his gaze.

He took her arm and smiled at her mother. "Good night, Mrs. Caulfield."

As they drove away he said, "I thought we would dine at the Black Swan. Do you know it?"

She did but had never been there, because it was the most expensive hotel for miles around. They drove for a quarter of an hour before reaching the high gates. The hotel was set back in its own grounds, the drive bordered by masses of rhododendron bushes, which, in summer, were a blaze of color. Now they were dimly visible in the car headlights.

They pulled up in front of the hotel. He came around and helped her out of the car and they proceeded to the brilliantly lit porch.

They were escorted to their table by an obsequious head waiter who used her escort's name ostentatiously. Kate guessed that even the Black Swan was not accustomed to the patronage of such wealthy customers. Not many people in Greyford came into the supertax bracket and there were no local millionaires.

She found the waiter's punctilious attentions embarrassing. Flushed and irritable, she avoided Marc Lillitos's eyes. Was this how he was always treated? Hovering waiters; flattering, bowing and scraping; continual observation by the other guests; curious whispers at each move he made? It must be abominable.

But if it was, perhaps it went some way toward explaining his air of arrogant self-assurance. How often had someone said no to him? How many times had he heard angry voices? Been told the truth? In his own way he was as warped as Pallas had been, twisted out of shape by the pressures his money created around him.

She was so embarrassed that she barely tasted the meal, but it was beautifully prepared and presented. She shook her head when Marc asked her to choose and left it all to him. He ran a quick eye over the menu and chose shrimp cocktail, duck, green peas, and orange sauce and creme caramel for her and cheese for himself.

She ate in almost total silence, answering only when he asked her a question. Kate was painfully aware of the other diners' stares and wished herself anywhere but there.

The dining room emptied as they reached the coffee stage and he leaned over to offer a cigarette, which she refused. Asked if she would mind if he smoked, she said that she did not, and watched him light his cigarette and push the lighter back into his pocket.

He had long, slender, shapely hands, beautifully cared for, and she stared at them with almost hypnotized awareness.

"Now," he said quietly, "shall we discuss my sister?"

Kate started and glanced up from her contemplation of his hands, her eyes wide. "Oh, yes . . . of course."

His look held hers for a second, one dark brow raised quizzically. Then he smiled slightly.

"Part of the problem is that I have no experience with young girls. Had she been a boy I might have understood her better. My mother, as I said, is bedridden for much of the time. My sister-in-law lives in the United States and only visits us occasionally." He spread his hands in an expressive gesture. "So Pallas is very lonely when she is at home."

"Surely you have some young friends?" she asked, surprised.

He shook his head. "I am a very busy man. My friends are all business acquaintances."

"Doesn't Pallas have *any* friends of her own?" She was not aware of the shocked disbelief of her own voice, but he looked hard at her.

"You find that strange? Yes, it is, I suppose. When she was small she used to play with the island children, but most of the girls in her age group are married now, or will be soon. Our girls mature early."

"No wonder Pallas feels cut off," Kate said slowly. "She's sent away to school while the girls she grew up with are regarded as adult women! When she first came to Cheddall she looked so sad . . . a young girl dressed like a middle-aged woman, very quiet and aloof. She was marooned on an island at a time when she should have been having fun with people of her own age."

"She had her music," he protested.

"Which you don't take seriously!"

He met her eyes. "She told you that?" And when Kate nodded, he said, "She was wrong, but that can wait. First, I want to know if you really like my sister, or if you are only sorry for her."

"I like her," Kate said. "I'm sorry for her too, but there's something appealing about her. She's so . . . eager. She wants to be happy. It's touching."

"Good, I am glad you like her. I want you and Sam to visit her during the Easter holiday."

She was shocked into an exclamation. "What?" Then, flushing, "I'm sorry, I was rather surprised. . . ."

He smiled, a little teasingly, which surprised her again. She had not thought he could look so human, his dark face relaxed and friendly. "You are impulsive, aren't you? But will you come? Our home is on Kianthos, a small Greek island. I have a private plane which will fly you there and back. Our villa is very secluded, but we have an excellent private beach, tennis courts, swimming pool . . . all the things young people like for a holiday."

She stared at him, feeling as unreal as a dream. "It's very kind of you . . ." she began, but again he cut her off.

"It will be a kindness in you to accept."

She shook her head. "I'm sorry, but it's impossible. I've already planned my Easter holiday."

He stubbed out his cigarette. "I would, of course, be happy to compensate you for any expense you might incur—"

"Please!" she broke in angrily. "You don't understand. I'm going on a dig in Sussex, with my fiancé. I couldn't break off the arrangements now."

He leaned back, his hands lying very still on the table. "Your fiancé?" he repeated, his eyes narrowed.

Kate held up her ring finger so that he could see the Victorian opals gleaming. She and Peter had chosen the ring together. He had liked the massive gold hoop, set with milky stones, and, although Kate had preferred a small sapphire ring, she had been happy to wear the one Peter liked.

Marc Lillitos stared at the ring impassively. "Did you say you were going on a dig?" he repeated.

"Yes, Peter is an archeologist. We always spend our holidays at archeological sites."

He raised a sardonic brow. "How unusual!" The smoothly derisive tone infuriated her once more.

"We like it!" she shot back angrily.

His smile doubted her, but he only said, "If your fiancé cares to come, he too will be very welcome."

She shook her head. "That's very kind of you, but I'm afraid Peter wouldn't be interested."

"I'm sorry," he said. "Pallas would have been so happy to have you there, but I am sure she will understand that you prefer to be with your real friends."

"That isn't fair," she said hotly. "I like her very much, but Peter is my fiancé, after all."

"Don't worry," he said blandly, "I'll explain it to her."

"I bet you will!" she seethed, "and hurt her feelings badly in the process." She stood up. "Will you take me home now? I think we've said enough."

He did not argue. They drove home in a frozen silence. When he stopped the car she fumbled with the door and he leaned over and put his hand over hers. "I'll do it," he murmured, looking down at her with the teasing smile which had surprised her earlier.

Kate angrily realized that her heart had once again performed that peculiar, inexplicable flip. Climbing out with dignity, she said good night and then took off as if the devil were after her.

Sam was waiting up for her, a jug of cocoa on the kitchen table at his elbow, his sketch pad open under his hand. She paused to look over his shoulder and felt a nervous shiver as she recognized the arrogant dark face he was drawing.

"Is it like him?" Sam asked without looking up.

"Very," she said offhandedly.

He leaned back so that his face was inverted and unfamiliar, smiling at her.

"What did he want? Or was it just a cover for wolfish advances? Did he offer you an apartment in Monte Carlo? Or a mink coat with diamond buttons?"

"Fool," she said, flushing. "He wanted you and me to visit their home during the Easter holidays."

"Wow!" yelled Sam, throwing up his charcoal and catching it. "Kianthos! Sounds great."

"I told him I couldn't go, of course," she said, pouring herself some cocoa and sitting down at the table.

Sam looked at her closely. "Couldn't? Or wouldn't?"

"You know I've fixed my holiday," she answered. "I'm going with Peter to that Anglo-Saxon burial site."

"Peter dropped in this evening," Sam said, irrelevantly. "He wanted to borrow some glue. He acted like a gundog after a pheasant when I mentioned Kianthos . . . seems there's an early Mycenean temple there that has never been properly excavated. The Lillitos family own the whole island and they won't let strangers land."

"Typical!" exploded Kate. "What right do they have to prevent people from seeing an important historical site. . . ."

"Keep your shirt on," Sam advised with kindly superiority. "You know, I bet if you mentioned this idea of going there for Easter Peter'd jump at it. He would really love to see that temple."

She drew a quick breath. He was right. Peter would certainly want to go there.

Sam yawned. "I'm off to bed now. Good night, Sis."

When he had gone Kate sat staring at the charcoal drawing he had made. It really was very like Marc Lillitos.

Some obscure instinct warned her against seeing too

much of that man. They were like people from different planets whose lives had touched by chance, and he had already had a disturbing effect upon her. Her life had been running smoothly for the past year. She had buried the yearning for a musical career, had settled down quietly at home, teaching and planning her life with Peter. And now, in one day, the smooth threads of her life were tangled and knotted.

She picked up the pad and tore the sketch off, holding it up to the light. The arrogant face seemed to smile at her. Angrily she crunched it into a ball and flung it across the room, then went up to bed.

Guiltily, she decided not to mention the projected visit to Kianthos to Peter. She had never practised deceit before, even by omission, and it upset her. But the thought of spending two weeks with Marc Lillitos disturbed her even more.

She was abstracted and dreamy at school next day. Even Pallas, during her daily singing lesson, teasingly commented upon it. Kate was relieved to find the girl still friendly, and decided that perhaps Marc had not spoken to her of his idea for the holiday after all.

When she reached home that evening she was in a more cheerful mood. She flung her coat over its hook and walked into the kitchen where, to her amazement, she found Peter and Marc Lillitos seated at the kitchen table, eating hot buttered scones.

There was something so odd about seeing Marc in that homey setting that her lips twitched with unguarded amusement, and, looking back at her, his gray eyes smiled in response. She looked away at once, thinking that it was irritating, the way he read her mind so easily.

"Hi, Kate!" Peter leaned back, offering his cheek, and she bent and kissed him, deliberately, on his mouth. He looked rather surprised, but accepted it calmly.

Mrs. Caulfield was getting another batch of scones out of the oven, and Kate exchanged a wry, inquiring glance with her. Her mother only smiled and shook her head, as though totally at a loss to explain the presence of the two men.

Peter took another scone and said, through a buttery mouthful, "I'd be eternally grateful, Lillitos. I've wanted to see that temple for years. I understand some of it is still standing *in situ*."

"Yes, it is partially restored," Marc said calmly, his gaze on Kate's flushed and angry face.

"I can't wait to see it," Peter said excitedly. "I could map out the general area of the site, then a full team could come in and do the serious work. I wouldn't disturb the site at all. Just work around, determining the limits of the building, if I could, and estimating the size of team needed for the job."

"Then it is settled," Marc said, still watching Kate with bland amusement.

"Peter!" Kate began, in a quiet voice. "We're going to Sussex for Easter."

He looked vaguely at her. "Oh, that doesn't matter! There'll be plenty of other workers there. But Kianthos . . . what a chance! I'll be in on the ground floor with this one. I'll get in touch with various people tonight, get them interested. . . ."

"I think that that should wait," said Marc firmly. "I would prefer you to keep the whole thing to yourself until you've seen the temple. Then we can discuss it in light of what you decide should be done."

"Right," said Peter amiably. "It might be better to have a definite plan in hand." He jumped up, wiping his buttery fingers on his handkerchief. "I'll be off now. I want to do some research on the temple." He offered

Marc his hand. "Thanks very much. I really am grateful for this chance."

Kate looked at him, seething. Suddenly noticing her again, Peter lightly kissed her cheek. "See you, sweetie," he observed vaguely. Then he was gone, banging the front door behind him.

Unable to trust herself to speak, Kate went into the sitting room where she flung herself into a chair and brooded furiously. She might have guessed that Marc Lillitos would get his own way. She could cheerfully have strangled Peter at that moment. All he thought of was broken pots and ancient bones. He didn't care that she was in emotional danger from this tank masquerading as a man!

The door opened again, and the human tank came in, and stood, watching her.

She glared at him. "Well, you've got what you wanted. Now go away!"

He raised his eyebrow. "Have I?" he retorted mockingly. "Do you know what I want, I wonder?"

She did not stop to examine this question too closely, but replied to it as though it were quite straightforward. "You wanted us to come to Kianthos. We're coming. You always get what you want, I suppose?"

He grinned, his hands in his pockets lazily. "Quite often. I am taking the night flight to Greece, but I will see you at Kianthos in two weeks. Give my regards to Sam." He smiled again and left.

Kate walked restlessly around the familiar room, feeling most uncomfortable.

It was ridiculous to be so nervous about a two-week holiday. She loved Peter, didn't she? Of course she did. So why should she be anxious about spending time with Marc Lillitos?

Annoyed, she said to herself, I'm behaving irrationally. The truth is that I've been influenced by the aura of glamor around him. He's rich, good-looking, charming; and I've never met anyone like him before. But those are surface things. Underneath I'm still the same person. I still feel as I always did about Peter.

She halted, staring out of the window. A blackbird was singing his evening challenge from the top of the garden shed. The lilac trees were already showing fat, green buds. It would soon be full spring. Daffodils were breaking out of their sheaths into frilly yellow under the hedge, and there was a flurry of pink blossom on the almond trees in the next garden.

She looked out for a long time, her face absorbed. It was all very real, very beautiful, very reassuring.

Of course I love Peter, she thought, with a surge of relief. She thought of him with warmth. He was absent-minded, thoughtless, vague, but basically kind and generous if one could only penetrate the mists of antiquity which filled his brain. He might not be dynamic or dangerously attractive, but he was real. She knew him, understood him and cared about him.

She turned on her heel and walked out of the room, mentally snapping her fingers at Marc Lillitos.

CHAPTER THREE

As the plane landed on the small airfield at Kianthos Kate peered nervously through the window, wondering if Marc were waiting for them, but there was no sign of him as they climbed down into clear, cool sunlight.

She and Pallas had gone shopping together a few days before they were due to leave and had returned laden with bags and parcels. Kate had felt guilty, squandering money on clothes for herself, but her mother had firmly insisted that she renew her wardrobe. "Think of yourself for once," she smiled, patting Kate's cheek. "You've done so much for us all since you started work. I don't know what I would have done without you. But it's time you had some really nice clothes."

Kate had suggested she make what she needed, as she normally did, but Mrs. Caulfield had shaken her head.

"No, dear. You may never have the chance of a holiday like this again. Buy them."

Kate was a competent seamstress, but she had to admit, as she gazed at diminutive bikinis and smart, multihued slacks, that she could never have produced anything half as professional.

Pallas was chattering to Sam, and Kate had time to look around while they walked towards the sleek black car which had come to meet them.

The airfield ran alongside the beach, the only flat part of the island, as far as she could determine. Above it rose green hills and rugged crags of stone, their peaks swathed in a lavender mist shot through with pink.

A man approached them, taking the bags from the airport manager while saluting Pallas with a grin. The airport manager slid away politely and began locking up the one building visible, a small modern pavilion built of wood.

"Hello, Jake," Pallas greeted the newcomer. "How are you?"

"Fine, Miss Pallas, just fine." He was a rugged Greek of middle years, with swarthy skin and a broken nose, giving him a slightly pugnacious expression. Stowing their bags in the trunk, he helped Pallas into the back.

All the details of the journey had been handled by the Lillitos family. Kate felt quite dazed as she sat back on the smooth upholstery of the limousine next to Pallas. Everything had been so troublefree that she almost doubted that she had really left England. Money certainly oiled the wheels when one was traveling.

Leaning forward, Pallas asked, "How is my mother, Jake?"

The driver turned his head to smile reassuringly at her. "Oh, she's okay! Just dandy, Miss Pallas . . . you know she always gets better in the spring!"

Pallas looked relieved and sat back with a sigh. The car glided along a winding beach road and mounted beneath dark cypress trees. Below them the airfield spread out like a green handkerchief beside the beach, and the air was filled with a fresh, salty tang.

"Is it far to your home?" Sam asked. He was rather pale. Kate suspected that the flight had left him feeling a little sick, but he had not mentioned it.

"A ten-minute drive," Pallas told him. "Our house is at the top of a cove, but we have to go up before we can reach it, because the cliffs cut it off from the airfield. My brother intended to build a large hotel near the airfield, but he hasn't got around to it yet. We don't really want strangers on Kianthos at all." She too was looking rather strained, and Kate guessed that she was nervous about the family reaction when she got home.

"Will it be just your mother and your brother who are at home?" she asked her.

Pallas shrugged. "Perhaps, but then Hélène might be there ... she often comes for Easter with some friends. Or Marc may have business friends of his at the villa. He often uses it to put them into a good mood before concluding a deal."

"Nice work if you can get it," said Sam, a little gruffly.

Pallas flushed and looked hurt, but Kate could see that her brother was feeling worse with each minute of the journey. His freckles stood out on his nose like microdots under a microscope. His mouth was thinned and taut and his cheeks white. She hoped he would not be sick before they reached the villa.

At that moment the car lurched downwards again, throwing Peter against the door. He rubbed his forehead resentfully, then bent to pick up the vast tome he had been reading ever since they left London. Kate watched him angrily. He had not spoken to any of them all morning. She knew that dreamy, abstracted expression. It meant that he was unaware of anything around him. Including her.

They stopped in a gully between dark rocky cliffs, with grass clinging perilously to little clefts, and wild yellow flowers blowing in the sea wind. The path was studded with lumps of stone, but the car reversed slowly, wheels churning up pebbles, and turned down a grassy track which ended on a paved patio.

Kate got out and stood with Sam and Peter, gazing in amazement at the view spread before them.

The Villa Lillitos was modern but built on classical lines; a two-story house, with flat, wide windows, a terrace running along the front, on which stood basket chairs and several small tables. The terrace was supported on smooth white pillars of stone, and in the center of it stood a portico, beneath which Marc Lillitos stood watching their arrival.

It reminded Kate of a colonial American house somewhere in the deep South, and the shady cypresses that surrounded it did nothing to dispel the illusion. The house stood on a sloping hill. Below it was a rough path that presumably led to the sea, for she could glimpse golden sand and curling blue waves some way below them. Behind the house were green lawns, spring flowers and the nets of a tennis court.

Before she had time to take more in, Marc was with them, giving a quiet order to the driver, taking Pallas's elbow.

"I am sure you would all like to rest before dinner," he said, politely smiling.

A short woman with smooth olive skin, dark hair and black eyes met them in the entrance hall and took charge of the visitors.

Peter hung back and Kate heard him say eagerly, "How soon can I see the temple, do you think?"

She did not wait to hear Marc's reply. Flushed and perturbed, she went up behind Sam to the room prepared for her.

"My name is Sophia," said the maid politely. "Please do not hesitate to ask me for anything you need." Her English was so good that Kate was quite taken aback. She had been wishing that she had had time to learn some Greek before her trip, but it was becoming clear that she was unlikely to need it. Everyone in the Lillitos household seemed to speak very good English.

She hesitantly tried out one of her few hastily learned phrases, "*Efharisto!*" which meant thank you.

Sophia smiled, with sudden real warmth, and replied in her own language.

Kate flushed. "I'm afraid that's almost the whole of my Greek vocabulary!"

Sophia laughed. "You will learn more, yes?"

"I hope I do," said Kate. "I would like to be able to speak Greek. I only speak French, and a little German."

"I speak fluent English," Sophia said proudly. "Marc taught me to speak it! I was his nurse. He learned at school, and I learned from him."

Kate stared in amazement. "His nurse? But you can't be old enough!" Then she flushed. "Oh, I'm sorry, I didn't mean to be rude."

Sophia was not at all offended, though. She beamed, "Why rude? It is very big compliment. I was 14 when I first come to work for the family. Marc was little baby, just born. I help the nurse, then nurse leave when Marc is two, and I carry on." She looked wistful. "He was very pretty baby. When he was eight, he went away to school. I stayed on as maid." She counted on her fingers, muttering under her breath. "You guess? I am 45 now."

"You don't look it," Kate said sincerely. "Your complexion is so good!"

Sophia smiled, very pleased, and after another moment or two went off, leaving Kate to change for dinner. She slipped into her new dressing gown and lay down on the bed for a while. The flight had been more tiring than she had expected. Half an hour later she got up and put on a turquoise dress she had bought in Greyford, then went downstairs and found Peter and Marc in a wood-paneled lounge, talking quietly.

She stood by the door watching them, feeling a surge of resentment against Marc Lillitos for the bored expression on his dark face. She forgot the number of times she had been irritated by Peter's passion for the past. It never entered his head that not everyone shared his interest, and even Sam had been known to ask him to shut up about ancient civilization. Now it was just another crime to chalk up against the name of Lillitos, and she illogically felt pleased to be able to do so.

Marc turned his head and saw her. Her heart did that annoying backward flip that she had only begun to notice since meeting him. There was something about the look in the gray eyes that disturbed her a good deal; a lazy, mocking intimacy, as though he not only knew and understood her, but could read her mind with a glance. It was alarming to feel so transparent.

She came forward, and Peter turned to smile at her. "Oh, there you are, Kate! I've made all the arrangements with Lillitos. He's kindly offered me camping equipment . . . a tent, blankets, sleeping bag, even cooking facilities."

"You're going to sleep on the site?" Kate interrupted. "But Peter, this is a holiday!"

He stared, in mild bewilderment. "Well, I couldn't make the journey every day, you know, there and back. The temple is up there," pointing out of the long window, which looked up at a green expanse of mountainous country, "on that hooked peak. Mr. Lillitos says you can see the whole of the island from the top; it's a good strategic position for a fortress. There must be more than a temple up there." His face glowed passionately. "Who knows what I'll find?"

"You're going to leave me here and spend the whole two weeks alone on that mountain?" she asked incredulously.

"You'll have Pallas and Sam to keep you company," he answered vaguely. "I thought the idea was that you should have fun with Pallas while I work on the site? You know you're never very interested in site work, Kate."

Angrily conscious of Marc's amused gaze, she was silent, and Peter took her agreement for granted. "Well, I'm very grateful," he told Marc. "I'll be off now, then." He shook hands with him, kissed Kate absently and was gone before she had time to think.

She looked at Marc coldly. He was leaning back in his chair, his face sardonic.

"You do not look too happy, Miss Caulfield. Your fiancé will be quite safe, I promise you. My car is taking him as far as the road goes. We do not have very many roads on Kianthos. Jake will help him carry up the camping equipment, and see the camp set up. He has plenty of food with him. And the goatherds will visit the peak once a day with their goats as they always do. If anything went wrong, they would let me know."

"Goatherds?" she asked curiously.

"There's a village on the other side of the peak. They keep goats and have some olive trees. Cheese and olives are the staple diet, you know. Goat's cheese and goat's milk, and fish, in season. They call the peak To Angkistri. It means The Hook. There is a local legend about it which I must tell you some time."

"How long have your family lived here?" she asked.

"Off and on for generations, I believe. My great-grandfather was a fisherman who left the island for the mainland when there was bad fishing for several years. My grandfather was successful enough to build up a good business, and my father bought the island thirty years ago. He built this house."

"Sophia said you learned your English at school," she said. "Was that in England?"

He nodded. "My mother is French, but English schools

are famous all over the world, so they decided to send me to England, and then to a French university."

She was startled. "Oh, you were at university?"

His dark face was suddenly alight with laughter. "That surprises you? You thought I was illiterate, I suppose?"

Kate flushed. "I hadn't thought about it," she said offhandedly.

"Well, I left without taking a degree, in fact, because my father was ill, and I had to take over the business. Then he died, so I carried on. I have often regretted it, but that's fate!"

She watched him curiously. His face had a fatalistic look as he said the last words. "Do you believe that?"

His brows rose. "In fate? Of course." His tone was suddenly brusque, as though he disliked the subject.

"Why have you never allowed anyone to visit the temple before?" she asked him after a long silence.

"My father would never have strangers on Kianthos. He felt they would spoil it. There are so few roads that it would be impossible to bring many cars here, anyway, and modern tourists love to go everywhere by car. The life of our people would change if we allowed too many outsiders onto the island."

"It's such a beautiful place," she said. "Isn't that a selfish attitude?"

"The villagers all agree with me. They are happy as they are."

"Are they? Living on goat's cheese and olives, with occasionally a little fish?"

"Does the technological society make men any happier?" he countered coolly.

"I think your attitude is too possessive," she said.

His eyes flashed across the room at her, and she felt oddly breathless, as though he had touched her. "But I am possessive," he said softly. "Any man worth his salt must be . . . the desire to possess is the root of love."

She was angrily aware of a weakness spreading through her body, a trembling and fluttering of the nerves. "That's a very old-fashioned idea," she said, trying to laugh, but too conscious of his masculine presence to be able to carry it off. "Nowadays we believe that to love is to be ready to let go. People have to be free."

"Hence divorce?" he said sarcastically. "And the high abortion rate in your country, not to mention the appalling tragedies of drug addiction."

She was grateful when, at that moment, Sam and Pallas came into the room. Sam was still very pale, but the blue line around his mouth had vanished, and some of his normal cheerfulness had returned.

"I am afraid you will not meet my mother this evening," Marc said to him. "She has a headache, but I hope she will get up for lunch tomorrow." He looked sharply at Sam's face. "You look ill. Was it a bad flight?"

Sam grimaced. "I'm the world's worst traveler. Don't worry, though, I'll be fine now I'm back on *terra firma*."

They dined quietly in a very modern room with mosaic tiling on the floor and pleasant yellow walls. Kate ate steak and salad, followed by a very sweet dessert made of figs and cream, after which black coffee seemed very appropriate.

Sam excused himself early, pleading a headache, and Pallas went up to sit and talk to her mother for a while. Kate intended to go to bed early, too, but Marc said that she would feel sleepier when she had walked around the garden for a while.

"The air is so pure here," he said, draping her cardigan around her shoulders, his fingers lingering on the nape of her neck a second longer than was necessary. She shivered at his touch, and he glanced down at her, gray eyes narrowed.

They walked around the garden without talking, listening to the cicadas and feeling the cool dusk stealing over the trees and flowers. The air was, as he had said, fresh and sweet, permeated by a faint scent of spring. One tree was covered with purple blossoms that Marc called Judas flowers. High up on the hills the mountain furze was in golden bloom, and a final shaft from the setting sun made the slopes glow like molten gold. Then the light died, and a purple shadow crept over them.

She was reminded of Peter and felt a pang of disloyalty. He had only been gone a short time, and already she was forgetting she was engaged to him. Marc was far too experienced in the small art of flirtation for her. She was not sure whether he was deliberately flirting with her, or if it was merely a reflex action, but from time to time she was aware that he was deliberately testing her reactions to him.

Perhaps he had been piqued by her attitude from their first meeting? Or perhaps he liked to have a row of scalps dangling from his belt?

Whatever the reason, those charming smiles, the light, meaning phrases and the way he touched her neck just now all added up to a flirtation. And she did not mean to get involved in that sort of folly.

"I think I'll go in now," she said, as they approached the terrace again.

"I'm not in the least tired," he said. "Are you really sleepy? You don't look it. Won't you play for me first? Something quiet and gentle?"

She played a piece of soft night music by Mozart, and the insidious intricacies gradually drove all disquieting thoughts from her head, and restored her sense of humor.

I'm a fool, she thought, her fingers moving delicately over the keys. Peter leaves me too much alone. I'm making mountains out of molehills, building ridiculous fantasies. Marc is just being polite. I must get it into proportion.

When she lifted her hands finally and sat back, Marc smiled at her. "You have a very pleasant touch."

"I'm a competent amateur," she said firmly, "but thank you."

He looked at her for a long moment, his face inscrutable. "What a girl for laying out the facts you are," he said at last. "You are unusually honest. I know many much less talented musicians who would claim a great deal more than competence."

She refused to be drawn, smiled and said good night, leaving him alone in the lounge.

Kate was up early next morning and met Sam on the stairs. He looked his usual self once more, clear-eyed and alert. He grinned at her, "I slept like a log! How about you?"

"Fine," she admitted.

They found themselves the first to arrive for breakfast. A pretty girl in a lavender uniform was going about laying the table, and looked around in surprise as they entered the room. She smiled, though, and said good morning in rather thickly accented English, then pointed out the food, waiting over steel hotplates.

There were scrambled eggs, bacon and sausages, but Kate stuck to her usual orange juice and slice of toast. Sam, however, greedily heaped his plate with a glorious mixture of everything, and grinned at her teasingly as he began to eat.

"I heard you playing the piano last night," he said between mouthfuls.

"Did it wake you? I'm sorry. Marc asked me to play something before I went to bed."

Sam shook his head. "It was quite pleasant, drifting off to sleep to Mozart." He shot her an acute glance. "Don't fall for Marc, will you? He's an attractive sort of chap, but Pallas says he has a girlfriend. French, apparently . . . a successful model. She won't give up her career, otherwise Pallas thinks they would be married by now."

Kate gritted her teeth and spoke very brightly. "A tough career girl should suit him! I hope she keeps him tied up in knots for years. His attitude toward women is as out of date as crinolines."

Sam laughed. "You're so right! Look, you don't mind my giving you the gypsy's warning, do you, Sis? It's just that I'd hate you to get hurt."

"You seem to forget I'm engaged to Peter," she said rather sharply.

Sam grimaced. "Yes, but then Peter isn't exactly a ball of fire in the romance department, is he? I mean, an Anglo-Saxon kneebone gives him more of a thrill than you do!"

"Really, Sam!" she snapped angrily.

Sam looked sheepish. "Oh, I'm sorry. It's none of my business, I know, but much as I like Peter, he does rather neglect you. Girls like a bit of attention from time to time."

"You should write a book on the subject," she said, "if you have so much valuable advice."

Pallas arrived while Sam was groping for a reply, and they dropped the subject, talking instead of what they should do that day. The sun was already bright but cold, and the sky was an unbelievable blue. The idea of a swim that morning was dismissed, and Sam suggested that Pallas show them around the island.

"I wonder how Peter is getting on," said Kate, sipping black coffee slowly.

"Would you like to go up and see?" asked Pallas. "Jake will take you in the car to where the track starts. Would you mind walking the rest of the way, though? It is very tough going."

"Of course I don't mind," Kate said easily. "I've done some hill walking. We went to the Lake District several times for our family holidays. Do you remember, Sam?"

"I remember you puffing and blowing when we got to the top," he teased.

Kate laughed. "Are you sure you don't mind my going off alone, though? It seems very rude. Your brother asked me to come to keep you company, you know. Actually, I would like to make a tour of the island with you. I just felt worried about Peter. . . ."

"I understand," said Pallas, smiling at her. "I'll have Sam to keep me company. Really, I don't mind. You go and put your mind at rest. I expect you would like to see the temple yourself. Then, when you know how Peter is coping, you can feel free to enjoy yourself with us."

Kate let out a sigh of relief. "Well, thank you, then. I'd like to go.'

Pallas went to the garage with her to find Jake, and he readily agreed to drive Kate up to To Angkistri. They set out ten minutes later, and Jake talked to her all the way. He had, he explained, learned his English in the United States.

"My name is Hector Hyakos, but over there they called me Jake for short. The States . . . a great country, Fifteen years I lived there. Very happy, earn lot of money. But then I met the boss and he says come to

Kianthos, be my driver-mechanic-man-of-work. Handyman, they call it in the States. I figure that I never manage to save enough to come home on my own. So I accept."

"And are you glad you came?" she asked him.

"Sure I'm glad. The boss is a great guy . . . generous, warmhearted, a real Greek. And I like cars. I was always homesick, you know? I mean, the States is great, but I'm a Greek." He pulled up with a jolt, and she looked around her with great interest. They were on the mountain slope now, the track nothing but a whitened ribbon between grass and rocks, pitted and scarred.

"This is as far as I can take you, miss. You want I should walk up there with you? You follow this track to the top. But it gets difficult as you get higher. You might slip or get dizzy."

"No, thank you," she smiled. "I have climbed before and I have a good head for heights. You'd better get back . . . I think Miss Pallas wants you to drive her somewhere."

He saluted. "Okay by me. I'll be back at four o'clock. You got a watch, miss?"

She showed it to him and he nodded. Then he stood by the car, watching her intently as she began the steep climb to the top. He clearly decided she was competent enough, because after a while she heard the sound of the engine and the grinding of the wheels on stones as he turned back the way they had come.

The climb was more difficult than she had anticipated. Several times she slipped, her hands clutching at the rock face, but each time she managed to steady herself. She kept going, breathing quickly, her hands scratched and bleeding slightly, her knees and back aching.

When she reached the top she sat down, panting, and

stared back the way she had come. From here the climb looked dizzyingly steep, and she wondered how she had had the nerve to attempt it—and also how she was to get down! Then she shrugged. Sufficient unto the day was the evil thereof. . . .

She found Peter lying on his stomach, stretched flat out, the only part of him that moved his hand, which was delicately scraping at the dusty covering of soil which lay everywhere over the ruins.

He turned his head to squint at her as she approached, and, without a sign of surprise or inquiry, said, "Careful! I've begun marking out the ground plan with string. Don't trip over it or you'll pull out the pegs, and I'll have to do it all over again."

"You've been busy," she commented, staring around her.

The site was laid out on a flattish plateau in a vaguely rectangular shape, with three broad stone steps running all the way around the building. The roof had been supported by the usual pillars, some of which still stood in more or less battered condition, rearing up toward the open blue sky, tapering to their plain capitals, their stone flaking away along the sides. Blocks of stone lay everywhere, among the wiry grass and yellow flowers. It was touching to Kate to see how the stone steps were hollowed out by generations of reverent feet, even though this place had been deserted for so long, slowly crumbling under the pressures of wind and weather.

"I only have two weeks to make this preliminary investigation," he pointed out. "Now you're here, Kate, pass me that plastic bag. I've found something interesting."

She ran and picked up the top bag from the pile laid ready, a stone keeping them from blowing away, returned and handed it to Peter, who gently pushed an encrusted object inside the bag.

"That was outside the temple area proper," he said. "Give me my map. Over there. . . ." waving a vague arm.

She fetched the map and Peter carefully marked the spot where he had found his first object.

"What do you think it is?" she asked, scrutinizing it. "A coin?" It was that shape.

He shrugged. "Possibly. We can't tell until it's cleaned." He grinned at her. "It's a temptation to look for other things, but I must get on . . . until a proper accredited expedition is organized, the site mustn't be disturbed. Because the coin was outside the temple it won't matter too much. Now, I want to finish my map today. I'll measure and you can jot down the dimensions."

"Have you had breakfast?" she asked resignedly.

"What?" He stared at her as if she were talking in a foreign tongue, then blinked. "Oh, breakfast. Yes, I had a roll when I first got up."

"At crack of dawn, by the amount of work you've done," she scolded. "What is there for lunch? I'll get you something."

He protested but she insisted, and at last he gave in and sat down with her to eat the stew she heated over the little camp stove. Marc had sent up a number of cans, she found, as well as eggs, cheese and bread. There was no reason why Peter should not eat well.

After lunch they resumed work. They continued to work for the rest of the afternoon, breaking only for a cup of black coffee at two o'clock, and soon had the whole site mapped out. Peter crawled around on his knees, measuring the ground, and Kate carefully marked down the measurements on his rough sketch map. Then they noted down all the positions of pillars, fallen stones and other objects, and measured the pillars, their heights, breadths, capitals.

Kate's shoulders and arms were aching. Her eyes kept blurring and she was hot and weary. But Peter seemed beyond such ordinary human weakness. Frowning, absorbed, intent, he worked on as the sun grew warmer, rose higher and higher, and then began to move down the sky again.

She glanced at her watch and found, to her relief, that it was half past three. She wanted to get back down the peak before Jake arrived, so she said goodbye to Peter, who answered briefly, hardly realizing what she had said, she suspected.

Kate was glad to see no sign of the car below. Taking a deep breath, she began to lower herself, clinging to the grassy outcrops of stone, her fingers clawing fiercely, feet feeling for support. She had to climb down backwards. It was impossible to walk down. She was only a short way from the top when she heard the car engine in the distance. It appeared to be racing along the bumpy narrow track. Stones rattled and flew as the wheels spun. She wondered if Jake had intended to get here early to help her down, and then, hearing the car stop with a ferocious jerk, turned her head to smile at him.

The smile froze on her face. It was not Jake, but Marc, who had leaped out of the driving seat of the khaki-colored jeep drawn up far below her.

His expression as he looked up at her was grim. She could see, even from this distance, the tight clenching of his jaw and teeth, the flash of the hard gray eyes.

He was bitterly angry, that much was obvious.

Shock made her move too quickly. She felt her hands slip, the tearing pain of the rock biting into her skin, her feet slithering helplessly down. Panic blotted out all thought for an instant, during which time she grasped desperately at the rock face and spreadeagled herself against it, toes curling into the niche they had somehow found.

Stones rattled downwards nearby. She heard quick, harsh breathing. Then an arm clamped around her and she was pulled against a cool blue shirt, her face buried against Marc's chest.

For a second there was a silence, then he asked roughly, "Are you badly hurt?"

Kate lifted her head, without looking up at him, and pushed herself back a little. "No," she whispered. "I'm so sorry. . . ."

She heard his teeth snap together and felt the raging fury inside him, although he said nothing. She felt singed and exhausted. He was right to be angry with her. She had been silly to attempt the climb.

"Do you think you can make the rest of the way with my help?" he asked tensely.

"Yes," she whispered.

Slowly, inch by painful inch, they descended. She felt his arm tensed permanently to grab her if she fell again, and dreaded the interview that must take place at the foot.

Then, at last, they stood upright beside the jeep. Marc opened the door without looking at her, and she wearily tumbled into the passenger seat. He slammed the door and walked around to the other side, got in and then sat staring at her, his arm along the seat.

"You stupid little fool!" he said harshly. "Were you crazy to attempt that climb? I thought you were out exploring with Pallas and Sam. It was only when Jake got back that I discovered the truth, and I tore the skin off his back for letting you go up there alone. I drove here like a maniac, expecting to find you in pieces at the foot, only to see you stuck up there like a fledgling bird." He glared at her with burning ferocity. "If you weren't in such a state already I would gladly teach you a lesson you won't forget! Never try that climb again. Do you hear?"

She nodded, silenced for once.

"Show me your hands," he commanded, after a long pause.

Trembling, she turned them palm up, and heard his breath drawn in explosively. "Good God!" he exclaimed. They were scraped and bloody, one deep gash at the base of her thumb, grass stains on the raw fingers.

"I wanted to see that Peter was comfortable," she muttered nervously.

"And I suppose he had you working with him up there?" he asked tautly. "Digging and scraping like a mole all day? Why didn't he see you safely down to the car? He must realize how dangerous that climb can be . . . or doesn't he care?"

"He was very busy," she said. "If I'd asked him to come with me he would have done, but I didn't ask. . . ."

"He's a selfish, irresponsible idiot!" Marc commented savagely. "No decent man would let his woman make a climb like that!"

"I'm not his woman," she snapped back, "I'm his fiancée. But the relationship is one of shared independence, not slavery! He's not a caveman, and I'm not in need of protection."

His gray eyes stormed at her furiously, the handsome features suddenly rigid and dangerous. "You make love sound like mild friendship. Is that all there is between you two? That isn't love as I know it!"

Something twisted inside her, and she lowered her eyes. "I'm sure it isn't," she said in a brittle voice.

His hands grabbed her shoulders, the curled fingers biting into her. For a second she was frozen with panic, then he released her with a thickly drawn breath, turned and started the engine.

CHAPTER FOUR

They made the return journey in less than half the time Jake had taken, tearing around corners and over bumps in the road, jolting and swaying furiously. She clung to her seat, eyes shut, aware of Marc's anger through every nerve in her body.

When they pulled up outside the villa Sam and Pallas, who had been sitting on the veranda, rose nervously and came to meet them.

Marc ignored them both, helping Kate out of the jeep with impersonal firmness. She shot a glance up at him and found his face under tight control again, but the gray eyes met hers with the glacial expression she always found so terrifying.

"Oh, your poor hands!" exclaimed Pallas, catching sight of them. "What have you done to yourself?"

Marc propelled Kate towards the building, his hand clamped on her elbow, taking no notice of his sister. He pushed her upstairs and into the large, luxurious bathroom.

"Sit down," he ordered, and left her alone for a moment, returning with a large bottle of iodine and some bandages. He ran warm water into the bowl, immersed her hands with the gentleness of a trained nurse, carefully washed and dried them, then anointed the grazes with iodine, while he put a bandage over the deeper cut.

Kate held her breath until the iodine had stopped stinging. "Thank you," she whispered, her blue eyes damp with tears.

He leaned over her, very tall and overwhelming, his eyes on her face.

"Did it hurt badly?"

She forced a wavering smile. "No, not at all."

"You're crying!" He somehow made that sound like an accusation and she felt, again, anger in him.

"I got some dust in my eyes on the road," she said quickly.

He washed her face delicately, wiping her eyes with wisps of cotton wool. She felt like a child again, sheltered, cherished, vulnerable. Why was it so pleasant to have your face washed, she thought vaguely, enjoying the sensation.

He took her chin in his long fingers and turned her face up to him. The savagery she had felt in him had evaporated. A warm indulgence shone in his eyes.

"What a silly child you are," he murmured, smiling quizzically. "You looked like a little girl with your eyes screwed up tight and your lip between your teeth. How do your hands feel now?"

"Much better, thank you," she said, very pink. In a way, he was more dangerous in this mood.

He lifted them in his, then bent suddenly and kissed them briefly. They quivered in his grip, then were pulled away.

He straightened, still smiling. "What else does one do with a hurt child but kiss it better?" he teased.

She turned blindly and stumbled out of the bathroom. In a moment she was in her own room, the door safely shut. She leaned against the door, heart pounding.

I mustn't let him get under my skin like this, she thought, eyes shut tight. He's only playing some game or other. I must keep my defences in place. I must hold on to my love for Peter.

That evening when she came down for dinner, she found Marc in the lounge with a small slender woman of 50 or so, whose thick black hair, dark eyes and elegant clothes had the mark of the Parisian.

Marc glanced up, smiling. "Ah, here is Miss Caulfield

now, Mama." He stood up. "Miss Caulfield, this is my mother."

Mrs. Lillitos smilingly held out a thin hand. "I am so pleased to meet you. Pallas has written to me of you so often that I feel I know you very well. But I cannot think of you as Miss Caulfield . . . will you let me call you Kate? Such a nice name. It always reminds me of Shakespeare."

Marc broke in teasingly, "Ah, yes . . . *Henry the Fifth*! What does he say, 'There is witchcraft in your lips, Kate. . . .' " His eyes provoked her openly, and Kate knew herself to be blushing.

His mother looked around at him, one delicate dark brow lifted in inquiry. "Marc! You must not be so teasing!"

He laughed. "Or did you mean Kate from *The Taming of the Shrew*, Mama? 'Kate, the prettiest Kate in Christendom, sometimes Kate the curst?' "

Mrs. Lillitos clicked her tongue. "That was not very polite, my son. I am surprised at you. Kate is covered with embarrassment. Say you are sorry at once!"

"Ah, Mama," he said lightly, "English girls are not brought up like our girls, to blush at everything! If Kate is pink it is because she wants to slap me, not because she is shy."

His mother looked from one to the other very slowly. A smile pulled at her lips. "Is that so?" she asked quietly. "I see."

"The first time we met," he went on gaily, "she spat at me like a cross kitten with its back arched. She almost stepped in front of my car, yet she flew at me furiously for daring to criticize her!"

Watching him from under lowered lashes, Kate

suspected that his light tone hid resentment. It was the first time he had ever referred to their first encounter.

"Perhaps you were rude to her, Marc," his mother said mildly. "Was he, Kate?"

Kate looked at her and was relieved to see that she was smiling warmly. "Very rude," she agreed, smiling back.

"Ye gods!" he exclaimed. "I was the very model of restraint! And when we met again she tore my character into strips, told me how to run my life and threw me out of her home as if I were a burglar!"

Mrs. Lillitos laughed softly. "The more I hear of her the more I admire her! Now, Marc, go away, and let me talk to Kate alone for a while. You are too disturbing."

He made a violent grimace, but did not argue. When he had gone, his mother smiled at her. "He was like that, even as a boy . . . it was like having a hurricane permanently in the house."

Kate laughed. "I can imagine!"

Mrs. Lillitos leaned back. "Tell me about yourself, my dear. Do you like teaching music?"

"I like teaching anyone as talented as Pallas," she said frankly. "It's a great pleasure to feel that one is able to help someone with her gifts."

Mrs. Lillitos did not reply directly. After a pause she said, "And yourself? Are you musically talented? Did you ever want to be a professional pianist?"

"How did you know I was a pianist?" Kate asked in surprise.

"I heard you playing to my son last night. It was very pleasant. You must play for me again some time. Did you enjoy exploring the island today?"

Kate blinked. "I . . . I didn't go with Pallas and Sam," she said slowly. "I went to the temple."

"To Angkistri?" repeated Mrs. Lillitos. "Are you interested in archeology? We have a young man here now, studying the temple."

"He is my fiancé," Kate explained, smiling in surprise. Why hadn't Marc told his mother that she and Peter were engaged?

Mrs. Lillitos stiffened and stared at her. "Fiancé?" she repeated. "Fiancé?"

Kate would have thought she did not know the word, but she remembered that Mrs. Lillitos was French and must be perfectly familiar with it.

"Didn't Marc tell you?" she asked. "Surely Pallas must have mentioned it to you?"

Then she saw that Mrs. Lillitos was very pale. Her frail hand was groping for the stick which stood propped against her chair.

Feebly she stood up, refusing Kate's offer of help with a silent shake of the head.

"I do not feel very hungry tonight," she said. "I think I will go back to my room. Will you call my son?"

Kate obeyed and Marc came in quickly, looking at his mother with natural anxiety.

"Give me your arm, my son," she said heavily.

He moved to her side at once and they left the room slowly. Kate sank back into her own chair, baffled. Why had Mrs. Lillitos suddenly altered? Was it just that she had begun to feel ill, or had something Kate said upset her?

Before she could think too closely about it, Pallas and Sam had come in together, talking loudly.

"Oh, you're alone," said Pallas, with obvious relief. "I thought Marc might be in here. Heavens, Kate, if you had seen his face when he discovered we had let you go up to To Angkistri alone! He practically burst a blood vessel.

Marc has such set îdeas about women. He likes to wrap them in cotton wool for safekeeping." She grinned at Sam. "Although these days he does seem to be making an effort to turn a blind eye to my new clothes and hairstyle. So perhaps he is improving."

"He's a throwback to the knights of old," Sam teased. "His recipe for life starts, first catch your damsel. . . ."

Pallas giggled. "Club her," she suggested, "and throw her over your horse."

Sam played up. "Gallop away with her to your castle," he added, twirling an imaginary moustache, "and shut her up in an ivory tower." He sighed exaggeratedly. "Ah, those were the days!"

"Nowadays," said Marc's cool tones from the door, making them all look round guiltily, "your knight would have a hard time telling the damsels from the other young men."

"But think what fun he would have trying to find out!" Sam countered impudently.

Marc's brows rose. "Really? Shall we go in to dinner now? Mama does not feel well enough to stay down, Pallas. She has one of her headaches."

They had moussaka for dinner—eggplants thinly sliced, rich dark minced lamb and a thick cheese sauce covering it all. Kate enjoyed it very much and determined to make it when she got home.

Marc peeled an apple slowly, his long slim fingers deft in all their movements. Kate watched him, remembering the gentleness of those fingers on her face earlier.

"By the way, Pallas, Hélène cabled today. She arrives at the end of the week," he said without looking up.

His sister looked up, frowning. "Alone?"

He shook his head and shot her a quick glance. "She is bringing Marie-Louise and Jean-Paul with her."

Pallas dropped the fork with which she was eating a confection of chocolate and cream. "Jean-Paul?" she repeated breathlessly. "Oh, why did you have to invite him here?"

"Why shouldn't he come here?" Marc demanded. "He is our cousin, after all. And he usually visits us once a year."

She pushed back her chair, standing up suddenly. "It isn't fair!" she wailed like a child, and ran out of the room.

Sam stared after her, then looked at Marc, who calmly continued to peel his apple, the rings sliding from between his fingers in symmetrical spirals.

Silently, Sam followed Pallas out of the room. Kate felt curious, yet nervous. She wanted to know why Pallas so much disliked the idea of a visit from this cousin of hers, yet she was intensely aware of being left alone with Marc once more.

He cut himself a slice of the apple, bit it with relish, and then smilingly offered her half. She shook her head. But before she could ask him about his sister's reaction to his news, he had said lazily, "Did you know that Spiro Pyrakis lived near here?"

She dragged her mind back from the thoughts that had been absorbing it.

"Spiro Pyrakis? No, I didn't. I have all his records at home. He's my favorite pianist. I went to all his London concerts last year, and I found his playing even better than I'd dreamed. Of course, a recording is never the same as the real thing."

"He's a friend of mine," he said casually.

She stared at him, too awed to speak.

"I was talking to him on the telephone this morning," he said lightly. "He asked me to sail over there tomorrow. Would you like to come?"

"I couldn't," she stammered, torn between delight and awe. "He wouldn't want to meet a stranger. . . ."

"I told him about you," Marc went on, "asked if I might bring you. He said it would be delightful to meet a pretty girl." He grinned at her, his gray eyes alight with wicked amusement. "Spiro loves the company of pretty girls, and he has been shut up on Epilison for weeks, writing a new concerto. He jumped at your visit like a hungry trout jumping at a fly."

Kate flushed. "I'm sure he didn't," she protested.

"Wait until you meet him. You'll see I am telling the truth. You'll come?"

"If you're sure . . ." she said nervously. "Are Pallas and Sam going, too?"

"No," he said firmly. "Too many people would irritate him. He hates a crowd."

"Pallas is a pretty girl," she suggested innocently, her eyes on his face.

He grinned at her. "Spiro has known her since she was knee-high to a cicada . . . he would squabble with her. There is something childlike about him, you know. He and Pallas always quarrel, but they are fond of each other."

Kate excused herself early, pleading fatigue, and he stood at the bottom of the stairs, watching her. "If your back is aching I have some liniment that might help," he offered, seeing her involuntarily holding her back.

She shook her head. "It doesn't matter. Thank you."

"I promise not to kiss the sore place again," he offered teasingly.

Red and furious, she did not answer but ran quickly up the stairs.

Next morning she was downstairs early for breakfast, wearing blue jeans and a loose matching jacket. Her thick, white, ribbed sweater gave her a boyish look, emphasized by the fact that she had tied her blond hair at the back into a ponytail. The severe style gave a new vulnerability to her face, of which she was unaware.

Marc was sitting at the table eating rools and dark red jam. He eyed her lazily. "You look about seventeen," he commented.

Kate took a boiled egg from the silver covered dish and came to sit down opposite him.

He leaned over and teasingly cut a slice of toast into thin strips for her. "Little girls like to have soldiers to dip into their eggs, don't they?"

She gave him a dignified frown. "What time do we leave?" she asked forbiddingly.

He laughed aloud, his mood clearly relaxed and carefree this morning.

They walked down to the small quay a quarter of an hour later. Marc helped her to climb aboard his neat little yacht, cast off and jumped on board himself. The wind took the sails and Kate looked up at them with pleasure as, white and free, they slapped to and fro above her.

"Watch your head," Marc ordered curtly, and she ducked down at once as the beam swung around.

The wind blew behind them all the way to Epilison, the neighboring island on which Pyrakis lived. They made the crossing in an hour and a half.

The island looked beautiful as they skimmed closer. Blue, shadowy hills, golden sand, white houses shimmering in the early morning sun, with an unreal beauty that reminded her of a postcard come to life. They tied up at a small jetty and walked up along narrow village streets, past the untidy white houses whose doors all seemed to stand permanently open. Old women in black sat on some of the doorsteps, shawls over their gray heads, their wrinkled, tanned faces smiling at Marc as he walked past.

He paused to speak to each one, gallantly, teasingly, and they giggled at what he said.

Fishermen mending nets waved to him, little boys begged for drachmae. Everyone seemed to know and like him.

They paused at the very top of the hill; then he pushed open high iron gates set in a flinty wall that ran around a charming, untidy garden, set with cypress and gnarled old olive trees.

The house was of an ornate, oriental design, the windows all curves and arches, the stonework fretted. Kate was so nervous that Marc, after a sharp glance, smiled and held her hand as if she were five years old. She did not protest, but clung to his protection.

"Suppose he's angry because you brought me?" she whispered. "He probably prefers his privacy, like most famous people."

He squeezed her fingers comfortingly. "Goose! I told you, he loves pretty blond girls!"

She giggled, and then the door opened and a fierce old man, his thick gray moustache quivering, glared at them from flashing black eyes.

Marc spoke to him in Greek, grinning affectionately, and the old man answered in a low, grumbling voice, his hands moving in vivid emphasis. Kate saw him shooting those black eyes at her, and looked nervously up at Marc.

He laughed, slipping an arm around her shoulders. "He says he does not like young ladies coming here because Pyrakis always falls madly in love with them, especially when they are blond and beautiful, like you!" And his gray eyes glinted wickedly.

She blushed and stammered, "I don't believe he said anything of the sort!" She moved away, so that his arm slid off her shoulder.

Marc's eyes continued to laugh at her. Grinning, he spoke again to the old man, who laughed deep in his throat.

He talked gutturally, gesticulating, and Marc laughed. Then they walked into the cool, shadowy hall and the old man shuffled away, his great hooked nose like an eagle's beak in profile.

Kate stared around her in fascination. The floor of the hall was tiled in black and white marble. A gold-painted tub stood in one corner, full of tall waving ferns, and opposite her hung a gilded mirror in which her own face swam, like a translucent mermaid's, against the dim background of the hall.

"That is Kyril. He has been with Spiro for years and is devoted to him, in a fierce, scornful way. They shout and swear to kill each other, but they are inseparable." Marc came up behind her, staring over her shoulder at her face in the mirror.

Their eyes met. Hers fell away, shyly, at something odd in his. Then Kyril came back and led them down the hall. The room they entered was long, austere and as shadowy as the hall. Beyond open french windows she could see a cluster of bushes and tall cypress whose branches darkened the room, giving it an undersea look, a cool greeny light filtering through and spilling over books, tables, chairs.

In a shabby old armchair sat Spiro Pyrakis, his leonine head turned toward them.

He rose, holding out his powerful fingers first to Kate. "*Mia kiria*," he murmured, his slightly protruding blue eyes appraising her. Then his polite smile widened. "Marc," he said, in charmingly accented English, "you lied to me, you dog!"

Marc raised an inquiring eyebrow.

"You told me she was pretty," said Pyrakis. "She is

enchantingly lovely!" And the blue eyes gleamed down on her. She was not so inexperienced that she could not recognize the glance of desired possession, and a hot blush rose to her cheeks.

Marc moved restlessly, but said nothing. Pyrakis raised her fingers, very very slowly, and kissed each one separately, his eyes still fixed on her pink face.

"What innocence, what delicacy!" he murmured. "To see her blush is like seeing a rosebud open."

Marc moved to the window and stood with his back to them, his hands jammed into his pockets.

"She is a pianist, Spiro, and an admirer of yours."

"Of course," purred Pyrakis, smiling. He turned Kate's hands over, inspecting them. "Your fingers told tales to me," he said, softly. "These little tips work hard. Either a typist or a pianist. I suspected a pianist, because of this . . ." and he delicately touched the pulse which beat at the base of her slender throat. "Sensitive, responsive little creature! Ah, if I were younger! To see that telltale beat stir at my touch!" He sighed romantically.

Kate looked helplessly at Marc's unresponsive back. "I . . . I teach, Mr. Pyrakis, I'm not an artiste . . ." she stammered, trying to withdraw her hands without seeming rude.

His face relaxed and a great charm flowed out toward her. "A good teacher is the bounty of heaven," he said gently. "I had a wonderful teacher!"

He released her hands and waved her to a chair. Much relieved, she sank into it, and Marc turned around and also took a seat.

Pyrakis glared at the door. "Where is that fellow, that thief, that rascal?" He bellowed in rapid Greek, and from somewhere in the house a loud voice replied in fierce tones.

Soon the old man reappeared, carrying a little table.

They sat around it, drinking black coffee and nibbling slices of honey-drenched pastry sprinkled with almonds.

Marc mentioned Pallas and Spiro Pyrakis bared his teeth.

"Has she begun to work yet, the lazy, idle girl?"

"Miss Caulfield is her teacher. Ask her," said Marc lightly, leaning back, his hands on the arms of his chair.

Pyrakis looked at her, one thick brow raised. "What do you think of her?"

"She is beyond me," Kate confessed. "I think she has great promise."

He gestured impatiently. "Of course, but the temperament! She will not work. A musician needs tenacity, humility, stamina. Pallas lacks them all."

"Kate has great confidence in her!" said Marc.

"Kate?" Pyrakis stared at her, his blue eyes caressing. "What a brusque name for such a feminine creature. I would call her . . ." he paused, looking her up and down slowly until she was once more bright pink. "Penelope!" he announced in triumph. "Yes, Penelope. She has that gentle, stubborn look of Homer's Penelope. Prepared to wait until eternity for her man. Fragile, delicate but unbreakable. That is what I like in some blond English-women . . . that look about the mouth that puts up the fence against all intruders." He grinned wickedly at Marc, his eyes acute. "You have seen it, eh? *Oriste?* It is so inviting. How can one resist that cool, sweet mouth? Any more than a little boy can resist the sign that says no walking on the grass, eh?"

Marc did not answer, but his face was set in rigid lines as he stared back at Pyrakis. The other man lifted his thick black brows slowly, speaking in Greek.

Marc reddened but did not reply.

Pyrakis turned back to Kate, his expression more

serious, and said, "So you have confidence in Pallas? Does she yet care about her work? Does she work hard for you? Does she worry?"

"I think she is so afraid to care that she pretends to be indifferent," said Kate, looking at Marc. "She thinks her family will never let her have a career, anyway."

Pyrakis turned to Marc, inquiringly. "Why does she think that, my friend?"

Marc shrugged. "We told her she would have to prove herself before we agreed. We did not say she could not try."

Pyrakis nodded and looked at Kate again. "You must make her work, little one. Be cruel, be ruthless, but make her work." Then he stood up, flexing his fingers. "Now I shall play for you."

He walked to the grand piano that dominated one side of the shadowy room, lifted the lid and laid his hands on the keys, flat and unmoving.

She had seen this odd trick of his before at London concerts. He said it was because he wanted to feel the piano before he began to play it, to sense the willingness of the keys.

He lifted his hands again and then broke into a series of fast, dizzying chords which startled her and were totally new to her ear.

"This is his own," Marc whispered.

Pyrakis played for an hour, totally absorbed, his untiring hands wrenching brilliant response from the piano.

When he stopped playing and swung round to face them, Kate was trembling with excitement. She could not speak, but her face spoke for her.

"I must go now, for my siesta," Pyrakis said. "You will lunch with me afterward?"

"I'm sorry," Marc apologized, "but I have just noticed the sky. A storm is in the offing. We must make a dash for Kianthos, I'm afraid."

Pyrakis shrugged. "A pity. I shall feel deprived. I was looking forward to more of Miss Kate's company. She is excitingly responsive, like a well-tuned violin." He kissed her hand; then, saying something in Greek to Marc, he bent and kissed her on the mouth.

Marc took her elbow. "We must hurry. I'll see you, Spiro."

He marched her back down to the harbor very fast, his face coolly shuttered, and helped her into the yacht.

They set off at once. Kate looked back at the island, its hills now dark and menacing with the approaching storm. Then she sighed. She would remember the meeting with Pyrakis all her life.

Marc shouted to her to come and help him; and she hurriedly obeyed.

She had done little sailing before but was light on her feet and quick-witted, so they worked together in comparative harmony.

"I don't like the look of that sky," he said anxiously. "I hope we get back before the wind veers, or we may be blown off course. I wish I had noticed the sky earlier."

They were within sight of Kianthos when the wind suddenly began to blow strongly, beating them to and fro as if the boat were a matchstick. Kate caught a glimpse of Marc through a turmoil of whipped spray and heard him shouting to her, but the wind blew his words away.

Then the boat seemed to fly upwards like a toy in the grip of a giant. She was thrown across the deck, cracking her head with such violence that she remained still with her eyes shut, the pain crashing over her unbearably.

CHAPTER FIVE

She lay crumpled against the side of the yacht for a moment or two, waiting for the pain to subside. Dimly, she heard Marc shouting anxiously, "Kate, Kate, are you badly hurt?"

She got herself up on one knee, staggering as pain shot through her head, and he bellowed at her to stay down.

"I can manage, but if you go overboard in this sea I won't be able to do anything about it!"

They fought their way doggedly, the coast shimmering through mountains of spray, but the wind was driving them off the whole time.

They rounded a sheer cliff, and Kate gasped in horror as she saw black rocks rising up, their jagged points like broken teeth above the water. Marc was desperately trying to avoid them, but the wind was too strong.

A grinding crash, the sound of splintering wood, and Kate again felt herself thrown about like a rag doll. This time icy water engulfed her. Panic made her strike out furiously, arms flailing. The cold water seemed to be dragging at her, pulling her downwards.

Then Marc swam up to her side, grabbing her by the throat from behind, turning her onto her back in a deft rolling movement.

"Keep quite still," he ordered. "Relax. Let yourself flop, but trust me. . . ."

Panic was choking her as she felt herself helpless, being towed like a stranded whale, but she forced herself to obey him.

He swam strongly, but she realized how tiring it must be. When they had passed the black rocks and were nearing the misty shoreline, she called to him to let her swim alone now.

"I can manage," she assured him.

He released her, and she swam beside him until they were in shallow water.

Panting, shivering, coughing, they lay on the sand, the sea flinging vengeful breakers after them. She heard a booming sound close by, like the breaking of waves, but realized it was her own heart.

Marc turned over onto his side and looked at her. "How do you feel?" he panted.

She laughed breathlessly. "Rotten. My chest is almost bursting after all that exertion."

"Can you walk? There's a goatherd's hut on the cliff. We'll get food and dry clothes there. The path is not as steep as the path at To Angkistri."

Kate flushed, remembering that day, and struggled to her feet. The wind whipped through her wet clothes and she shivered.

Marc was watching her with concern. "Perhaps you ought to wait here," he said.

She felt panic sweeping over her again. "No," she said quickly, "don't leave me here alone...."

His face softened and he held out his hand. "Let's go, then."

What, she wondered, as she climbed the cliff path at his side, had happened to her hatred and resentment? From their first meeting she had had a picture of him as an arrogant, overbearing tyrant whose every word put her back up. She had detested his self-assurance, his sarcasm and scornful dismissal of women as mere playthings. When had all that changed?

She flinched away from too close an examination of her new feelings. That she no longer bristled at the sight of him was sufficient food for thought, at the moment.

The goatherd's hut was built of creamy stone, rough and unfaced, but as solid as the rocks beneath it. The one small window was shuttered and the door closed.

There was no answer to their knock, so Marc pushed the door open and shouted. No reply came. The small room beyond was empty. A wooden ladder led up into the tiny attic bedroom from which wisps of straw protruded, leading Kate to conclude that it was a hayloft as well as a bedroom.

Marc went out again and walked around the hut, shouting. Then he came back and shrugged. "Nobody in sight. I'll get a fire going. There's an outhouse with plenty of dry wood stacked up." He opened a large wooden cupboard that took up the whole corner by the fireplace and produced a thick, natural wool sweater. He flung it to her, telling her to put it on while he got the wood.

Gladly she slipped out of her wet clothes and into the sweater. It was obviously intended for a huge man and fell to her knees, the sleeves hanging far below her wrists. But it was comfortingly warm, and she huddled into it with gratitude. She rummaged in the cupboard when she was dressed and found a pair of rough pants and a long white shirt that she thought would fit Marc.

He came back laden with wood, and grinned at her, his glance running over her sweater and the long bare legs beneath. "You do look funny," he teased.

Shuddering, she slipped her feet back into her sodden running shoes, then took her wet clothes outside to hang on the wire line that stretched between two small posts. When she got back, Marc had coaxed the fire into life and was standing beside it in the goatherd's baggy pants, the shirt in his hand.

She stood at the door, looking at the bare brown

shoulders turned toward her. Under the smooth tanned surface of his skin, the muscles rippled as he moved. Her breath caught as she felt an insidious warmth deep inside her, and Marc, hearing the little sound, turned quickly.

"You don't mind being alone here with me like this?" he asked, slipping into the shirt.

"Why should I?" she answered offhandedly.

He buttoned the shirt front, staring at her with narrowed eyes. "Some girls might feel . . . threatened . . . being alone with a man in such circumstances. This is a very isolated spot."

She forced a laugh. "I have too much common sense. You've just narrowly escaped drowning, after all. You're cold, tired and hungry. The last thing on your mind is sex, I would say."

He grimaced. "I see," he said on a strange note. "It is just as well you have so much . . . what did you call it? Common sense. Rather uncommon, I would have said. But I would hate to be stuck here with a female who expected rape at any minute."

"What we both need is food," she said lightly. "I wonder where the goatherd keeps it?"

Marc opened a drawer and produced a flat loaf of dark bread, sugar, a tin of anchovies and some goat's cheese in a yellow dish.

"Giorgiou always keeps his food there," he explained, "and there is coffee here . . ." producing a wooden tub. While Kate sliced the bread on the small, homemade table, he ground the coffee and opened the anchovies.

She toasted the bread, spread it with cheese and anchovies and held it in front of the fire until the anchovies curled slightly, and the cheese bubbled.

They ate the meal by the fire, sitting on low stools. The black coffee was hot and sweet. It ran through her like fire, making her sleepy and content.

"Are we going to try to get back to the villa tonight?" she asked.

Marc shook his head. "We wouldn't make it; the terrain is too difficult. I would not care to try in the dark."

"You would try if you were alone," she guessed.

He shrugged his shoulders. "As that situation does not apply, there is no point in discussing it. We must stay here until dawn. Giorgiou is bound to be back then. He is probably visiting his sister in the village." He threw some more wood on the fire and the flames leaped upwards. She watched them, feeling lazy and at ease.

"You can sleep upstairs," Marc told her. "The bed is only a straw mattress, but you must have some sleep."

She looked at the wooden ladder. Yawning, she got up and went toward it, then heard a distinct scampering above her head.

Marc leaped toward her as she screamed, and she flung herself into his outstretched arms without thinking, clinging to him, shuddering. "Rats! I saw one . . . its tail. . . ." She was almost physically sick, her teeth chattering with repulsion and horror.

He held her tightly, one hand clenched on her shoulder, his thumb moving over her delicate shoulder blade. "You're quite safe," he whispered, his mouth just above her hair.

"I hate them," she stammered. "Horrible, creeping things . . ." burying her face in his chest with tightly shut eyes.

"Kate, stop this," he said in suddenly hardened tones, holding her away from him. "You have been brave up till now. Stop it!"

The shock of his sudden coldness snapped her back to self-awareness. She was scarlet at once, realizing what she was doing. "I'm sorry," she said stiffly and drew away from him, her eyes on the floor."

"I am relieved to see you have some feminine reactions," he said, reverting to his teasing. "For a girl who came so calmly through a violent storm, shrugged off the possibility of rape with the utmost scorn and has been so levelheaded and sensible all day—you amaze me! Who would have thought you would draw the line at rats!"

She could not control the quick shiver that ran over her. "I . . . I don't like them," she said.

"Obviously," he nodded. "But they are clever little creatures, you know. I would have expected you to be more tolerant of them, the English are such animal lovers!"

She saw that he was attempting to put things back on a normal footing, and tried to respond. "They're like some men," she said lightly, "clever but loathsome!"

He grinned. "Present company excepted, I hope?"

Kate laughed. "Did that come too close to home?"

He grimaced. "I'll get some straw and make a bed on the floor."

Within ten minutes they were both lying on warm dry straw near the hearth, covered by a heap of thick blankets.

The room was dark except for the glow of the fire, and Kate felt her eyes growing heavy. She could feel every little movement Marc made, hear his regular breathing. How strange, she thought sleepily, to be here like this with him. She giggled at the thought of what Miss Carter would say if she could see them.

"What's so funny?" Marc asked softly, turning his head toward her.

She told him, still laughing.

"And your fiancé?" he asked. "Would he be shocked?" He paused, then added, "Jealous, perhaps?"

"Peter? Good heavens, no, why should he be? He trusts me."

Marc was silent for a moment, and she thought he had gone to sleep, but then he spoke again, making her start, his tone sharp and unpleasant.

"Oh, he trusts you, does he? But what about me? Does he trust me? A stranger of whom he knows nothing?"

She opened her mouth, but how could she bear to let him know that Peter was too absorbed in his work to care what she did?

He waited for her to answer, then said, "You have been engaged for a long time. When do you plan to marry?"

"Oh, some time next year," she said vaguely. "We haven't actually fixed a date."

He spoke abruptly, his voice hard. "When I get married it will be with all possible speed. No long engagement for me. I want to be certain of my girl."

Was he thinking of his French girlfriend, the model? "Do you hope to marry soon?" she asked.

He hesitated for several minutes before replying. "It is in my mind," he said slowly, at last. "But there are . . . problems."

"Your girlfriend isn't ready for marriage yet?" she suggested. So he was thinking of the French girl. Kate wondered what she looked like. Very beautiful, suavely dressed and sophisticated, she decided, with hard eyes.

He seemed to be choosing his words very carefully. "There is someone else," he said. "I have a rival!"

She heard the roughness of his tone and felt a knife twist in her heart. He was jealous of this girl. He must love her very much to reveal his pain to a comparative stranger like this. She forced herself to continue to talk, although she was feeling dull and miserable.

"I'm surprised you allow that," she said teasingly. "I would have expected you to sweep him away."

"Oh, I would like to," he said harshly. "But I am not sure of her. . . ."

"You're not sure you love her?" she asked involuntarily.

"Oh, I love her," he said, in a deeply shaken voice, "more than I thought possible. But it is she who . . ." he paused, taking a deep breath.

"Who can't make up her mind?" she suggested brightly. "I'm sorry." A thought struck her. "She won't mind about us, will she? About us being here like this, alone?"

He laughed bitterly. "I wish I could believe she did mind. But she would be totally indifferent." He paused, then added contenptuously, "As indifferent as your Peter."

Kate flushed and did not answer. They said nothing more, and she gradually fell asleep.

When she woke she found the fire out, the room cold but filled with cool gray light. Marc had gone, but her clothes, now bone-dry, were laid out for her on the little table.

Shivering a little, she dressed quickly and looked down with a grimace at her clothes. They were dry but needed ironing, and the salt had stiffened them so that they crackled slightly as she moved. A pale sheen covered them, a salt bloom that flaked away as she brushed at it with her hands. It was lucky she had been wearing practical denim, she thought.

She found Marc outside, walking to and fro with his hands in his pockets. He too wore his own clothes again. His white terry shirt and blue jeans were as crumpled as hers, but she felt a quick tug of her heart at the sight of him. It was strange how quickly she had grown accustomed to being with him. There was a dangerous sweetness about being here alone with Marc.

"Giorgiou came back two hours ago," he said. "He woke me, and I sent him to fetch Jake. He only has an old donkey that wouldn't carry two of us, and it is too far to walk."

"I'll tidy his house for him," she said.

"There's no need," Marc said brusquely. "I will compensate him for everything."

She felt herself going hot. "Money isn't the answer to everything, you know!" she snapped. That ill-advised remark of his somehow brought all her old resentment rushing back. Last night in their shared danger and discomfort, she had forgotten how wide the gulf between them was, but she remembered now.

Marc gave her a long, hard stare. "Giorgiou will be quite satisfied," he said harshly. "Do you think he would like you to act as an unpaid servant in his house, sweeping and washing? He would be embarrassed and bewildered."

"Who do you think does all the housework in my home? We have no servants. We do it ourselves." She turned towards the house, but he caught her wrist.

She looked down at his long brown hand contemptuously. "Let me go!"

His eyes were savagely angry. "You are not going to do any housework while you are on Kianthos! I will not allow it!"

"You? What gives you the right to order me about?" she gasped furiously. "You live in a private dream of your own, but I live in the real world, and a little sweeping and cleaning up will do me no harm at all."

"It will do me harm," he said forcefully. "You are my guest. I will lose face with my own people if they think I have guests who work like domestic servants."

Kate was almost in tears yet could not help laughing wildly. "I can't believe it! What a Victorian attitude!"

The blare of the car horn made them both jump. Marc dropped her wrist with a contemptuous glare. "There's Jake," he said, and she wondered if she was wrong in fancying there was a note of relief in his voice.

She looked at the little hut, hesitantly. Marc saw her glance and took her by the elbow, propelling her towards the waiting jeep.

"There isn't time now, anyway," he said with satisfaction.

"I ought to kick your ankle for that!" she hissed as they marched towards the jeep.

He laughed, with one of his bewildering changes of mood. "Try it, my girl, and see what happens!" He looked down at her. "Your jeans have shrunk a little. I'll get you some new ones. The seawater always ruins cloth."

She flushed. "There's no need, thank you. Denim is meant to stand up to salt water."

"What a proud, stubborn creature you are!" he murmured. "I am responsible for ruining them, remember? It was my yacht you were on when you fell in the sea. . . ."

"I'm responsible for myself," she retorted, "and they'll be fine when they have been washed."

Jake greeted them with a broad grin, which disappeared when Marc curtly told him to hurry back to the villa. "I've some business calls coming through."

The journey passed in total silence. Marc stared out of the window, his profile rigid. She glanced at him under her lashes, wondering what he was thinking about. He looked angry.

She was angry with him. His automatic gesture of money had offended her. Did he think he could buy everything? They had come through threatened death, spent the night alone, eaten a scratch meal cooked by both of them in harmony, and yet now he spoiled it all by offering to buy her new clothes. It seemed an attempt to reduce her to a lower level once again—to make her a subordinate, an employee, one of his small responsibilities.

It stung badly. All right, she thought, he's a millionaire and I'm just a schoolteacher whose salary wouldn't keep him in shoe leather! But I won't stand for a situation in which he is King Cophetua and I'm just the beggar-maid.

She brooded all the way back to the villa, ignoring the rugged scenery through which they passed, the tangled glory of yellow furze, the gray rock and tumbling green slopes. The cool mists rolled away and the sky grew bright, burning blue.

"Going to be a great day," Jake said hopefully as they climbed out of the jeep.

Marc ignored him, but Kate gave him a warm smile. "A lovely morning," she agreed.

Jake shot a wary glance at Marc's back, then winked.

Kate followed Marc up the steps onto the porch. As he held open the door for her to pass into the house, she looked up with a deliberately cool expression and said, "By the way, we never did decide how much we were to pay you for our holiday. You'll let us know, won't you?"

His face looked first amazed, then black with rage. She felt her nerves leap at the look he gave her. "You little . . ." he began violently, grabbing hold of her shoulders and shaking her.

"Marc! My son, what are you doing? Have you taken leave of your senses, to shake a young girl like that?"

Marc's hands dropped like stones, and he turned to confront his mother stiffly.

Frowning, she stared from one to the other, very pale and fragile in a black satin housecoat.

"Well?" she demanded. "What is the matter? Will neither of you tell me?"

"I'm sorry, Mrs. Lillitos," Kate said quietly. "It was my fault, I'm afraid. Marc offended me and I insulted him to . . . to get even." The words sounded childish and stupid as she said them, and she flushed hotly.

His mother threw up a protesting hand. "I am at a loss for words! But I am too relieved to see you both to be angry. Come, my son, kiss me!"

Marc obeyed, and she clung to him.

"I hope you were not too anxious, Mama," he said gently. "We were quite safe once we reached land, but I had no means of letting you know."

Sam tumbled down the stairs, dressed in a sweater and jeans. "Glad to see you, Sis," he muttered, hugging her clumsily. "We began to think you were in Davy Jones's locker." Then he threw a nervous look at Mrs. Lillitos and bit his lip.

She held out a hand to Kate. "My dear, I hope your holiday has not been totally ruined by such an unpleasant accident. I am so sorry this happened."

Kate smiled, shaking her head. "I'm pretty tough, Mrs. Lillitos. I was frightened at the time, but I'm fine now."

"But there is a bruise on your forehead. How did that happen? It looks very painful."

"I'll phone the doctor," Marc said brusquely.

"There's no need," Kate protested.

He turned on her, his dark face savage. "You'll see him! Even if you pay him yourself!"

There was an astounded silence as he slammed out of the room. Kate forced a laugh, conscious of her burning cheeks.

"I'm afraid he's angry this morning. The boat is a total write-off, you know." She looked at his mother nervously.

Mrs. Lillitos watched her thoughtfully. "Don't worry about it, my dear. Marc is a man of great depths of emotion. He is quickly angry, quickly calm. Next time you see him he will be his usual self, I'm sure."

Kate doubted that. After what she had said to him, Marc would dislike her intensely. His expression had been dangerously violent when he turned on her just now. She had the impression that he could almost have killed her.

She went to her room, meeting Pallas on the way. After a short chat with her, she had a long, hot bath. Gratefully, she lay soaking in the water, thinking back over the events of the last few hours. She must try to keep her temper. Marc couldn't help treating everything as a commodity to be paid for, could he? It was the way he had grown up, in a mercenary world.

I must see Peter again, she thought. Already the day she spent with him seemed an eternity ago, as though she had traveled hundreds of miles and changed totally in the meantime.

She must reassure herself. She got out of the bath, dripping wet, and stared at herself in the full length mirror on the wall. She even looked different. She could not be sure what it was, but her eyes had a new expression. They were more alive, more secretive, as though concealing something, even from herself. That look of youth was beginning to go. Her mouth had an adult bitterness in its curves.

She shivered, and began to dry herself vigorously. Slipping into her new dressing gown, she padded toward her own room, and met Marc coming out of his. He still wore his jeans and sailing shirt. They looked at each other in silence for a moment.

"I've phoned the doctor," he said curtly. "He'll be here in four hours. He has to come over from Epilison and this is not his usual day for visiting Kianthos."

Kate shrugged, "There's no hurry." She swept past him in a cloud of perfumed talcum, and he caught her arm.

"Kate," he said huskily, "why do you fight me all the time?"

She couldn't look up at him. She was too painfully aware of him, big and dark and dominating, standing very close to her. He waited for a moment, then dropped her arm and stalked away down the stairs.

He did not appear at lunch; nor did his mother, who was recovering from the shock of believing them both drowned yesterday. Sam, Pallas and Kate lunched quietly together. Then the doctor arrived, examined her and pronounced her perfectly fit but suffering from mild shock.

"No more excitement," he ordered. "Rest, relaxation." He spoke little English, but Pallas translated for him, while also acting as chaperone.

Kate spent the afternoon on the stone patio with Sam and Pallas, lying on comfortable canvas loungers and enjoying the sunshine.

The storm seemed to have blown quite away, leaving the island calm and peaceful. Out of the wind, the air was warm and still. The sun seemed almost hot on her bare back and legs.

She wore her new bikini, two delicate scraps of black cotton which emphasized her slender waist. Sam rubbed sun tan lotion into her skin, offering to perform the same task for Pallas.

"My complexion is intended for this climate," she claimed triumphantly. "The sun is kind to me. I never use those things."

Kate was very tired that afternoon. Her experiences of yesterday had left her weary, and she drifted off to sleep as she lay on the lounger. She did not hear Sam and Pallas get up and leave to play tennis, and they, considering her, decided it would be kinder to leave her.

She slept on for several hours, her skin beginning to redden as the sun poured down upon it, then woke with a stifled cry of pain as a hand touched her red shoulder.

Marc was crouching beside her, his face set grimly. "Now look at you!" he said furiously. "You have given yourself sunburn! I can't take my eyes off you for five seconds without you getting into some scrape or other!"

She turned and sat upright, wincing at the agony of her reddened back and shoulders. It felt as though red-hot needles were stinging her skin. Her head swam dizzyingly. She looked at Marc, her eyes filling with tears.

"Oh, good God!" he groaned, and the next minute had picked her up in his arms and was carrying her like a child into the house.

CHAPTER SIX

The doctor was back the next day and tut-tutted over her, waving his small hands and talking rapidly in Greek to Pallas.

"He says you have been very silly," Pallas translated, smiling sympathetically.

Kate had had a bad night. She had tossed restlessly, her whole body apparently on fire. "I didn't realize the sun was so hot," she said wearily, on the point of tears again. She could not understand why she felt so emotionally disturbed. The slightest thing made her burst out crying.

The doctor bent over, shaking his head and spoke again.

Pallas translated again. "He says that the sun was unusually hot yesterday, but you should never go to sleep in the sun at any time. And he says," she paused, listening, "he says that the lotion should help, but the pain will be bad for another day or two. And you are to stay in bed and do absolutely nothing until he comes again. It is an illness that makes you depressed, like the flu, so try not to cry."

Kate looked up at the doctor and smiled faintly. "Thank him for me," she told Pallas.

The doctor nodded as Pallas spoke and smiled back. Then he left, and Pallas gently tucked her in again. "Would you like to sleep now, or shall I stay and talk?"

"I think I'll try to sleep," Kate said. "This lotion has made me more comfortable. I didn't sleep at all last night."

"Poor Kate," sympathized Pallas. When she had gone Kate lay in the semidarkness of her room, gazing at the white shutters which Pallas had closed. Faint beams of light struggled through them and lay in bars across the floor. Her headache was better now, but her eyes felt hot and dry, and she was grateful for the cool shadows around her.

Marc had carried her up here yesterday and laid her gently on the bed. Through the hazy mist of pain she had stared up at him, wondering why he looked so savagely angry. She couldn't help getting sunburn. Then she had been suddenly, violently sick, and when she came back from her desperate race to the bathroom, found him gone and Sophia waiting with cool water and gentle, soothing hands.

Her eyes closed. She preferred to forget what had happened yesterday. It had been a traumatic experience.

The next few days were quiet and peaceful. Pallas and Sam came in every morning. Sometimes they played cards with her, or just sat and talked. Sometimes she slept for most of the day. The burning sensation had lessened gradually. Her skin was now merely hot and dry. It was beginning to peel in places, and she watched it discontentedly. She was going to look terrible when it flaked off on her back. She would not be able to wear her bikini for the rest of the holiday.

On Friday morning the doctor said she could get up. "But," he warned sternly, "no more sunbathing. No exertion."

She promised eagerly. "It's been such a waste of a holiday," she said to Sam.

He was looking pleasantly tanned, his freckles merging with his healthy brown skin.

He gave her his hand. "Come on," he said, "I'll help you downstairs."

"I'm not an invalid," she protested.

Sam grinned at her. "You've been acting the part pretty well, then!"

To give herself confidence Kate had put on one of her new dresses, a cool white voile, very feminine and delicate, with a full skirt which reached halfway down her calf, soft frills which left her throat bare, and tight-fitting sleeves.

She met Mrs. Lillitos as she and Sam were going down, and the older woman smiled delightedly.

"My dear child, how enchanting you look! A vision from the past. But you need a hat." She smiled. "I have just the hat you need, *ma chère*." She walked stiffly back to her room, leaning on her cane, and returned in a short time with a large picture hat of white straw, trimmed with one very floppy pink rose.

Kate stood still while Mrs. Lillitos adjusted it. Sam watched, smiling.

"Great, kid," he enthused. "You look . . ." he hesitated, lost for words.

"Beautiful?" Mrs. Lillitos suggested teasingly.

Sam grinned. "You took the word out of my mouth, Mrs. Lillitos."

"And it covers up my sunburn," Kate told them confidentially. "My back and arms are still very unsightly. I wanted to hide them."

They sat on the porch out of the treacherous sun until lunchtime. There was no sign of Marc, and Kate did not dare to ask after him, but she gathered later that he had been engrossed in business during her illness, and had rarely emerged from his office, which was at the far side of the house.

They were about to move in for lunch when Marc came out onto the porch. He stopped dead upon catching sight of Kate, and stared at her in silence for a moment, then said politely, "You look much better. How do you feel?"

She murmured a vague reply. Sam and Pallas discreetly wandered into the house, leaving them alone. Kate stood up, feeling ridiculously overdressed. Marc was wearing a light blue shirt and casual gray slacks.

"I went up to the temple and told your fiancé about your illness," he said abruptly.

"That was very kind of you," she said stiffly.

"He would have come down to see you, but he had to finish his survey, and as sunburn is hardly a dangerous illness. . . ."

"I see his point," she said, quickly breaking in. "Of course he wouldn't come until he had finished.

Marc's lip curled. "You don't mind?" he asked. "You lack the usual feminine vanity, then. Doesn't it worry you that he couldn't care less whether you are ill or not?"

"You don't understand Peter," she said hurriedly.

During her illness she had had plenty of time in which to think about herself, and she had come to a decision about Peter. She had made up her mind to ask him if he would release her from their engagement, but she had no intention of letting Marc Lillitos know that. She did not want to discuss the subject with him.

Marc was watching her with narrowed eyes. "Do you understand Peter Hardy?" he asked her coolly. "Do you realize what a selfish, irresponsible, coldblooded fish he really is?"

She flushed and walked past him without answering. She was still engaged to Peter. She would not be disloyal to him now.

That afternoon the other visitors arrived, and Marc drove down to the airfield to meet them.

Pallas was sulky as she sat with her mother and Sam, waiting for the black car to return. Mrs. Lillitos kept a stern eye on her and checked an attempt she made to escape with Sam to play tennis, while Kate sat back watching, wondering why Pallas was in such a strange mood.

The visitors arrived, talking in a French that sounded like machine guns rattling away, and Kate hoped that they spoke some English, or the rest of the holiday was going to become a nightmare.

Marc came in, ushering two women before him, smiling down at one with great charm and courtesy.

She looked around and gave a little cry, "Madam!"

Mrs. Lillitos held out her arms, and the other woman hugged her warmly. "*Ma belle* Hélène," murmured Mrs. Lillitos, smiling.

She was a tall, slender woman, with deep brown hair, brown eyes and a look of quiet sophistication. Her coat and dress were cut very plainly, but with exquisite taste, in a striking violet. They looked superb on her.

Mrs. Lillitos looked past her to the other woman standing beside Marc, one hand clinging to his sleeve, smiling up at him from wide brown eyes fringed by very thick black lashes. Her eyes were too heavily made up, giving her the appearance of a panda, with her white skin and black hair. She wore a figure-hugging black suit, very demure and yet very sexy. There was no blouse beneath it and the deep lapels revealed the white curve of her breasts and her slim white throat.

She was whispering to Marc and he bent his head, seeming amused, his eyes flickering over her appraisingly.

"Marie-Louise, *ma chère*," said Mrs. Lillitos firmly, and the other woman turned and walked over to her, still holding Marc's arm.

Kate stared at her. Was this, then, the French model with whom Marc was in love? She could not understand why he felt uncertain of her. She seemed madly in love with him, judging by her practised arch looks, her smiles and her air of possession.

She was very attractive, Kate had to admit. The silky dark hair was sleek and straight, drawn back from her face in a chignon. Her mouth was painted glistening red, her chiseled cheeks almost classically perfect. Yet there was a falseness, a coldness about her which made Kate dislike her.

Mrs. Lillitos introduced Sam and Kate to them, and Marie-Louise stared at her with insolence.

"A schoolteacher?" she repeated, then laughed, looking at Marc. She turned her head aside and whispered to him. Kate caught the words, "How irritating for you to have to put up with them, *mon cher*."

Marc did not reply. A man had come up the steps into the house and stood watching them all with a smile. He was tall, dark and about 24, with curly hair, pleasant brown eyes and a relaxed air.

"Jean-Paul," said Marc, "come and meet my sister's friends."

Pallas sat like a frozen statue, staring at her feet. The newcomer glanced at her, then at her brother, his brown eyes inquiring.

Marc said Kate and Sam's names. "This is Jean-Paul Filbert," he told them, "a cousin of ours."

He smiled at them, but his eyes rested longest on Sam, with curiosity and intentness. Sam was rather red, Kate saw. She wondered suddenly if this could be the man Pallas had told her about, the man Marc intended her to marry when she left college. Surely not, she thought, he's much older than Pallas. But she knew that, even now, arranged marriages were common enough in Greece. And families always liked to keep their money in safe hands.

"Marc darling," drawled Marie-Louise, "give me a cigarette. I've run out."

He brought out his cigarette case and held it out to her. She took one and put it into her bright red mouth. Marc flicked open his cigarette lighter and held it to her cigarette, bending down. She took his hand in hers and held it steady, gazing up at him with provocative eyes.

"Thanks, angel," she murmured, leaning back.

Marc straightened. "Now you must excuse me. I am expecting a phone call from New York."

"Angel, you'll kill yourself," complained Marie-Louise. "Work and no play, you know. You don't want to be a dull boy, do you?" Her lashes flickered teasingly. "Why don't you relax and enjoy life?"

"I cannot afford to," he said, lifting his shoulders in a shrug. "Money, like children, needs constant attention."

"But so do I, my darling," she said, opening her eyes wide. "I am going to compete like mad, Marc. Business must be prepared for a battle."

"With me as the prize?" he asked lightly, grinning.

"Of course!" she said softly. "And a very valuable one. I will not share your attention with anything, especially not a telephone!"

Marc laughed. As he walked toward the door he passed Kate. Their eyes met. Hers were deliberately blank. He gave her a mocking, derisive flicker of a smile.

She understood what he meant without needing it put into words. That is how a feminine woman behaves, he was telling her. That is how a man wants his woman; flirtatious, flattering, attentive.

Mrs. Lillitos rose soon after Marc had gone and said that she was going to her room to rest.

"I will come with you, Maman," said Hélène, slipping an arm around her. "We have so much to talk about, you and I."

Marie-Louise yawned. "I might as well have a nap myself. If Marc is going to be boring, I might as well not have come."

Sam and Pallas stood up, too, as Mrs. Lillitos walked slowly out of the room. Pallas said, "A game of tennis, Sam?" and Sam nodded.

Kate was taken aback to find herself thus left alone with Jean-Paul.

"You are also going to sleep?" he asked her, as she rose instinctively.

She shook her head, smiling. "I think I'll take a stroll in the garden. I've been ill for a few days and I need the fresh air."

"May I come too?" he asked, head to one side, scrutinizing her.

"Why not?" she returned politely, and they went out into the garden.

They walked beneath an arched trellis hung with vines out onto the lawn. The cypress trees and flower beds gave a quiet grace to the little garden, which was framed by a thick hedge.

"Tell me about yourself," said Jean-Paul. "A school-teacher, Marc said . . . how did you come to meet him?"

"I teach Pallas," she explained. "I teach music at her school, Cheddall."

He shot her a sidelong look. "Ah, yes, Pallas. And do you get on with her?"

"Very well," Kate said. "That's why I am here."

"And . . . the young man? He is your brother? Is that why he is here? Because of Pallas?"

"They're friends," she said carefully.

Jean-Paul lit a cigarette, after offering them to her. For a while he smoked in silence. Then he said, "Pallas thinks herself in love with him, perhaps?" His tone was diffident, almost embarrassed.

She shrugged. "I really couldn't say. I don't have her confidence in this matter."

He looked sharply at her. Kate met his gaze directly and frankly.

He sighed. "I see. But perhaps you have your brother's?"

"No," said Kate firmly, "I've never discussed her with Sam. After all, it's a very private subject."

He laughed incredulously. "Love is never private, Miss Caulfield. It is, above all else, a family matter. That is why, as soon as I knew I loved Pallas, I spoke to her brother on the subject."

She came to a halt and stared at him with total disbelief. "You love Pallas? But she's only 16; years younger than you. Almost a child, still."

"She will be 17 in two months," he said. "My mother was married when she was 16. I was born when she was 17."

"You are Marie-Louise's brother, though, aren't you?" she asked, puzzled. She had been sure Marie-Louise was older than him.

"I am her half-brother," he said. "My mother was Greek, a Lillitos. Her mother was French. Marie-Louise is five years older than me."

"Oh." Kate considered the information for a moment, then went back to Pallas. "Does Pallas know you love her?"

"She knows I wish to marry her," he said quietly. "I have not, of course, approached her alone. It would not be fitting."

Kate almost reeled with hilarious incredulity. "I can't believe it!" she exclaimed. "You talk like a Victorian novel!"

He flushed. "You are laughing at me," he said.

"I'm sorry, but I can't help it. No wonder Pallas was so awkward when you arrived!"

He was silent for a moment. Then he said, "You think she does not like me? Finds me unattractive?"

She looked at him, embarrassed, and saw the hurt look in his brown eyes. "Look," she said frankly, "Pallas is a modern girl. She doesn't want to be married off like a prize cow. She wants to—" she guestured vaguely "—live her own life."

"And I am not part of the life she wants?" he asked quietly.

"How do I know? How does she know, when she's never been given the chance to choose freely? Perhaps you might be the man for her. But if you marry her against her will you'll never know if you are."

"I see," he said slowly. "You think I should back out now? Tell Marc I have changed my mind?"

"I shouldn't really advise you," she said. "You may think me prejudiced on my brother's behalf. To be honest, I don't believe that he and Pallas are in love. I don't believe they will ever be in love. But I think that if Pallas feels under pressure from you and Marc, she may convince herself she does love Sam, and that will be a disaster for everybody, including my brother, because I think Sam is the wrong man for Pallas. They're good friends, but they are too far apart for anything more intimate."

"O wise young judge," he said gently, taking her hand between both of his and kissing it. "Thank you. I will speak to Marc tonight."

"And make sure he passes the word to Pallas," she said. "Insist on that being done immediately. Marc is capable of playing it by ear, and that might push Pallas too far."

He nodded. "I will be firm with him. And I am grateful to you for your advice; several things Marc had said to me in his letters had made me suspicious of some other intervention. I was not surprised to see a young man here."

"Marc didn't tell you?"

"He never mentioned Sam to me," he said. Then, by common consent, they dropped the subject and walked around, talking of the weather, Kate's sunburn, the world situation and other very natural subjects.

Dinner that evening was a far more lively occasion. Hélène and Marie-Louise talked to Marc throughout the meal, ignoring everybody else. Pallas and Sam ate silently, and Jean-Paul devoted himself to Kate.

Their frank discussion had left them on a comparatively intimate level of friendship. He had discovered a shared love of Bach, and discussed various recordings with her with almost professional enthusiasm and knowledge.

Kate felt Marc's eyes upon them from time to time, probing, curious, watchful. He was flirting lazily with Marie-Louise most of the time, fencing easily with her when she tried to provoke a show of jealousy by referring to her many admirers in Paris.

Her boasts of her conquests made Kate wonder if Marc were wise in not marrying her quickly. She could not believe that Marie-Louise did not desire to marry him. Everything she said, every look, said that she was ready and eager to be his wife. But was Marc not content, perhaps, merely to own the lovely French girl? Did he want to be certain of her fidelity? Perhaps he took her boasts of conquests too seriously, not seeing them for what they were, blatant attempts to make him declare himself jealously.

After dinner Marie-Louise put a sleepy record on the turntable and she and Marc danced in the lounge, her black head upon his shoulder, her body leaning close to him.

Jean-Paul leaned over and asked Kate to dance. She smiled and stood up, going into his arms. She caught the exchange of looks between Pallas and Sam, her brother's raised eyebrows and grin. But Pallas was not looking as triumphant as she ought to do if she was really indifferent to Jean-Paul. She was, interestingly, frowning.

Jean-Paul looked down at Kate. "How am I doing?" he asked with a mischievous grin.

"Is this part of your plan?" she asked, laughing. "To use me as a tease for Pallas?"

"You object?" he asked anxiously. "Your fiancé will mind, perhaps?"

"No," she said quickly, smiling, "he won't mind. And neither do I. It's in a good cause."

Jean-Paul looked relieved, and pulled her closer, bending his head to whisper in her ear, "You are a most unusual girl, Kate."

She smiled, then met Marc's glance over Jean-Paul's shoulder. Marc was not smiling. He was looking savagely angry again, the arrogant features dark and saturnine, the gray eyes biting.

Kate looked away. He was angry with her, of course, for flirting with his sister's promised husband. He probably thought her contemptible for attempting to steal Pallas's lover. She felt chilled but tilted her chin defiantly. Let him think what he liked. She and Jean-Paul were going to set Pallas free to choose for herself.

Later, Jean-Paul spoke discreetly to Marc, who looked a little surprised but gestured politely toward the part of the house in which his office lay. They walked out in quiet conversation. Jean-Paul returned alone. He spoke softly to Kate, his face grave. "I have done it. I told Marc I had changed my mind."

"What did he say?" she asked involuntarily.

He shrugged. "He said very little . . . I was rather surprised. But he seemed displeased. Of course, there had been no official announcement. It was just an understanding between us, so there can be no gossip."

"Did he ask you why?" she queried, wondering what Marc had thought of Jean-Paul's unexpected change of heart. She could imagine him being very angry, particularly after the savage way he had looked at her while she was dancing with Jean-Paul.

"No, he seemed very thoughtful. Perhaps he has some business worry on his mind. Marc and I are old friends, but I felt a certain . . . how shall I put it . . . distance between us. I did not explain my motives to him; I know he would try to persuade me to change my mind." Jean-Paul grinned at her. "He is an autocrat, as you must have realized. The Lillitos family obey him without question. And his business interests are so vast . . ." he lifted his shoulders in a Gallic gesture, "it is not surprising he is so dictatorial at times."

"It is irritating, though," she said, "and I don't think one should pander to his god complex. He isn't a little tin god, whatever he thinks."

Jean-Paul looked both astounded and deeply amused. "A little tin god? Is that how you see him?" He stared into her blue eyes, smiling. "As I said before, you are a most unusual girl."

Next morning the sky was a little overcast and Kate decided to take the opportunity of sitting out on the beach again, while the sun was not so hot. Pallas and Sam walked down with her, carrying huge sun umbrellas, beach balls and towels, and they spread themselves out in luxury on the deserted sand of the little bay.

There was a pearly mist on the water, hiding the sun, but no wind, and Kate stretched out on a towel, gingerly lowering herself in case her back began to hurt again.

Her peeling skin was well coated with the doctor's soothing lotion. She slipped sunglasses on and lay with her face in the shade of a multihued umbrella, a plastic air cushion under her shoulders.

The sea murmured soothingly, flinging whitecapped fingers upward toward them, then falling back again in little ripples, leaving the sand ribbed and pale.

Pallas was reading a biography of Beethoven; Sam was playing chess with himself and occasionally commenting rudely on his own weak moves. Kate did nothing at all, feeling her whole body limp and relaxed in the soft air.

She felt Pallas stiffening beside her, and looked up to see Jean-Paul and Marc coming down the beach.

"You look very comfortable there," Jean-Paul told Kate, lowering himself beside her, "but should you be out here in the sun so soon?"

She peered up at the sky. "The sun is still hidden in cloud," she pointed out. "I have to venture forth sometime, you know. I can't live in a tunnel like a mole."

He laughed and picked up her lotion. "Let me rub some of this into your arms before the sun comes out then."

She had already done so, but she meekly allowed him to do as he pleased.

"Your skin is so fair," he murmured, his hand slowly stroking up to her shoulder. "It is like peaches and cream. I always thought that a silly expression, but now I know what it means."

Pallas leaped impatiently to her feet, sending up a shower of sand. "Sam, come and play beach ball!"

Obediently, Sam closed his pocket chess game and followed her down the beach.

Marc was leaning on one elbow, watching Kate and Jean-Paul like a cat at a mousehole, his gray eyes narrowed. She found his unmoving, unreadable gaze disconcerting. What was he thinking?

Pallas and Sam were running closer to them, shouting as they threw the ball from one to the other. Suddenly the ball landed with a thud on Jean-Paul's back, sending him sprawling over Kate. He landed with a hand on either side of her, almost knocking the breath out of her body, and after the initial shock they both began to laugh.

"I'm so sorry," Jean-Paul apologized. "I hope I did not hurt you."

"Not at all," she smiled.

He withdrew slowly, looking down at her with a crooked smile. Over his shoulder Kate saw Pallas's sullen face as she took back the ball. Jean-Paul was about to lie down again when Sam said cheerfully, "Care to join us, Jean-Paul? Beach ball is more fun with three."

Pallas turned away, her dark hair swinging as she tossed her head, as though to emphasize her indifference as to whether Jean-Paul played or not.

He hesitated, his face uncertain. Kate smiled at him, "Yes, do play. I mustn't because of my back. I think I'll go to sleep for a while."

He stood up and slowly joined the other two. Pallas flung the ball at him, very hard, and it hit him in the stomach. Kate knew that Pallas had done it deliberately and felt like shaking the girl. But Jean-Paul straightened, looking steadily at her, and threw the ball back without a word.

Kate pulled her straw hat over her face and let her body

relax. The sound of the sea and the balmy air made her drowsy. Vaguely she heard the high voices of the ball players drifting away. The sea murmured on, gulls cried overhead and the sun came out mildly, caressing her skin. Behind her closed lids a warm orange flood of light seemed to focus, spreading through her like wine. She was lazy and content. Even Marc's silent presence seemed distant.

Then she heard a movement beside her. Sand scattered over her bare legs. She opened her eyes and saw Marc, still lying on one elbow, casually ladling handfuls of sand over her like a child.

"What are you doing?" she asked resentfully, lifting her leg so that the sand fell away.

"What are *you* doing?" he asked, with an odd emphasis.

"Trying to sleep," she snapped. Was it impossible to stand still in any relationship, she wondered. One always seemed to move either forward or back, certainly in a friendship with the opposite sex. With Marc she moved between hostility and attraction. Were the two interchangeable, like two sides of one coin? Today, again, she did not like him.

"Last night," he said conversationally, "I had a rather startling discussion with Jean-Paul."

Kate closed her eyes, straightening her leg again. "Oh?" She tried to sound bored, even indifferent.

"He was unofficially betrothed to Pallas," Marc said softly, "but last night he told me he had changed his mind."

"Really?" Kate yawned, flapping her hand over her mouth in a lazy gesture, her body stretching pleasantly with the movement. "Well," she went on, "Pallas is rather young for a man like Jean-Paul, I suppose."

Marc moved like a spring uncoiling, a hand on each

side of her, bending to whisper forcefully. "What do you know of a man like Jean-Paul? You only met him yesterday!"

She could not pretend to be sleepy now. She lay staring up at him with a suddenly dry mouth. He was very close to her, his dark face tense and menacing, the strong muscles in his brown shoulders rippling as he pressed his hands down on the sand. He looked very handsome, very dangerous and more attractive than she could bear.

"What does any woman know of any man she meets?" she countered warily, grateful for the sunglasses which helped mask her expression. "I just made a snap judgment, I suppose."

"You walked in the garden with him for an hour," he said bitingly. "I saw you from my office window. He kissed your hands. Rather fast work on his part . . . he was never the wolf type. You must have given him a lot of encouragement."

He was furious because Jean-Paul had broken his engagement to Pallas, she thought. But why take it out on me? He's looking for a scapegoat, but I'm not volunteering.

Aloud, she said, "He is a Frenchman, isn't he? They kiss hands to be polite."

"He hasn't been able to take his eyes off you since he arrived," Marc said tightly, his lips curling at the edges.

"Is that my fault?" she retorted. "What am I supposed to do? Hang out a sign saying 'don't look'?"

"You put up one saying 'don't touch,' " he sneered.

"That was only for your benefit," she flung, suddenly too angry to care, and then realized, with a sinking heart, that she had gone too far, made him blazingly angry.

His dark face tightened as though she had struck him. He glared down at her, eyes glittering like points of steel, and his mouth swooped, closing on hers savagely, his hands gripping her sore shoulders.

For a second her heart seemed to stop, then it thundered into life again, pounding in her ears. Her eyes seemed darkened and aching. Her fingers curled imploringly, arms rigid at her sides as she fought the impulse to reach up and touch him.

Whatever happened, she must not let him guess what that cruel, punishing kiss had done to her. As he drew away, breathing hard, she kept her eyes and lips tightly closed. After a moment she heard him walking away, his feet crunching on the sand.

Tears began to trickle down her face. So now she knew what she had always known since their first meeting. She loved him. But now she had been forced, by her body's treachery, to admit it to herself.

CHAPTER SEVEN

When the others came back she pretended to be asleep and let them wake her, so that her silence could be put down to the drowsiness of someone suddenly dragged back to a wakeful condition. She trailed after them back to the villa, dreading the first meeting with Marc, but when they arrived they found Sophia busily supervising the laying of the table, and she told them that Marc had taken Marie-Louise to Epilison to visit Pyrakis.

Kate felt a pang of unbearable jealousy at the news. She knew that when he kissed her, Marc had only been reacting angrily to what he believed to be her interference between Pallas and Jean-Paul. The furious glitter of his eyes had confirmed that. But she stupidly felt hurt that he should take Marie-Louise to see Pyrakis so soon after taking her there.

She went up to change for lunch and chose a plain green linen dress which somehow expressed her depressed mood.

After lunch she played cards with Hélène Lillitos, who was bored. She found the other woman quite pleasant, out of the company of Marie-Louise. Hélène seemed to make an effort to be polite to her. Kate had noticed that she always wore black or lavender, and wondered if she were still in mourning for her husband. But Paul Lillitos had died several years ago, so perhaps it was just that Hélène knew that somber colors suited her best.

Occasionally, Hélène's slight French accent was tinged with an American twang, which reminded Kate of her usual residence in the United States.

She asked Hélène where she lived when she was in the

United States, and Hélène explained that she had two homes.

"An apartment in New York and a little place in the hills in California. New York used to be an exciting place, but it is becoming a nightmare. One hardly likes to go out after dark, and never goes out alone." She shuddered. "So many of my friends have been mugged . . . you know, robbed in the street. It is incredible that such things happen in such a civilized city."

Kate asked her about California, and Hélène went on to describe her other home. "In the spring and autumn it is beautiful, but it is too hot in summer."

"The Americans call autumn the fall, don't they?" Kate asked.

Hélène laughed. "Yes, the fall."

"It is such a descriptive word," said Kate. "It conjures up falling leaves, the dying summer, everything."

Hélène looked at her carefully. "You like words?" Then she smiled. "Of course, you are a schoolteacher."

Kate flushed at the slight condescension of the words. "I teach music, not English literature," she said, a little more sharply than she meant.

Hélène said quickly, "I am sorry, I did not mean to offend you."

Kate relaxed. "I shouldn't have snapped," she apologized in her turn.

Marc and Marie-Louise returned just before dinner. Kate saw them walking up toward the villa, holding hands and talking with animation, and she had to fight down a wild impulse to run away.

She was sitting beside Sam on the porch, drinking an aperitif, and wearing her white voile dress. The weather had been rather sultry that afternoon. When the early morning mist lifted the sun shone like a brass coin in the sky, and as the day wore on the heat grew more and more oppressive.

Sophia darkly prophesied a thunderstorm that night, and Kate was inclined to agree with her. The lowering sky, the humidity, seemed to make one inevitable. Something of the same atmosphere oppressed her own spirits. She felt tense, restless, nervous.

Marie-Louise gave Sam and Kate a brief, indifferent glance as she walked past, but Marc nodded to them, his eyes sliding over Kate without meeting hers. He was looking rather serious, she noticed. She felt relief flood over her when the other two vanished inside. The first encounter had passed somehow, and now she need not dread having to speak to him.

At dinner Jean-Paul was unceasingly attentive, talking to her, watching her, smiling at her. She was grateful for the shield of his presence. Behind that shield she could build up her defences again. Marc must not be allowed to bulldoze them down again.

She and Jean-Paul had need of each other. She was under no illusions about his flattering attentions. He wanted to heal his pride, wounded by Pallas.

The rest of the table was more divided. Pallas barely spoke at all. Sam was absorbed by his shishkebabs and sweet, orange-flavored gateau. Hélène seemed distraught and nervous, and Mrs. Lillitos was apparently quite without appetite. Marc spoke anxiously as she sent away her plate barely touched, but she unsmilingly shook her head, obviously telling him that she was quite well.

Kate remembered the time before the arrival of Marie-Louise and Hélène, and wished it was back. There had been more ease in the party then; they had been quite happy.

After dinner Marc retired to his office. His mother

went to bed with Hélène in attendance, and Kate soon followed, feeling very low in spirits.

She heard voices from Mrs. Lillitos's bedroom, and thought that it was charming to see such affection between Hélène and her mother-in-law, particularly since Paul Lillitos had died so long ago. Would Marie-Louise get such a warm welcome into the family? She felt somehow that Mrs. Lillitos did not like the other woman. She was always polite to her, yet there was a coldness between them. Marie-Louise was always cloyingly eager to flatter Mrs. Lillitos. Perhaps the older woman found that distasteful. Certainly, Kate thought, the quiet warmth between her and Hélène was based upon respect for each other.

She washed, cleaned her teeth and got undressed, then sat in her frilly white nightie, staring at herself in the mirror. She was thinner, she thought. There were new hollows in her cheeks, a blue shadow beneath her eyes. Of course, she had been ill. Her appetite had not yet recovered since her attack of sunburn. But that did not account for the little droop at the corners of her mouth, or those telltale shadows in her eyes.

A soft knock on her door startled her. She slipped on her dressing gown and went to open the door. Her heart leaped into her throat as she stared, blue eyes wide and frightened, at Marc.

He was wearing an elegant dark lounge suit, formal white shirt and dark tie. He looked more like a successful businessman than ever tonight.

"Yes?" she asked, holding her voice steady by an effort.

He looked at her dressing gown, which she had not buttoned, that revealed the scanty white nylon nightie beneath.

"I'm sorry," he said, his voice deep, "I did not realize you had gone to bed."

She pulled the dressing gown closer. "What did you want?"

"To apologize," he said abruptly. "May I come in for a second? We need not close the door, if you are nervous about conventions." Without waiting for an answer, he walked past her into the room. Kate looked down the corridor, saw nobody, and followed him, leaving the door ajar.

He stood by her dressing table, looking down, his fingers lightly touching the lids of cosmetic jars, perfume bottles, her hairbrush. She waited, a few feet away, looking at the back of his dark head.

Then he seemed to jerk himself together, turned and looked at her, his face unreadable.

"I am sorry about that incident on the beach," he said formally. "I lost my temper."

"You blame me for Jean-Paul," she said quietly. "You're wrong. You should never have agreed to that arrangement, you know. It's that that has been at the bottom of the trouble with Pallas all the time . . . she felt she was under pressure, being forced to marry him."

"Arranged marriages work very well," he said defensively, "and I am certain Pallas liked Jean-Paul very much. I should never have sent her to school in England. It has given her crazy ideas."

She flushed. "Like falling in love and choosing whom one marries?"

"Exactly so," he retorted. "You chose whom you should marry, and see what a mess you have made of your life!"

"You have no right to say that!" she said angrily.

"Isn't it true?" he asked thickly. "Can you deny that

Peter Hardy is selfish and indifferent to you? All he thinks of is his work. He doesn't love you. He probably never has . . . or only for a short while. I do not suppose he will ever fall in love with anyone. He is too self-obsessed."

"You mustn't say this to me," she said weakly, unable to deny what had become obvious to her with every day that passed since their first meeting. No man who loved her could have abandoned her in a house where she would be thrown into Marc's company. Peter had not even noticed that she was uneasy with Marc. He would have been aware of it if he had loved her.

"Your mother should have said it long ago," Marc said coolly. "Even Sam is aware of it. It is obvious to everyone but you. Peter does not love you, Kate, and I do not believe you love him."

She felt her cheeks flame scarlet and her eyes seemed to lose the ability to focus. When her breathing settled a little, she said huskily, "My feelings are my own business. Was that all you wanted to say?" She was suddenly terrified that he might guess her feelings for him. He must go, she thought desperately. He must leave her alone before she betrayed herself.

Marc thrust his hands into the pockets of his elegant suit. "You won't listen to common sense, then? You hand out free advice to Pallas, to Sam, to me . . . why won't you take some back? Break off this ridiculous engagement and find someone you can really love who is a man, not a dedicated scientist."

She was so afraid that he would read her love in her eyes that she said fiercely, "Perhaps I have . . . perhaps Jean-Paul is the answer to a maiden's prayer. Do you mind going? I'm sleepy."

Marc turned like an automaton, his face rigid. "Very

well, good night," he said stiffly, then the door was shut and Kate was alone.

She rammed her fists into her mouth, quivering with agony. She could not possibly sleep now. She dressed again in jeans and sweater and slipped out for a stroll in the garden, but the thick heat of the air was no relief. After ten minutes she went back indoors, where it was cooler.

As she passed Mrs. Lillitos's room the door opened and Marc came out, his shoulders unusually bowed. He straightened as they met, his eyes running over her jeans and sweater in surprise.

"You've been out?" he asked sharply. "Alone?"

"I was too hot to sleep," she said uncomfortably.

He moved closer and looked down at her, the gray eyes narrowed. "Have you been thinking about what I said?"

Before she could answer, his mother called from within her room, and he turned back to answer her.

"Is that Kate?"

Kate looked in at the open door. "Yes, Mrs. Lillitos. I couldn't sleep; it was so hot."

Mrs. Lillitos was sitting in a deep armchair with a jigsaw puzzle on a tray in her lap.

She smiled. "Come and do this with me then, my dear. I cannot sleep, either. I am afraid there is going to be a storm tonight, and I do hate them so."

Kate went into the room. "I'm not very good at jigsaws," she said, "but I would like to talk to you for a while. I hate storms, too."

Marc had followed her in, and was standing watching them. His mother looked at him severely.

"Go to bed, my son. You look very tired. I shall be quite all right with Kate to keep me company. Young company makes me cheerful, and Kate is such a pretty child."

He nodded. "Very well, Mama. Good night." He hesitated, then added coolly, "Good night, Kate."

His mother picked up a piece of blue sky. "Now, where does this go, I wonder? All these blue pieces look the same shape."

Kate hunted for a moment or two, then at last managed to fit the piece into place.

"It's a hard puzzle," she said. "Do you do many of them, Mrs. Lillitos?"

"It helps to pass the time. Marc is so absorbed in the business, and Hélène is always in the States. Even my little Pallas is away at school."

Kate felt herself flushing. Did Mrs. Lillitos know about Jean-Paul's change of mind? Had Marc told her that he blamed Kate?

The older woman's fragile hand suddenly reached out and took hers.

"*Ma chère*," she murmured gently, "there is no need to look so tragic. You are worrying about Pallas, no? Comfort yourself. I have had a long talk with Jean-Paul today. He told me everything."

Kate looked up, eyes wide. "Oh!" she breathed with relief. Then, "You haven't told Marc?"

"Of course not, as Jean-Paul asked me not to do so, but I think you are both wrong. My son is quite capable of understanding the matter, if it is explained to him carefully. Pallas is a girl of temperament. Like a wild bird she flies hither and thither, struggling. She needs Jean-Paul's steadiness, his gravity, his French formality. He would be the perfect mate for her."

"But, madame—" began Kate, and the other woman smiled and shook her head, interrupting her.

"I know, I know . . . Pallas must think she has chosen him herself. I agree."

"You do?"

"Of course," Mrs. Lillitos smiled. "Pallas wants to be hunted, to be caught, but only with her consent. She does not want to be sold like a cabbage in the marketplace."

Kate sighed with relief. "Exactly what I think."

"But you do think it wise for Jean-Paul to flirt with you in order to provoke her into an interest in him?" asked Mrs. Lillitos seriously. "People may misunderstand." She carefully fitted several pieces into her puzzle without looking up and added, "As Marc does."

Kate's fingers trembled as she tried to fit another piece into an odd-shaped hole. Mrs. Lillitos gently took the piece away from her.

"No, *ma chère*, not there. . . ."

Kate looked up and their eyes met. Mrs. Lillitos searched the wide blue eyes thoughtfully, then Kate looked down again. They went on doing the jigsaw puzzle in silence until a sudden crack of thunder heralded the awaited arrival of the storm.

Kate saw her hostess flinch. "What we need," she said cheerfully, "is some soft music, to drown the sound of the storm. Have you got a radio?"

"We would waken the others," Mrs. Lillitos said regretfully. "But there is a record player in Marc's office. We could go down there, couldn't we? And his office is so far away from the bedrooms that we would disturb nobody."

"Won't he mind?" Kate asked anxiously. She did not want to run the risk of another row with Marc tonight.

"Why should he?" asked his mother, raising one fine eyebrow. She groped for her stick. "Give me your arm, *ma chère*, and we will solace our souls with music."

Kate laughed and guided her down the stairs and along the corridor which led to Marc's office. She had never been there before, and for a moment her curiosity mastered her manners. She stared around her, taking in the long, red leather-topped desk, the steel filing cabinets, the bookshelves and cupboards. It was a long, wide room, probably the biggest in the house. The windows were covered with wooden shutters. There was discreet strip lighting down the middle of the room, and a thick gray carpet on the floor. Leather arm chairs stood about the room. Everything was very tidy, very businesslike.

Mrs. Lillitos was watching her with a faint smile. "You are interested in the room?"

Kate flushed. "I'm sorry, I was being curious."

"Naturally. *Ma chère*, my son works very hard. He is the head of a vast modern business complex. It is not a . . . what do you say? A nine-to-five job. He works all hours of the day, sometimes. He gets very tired, very irritable. Because, of course, he is only a man. And men have needs they are sometimes too proud to reveal."

Kate plunged across the room, desperate to change the subject, afraid of what she might hear. "Is this the record player?" She knew that she was behaving rudely, but she had to protect herself at that moment against the pain of hearing his mother tell her about his need of Marie-Louise.

Mrs. Lillitos did not attempt to reopen the subject. She sat down in one of the thick leather chairs, and listened to the record Kate chose, a crashing piece of Wagner which rode down the storm and made it seem irrelevant.

When the music ended, the storm seemed to be blowing itself out, although rain still rattled against the shutters, and the wind blew the cypresses until their branches scraped along the walls.

Kate put on another record, since Mrs. Lillitos seemed reluctant to go to bed. This one was quieter, more conducive to a state of drowsiness.

"Ah, Bach," Mrs. Lillitos sighed, smiling. "Jean-Paul told me of your fondness for him. Marc too loves Bach, especially the Brandenburgs."

Kate forced herself to smile. She wished she had not been told that Marc loved her favorite composer. She wanted to be able to listen to Bach in the future without being reminded of her brief, unhappy stay here on Kianthos.

They heard the record to the end and then went up to bed. Mrs. Lillitos smiled and touched Kate's hand as they said good night at her door.

"You have been very kind to me, *petite*. I have never enjoyed a thunderstorm before!"

Kate laughed. "I'm glad you enjoyed this one . . . I did, too."

They had turned to part when a loud hammering startled them. It went on, growing in volume, and Marc's door burst open. He plunged out, wearing dark red pajamas, his black hair on end.

"What is it?" asked his mother.

He shot her a look. "Someone on the porch. . . ." He vanished downstairs, and they followed more slowly.

"Who can it be at this hour?" Mrs. Lillitos wondered.

Behind them doors opened, but, as the banging had now stopped, closed again. They found Marc standing in the hall with a young man wearing a soaking-wet jacket. As they arrived he ran out again into the rain, and Marc came towards them, frowning.

"There's been a serious rockfall on the Etrusci road," he said grimly. "Alex is going to try to get across to Epilison by boat . . . the telephone lines are all down here." He turned towards the stairs. "I'll get over to Etrusci now," he said. "The worst of the fall crashed on the roofs of the side street. There are a number of people injured; Alex doesn't know how badly. They are just digging them out."

"I'll come with you," Kate said urgently, as he turned to go.

He stopped and looked at her, expression inscrutable. "You?" His mouth twisted oddly. "No, stay here. It will not be a very pleasant sight."

"I did a first-aid course last year," she said quickly. "I learned how to cope with civil disasters. I can bandage, diagnose . . . do all sorts of things."

He grimaced, hesitating. Over her head he looked at his mother. Then he said, "Oh, very well!"

Kate ran upstairs and got out her jacket, put on a pair of rubber boots that Marc threw at her as she passed his door, which were rather big, then joined him as he came out of his room in sweater and slacks, a thick raincoat in his hand.

He looked at her, one brow arched. "Where is your raincoat?" And when she explained that she did not have one, he went off and came back with one of his mother's. He pushed her into it as if she were a child, buttoning it quickly. Then he waved her down the stairs and followed.

Mrs. Lillitos hugged them both. "Be careful, my dears," she said, and shut the front door behind them.

They took the jeep and drove through the blinding rain at a speed that terrified Kate. She said nothing but sat beside him, twisted into a corkscrew of fear, grinding her teeth and clenching her fists on the side of the door.

They stopped, suddenly, as the jeep ran over something in the road.

"This is as far as we can go," Marc said, peering through the darkness and the sheeting rain. Kate could see practically nothing, but she followed him out of the jeep, carrying one of the boxes he had brought down with him.

They stumbled over rocks for a while until they came to a place where the road was completely blocked. They had to climb down from the road on slippery, muddy grass, Kate clinging to Marc's firm hand to guide her.

The village of Etrusci lay at the base of a sheer cliff. The storm had dislodged rocks from above, sending them crashing down on the end of the village. Fortunately, only some 12 houses were involved, but the people who had been in them were only now being dug out of the ruins of their homes.

When Kate and Marc arrived they found the local priest directing operations, his long black beard wagging furiously as he kept the men working. He turned aside to greet them, staring curiously at Kate, then smiling when Marc said something in Greek to him.

"I've told him you know some nursing," he told her. "He says the injured are being taken to his house. I'll take you there."

The men were working like demons, shifting the rocks and fallen walls with every tool they could find, even using their bare hands. The rain poured down on them as they worked, soaking through their clothes and running down their faces.

The priest's house was already full of crying women, white-faced, terrified children and shocked old men who sat rocking themselves like babies in corners.

Kate took off her raincoat, rolled up her sleeves and set to work. Marc left one of the first aid boxes with her, took the other and shot off to the site of the disaster again.

There were already two women working with the

injured, a small middle-aged woman with a tight mouth and snapping black eyes, who seemed very efficient, but whose curt manner distressed the children even more than they were already; and a plump, slow woman with a sweet smile who moved very lazily around the crowded room. They looked at Kate, spoke in Greek, and then went on working when she answered in English, shrugging.

Kate began to wash and bandage the arm of one weeping woman. She comforted her, wishing she knew some Greek, then moved on to a child with a blood-soaked dress who lay nearby. She found that the blood had apparently come from somewhere else; the child was not hurt at all, only shocked into a state of complete disbelief. Kate stripped off the bloodsoaked dress, washed the child gently and wrapped her up warmly in a blanket before giving her a small glass of pure glucose and water. The little girl coughed, made a disgusted face, but seemed less stupefied as the glucose took effect. Kate patted her cheek, smiled and went on to an old man who needed help.

She worked for what seemed like hours until she found that Marc was at her side, taking her arm.

"The doctor is here, with the Sisters from the convent at Epilison. They will cope from now on . . . come home, Kate. You look worn out."

She straightened wearily, pushing back a damp hank of hair from her perspiring forehead. Her back ached, her head was throbbing; without a word she let him guide her out of the crowded house.

The doctor turned and smiled at her, shaking his head, and speaking severely, but with a great warmth and kindness in his black eyes. The two nuns with him nodded in approval like smiling children.

Marc slid his arm around Kate as she swayed a little.

"The doctor says you are a silly girl, but very brave and very kind. You have done excellent work tonight, but now you must rest."

She managed to return the doctor's smile, then Marc led her out of the house, where the cool freshness of the night made her head swim.

"Hey—" Marc caught her, as she stumbled drunkenly "—you aren't going to faint, are you?"

She laughed, her voice sounding high and unstable even to herself. "I feel quite drunk!" she confessed, giggling. "Everything is going around like a fairground."

Marc supported her gently. "Can you walk to the car? The road is still blocked."

"I think so," she said, trying to stop giggling. The road was awash with rain, but the purple sky was now clear and cloudless. To the east there were a few gray wisps of light, heralding the coming dawn, but the stars still flashed like tiny diamonds, and the moon sailed lemon-yellow above the shadowy hills.

They picked their way back carefully over the rock-littered road. Marc helped her into the jeep, climbed in and began backing up slowly, honking his horn to warn anyone coming up the road behind them. At a convenient widening he managed to turn the jeep and they drove home quickly.

Kate swayed with the movement of the jeep, her head feeling almost loose on her shoulders. So much had happened tonight! She had worked with such intense concentration that she had lost sight of everything but the job in hand; now the loss of sleep was catching up with her. Her eyes were raw and dry, as if rubbed with sand, and her throat hurt.

The grayness in the sky grew as they drove. "It will be

morning soon," Marc murmured as they drew up outside the villa.

Kate climbed out and stretched, yawning. Through the trellised tunnel at the side of the house she could see the green lawns of the garden glistening with rain, and on a wild impulse she ran around in the cypress-lined garden, then stood, breathing deeply, enjoying the fresh night scents.

Marc came up behind her. "You English lunatic," he said softly, "come into the house. You have been up all night and you are asleep on your feet."

She laughed and turned back. "I wanted to feel . . ." she paused, not knowing quite how to describe the feeling she had been possessed by at that moment.

"Alive?" he suggested gently. "I understand. It was grim, wasn't it? Nature can be very cruel."

"Yes," she whispered, remembering the child in the bloodstained dress. She had found out later that the child had lost her father in the rockfall. His body had been found in the ruins of his house. Only the arrival of her weeping, white-faced mother had snapped the little girl out of her dangerous state of suspended grief. They had clung together, loudly weeping, yet finding some comfort in each other.

Marc propelled her by the elbow into the villa. They went into the kitchen, which was large, beautifully equipped and tiled in orange and black.

Marc made Kate sit down while he put the kettle on the stove. "A cup of tea is what the English love most," he teased. "That will restore you!"

She sighed longingly. "It sounds heavenly! My mouth is as dry as a kiln."

He stood over her, very tall and dark. "Pyrakis said

your mouth was cool and sweet and inviting," he reminded her softly,

Kate was too weary to respond. She shook her head so that her blond hair fell loose from the band that had held it in place all evening.

Marc knelt down beside her and took off her muddy boots and damp socks, flinging them behind him carelessly. He treated her, she thought, as if she were a small child. Then he brought her a bowl of warm water and some soap. "Wash your face . . . it will make you feel better," he said, "and then soak your feet. We don't want you catching a chill."

He stood with his back to her, making the tea with deft movements. She carefully washed her hands and face, feeling relief as the sticky grime and perspiration sponged off, leaving her skin cool and clean. Then she put the bowl on the floor and let her feet soak gratefully. They were sore and hot, and the water lapped around them deliciously.

She looked down at her clothes with a grimace. Her white sweater was filthy with bloodstains, mud, and green streaks of grass. The jeans were in no better condition. One leg was matted with dried blood and the bottoms of both were black with mud from the wet roads.

"I look a sight," she said with a yawn, uncaring.

Marc put a fragrant, steaming cup of tea in front of her, with a slice of lemon floating on the top. She yearned foolishly for English tea, milky and sweet, but this was better than nothing. As she lifted the cup to her lips Marc muttered something, and she looked up, eyes inquiring.

"The veins are standing out on your wrist like whipcord," he said curtly.

Kate looked incuriously at her wrists. He was right. Beneath her pale skin blue veins stood out visibly. "They always do when one is tired," she pointed out. "I expect yours do, too."

He shrugged. "I am more used to late nights, perhaps. You must stay in bed all day tomorrow. We do not want you to be ill again. This has been an unfortunate holiday for you."

In more ways than one, she thought miserably. She drank her tea and stood up to reach the towel he had placed on the table for her. Marc walked to the side of her chair and took it from her grasp, crouched down and lifted one of her feet. She sat down again suddenly, in case she fell over.

"I'll do that," she said quickly.

He took no notice of her. Gently, slowly, he wiped the foot dry, holding it on his knee. Then he put it down on the floor and took the other, and did the same.

Kate stood up quickly, her heart quickening. She suddenly could not bear to be here with him any longer. It was too agonizing to have him being so kind in that impersonal fashion. She did not want him to treat her as a child; she was a woman.

"Good night then," she said brightly, edging towards the door.

He smiled at her. "Sleep well. I'll tell Sophia not to wake you. You can stay in bed as long as you like."

She nodded and opened the door.

"Kate," he said suddenly, moving toward her. She halted, looking around uneasily at something in his voice which she could not quite identify.

"I haven't thanked you yet," he said quickly. "You worked like a Trojan tonight. I am very grateful to you."

"It was nothing," she dismissed. "Anyone would have done it."

"Not quite," he shook his head. "Only someone kind

and brave. You got filthy and exhausted, and you were very upset by some of the things you saw. Don't push my thanks away, Kate."

She blushed, then smiled. "I'm sorry, I didn't mean to be curt."

"You are tired," he nodded. "Go to bed, my . . . my dear."

Kate looked up, smiling at him, and he slowly bent his head toward her. Her heart quickened into a thunder as she waited, lids drooping, lips slightly parted.

Then a voice behind them said sharply, "Marc, what is going on here?"

Marc straightened, stiffening, and his eyes went over Kate's head to the woman standing beyond her in the open doorway.

Marie-Louise repeated her question in a high, shrill tone. "Why are you here, in the middle of the night, dressed like that? Where have you been?"

Kate turned blindly and pushed past her without a word. As she fled up the stairs she heard Marie-Louise say, "You haven't been making advances to that little schoolteacher, have you, darling? You really must not flirt with people like that . . . they don't understand your little games! They take them seriously and get hurt."

CHAPTER EIGHT

She slept all the next day, dreaming constantly of Marc. She seemed to be fighting her way towards him through thick jungle, continually aware of hissing snakes underfoot that uncurled and slid away from her, making terror flare inside her. She kept catching sight of him, tall, dark and elegant in formal clothes, with a woman on his arm. Jealousy and despair made her fall back, sobbing, but then she would hurry onward. Always he was just beyond her reach.

Then, just before she awoke, she finally caught up with him, but he turned and looked at her with cold, indifferent eyes. She gave a cry of pain—and woke up, the cry still on her lips, to find herself in the darkened bedroom.

She sat up and looked at the tiny jade clock that stood on her bedside table. It was four o'clock, she noted. She swung her legs out of the bed and went to the window. The shutters swung back, letting the sunshine stream into the room. The light made her blink and her head throbbed. She sat down on the end of the bed, stretching sleepily.

There was a knock on the door a moment later. Kate called, "Come in," expecting Sophia, but it was Mrs. Lillitos who entered, smiling at her as she slowly limped across the room.

"I was in my room when I heard your shutters open," she said. "I have sent down for your breakfast, my dear."

Kate laughed. "Breakfast? I'm afraid I've slept later than I intended. I'm so sorry."

"Nonsense. You had every right to sleep after being up

all night. I slept very late myself. I thought we might eat together in here."

Kate smiled, "That would be very pleasant."

Sophia came in shortly afterward with a large tray and smiled warmly at Kate.

"*Kalimera, kyria!*"

Kate had begun to learn a little Greek from Sophia after her arrival, and was able to answer. "*Kalimera, Sophia!*"

Mrs. Lillitos laughed. "Ah, you are learning Greek. That is very good."

"I only know a few phrases Sophia has taught me . . . good morning, good night and so on. . . ."

"One must make a start somewhere," said Mrs. Lillitos, looking oddly delighted.

Sophia put the tray down on the long table under the window. She whipped off the cloth that covered it, revealing orange juice, toast, coffee and boiled eggs. A pot of English marmalade made Kate laugh.

"It looks delicious, Sophia. *Efharisto!*"

"Thank *you*," Sophia emphasized, smiling, and went out.

"We are all grateful to you for what you did last night," Mrs. Lillitos explained. "Sophia has a nephew who lives in Etrusci. You comforted his wife while she waited to hear if he had survived."

Kate thought back to the horror of the night before. "The tiny, dark girl who was very pregnant? Oh, I wish I had known she was related to Sophia; I might have said something more comforting. I felt so helpless, not being able to speak the language. But her husband was safe, so all ended well."

Mrs. Lillitos smiled. "I think she understood your feelings, even if she did not know what you were saying.

You have such very expressive eyes, Kate. They are the mirror to your heart."

Kate blushed hotly. Were they, she wondered uneasily. And if so, had Marc read their message last night, and seen her helpless love for him? Humiliation and shame burned in her chest. She made herself eat her breakfast, although it almost choked her.

Marc tapped on the door as they finished. He was looking very alive and vital this morning, his blue sweater and casual, dark blue slacks very neat compared to the clothes he had worn last night. He grinned at Kate. "How are you? You look very pretty."

She became embarrassingly aware of the scantiness of her nightdress and looked around for her dressing gown.

"Come back later, my son," his mother said sternly. "Kate is *en déshabille,* and not ready to receive male visitors."

"I only came to tell her that her fiancé has arrived. I sent for him this morning." His gray eyes danced challengingly. "I thought she might want to see him."

Kate felt her nerves jump, but she kept her face under control. "Thank you," she managed to say stiffly.

His mother went slowly to the door. "Come down when you are ready, my dear," she said gently. "There is no hurry."

The door closed and Kate was alone. Now there could be no doubt left in her mind about Marc's feelings toward her. If he had cared about her at all, would he have sent for Peter? Was this his way of telling her he was not interested and that she should concentrate on her fiancé?

Of course, he did not know, and she would never tell him, that she had decided to break her engagement.

She had faced her decision days ago. It had been a mistake to become engaged to Peter. It was fortunate that she had realized it in time. It would have been a disaster if she had married him and only then discovered their total indifference to each other. Marc had been so right when he said that Peter did not love her, nor she Peter. But, believing that, why had he brought Peter here now?

A flash of intuition came to her and she bit her lip. Of course! He was trying to protect his sister. He thought that she was interested in Jean-Paul and had brought Peter here in order to put a stop to all that.

Dully, she dressed in her plain green linen dress and went downstairs. She found the lounge empty. Sophia bustled past and stopped to tell her that Peter was in Marc's office and the others were all down at the beach.

The storm had left the weather golden and sunny again. Kate stood on the porch staring up at the bright blue sky. It seemed cruel that the world should be in such a holiday mood when she was so miserable and depressed. It ought to be raining all day.

Then she laughed at herself. What a conceited, self-obsessed thought! As if she was the only person in the world!

Peter erupted onto the porch beside her, his fair hair standing wildly on end, his eyes furious.

"Kate," he began hotly, "you must go and talk some sense into Lillitos!"

She looked at him in startled amazement. "What?"

"He says there's to be no expedition," Peter shouted. "He just said he's changed his mind. He won't allow anyone else to dig up there. He doesn't want strangers on the island. The man's insane. It can't be allowed!"

Kate looked at him silently for a moment. He had not seen her for over a week, she thought with wry resignation, and in that time she had been very ill with sunburn, been involved in a disaster, and for all he knew, was still weary. Yet he did not even greet her. No kiss, no word of pleasure in seeing her again. All that interested him was the temple up there on To Angkistri.

"I can't interfere," she said quietly, at last. "You must cope with it on your own, Peter."

He glared at her. "Kate, this is vitally important. The temple is the most wonderful thing that's ever happened in my life. It shows clear signs of a number of periods, so it's been in continuous occupation for generations. It was first founded in Mycenean times, but the pillars and roof were obviously much later. Oh, Kate, for God's sake . . . can't you see what it means?"

"Peter, I want to ask you a question," she said clearly.

He shut his mouth on what he had been about to say. Impatiently he waited, fidgeting.

"Do you love me?"

He gave her an incredulous look, running his fingers through his hair. "What? My God, Kate, don't drag in irrelevancies at a time like this! I have too many important things to think about!"

"Aren't I important, then?" she asked.

He looked embarrassed. "Oh, I'm very fond of you, of course, you know that! We're engaged, aren't we? What's the point of these questions, Kate?"

"Never mind your damn temple," she snapped, suddenly angry. "Listen to me for a moment. You don't love me, Peter. You are, as you said, mildly fond of me, but if I vanished tomorrow, I doubt if you would even notice."

"Oh, really," he said with distaste, "how like a woman to try to put everything on a personal level! Can't you think of anything but yourself? This is a crisis in my life. I need your help, and you're trying to make me pay for it with declarations of undying passion, I suppose."

Kate was so angry she could hardly speak for a

moment. "I'm doing nothing of the kind! I only want a little honesty between us. I'm trying to be honest with you."

He looked at her then with dawning awareness. "Oh, I get it! You want to break off our engagement? You've found someone else?"

"No!" she said roughly, "I haven't found anyone. I just . . . want to sort things out honestly."

"You do want to end things, though?" he asked.

She hesitated. "Oh yes," she said on a quick breath. "Yes, I do. I don't love you. I'm fond of you, but I don't really love you."

He shrugged. "Well, now that's settled, can we talk about the temple?"

She glared at him. "You don't give a damn, do you, Peter?" She pulled off her ring and threw it at him. He caught it awkwardly, looked at it with amazement and stuffed it into his pocket. "The temple—" he began, but Kate had fled.

Peter stared after her, grimacing. "Women! Really!"

Marc came out onto the veranda, smiling gaily, and Peter grabbed at his arm.

"Look, Lillitos, about this expedition. . . ."

Marc grinned at him, eyes dancing, "Try again next year," he said. "Perhaps I'll change my mind again. By the way, if you wish to leave right away, my plane is waiting on the airfield. I have had all your gear put aboard. When you have drawn up all your plans for the expedition, write to my office in Athens, to my personal secretary, Achille Danelos. He will get in touch with you and make the necessary arrangements. If there is an expedition, it must be a small one, and for the summer months. Right?"

Peter let out a long, relieved sigh and grinned. "Thank you very much. I'm very grateful."

"Jake will drive you to the airfield," said Marc. "Off you go."

Peter looked a little startled. "Now? But I wanted to see Kate...."

"I think she has said all she wants to say," Marc said politely. "If you do not leave now it will soon be too dark. My plane will take you to Athens, where I have booked a flight for you tomorrow at noon. You can pick up the ticket at the airport, it's in your name. Goodbye."

Stunned, Peter obediently walked toward the spot where Jake was waiting with the car. Suddenly he stopped, holding out the little ring. "Will you give this to Kate for me?" he asked Marc.

Marc looked at it, lying sparkling on his palm, and his lip curled scornfully. "I do not think so," he said with hauteur. "Keep it for your next fiancée."

Peter reddened, looked angry, then drew himself up and walked away. He did not dare antagonize the man, he thought. The expedition depended on the whims of this rude, spoiled millionaire. And anyway, Kate was right. They had not been compatible. She had never really been interested in his work. And if a man couldn't depend upon his wife to share his interests, what point in marrying? He looked forward to the excitement there would be in archeological circles when he dropped his bombshell, and he broke into happy whistling, forgetting Kate and everything else.

Kate wandered for a long time around the cliffs, then turned back and found herself in a myrtle grove. She stood, breathing in the fragrance of the cooling air. The heat of the sun was slackening and the moths had begun to flit over the thyme, their dusty wings glowing.

She thought back over the six years of her relationship with Peter. How had she come to think herself in love with him? She remembered how different he had seemed when she was a young girl, with his blond beard and vague professorial air. The boys she had known then had all been crazy, immature youths. Peter had seemed so much older, more responsible. And from a girlish crush she had let herself drift into a longterm relationship with no solid base.

She knew now that she had never been in love with him. He had never made her heart stop, as Marc did. His kiss had never exalted and petrified her. She could not blame Peter. It had been her own fault for allowing herself to be fooled by such a vague response. He had been too amiable to hurt her, and she had never seriously thought about his feelings.

Well, they were both free now, to find real love. At least, Peter was. She was not free; she knew that she would never love anyone as she loved Marc.

She heard a twig crackle nearby and turned to see Jean-Paul, looking lost and fed up, wandering toward her.

He smiled politely. "How are you today, Kate? You look pale. Marc told us how brave and good you were last night. I admire your courage."

She shrugged his compliments away. "Thank you, but really, it was only a little thing. You're looking rather annoyed yourself," she said, adroitly changing the subject.

He grimaced. "Pallas barely speaks to me. How can I woo her when she will not let me near her?"

"She's jealous," Kate explained, "and uncertain of herself. After all, she isn't even 17. Give her a chance. You're in too much of a hurry, wait a while."

"Easy for you to say," he said forcefully, "but hard for me to follow your advice. Do you really think she is jealous?"

"I'm certain of it. She's been very offhand with me since you arrived."

Jean-Paul looked delighted, "Then you think she cares something for me, after all?"

"I'm almost sure she does. It might only be pique, of course. But time will show you the truth."

He took her hand, stopped and held it up to stare. "Your right? You have lost your engagement ring!"

"I'm no longer engaged," she said, looking away.

He looked appalled. "*Ma chère*, I hope this is not my doing! I would not have done that for the world."

"It has nothing to do with you. My fiancé did not even know of your existence. It was a mutual agreement; we just did not suit."

He looked a little embarrassed. "I see. . . ."

She looked up at him and laughed. "Really, Jean-Paul, you are quite irrelevant, I assure you. I am not in the least attracted to you, which is what you are afraid of, I think?"

Very red, he met her teasing eyes. He laughed, a little shamefaced and embarrassed. "Pardon! I was nervous for a moment. The freedom of English girls astounds me. You are so . . . forthright!"

She grinned. "Well, it clears the air to know how you stand, doesn't it? Shall we go in to dinner?"

Dinner was, oddly enough, a very gay occasion at first. Marc was in volatile spirits, keeping up a barrage of teasing humor, his eyes constantly dancing.

But as the meal went on his mood seemed to deflate a little. Kate, who was quietly talking to Jean-Paul most of the time, was curiously aware that Marc's smile came less and less often, and that he was more and more silent. She wondered if he were feeling the effect of his very late night. Had he slept at all since? Glancing furtively at him she saw shadows beneath his eyes and tension lines around his mouth that seemed to show he had not.

Jean-Paul poured her another glass of retsina, his fingers touching hers as she held her glass toward him. He smiled at her gravely and she smiled back with warmth, liking him very much.

It was comforting to feel that she need not be forever nervously on edge against the probing intelligence Marc always aimed at her. With Jean-Paul she could relax, be herself, unconscious of herself. He was a very quiet, steady young man without Marc's vitality and tension.

She saw Pallas sullenly pushing her unfinished meal away, pouting, her small dark face all angles and frowns. What Pallas needed, she thought, was the sort of calm background Jean-Paul would give her.

"Shall we dance, *chéri?*" Marie-Louise asked Marc, as they drank their coffee in the lounge later. "Put some records on and let's dance!"

Marc shrugged, "Why not?"

He crossed to the cabinet and selected some records. As the music swirled out, sweet and soft, Marie-Louise archly turned out most of the lights around the room.

"Dancing in the dark is more romantic," she said to Marc, her thick lashes fluttering invitingly.

The room was shadowy now, the only lights left on being one at each end. Marc and Jean-Paul cleared a central space, moving the furniture back against the walls. Then Marc turned to Marie-Louise with a brilliant smile, and she glided into his arms. Pallas looked up at Sam, her face urgent.

"Shall we dance too?"

"What? This is music for the oldies," Sam said scornfully. "I don't know how to dance to it."

Kate laughed. "Just put your arms around Pallas and

let your feet move in time to the music," she advised, and added teasingly, "I won't tell your friends when we get back home. Cross my heart!"

Sam grimaced at her. "I'll feel stupid!"

"I know how to dance to it," Pallas said shyly. "I learned at my last school . . . the waltz, the polka and the military two-step."

"Good grief!" Sam shuddered. "Did they wear chastity belts, too? What a freaky establishment!"

Kate kicked his ankle. "Dance!" she commanded.

He grinned, shrugged and got up, giving Pallas his hand with a grimace of resignation.

Jean-Paul had watched and listened in silence. Now he moved nearer Kate and said steadily, "And shall we dance now, Kate?"

She nodded and they moved off, dancing very formally. He danced as he did other things, with precision and care. His feet slid neatly from step to step. He revolved, reversed, guided her through the dance, a slight polite smile on his finely chiseled lips, but not speaking.

Kate looked up at him. "You look as if you're hating every minute!" she said gently.

He looked down and the gravity of his expression melted a little. "You dance very well, *au contraire*," he murmured, smiling.

She stood on tiptoe and whispered in his ear, her face very close to his, "When you dance with Pallas tell her how pretty she looks tonight."

He looked puzzled. "I thought I was not to dance with her? I thought I was to . . . be indifferent?"

"Alter tactics now and then," she advised, still whispering. "See what a little change brings."

The record came to an end. Kate moved out of Jean-Paul's arms, nudging him discreetly. He turned to Pallas and asked her to dance with him next, and she flushed and glanced uneasily at Kate, who smiled cheerfully and took Sam's hand.

"Come on, brother, let me teach you how to do these oldie dances now!"

Marc interrupted her abruptly, leaving Marie-Louise and pushing Sam aside.

"No, no, we cannot have brother and sister dancing . . . Sam can learn the steps from Marie-Louise." He slid his arm around Kate's waist and she felt her heart squeezed inward, as though by a giant hand.

Marie-Louise looked hard at them, her eyes brilliant with fury. Sam stood awkwardly, trying to smile at her, but she pushed past him, flinging a careless, "I am going to get myself a drink . . ." as though he were a little boy.

Kate looked up at Marc. Didn't he realize how Marie-Louise resented his dancing with her? He was gazing past her, his jaw taut, the gray eyes hidden by drooping lids. She could not read his expression at all.

Anyway, she thought defiantly, why should she worry about Marie-Louise? Let Marc deal with her. She was here, in his arms for a brief while, and she determined to enjoy it.

As though he read her thoughts he glanced down, the arrogant mouth relaxed. "We dance well together, don't we?" he said very softly, his arm tightening around her waist.

She laughed, a little breathless with excitement, and a pink flower bloomed in each cheek.

His left hand gripped hers more firmly, his thumb sliding over the back of her hand and touching her ringless finger. "There is a white band where your ring was," he said teasingly. Over dinner he had very casually mentioned that Peter had already left the island.

Kate threw a glance up at him. "You know I've broken my engagement, then?" she asked unsteadily.

He grinned wickedly. "I heard every word," he admitted shamelessly. "I was eavesdropping."

She flushed hotly. "How could you?" she burst out. "You had no right," she said, remembering the conversation between herself and Peter.

He pulled her nearer to him, bending his head to whisper to her, "You took my advice, though," he said with irritating self-assurance. "I knew you did not love that fellow."

Burning with humiliation, she tore herself away and ran out of the room, through the front door and out into the quiet garden. As she plunged beneath the cypresses she heard him following her and turned angrily to face him, chin tilted defiantly.

"Please leave me alone," she said, her voice wavering.

Marc stood facing her, very tall and dominating, his hands in his pockets. Over the top of the hills the moon swam like a silver crescent, trailing misty clouds. The wind stirred slightly in the branches of the trees. From the house she could hear the faint sounds of sweet music, and a patina of yellow light streaked the darkness by the door.

"You don't mean that," Marc said, his accent sounding foreign for once, his voice thickened and uneven.

"I do!" she flung bitterly, hating him for that moment. She was so afraid he had guessed her love that she could almost have killed him at that moment. Her pride fought bitterly against her love, poisoning it.

He stepped closer and looked down, eyes glittering in the moonlight. His profile was dangerously masculine, the light shafting on the narrow planes of his cheekbones and jaw. "If I thought for a moment that you did . . ." he began slowly.

"Go away!" she whispered frantically, her hands pushing at his chest.

But at her touch, as though a dam burst, he grabbed her shoulders and pulled her close against him. She trembled, feeling his hard litheness pressing against her. "No, Marc," she whispered in terrified appeal.

"I've had enough of being treated like an old-fashioned villain," he retorted harshly. "Like all women, you aren't honest enough to admit your own motives. You make up fantasies and hide behind them. Well, I will not let you fashion a fantasy about me. I'm real." He bent her backward, his hands cruelly hurting her shoulders. "Look at me, Kate!"

She nervously obeyed him. His face was very close, the features etched sharply in the moonlight. His mouth had a cruel tightness below the mocking eyes. Then he slowly lowered his mouth until it touched hers. She gasped, trying to shrink away, but he pulled her nearer. His lips whispered against hers, "You want this as much as I do . . . do you think I don't know that? You can't hide from me forever, Kate. I want you. . . ."

Then his mouth was moving, hotly, urgently against hers, and she felt her body melting in passionate response. Through the rising passion and clamor of her pulses she dimly tried to reason with herself. He had not said he loved her. But her own desire was breaking loose from the bonds she had placed on it, and she knew she would not be able to resist much longer. She loved him too much.

The sudden interruption was like a splash of cold water on inflamed nerves. From behind them came a peal of silvery laughter, and Marc's arms dropped from Kate, his head jerking upward, a blind look on his face.

Marie-Louise stood there, head to one side, an artificial smile of amusement painted on her red mouth.

"*Chéri*, I am so sorry to spoil your fun, but there is an urgent call for you from New York. They said it could not wait."

He muttered furiously beneath his breath, hesitated as he looked at Kate, then walked quickly into the house.

Marie-Louise smiled at Kate, her eyes hard and glittering. "Marc is an exciting lover, *n'est-ce pas?* I hope you enjoyed your little interlude with him." She held up a hand as Kate stirred in restless anger, "*Mais non,* I am not jealous, *ma petite.* There have been so many pretty little girls! Marc likes his girls blond sometimes for a change, but he prefers brunettes. I would not want you to misunderstand him. He is a flirt, you understand? He likes to conquer. You say in England . . . he collects scalps!"

Kate was aching with bitter misery but she managed to hold up her head scornfully. "Why are you telling me all this?"

"To save you from being hurt. I know how serious you English girls can be . . . you might think he meant his little attentions. When I marry Marc all this will stop, of course, but until I am ready to give up my career I do not feel I can interfere with his pleasures. After all, he is a man! So please enjoy yourself with him as you wish, but remember . . . be prepared for dismissal when he is tired of you."

Kate's face was burning with humiliation now. She laughed fiercely. "Thank you, Mademoiselle Filbert. You are too generous."

"Ah, you are upset," said Marie-Louise sweetly. "I did not mean to hurt your feelings, or make you feel ashamed. Believe me!"

Kate walked away with her mocking laughter ringing in her ears. She went to her room and sat on the bed, clutching her head in her hands. Humiliation, pain, shame drove her wild. She bit her inner lip until it bled, then threw herself down onto the bed and gave herself up to a silent sobbing, her head buried in the pillow.

Echoes kept reaching her inner ears. So many pretty little girls, that woman had said. And, Marc is a flirt, you understand, he collects scalps. Well, she had suspected as much from the beginning. It was only confirmation of what she already knew. But how it hurt! She had revealed herself to him, left herself exposed to his mockery. Now he knew that he could have her if he wished . . . what next?

She must get away, she thought. But how? She was forced to wait until Marc allowed her to leave, and every moment she spent in his company was dangerous. She never wished to see him again.

So he thought he would amuse himself with her, did he? Play until Marie-Louise condescended to marry him? What had she said? Be prepared for dismissal when he tires of you? The insolence of it!

Then her blood ran hotly as she remembered the way he had whispered that he knew she wanted his kisses. She had noticed at the time that he had not mentioned love, only said that he "wanted" her. Well, now she knew what he had meant!

She had locked the door of her room. Suddenly she heard the door knob turning. Someone knocked. She sat up, rubbing her face.

"Who is it?" she whispered.

"Marc! Let me in!"

She stiffened. How dared he come here like this! Scarlet, hollow-eyed, she went to the door. "Go away!" she hissed. "Leave me alone!"

She heard him groan, "Oh, for God's sake, not again! I thought we got that straightened out!" And there was a note of tender amusement, of indulgence, in his voice that stung her.

"I meant it the first time," she said, "before you forced your disgusting attentions on me!"

There was a silence. "Kate," he said, his voice sharp now, "open this door!"

"I certainly will not!"

Again a pause, then he said almost pleadingly, "Kate, I have to fly to Athens tomorrow morning at dawn. I have to go to the States. I won't be back for a week at the earliest. Let me in, please. I must see you."

"We have nothing to say to each other. Now go away. You're boring me." She yawned noisily.

He rattled the door again, loudly. "Kate, for God's sake . . . I need you!" His voice seemed muffled by the door, strained and uneven.

"All I need is some sleep," she said lightly. "Don't you know when you're not wanted? Now, good night!"

The silence this time was so long that she pressed her ear to the door, to see if he was still there, and jumped away when she heard his breathing.

"For the last time, Kate," he began thickly, and she cut him short.

"Good grief, you're worse than a tax collector! Haven't you gone yet?"

She heard his heavy footsteps move away, then the slam of his own door.

He had gone, and tomorrow he would not be here when she got up. She would probably never see him again. She sat down on her bed, looking at herself in the mirror. Hollow-eyed, pale, her blond hair made her look like a negative, strangely ethereal and poignant. How long, she wondered, would this pain last?

CHAPTER NINE

The rest of the holiday passed in a dull dream for Kate. She walked, sunbathed and talked to the others without ever noticing anything around her. Pallas and Sam were comfortable companions by that time. They asked little of her, hardly seeming to notice the depression that was making her silent and withdrawn.

Jean-Paul's grave company was equally peaceful. He would sit for an hour without speaking to her, his smile calm and reassuring when she made the effort to speak. It was with him that she walked over the cliffs, swam and played a slow game of tennis. He was, she sensed, as inwardly troubled as she, and equally grateful for her undemanding company.

Sam did once mention Peter to her casually, with a brotherly pat on the shoulder. "I can't pretend to be sorry you've broken it off, Sis . . . Peter's a decent chap, but I never thought he was for you. You want someone with a bit more zing."

She had smiled briefly, without answering. Peter seemed like someone from the distant past now. She never thought of him, and Sam's comment was an irrelevant intrusion into the turmoil of her emotions.

The two Frenchwomen, Marie-Louise and Hélène, grew bored with Kianthos once Marc had gone, and two days later took off in Marc's plane, which had returned from ferrying him to Athens.

Marie-Louise tried to persuade Jean-Paul to accompany them on her last morning on the island.

Calmly finishing his rolls and cherry jam, her half-brother shook his head. "I am enjoying myself," he said.

146

His sister threw Kate a hard look. "Why do our men always like to play with pretty blond dolls?" she asked Hélène, her high voice insolent.

She had spoken in rapid French, thinking Kate would not understand, but Kate's French, though not perfect, was quite good enough to understand the insult.

Jean-Paul laid down his knife, wiping his fingers slowly on his napkin. "*Ma chère soeur*," he said coldly, "*tais-toi!*"

The sharpness of the command to shut up made Marie-Louise go rigid with fury, but she said nothing. When she came down with Jake, later, her cases packed to go, she said goodbye to Kate with forced politeness.

Jake struggled off, laden with baggage. Marie-Louise kissed Mrs. Lillitos, gave Jean-Paul a whispered comment about not forgetting that Kate was ineligible, and departed in a swirl of perfume.

Hélène embraced her mother-in-law more naturally. "I will see you again soon, Manan; sorry this has been such a short visit. Next time I will come alone."

Mrs. Lillitos touched her cheek gently. "You must marry again, my dear, and bring your new husband to see me. Paul would want you to be happy. No woman can go through life alone, you know."

Hélène flushed and did not reply.

Kate wished she were going with them. She was aching to leave the island before Marc returned.

"Kate, my dear," his mother said quietly, "will you help me back to my room?"

Reluctantly she obeyed. She had no wish to discuss Marc with his mother, but she sensed that Mrs. Lillitos wished to talk to her about something. Perhaps she is still worrying about Pallas, she thought hopefully.

Mrs. Lillitos sat down with a sigh of relief. "Ah, that is

much better. Kate, sit down near me. I want to talk to you."

Kate drew up a chair and sat down, hands folded in her lap, face under control.

Mrs. Lillitos smiled at her, dark eyes soft. "I have grown very fond of you, child. You have a soothing gentle presence . . . that is why it makes me sad to see you look so pale and unhappy. Won't you tell me what is wrong?"

Kate tried to laugh. "Nothing is wrong, madame. I am enjoying my stay here very much. I like to see Pallas having fun. She—"

"Please!" The older woman held up a hand. "Do not try to throw me off the track by talking of my daughter. It is you for whom I am concerned. You look ill. I see that you no longer wear your engagement ring, for instance." The dark eyes rested on her hands, then rose to search her face. "Is this why you are so sad? I had gathered that it was you who broke off the engagement and that you were relieved to do so. Yet you look depressed and lonely. Why is this, Kate?"

"I—" Kate broke off, catching her breath, then went on after a moment "—I expect I have not yet recovered from the attack of sunburn, madame. You have been so kind to me since I arrived. Kianthos is a lovely place. How could I not be happy here?"

Mrs. Lillitos sighed. "How reticent you English are! Well, if you will not discuss the matter with me, I cannot be ill-mannered and press you. But remember, Kate, I am ready to talk to you, to listen. And I am very fond of you."

Kate blushed. "Thank you, madame. I . . . I am fond of you, too." She stood up. "You look tired. Shall I call Sophia for you?"

"No, no, I shall sleep later. But run along, by all means, and enjoy your last days here, child. By the way, did Marc tell you that we have decided to take Pallas away from Cheddall?"

Kate was stunned. She halted, freezing on the spot. "No," she stammered. "No, I hadn't heard. You . . . you're not happy with the school? I thought. . . ."

"We are very happy with the school, but Marc has decided that Pallas should study music in Paris. He feels she would prefer the Paris Conservatoire to a London school. She is to have special tuition until she is 18."

Kate nodded. "I think that is an excellent idea. Pallas will be delighted. Does she know yet? She's said nothing to me."

Mrs. Lillitos shook her head. "No, we have not told her. You can do that if you like. She will take the news better from you. She is very fond of you, too, and I think she will miss you."

"I'll certainly miss her," Kate admitted.

Mrs. Lillitos smiled at her. "But perhaps, who knows, we will be able to see something of you from time to time?" She leaned back, closing her eyes. "*Au revoir, chérie*."

Kate went downstairs, feeling stunned. If Pallas left Cheddall she would certainly never see Marc again. Had he decided on this change of plan to spite her for refusing to let him come to her room the night he left for Athens?

She found Pallas and Sam playing a strenuous game of tennis, and watched them until Sam won. They wandered toward her, flushed and panting.

"I am exhausted!" Pallas puffed, throwing herself down on the grass.

Sam grinned at her. "Weakling! I could play another game and still win!"

Pallas grimaced at him. "The conceit of him! Did you hear that, Kate? Your brother is absolutely the most conceited boy I ever met!" She aimed a lazy blow at his leg with her racquet, not intending it to land. "Take that, you scoundrel!"

Sam danced nimbly out of reach. "You're just jealous," he observed loftily. "Women aren't called the weaker sex for nothing."

Pallas howled at him, "Male chauvinist pig!"

"Language, language!" Sam teased.

Kate interposed lazily, "Children, children, don't squabble!"

The remark had the desired effect of silencing them both.

She looked from one to the other of them, smiling. Their behavior strongly confirmed her belief that there was no romantic attachment between them. Only a brother-and-sister relationship could explain the squabbling, the rudeness, the teasing. They were too casual with each other for anything else.

"I just had a chat with your mother, Pallas," she said.

Pallas sat up, tossing back her long black hair. "Oh, yes?"

"She tells me that she has decided to send you to Paris to study music."

"Oh?" Pallas flushed. "When I am 18, I suppose, instead of going to a London music college?"

Kate shook her head. "No, not when you are 18. Now. Right away."

Pallas stared at her, eyes wide. "You mean . . . instead of going back to Cheddall?"

Kate nodded. "Yes. Are you pleased?"

Pallas gazed around, mouth open, eyes troubled. "I . . . I do not know. I prefer to concentrate on my music, of course. You know I detest my other lessons. But . . ." she looked at Kate, smiling a little, "I shall miss you, Kate." She grinned at Sam. "And you, you conceited boy!"

Sam said seriously, "I'll miss you too, Pallas. You must write to us from Paris. Lucky you! Imagine . . . Paris in the summer! A lot better than Greyford, I can tell you."

Pallas murmured, "Paris in the summer . . ." Her eyes were dreamy and far away.

Kate wondered if she were thinking about Jean-Paul. He lived in Paris, she remembered. Was that why Marc was sending his sister there? It would be just like him to have thought out such a devious plan.

They went back to the house in a cheerful silence. Watching Sam, Kate was convinced that her news had not upset or worried him. He seemed sorry to be parting with Pallas, but not unhappy.

Jean-Paul was sitting on the porch. His grave glance rested on Pallas, slight and cool in her white tennis dress, her racquet swinging, her long brown legs moving gracefully.

Kate saw a serious expression move over his face, then he smiled politely, as if at a stranger.

"Good morning again! A good game?"

Pallas linked her arm in Sam's, leaning against his shoulder with an unusually demonstrative gesture. "Wonderful!" she gushed.

Sam gave her a curious look, but said nothing.

When they had gone in Kate looked down at Jean-Paul's bent head. He was frowning slightly, his mouth drawn in at the edges.

"That was for your benefit alone," she said.

He jumped and looked up quickly. "I beg your pardon?" he mumbled, flushing.

Kate smiled at him. "You heard what I said, Jean-Paul," she said dryly.

He shrugged. "I wish I could believe you, but I am

afraid I do not agree with your diagnosis. Pallas, it seems to me, is far too interested in Sam. And after all, why not? I like your brother, Kate. A nice boy." He stood up, smiling politely at her. "As pleasant as his sister. I am very glad to have met you, Kate. It has made my stay here a charming one, after all."

"You make it sound so final," Kate said, watching him. "Are you leaving Kianthos soon?"

"Very soon, I think. But I hope I will see you again, Kate. Will you give me your address? If I am in England I might call and see you, perhaps. Or would you object to that?"

"No, of course not, Jean-Paul. I would like to see you again." She wrote it for him on a piece of paper he found in his pocket. "There you are!"

He put it carefully away. Pallas came out onto the porch and looked from one to the other, her face still very flushed. Kate wondered if she imagined the hurt look in the other girl's dark eyes.

They flew back to England as scheduled, but Pallas did not go with them. She was to proceed to Paris with Jean-Paul, it seemed. She did not appear to find the news unpleasant when her mother told her about the plan, although she did give Kate an uncertain look. Kate deliberately avoided any discussion of the subject. Pallas clearly wished to mention it to her, but Kate had decided that the less said the better.

If Pallas ever did marry Jean-Paul, she thought, it would be much later than her family had at first intended. That the girl had a great fondness for him she no longer doubted. She had watched her carefully and come to the conclusion that Pallas was attracted to him and valued his friendship. She would probably learn to love him maturely as she grew older, but there was plenty of time for that.

Arranged marriages might have worked well once upon a time, but Pallas had a more modern life in front of her. She would be working like a Trojan for the next five years at least and would have no time for romance. It would be much better to let her discover for herself whether she wanted to marry Jean-Paul or not.

While they were saying goodbye, Pallas unexpectedly flung her arms around Kate. "Goodbye, Kate. Thank you."

Kate hugged her back. "I expect I'll see you again some day, Pallas. It's been a wonderful holiday. I'm very grateful to you and your family."

"After what you did for me?" Pallas made a face at her. "You changed my whole attitude to life. Even Marc had to agree that that was so! Now look, he is letting me study in Paris. A year ago he wouldn't hear of it! It is all your doing!"

"I'm glad I helped," said Kate. Her throat was dry. So Marc agreed that she had changed Pallas? She could believe that, but he had not intended to be flattering, no doubt. He did not approve of the changes in his little sister.

It was difficult for her to say goodbye to Mrs. Lillitos. The older woman seemed quietly disapproving, as though Kate had hurt her in some way. Not that she said anything to her, but there was a puzzled, sad expression in the dark eyes as they said their farewells.

She looked down at the island as they flew far above it. The sea encircled the shores, as deeply blue as the sky, with white frothy foam topping the waves. The hills and valleys were leveled from up here. It looked unreal, dreamlike. That was what it was, she thought. An island of dreams. For her they had been unhappy dreams, but they had been beautiful, all the same.

She did not, in the long run, repent or regret anything. She still loved Marc even though she despised him. He was, after all, a rich and attractive man. No doubt many women in the past had been only too happy to amuse him. He could not have realized how differently she felt. She remembered the evening when he had taken her to the Black Swan, the obsequious waiters, the curious stares, the whispering. Living as he did in that artificial atmosphere, it was not strange that for him love should merely mean pleasure, a commodity to be bought like any other.

At least the visit had cleared her mind, shown her the falseness of her relationship with Peter. She might have married him and been disastrously unhappy.

England was oddly noisy when they got to London. Traffic deafened her. People were frighteningly busy and bustling. Cars hooted, pavements were crowded. It was a nightmare.

How quickly one became accustomed to the peace and quiet of an island like Kianthos, she thought. She had lived in an urban atmosphere for most of her life, yet after only two weeks away, she found her eardrums banging with the noise, her head aching, her eyes shrinking from the vivid colors.

It was not that Greeks did not talk loudly. They did. They shouted at each other in the kitchen at Kianthos. She had often heard the servants arguing, discussing, their gestures and faces lively and dynamic. But somehow it had all been more good-humored, less hurried. The pace of life was different.

Her mother embraced her warmly, then held her away from her to stare. "My goodness, you do look well!"

Kate laughed, "Do I?" She did not think that it was true. She felt tired and mentally worn.

Then Mrs. Caulfield looked at Sam and exclaimed over him. Brown, healthy, cheerful, Sam looked the very picture of health.

Later, Kate explained to her mother that her engagement was broken. Mrs. Caulfield took it calmly. She did not seem surprised, nor did she ask questions. Kate was relieved, yet wondered why her mother took it so well. Mrs. Caulfield had never, by word or look, hinted that she did not thoroughly approve of Peter. Yet she just smiled and said, "I see, dear," without so much as a blink of the eyes. Kate was puzzled.

On returning to school, Kate had an interview with Miss Carter. The headmistress seemed quite resigned to the fact that Pallas had left so suddenly after such a short stay at the school.

"I think we did her good, Kate," she said, smiling. "Don't you think so?"

"I hope we did," Kate agreed.

"I'm sure of it . . . she was very depressed and difficult when she came here, but at the end of term I thought she looked a changed girl, lively, cheerful, full of beans. A great improvement, and I must congratulate you. You did what I expected you to do. Now, did you enjoy your holiday in Greece?"

"Very much," Kate said politely.

After a few remarks about her own holidays in Greece in past years, Miss Carter dismissed her, and Kate went down to her class with a heavy heart. Now, she thought, it's all over. I can forget the entire episode. With Pallas gone, there was nothing to remind her of Marc.

She met Peter in the High Street some weeks later. He was talking abstractedly to a thin, brown-faced girl whose untidy clothes and intense face put her in the student body.

Kate's eyes met Peter's, and he blinked, then smiled without rancor. "Hi, Kate!" he called, lifting a hand.

She smiled back but did not stop. Some other girl, she thought, was going to have to learn that for Peter, the only thing in life was archeology. At least the little incident cleared her conscience. It was obvious that Peter was not suffering at all. He seemed perfectly normal.

The next weekend she went to the Lake District with one of the other teachers to do some hill walking. The weather was splendid, warm without being humid, and never too hot.

The weekend was very pleasant and, congratulating themselves, the two decided to do it again sometime. They met a party of fellow enthusiasts on the hills on the Sunday and spent the day with them. All in all, Kate came home feeling very much better.

But her mother looked up as she came into the kitchen, still smiling, and said, "Mr. Lillitos was here yesterday, Kate!"

Kate froze, her eyes out of control for a second, the pain flashing into them before she had time to force a smile.

Mrs. Caulfield straightened. "Kate!" Her eyes filled with concern. "My dear girl, whatever is it?" She frowned. "Something he did while you were there? Kate, he didn't hurt you in any way, did he?"

Kate laughed artificially. "Of course not, Mother. What an imagination you've got!"

"Kate, don't pretend with me," her mother said, stricken.

Kate sighed. "I'm sorry, but please, let's not discuss it. What did M . . . did he want?"

"He wanted to see you," said her mother, watching her uneasily. "He seemed angry when I told him you were away climbing. Wanted to know who you were with . . . I thought it odd, his asking in such an abrupt fashion. Kate, what's going on?"

"He . . . I . . . Oh, Mother, I don't want to talk about it," Kate burst out. "Really, I'd much rather forget him."

She ran out of the room, leaving her mother staring after her with a disturbed expression. She wondered what had happened between her daughter and the tall, dark Greek to make Kate behave so strangely.

Next morning, as Kate was leaving the house, the telephone rang. Mrs. Caulfield hurriedly shouted after her that she was wanted on the telephone. Kate stood, hesitating. "Who is it?" she asked warily.

"A man with a foreign accent," said Mrs. Caulfield.

Kate looked at the phone with loathing. "Ask who it is, and if it's Marc, tell him I just left for school."

Her mother obeyed with a worried look, and then said, "It's someone called Jean-Paul, I think."

Kate came back. "Hello, Jean-Paul!"

"*Bonjour*, Kate," he said quietly. "I am ringing from London, but I am just flying back to Paris. I have a little time. I want to ask you if you could come to Paris next week. Pyrakis is giving a concert and I have two tickets. I would be happy if you would come with me."

Kate was astonished. "Well, I . . . Thank you very much, Jean-Paul, but I—"

Quickly he interrupted, "I have English friends who would be pleased to put you up for the night. They have a large apartment and only one child, so there is a spare bedroom you could use."

Kate thought hurriedly. "That's very kind of them. Are you sure I would be no trouble?"

"They have said they would be delighted," Jean-Paul assured her. "They are very ordinary people, you understand, a family, but charming and kind. Henry Murray works with me."

Kate said, "I didn't even know you had a job, Jean-Paul!"

He laughed. "You thought I was a parasite? *Mais non,* I am a worker bee, I assure you. I run one of Marc's companies."

"Oh," said Kate flatly.

Jean-Paul was silent for a second, then he said, "But you will come, Kate? I would so like that. And Pyrakis would like to meet you again. I saw him yesterday and he mentioned you with great admiration."

Kate felt herself blushing. "Well, thank you very much then, Jean-Paul. I would like to come."

"You will fly? Shall I arrange your ticket?"

"No," she said hastily, "I'll do all that. When shall I arrive?"

"Saturday morning, perhaps? I will meet you at Orly if you give me the time of your flight. Drop me a postcard. I must run now. *Au revoir, ma chère.*"

"*Au revoir*, Jean-Paul," she said, as the phone clicked.

She turned to face her mother, still flushed. Mrs. Caulfield looked dazed.

"What was all that about?" asked her mother.

"Someone I met in Greece, asking me to Paris for the weekend." Kate kissed her quickly. "Must fly or I'll be late."

"Kate!" her mother called after her, protesting, but she was gone.

Mrs. Caulfield shut the door with a bang. Visits to Greece, trips to Paris for the weekend with strange men! What was happening to her daughter?

When Kate got home, her mother asked her about

Jean-Paul, and Kate told her enough to set her mind partially at rest. Kate could see that she was still longing to ask questions about Marc Lillitos, but with Kate obstinately set against discussing the subject, there was little her mother could do but accept the fact.

Kate managed to book a seat to Paris very early on the Saturday, and wrote to Jean-Paul's Paris address giving the time of arrival.

She was curious about his invitation. Why did he want to see her again? He had no interest in her, she was sure of that. But if so, what was his reason for inviting her?

She left for London Friday after school and spent the night in a small hotel near London Airport. Her flight to Paris arrived on time and she came through Customs to find Jean-Paul patiently awaiting her.

He took her bag, smiling. "I am glad to see you again, *chérie!*"

She glanced at him oddly. Suddenly she had a suspicion that he was up to something, but what?

They went directly to his friends' apartment to drop off her bag, and Kate liked the friendly English couple on sight. Henry Murray was short and sturdy with brown eyes and a quiet smile. His wife, Clare, had a French elegance combined with British informality. She chattered easily to Kate as she showed her to her room.

"It's nice to have someone to talk to now and then. Have you known Jean-Paul long? I like him a lot, but he is a bit deep, isn't he? Doesn't give away much. I wish you could stay longer than one night, but I suppose you've got a job like the rest of us. Although my job is Sacha. You'll meet him tomorrow morning, I expect. He's a devil . . . four years old and knows everything! Of course, we christened him Stephen, but everyone calls him Sacha, I don't know why. What lovely hair you've got. Do you mind my saying that? I hope the bed is comfortable. I do hate a lumpy bed, don't you?"

Kate was kept busy just nodding or shaking her head. She did not even try to get a word in edgewise.

After a cup of strong French coffee, Jean-Paul took her out to lunch at an expensive and luxurious restaurant, where she ate a shrimp omelette with green salad and frothy zabaglione. Afterward they walked through the shopping district, Jean-Paul patiently amused as she studied the windows with rapture.

He took her on a lightning tour in his little red sports car to all the famous landmarks, then drove her back to the Murray apartment to change.

Clare Murray greeted them cheerfully, carrying a small boy whose freckled face bore traces of jam and butter.

"Hello, can't stop. Sacha has disgraced himself again . . . more food on the outside of his face than the inside! Help yourselves to a chair. I'll see you later."

Kate laughed. Jean-Paul stared after Clare with awe.

"She always talks like that," he confided. "And when she speaks French, *ma foi*! It is ten times worse. French is a much faster language than English, of course!"

He left for his own apartment and Kate went to her room to change for dinner before the concert. She had not yet managed to discover why Jean-Paul had invited her. He had not mentioned Pallas or Marc or anything except the merest polite small talk. Yet she still felt that he had invited her here for a specific reason.

She wore her white voile, now her best dress, and Clare Murray admired it volubly.

Jean-Paul arrived on time, kissed Clare Murray's hand and took Kate off with him to dinner.

"Why did you ask me to come to Paris?" she asked

over their coffee, having decided it was time to be brutally frank.

Jean-Paul's hand hesitated as he lit his cigarette. Then he smiled at her. "I wanted to see you again."

"Will Pallas be there tonight?" she asked flatly.

He flushed. "I . . . I do not know," he murmured without meeting her eyes.

"Jean-Paul!" she reproached him. "It was a good idea for you to make her jealous, but not yet! You really must be more patient. I thought you agreed that you might try again in a few years?"

He smoked nervously, rather red around the ears.

"Well," he began, "you see, Kate, I met her accidentally last week at a party. Pyrakis was talking about you to Marc, and Pallas kept looking at me. She made a joke about you and me! But she was not really laughing, you know? And I thought she seemed . . ." he shrugged deprecatingly, "well, I thought. . . ."

"She was jealous!" Kate finished the sentence for him.

"Yes," he admitted. "Kate, I am afraid she will meet someone else at this Conservatoire. She will forget me. I cannot wait!"

Kate said soberly, "But is it right to use me as bait?"

He looked at her apologetically. "You are angry with me? I do not find it easy to talk to most girls, but you are different. I thought you would not resent it."

She sighed. "Well I don't, as a matter of fact, but I do feel you're trying to rush things. Why don't you just start dating Pallas and go on from there? Take her to concerts, not me."

He stubbed out his cigarette. "I am afraid she will refuse," he said simply.

"You're far too self-deprecating. You're an attractive man."

They discussed it as they drove to the concert, but Kate

saw that nothing would make Jean-Paul brave enough to expose himself to Pallas's tongue. His formal education had made him shy and backward with the other sex.

The concert was extremely enjoyable. Kate had never heard Pyrakis play so well. She sat beside Jean-Paul, listening intently and remembering the day she had heard Pyrakis play just for her and Marc. It seemed light-years away now.

As they drifted out afterward she caught a glimpse of a dark head. Her heart thudded harshly and she stumbled slightly, clutching at Jean-Paul's hand.

So it was that when she came face to face with Pallas and Marc, she was hand in hand with Jean-Paul.

Pallas gave them a cold nod. Marc's glittering gray gaze rested on the linked hands, then rose to encompass Kate, contempt and anger in his face.

CHAPTER TEN

Pallas spoke first, breaking the silence that seemed to lock them all together.

"Hello, Kate . . . I didn't expect to see you in Paris!" Then she bit her lower lip, blushing, as if she would like to recall the words.

"The concert was very exciting, wasn't it?" Kate said with artificial enthusiasm. She felt Jean-Paul's fingers growing cold against her own, but he held on tightly, as though afraid to let go.

"Marvellous! How's Sam?" Pallas smiled sweetly. "I do miss him terribly, you know! And he misses me, I know, according to his letters."

Kate blinked. She had asked Sam only the other day if he had heard from Pallas, and he had said he had not. She knew her brother too well to doubt his word. He would never write to a girl unless she wrote to him first. She smiled, however. "Oh, yes, I expect he does! But he's back at college now, of course." She did not add, as she could have done, that Sam was dating two entirely different beauty queens, one a redhead, the other a statuesque blond with a Swedish accent and strong Women's Lib views of the world.

It interested her that Pallas was refusing to look at Jean-Paul. He might have been invisible for all the notice she took of him.

Pallas looked sideways at Marc, who was standing silently listening, his hands jammed in his pockets. "Well," she said, laughing rather falsely, "we must go, Kate. See you some time."

Hating herself yet unable to stop, Kate let her eyes

flicker over Marc's dark, rigid face. Their eyes met. Hers shrank and fell before the look in his. Then he and Pallas had vanished and she was walking out of the theater with Jean-Paul.

They drove along the riverside slowly, neither in a mood for talking. Kate hardly noticed where they drove after that. By common consent they seemed to drift on in the red sports car, through street after silent street.

When the car stopped Jean-Paul looked up at the narrow house, then back at her with surprise. "Oh, I am so sorry, Kate . . . I have brought you to my own apartment by mistake." He grimaced. "And it is an error, I assure you, not a trick."

She smiled. "I'm sure it is, Jean-Paul." Then she looked at her watch and gasped in horror. "Good heavens, look at the time! It's two o'clock! What will the Murrays think? I haven't got a key. I'll have to wake them up."

He exclaimed apologetically, "It is my fault, I forgot the time! I am so sorry. But look, come in for a cup of chocolate before you go. I am too tired to think properly but too depressed to sleep. The Murrays will understand. After all, one is not in Paris for nothing! They will make assumptions, yes, but charitable ones!"

She hesitated. She did not suspect him of any ulterior motive, but she was wary of all men at the moment. Then she shrugged. Why not? She, too, was too depressed for sleep.

She followed Jean-Paul up into the old-fashioned elevator and they whined slowly upward, coming to a stop with a shudder of machinery. He unlocked a door along the dark corridor and stood back to let her enter.

It was an elegant apartment, very obviously that of a man, yet furnished, she suspected, with the help of Marie-

Louise. The curtains and carpets were of a traditional French Empire style. There were delicate pieces of porcelain along the white and gold mantelshelf. But the furniture was solid and masculine and fitted oddly with the more feminine furnishings.

Jean-Paul gestured at her to take a seat, but she said that she would help him make the chocolate. He led her into the tiny kitchen and they companionably heated the milk, talking very little.

"You were right, Kate," he sighed. "She barely looked at me. Well, I am finished after this. I shall ask Marc for a job elsewhere . . . in England, perhaps."

She stirred the chocolate. "Be more patient," she advised again. "Wait and see. Ring her in a few weeks and ask her out. If she refuses, don't make a big thing of it . . . wait and ask again."

They carried their cups through to the sitting-room and were just sitting down when the door bell rang.

"Who can it be?" Jean-Paul said, staring in surprise. "It's two-thirty in the morning."

He left Kate seated on the sofa, her head back against the fat striped cushions. She ran her fingers wearily through her hair. It was very untidy. Their long drive in the convertible sports car had whipped her blond hair into a positive birds' nest and she had not yet had time to comb it.

She sipped her chocolate and choked on it as she heard the voice of the new arrival behind her. Spinning around, with a scarlet face and wide, panic-stricken eyes, she faced Marc.

He was grim and furious, his eyes sparking at her. "Quite a surprise," he drawled, jamming his hands into his pockets. "Who would have expected to see you here at this hour?"

"Let me explain, Marc," stammered Jean-Paul, very red.

Marc raised a lazy, sardonic eyebrow. "Do, by all means. I am in the mood for fairy tales."

Jean-Paul looked aghast. "No, no, you misunderstand! It looks odd, I suppose, but truly. . . ."

"Looks odd?" Marc bit off his words with a fierce snap of his white teeth. "You're damned right it looks odd! Let me guess . . . Kate got locked out and had to beg a night's lodging here? Or she couldn't find a hotel in Paris ready to take her?" He laughed unpleasantly. "Or would it be more accurate to guess that this—" he gestured around him "—is the hotel at which she is staying?"

"I am staying at the apartment of Henry Murray," Kate intervened in a clear, cold voice. Her own anger had got the better of her now. How dared Marc burst in here with these wicked insinuations? What right had he? Just because he led an irregular and immoral life, there was no reason to imagine everyone else was the same.

Marc stared at her. "Henry Murray?" he repeated blankly.

"We went for a drive," she explained, "and were just having a drink before we went to bed." Then her last words echoed in her brain and, with a feeling of panic, she added hastily, "Before I went back to the Murray apartment, I meant."

Marc's face twitched suddenly, as though he were laughing at her. He looked at her slowly, his gaze mocking. "You need a comb. May I?" And offered her a comb from his inside pocket.

She knew from the derisive smile that he would not believe her hair had got rumpled driving around Paris. He was quite determined to believe the worst.

Jean-Paul swallowed audibly. "It is unfortunate, the appearance we present, Marc, but you must believe me that Kate and I . . . we were not . . . I mean, there is no . . ." he stammered to a silence, scarlet under Marc's sardonic, cynical gaze.

Kate stood up. "Oh, never mind, Jean-Paul. Let him think what he likes. I'd better go back to the apartment, I think. Will you drive me or shall I call a taxi?"

"At this hour?" drawled Marc. "Allow me . . . my car is outside."

"No thank you," she snapped, "I'd rather walk!"

He took her arm in an iron grip. "Now, don't be ridiculous. Why will women take these little things so personally? Good night, Jean-Paul. By the way, are you free tomorrow afternoon? My mother is in Paris shopping and would like you to go for tea with her and Pallas."

Jean-Paul looked at him incredulously, eyes alight. "Tea? Why, yes, I should be delighted! What hour?"

"Three o'clock? Good. Afterwards you might take Pallas for a drive to Versailles. She needs some fresh air."

Jean-Paul clasped his hands behind his back and swallowed. "I . . . yes . . . I . . ." he stuttered, visibly shaken.

Marc looked down at Kate, his gray eyes mocking her. He marched her to the door and pushed her out in front of him. She maintained a frozen silence while they were in the shuddering, droning lift, but when they were out in the street again, she shook his arm away.

"I'll walk," she announced, turning on her heel.

"Oh, no, you don't," snapped Marc, grabbing at her.

He pushed her into his car and slammed the door. Rigid with fury, she stared straight ahead as he started the car. But within minutes she realized that he was not driving her to the Murray apartment, which was only two streets away from Jean-Paul's, but was heading out of Paris altogether.

"Where do you think you're going?" she asked him angrily.

He did not answer, his face cool and remote in the dim interior of the car, but some minutes later he pulled up at the curb, near a small, tree-lined square. The wind gently moved the branches of the lime trees, and their cool scent floated in through the open windows of the car.

He turned, one arm along the seat, and looked at her. Her heart shook. It just wasn't fair that any man should make me feel like this, she thought. With a determined effort she made herself sit upright, her chin tilted defiantly.

"Take me back to the Murray apartment," she ordered. She was only wearing a thin shawl over her white voile dress, and it kept slipping down. "I'm cold," she said, her voice reproachful.

He put out his hand and ran it lightly along her thinly covered arm. It burned through the fine material and she jerked away.

"Don't touch me!"

He stiffened and a glint came into the gray eyes. "I'm tired of this game of yours," he said thickly. "As you seem to expect me to try to seduce you, I might as well be hanged for a sheep as for a lamb, as you say in England!" He leaned over her, holding her back against the seat.

Vaguely she thought of struggling, of pushing him away, but the clamor of her senses drowned the voices of common sense. When his mouth lowered to hers, she abandoned herself, heart pounding, and allowed her arms to creep around his neck and touch the dark hair at the back of his head.

He groaned and pulled her closer, kissing her throat and her closed eyes.

"Kate, my dearest," he murmured, "you love me, I can feel it! You couldn't kiss me like this if you didn't love me." His mouth moved back to hers, burning and dry on her lips.

She half sobbed but responded passionately, unable to resist him. When he drew away again she was weak with pleasure. Eyes huge, she stared up at him as he thrust a hand through his hair.

"Why the devil did you hold me off?" he demanded. "Why did you refuse to talk to me the night before I left Kianthos? I was almost out of my mind over you."

"I can't have an affair with you, Marc," she whispered through dry lips. "I love you . . . I admit it. I wish I didn't. But I'm just not the sort of girl who has casual affairs."

He stared down at her. "Casual affairs? What the hell do you mean? I want to marry you, you featherbrained female!"

She began to tremble violently. "Marry me . . . you . . . but . . . she said. . . ."

"She?" His voice was sharp. "Who said?"

"Marie-Louise," she said miserably. "Oh, Marc, what about her? She said . . . everyone thought. . . ."

"I wouldn't marry her if she was the last woman in the world," he said forcefully. "She is fun for a party, but hardly the sort of girl one marries. She is all surface, like a painted doll. In the rain the paint comes off. And with Marie-Louise, the glitter comes off when one knows her well enough. So what did she say to you, my silly darling?"

"She implied that you only wanted to seduce me," she said softly, half dazed by her joy, "that you would throw me away when you were tired of me. I couldn't bear it. I was so miserable."

"And that's why you wouldn't let me in that night? You thought I'd come to drag you into bed with me?" He grinned at her. "Was it a struggle, my sweet? Or did you righteously lock your door without a second thought?"

"Don't laugh," she pleaded. "I was desperately unhappy."

He wound his fingers in the silky blond hair and pulled her close to him, kissing her ear. "I felt pretty fed up myself. I came to ask you to marry me. When you wouldn't even talk to me I felt like smashing the door down. You don't know how close you came to being pretty savagely kissed that night. I lay awake thinking of what I would like to do to you. I couldn't understand your sudden changes of mood."

"I didn't want to love you," she said, sighing.

"That was obvious. I thought that once I had got Peter Hardy out of your life it would be plain sailing. It was a big shock to find I was still not home and dry."

Kate sat up indignantly. "How conceited! You thought that as soon as I was free I'd fall into your arms, I suppose?"

"Something like that," he grinned unrepentantly. "You see, my dear girl, I fell in love with you on our second meeting, when you threw truths at me like poisoned arrows. Your eyes fascinated me. They were so blue and so furious!"

"You deserved every word!" she said.

"So I did," he agreed lazily, with disgusting complacency. "I knew then that I had to marry you. I had been in love before, but never like that . . . it was like a thunderbolt. When you told me you were engaged I felt the first qualms. Jealousy was a new experience, and not one I enjoyed. I felt a little better after I had met the gentleman." His derisive tone irritated her.

"Peter is very nice," she said. "I just didn't love him."

"I've no axe to grind about Hardy," he shrugged. "I found him boring, personally," he grinned. "I enjoyed listening to you giving him his marching orders. I knew then that I was right . . . you didn't love him."

Kate pinched the hand that was fondling her neck. "Vanity again . . . you're too sure of yourself!"

Marc looked down at her, his face darkened by a look that turned her bones to water. "I wanted you so much that I just dared not believe you wouldn't feel the same," he said thickly, kissing her throat.

"Oh, Marc," she murmured joyfully, stroking the black hair.

"My mother gave me some hope when I came back from the United States," he went on. "She was sure you loved me. I came to England after you, but you were away, and your mother seemed so vague about who you were with. . . . I wasn't certain you weren't seeing Hardy again. I meant to come back again soon. Then I saw you with Jean-Paul."

"Jean-Paul was using me to make Pallas jealous," she explained.

Marc grimaced. "Stupid fool! But why did he break off his engagement if he still loves her?"

She explained and he groaned. "You again! I might have known! But Pallas adores Jean-Paul, you little fool. She has been miserable since we left Kianthos."

"I was sure she was reluctant to marry him, though," she explained anxiously.

"I talked to her about that," he said. "She said she was only unhappy because she thought it was a business arrangement . . . that Jean-Paul did not really love her.

He had never breathed a word of any affection to her, of course. It was all done through me. And Pallas hated the idea of an arranged, loveless marriage. But she is attracted to him, all right."

"Oh, dear, I hope I haven't harmed them," said Kate, biting her lip.

"I doubt it," Marc said. "Jean-Paul must convince her he loves her, that's all. She is still very young. He will have plenty of time." He reached for her and kissed her hard. "Never mind them. What about us? When will you marry me?"

"I don't know. . . ." She wriggled uneasily. "Marc, we come from such different worlds. Do you think we could make a marriage work?"

He looked very seriously into her eyes. "It has got to work. I need you too much to let you go. Don't start all that again, Kate, I couldn't bear it. When I saw you with Jean-Paul tonight at the concert, holding hands like a pair of lovers, I almost killed him. And I drove back to his apartment only to find him out. I waited around the corner, where I could see when his lights went on, and then when I got up there, and found you with your hair all tousled as though he'd been making love to you . . ." he drew a deep breath, looking savage. "I am amazed at how well I controlled my urge to knock him down."

Kate shivered at the look on his face. "Don't!" she said sharply.

"Then don't you ever again suggest that I could live without you," he said deeply.

She relaxed against him. "Just as you say, my darling," she whispered.

And Marc laughed softly and began to kiss her again with a passion that convinced her any further argument would be a waste of time.

Next day he called for her at the Murray apartment, and drove her to his Paris home to meet his mother again. Mrs. Lillitos was overjoyed by their news. She welcomed Kate with open arms, her eyes filled with tears.

"I am so glad! I knew you were the girl for my son when I first met you. The way he looked at you, spoke to you and of you . . . I could not be mistaken. But then you told me you were engaged, and I was worried and unhappy. I foresaw grief for Marc."

Marc looked down at Kate with amused eyes. "How right you were, too, Mother! She has given me more headaches than any business deal I ever put through. But I've got her now, and I mean to keep her!"

Kate grimaced up at him. "You talk as though I were a valuable piece of property instead of a person!"

"You are valuable, to me," he teased, and his mocking eyes brought hot color into her cheeks. "And as for not being a person . . . if you have forgotten how human I can be then I'll have to take you out and show you all over again, and it will be a pleasure, I assure you!"

"Children, children," said his mother gently, smiling at them, "I am too old for such a conversation! So, Marc, you have invited Jean-Paul to tea? Have you told Pallas that he is coming here?"

Marc shook his head, grinning lazily. "Let it be a surprise for her. I will even ask him to be my best man at the wedding. Will you let Pallas be a bridesmaid, *chérie?*"

"Of course," she said, still very flushed.

Three months later they were married from her home. At the reception she watched Pallas, glowing like an apricot in her orange bridesmaid's dress, toasting their health at Jean-Paul's side.

Marc grinned at her, his eyes intimate. "I do not think

Jean-Paul will wait too long before following our example!" he whispered.

She nodded, watching smilingly as Jean-Paul put an arm around Pallas and said something to her which brought a flush to her cheeks.

She had seen nothing of Marie-Louise after their engagement was announced, but she was here today, elegant and provocative in a vivid flame-colored dress. She had a handsome escort with her and seemed to be enjoying herself. But Kate had no doubts as to Marie-Louise's attitude toward herself. Once or twice the French girl had looked at her viciously, eyes full of hatred.

Nothing could mar her happiness today, though. She slid her hand through Marc's arm and he turned his head to look down at her with that intimate, smiling glance which made her heart turn over.

"Shall we slip away now, darling?" he whispered. "I'm in a hurry to be alone with you. Three months is a long time to wait for what you want."

Kate blushed and laughed. Moments later she had shed the lacy white bridal gown and was slipping down the back way of the hotel in which the reception was being held.

Marc grasped her hand and they ran to where his car was secretly parked. Behind them they heard whooping cries of pursuit, but they were in the car and away before the guests could catch up with them.

Looking back, she saw Sam waving and her mother tearfully smiling. Pallas and Jean-Paul stood close together, their hands linked.

"We have both got nice families," said Marc softly, as the car left them all behind.

"Yes," she agreed. "But I know a nicer one!"

He glanced at her, brows lifted.

"The one we're going to start some day," she said, smiling at him.

He drew into the curb, brakes screeching, and reached for her. "For that remark, my sweet, you must pay the forfeit!" he whispered as his lips reached hers.

And she gladly paid it.

MAN IN CHARGE

Man
in Charge
Lillian Peake

Juliet had more enthusiasm than experience. She was excited about running the boutique and full of new ideas.

Then she found herself in constant conflict with Drew Major, son of the department store chairman. She wanted to keep her job, but was afraid it meant fighting him every step of the way.

To Juliet, Drew was a conceited, cynical playboy with old-fashioned ideas about running the store and its employees. Yet she had to admit, he had more personal magnetism than anyone she'd ever met.

Furious about the feelings Drew aroused in her, Juliet was determined not to be his next conquest!

CHAPTER ONE

Cynthia Bourne suppressed a shudder and said to her daughter, "If they don't answer the bell soon, I'm sure we'll be eaten alive by those two horribly pretentious predators sitting there staring at us. They look ravenous and I'm sure they're getting ready to spring!"

Juliet laughed. "Now that you mention it, they do look hungry."

The sphinxlike stone lions her mother referred to stood guard over the entrance like two formidable and socially selective butlers. Their petrified scowls, forever fixed, were plainly intended to impress on would-be visitors that only the most favored were allowed to go unmolested past their watchful eyes and escape injury from their outspread, sculptured claws.

The Major residence was a rambling, two-storied building that had been constructed almost 200 years earlier in the manner of the great country houses of the day.

Its dusky red brick was time-mellowed and soothing to the eye. The white-pillared front entrance, in common with the lions, seemed to convey the impression that it was decidedly fastidious about the people it allowed to cross its threshold. No irreverent feet, it seemed to say, would be allowed to tread on the sacred pile of the deeply luxurious carpet revealed as the door came open at last.

Warren Major, in his fifties, eyes alert and questing, passed his glance lightly over the girl on the doorstep to rest with ill-disguised eagerness on the face of the woman at her side.

His hand came out. "Cynthia! Thirty years, isn't it?"

"Must be," Cynthia Bourne replied, stepping into the hall and putting her hand in his.

"Unbelievable," said their host. "You've hardly changed."

Cynthia laughed. "Nor you, although," she eyed him, "there's a little more of you now than there used to be!" With some pride she added, "This is my daughter, Juliet." Her face grew serious. "It was good of you to see us, Warren. I hate having to ask favors of you, but in the circumstances. . . ."

"Think nothing of it." He took Juliet's hand. "Looking at you, my dear, takes me back 30 years." He led them into the main drawing room. Juliet rose to the occasion and gazed around with the admiration obviously expected of visitors to the house.

There was a nebulous impression of gold and gilt, velvet and satin, the kind of comfort—if such a word could be applied to such an atmosphere—that only genuine affluence could achieve. Her gaze adjusted and she found herself caught unawares, like the click of a camera shutter, by two quizzical eyes belonging to a man standing in the doorway.

"My son," Warren said. "Drew, Cynthia Bourne, my very old friend. Her daughter, Juliet."

With studied politeness the son's hand rested first in the mother's, then in the daughter's. He seemed aloof but, Juliet decided, charitably trying to find excuses, it could have been his height that gave a false impression.

"My wife." Warren's voice was abrupt and his hand moved toward the woman on the couch. "Mildred."

Mildred Major stretched her thin lips only so far, as though a broader smile might crack the parchmentlike material her cheeks seemed to be made of. She lifted her right hand a few inches in greeting, but did not proffer it to be shaken.

"Good of you to ask us," Cynthia said to break the awkward silence.

"Not at all," said Mildred in a high, birdlike voice. "It was Warren's idea, not mine."

"Yes, well," said Warren, over-hearty, "what shall we do first?"

"Show them around," his wife advised, rising from the couch, "while I supervise the tea."

"Drew," his father moved his hand with a flourish toward Juliet, "be this young lady's guide. I'll be her mother's."

So Drew Major, tall, black-haired, in his early thirties, strolled beside Juliet, his good looks sharpened into arrogance by the aristocratic way he held his head. His manner was nonchalant, his air slightly bored, as if he could have thought of many better things to do than show a wide-eyed young woman about his father's residence.

His eyes were a little derisive as he raised first his right hand then his left to indicate the elegance and luxury of one bedroom after another, the elaborate furnishings of the small drawing room, the equally imposing living room and the long and austerely gracious dining hall.

He smiled slightly. "I'm sorry to inflict all this on you, but I trust you're suitably impressed? My father intends you to be. He never tires of showing his visitors the concrete evidence of the fruits of his lifetime of effort, the rich rewards of his self-taught business acumen. You're his guest, so you must show the appropriate appreciation. You mustn't let him down!"

He was being cynical, but Juliet replied with sincerity,

"Of course I'm impressed. I think the whole place is beautiful, the building as well as its contents."

He looked into her face. "I do believe you mean it. Tell my father that and he'll give you anything you ask for—even the job you seem to be after in the family business."

She flushed. "You've heard about that?"

"Of course. I'm the company manager, in other words, the man in charge. My father's the chairman of the company, but his desk is as innocent of work as the tray of a baby's highchair. He sits—metaphorically—with his feet up all day. I do the work. I hold the reins and occasionally, but only when necessary—" his voice altered subtly "—wield the whip."

"I see." She was silent for a few moments. "In that case, Mr. Major, I'm sorry."

"What about?" He looked surprised.

"My mother's request. You don't have to give me a job in your firm just because she asked you to. I don't believe in nepotism and this is really a form of it."

"And of course—" his eyes were mocking "—you wouldn't go against your principles, even when you would be the beneficiary, would you?"

"I . . . I. . . ." She squirmed at his sarcasm and knew he had caught her out. Of course she would take any job he offered her. In the circumstances she had to.

He knew it, too. He smiled with satisfaction. "Don't worry about your principles. We'll find room for you somewhere and I promise you that the job won't be a sinecure. If you're employed in a Major department store, you have to work. I'll make damned sure you earn your money like all the others. You'll have me to reckon with if you don't come up to expectations."

He smiled, and it was then that she realized how much this man irritated her. Something in his manner made her prickle like the bristles of a brush rubbed against skin. He was plainly tiring of her company, because he slowed down to let her mother and his father to catch up with them.

They returned to the main drawing room and tea was wheeled in on a glass and gilt trolley by a large-boned grayhaired woman, who smiled with trained subservience—Mildred Major had obviously proved herself an excellent tutor in teaching the woman her place. The woman withdrew and Cynthia complimented Mildred on the scones, pastries and savory delicacies with which Warren was insisting they fill their plates.

"I didn't cook them," Mildred said in her harsh, unfeminine voice. She added smugly, "Kate's a cook as well as maid. They're her handiwork. I couldn't do without her. Warren's so particular about his food I don't even try to rise to his standards."

"Do you still cook as well as you used to, Cynthia?" Warren's question, as it was intended, wiped the smugness from his wife's face. "I still remember with pleasure the meals you cooked me in the old days."

Cynthia laughed. "Ask my husband and daughter. I find it hard to judge."

"And like any true artist," Warren took her up, "you find it difficult to judge your own work?"

Mildred Major's eyes glazed at his words and a pinched look crept into her face, like someone who had been out in the cold a long time.

They had barely eaten the last crumb when she gathered the dishes together and piled it noisily onto the trolley. Juliet rose to help, but Mildred flapped her hand, urging her back to her seat. As if the mistress of the house had sent a telepathic message, Kate appeared and trundled the trolley away.

There was a brief silence. Warren Major, successful

businessman and more than halfway to being a millionaire, spread himself expansively across a corner of the long settee, drawing himself as far away from his wife as he could. He crossed his expensively trousered legs and, running a heavily-ringed hand over his smooth grey hair, he said, addressing Juliet,

"If your mother had married me, she would have been mistress of all this—" his sweeping arm took in not only the elegant room but his entire estate, "—and inheritor of my considerable fortune. I say 'inherit' because most wives outlive their unfortunate husbands. She's sturdy enough. Look at her now, even at fifty."

At his bidding, everyone looked at Cynthia, while Mildred, his wife, folded into herself like an ageing flower closing up for the night.

Cynthia Bourne, dressed becomingly in a deep mauve pant suit and white polo-necked sweater and looking ten years younger than her actual age, bore their scrutiny with smiling tolerance. Her brown hair was tinted where she had determinedly covered the gray, and her smile revealed that the fact that she was not the inheritor of Warren Major's fortune nor mistress of his estate did not worry her unduly.

"I've no regrets, Warren. I'm too happily married, ailing though my husband at times is, to let the thought disturb me."

Warren smiled as though she had spoken on cue. He addressed Juliet again. "I suppose she told you we were once engaged, but that she objected so strongly to my driving ambition and my ruthlessness, as she called it, that she cruelly and irrevocably broke off the engagement? And also that she broke my heart?" His smile flicked like a whip over his wife as though he was secretly punishing her for an unforgivable crime. Then it changed and settled challengingly on Juliet's mother.

Cynthia was unperturbed. "My dear Warren," her voice was gentle, "let's face it, in those days you had no heart to break. And to be honest," the warmth in her smile was intended to soften the impact of the words, "I rather doubt if you've ever had one. Otherwise how could you have amassed the fortune you're now so proud of? No one does that without riding roughshod over hundreds of people."

His laughter was hearty and he enjoyed the joke at his own expense. "My word, she's still got the old fire! I remember the violent arguments we used to have. Have you passed on your fieriness to your daughter, Cynthia?"

He dwelt with indulgent interest on the girl sitting beside him. "She's like you were, you know. Brown hair with auburn lights—only hers is longer—roses and cream complexion, lips red and pouting and asking all the time to be kissed."

Cynthia laughed and the lines around her eyes crinkled. "The passage of time has certainly lent enchantment to your view of me, Warren." She turned to his wife and her eyes held apology for the indiscretions of Warren's memory. "I wasn't a bit like that, Mildred."

Mildred merely turned her head away with a lifeless, disinterested gesture.

"All the same," insisted Warren, "Juliet's the image of what you were in the old days, no doubt about it." He swivelled around and faced Juliet. "Tell me, girl, do you think I've got a heart?"

Juliet smiled. "Obviously you have, Mr. Major. You wouldn't be a living, breathing man without one, would you?"

"Tact. That's good. A good answer, eh, Drew? Think she's inherited her mother's fire?"

The son's eyes moved languidly over the girl in question. He took his time, dwelling on the antagonism she could not suppress, the quick but becoming flush of resentment at his scrutiny, the tightening of the lips as she awaited his verdict.

"I would say," commented Drew at last, having looked his fill, "although I merely hazard a guess from the surface appearances, that it's not just the fire she's inherited, but the whole darned furnace. From the look of her at this moment," he backed away with a provocative jerk, "you'd just have to get a little too near and you'd be set on fire."

Warren laughed loudly again. "My word," he looked at Cynthia, "hearing Drew say that brings back memories. Pleasant ones, too."

Cynthia smiled without embarrassment. Mildred's face did not flicker. She sat motionless, her body small and painfully thin, her short gray-black hair doing nothing at all to enhance the pale rigidity of her features. Her clothes were hopelessly out of fashion. She seemed as incongruous beside her well-fed, immaculately dressed husband as a scarecrow sharing a sofa with a fashion model. She looked at Cynthia, and self-righteous disapproval pushed her thin lips out as she contemplated the other woman's bright, optimistic face and well-rounded, still-attractive figure.

"Well, Juliet." Warren was determined, wife or no wife, to develop his theme, "having established that I do indeed possess a heart, you've got to believe me when I tell you your mother broke it once."

"All the same, Mr. Major," Juliet smiled, "I'm quite sure that, unlike Humpty Dumpty, it was soon put together again."

The astute gray eyes, an older version of his son's, considered her. "What makes you so sure?"

She shrugged. "Well, it didn't stop you making a

success of your life. Also, you found another woman to love—" Warren's eyes rested on his wife as a diner regards a caterpillar in his lettuce—"and to marry. You didn't exactly pine away from unrequited love. And," her eyes moved upward to the younger man who was standing beside her chair, "you had a son. All those things are positive signs of a heart well and truly mended. You also have what many men long for but never have—an heir," she smiled at her host, "who, unlike my mother, will one day inherit your fortune."

The heir in question stirred and folded his arms. He asked softly, "Since you're so articulate on the subject, not to say loquacious, Juliet, where do I stand in your estimation? Would I be rated by a woman as an excellent catch, do you think? And would any woman break my heart as my father's apparently was, because of my stable financial background and the money that will one day come my way?"

She grinned up at him. "With so much to inherit, what woman could resist you?"

"Do you find me irresistible, Juliet?"

She shifted her eyes away from his. "Unfortunately, no."

His father gave a short, sharp laugh. "Her mother all over! Out she comes with the truth, right below the belt."

"But," the son persisted, apparently unaffected by the blow he was supposed to have received, "think of all the money, the property that will be mine one day. Doesn't that tempt you, make me irresistible, even in your jaundiced eyes?"

"No." This time she spoke with irritation. "And I'm not jaundiced, I'm just speaking the truth." She recovered her good humor and shot at him, smiling, "You aren't by any chance proposing to me, are you?"

He threw back his head and laughed, and there was grudging admiration in it.

Cynthia laughed with Warren, who said to his son, "First she insults you, then she's cheeky. My word, Drew, if we give her a job, you'll have to keep her in her place, otherwise she'll be taking over from us and running the firm herself!" He slapped his leg and seemed to enjoy the idea." "She's got spirit, your girl, Cynthia. She'll break a few hearts before she's finished."

Juliet shook her head. "I'd never break the heart of a man I loved. And I'd only marry him if I loved him. Even if he were penniless it wouldn't stop me. Look at my mother. My father was an impoverished young clerk when she married him and they've never had much money, but anyone can see how happy they are, even now." She gave Drew a look that was by no means flattering. "Men with money don't attract me. In fact, they repel me."

"There's no doubt," came softly from Warren, "she's her mother's daughter."

Drew smiled mockingly. "You've wounded me to the heart, Juliet."

She smiled up at him derisively. "I doubt if you've got a heart to break."

He bowed. "You flatter me."

She was still smiling. "Anyway, Mr. Major—"

"Oh, call him Drew," said his father. "After all, if things had been different, he could have been your brother."

"Anyway, Drew," the man she was addressing smiled slightly at her easy use of his first name, "men's hearts aren't made to be broken these days. Women come and go in their lives with such rapidity that their hearts are unaffected, aren't they? Now be honest!"

He hitched his elbow onto the ornate stone mantel-piece and rested a foot on the highly polished brass fender. His smile challenged her. "You aren't by any chance inviting me to pour out the secrets of my love life? Tell you how many women—?"

"Drew!" His mother's twittering, high-pitched tones cut him off. "You really mustn't talk like that. You know how much I dislike it."

Her protests passed over him, and Juliet had the feeling that Mildred Major played a very insignificant part in the lives of these two men who were so alike in feature and manner. He went on, "I will if you like, but unfortunately it would take so long. . . ."

His father threw back his head and laughed. "So many of 'em, eh, Drew? That's the stuff, boy, but take care not to get caught!"

Shocked, Juliet glanced at Mildred. That he could talk in such terms in front of his wife appalled her. But Mildred might have been deaf for all the reaction she showed. Was she perhaps used to the scarcely veiled insults which her husband seemed to take such pleasure in flinging at her?

Cynthia looked at her, too, and Juliet recognized the rage, firmly controlled though it was, as her mother said, "Do you know, Warren, I'm coming to the view that I had a remarkably lucky escape when I broke off our engagement."

Now Warren looked as though he had received a blow, but the grimace of pain passed so swiftly it might never have been. He smiled weakly. "Runs in the family, doesn't it? Punch drunk, they are. Below the belt every time. Watch out, boy," he said to his son, "don't get involved with that one," he indicated Juliet, "otherwise you never know where you might end up. Out stone cold on the floor of the ring, while the referee counts ten."

Drew grinned. "No fear of that. No woman has ever yet got me where she wants me."

Juliet raised her eyebrows. "The other way around, perhaps?"

Drew smiled. "Most definitely the other way around."

"Another of my pet hates—" Juliet murmured, "—womanizers who never take women seriously. That, plus your money—" She shook her head. "You're simply not my type."

"So we're completely incompatible, Juliet?"

"Absolutely."

He pretended to mop his brow. "My word, that was a lucky escape! Now, having got that little matter cleared up, perhaps we can talk business."

"Excellent idea," said Warren. "Take her for a walk, Drew. You do the honors. You run the firm, so you ask the questions. I'm just the figurehead. There's a permanent dent in my desk where I put my feet!"

Cynthia was laughing as Drew motioned Juliet out of the room. "I don't believe a word of it, Warren," she was saying.

"So," Drew said as he showed Juliet through the French windows into the gardens, "I've been detailed by the chairman of the company to ask you a few questions."

"Is this an interview, Mr. Major?"

"It is. Consider yourself highly honored, Miss Bourne, that it isn't the personnel manager who is doing the interviewing, but rather the company manager himself. Now, have you any past experience in retail distribution?"

"None at all. I shall probably be quite useless to you."

"That's the first time in my experience that an applicant has ever tried to talk herself out of a job."

"I'm being honest. I am . . . at the moment . . . an art student."

"Commercial art?"

"Graphic design."

"M'm. Might come in useful." He smiled. "So you're an art student. Do you ever do any work at the college?" When she looked indignant he explained, with a smile, "I've heard it said that all art students learn is how to make love and how to make trouble."

He drew back with mock alarm at her furious expression. "I suppose," she said bitingly, "you're going to ask me next whether I've seen any good sit-ins lately?"

He was unaffected by her sarcasm. He smiled again, but it faded as he asked, "I'd like to know why . . . let's be blunt . . . your mother had to lower her pride and ask my father, a man she had rejected years ago to give her daughter a job."

"I don't really see that it's relevant." She frowned. "If you haven't got a job to offer me, then would you please say so and bring an end to this inquisition? Do you pry into the private lives of all your would-be employees?"

"I resent that. Every employer has a right to ask questions of any candidate, especially someone who has taken the unusual step of asking for a job to be created for them where none exists."

She could not hide her disappointment. "You mean you're trying to tell me politely that you haven't got a suitable job available?"

"In a sense, yes."

She felt like crying. "Sinecure was the word you used earlier, wasn't it? Now I see what you meant." She sighed with resignation and turned back toward the house. "We might as well go in."

He caught her arm and turned her back. "It's usually the prerogative of the potential employer to end the interview, not the applicant."

"I'm sorry, but I wouldn't want to be a liability to anyone."

"Stop being sarcastic, or bitter, or whatever that self-deprecating statement was meant to be.

"I wouldn't want to be a burden—"

"I said shut up, Juliet." His quiet, authoritative tone effectively subdued her. "Now, whether you were an asset or a liability would depend on how much you pulled your weight. And don't worry, we'll know. We don't spy on our staff, but we have means of checking up on the progress of a member of the sales personnel. If you don't come up to scratch in the firm of Major and Son, you'll be out," he clicked his fingers, "just like that."

"No second chance? I'm not surprised. With you at the head of it, I can believe that the firm pursues a policy of intolerance and instant dismissal without compassion!"

He bowed his head in a mocking gesture of thanks. "Your good opinion of me, based of course on years of an intimate knowledge of my character flatters me inordinately. However," his tone hardened, "if you want a job with us, you'd better become a little more submissive, not to mention polite."

She wasn't quelled. Her mood switched and she grinned up at him. "Talking of politeness, if you give me a job, would I have to call you 'sir'?"

"Most of my employees do." She glanced at him to see if he was joking, but his face was perfectly serious.

"Sorry, even if it costs me the job it's not on. I've never in my life called a man 'sir', and I don't intend to start now."

"In that case," he smiled, "I'll have to issue a directive

to the entire staff, including everyone from the general manager down to the youngest, newest and most insignificant member of the staff that Mr. Drew Major is henceforward to be addressed only as 'sir.' "

She smiled up at him. "Yes, Drew. Of course, Drew. Sir."

"My father," he said, looking down at her with a faint smile, "was right when he warned me you would need to be kept under my control."

"Sorry. I'll try to behave." She smiled disarmingly and he nodded, amused like someone watching the antics of a very young child.

They came to the end of the paved pathway and turned to look back at the house. What they saw was a perfect example of perspective and symmetry. There were beds of roses on each side of the path which thrust arrow-like in a narrowing line to the very center of the red brick mansion. Pyramid-shaped cypresses, trained and trimmed by the loving hand of the gardener, sprang like dark green cones from behind the rose beds, giving even greater emphasis to the feeling of perspective. With the profusion of colors, the heady scents which tantalized the nostrils like the smell of wine to a hardened drinker, the greens of the lawns and leaves and, at the end of it all, the mellow red brick and the small white-painted casement windows of the house itself, gave the scene a birthday card perfection.

"Where to now?" She looked up at him.

"Over there," he pointed, "is the sun lounge and there the swimming pool, but," he looked her over, "since you aren't appropriately dressed for swimming . . . no enticing bikini to tempt me—"

"I can't swim anyway," she said.

"Then we'll go through the rose garden to the pond."

He turned her in the right direction as if she were a robot and, as they walked side by side, he said, "Tell me why you want this job."

His voice was serious with a touch of command she could not overlook.

"Why, for instance," he went on, "aren't you continuing your art training and going on to better things?"

"Domestic circumstances. In short, lack of money in the family."

"I see." He looked thoughtful.

"My father suffers periodically from asthma. As he gets older the attacks get more frequent and he's often forced to be absent from work. Then only his sick pay is coming in. That isn't much, so—" she sighed "—in the circumstances, I can hardly go on being a student when I should be bringing in money to supplement my father's meagre allowance." She hated telling this man, this rich man, so many private facts about her parents' and her own circumstances, and confessing to him the true state of their finances. "In short, we're hard up. We need money desperately. Any money I earn will go into the family kitty and help us live." She lifted a proud, pale face to his. "So now you know our family secrets, secrets you were so determined to get out of me."

They came to a circular, lily-strewn pond, which was encircled by even more roses—scarlet, gold, white, as rich in scent as this man beside her was in money. From the center of the pond spurted a tall, misty blue fountain shooting left and right as the wind drove it.

Some of the spray pelted momentarily over Juliet's hair and dress and she stepped back, searching for a handkerchief to wipe herself dry. He stood watching, making no move to assist. A lump came into her throat at the unfairness of it all. That he did not apologize for what had happened—though he had no control over the direction of the wind she felt irrationally that he was responsible because it was after all his fountain—that he and his father should be so wealthy, own so much beauty and live in such luxury while her parents had to count every penny brought her to the edge of unreasonable anger.

She nearly burst out, "I don't want your rotten job," but with the most stringent self-control held her temper. Of course she wanted it. She needed it; she should really be begging him for it.

"This way." He turned her toward the house. They were nearly there, yet he still had not told her the result of their unconventional interview. Should she ask him? If she had failed to convince him of her capabilities, if the answer was "no," she would rather be told now.

"Drew?" He looked at her. "Have you . . . will you . . . will there be . . . ?" She was making a mess of it.

"A job for you? Yes. We'll push you in somewhere." He smiled. "Even if it's operating the elevator or sweeping the floors."

She couldn't keep the relief from her eyes. "If it would bring in some money, I'd do even that."

"My dear girl," there was a hint of exasperation in his voice, "do you really think my opinion of your potential is so low that I'd direct you to those jobs? You need the money. We have it to give."

Juliet bristled. "I don't want charity."

He laughed shortly. "Charity? Not on your life! If you come to work for us, you work. Understand?"

Drew took them home. As they were leaving, Mildred stood on the doorstep with her hands clasped primly in front of her while Warren leaned against the lowered window of Drew's car. Cynthia was in the front seat. Mildred called a tight-lipped "Goodbye" and went in.

As Drew prepared to drive away, Warren opened the

car door, pulled Cynthia toward him and kissed her cheek. "Old times' sake," he mumbled, slamming the door. "Some day I'll tell you just what you did to me."

Cynthia seemed overcome, but recovered quickly. She reached out and squeezed his hand. "Can't turn back the clock, Warren. To be honest, and at the risk of hurting you, I wouldn't want to."

"She's at it again," he said to his son, smiling ruefully. "Slap bang, out with it. Whatever the consequences, it must be the truth."

They laughed and waved as they drove away. Juliet, staring out of the window during the drive home—they lived on the other side of the town—wished they could have taken the bus, as they had come. She hated the thought of Drew seeing the modest little house they lived in. They had roses in their garden, of course, but there any resemblance to the Major residence ended.

Drew didn't seem to notice the shabbiness of the street he was directed to, however. Juliet and her mother stood on the sidewalk and waved as he left them.

Cedric Bourne lowered his newspaper as they entered. "Enjoy yourselves?" he asked with a touch of irony in his voice. "What was it like mingling with the moneyed classes?"

His wife shrugged. "Warren hasn't changed. I'm sorry I had to go running to him for help."

"When a man's as knee deep in money as he is," her husband remarked, "there's no need to have a conscience about asking favors of him."

Cynthia looked at her husband with the eyes of a woman accustomed to searching a well-loved face for signs of physical suffering. Finding none, she consciously relaxed. "Warren's not an easy person to talk to. Never was. And his wife!"

"I thought he treated her abominably," Juliet commented. "The things he said, not exactly to her, but with insults wrapped up like a booby-trapped package."

"Perhaps he had a good reason, dear," her father said. "You never can tell with some couples. Hasn't he got a son? I saw him in the store once. An assistant pointed him out. Tall fellow, dark hair, holds his head as if he were a member of the aristocracy."

"A good description," Juliet agreed. "I can't stand the man. Unfortunately, he seems to be in charge."

"Did he give you a job? That was the object of the exercise, wasn't it?"

Juliet shrugged. "Don't know. He said he'd probably create one if there wasn't one available."

Cynthia said, "Well, that was nice of him. You must admit he was being considerate in saying that."

"If he meant it. Personally, I think he'll forget all about it and I won't hear any more from him."

Cynthia stood beside her husband, her hand resting on his shoulder. It was broad and solid, like his personality. He looked up at her and smiled, his long narrow face lighting up at her touch. He put aside his paper and pulled her onto his knee. "Glad you married me and not Warren?"

She whispered her answer in his ear and he laughed. The phone rang and Juliet answered it.

"Am I speaking to Juliet Bourne?"

"You are." She recognized the precise, businesslike tone immediately.

"Drew Major here. I've been thinking about your request for a position with our firm." *Good heavens*, she thought, *it can't be half an hour since we parted.* She told herself she should be flattered. Then she reminded herself that it must be the firm he had in mind. Here came the polite refusal. "I'm sorry but—" Better to say it over the phone than to her face. . . .

"I'd like to meet you for lunch some time to discuss the matter. You must understand that I can't commit myself to anything before knowing something about your education, your past experience and so on."

Good heavens, she thought, *I only want a job as a salesperson.*

"Well, I . . . I'm still at college. Term doesn't end until next week."

"I see. So lunch would be difficult? Would you prefer us to have dinner together?"

"Oh no, thanks." An evening spent in that man's company? "I can manage lunch whenever you like." If she played the subservient sales assistant in advance, maybe he would more easily "commit himself."

He must have consulted his diary. "I'm free the day after tomorrow."

"So am I," she answered, as if it were a great coincidence.

"Where should I pick you up? At the college?"

"Well, yes, thanks. You know where it is?"

He said he did, only too well. She wondered what that meant. They arranged a time and hung up.

The day Drew called for her was pouring with rain. She was wearing her bright red pants and multicolored tunic and had left her raincoat at home. She dashed down the steps of the art school, feeling dozens of interested eyes boring into her back from the hundreds of windows behind her.

Drew threw open the door without getting out of the car and she tumbled into the passenger seat gasping for breath and apologizing for getting the luxury carpets on the floor wet.

Once again she tried to dry her clothes with her handkerchief, but this time, instead of looking on, he reached into his pocket and produced his own.

"Sorry about this," she apologized again as he drove away from the curb.

He smiled. "If the colors you're wearing now ran into each other, you wouldn't even notice. They're so startling anyway you look like an artist's palette."

"Thank you for the compliment. But if I'm not dressed in tune with your mood or for the place you have in mind for lunch, then you'd better turn around." She wondered if she had gone too far in speaking to him so presumptuously. He was, she hoped, her future employer. She made her tone a fraction more amenable. "I think you must be out of touch with modern youth."

He gave a short, disclaiming laugh. "This stuff," she indicated her clothes, "is the norm. If I dressed otherwise, as an art student, I'd be decidedly odd. You're expected to express your individuality, your difference from those around you, in the clothes you wear."

He laughed loudly. "Difference? All around me every day in the street I see young people dressed like you. So where's the difference? It's just a uniform."

Because she wanted—no, needed—to work for him, she bit back the retort she would have made. They went to a restaurant which even in the middle of the day was dark as an underground cave. The place was illuminated by candles flickering deep inside large red bowls. "It wouldn't have mattered," Juliet told herself, "if I'd been wearing a nightgown."

"Does this suit your artistic sensibilities?" he asked mockingly, and she nodded her appreciation.

He sat opposite her on a bench seat. His face glowed red, his white shirt had turned pink and even his expertly cut suit had a roseate hue about it. "In this light," she reflected with a smile, "even you might pass as one of 'us'."

"Me, look like an arty type?" He laughed derisively. "Heaven preserve me from such a calamity!"

She asked indignantly, "What's wrong with artists?"

"A lot—with those I have to deal with. And a large number come from your art school. Oh yes," at her look of surprise, "I employ them—in the art department of the store, in display and so on."

She grew excited. "Is that where I might . . . ?"

"Sorry. No vacancy."

"Oh." She bit her lip with disappointment.

He ordered, after consulting her wishes, and said, "But the object of this outing is to discuss you, not artists in general. Tell me about your subject."

If talking to him about her studies would enhance her chances of becoming an employee of his, then talk she would, and volubly.

"Graphic design covers a lot of things, like designing gift boxes, posters, packaging, even notepaper. You have to have a feeling for design to be any good at it. It teaches you the use of color, the aesthetics of good and bad design. An object must be attractive to look at, but you also have to ask yourself 'could it be made?' And if so, would it stand up to use?

She tried to guess what he was thinking, but the flickering scarlet glow frustrated her efforts. He seemed prepared to let her go on so she did. The food was put in front of them and she went on talking.

"You learn about printing techniques and color printing, too. Will it, for instance, be possible for the packaging you've designed to go through the post? Can it be manufactured cheaply? You're taught lettering, photography, and window display."

"And all this leads to what?"

"If you're good enough, a diploma. Then you start trudging around looking for jobs. You have a large portfolio and show people pictures of work you've done at the art school, color transparencies you've taken of your stuff, and so on. You show them notepaper you've designed, boxes, book jackets, cardboard cutouts, logos you've thought out for firms." She looked at him, trying to judge his response, but he merely nodded. "Have I . . . have I talked myself into a job in your art department?"

He laughed, shaking his head. "I told you, no vacancy." He saw her disappointment. "Sorry. But if it's any consolation, I'll give you a job in another department. When can you start?"

"Next Monday."

"What about your summer vacation? I'd prefer you to have had it before you start with us."

"I . . . I'm not having one."

"But everyone needs a summer holiday."

"You're probably right. But I couldn't afford it."

"I see." He was silent for a while as if trying to work something out. He must have given up, because he shrugged. As coffee was served he said, "If you will report to the staff manager next Monday morning, she'll direct you to the department you'll be attached to."

Juliet looked at him, gratitude lighting up her eyes. "Thanks."

He nodded and stirred his coffee. "Pity," he said, "that you have to leave college. Wouldn't it be better for you if you were to get this diploma you talked about? Wouldn't it improve your career prospects and so on?"

"Of course it would, but I told you before, the money's just not there to let me do it. I can hardly exist on my grant as it is. And I certainly can't give any money to my parents to help them. I've got to start earning, and the sooner the better."

"You realize that the pay you'll get won't be very high? With no past experience in retail selling—"

"I understand that," she said quietly. "But whatever I get, no matter how small, will be a help." She paused. "Drew." He looked up. "I'd like to tell you how grateful I am to you and your father—"

He shook his head, silencing her. "Don't go on." He smiled. "Who knows, after a week of Major and Son, especially the 'Son,' you might want to hand in your notice. You haven't seen me in action yet. I've only got to appear in the store and everyone shakes with terror." She laughed. "You don't believe it? Wait until the other employees start talking. I know exactly what they think about my methods. But they have to admit I get results." She laughed again, but stopped at the change in his tone as he said, "Nor will I make any exception of you."

She frowned. "I wouldn't expect you to."

"Just as well. You may not like me much now. . . ." he looked into her eyes, "in fact, I can see you don't, but you'll like me even less before you're finished. My father has made me in his own image. Hardened me up, he said, so that I wouldn't be fool enough, as he was, to fall for any girl, especially one who might reject me because of my ambitions." She tightened at his callous reference to her mother. "He sent me to boarding school . . . thought that would help the process of hardening me. He had me educated, made me into everything he would have liked to have been. Under his tuition, I've been ruthlessly gutted of all sentiment. A sign of weakness, my father calls it. So I'm warning you." He moved back his chair and pulled out hers as he rose.

"You mean I'm going to work for a tartar?"

He smiled. "You'll discover that for yourself soon enough." He settled the bill and they left the restaurant side by side. "Tell me," he said as they got in the car and drove away, "has Juliet got a Romeo?"

Juliet smiled out of the window. "Yes, she has a Romeo. His name's Malcolm. Malcolm Watling."

"Older than you?"

"No, same age. Twenty-one."

"Art student?"

A slight pause before she answered, then, "No." He seemed to be waiting for more. "He's a sales assistant." She looked at his profile, a little forbidding as he frowned. Could he guess what was coming? Dare she tell him? How would he react? "At Curlews."

He reacted violently. His head shot around. "What? Our deadliest rivals?"

He sounded so angry she thought it was the end. "I'm sorry," adding wearily, "You can withdraw your offer of a job, if you like."

He took so long to answer she thought he must be seeking a way of softening the blow. She would make it easy for him.

"I'll look somewhere else for a job. You can be blunt. I don't mind. . . ."

He said slowly, "No, I won't withdraw my offer, I'll take you on as an employee on one condition. Let me warn you that if anything you hear about Major and Son, like business deals, policy matters and anything else that might be classified as confidential, is passed on by you to any member of Curlews' staff, however junior he may be and even if he seduces you to get the secrets out of you, you will be fired! Have you got that?"

She flushed at his innuendo and his objectionable manner and held back a vicious retort. In the circumstances she had to be polite to the man, because he held the purse strings. "Yes, Mr. Major." But subservience was foreign to her nature. She burst out, "Thanks for your faith in my integrity. I have got the message. How could I have missed it? It was put so . . . so succinctly, so tactfully. And Malcolm is my boyfriend, not my lover."

He remained maddeningly calm. "Thanks for that bit of information. I'll sleep all the more soundly in my bed at night knowing that." His sarcasm grated on her like a piece of music played out of tune. "Are you serious about him?"

"Is this an extension of my interview for the job?" she asked, between her teeth.

"You could put it that way," he answered blandly.

She replied grudgingly, "My affairs, in the social as opposed to the sensual meaning of the word, are really my own business, but if you insist on knowing, I don't even know myself."

He nodded noncommittally as he turned left and stopped outside the art school. She looked into his face, trying to judge his mood. Still smarting from his prying, but knowing at the same time she had no business to be questioning him on the subject, she said, "Because you've asked me and because you're not yet my employer, can I ask you a similar question? Have you got a girlfriend?"

He rested his elbow on the back of his seat and turned to look at her. He raised his eyebrows, smiled and half echoed her own words, but with greater emphasis. "My affairs, both social and sexual, are my own business. Not yours."

She flushed with annoyance at having allowed herself to be put so firmly in her place. She thanked him coldly for the meal.

He nodded. "Monday morning, 8:30 promptly. Report to the staff manager, administrative section, sixth floor." Without another word, he drove away.

CHAPTER TWO

The day before Juliet started work at Majors' department store, she went for a long bicycle ride in the country with Malcolm. They hid their bicycles in a hedge and wandered through the woods hand in hand.

They were talking about Juliet's new job. "Wonder which department you'll be in?" Malcolm said. "One place they won't put you is the carpet department, like me. A girl wouldn't be any use there. Ever tried to lift a carpet? The really big ones weigh a ton. Then a customer comes along and wants to have a look at the one at the very bottom of the pile and you have to flip them up one by one. After your arm feels as though it's going to fall off with the weight of the ones on top, she says, 'Thank you, I'll think about it.' "

She laughed. "Heaven knows where I'll be working. He said there wasn't really a vacancy to suit me. I'll probably end up operating the elevator!"

"I've done that before now and let me tell you," they were lying between the bushes and he kissed her swiftly, "it's no laughing matter. By the end of the day you feel dead on your feet."

She lifted a hand and pushed back a lock of his fair hair that had fallen across his eyes. "All the same, I'd even do that if it means earning some money. I'm sick of struggling along on a miserly grant, with nothing to spend on things I want and nothing much to give my parents for my keep at the end of the week."

"You won't earn a lot at Majors. They're rotten payers. Now if you came to work for Curlews—"

"No, thanks," she said, grinning. "With a certain

Malcolm Watling working there, even if they offered me a fortune for my services, I wouldn't—" The rest was lost as she struggled to get away from him. Laughing, he let her go and they made their way back to their bicycles.

"Anyway,", they pedaled home side by side along the country lanes, "I'm only being allowed to work at Majors on certain conditions. Drew said—"

"Who's Drew?" came sharply from Malcolm.

She colored at her slip. "Drew Major. My mother used to know his father. We went there for tea."

"On first name terms with the top brass, are you?" He sounded displeased.

"Don't be silly, Malcolm, it doesn't mean anything. Anyhow, it'll be Mr. Major, sir, from tomorrow on, when I'm an employee. Can you imagine me calling the man in charge 'Drew'? He told me everyone calls him 'sir' anyway."

"So I suppose you're going to bow to him like the rest every time you meet."

"Not likely. You should know me better than that."

All the same, next day as she joined the flow of people passing through the staff entrance at the side of the great beige-colored building, she realized what a small component she was in the thriving business that was Major and Son. Of course she would have to toe the line, and even, if necessary, address the company manager as 'sir,' although the word would probably turn rancid in her mouth.

Up she went in the swift silent elevator pressed tight between a dozen other staff members, whose faces were unwelcoming and disinterested. The number six flashed on the floor indicator and the doors slid open. Juliet breathed deeply and she pushed her way out, to be left alone as the elevator doors closed again.

She walked a few paces, hoping someone would come along. No one did. She walked on, her heart jolting at the words on a door. Drew W. Major, Company Manager, they said. She passed by, dreading that the door would open and he would come out. But, she told herself, he was probably still in bed. It was, after all, only half-past eight.

Then she heard his voice inside the room and scuttled past as fast as she could. She walked to the end of the corridor and back. A door opened. A man appeared, staring at her.

"I told you to see the staff manager," said the man in charge. "Can't you read?" He pointed at the door opposite his own.

"Sorry, Mr. Major," she said, coloring furiously. Did he have to be so unpleasant on her first morning as an employee of his? "I must have missed it."

He shook his head irritably and watched as she raised her hand and tapped on the door. There was a mumble from inside the room, but she couldn't decipher the words. She hesitated.

"Well, go in, Miss Bourne. Are you deaf as well as blind?"

She gave him a look of concentrated fury, pulled herself together, dug up a smile from the depths of her being like a miner hewing coal, and went in.

A middle-aged woman with a bored expression lifted her head and said, "Yes?"

Her name, Mrs. Audrey Arthur, was printed on a notice standing on her desk.

Under the slightly hostile stare, Juliet began to wilt. "I'm . . . my name is Juliet Bourne. I—"

"I was expecting you. I've been instructed to direct you to the marking-off room. Eighth floor, turn right through a swinging door and you're there. They'll tell you what to do."

Juliet thanked her, followed the woman's directions and pushed her way into a vast dimly lit area. It was a great depressing wilderness, with the walls covered in peeling yellow paint, the ceiling a dirty white, the lighting resembling a guest house lounge in a poor season. There seemed to be cages everywhere, all padlocked to guard against theft, containing merchandise which would one day find its way to the counters and display stands of the main store. Behind the wire mesh were pillows, washing bowls, hardware, shopping carts, toy guitars, toys—all unrelated but gathered there for one purpose only—to be price tagged.

There were about a dozen women at work. They were chatting and laughing, but not one of them raised her head and noticed Juliet. She stood there for nearly five minutes wondering how to announce herself. Finally she coughed and one of the women looked up. "Yes?" came the same flat, disinterested tone that had greeted her in the staff manager's office.

"I've just come," said Juliet feebly. "I'm new."

"Come and join us," sang one of the brighter souls standing at a large table.

"All are welcome," said another. "Take off your coat, dear, and get down to it."

Juliet removed her coat and, looking in vain for a hanger draped it across a pile of wheelbarrows, hoping it would still be there when she needed it later.

The women at the table were pricing large gilt chandeliers. One of the women, who introduced herself as Madge, pushed a box of price tags towards Juliet and showed her how to fix them.

"Nearly finished with these," she said. "After this there's the purses."

"Not the purses," said another woman called Pat. "The buyer of hardware keeps asking us for his canteens of cutlery. Ought to do those before purses."

Madge shook her head. "Let him wait. They're too heavy for us to lift. After all, we've just done these chandeliers without Mr. Wilkes to help us, and they're heavy enough."

So they worked on purses, which had to be priced with adhesive labels. Mr. Wilkes, it seemed, was the marking-off room supervisor, whose job it was to lift heavy objects to the table for pricing.

"He's away more than he's here," said Madge with disgust. "He's always taking extra long coffee breaks. That's why the big things get left and the buyers come shouting for the stuff." She laughed. "We just let 'em shout!"

After the purses came racks of dresses, to which Juliet was told to fix swing tickets bearing price, size and code number. Piles of plates and dishes had to be marked with grease pencils, cardigans priced with special pin tickets. It was toward the end of the afternoon that Juliet began to wonder how long she could stand the job.

The incessant chatter of the women, the constant taped music, the roar of the air-conditioning which was nerve-racking, and the mindless, repetitive nature of the work depressed her beyond words. It was not as though the surroundings acted like an antidote to the monotony of the work. The poor lighting, the badly painted walls, the absence of windows providing natural light, and the wire cages reminding her of a prison all played upon her imagination to such an extent that even the shadows took on a grotesque shape.

At the end of the day she felt like knocking on Drew Major's door and telling him she had had enough of his department store. She knew, however, that she would do no such thing and that she would arrive next morning and make her way to the marking-off room.

That evening while she was telling Malcolm on the phone about her first day at work an idea came to her. She was explaining how it was the surroundings above all that got her down when the artist in her whispered a solution.

She worked through the following day, pricing wash bowls with adhesive labels, hats with swing tickets and shoe boxes with ball point pens. She priced and carried the articles to the shelves, unlocked the padlocks which fastened the wire cages and took out more goods for pricing. She placed merchandise on the bucket which moved down to the appropriate departments in the store. All the time she talked and laughed with the other women, but she kept her secret strictly to herself.

When the day's work was over and the staff had gone home, she would stay behind and cover the peeling dirty walls with posters she had made in art school. She had brought them from home that morning in a large travel bag where they now lay hidden. She had decided not to ask permission. That would be courting a refusal, which she was not prepared to risk. She believed in the maxim "act first, ask afterward," which since childhood had reaped dividends for her in her dealings with her parents.

When everyone had gone and she was left alone in that dim, uncanny stillness, she brushed off the cobwebs of fear her imagination had started to spin around her and began her task.

She applied a special adhesive to the backs of the posters. Then, with joy rising in her like the sun at dawn, she decorated the walls with paintings of the British countryside which she had designed for a travel firm; with abstract patterns; with portraits of fellow students; still life, and even a self-portrait she had once painted as an exercise.

She stood back to admire the effect. Her efforts had been worth while. Of course the great room was still dingy and shadowed, the goods were still stacked high and the atmosphere remained one of a wasteland of man-made goods, but at least it was possible to escape for a few enchanted moments into the color and fascination of dreamy, impressionist landscapes, bowls of fruit, flower arrangements and drawings of young people. She went home at last, her artistic sensibilities deeply satisfied, her social conscience assuaged, experiencing not a single qualm.

Next morning she arrived early, anticipating her colleagues' gasps of astonishment and disbelief and, she hoped, a little praise. One by one the women drifted in, and she had her share of compliments on her skill as an artist and their gratitude for her attempts to introduce color and diversion into their wo king lives.

"Don't know whether you'll be able to leave 'em up though, love," Madge said regretfully. "Mr. Havering . . . he's the general manager . . . can be a stubborn so-and-so when he likes. He don't hold with what he calls initiative in the staff. Says they're all paid to do what they're told, not what they want. If he comes in, don't be upset if he orders you to take 'em all down."

"I don't see what's wrong with trying to hide these horrible walls," Juliet complained.

"Couldn't agree with you more, dear," Madge answered, "but you just convince the management of that."

They started work discreetly pricing birthday cards with a pencil on the back. While they were lifting coffee makers from the wire cage to the marking table, the door opened.

"Watch it, love," hissed Madge. "Here comes Mr. Havering."

But Juliet nearly dropped the expensive item of electrical equipment she was holding. It was not Mr. Havering.

"Gawd," whispered Madge, "it's the heir to the throne himself?" She murmured out of the corner of her mouth, "To what honor," she pronounced the "h," "do we owe this visitation? Can't say I've ever seen him in here before."

The "heir to the throne", as she called the company manager, was gazing around the room like a man who had woken from a nightmare to discover that his bad dreams were a reality.

He looked at Juliet. "You'd better put that thing down, Miss Bourne, before you drop it on your foot. I'm not worried about your foot, but I am concerned about the delicate piece of equipment you're handling."

Mutinously but with care she placed the heavy box on the table. Then she stood still and waited for what she knew was coming.

"I take it," said Drew Major tersely, "that it's to you we owe this very exclusive exhibition of modern art. What were you trying to do, turn the place into a poor relation of the Art museum?"

"No, Mr. Major," she said quietly. "I was merely trying to introduce into the lives of the unfortunate staff who work in this . . . this dungeon, a little color and brightness, to remind them in case they've forgotten by the end of the long, long day that there's a more attractive and exciting world beyond these four walls."

"Dungeons, Miss Bourne," Drew said dryly, but with a warning note beneath his sarcasm, "are, for your information, usually deep in the earth, not poised on the eighth floor of a 12-story building. And if the people employed here have any complaints, they know where to take them—to the personnel manager."

Juliet was conscious of the rustle of the women working at the table. They were pretending feverishly to be deaf to Juliet's exchange with the man in charge.

"Did you get permission to put up these works of art?"

"No, Mr. Major."

"Not from the general manager? Not even from the supervisor of this section?"

"No, Mr. Major."

"Then you will kindly take them down and put them where they belong—in your portfolio at home."

Forcing her antipathy aside and remembering only her desire to brighten the lives of the people who worked in that comfortless room, she tried to persuade him.

"But why, Mr. Major? What harm does it do to have a few pictures on the walls to cover the cracks? I admit that as works of art they're not very good, but they're better than nothing." She moved toward him, but he retreated as if he was afraid that she would fling herself at his feet. "Please, Mr. Major," she pleaded, "can't I leave them up there, just for a little while?"

"I'm afraid not, Miss Bourne."

Furious at her inability to move him, she scowled and their eyes became entangled like two boys fighting. She withdrew hers, battle-scarred. He was the victor.

She held in her anger. "All right, Mr. Major. I'll take them down, Mr. Major. At the end of the day."

When he had gone, the others didn't speak, but she felt

their sympathy and saw in their covert glances astonished admiration for her courage in standing up to him. The admiration seemed to be muted by the fear of what might happen to her now.

At the end of the day, when the others had gone home, she looked at her pictures and her anger returned, bringing with it a twisted desire for retribution. She would show Drew Major! Motivated now by a fierce mindless passion, she tore down the paintings one by one. And, one by one, with vindictive, furious fingers, she crumpled them into tight balls and threw them into the waste basket.

Then she grasped the basket, ran along the corridor, raced down two flights of stairs to the administrative section, rapped on Drew Major's door and burst in. He was alone.

She lifted the bucket and dumped it on top of the papers on his desk. "Now are you satisfied?" she cried. "The walls in the marking-off room are back to their miserable darkness and filth, and everything is back to normal!"

He had not moved a muscle. She looked at the destruction she had wrought and it came to her just what she had done. She had destroyed some of her most cherished possessions. She began to cry.

"You can have my paintings, you can take them home and unravel them. Then you can pin them up and desecrate the immaculately decorated walls of your luxury home and spend the rest of your life laughing at them till you cry!" She began to laugh at herself, overwrought and hysterical, and turned toward the door.

But Drew was there before her. "You little idiot, what have you done? Why did you do it? To hurt me? Because you haven't. You've only hurt yourself instead, and you know it." He grasped her arm and shook it to bring her to her senses. "Stop it! Pull yourself together, girl!"

He pushed her into a chair and stood over her until she quietened down, mumbling her apologies. She wished she could take every one of those pictures and smooth them flat again. They represented days of work. She had spent hours perfecting them and now they were gone.

"My God," he whispered, "my father said your mother had fire. He didn't know when he was lucky. Compared with her you're a blazing inferno!"

He sat down and watched her until she grew calmer. Then he spoke. "Look, Juliet, I gave you a job. Out of the kindness of my heart I found a place for you in the firm. I could have said, 'Sorry, no vacancy.' But I didn't. I think the least I can expect from you is an observance of the rules of the firm, a respect for those above you. Initiative is fine. Normally, I welcome it, but for heaven's sake let it be after consultation with others who know better than you. If I had let you get away with that, how could I have stopped any of the others doing the same thing all over the building where there may be paint peeling off?"

"I'm sorry," was all she could say.

"You may like to know, and I'm telling you this even though there's no need for me to do so, that I'm quite aware that the marking-off room is in need of alteration, rearrangement and decoration. In fact, it's on the list. Its price has been estimated, its cost approved. It's moving upward gradually in the list of priorities. Before very long, work will start. Does that satisfy you?"

"I'm sorry," she said again, and stood up. "Thank you for telling me."

"Sit down." She sat. "Don't you like your work in the marking-off room?"

"I hate it."

He smiled slightly. "Right out with it, as my father would say." He leaned back and hitched an arm over the back of the chair. "Do you want to be moved?"

She moistened her lips. "Yes, please." Her voice was hoarse.

"Why? Don't you like your colleagues?"

"They're very nice. It's the monotony, the boredom, the—"

"All right, don't go on. So you want to be moved?" She nodded. "If I moved you, once again I'd have to create a vacancy." She waited, holding her breath. He was thinking, drumming his fingers on the desk top. "Fashion?"

Her eyes, red with weeping, grew bright. "Wonderful," she said.

He smiled and rose. "All right. We'll try fashion, if you promise not to fling paint all over the walls of the fashion department with a view to 'brightening it up.'"

"I promise," she whispered, eyes shining. "When can I start? Tomorrow?"

He nodded. "I'll let them know in advance just what's coming to them. Via the general manager, that is. If I were to appear in the fashion department, they'd all suffer from shock as the women in the marking-off room did this morning. They might even start salaaming . . . all, that is," he smiled mockingly, "except one. The newest assistant."

"I'll try to . . . to behave, and toe the line, Mr. Major." She grinned. "Sir."

He clenched his fist at her and moved his head in the direction of the door. "Out!" Juliet grasped the waste bucket containing her paintings. "Leave those, Miss Bourne. I'll dispose of them. The cleaners will be around soon."

She took one long, sad look at the remains of her pictures and left him.

When Cynthia asked her daughter apprehensively—knowing her volcano-like nature—how she was getting on at Majors, Juliet was evasive. Cynthia recognized the danger signals and her heart sank.

"Trouble already, dear? Whatever job they give you to do, you must remember it was good of them—"

"I know that," Juliet said irritably. "It's just that I had a . . . a difference of opinion," a delightful euphemism, she told herself, for a violent quarrel, "with Mr. Major . . . I mean Drew." Cynthia started to speak, but Juliet went on, "If you want to know who won, in a sense we both did."

When Cedric Bourne came home from work that evening, looking tired as he usually did, he brightened considerably when he heard that Juliet had had an argument with the boss.

He laughed heartily. "Delighted to hear that my daughter is standing up to the son of my wife's objectionable ex-fiancé."

"That's a little strong," Cynthia protested. "He's not objectionable, he's just—"

"A conceited bighead," her husband finished.

Cynthia laughed and put her arms around him. "Don't tell me you're jealous of him after all these years?"

"Jealous?" He kissed her cheek. "Of course not. I just hate his guts. What else am I supposed to feel toward the man you thought you fancied enough to marry?"

"But, darling, that was years before I met you and I was too young to know what I was doing." She saw that he wasn't appeased and switched the subject to safer territory. "What," she asked Juliet, "did you mean when you said you had both 'won'?"

"Well, in the first place, Drew got his way. Then I got mine." Her father applauded. "He's moving me to fashion."

When Juliet reported to the staff manager next morning, Mrs. Arthur sighed. "Second floor," she said. "Coats. See the buyer, tell her I sent you." She eyed Juliet's pink sleeveless dress. "You can't wear that."

"But," Juliet pointed out, "it was all right to wear it in the marking-off room."

"Maybe, Miss Bourne," the staff manager said wearily, "but you were behind the scenes in that department, hidden from the public. The House rule dictates a black dress. Take one from stock. You can have it at cost price. That's another rule."

"A black dress?" Juliet wailed. "But I hate black. Why should I spend money on something I dislike? Can't I wear—?"

"Black dresses for women staff," Mrs. Arthur repeated slowly, "is the policy of the management. If you object, take the matter up with Mr. Major. But I know you won't make him change his mind."

All right, Juliet conceded as she swept down to the second floor, *black it will have to be. But it's going to be a style of my choice.*

She hadn't reckoned with the dictates of the management.

"Black dress," said Miss Skimpton, buyer of coats. Her white hair was tinted mauve, her spectacle frames shaped into Machiavellian points, her manner offhand. "Regulation short sleeves, high neck, skirt length at or just below the knee, black belt at waist. Go to Dresses. They've got a rail of them behind the scenes. Find one to fit you. They stock all sizes."

Controlling her outrage with difficulty, Juliet went across the fashion floor to the dress department. "In the office," she was told. "Try on one or two in the fitting room."

The full-length mirror she looked into reflected a pale sullen sales assistant, her skin already becoming allergic to the high collar which hugged her neck "Nineteen fifties," she thought, disgustedly. "If my friends come and see me, they'll die laughing."

"It goes with the atmosphere of the store," said one of the assistants. "Early nineteen hundreds."

Still eyeing herself with loathing, Juliet said absently, "I don't know why Majors don't alter their policy and start catering for the sort of people who go to Curlews. My boyfriend works for them and—"

The girl called Penny nudged her. "Better go back to Coats. Miss Skimpton's looking like thunder."

Juliet turned and looked at the buyer of coats. "You're right," she said.

Miss Skimpton stormed, "Why were you away so long, Miss Bourne? It can't take half an hour to find a dress to fit a stock size like yourself."

"No, Miss Skimpton," said Juliet meekly. After all, she had promised Drew to toe the line. She ran a finger between the collar of the dress and her neck. Her skin was beginning to feel irritated.

Miss Skimpton introduced Juliet to the other assistants, all of whom seemed to be replicas of their supervisor in looks, bulk and manner. One or two tried to be friendly. On discovering her inexperience, a woman who introduced herself as Edna tried to teach her some sales technique.

"But don't worry, dear, we have half-hour training sessions once a week. Some of the sixth-floor admin mob lower themselves to come down and lecture us on how to increase our sales by telling the customers bigger and better lies!" She shrieked with laughter and Miss Skimpton hushed her as a customer approached.

Edna went forward. "Watch me," she muttered, plastering a welcoming smile on her face and asking the customer, "Can I help you?"

Fifteen minutes later, the customer walked out, a Major's carrier bag in her hand bulging with the coat she had just bought, a satisfied smile on her face.

"That's how you do it, dear," said Edna. "You advise, you reason, you praise, you coax, you admire and last of all you put on a little bit of pressure. Then you take their money." She thrust her hand, palm upwards, toward Juliet. "Easy. I've sold a woman a fur coat in the middle of summer, just by talking."

Miss Skimpton enthused, eyes alight, her throaty voice full of emotion, "Edna's our best saleswoman. Copy her, Miss Bourne, and you won't go far wrong."

"Copy her?" thought Juliet. "No, thanks. I'd never live peaceably with myself again if I used her tactics. That customer looked atrocious in that coat."

"The higher our sales," Miss Skimpton went on, "the bigger our profits. That's the maxim we all memorize in this department."

Then I'm going to be the exception, Juliet decided. Thus it was a few days later she was reprimanded by Miss Skimpton for not having sold one coat since she started in that section.

"I'll have to have you moved, Miss Bourne, if you don't buck up your sales. Mr. Major was asking the other day how you were getting on. I'm afraid I had to tell him, 'No sale.' 'Not one?' he asked. 'Not one,' I had to say. I can tell you, he looked pretty fed up."

Juliet's heart sank. In trouble again with Drew? "But I do try, Miss Skimpton. I just don't seem to have the right touch."

She was also finding it difficult to fit in with the other sales assistants. They all seemed to be trying to pretend she wasn't there. They were all twice her age, and the generation gap hit her more and more forcibly when she attempted to talk to them. They excluded her from their conversations and when she tried to join in, they made her feel like an interloper.

The black dress with its choking collar was making the skin of her neck break out in a rash. The warm weather made the length of the skirt intolerable. And she was beginning to hate the sight of coats. Trade was slack because the weather was so warm. Miss Skimpton was panicking because so many styles were being left unsold.

"We'll have to mark them down," she fussed. "Think of the loss in profits!"

Having no one else on whom she dared vent her feelings about the unexpectedly hot summer, she poured out her ire on Juliet, who didn't seem able to do anything right.

"Tomorrow," she said to the assistants, picking out Juliet with gloating eyes, "we have our weekly staff training session. It might be Mr. Havering, the general manager. Or it might be Mrs. Arthur." She caught her breath. "It might even be Mr. Major, Mr. Drew Major himself. Sometimes he honors us with his presence."

Years of practice in servility had taught this woman to worship those in authority, and to her Drew Major was a man to idolize because of his position of power within the firm. Juliet, whose generation, on principle, venerated no one, was disgusted by the woman's subservient attitude.

That evening Juliet went home and phoned Malcolm, hoping to arrange to see him. But he had a meeting to attend—he was the secretary of a local youth club—and said he was sorry, he couldn't make it, but that wild horses wouldn't keep him from her the following day.

In a vicious, impulsive mood, she looked at her work dress which she had flung on the bed. If the scissors hadn't been lying on the dressing table she probably wouldn't have done it, but there they were, challenging her. She picked them up, seized the dress and with an exquisite feeling of revenge, started chopping at the neck of it.

The high collar disappeared, the scissors cutting lower and still lower and up the other side. There it was, a becoming neckline which needed only the removal of the sleeves to balance it. The sleeves were snipped out, and she held up in front of her a stylish dress. *Three inches off the skirt,* the artist in her murmured, *and it would be perfect.*

She went downstairs for her mother's workbox and without telling her why she wanted it, took it upstairs. An hour later the alterations were finished. She tried the dress on and was so pleased with the result she went down to show her mother.

Instead of praising her, Cynthia blanched. "What have you done? You won't be allowed to wear that if it's against the policy of the management."

"Then," said Juliet, "the management will just have to change its policy."

Her father laughed, "Good for you!" He turned to his wife, eyes approving. "Where did she get her fight from, Cynthia? She's got spirit, you must admit."

" 'Fire,' Warren called it," Cynthia mused.

226

Her husband closed down. "Did he?" His voice was as flat as a punctured tire. Then, sarcastically, "He should know, shouldn't he?"

"Darling," Cynthia placated, "don't be like that."

Cedric raised his newspaper between them.

Juliet wished her defiance of the previous evening had persisted through the night. Somewhere between the hours of sleeping and waking her courage had deserted her. She felt like a swimmer on the top platform of a diving board suddenly taking fright at the idea of jumping. She looked with dismay at the altered dress. She put it on and ran to the waste basket in a hopeless attempt to salvage the material and replace it like pieces in a jigsaw puzzle.

As a result she was late. She slipped into the office attached to the fashion department and hung up her coat. She spread out guilty fingers against her neck, feeling the bareness of her skin. She felt half-dressed. Her uncovered arms prickled and her legs seemed to stretch for miles from the hem of her shortened skirt.

The mumble of voices was dying down. The speaker must have arrived. Drawing herself to her full five feet five and swallowing a deep draught of courage from the conditioned air around her, she walked out into the fashion department to find that the chairs had been arranged in a semi-circle. She searched for an empty seat. There was one left. It was in the front row.

There was nothing to do but brave the astonished stares of the assembled staff and make for that chair. The women gasped. The men—there were less than half a dozen—gazed, and the appreciation in their eyes was unmistakable. When Juliet felt brave enough to look up and identify the member of the staff who was to address them, it was she who gasped.

Drew Major stood at the table, papers spread out in front of him. But he was staring at her, not his papers, his eyes unbelieving, his jaw square and belligerent, his lips compressed. Among those conventionally dressed, dowdy-looking women in their store uniform, he made her feel as unwanted as a discontinued line of merchandise.

The company manager, having allowed his gaze to look her over and hammer her down like the flap of an envelope, removed his eyes and concentrated on the job in hand.

"You may wonder," said the speaker, "why I am giving the training session this morning. I'm deputizing for the general manager who is away at a meeting. I'll begin with a statement which you've probably heard before, but which I feel is worth repeating. It is that stock well looked after is stock more than half sold. Sometimes the task of looking after stock is entrusted to the newest assistant. Without supervision, this practice could be risky, bearing in mind," he raised his eyes and stared at Juliet, "the dubious quality of the new assistants we have in these days of staff shortages."

There was an amused titter and everyone leaned forward to stare at the girl to whom the company manager was unmistakably referring. She flushed deeply, but her eyes stared courageously back at him. She would not be cowed into subservience by his sarcasm, nor would he reduce her to servility and groveling by deriding her in public. She was no second Miss Skimpton.

He had returned to his subject. "The care of stock is important because markdowns due to bad stock-keeping have a tendency to eat into the profits and with good management should be completely avoidable. Such apparently trifling things as sewing on loose buttons and repairing slight damage resulting from customers trying on garments are important too. This job should ordinarily be given to the youngest assistant to tackle, provided," he paused, but Juliet did not dare look up this time, "that that assistant can be trusted to carry out the work thoroughly and responsibly.

"Other things can damage existing stock—too much heat, for instance, strong sunlight, dampness in the atmosphere, soiling of the garments through too much handling—all of which tend to bring down the sales value of the goods on display."

He paused and turned a few pages, Juliet looked up and he raised his eyes and looked through, not at, her. "There is, of course, the unpleasant subject of loss of stock. Some way of safeguarding it is essential, which is why we have a security officer and other ways in which we can detect either pilferage by staff—a rarity, but it does unfortunately happen—or shoplifting. As you probably all know, we operate closed circuit television in this store. We use special mirrors, which are transparent from the other side. We have members of staff specially trained for purposes of detection, and we also employ outside help in this respect. This is an unpleasant subject to dwell on, but unfortunately it's such an important one that I have to do so."

Drew continued with his lecture for a while, then shuffled his papers together, indicating that the training session was over. The audience rose stiffly, reluctant not so much to leave the meeting as to shake off the torpor that had settled on them while listening.

Juliet noted with some fear the sluggish movement of the crowd. It hampered her attempts to get out of reach of the man in charge. With as much speed as the others would allow, and abandoning any attempt at politeness, she pushed her way through them, making for the sanctuary of the fashion buyer's office. But her bid for freedom was thwarted as sharply as a warning shot fired over the heads of a riotous mob.

"Miss Bourne!" rang out, and the command in the familiar voice stopped her in her tracks and made her hold her breath.

The others, dispersing slowly, regarded her with some pity, although not all of them were on her side. Older women, mostly, stared at her with self-righteous disgust. After all, hadn't she asked for trouble turning up for work dressed like that? They glared at the bare white skin of her throat and her uncovered, slightly tanned arms with such distaste that she felt she couldn't have committed a greater sin had she arrived for work in her swimsuit.

"I wish to see you," the voice said, abrasive as a nail file. "Come upstairs to my office, Miss Bourne."

He went towards the swinging doors and she had to follow. With cold courtesy he held the door open for her and then preceded her up four flights of stairs. She trailed him all the way like an apprentice mountaineer following an expert. By the time they had reached the sixth floor, she was gasping for breath. She concluded that he had subjected her to the long climb instead of taking the lift as any considerate employer would have done to deprive her of the powers of speech on arrival at his office.

He unlocked his door and she followed at his heels. He phoned his secretary and told her he did not wish to be interrupted for the next ten minutes. Juliet wondered dully if that was how long it would take to fire her from her job. She sat down without invitation. He sat too and clasped his hands, elbows resting on his blotter, while his eyes did a quick but thorough examination of her person.

She winced. Any other man's gaze wandering over her she could take with equanimity—she had had a few wolf whistles directed her way in her time—but not Drew Major's. His eyes, detached and cool, were spiced with such a strong seasoning of male evaluation that she turned a deep, uncomfortable pink.

"So," he murmured, "you've done it again. With your customary contempt for authority, you've snapped your fingers in the face of conformity and done your own thing as dramatically as only you know how."

This time she did not flinch from his steady gaze. "Yes, I admit it. But I'm not sorry. Something inside me made me do it."

"And," his sarcasm began to seep through, "that 'something inside you' was quite untameable, in fact it had such power over you that your reason and your common sense were hopelessly overruled? Like an unthinking child you were seized by an ungovernable impulse, disregarding all thoughts of the consequences—" she winced again at his too near approximation to the truth "—and grabbed some scissors and proceeded to hack your way through the material of the firm's dress—"

"I paid for it," she interrupted, like a sulky child.

He ignored her comment. "—and, extracting a sadistic pleasure out of every snip of those scissors, (you were hitting out at authority all the time, remember, for 'authority' meant 'Drew Major') you created out of the original design something far more suited to your artistic sensibilities, your ego and—" his eyes wandered again over her shapeliness, "—your figure, the attractiveness of which you are only too well aware."

She lowered her eyes. "I'm still not sorry."

"Well," he leaned back, "where do we go from here?"

"That," she said, clasping and unclasping her hands, "is for you to decide."

"What would you do, I wonder, if I ordered you to go

away and take that dress off? Would you do to it what you did to your paintings, tear it up into tiny pieces like a truculent child and throw it in the waste basket? Destroy it utterly, as a substitute for destroying me, because I represent the authority you so despise?"

She whispered, defiance staring out of her eyes, "Yes, I would."

"I'm sure you would. And is this," he motioned to the dress, "what you call 'toeing the line,' as you promised to do the other day? Was this what you meant by 'behaving'?" She was silent. "Suppose," he persisted, "I told you to discard that dress and go and buy another, making absolutely sure that this time you didn't meddle with the design, but wore it as it should be worn, during working hours, like all the other women members of staff?"

"I'm sorry," she said dully, "I wouldn't do it."

"And if I said the alternative was that you'd lose your job?"

Juliet touched her lips and found them wrinkled with dryness. She took a breath. "I still wouldn't do it."

He tapped a pencil on the desk top. "Stupid of me to ask such a question, wasn't it? I should have anticipated such an answer. Rebellion for the sake of it." She opened her mouth to protest, but he went on, "Some call it 'fire,' some call it 'spirit.' " He rose. "I, Miss Bourne, would call it rank disobedience." He walked around the desk and faced her. "Tell me, why the revolt against such a trivial thing as a dress?"

Now her ire was raised. "Trivial? You call the compulsory wearing of a garment at least 20 years out of date trivial? Not only do I object to a rule which, as I see it, arises out of a management policy which can only be described as a form of dictatorship—"

He raised his eyebrows. "So we're getting political

now, are we? My father was so right when he said, as a joke, that you would probably try to take over running the firm. You may not know it, Miss Bourne, but your anarchy is showing, an anarchy born no doubt of the teaching you received at art school, which was to make an impolite noise at all forms of law and order."

"Just how stupid can people in your position get?" she burst out. "You and your executive brethren seem to take a delight in perpetually regarding all artists as the lowest form of animal life!"

"Well," he smiled, provoking now, "aren't they?"

She was scarlet with anger, goaded all the more because he was watching her with an inscrutable expression in his eyes. "No, they are not! Without artists, the world would—"

"Spare me that, please. Don't go into touching details about the so-called virtues of your artist colleagues and how the world would be an unbearable place to live in without them. I question that, anyway."

She said coldly, trying to ignore his goading smile which, in its complacency, gave away that he had achieved what he had set out to do—arouse her to anger, "If you'll allow me to return to the subject under discussion—" He inclined his head mockingly. "I object not only to the color and the outdated style, but most of all to the ridiculously high neck which in this hot summer weather makes me feel like I'm suffocating. No doubt in winter, with the central heating going full blast, it would have the same unfortunate effect. It also irritates my skin and makes me break out in a rash."

He lounged against the desk, crossing his legs and folding his arms. "Why don't any of the other women members of staff suffer similar symptoms? I'll tell you why. It's your emotional state that creates the rash, your squirming dislike of having to obey the rules that are imposed on you from above. It's not the style of dress at all. It can't be, otherwise all the other women would be scratching away merrily at their necks, wouldn't they?"

"Are you trying to tell me in a roundabout way that I'm unbalanced, that I'm neurotic?"

He shrugged. "I'm not a psychologist, so how am I to know? But, as they say, if the shoe fits—"

"Well, it doesn't! If you must know, I am rebelling against the stuffy atmosphere of the whole store, and I'm not referring to the air conditioning." Now she had started, nothing was going to stop her, not even if he clamped his hand over her mouth to force her to be quiet. He made no such move, so she went on, "You might say that the dress was symbolic. Its style typifies the 'high class' aura this establishment has around it like the rings round Saturn. The prices you charge are enough to keep away most of the women, the ordinary women, of the town. You may not know it, but you've got a name for being expensive."

"That may be so," he said evenly, not seeming to resent her remarks, "but Majors aren't exactly bankrupt."

"But, don't you see," she persisted, wishing she possessed the verbal expertise to convert him to her point of view, "Curlews are cashing in on your 'expensive' image. In almost every case, their prices are cheaper than yours."

"I'm more aware than you think, Miss Bourne, of the image of cheapness that Curlews have put about. It's largely a myth, as you would have discovered if you'd gone into the whole subject of Curlew's prices from a professional standpoint as I have, instead of the very amateur, 'customer' angle from which you viewed the matter. Experience has taught me to look at other people's prices with a discriminating, not to say suspicious, eye, which you with your ignorance of the ways of the retail world could not do. The goods Curlews sell in every department at a low price are purchased solely for that purpose, to create a 'cheap' image. Their other goods are sold at prices comparable with ours."

She felt she was losing ground. "All the same, Curlews have a name for being the shop where 'ordinary' women go, and Majors are regarded as the 'high-class' women's shop. Malcolm told me—"

"Ah yes, the inestimable boyfriend. Tell me, is he an executive of the firm?"

"You know very well he's only a junior assistant."

"You surprise me. I thought he must at least be a director." He watched the color sting her cheeks.

"Well, they adopted the slogan he suggested and gave him a pay raise for it: *The Call of Curlews*."

"And did he also suggest that they use that maddeningly repetitive sound that greets you as you enter the store, the call of the curlew itself? A beautiful, winsome, poignant sound when heard in the right place—high up on the moor—but enough to drive you mad when heard constantly above the din of the customer's chatter."

"Yes, he did."

"Ah, a real 'ideas' man. They should put him on the advertising staff. Or even promote him to administration."

"Well, he's not in either. He's in the carpet department."

"Carpet department? What a waste of a brilliant brain. Someone should tell them what they're missing." He grinned sarcastically.

"He may only be a carpet salesman," she said defensively, "but the people at the top do listen to him when he tells them things, and to all their assistants with ideas, however junior they may be."

"A gentle hint, I suppose, that Majors should do the same?"

"Why not? It's the young people who've got the ideas these days." He laughed sardonically at that. Nevertheless she continued, "If you invented some slogans yourself, like . . . like," she groped, "Like 'Major reductions, Make Mine Majors' or—or 'You get more for less at Majors', you would get the ordinary people to come here, too."

He paced the room. "You've done it for me, Miss Bourne. Do you want a pay raise on the strength of your commendable but slightly feeble poetic efforts?"

She stood up angrily. "I might as well hand in my notice. It's obvious I don't fit in here. I never will, wherever you try to place me, whatever department you let me join. I'll relieve you of my irritating presence. I'll go to the employment exchange, I'll join the queue for jobs. . . ."

He pulled her hand from the handle and held on to it. "Don't be such an impetuous little fool, Juliet. What are you trying to do, tear yourself up into little pieces, like you did to your paintings, because you consider yourself a failure? You're such a damned rebel you'd refuse to knuckle under to any kind of authority, no matter where you worked!"

She tried to remove her hand from his, but failing, let it rest there slackly. "I can't help what I am. When I see things that are wrong, I want to put them right. Is that such a crime?"

He dropped her hand and shook his head. "A law unto yourself, aren't you? What are we going to do about you?" His fingers closed around her bare arms and he looked her over. "The dress suits you like that, there's no doubt about it." Her heart leapt. There was appreciation in his eyes which he didn't even try to hide. Then they narrowed. "The new image." Her heart settled down. He was seeing her not as a woman, but as a new kind of Major employee.

"May I . . . go on wearing it like this?" He didn't answer, just looked. "Please, Drew?"

He scanned her face, saw the appeal there, removed his hands and turned away. "It's difficult. There are all the others to consider." He stood at the window, his legs stiff, hands in pockets, his back rigid. "In the circumstances, I'm afraid I'll have to say 'no.' "

She had lost. She bit her lip, hesitated, then ran to the door. "Goodbye, Drew."

He called her back, but she had gone.

CHAPTER THREE

Juliet stayed away from work the next day. What was the use? she asked herself. She decided not to tell her parents. She played truant, leaving the house at the usual time but taking a bus going in the opposite direction and getting out in the heart of the countryside. Then she walked, fretting, worrying, trying to think, stopping only for a few sandwiches and a cup of tea at a snack bar.

She walked until her legs refused to carry her, then she sat on a milestone at the roadside, ignoring the curious looks of car drivers as they sped past. One or two slowed down, thinking she wanted a lift, but she waved them on.

With her elbows on her knees and her chin in her hands, she didn't even try to fight the depression that weighed her down. If she resigned from Majors, she would have to find something else to do. No other job would fall into her lap as this one had.

She would have to go on interviews and fight for any position in competition with other girls. And she needed the money to help her parents. The whole point of leaving art school had been to earn her living and pay her way.

Perhaps Drew had been right in saying she was too rebellious and would refuse to bow down to any authority, no matter who it was. But that was her nature and she couldn't alter it. She sighed, finding no solution.

Her watch told her it was safe to return home on the next bus without arousing her parents' suspicions. But she arrived to find her mother frantic with worry.

"I've been out of my mind! Where have you been all day? Drew phoned. He wanted to know why you hadn't gone to work. When I told him that was where I thought you were, he grew frantic with worry, too."

Juliet smiled. She could imagine Drew being frantic—with delight at her absence!

Cynthia went on, "If you didn't go to work, where did you go?"

She answered her mother's outburst with one word, "Walking."

"Walking? Darling," Cynthia sounded deeply worried, "they haven't given you the sack?"

Juliet winced at the anxiety in her mother's voice. It was too much an echo of the uneasiness which had stalked her all day like a criminal doggedly pursuing a victim. "I don't know, Mom. If they haven't then I'll probably have to quit." Her voice was strained and she flopped down, white-faced, into an armchair. "Yesterday Drew called me in. I'd transgressed again, overstepped the limits beyond which the policy of Major and Son won't allow their employees to go."

"Was it your dress?"

Juliet nodded. "Then you can hardly blame Drew for telling you off, can you? I thought you'd been far too drastic with it."

When Cedric came in, Cynthia told him what had happened. To Juliet's surprise and chagrin he advised caution. She had thought that at least her father would be on her side.

"You've got to have a certain amount of discipline among the staff to run a business successfully, dear," he said. "You can't have employees behaving like anarchists."

Juliet flinched. Anarchy was Drew's word, and in using

it her father was as good as putting her in the wrong. "Staff can't make their own rules and flout those of the management. Be reasonable."

But she was incapable of seeing reason. In her present mood of self-pity, brought on partly by fatigue and partly because there seemed to be no one who was prepared to give her the sympathy and support she craved, she would admit that no one was right but herself. She chafed against the necessity to conform and thus lose her identity, identity which she cherished because it was such a vital part of her development as an artist.

"But they're so inflexible, Dad. They won't give an inch in any direction."

He said with a smile, "You mean they won't give in to you. Knowing my daughter, she probably went about things in a rash, tactless way—"

The phone rang and Cedric went to answer it. Juliet called, "It's probably Malcolm. I promised to go out with him tonight. Put him off, will you, Dad?"

But it wasn't Malcolm. Her father called her, handing over the receiver. "Your boss. The 'and Son' part of Majors."

Her heart thumped as she took the phone. What excuse could she give for her absence? She could hardly plead illness because he knew she was perfectly fit. Tell him the truth, that she couldn't face another session of censure and reprimand with him.

"Juliet? Where the devil have you been all day?"

"I took a bus ride."

"Playing truant?"

She sighed. "If you like to put it that way."

"People who play truant are usually afraid."

"I wasn't afraid. I was—" She thought the words, "I

was fed up, miserable, depressed, hating myself, hating you—" But they stopped short at her lips.

"I want to see you. Tonight."

"Sorry," she snapped. "I've got a date."

"Then you'll have to break it. I told you, I want to see you. Have dinner with me. I'll give you half an hour."

He slammed down the phone and she looked at the receiver as though it was a poisonous snake. Then she dialed Malcolm's number, excusing herself from their meeting and saying she would explain tomorrow.

Dressing to go out with Drew put her in a defiant mood. She chose the most flamboyant outfit in her wardrobe, a long-sleeved heavily embroidered blouse, fringed suede waistcoat and scarlet tight-fitting trousers. Black dress indeed! She would show Drew Major.

Her mother frowned. Her father asked her whose country's national dress she was wearing and could she still speak the language of her motherland? She ran out to Drew's car. She didn't want him to see the inside of the house she lived in. She could imagine his disdain if he were to see the poverty of her home in comparison with the richness of his.

She watched hopefully for his shocked reaction to her clothes, but apart from the merest flicker of his eyebrows, nothing happened. Disappointed, she provoked him.

"In these things I'm wearing you can't take me to one of your high class places, can you?"

"My dear Juliet, as my guest you really have no right to speak to me like that." His tone was deliberately high-handed.

He had successfully wielded the newspaper and she had contracted, squashed, like a fly on the window pane. She stole a look at his clothes. She was shaken to discover that he was not dressed in his usual impeccable executive style. His shirt was floral, with matching tie, his jacket, tailored to perfection, was suede, his trousers the most up to date in men's wear.

"I'm sorry." Her apology was belated and just a little flat. Her provocation had misfired.

The restaurant he took her to was along a seemingly endless passage. The entrance doors bore stained glass windows depicting various aspects of modern living—aircraft, sports cars, space capsules, long-haired youth of both sexes fixed in the many twisting, writhing, almost primitive attitudes adopted by modern youth at play.

The paintings around the walls which could hardly be discerned in the half-light of the long, low room, were unintelligible enough to gladden the heart of any modern artist. Juliet looked across the table at Drew and wondered how he knew of the existence of such a place.

"Well?" he smiled. "Are your aesthetic sensibilities pleased by the surroundings? Is your artistic temperament pleased, your appetite for the new and the different satiated?"

He was laughing at her, of course, but she smiled nevertheless. "I was wondering how you knew about it. I suppose you bring your women here regularly."

He raised a corrective hand. "Singular, please. Never plural. Woman, not women. I never complicate my life by having more than one girlfriend at a time."

"That's such a relief," she was sarcastic back, because for some reason his admission, whether true or false, pained her. "Don't let your current lady friend know you took me out to dinner tonight, will you? She might be jealous."

He looked at her eyes, full of spirit, her face, full of fire, her figure, too conspicuous to be overlooked, and murmured, "You could well be right."

They ordered and when they were alone again, she said, "May I ask who she is?"

"My current girlfriend? Her name's Camille Wyngard. Her father's a highly placed civil servant, something important in the Treasury; her mother's a socialite."

"What's she like?" Her brain felt oddly numb, enabling her to speak only in monosyllables. "Is she rich?"

"Very. Now, let me see, what is she like?" He rubbed his chin and studied Juliet's face as if seeking inspiration there. "Beautiful, naturally. Shapely, naturally. Brown-haired, brown-eyed, medium height. And . . . er . . ." he withdrew his eyes from hers, "all woman."

Juliet searched frantically for the waiter. When would he bring the food? There must be something else she could do with her hands besides clasping them like this under the table.

Failing to find him, she returned to the subject, drawn despite herself like a murderer returning to the scene of the crime. "Intelligent?"

"Of course. I never take out a dull-witted woman. They have nothing to talk about."

"Does she . . ." she squeezed out the words like juice from a lemon, "does she conform, unlike me? Does she do everything that's expected of her, unlike me? Does she accept everything at its face value without questioning it, as I do?"

"She gives me no trouble." He smiled. "She's tractable, pliable, and responsive . . . very." He eyed her. "Shall I go on?"

For a painful moment she imprisoned her bottom lip between her teeth. "No, thank you."

The food arrived and as they started eating, he asked, "Tell me, why the dramatic absence from work today?"

"I wondered when that was coming." Juliet concentrated on her meal. "You know very well why."

"Unless your excuse is really watertight, you'll have to lose a day's pay, you know." He sounded as if he was smiling, but she wouldn't raise her eyes to confirm it.

"What's the use of coming back? I'll stay away until the end of the week, then you won't have the embarrassment of calling me into your office and paying me off and telling me you have no further use for my services."

"They're the staff manager's and cashier's jobs, not mine." He was being deliberately difficult.

"I've failed in everything you've given me."

"You're beginning to tear yourself apart. I should have expected it. It's in character."

"Everything I do is wrong. You know that."

He put down his knife and fork. "Are you trying to talk me into dismissing you, thus completing the process of self-destruction?"

She shrugged helplessly, finding her food difficult to swallow. "There's no need for me to do that. You've already made up your mind to get rid of me. That's why you've asked me out tonight, to soften the blow."

He resumed eating. "My dear girl, I'm a businessman. Where the interests of the firm are concerned, I never 'soften the blow.' Do you think I'd really be such a despicable hypocrite as to dine and wine a girl I was about to throw out of her job?" She would not look at him. "Juliet!"

At the sharp note in his voice she looked up.

"I was going to offer you a promotion."

It couldn't be true. She searched for mockery in his face, but there was none. For a moment her spirits soared, like a lark rising joyously into a blue, limitless sky. Then, like a lark descending from the heights, they dropped like a stone, scooping out a crater in her hopes.

"You're joking."

"I swear I'm not."

"Then you're doing it because of who I am, because my mother was once engaged to your father."

"What do you take me for? I told you, I'm a businessman. I know ability when I see it, latent and undeveloped though it may be."

"And, in your opinion, I've . . . got it?"

"I think so. I think that embedded deep down in all that show of rebellion is something of great promise." He paused while the waiter removed the empty plates. "I'm convinced that you possess that priceless thing called 'vision,' an attribute so rare that it's misunderstood and abused by those who haven't got it. People with vision . . . and they're few enough . . . can somehow project their minds into the future and see things as they could be. They spend their time, like you, fretting because things aren't changing fast enough. Others . . . usually those who are afraid of change and, by heaven, there are more than enough of those types around . . . exist in the present, seeing things only as they are or were, and denying that the future exists."

She looked away, not knowing whether to thank him for the compliments he was paying her, or accept what he was saying as matter-of-factly as he was saying it.

"For some time now," he went on, "my father and I have been toying with the idea of opening a boutique." Her heart began to hammer unmercifully. "We want somehow to get the younger age groups into the store. Up to now they've made themselves conspicuous by their absence. You're one of them. Can you tell me why?"

"I think," she said slowly, trying to keep the excitement out of her voice, "it's because there's nothing there for them, nothing to bring them in."

"Exactly. We thought a boutique, geared to their needs, might do the trick. Am I right?"

"If it were run in the right way, and by . . . by the right person, yes. Who. . . ." Dare she ask? Would she be snubbed if she did? She decided to risk it. "Who did you have in mind?"

He smiled. "You. After all I've been saying, who else? With your artistic training, your flair for design, your impertinence . . . no, in the circumstances let's be kind and call it courage in the face of established custom, you should be able to make your point and your presence known among the age group to which you have the fortune . . . or some might call it misfortune . . . to belong."

"You mean . . . I'd be in charge? Of the whole thing?"

"Yes. You'd come into the category of buyer. Compared with the very junior sales assistant you are now, it would mean a considerable increase in salary and status."

"But," for the life of her she couldn't think why she was raising obstacles to her promotion, except perhaps to test the sincerity of his proposition, to make quite sure, like a child being offered a longed-for present, that it was really meant for her, "but suppose the other members of staff don't like it? Because I'm so new they might regard it as favoritism."

"You? A favorite of mine?" He laughed loudly. "That's rich, after all the fights we've had! Anyway, I'd soon disillusion them. If you make a mess of things or put a foot wrong, I'll be down on you like a building collapsing in an earthquake. There's no sentiment in business, my girl, nor in me, as I've told you before."

She smiled, bold now in her elation. "I told you before that I didn't think you had a heart to break. It seems I was right."

He raised an eyebrow. "So you have X-ray eyes. You

can see through the walls of my chest and have disco-vered that I'm a heartless automaton, devoid of feelings and anything resembling emotions?"

"Yes." She grinned, pleasure at the new life within her grasp giving her eyes the sparkle of sunlight on water. "You've got an automatic pump where your heart should be. Even if you had one, you'd never give it in love, would you? If a girl came along who threatened to steal it, you'd lock it in a vault with walls seven feet thick and throw away the key!"

"My word," his eyes narrowed, "In more appropriate circumstances I'd make you pay for that colossal piece of impudence. As my father said, you need to be kept under control."

"Sorry." She was smiling as she said it. She was floating on air and hardly aware of what she was saying. "Will there be papers to sign or a letter from you confirming my change of position within the firm?"

"You're taking a lot for granted. You haven't got the job yet."

She frowned and her heart raced, this time with fear. It was like a curtain coming down in the middle of an act. "What do you mean?" She underwent a complete change of mood. Her elation vanished, her eyes dulled over like a curtain being pulled across a lighted window. Had she talked herself out of the job?

"I've said I'm sorry," she told him heavily, uncertain now and apprehensive. "If it does any good, I'll say it again. And again." She moved to stand up and leave him. It had been a long day. She was tired from her miles of aimless walking, from the strain of fretting and worrying as she had tramped miserably through the countryside. She had been given a vision of the Promised Land and had had it snatched away. She had failed again. She couldn't take any more. "Good night."

He wrenched her down into her seat. "My God, what a temperament for some poor man to have to keep up with one day! Mercurial is hardly the word. Does wonder boy Malcolm know what he's taking on when he marries you?"

"I'm sorry," she said again, trying to disengage her wrist from his fingers.

"It's no good doing that," he said. "If I let you go, you'll be off again. And I'm certainly not chasing you across the restaurant and out into the street like a man after a woman he's madly in love with."

"I'm s—" He closed her lips with his fingers, preventing her from saying the word.

"Listen to me, my girl. I'm going to ask you a question and your whole future depends on the answer. If I promote you to the status of buyer . . . a very responsible position . . . will I be able to trust you? Will you sober up and stop being so damnably impetuous?"

"I'll try." She raised her eyes to his, but there was no elation in them now. There was nothing she could do to recapture the euphoria which had swept over her earlier. "Really try. I promise." She looked down. "And you can take your hand away. I won't run off."

"I don't know that I want to take my hand away."

She asked bitterly, her mood changing again, "What are you trying to do, make me one of your women? Haven't you got enough already? I told you before you're not my type. I don't like men with money. We agreed we were completely incompatible."

He drew in his lips like a man exasperated. "You can say that again! Isn't it ever possible for the two of us to carry on a normal conversation without this constant backbiting and the petty, meaningless arguments you somehow get us involved in?"

She opened her mouth. "I'm—" She stopped at the ferocious look he gave her.

"Come on." He rose. "We'll carry on this discussion in the car. There we can fight like cat and dog without the fear of being overheard or interrupted."

As they drove through the streets she asked, "Where are we going?"

"Since it's not late, not even dark yet, out to the country."

They didn't speak again until there were green fields on both sides of them. The sun, a golden ball, hovered tantalizingly above the horizon, shedding a golden glow more brilliantly as the minutes passed, like a last fling before final extinction.

Juliet shivered in anticipation of the loss of the sun's warmth. "I'd rather go home."

"All in good time. You'll have to put up with my company just a little longer." He drove on for a while. "I spoke to Romeo on the phone this morning."

"You mean Malcolm? What for?"

"To find out whether you had run to him for sympathy, and to Curlews for a job. He said," he glanced obliquely at her and in the dusk his eyes were sardonic, "much as he loved you, he didn't keep a detailed diary of your movements and whereabouts at any given moment. He didn't think you were the sort to run off with another man. He said he'd hazard a guess that you had run off, though, away from me. Was he right?"

She wondered if he was. It was true she'd run away, but not from her problems. She had taken them with her, but had taken them home again.

"I suppose in a sense I was running away from myself. I didn't get far." She smiled at him. "I soon caught up with me again."

He laughed. "I'm relieved I wasn't the one you were running from."

"Oh, but you were," she told him with disarming honesty. "You scare me stiff."

"Why, Juliet?" His voice sounded odd.

"Because . . . because you seem to have such power over me, and I fear you because of it." How could she tell him that? Just knowing it would increase his power. She shrugged. "I don't know."

"I think we'd better change the subject." He pulled off the road onto the grass bank, switched off the engine and rested his arm along the back of her seat. His hand found her shoulder, then moved under her hair to rest against the bareness of her neck. She held her breath at his touch.

Apart from the twitter of the birds dying down with the approach of darkness, the occasional swish of a passing car, and the hum now and then of a night insect, the silence was intense.

She looked at his profile and felt her fear of him tautening her muscles. It was fear of a different kind this time, a fear of the emotions the feel of him was awakening in her and of what his hands might persuade her to do if they chose to make demands.

His hand moved back to the upholstery which he stroked and moulded between restless fingers. As he began to speak, the movement stilled.

In the darkening silence his voice, though soft, sounded loud. "By promoting you to this new position, Juliet, I'm putting a great deal of trust in you." He looked at her. "You realize that?"

"Curlews have a boutique," she told him, "but Malcolm says it's not very successful."

"But," he smiled, "with your inventiveness and good ideas, ours will be." His fingers rested momentarily on her neck again. "Won't it?"

"I hope so. I hope . . . I don't let you down."

He laughed and withdrew his arm, leaning forward and switching on the lights. "So do I, considering all the capital we'll be sinking into the set-up. You realize you'll be handling a great deal of money? You'll have to buy fitments and stock. You'll be in charge of ordering, making sure deliveries arrive when promised. You'll have to cope with reps, serve customers, handle complaints with tact. It'll be necessary for you to dovetail with other departments, consult with display and advertising, and deal gently with your fellow artists in the art department. A lot of money will be passing through your hands. You'll be allocated certain sums of money which you, in turn, will have to allocate to the various sections of your department." He faced her and she could only see the outline of him now. "You realize what you're taking on? Or have I said enough to make you want to get out of the car and run a mile?"

"The prospect is daunting," she said softly, "but it's a challenge I'm going to accept."

"Good," he said, and drove on.

"Does your father know about this idea of a boutique?" she asked.

"Of course. After all, he's the chairman."

"Did he agree to my taking charge?"

"Absolutely. He said you've got what it takes."

She colored in the darkness. "That was very nice of him." She asked playfully, "Did you agree?"

He answered softly, "I do believe you're provoking me. So, just to annoy you, I'll evade the question and say it remains to be seen."

The car moved past the dark shapes that became trees growing beside the hedgerows. Juliet mused out loud, "I'm glad your father at least has faith in me. Does he," she asked, "play a very big part in running the firm?"

"No. He takes a back seat. What he said when you came to tea was pretty near the truth. When he's in his office . . . and he's more often out than in . . . his feet do find their way to the desk!"

"Your mother, does she . . . ?"

"What about my mother?" His tone was hard.

She wondered what she had said to upset him. "Does she take much interest . . . ?"

"In the firm? None at all."

"I'm surprised. I'd have thought she might have been a help to your father in some ways." He was silent. "I mean, for instance," she stumbled on, "on the fashion side? Or the furnishings? Giving a woman's viewpoint. . . ." Her voice trailed off.

"My parents," he said curtly, "are barely on speaking terms." Now Juliet was silent. "They've hardly exchanged a polite word for months."

She was beginning to understand Warren Major's harsh attitude toward his wife the day she and her mother had gone there to tea. "Perhaps," she ventured, "if your father encouraged her—"

"Don't put the blame on my father," he interrupted curtly. "If you knew the truth you would apportion the blame to the right quarter."

"But surely," she said tritely, "it usually takes two . . . ?"

He interrupted with violence, "But it only takes one to wreck a marriage. My mother's son I may be, but I'm not blind. She's driven my father so far away from her that I wonder he hasn't left her long ago. If you think he's been

faithful to her all these years, then you can think again."
His voice deadened. "He's had one woman after
another." There was an anguished silence. She felt his
pain, the suffering that only a child of an unsuccessful
marriage can feel.

"So now I know," she said quietly, "the fate my
mother escaped."

Without emotion he said, "If my father had married
your mother, he would have remained faithful unto death.
He was madly in love with her . . . a love which would
have lasted through his life."

"How do you know?"

"He's told me often enough. She broke his heart."

"But only," she had to defend her mother, "because of
the sort of person he was. He was crazy with ambition.
That much I did gather from her when she told me about
him."

Softly he said, "She would have changed him."

"But," she protested, "at what expense to herself?
Anyway," she went on unconvinced, "let's be realistic.
He would have reverted. And then he would have broken
her heart. He would still have had his women. He's the
sort of man who couldn't help it. It's his way of proving,
if only to himself, his virility, his continued attractiveness to the opposite sex."

He repeated bitterly, "If you knew the truth, you
wouldn't find it so easy to blame him for what he's done
with his life. Who can stand in judgment on a man who
has been forced by his wife . . . my mother . . . out of his
rightful place beside her, first into another bed and then
into another room?" There was a poignant silence with
only the hiss of the tires on the road to break it. They
were nearly home now.

Drew went on, "His life with a deadly cold, incompatible woman has soured him completely in his relations with women. It could, I suppose, happen to any man."

"Even you?" He turned his head briefly and she gave him a flickering half smile which he caught through the darkness.

"Not on your life! When ... if ... I marry, the woman I take to bed with me will be made to measure, all a woman should be. She won't fail me in any way because I will certainly not fail her. I would want my passion to be reciprocated in full. But," he became cynical, "there's little possibility of my ever marrying, of my ever legalizing any liaison I might have with a woman. I've learned the doctrine my father has preached to me since puberty. It was a doctrine he formulated after losing your mother, when bitterness set in ... that women exist only to satisfy a man's physical needs and for that alone. He told me to take one and go on to the next, and the next. ..."

The car drew up outside Juliet's house. "And," she tried to smile but her lips were tight, "did he succeed in getting his message through? Did he successfully indoctrinate you? Have you followed his illustrious example, without fail, without scruple?"

His next words came like a slap across her face with the back of his hand. "Wouldn't you like to know?" His tone was challenging and in the light of the street lamp she could see that his eyes were diamond bright and his smile hard and cynical.

It incensed her. "Speaking purely as a friend of the family," she said, keeping her tone silky, "and not as an upstart employee of yours, all I can say is that if Camille Wyngard is in love with you ... though how any woman could be in that condition is beyond me . . . then I'm sorry for her from the bottom of my heart. I wouldn't be in her shoes for a million dollars!"

"Don't worry, my dear acid-tongued Juliet," he leaned across and opened the door for her, "you never will be." She scrambled out. "If Malcolm ever deserts you, and you find yourself in need of another Romeo, count me out."

Juliet slammed the car door. He wound down the window. "Thank you for the meal," she forced out, the prickle of tears behind her eyes stinging her like a nettle, "and for the enlightening lecture on the place of females in your life. But I didn't need the warning it contained. The man I marry will be as unlike you as a . . . as a sparrow from a vulture!"

His laughter followed her to the front door. He got out of the car and called out, "Come to my office in the morning, nine-thirty prompt."

To that she didn't have an answer. He had had the last word.

Juliet had to pacify the rebel inside her when she presented herself to Drew Major the next morning.

"Sit down, Miss Bourne." His tone was offhand. The quarrel that had taken place in the car the night before might never have happened.

"This boutique," he said. "As a buyer, your salary will be increased." He named the sum they were prepared to pay her and she was so staggered by its generosity she nearly rejected it. "Do you really think," she asked shakily, "that I'm worth all that?"

He gave her a calculating look. "Personally no, but my father insists that is the correct amount for the job."

She looked down. "I'll have to thank him. As I said

before, I'm extremely grateful to him for his faith in my abilities."

"I'll have faith in you, Miss Bourne, when, and only when, you prove yourself worthy of it."

"Perhaps," she said, smiling and knowing she was provoking him, "your father has more vision than you, and is a better judge of character?"

"I suggest we leave the chairman of the company out of this discussion," he responded icily, "otherwise you might find yourself in very deep water. Floundering around, in fact, in the cold world without a job!"

"I'm sorry," she said wearily. The two words were beginning to sound as monotonous as water dripping from a leaking tap.

He told her the amount of money the company was prepared to sink into the proposed boutique. It was a very large sum. When she protested that it was almost certainly far more than she would require he replied, "Don't worry, it won't be long before you come screaming to me, like all your other buyer colleagues, that it's simply not enough. But in your case, unless you can prove to me not only in black and white but also in the form of turnover that you really deserve more, you won't get it."

"So I'm on trial?"

"You are. The verdict is in your hands, and yours alone."

Somehow she would have to find the confidence to meet this challenge. She had a sudden vision of sleepless nights worrying about her job and about whether she would rise to Warren Major's high opinion of her. She nearly turned the job down on the spot. But something in Drew Major's face, as though he was daring her to take it on, renewed her fighting spirit and she asked where they had decided to put the boutique.

"We're prepared to allocate a reasonably large area of the fashion department to the venture. We feel it will fit in, being a branch of fashion itself."

Now doubts were creeping in. "But it's a very specialized form of fashion."

"I'm aware of that, but the money we can devote to this project isn't limitless."

"Can I be assured that I'll have a free hand in the design of the boutique, and in the style of clothes I stock for sale?"

"Within reason. As you're so inexperienced, you'll have a greater need for consultation than our other buyers."

"With whom?" she asked, her heart sinking slowly like a torpedoed ship.

"The buyer of the more conventional fashions, display, the accessories buyer and so on."

Already she felt the stirrings of rebellion. "I don't see why." Her own ears told her she sounded sulky.

"Look, Juliet," he sat down at his desk opposite her, "I'm doing my damnedest not to bring out that fighting spirit of yours. I'm keeping calm, I'm being gentle. But by heaven, if you start any of your tricks, if you rebel against the advice I'm giving you which is based on years of experience, and what's more, if you start abusing me, I'll fire you. Understand?"

She opened her mouth to protest at the unfairness of it, took a breath, opted for discretion and started to mouth the words "I'm sorry." But before she could get the second word out, he was around the desk with his hands at her throat.

"If you apologize to me again, woman, I swear I won't be able to stop myself, I'll throttle you! Then I'll put you across my knee!"

She colored violently and tried desperately to remove

his hands, but they slipped upward until his fingers burrowed into her hair and gripped her head. He tipped it backward and looked into her eyes.

"My word, I see your mother there," he murmured.

Their gaze locked for a few seconds, then his hand fell away and he returned to his seat. She was left with a scarlet face and with nervous hand she tried to smooth down her hair.

It took her a few moments to compose herself, then she asked, "What's the next move?"

His voice was normal and controlled when he answered, "We've already contacted contractors to come and erect partitions. They start tomorrow. Your first job is to order stock. You understand that we always add to the wholesale price and that the price at which we actually sell the garments must represent a profit?"

"Of course. Any fool knows that."

He raised an eyebrow at her tone. She hissed, "S . . . s . . ." closed her lips and held her breath. But he merely smiled and went on, "The best way to go about things in the initial stages is to contact firms by phone and ask their representatives to visit. They'll show you their wares and you can make your first orders that way. I warn you that once it gets on the salesmen's grapevine that you're in business, you'll have a stampede on your hands. The queue of sales reps may stretch all the way down the stairs to the ground floor!"

She rose and he said, "Miss Skimpton, buyer of coats, and Mrs. Rouse of separates will be able to give you a list of wholesalers you can telephone."

He saw her to the door. His hand came out and grasped hers. "Good luck, Juliet. You'll need it!"

She had a date with Malcolm that evening. As she put on her make-up and combed her shoulder-length hair, she recalled what had happened when, after seeing Drew, she had asked the other fashion buyers for the names and addresses of sales representatives.

First they had wanted to know why. Miss Skimpton had turned purple and had refused to believe it. Mrs. Rouse had been sceptical and had kept probing, trying to find out why it was that she, Juliet Bourne, had been chosen out of all the other members of the fashion staff to receive such a promotion. "You're new," she had said. "It's hardly fair to the others who've been here much longer."

"I think," Juliet had told her feebly, "he wanted someone with new ideas." But that had been the wrong thing to say. The two women had bristled and only with the greatest reluctance had they given her the information she required.

It had taken shorter than an hour for the whole fashion floor to hear about it. She saw groups whispering in corners draw apart and watch her as she passed. They looked at her as though she was something that had crawled out of a piece of cheese. It occurred to her to wonder if they were speculating about a possible liaison between herself and the company manager. This, to them, would have explained her sudden promotion.

"How are you making out with boss man?" Malcolm asked as they cycled side by side toward the open country. "He sounded pretty sharp on the phone the other day when he was checking on your movements. A bit like a probation officer keeping an eye on a young offender! You'd obviously offended him."

"Well," she laughed, "if you can call being threatened with the sack almost every time we have a business chat 'making out' with him, then we're doing fine! Actually, he's promoted me."

Malcolm wobbled and nearly fell off his bike. "What? You've only been there a few days! You're fooling."

"I'm not." She drew in behind him to allow a car to pass, then joined him again. "Meet Miss Juliet Bourne, fashion buyer, in charge of Major's new boutique. It doesn't exist yet, but it's more than a twinkle in its father's eye. Work starts on it tomorrow."

"You don't mean it!" He glanced across the road at a clearing in the woods. "Over there. Let's pull in. I need a rest to assimilate that piece of information."

They propped their bikes against a bush and sat down. "I bet that caused a stir among the Major retinue. What did the old hands say?" His tone changed to that of a crotchety old man. " 'We've been here 50 years and our fathers before us. You're just an insignificant young upstart. Why shouldn't we have got promotion?' "

She laughed. "You're dead right. Filthy looks by the dozen. They all started whispering. I'm sure they think Drew Major's made me his mistress and that's how I got the job."

Malcolm looked shocked at her flippant manner. "You keep away from boss man, Juliet. I wouldn't put it past him to try even that."

"He's not that sort," she said, but even as she spoke she knew he was. Hadn't he told her about his attitude to women, how he regarded them as objects who existed merely to satisfy men's physical needs?

"Anyway," Malcolm pulled her close and kissed her, "you're my woman." After a few minutes he said, "So Majors are having a boutique now? Curlews have got one, did you know?" She nodded. "Not very successful from all I hear. Too out of the way. No one seems to know it's there and the girls who do don't like patronizing it because it's tucked away in a corner of the fashion department."

"But," she said, concerned, "that's where Majors are going to put theirs."

"Then make them change their minds. It won't work. Glenda, who's in charge of Curlews' boutique, told me the reason. She said young girls run a mile from the older women on the fashion department staff. And if the boutique's placed so that they have to walk through the conventional fashion section and past all those bossy ladies to get at the things they've come for, they just won't come."

"Now you've got me worried." Juliet, chin in hand, stared at the tangle of bushes in front of them. "In that case, Majors have either got to give me a better site, or abandon the whole idea." She stood up. "I'm going straight to Drew in the morning."

Malcolm pulled her down again. "Are you really? Well, at the moment it's this evening, and you're with me. You say much more about that big-headed business tycoon called Drew Major and I'll begin to think things, my dear. We can't conduct a single conversation these days without your dragging his name into it."

He pulled her against him, but she struggled away. "Don't be silly, Malcolm. He's just my boss."

"And don't you forget it," Malcolm said, pulling her to her feet.

"I don't know why you're so worried. Drew and I have only got to meet and we start quarreling."

That pacified him a little and he kissed her as though he forgave her.

But that night in bed she realized how much Drew Major occupied her thoughts these days. She tossed and turned because the knowledge worried her. Why did she think about him so much? "It's only because he's the man

I work for," she told herself as she drifted into sleep.

Next morning she arrived at the store to find the workmen assembling their materials and carrying in their equipment. Miss Skimpton fussed and tutted, afraid that their dirty overalls and their saws and their ladders would brush against the clothes on display.

The sight of the workmen dismantling the corner which had been set aside for the new boutique made Juliet panic. She would have to see someone about it at once. She picked up the phone and dialed Drew's extension. His secretary answered.

"I'm sorry, Miss Bourne, but Mr. Major is out all day. Try Mr. Havering, the general manager."

Juliet fretted. She didn't want Mr. Havering, she wanted to see the man in charge. But she would have to make do with second best and hope that the general manager was empowered to authorize the change of plan and stop the workmen before they did too much damage.

Mr. Havering was in and she was invited to go and see him. He was a short man in his early forties, with a clipped moustache and a straight-shouldered, almost military bearing which he plainly hoped would make up for his lack of height.

He listened to her with a kindly interest and she thought she had succeeded in making some impression on him.

"I understand what you're saying, Miss Bourne," he said, "and sympathize with your point of view."

Her spirits lifted. She had made contact with one of the top men and now he was on her side.

"But," her spirits fell as sharply as a shooting star, "I disagree with you completely. The site for such a place as a . . . as a boutique," he tried out the word as if it were a new food and it tasted odd to him, "concerned with fashion as it is, is in the fashion department. I can't see how you can challenge the logic of that statement."

So the military bearing was no sham, it was there, a hard core beneath that show of kindliness. Juliet was annoyed with herself for having been taken in. She should have known that, as one of the Major hierarchy, he was made of the same unmalleable material as the others at the top.

She rose; she wouldn't waste her time. Because the 'and Son' part of the establishment was not available she would go to Warren Major, the chairman himself. She knew that he, also, was hard at the core . . . hadn't his son told her so? . . . but she was willing to take the risk and confront him. Perhaps by talking persuasively to him she would be able to mold him to her own wishes.

The secretary said that Mr. Warren Major was in and that he would see Miss Bourne.

As Juliet entered his office, the chairman of the company lowered his feet to the ground. The smile with which he greeted her was genuine and warm and Juliet felt that such a gesture of friendliness from him was rare enough to be remembered and cherished.

He seemed, Juliet thought, to be a man who was buoyed up by his own success. Like a giant plane speeding through the skies, magnificent in its remoteness, revered for its power and size, he roared through life above people's heads, reveling in his influence.

But, Juliet sensed as she sat down and looked at him, like an aircraft that had come crashing to earth and shattered to a pitiful stillness, so if he were to fall, through the ill turn of fortune, misjudgment or the thwarting of his plans, he would be brought down and lie scattered under the ruins of his own personality.

She glanced around the well-equipped office and, lavishly decorated and richly carpeted though it was, it had about it an air of rest and refuge rather than of the rhythm and bustle of meaningful work. She eyed the desk where his feet had been.

He threw back his head and laughed, his whole body shaking. "Looking for the dent?" He pointed. "There it is. I told you, didn't I?"

She laughed too. "I hope you didn't mind my coming to see you."

"Mind? My dear, I'm delighted." He sat forward, hands clasped, the gold of his rings glinting in the reflected sunlight. He seemed prepared to enjoy himself. "I wondered how long it would be before my son's most awkward, recalcitrant employee would have the impudence to make her way to the summit and demand the chairman's attention! After all, as I've said before, you're your mother's daughter."

Friendly though he was, she found herself just a little intimidated by what she had done. "You . . . you know about my new appointment, about the boutique?"

"Naturally. I negotiated your salary with my son, and much to his annoyance pushed the figure up and up until he wouldn't budge another penny! He said if we were going to pay that much, we might as well put someone in the job who was really worth it. I said I refused to let him talk like that about Cynthia Bourne's daughter."

She flushed at the son's low opinion of her, having to admit that it hit her where it hurt. "It was very good of you," she said inadequately. "I wouldn't have troubled you, but Drew . . . I mean your son . . . is out and the matter is urgent."

He looked concerned and said in a kindly way, "Tell me about it."

"How different he is from his son," she thought.

He listened sympathetically, but Juliet would not let herself be fooled by his understanding expression. "I know these Majors," she warned herself. "Dig down a few inches and you come up against granite."

"My boyfriend works for Curlews," she told him, "and he said their boutique is doing badly because they've placed it exactly where you have decided to put ours."

"And you, quite rightly, think we should learn from other people's mistakes, especially our rivals?"

"Well," she said, on the defensive, "don't you?"

He made a patting gesture in the air with his hand. "It's all right, my dear, don't bristle at the least provocation." She laughed and relaxed. "You see," he smiled, "I know how to deal with you, having learned by experience with your mother more years ago than I care to remember."

"So, Mr. Major," she pressed him, "could a decision be taken now about moving the boutique? The only reason I'm asking is because the builders are already working on the fashion floor. The sooner they're stopped the better."

He lifted the receiver and dialed the general manager's extension. He gave orders for the work on the new boutique to be halted at once. The builders were to be told to await further instructions.

She thanked him as he put down the phone and he asked her where she thought the new department should be sited.

"On the ground floor," she answered at once, "not too far from the entrance, built on a walk-in, walk-out basis, and designed so that as people pass by they can see the goods on display."

He beckoned her to sit beside him and, looking at a plan of the store, they discussed possible positions and agreed on a site.

He leaned back and laughed. "You know this is all highly irregular. This shouldn't be a decision arrived at by a committee of two, with one being a young, very inexperienced employee."

She said anxiously, "I don't want to do anything unconstitutional...."

"Don't you, my dear?" he laughed. "Well, I can assure you you've already done it! What my son will say when he returns tomorrow ...!" He leaned forward and whispered, "Shall I tell you a secret? I'm terrified of him!" She laughed as if she knew he was joking. "Well, perhaps I am overstating the case a little, but I can assure you on one point, I'm passing him over to you lock, stock and barrel. You've used your charm on me, now you'll have to use it on him. And my goodness, you'll need all the charm you possess to get around him!"

She laughed again, more to cover her apprehension then to express amusement. She rose to go, but he motioned her to remain seated. "Tell me, Juliet," he fiddled with a letter on his desk, "you must promise not to take umbrage at my question?" She nodded. "How is your mother placed for money? Is she reasonably comfortable financially? Can she manage to pay her way?"

Juliet was puzzled. Why was he referring to her mother as though she were a widow? "She's not alone, Mr. Major," she pointed out gently, "she has my father."

A flicker which might have been pain passed across his eyes. "I beg your pardon, my dear. Of course she has her husband. Somehow I still can't think of her as anything other than a woman alone. But the question still stands. You see, I can't ask her, so I have to ask her daughter."

"They're ... they're reasonably comfortable, thank you. Now I'm earning, I can help them."

"It's you who's had to make the sacrifice. You gave up

your studies to do that, didn't you?" She nodded. "I only wish it were within my power. . . ." He shook his head. "With my fortune. . . ." He shrugged hopelessly and it was what he did not say that caught at her throat.

A man with his wealth, his position and his influence was helpless to aid those he most wanted to because of etiquette, convention and the barrier of pride.

He was silent, lost apparently in a dream, and she cleared her throat and said, "What's the next step, Mr. Major?"

He straightened his shoulders and came back to earth. "Sorry, my dear, I was drifting. The next 'step' is hardly the right word." He smiled. " 'Obstacle' would be more appropriate, and that in the shape of my son. We tackle him next. He'll be in tomorrow." They stood up and he patted her shoulder. "I promise to try and soften him up before I pass him on to you!"

He took her arm and pulled her gently toward him, kissing her cheek. "I can't kiss your mother, so I kiss her daughter instead."

She turned at the door to thank him again for his help and support, and caught him off guard. His shoulders were sagging, his body drooping, his face corrugated with misery. He was like a fish caught in the net of his own unhappiness and who knew he was doomed to stay enmeshed for the rest of his life.

CHAPTER FOUR

Juliet's father was ill during the night. He had trouble with his breathing, and at one point was actually fighting for breath. Juliet was unable to sleep. She sat with her mother at his bedside, and they gave him all the comfort they were capable of.

Cynthia was torn in two about whether to phone the doctor and disturb him in the early hours or wait until morning. She decided to cope until breakfast time and then ask him to come over.

Consequently Juliet, when she did crawl into bed for a couple of hours' sleep before going to work, awoke late. Her mother had let her sleep longer than usual, thinking she was doing what was best for her.

But Juliet was horrified when she saw how late it was. She skipped her breakfast and decided to cycle to work because she had missed the bus and the next one was not due for half an hour. She cycled around the back of the store where the delivery vans parked to unload, leaned her bicycle against the wall, padlocked it and raced up the stairs, terrified in case Drew had sent for her.

Miss Skimpton greeted her joyfully with the news that she was wanted at once by Mr. Drew Major, and that he was livid with anger at discovering she had not yet arrived.

"He said," Miss Skimpton crowed, "that you were to go up to him the moment you arrived." She looked at her watch and beamed, "An hour late. You'll find him in a good mood!"

Without waiting to remove her jacket or look in a mirror, Juliet made for the stairs again . . . the lift would

267

have been too slow . . . and sprinted two at a time up the four flights. As she reached the sixth floor, gasping for breath, Warren Major came out of his room.

He saw her dishevelled appearance and put out his hand to stop her. "Something wrong, my dear? You don't look up to par."

She shook her head, eyeing Drew's door and breathing heavily. "I'm late. I was up most of the night with my mother—"

He cut in at once, "She's ill?"

"No. My father . . . he had a bad attack. I'm sorry I'm late, Mr. Major." She moved towards Drew's door, but Warren stopped her again.

"If there's anything I can do to help your mother, or," as an afterthought, "your father . . . ?"

She shook her head, thanking him. "The doctor's coming this morning. He'll prescribe something."

Drew's door opened. "Miss Bourne!" he thundered, "not only do you arrive at a disgustingly late hour, but you stand there chatting with my father as if you were paying the firm a social call instead of reporting for duty."

Warren walked toward him raising his hand as if to caution him. "Son—" he began, but Drew interrupted.

"I'll deal with this, Father." Warren started to speak again, but Juliet turned to him.

"Please, Mr. Major, it doesn't matter."

Warren shrugged and walked away.

"Crawling again, Miss Bourne?" were the words that nearly knocked her sideways as she sat down.

"Crawling, Mr. Major?" She shook her head, which was beginning to throb. "I'm sorry, I don't know what you mean."

"Yes," he said nastily, "you look as though you're

barely awake. Got a hangover, Miss Bourne, after a night out with the boyfriend?" Her head drooped and she let his sarcasm pass over her. "Chatting up the chairman at every opportunity is what I mean by crawling. Running to him when you're in trouble, going to him over my head and when I'm out of the way in order to get exactly what you want, knowing I would oppose your ideas and your demands every inch of the way."

"I'm sorry," she answered wearily, "that you think of it like that. But you were out and I tried the general manager—"

"That was exceedingly considerate of you."

"And since immediate action was necessary, because the workmen had already begun, I thought the best thing to do was to go to your father. I realize what I did was unconstitutional, and I'm sorry."

"Unconstitutional? It was outrageous! What should have been a decision by the management committee was arrived at by two people, one of whom should have known better and the other so insignificant that if she never put in an appearance in the store again no one would miss her! I've never, in all my time with this firm," he thrust his hands into his pockets and came around to stand in front of her, "had as an employee anyone who's given me so much trouble in so short a time. Your wilful and constant refusal to abide by the rules is such that if there were a rule against having rules, you'd rebel against that." He walked up and down the room. "What peculiar chemistry did your parents use to produce such a creature as you? All I can say is, heaven be praised that they don't come like you very often!"

Hoping to distract his attention from herself and longing to know his verdict on the removal of the proposed boutique to the site she and his father had chosen, she asked, "Do you approve of your father's decision, Mr. Major? Will you allow—"

"No, I will not allow! And you dare to call it my father's decision? That's rich! Your decision, you mean. You knew very well that if you went to see him you'd get exactly what you wanted. He'd give you the earth if you asked for it."

She stared up at him, whispering, "But why?"

"Because of your mother, that's why. He's still in love with her, didn't you know?"

She paled. "You can't mean it?" She put her hand to her head as though a brick had hit her. The room had started spinning. She wondered if she was going to faint.

He paused in his walking. "Is there something wrong?"

She closed her eyes. "It's probably because I didn't have any breakfast. I was so late I—"

"If you're stupid enough to come to work without food, then you deserve everything you get. Don't expect any sympathy from me."

His unkindness, his callous disregard of her feelings which, in the circumstances, amounted almost to cruelty, drove her to her limits. She felt the tension inside her snap like a rubber band being pulled beyond its strength and her anger knew no bounds.

She hammered with her fist on his desk and shrieked, "No, I don't expect any sympathy from you! Or compassion. Or understanding. What you haven't got you can't give, can you? I don't expect anything from you in the way of feelings. I was right that day when I said you hadn't got a heart. . . ." The anxieties of the night, the lack of sleep and food caught up with her and she began to sob, lowering her arms onto his desk and resting her head on them.

"If you think you're going to get around me as you got around my father by putting on an act—"

Unable to stand another moment in his presence, she jerked herself off the chair and lurched to the door. It was opened and Warren stood there. Unsteady as she was she fell against him, and he put his arms around her and offered her comfort. She sobbed against his shoulder.

"It's my father," she whispered, "it's my father," over and over again.

"What's the matter with her father?" she heard Drew ask.

"Taken ill in the night," Warren told him. "She and her mother have hardly had any sleep."

"But why the hell didn't she tell me?"

"I don't suppose you gave her a chance, son. I heard her shouting. What have you been saying to her to bring her to this state?"

She heard Drew move as if he had slumped into a chair.

Warren stuffed a handkerchief into her hand and she took it gladly. He said over her head, "You never talk to any other member of our staff as you talk to her." His voice softened. "Why her, son, why her?"

There was no reply.

"Are you," Warren's voice persisted, "punishing me for the life I've led? Hurting me through her, knowing how I feel?"

Juliet could not bear to hear any more. She pulled away from him and, her sobs growing less, hid her face in his handkerchief. She knew she must look a sight and she could not let Drew Major see. He thought little enough of her already.

"You'd better come to my room, my dear." Warren turned her by the shoulders.

"She can stay here," Drew snapped.

"No, thanks, son. I wouldn't leave her to your tender mercies now any more than I'd leave a newborn baby in your care."

Warren led her into his office, sat her in the visitor's chair, fussed around her. "Would you like a drink?"

She raised her head and gave him a watery smile. "I don't dare. I haven't had breakfast. I overslept and I was so late I rushed straight out."

He gave an exasperated sigh. "It's a wonder you haven't passed out, what with one thing and another." He went to the door. "Will you be all right if I leave you for a few moments?"

Julied nodded and when he had gone, rested her head on the back of the chair and closed her eyes. Her head was aching, her face felt blotchy, her eyes swollen, but she didn't care any more.

Some time later the door opened and she sensed it wasn't Warren who came in. Drew was holding a tray of sandwiches and coffee. "My father sent these." He lowered the tray to the desk and stood there watching her. After a moment he said stiffly, like a man unused to apologizing, "I'm sorry. If you'd told me about. . . ."

She turned her head to one side. "You're not really sorry. You hate me, I'm sure you do." He had nothing to say. "We can't go on like this. Our relationship just isn't workable. I'll have to leave . . . there's nothing else to do. As you said the first time we met, we're incompatible. How right you were!"

"You're not leaving, Juliet."

She opened her eyes. "You can't stop me. I resign as from now, this minute." She got up. Her legs felt weak, but she made for the door. His arm came out and caught her across the waist.

"You're staying right here," he said softly, facing her. "Your resignation has not been accepted. And, what's more, I'm prepared to reconsider the whole question of re-siting the boutique."

She shook her head. "It doesn't matter to me now where you put it. I won't be in charge. I'm leaving."

His fingers tightened around her waist. "I'll go further. I'll agree to the chairman's decision to move the boutique downstairs and to put it exactly where you want it, without insisting on referring the matter to the board of management."

She stared. "You don't mean it?"

He took her by the shoulders and moved her gently backward into the chair again. He smiled. "You've forced me into it, haven't you? Inch by inch, you're getting your own way. You're an unscrupulous little minx, do you know that?"

She shook her head again. "But I told you, I'm leaving."

"You're not leaving. When you've eaten that food, you can go back to work and start ordering the stock for your new boutique."

He put the tray on her lap and she picked up one of the sandwiches.

"Unfortunately," he said, watching her eat it, "I can't promise not to shout at you again. I wish I could. But somehow you have that effect on me."

She smiled up at him. "And you on me!"

"At least we're aware of each other's shortcomings."

"And that," said Warren, coming in, "is halfway toward a reconciliation."

"I doubt it," said Drew, lingering in the doorway. "We've just decided we hate each other."

"Well," Warren said briskly, "that's as good a start as any. Who knows where that might lead?"

"The road to hell," said Drew. "You should know." He snapped the door shut behind him.

Juliet spent the day studying catalogues of display stands.

She knew they had to be practical as well as eye-catching and it was not always easy to combine the two. Her studies at art school had taught her that it was not only the clothes she would stock in the boutique which would attract customers, it was also the way they were displayed.

Men were working on the ground floor erecting the partitions which would separate the new boutique from the other departments. Their hammering could be heard above the chatter of the customers who moved around the counters. People, Juliet thought, were the life-blood of a department store, circulating through its veins and arteries like blood around a human body, keeping it healthy and alive. Without people a store would fail and die.

When Juliet had told Miss Skimpton that the boutique would not be part of the fashion floor after all, she had been surprised and, in a grudging sort of way, pleased. She had thanked Juliet for being so considerate. It hadn't occurred to her that Juliet might have requested the boutique's removal from the fashions department for any other reason than that of gratifying Miss Skimpton. Tactfully, Juliet did not enlighten her.

Her father was a little better when she arrived home. The doctor had come and the medicine he had prescribed had brought some relief.

In the kitchen her mother told her, "Warren phoned. He said you'd told him about Cedric. Juliet," she looked troubled, "he offered his help."

"He asked," Cynthia went on, "if Cedric had seen a specialist. I said yes, one our own doctor had recommended. Then Warren offered to pay for Cedric to see one of the top specialists in London. I was so over-whelmed I didn't know how to thank him. He told me to phone him back when we'd talked it over."

So that was the way Warren had calculated he could most effectively offer financial assistance without fear of offending. Surely, Juliet thought, her father would overcome his antipathy to Warren sufficiently to accept such a chance.

But Cynthia flopped into a chair. "Cedric wouldn't hear of it."

Juliet was dismayed. "Why not?"

"Pride, stupid pride. He dug in his heels as only your father can. He said he didn't want help from any ex-boyfriend of mine. I asked him how idiotic could he get being jealous of a man I'd thought I was in love with 30-odd years ago? I said it didn't matter who it was offering help, in our position it was the money that counted."

"Then what happened?"

"We had a ridiculous argument." Juliet was appalled to see her mother start to cry. "He said . . . he said was I saying that he didn't earn enough to please me and was I blaming him for not making a fortune like my ex-fiancé?" Juliet put her arm around her mother, feeling more helpless than she had ever felt in her life. She had never been the one to offer comfort before, it had always been the other way around.

"Then we had a quarrel. It didn't matter that I said I'd take any steps to help him get better, even to accepting money from Warren Major. He wouldn't budge. Oh, darling!" Her mother rested against her daughter as Juliet had rested against Warren for comfort that morning.

She stroked her mother's hair and let her cry, then she said, "You go to bed. You're tired out with your broken night. Mom, I . . . I cried this morning. I was in Drew's office," she didn't tell her why, "and I was silly and let things get on top of me. Mr. Major . . . Warren . . . was so good and offered me a shoulder to cry on."

They hugged each other. "You shouldn't get so involved in our troubles, darling. You've got your own life to lead." She sighed. "I might do as you suggest. I'm worn out. You don't have to worry about the meal. The food's cooked."

"I'll bring it up to both of you."

Some time later, Juliet tapped on her parents' bedroom door and took in their trays. They sat side by side in bed, and Juliet could see that their quarrel was over. She said they looked like two turtle doves and they called her 'nurse.'

Cynthia drew her daughter down to whisper in her ear, "Will you phone Warren? I haven't had the heart."

Juliet agreed, at the same time dreading it. Warren answered. Stumbling over her words, she told him as tactfully as she could that her father had felt unable to accept his offer.

He cut in, "I know what you're going to say. I've come across stubborn pride before, and I know it when I see it."

"It wasn't my mother," Juliet hastened to explain. "She would have accepted gladly."

"I'm sure she would. No woman likes to see the man she loves struggling with an illness which might be alleviated by the expenditure of money in the right quarter." He paused and his voice softened. "Just as no man likes to see the woman he loves desperately worried and unhappy."

Drew must have taken the receiver from his father because his voice said curtly, "There's no need for you to come in on time in the morning, Juliet. In the circumstances you have my permission to arrive late."

Unreasonably irritated by his high-handed manner, she snapped back, "Thanks for your concern, but as you're never tired of telling me, if you did that for me, you'd have to do it for others, wouldn't you? And that would never do, would it? In any case, I don't want your charity."

"Charity?" He sounded puzzled.

"Yes, in the form of time off with pay." She banged down the receiver.

Then she stared at it, conscience-stricken. Now what had she done? Snubbed the man in charge, thrown back in his face his thoughtful gesture, his consideration for her in the light of difficult circumstances at home.

She lifted the receiver and dialed his number. He answered.

"Drew? I want to apologize for what I said. You're right when you say I'm too impetuous. I . . . I really will have to curb it as you say. I'm very sorry."

"Stop groveling," he snapped back. "And you can save your breath . . . your apologies are getting monotonous!" His receiver crashed down.

Until the boutique was ready, Juliet had been given permission to share the office belonging to Mrs. Rouse of separates. She used her phone next morning and dialed Drew's extension. As she waited to speak to him she hoped he had forgiven her for her rudeness the previous evening.

His voice was businesslike and brisk, but there was nothing unfriendly about it, so she supposed he had. She asked him when he thought the boutique would be finished.

"The men are making good progress, as you've probably seen for yourself. Provided you have the display equipment delivered on time, the official opening could take place in a couple of weeks. You know you can store stock and equipment in the marking-off room for a limited period until you're ready for it? Which means you're free to order in advance."

She said she did know. "I worked up there for a time, Mr. Major," she reminded him stiffly.

"All right," he must have been smiling, "don't take umbrage. My memory's not that short."

"Sorry," she said, then wished she could have swallowed the word. "Sorry I said 'sorry.' "

He laughed. "Have you thought about publicity? We could take some space in the local paper and give it a splash. You know, new venture and so on. Contact the advertising department."

Malcolm called that evening. Juliet told him about the progress of the boutique. "We're taking a couple of half columns in the local paper to advertise the opening."

"Getting a big name to come and do the honors?"

She hadn't even thought of it, she said. "Doubt if it's worth it. And they cost a lot in expenses. To start with, until I can prove my worth, I'm on a limited budget."

Things were back to normal at home now. Her father had recovered from his latest asthmatic attack and had returned to work. Her mother's anxiety had once more receded into the background and she was happy again.

On the day the advertisement announcing the opening of the boutique was due to appear, Juliet seized the local newspaper and turned the pages. It was there, small but, she hoped, effective. Idly, she turned another page and her eyes were riveted by a half-page advertisement. Curlews's boutique, it announced, was the finest in town. Its clothes were the trendiest, its prices the lowest, its value the best that money could buy. You can't resist, it said, the call of Curlews's boutique.

All around the edges of Curlews's advertisement were sketches of newly arrived models. Across the center were the words in giant-sized lettering, "S-p-l-a-s-h!" followed in smaller letters by the words "Your money at Curlews".

Compared with this ostentatious piece of publicity, Major's restrained promotion of their product was weak and puny.

Barely able to restrain her fury, Juliet phoned Malcom. She caught him just before he left for work. She accused him of treachery, disloyalty. "Why did you do it?" she demanded, adding in dramatic tones, "And I thought you loved me!"

He swore that he had not done it intentionally. "I happened to mention to the buyer of carpets what you'd told me about Major's announcement of their new boutique. He's in touch with the great high-ups and must have passed the information on. I wasn't to know he'd do that, was I?"

"You may have lost me my job," she wailed. "If not that, then my position as buyer. I'll have to take a drop in salary and be demoted—"

Malcolm cut her short, said he was sorry but that it was just one of those things, and that if he didn't go he'd miss the bus. She said bitterly that she hoped he did.

On her way to work she wondered how she was going to break the news to Drew. She met him on the stairs and decided to brave his anger there and then. He was about to sweep past her, but she put out a hand and stopped him.

"What now?" he asked wearily.

"About the advertisement—" Some members of staff hurried past and Drew pulled her to one side.

"You're blocking the stairs. Don't bother to explain. I

know exactly what you're going to say. The boyfriend came. Am I right? You poured out your heart to him about the boutique. Right again?"

"I'm afraid so, Mr. Major. I didn't do it on purpose, nor did he."

"Of course you didn't. No one in their right mind would. Nor would a woman's beloved give away her secrets and deliberately spoil things for her. But you'll have to be a damned sight more careful in future. Next time it might be much more serious. You would have to have a boyfriend in the enemy camp, wouldn't you?" She opened her mouth automatically to apologize, but he reached out and closed it effectively with his fingers. "Spare me that, Miss Bourne." He continued on his way, calling back, "But remember, don't let it happen again."

After supper, Malcolm called for her. He said he was sorry and kissed her on the doorstep. With a show of reluctance she let him in.

"Still love me?" he asked sheepishly.

"That assumes," she answered, with dignity, "that I loved you in the first place."

He winced, and her mother, overhearing, said, "My goodness, Malcolm, you really are in the doghouse tonight!"

He laughed. "If I sat up and begged, do you think she'd forgive me?"

The phone rang and Cynthia went to answer it.

"Dad's out," Juliet said, "so we can go in the living room."

Malcolm asked if she'd got into trouble with her boss.

"He said in a roundabout way that he understood, but that it mustn't happen again."

When Cynthia came in, her eyes were shining. She told them, "That was Warren."

Juliet's heart bumped. Why was her mother so happy about it?

"He asked me if I'd like a freezer. I said I'd love one, but I'd love the money to pay for it better! So he told me they were expecting a bulk purchase of deep freeze cabinets any day at a ridiculously low price and if I wanted one I could have it."

"Did you accept?"

"On the spot. I've wanted one for years. We could rearrange the kitchen and make room for it."

"But what will Dad say? Won't he call it being offered charity again?"

"He'll have to agree. It's a chance I can't miss."

"That was a bit of luck for Major's electrical department," Malcolm said thoughtfully. "I wonder which wholesaler did them that good turn?"

"Malcolm!"

He started guiltily. "Sorry, Juliet. It's a case of keeping up, not so much with the Joneses as the Majors. It's the loyalty in me coming out. If you work for Majors long enough, it'll get you, too."

"I doubt it. Anyway," she said loftily, "shouldn't loyalty to your girlfriend come first?"

"You win." He moved nearer and took her hand. "I promise to try to keep it to myself."

"You must," she wailed, "otherwise I really will lose my job. Drew's given me two warnings already about passing on information to my 'Romeo' as he calls you."

The others laughed. "A lot of encouragement I get from 'Juliet,'" Malcolm complained. "The real Romeo did a lot better. Look at you this evening. Talk about turning the other cheek when I kiss you and giving me the cold shoulder!"

"When you've finished trotting out tired clichés about different parts of my anatomy, we'd better go."

He turned up a nonexistent coat collar and pretended to shiver. "Next time I come I'll wear my winter woollies!"

Cynthia laughed and waved them off. They went to a film and when Malcolm left Juliet on the doorstep, she let him kiss her without drawing away and even condescended to kiss him back for a few moments.

Drew was on the phone to her again next morning. "I want to have a talk with you some time. Since you're such a babe in arms when it comes to the art of buying, I feel you need a bit of tutoring."

She began to thank him, but he cut her short. "Don't run away with the idea that it's you I'm worried about. If it were I'd let you flounder at the deep end until you learned to swim. It's Majors' financial standing that concerns me. I'd hate us to go bankrupt because of the ignorance of a very young buyer called Juliet Bourne. Some of those reps you'll be dealing with are reasonable types and only want to earn an honest living. But some are wolves in disguise. If that sort spots your innocence of the ways of the commercial world, and with their experience they're bound to do so, they'll rob you right and left. So a word in your ear would, I feel, be not only advisable but absolutely essential if you're not going to be allowed to let those reps devour your profits before the goods you order are on the display stands."

She said dutifully. "Yes, Mr. Major," and waited for the pause to end.

"Now," he said, "looking at my desk calendar, I see tomorrow is Saturday. It's asking a lot of you—and knowing you you'll probably demand overtime—but could you come to my father's house tomorrow after lunch? That is if it isn't depriving you of the company of your Romeo."

"Well, he was coming around, but we were only going for a bike ride. Yes, Mr. Major, I'll do as you say."

"My word," came softly into her ear, "you unnerve me. Such docility so early in the morning!"

She laughed. "I do occasionally go against my principles and obey orders, Mr. Major!"

He laughed with her. "That really is good news, Miss Bourne. May you long continue to break that particular principle. It would make life so much easier for me." He hung up.

Saturday was cloudless and unbearably warm. Juliet wondered what to wear. She tussled with her longing to put on her sundress, deciding in the end on something a little more formal. She was after all going to the Major residence for business reasons, not pleasure. She wore a thin sleeveless top and lightweight skirt and, remembering the cold splendor of Warren's house, pulled on a cardigan in case her outfit was still too informal.

Mildred Major opened the door. Her royal blue dress was long and hung limply from the waist. The neck was conventional, the front fastening discreetly to the top button. It must have been a dress in vogue ten years before and Juliet knew that the changing fashions of the ensuing decade had passed her by.

"They're in the garden," Mildred said in her lifeless way. "You'll have to look for them. Go around the back." She pointed her finger vaguely to the left and closed the door in Juliet's face.

"It's a wonder," Juliet thought disgustedly, "she didn't tell me to go to the tradesmen's entrance."

Feeling as let down as someone who had had a chair snatched from under them, Juliet wandered around to the back of the house. She walked through the rose garden and was passing the fountain feathering out over the pond when a shout hailed her. She turned. Of course, the swimming pool!

Warren Major was standing and waving his arm. As she approached, he said, "Welcome, stranger. What brings you here?"

"I did," said a lazy voice a few yards from Juliet's feet.

Drew was lying on a large towel beside the pool, wearing only his swimming trunks. His tanned, lean body was glistening with water. He had obviously just come from the pool and had not bothered to dry himself. He was letting the heat of the sun suck up the moisture from his skin.

"Sit down, my dear," Warren invited, taking the garden chair beside her. He too was in swimming trunks, but there was no leanness about his body, which bulged with spare flesh. Even his physique reflected his affluence and his informality seemed to drive an even bigger wedge between himself and the woman who was, in name only, his wife. "How's your mother?" betrayed the line of his thoughts.

"Very well," Juliet answered, adding, "my father's fine, too, at the moment."

Warren nodded without comment, his interest waning after her first reply. *Why does he keep pretending I haven't got a father?* Juliet thought, fiercely resenting his attitude. But the feeling passed as she looked at the restless, unhappy eyes that raked the grounds as though he were searching for something just out of his reach. Something his money couldn't buy.

"This," Drew addressed his father, arms raised behind his head, eyes masked by sun-glasses, "is a business call, believe it or not. Not a social one."

"You disappoint me, son. I thought she'd come for love of you, not the firm."

"Love?" Drew raised his head, then lowered it again, closing his eyes behind the darkened lenses. "There's little love lost between us, is there, Juliet? Give us a few more minutes and we'll be quarreling again. In fact, I'm surprised we haven't started already. It's probably only your presence as an intermediary that's having a restraining effect on us both."

Warren rose, laughing. "I'll bow out and leave you to it. I wouldn't want to interfere. Chairman of the company I may be, but I should hate to put my nose in where it isn't wanted!"

"The only time he does interfere," said his son idly, "is when it's to the detriment of the firm, when the man who runs the outfit is conveniently out for the day and a rebellious young woman pushes her way into his office and makes impossible demands, to which he agrees totally and unreservedly."

Juliet flushed, guessing his meaning.

"All right, son, point taken." Warren raised his hand and went on his way.

"Come and sit next to me, Juliet." Without rising or opening his eyes, Drew patted the towel.

With reluctance she sat beside him, feeling the overpowering attraction of him pulling at her like a magnet.

He raised his head and looked at her disparagingly. "My word, you're too well dressed for words! Can't you take some clothes off?" He lifted his hand and tugged at her cardigan, removing it from her shoulders. She slipped her arms out of the sleeves and he threw it to one side.

"I may look well-dressed," she said, "but I'm quite cool. I haven't got much on underneath."

He raised himself on to his elbow and looked her over. "Now you've got me interested." He whipped off his sunglasses. "yes, I see what you mean." He indicated her sleeveless top. "Isn't that what they call a see-through blouse? The name's appropriate. It doesn't leave much to the imagination. All the same," he replaced his sunglasses and stretched out again, "you should have come in a two-piece swimsuit, then you could have joined me in the water."

"What would have been the use? I told you, I can't swim."

"You'll have to get Romeo to teach you." He smiled provocatively. "I bet he's taught you a few things already."

Indignantly she answered, "It's not like that between us."

He turned to face her, his eyes hidden. "Are you trying to tell me you're young, innocent and unblemished? And you an ex-art student? I can hardly believe it." His hand groped for hers and found it. "You tempt me to find out just how experienced you are in . . . er . . . certain matters."

She tugged her hand away. "I came here to work, Mr. Major, not to play."

He sighed and sat up, his skin almost dry now. "That's Drew Major put in his place! Now, Miss Bourne, since you insist on being so formal, have you any queries, any questions you'd like me to answer?"

"Yes," she said promptly, "how will I know, when a salesman shows me his stock, which clothes to choose? I imagine that at first I'll want to buy everything I see, and I know I can't do that."

He laughed. "Glad you realize it. Well," he poured a drink from the jug of lemonade which stood on a folding picnic table beside him and gave her the glass, then took one for himself, "first you think of your most typical customer, then you think of her requirements and then you select garments which will most closely answer those requirements." He drank deeply. "There are really three guiding principles that govern the selection of fashion goods—the buyer must have 'feel', flair and taste, all of which you should possess already as a result of your art training." She nodded. "All the same, even when you've decided on your typical customer, the choice could still be embarrassing. At which point you'll have to use what is called, for want of a better term, 'know-how.' It's something you'll develop as you become more experienced."

"Oh dear, you make it sound a bit daunting!"

"I don't think so. As long as you've got common sense, and I think you have—"

She bowed her head graciously. "Thanks for the compliment. I'm not used to praise from you."

"This, Miss Bourne, is a business discussion. So you can stop being cheeky."

She peered at him to see how serious he was, but the dark lenses were disconcertingly blank.

"First," he went on, "you must consider in which order you're going to examine the garments the rep shows you. You might decide, and in your case, I think it would be wise since the clothes you'll be stocking won't be in the higher price ranges, to see the cheapest articles first, going through the range until you reach the most expensive."

He refilled her glass, then emptied the jug into his own, tossing the contents down his throat. "Once you've made your decision, you must stick to it, no matter what the salesman says. He'll probably want to show you the most expensive lines first, because they're what he wants to sell most. But it's the buyer's requirements that matter, not his, and even if he argues, you must argue back. Salesmen are trained to take the lead in a sale, but a successful buyer sticks to his guns and wins. In other words, you must put the salesman in his place." He smiled at her. "That shouldn't be difficult for you. You can employ that so-called 'fire' my father insists you possess, and which I call impudence. If you show a rep what you're made of from the start, he'll soon learn to respect your judgment."

"From the way you're talking," she put down her empty glass and hugged her knees, "it sounds as though a buyer needs to know a certain amount about psychology. You've got to know the salesman's mind well enough to be a jump ahead of him all the time."

He frowned into the distance. "In a sense, that's right. You, the buyer, have a fixed budget . . . that is, a certain sum of money you have been allocated. He, the salesman, wants to get you to spend as much money and to order as many of his goods as possible. You have to learn to recognize when he's putting on the pressure to such an extent that if you listen to him, you'll be overspending. That can lead to all sorts of complications where your budget's concerned. Sales reps are just one side of your job, though."

"Oh dear, what have I taken on? You're making me nervous!"

"It's about time you realized the amount of trust I've invested in you in promoting you to this position." His tone was almost a reprimand. "Don't fail me, Juliet."

She clasped her fingers around her knees, infinitely touched by the sudden appeal in his voice. More than anything she wanted to please this man, to gain his respect and admiration, to make him think of her not as an unworldly artist but as an accomplished business woman. She wanted to justify the trust he had placed in her. Would she ever manage it?

"You'll be handling large quantities of stock and cash," he went on. "You'll need the courage to take risks by buying fashions not yet in vogue but which you think may become popular. You have to know how to deal with people. You must be patient with the complainers, and there are plenty, and receive little in the way of gratitude. You must get your sums right, otherwise your profits will be nonexistent. You must realize there are seasonal fluctuations. You must not only have the right touch to keep customers, suppliers and staff happy, but also know how to communicate effectively with them. You also," he turned and smiled, "have to keep on good terms with your superiors. You must know not only when to be aggressive . . . no difficulty there! . . . but also when to be polite and know how far you can push people, at the same time knowing how much you can give."

"So," she smiled back at him, "from now on I've got to be a sort of superwoman."

"Yes," he agreed, then softly, his eyes moving over her, "but whatever you do, Juliet, don't lose your femininity. That way you'll not only gain a man's admiration, but his respect, too." He lay back, closing his eyes.

The sun beat down, the breeze stirred the roses, tampered with the bushes and shrubs which edged the path around the swimming pool and rippled across the suface of the water.

"Thanks," she said, "for your advice. I appreciate it very much."

He was so quiet that she thought he was asleep, but he turned onto his front to let the sun tan his back. "Lie down, Juliet," he murmured. "Relax. You need some rest after that prolonged lecture."

With some hesitation and a large measure of self-consciousness, usually alien to her, she lay back beside him and turned her face away. She didn't know why, but her heart was thumping . . . there was an odd tension in her limbs. She found that her hands clasped under her head were moist.

The silence, broken only by the occasional passing car in the road at the front of the house, induced sleep, but she resisted it without too much trouble. Her body felt too alive, her mind too alert to relax completely. If he had touched her, merely stretched out a hand, she knew for certain that the invisible barrier between them would crumble to nothing and. . . . But her mind cowered from the consequences like a child being pushed alone into a dark room.

"Juliet." The word was a whisper. She turned her head and wished she could see his eyes. "Since you have nothing better to do, you wouldn't care to spend the rest of the afternoon here, and have supper?"

She sat up and looked around. There was a spurt of longing inside her that made her want to do just that. The beauty all about her, the peace, the solitude, the company of the man beside her . . . what about the man beside her? He was her boss, he meant nothing more to her than that.

She must not let herself even begin to love him, the son of the man her mother had rejected so many years ago. It was unthinkable. She knew his views about women, his refusal ever to be tied down to one woman.

Nothing better to do? It was typical of his arrogance. She knew she was whipping herself into a state of anger toward him as a form of self-defence, or even self-preservation.

"Thanks for the invitation," her tone was intentionally abrupt, "but I think I'll go for that bike ride with Malcolm after all." She stood up, smoothing her skirt, fighting the sun-drenched lethargy of limbs and pleased with herself for her successful battle with her feelings.

He sighed, rose and pulled on his shirt. It hung loosely

over his swimming trunks. As he stood, towering over her, lithe, athletic-looking, she could not believe he was the same man who, immaculately dressed, executive to the finger tips, ran the firm of Major and Son.

He folded his arms and gazed down at her. "I've never before had dealings with a woman who disliked me." His fingers raised her chin and his eyes, still hidden, scanned her face. "It's a novel experience." He put his arm across her shoulders and she had to pretend that she could barely tolerate his touch. He got the message and his arm fell away. "I'll see you out," he said abruptly.

"No need," she murmured, walking at his side.

"Better still, if you wait until I've got a few more clothes on, I'll give you a lift home."

"There's no need," she repeated. "I'll go back the way I came, by bus."

"Wait in the hall." He sprinted up the stairs. She was beginning to wonder where his parents were when he reappeared, having added trousers to his shirt.

A car pulled up in the driveway and he frowned. "Who the—?" he said, and answered the heavy, commanding knock.

"Darling," said a feminine voice when the door was opened, "I was at loose ends. Then I thought of you. I knew you wouldn't mind." She held up her face. "Aren't you going to kiss me?" Then she saw Juliet and her frown made a petulant pleat between her brows. She turned large, wondering eyes up to Drew's. "Darling, been amusing yourself in my absence?"

"Juliet, Camille Wyngard. Camille, Juliet Bourne, friend of the family."

"Only of the family? But darling," the word grew softer every time the pouting lips uttered it, "you've never spoken about her before."

The eyes that ran, like mice, up Juliet, from her

sandaled feet, over her flimsy blouse to the untidiness of her hair, were puzzled and disturbed. The face that refused to smile was oval-shaped and heavily made up, the figure from the shoulders downwards a temptation to any man. The fair hair curved into the hollows of her neck and the sun-dress she wore was designed to catch far more than the sun's attention.

"Go to the pool," Drew told Camille. "I'm driving Juliet home."

"It doesn't matter, Drew," Juliet said, her voice coming out as dry as an autumn leaf. "I'll make my own way home."

"You heard what she said, darling." Camille caught his arm.

Juliet began to move down the steps, but Drew pulled his arm from Camille and clamped his fingers on Juliet's shoulder, swinging her around. He had an odd look in his eyes which she mistrusted.

A few seconds later her lack of trust was justified. Drew had bent down and kissed her mouth. She jerked away, scarlet. "What do you think you're—?" He cut off her words with another kiss.

"Thanks, sweet, for your delightful company. Don't keep me waiting too long before you come again, will you?"

This time Juliet ran down the steps out of reach. What game was he playing? She looked back to see his mocking grin. Camille slid her arms around his neck. "What are you doing, darling?" she murmured against his lips. "Giving me notice to quit?"

Out of the corner of her eye Juliet saw the two lions, enigmatic and supercilious as ever, gazing into the distance as though nothing catastrophic had happened.

But it had. Two kisses from Drew, and she was wanting more.

Drew showed Camille into the house and closed the door. A last look back at the entrance made Juliet swear she saw the ghost of a smile on the lions' faces.

CHAPTER FIVE

On Monday morning, Juliet was summoned to the company manager's office. *What now?* she wondered.

He was smiling as she entered and held out her cardigan. "You left this behind on Saturday." He tutted. "Forgetfulness is a bad characteristic in a buyer. One you'll have to eradicate."

She snatched it from him, thanking him grudgingly.

"Did you enjoy your bike ride?" he wanted to know.

"Yes, thank you." She asked spitefully, "Did you enjoy—?"

"My girlfriend?" he grinned. "Yes, thank you."

He had got the better of her. "The next time," she snapped, "you want to make your girlfriend jealous, choose someone else, someone from your own social circle, not me!"

She slammed out of his room, away from his malicious grin.

A sales representative was waiting for her when she returned to the fashion department. She invited him into Mrs. Rouse's office.

"I thought it was usual for a rep to make an appointment before calling," she said, acting on the old saying that attack was the best form of defence. She also did it to hide her nervousness.

The thick-set, red-faced man whose eyes were roving appreciatively over her slim figure, smiled. "Point to you, Miss ... er ..."

"Bourne, Juliet Bourne." They shook hands.

"Fresco fashions." He produced his card. "Dermot Edmond."

"As you probably know, Mr. Edmond," she spoke in her most businesslike manner, "the boutique I'm buying stock for isn't open yet. I have nothing at all in the way of supplies—"

"Which gives me a clear field? That's heartening, for my commission as well as for my firm!" He rubbed his cheek. "Since you want so much in the way of stock, I think the best thing is for you to come to the factory with me. It's in the industrial estate on the outskirts of town. We've got the whole range there. You know we specialize in separates?"

"That's just what I want. If you'll wait until I confirm that it's all right for me to go with you—" Immediately, she regretted the words. To a man as astute as he was, having to get permission to leave the store revealed her inexperience and gave the man the advantage.

She dialed Drew's extension. His abruptness, following his earlier good humor, took her by surprise. "Go out to the factory? Yes, I suppose so. But remember what I told you. Some of them are wolves, in more ways than one. They're after your money, as well as the other thing. Keep a tight hold on it . . . them. Your budget isn't elastic. Oh, and," he paused, "don't keep running to me asking permission to do what is after all your job. You don't need your hand held!" He rang off with a slam.

Flushing, she turned back to the man. He didn't miss her high color. He grinned, "Had words with the boss? Rumor has it he's an awkward devil. Never met the man myself."

As he drove her through town, he became a little too personal. He wanted to know if she had a boyfriend and if she ever had an evening free.

"Very rarely," she said firmly. If he took it as a snub, that was all the better.

The factory was modern, freshly painted and pleasant to work in. The building was typical of those usually found in new industrial developments. The showroom was well designed with subtle lighting to enhance the firm's products.

Remembering Drew's advice, Juliet insisted on seeing the cheapest end of the range first. The salesman remonstrated with her as expected . . . Drew had been right again . . . but she won her point.

From the moment the first garments were shown to her, she worked by instinct.

She sorted the collection of separates into "certainties," "possibles" and rejects." Some she found difficult to classify, and it was then that she longed for the experience she lacked. Some of the styles were so new she rejected them at once, although she wondered afterward if she should have done. Had she failed to use the vision that Drew seemed to think she possessed?

As soon as she had made her final decisions on the items she wanted, she wrote them down in her order book as Mrs. Rouse had advised her to do. "Never rely on memory," Mrs. Rouse had said. "You're bound to forget something that way."

Dermot Edmond produced a bottle of wine and a couple of glasses from a cupboard and suggested a toast to their mutual success and future co-operation. He eyed her over the top of his glass as if sizing her up.

"I'm free this evening. Are you?" he asked. "Would you have supper with me somewhere?" As if to encourage her he added, his eyes ingenuous, "I could give you a few tips on the gentle art of buying, and dealing with obstreperous reps."

The bait was too strong for her to resist. She took the

offer at its face value and could find no harm in accepting the invitation.

She thought about Malcolm, but he couldn't be annoyed because in a way this would be a business engagement. She thought about Drew, and how contemptuously he had spoken of some of the salesmen's morals. She thought about those kisses Drew had given her and the way he had used her for his own ends.

"Yes," she said defiantly, "I'm free."

Dermot Edmond's eyes glistened. "Eight o'clock. Give me your address and I'll pick you up."

She wondered what her parents' reactions would be, but she would tell them she was capable of taking care of herself. In any case, Drew wasn't right about everything.

She told Mrs. Rouse that afternoon that she was going out with a sales representative. "Which one?" Mrs. Rouse asked. Juliet told her. Mrs. Rouse said she didn't know him. "I don't deal with way-out clothes like you'll be doing, only the more conventional styles. All the same, I wouldn't go out with him if I were you. It might be a bit like favoritism. If you go out with one rep, you'll be expected to go out with the whole lot." She frowned. "Might get yourself a bad name, dear. And you don't know the man, do you?"

"But I'll have to go, Mrs. Rouse. I promised. The only trouble is I don't know what to wear. My clothes are all a little 'way-out' as you put it."

"Borrow a dress from the racks. It's allowed, as long as you bring it back next morning. No one's said we could, but on the other hand it's well known that it goes on, and no one's said we can't. So we all do it. Look," she beckoned to Juliet to follow, "here's one that'll suit you." She took it from the hanger. It was bright red, with a low-cut neck, draped skirt and wrist-length sleeves. "Try it on."

Juliet took it into a fitting room. The dress transformed her into a sophisticate, and she imagined it was the style of dress which Camille Wyngard might wear.

"A bit of make-up and your hair done, and you'll be a treat," said Mrs. Rouse.

There were voices outside the fitting room. One of the assistants said, "Miss Bourne's in there with Mrs. Rouse."

Drew appeared at the fitting room door. Mrs. Rouse saw his hostile expression and melted away, leaving Juliet to her fate.

"Whose dress is that? Yours?"

Embarrassment reddened her skin until it almost matched the color of the dress. "No, Mr. Major."

"Are you buying it?"

"No, Mr. Major. I was just trying it on."

"For what purpose? Are you, by any chance, training to be a model to augment your salary?"

It was plain that her explanation would have to be good, so she told him the truth. "I was going to borrow it, Mr. Major. Only for this evening. I was told that it was allowed. I'd . . . I'd meant to return it."

She was up to the chin in guilt, and it was sucking her in like a bog. Now suspicion had crept into his eyes, like a cat on the prowl, and his frown held disbelief and dismay. Her color deepened. Was he thinking she had intended to steal it? She wanted the floor to open, she wanted to tear the dress off and throw it at him.

His eyes narrowed. "Who told you it was allowed?"

She couldn't give Mrs. Rouse away. "Someone." That sounded even more incriminating. "I was told it was an . . . an unwritten rule."

"Were you, indeed? Then it's an unwritten rule I shall revoke in writing. I suppose you know what I'm thinking, Miss Bourne? You may not realize that petty pilfering by the staff is one of my worst headaches, second only to shoplifting."

She was silent. Nothing she could say would exonerate her from the blame he seemed so keen to attach to her. But she was also aware that her silence didn't help, either.

He changed the subject. "Where are you going tonight that you feel the need to dress up?"

Sulkily she replied, "I'm going out."

"With whom? Malcolm? If so, he'd hardly appreciate you in that dress. It makes you look . . . like something I assumed up to now that you were not. Easily available. Seeing you in that dress makes me wonder if I'm wrong."

She felt his sarcasm was quite unfair. She rallied, her clear conscience loosening her tongue.

"I haven't committed a crime, Mr. Major. I've only tried on a dress. Customers are doing it all the time." Her voice wavered. "You can't really mistrust me as much as that?"

He heard the appeal, but his voice was hard as he said, "Don't change the subject. Where are you going this evening?"

"Out." But she could see he was not satisfied. "With . . . with a man." That sounded terrible. "With the rep who called this morning, the one who took me to his factory."

He walked toward her and his hand gripped the neck of the dress as if he was about to tear it off. "Oh no, you're not! Unless you really want to be seduced? If so, there are men much closer to home whom you know a little better and who would be only too willing to oblige." He gave the dress a tug. "You can take that off. Not only do you agree to go out with a man you've never met before today, but you were thinking of wearing a dress that unmistakably says 'Come and get me.' "

"But I promised. He seems like a nice enough man, Mr. Major. He said he'd give me a few hints on being a buyer."

"Good grief," he looked disgusted, "were you born yesterday, woman? You fell for that line? Run back to your Romeo and ask him to tell you the facts of life." He went to the door. "It's no good trying to exact a promise from you that you won't go out with the man, so I'll threaten you instead. If you keep that date tonight or any other night with any sales representative who comes to see you, I'll fire you. Understand?"

She understood, she said, and he went away. That evening she did run to her 'Romeo' as Drew had suggested, leaving her mother to apologize and explain her absence to Dermot Edmond.

The day the freezer arrived, Cynthia was as happy as a woman with a new engagement ring. Her husband was disapproving but grudgingly pleased that she was happy.

"Now," he said, "you'd better ask your ex-boyfriend where we're going to get the money to fill the thing. I suppose you know you purchase in bulk when you're buying frozen food?"

She put her arms around him as winningly as a young girl and said, "We'll fill it a bit at a time." He held her to him for a few minutes, then left her.

Malcolm came and admired it and a brooding look came into his eyes. "I'd love to know their source of supply. It's a bargain at the price."

Juliet told him quickly, "It was a special price to Mother, wasn't it?" she appealed to Cynthia.

"A very special price, darling. I think he must have knocked off far more from the price than he said he would."

"All the same. . . ." Malcolm murmured, but Juliet gave his arm a shake.

"You promised not to tell anyone at Curlews."

"All right." He kissed her forehead. "I'll keep the promise, but Majors don't deserve it. If you weren't working for them—"

"Then you wouldn't have known about it, would you?"

The phone rang and Juliet answered. "Is your mother there?" Warren's voice was eager.

With an equal eagerness, Cynthia ran to the phone. "Warren?" Her voice was high and excited and she must have sounded to him as she had years before when he used to phone her. She thanked him twice for the deep freeze and they chatted for a long time.

Troubled, Juliet left the house with Malcolm, waving to her mother as they went. Cynthia waved back absently as though her thoughts were back in the past too.

"My father's still in love with your mother," Drew had said. But what of her mother's feelings? Surely she didn't reciprocate Warren's love after all these years?

Juliet was growing excited about the opening of the boutique. The special lighting effects she had asked for had delayed completion by a week or so, but she had insisted that they be at least as good as those she had seen at the boutiques she had patronized in the past.

Drew had argued that the money they were able to devote to the enterprise was not unlimited.

"What's the need for all this nonsense?" he asked one morning as they stood together watching the electricians put up the colored lights which, when finished, would move enticingly over the clothes, subtly changing their colors and highlighting the fashion trends as conventional lighting never would.

"It's not nonsense, Mr. Major. It's as vital a part of the boutique as assistants are in the main store. It's what my customers will expect. You told me the other day that I must cater for the typical customer when I'm buying stock."

"But this," he raised his arm, "isn't stock. It's like the icing on a cake. Pretty but superfluous."

She shook her head pityingly. "It creates good will, can't you understand?"

He laughed. "Spoken like a hardened professional buyer! What do you know about good will?" He lowered his voice. "Especially where I'm concerned. I suppose you'll be telling me next in your typically blunt, not to say rude, way that I'm too old to understand all these modern ideas."

"You've said it for me," she answered with a grin.

"Straight below the belt, as my father would say. The truth of the matter is that I find it difficult to get down to the level of your potential customers."

"Now you're being rude," she said, offended.

"It's my prerogative. I'm the boss, so I can be rude as I like!"

They watched the electricians for a few more minutes. She pointed. "Why the television screen?"

"You should know why. It lets the customers know in a polite way that there's closed circuit television operating inside the store. As I told you at that morning training session, it guards against shoplifting. It's vital for security purposes."

He left her. Later she was informed by the receiving room that there had been a delivery of her stock and where was it to go?

"The marking-off room, please, for pricing," she told the porter. She took the lift to the eighth floor and supervised her stock being stored on hangers in the wire cages with which she had grown so familiar while working up there. The other women hailed her like an old friend and she chatted with them for a while.

Looking around the marking-off room, still dull and depressing with its unattractive bare walls, reminded her ruefully of her efforts to brighten the place when she had first joined the firm. Then a thought struck her with such force she nearly cried out. She had a place of her own now—the boutique!

She left the others with a wave of her hand and sped down eight floors to her own little corner which, deserted by the electricians, was almost ready to be filled with stock.

What couldn't she do with a paintbrush and some paint? Her pent-up artistic feelings started hammering on the walls of her mind like a prisoner crazy to get out. She would buy her own paintbrush so that Drew couldn't criticize her for unnecessary expenditure, then she would bring those bare, uninteresting walls to life. This evening, she promised herself, she would stay on after hours and start painting. It must be done tonight, before the display stands were fitted and clothes filled the racks.

She seized her handbag and walked swiftly through the ground floor, passing the perfume, radio and electrical sections and found the area devoted to home decoration. She bought four cans of paint and a couple of brushes, asked the assistant to wrap them so that she couldn't be accused of taking them without payment and carried them back to the boutique, stacking them in a corner. Then she phoned her mother to tell her she would be home late.

When the last customer had gone and the doors closed

for the night, she sighed with relief. The anticipation she had dammed up inside her all day had burst its banks and she could hardly wait for the last member of staff to call "good night."

She went out into the main store to make sure she was alone and the stillness filled her with a sense of awe. The goods on the counters—perfume, handbags, jewellery—lay, like a beautiful woman, waiting to be admired, but they waited in vain. The admiring, covetous eyes had gone until morning. There was no hustle now, no chatter, no coming and going of people, and the place was lonelier for their absence.

But Juliet, her instincts sharpened by solitude and alert for the slightest sound, threw off her momentary apprehension and went back into the safety of the boutique like a burrowing animal making for cover.

She opened the cans of emulsion pain, unwrapped one of the brushes and dipped it into a can labelled "orange glow." She held her hand in mid-air, uncertain, inhibited by doubt, but the hesitation lasted no longer than a few seconds. The artist in her, the vision she carried in her mind of the transformed walls, overrode all rules and regulations. The paintbrush was lifted and applied and a great curve of orange swept over the insipid cream wash with which the partitions were covered.

Now she had started, she felt reassured. It looked better with every stroke of the brush. She followed no set pattern, applying the mixture of colors at random, guided all the time by her inborn feeling for design and the lessons in disciplined self-expression she had learned as a student.

She must have been painting for half an hour and had covered an entire wall when she began to feel the effects of missing a meal. But she was so carried away by her work that she pushed aside all thoughts of food.

A sound from the main store, soft thought it was, stood out three-dimensionally from the intense silence. Oddly frightened, she stopped, brush poised, to listen. There were footsteps stopping, moving, pausing, and . . . were they creeping? Fear had her skin prickling and trapped her breath in her throat.

Quietly she rested the brush across the top of a paint can and crept to the boutique entrance. A man stood a few yards away behind a counter, staring at her. He was wearing overalls, and relief nearly made her faint.

" 'Evening, miss." He was one of the caretakers. "Workin' late, miss?"

She said, "You gave me a terrible fright. I thought it was a thief, someone who'd broken in to rob the store!"

"Just doing the rounds, miss, making sure all's well. Will you be staying much longer, miss? I'll have to lock up in half an hour or so."

"I'll be through by then, I expect. Give me half an hour and I'll be off. All right?"

He raised a finger in a salute. "Fair enough, miss. Good night, now."

Her heart had still not settled down to its normal beat, but she picked up the paintbrush, took a few deep breaths to steady her nerves and carried on. It must have been five minutes later that she heard footsteps again. Had the man come back? But these footsteps were different. They were decisive and fast, they knew where they were going. And they were coming straight toward the boutique. A different kind of fear had her heart thumping again, and a sickening feeling of guilt, of being caught in the act, spread through her body like the roots of a tree. She stepped back without turning her head and knocked over a can of paint which, in toppling, knocked another over.

"Oh," she cried, almost in tears. "Now look what's happened!"

"What the devil are you up to now, you little idiot?"

Only one person in the world could have spoken those words in that unpleasant tone, and she turned and faced him.

"What the blazes do you think I'm doing?" she cried, politeness and protocol flung aside like restricting bed-clothes.

"Knowing you, I don't dare think." He looked around. "You're not painting the walls?"

"What does it look like? And now the floor, too. It was all your fault, coming in so quickly, giving me another terrible fright. First the caretaker, now you. . . ."

"Be careful what you're saying, Miss Bourne. You don't speak to me in that tone. My name is not Malcolm Watling."

"Oh, I'm sorry." She dismissed his reprimand as though it was entirely irrelevant and stared horrified at the mass of paint merging into a rainbow of colors and creeping unchecked across the floor. She was tired, she was hungry and she was still suffering from the electrifying effect of two shocks following each other in quick succession. "Now what do I do? What a terrible mess! And all that money wasted."

She crammed the tears back down her throat and looked at him. He saw the hopeless appeal in her eyes, heard the despair in her voice, and softened his tone a fraction. "Obviously it has to be cleared up, right? What paint is it and what's its solvent?"

"Water . . . it's emulsion paint. But where do I get

water from at this time of night? And a mop and bucket?"

He shook his head. "And I've just sent the caretaker home. With you around, I must have been mad!"

"You saw him?"

"He came to see me. He said there was a young woman down here, looking suspicious. Said he didn't entirely trust you and thought you were up to no good."

She reddened indignantly. "What did you think I was doing? Robbing the place? So you came down to catch me red-handed?"

"I had an idea who it was as soon as he described you, and when he said you were hiding, as he put it, in the boutique, I knew for certain."

They looked down at the pools of paint inching across the floor. "I'll get the necessary," Drew said, "while you put away what's left of your precious paint." He looked around the walls. "What a crazy idea, staying after hours to slosh paint all over the place. Is this your idea of beauty? And at the firm's expense?"

His sarcastic comments, after all her efforts, unraveled the frayed edges of her temper. "No. If you must know, I paid for the paint myself. And for the brushes. So it's cost the firm nothing. It's my money that's been wasted, not yours."

She remembered the excitement she had felt all day and the enthusiasm with which she had started the work. She sank down on the floor and put a hand over her eyes, but his compassion was not stirred.

He said in a bored tone, "If you must weep, Juliet, do it after we've cleared up the mess, will you?"

He went for some water and she mopped up her tears and waited, sitting back on her heels, staring helplessly at the sprawling stain the paint had made. In his absence she felt contrite and when he returned with buckets of water, scrub brushes and cloths, she said, "I'm sorry I was rude."

He shrugged and rolled up his sleeves. "Let's chalk it up to artistic temperament, shall we?"

"No, it is not artistic temperament! It was tiredness and disappointment and . . . hunger."

"Haven't you eaten?" She shook her head. "Nothing since lunch? No wonder we had the histrionics. Nobody can be reasonable on an empty stomach. When we've cleared up this mess we'll have to do something about it."

She said quickly, "I'm not having dinner with you."

"I haven't invited you to dine with me." The coldness of his tone made her want to creep into a corner.

"Sorry," she muttered, seizing a scrub brush and dipping it into a bucket of water. They worked in silence for a while. When the paint had gone, leaving only faint stains on the floor, Juliet sighed and Drew laughed.

"If the staff could see me now, the company manager on his knees helping to clear up the mess created by the most maddening and unruly employee in the firm!"

She protested, "I may be maddening at times, but I'm certainly not unruly. How can you say that?"

He stood, pulling her up with him. "How can I say that? Because you are unruly. You're an anarchist, my girl. You flagrantly disobey all rules, you refuse to acknowledge any form of control, and you believe in revolt for the sake of it. You're the most disobedient, undisciplined young woman I've ever come across." He gripped her chin and a quantity of hair at the back of her head. "There's a ruthless streak in me, so you'd better watch your step, because if you bring it out by going too far, I won't be able to help myself. I'll do something drastic to you." His face came nearer, his eyes searched hers, his lips seemed to hover. He saw the tiredness and the touch of fear she couldn't hide. He dropped his hands.

Bitterly disappointed, longing for his kiss to ease away her tiredness and that haunting sense of failure which reared its head like a snake ready to hiss at the slightest setback, she turned away.

"Would you like some food? I'll look for a sandwich or two in the canteen, if you like."

"No, thanks. My mother will probably have a meal waiting for me when I get home."

He looked at his watch. "I'll give you a lift."

"No, thank you." It came out a little too quickly for politeness. She didn't want to give him the impression that she was asking for a lift as she had assumed earlier that he was inviting her to dinner with him.

"All right, all right, I only offered. As a matter of fact, I am in a hurry." He unrolled his shirt sleeves and buttoned them.

"Camille?" she asked, knowing as soon as it was out that the question was impertinent.

"If you must know, yes," he said in a tone intended to squash her.

He reached for his jacket which he had hung on a hook, but put it back again saying "Damn! I've got some paint on my sleeve." He held it out as if asking her what to do about it.

She laughed and somehow it eased the tension. "Just like a helpless male! I'll get it off for you. What would men do without women?"

"I wouldn't know," he answered laconically. She picked up a rag and dipped it in some water. "I'm hardly ever without one."

She tightened up at once. With a cynical smile he offered her his wrist and she rubbed at the paint stain on his sleeve, holding the back of his hand in hers. Her eyes strayed to his slightly curled fingers and she fought a crazy desire to lift the palm of his hand to her cheek, her lips, to feel it caressing her body. She stopped, horrified at where her thoughts were taking her.

She said, her tone deliberately flippant to keep at bay the powerful emotions clamoring, like an unruly mob, to have their demands met, "Your girlfriend would disown you, wouldn't she, if you took her out to dinner with a paint-stained shirt?"

There was no reply and she looked up at him, smiling. But he wasn't smiling. His expression as his eyes met hers was more intensely serious than she had ever seen it and her smile died a slow, painful death. She held her breath. What was he going to say?

Nothing, it seemed. He frowned instead and pulled away his hand with some impatience. "Thanks, that will do. I'll change when I get home." He swung into his jacket, looked at his watch again and said, "I must be off. You, too. I want to lock up."

She tidied the paint cans, put the brushes in water and, picking up her belongings, walked by his side through the silent store to the exit. Before he left her he said, "Claim for the paint you bought through petty cash. Go to the cashier, produce the receipts and she'll give you back your money. Good night." Abruptly he left her.

She went to work the next morning oddly happy. It wouldn't be long now before the boutique would be ready. She had even decided on the name: *Girl Major*. She hoped Drew would approve. In a day or two the display stands would be in position. Some of the stands she had chosen were conventional racks. A few would be suspended from the ceiling by long chains, so that the clothes handing on them would swing and twirl. Others would hang low from flat, round table-like tops on which would sit dummy figures displaying clothes.

As she entered the boutique she saw the stain left by the paint spilled the evening before. Her heart beat a little faster when she remembered how Drew had helped her clear away the mess. Then she thought about Camille and how he had spent the evening with her. She wondered if he intended to marry her one day and the idea hurt her like a wound.

Her name being called out over the internal public address system gave her a shock. "Miss Bourne," the voice said, "Miss Juliet Bourne to go to the company manager's office immediately."

Her first reaction to the summons was one of pleasure that Drew should want to see her. But as she went up in the elevator she wondered why he hadn't phoned. *He must have been too busy*, she thought.

When she knocked and entered he was seated at his desk. He raised his head and he might have been looking at a stranger for all the recognition there was in his eyes. His cold, evaluating scrutiny misted her vision like frost spread over a window pane.

"You . . . you sent for me, Mr. Major?" He motioned her to a seat.

She became aware that there was someone else in the room, a man she had never seen before. Drew indicated him. "Mr. Cunningham, our chief security officer."

Security officer? Why did he think she would be interested in meeting the security officer? Mr. Cunningham nodded but did not rise, nor did he proffer his hand. Instead he scrutinized her as closely as Drew had done. What was the matter with them? Did they think she was an escaped criminal? Was this an identity parade and she a suspect?

She knew the answer as soon as Drew spoke. "Overnight," he leaned back and fixed her eyes with his, "an expensive transistor radio disappeared from the radio and electrical department."

Juliet frowned. "Did it? I'm sorry to hear it." The trite expression sounded weak, but she could think of nothing else to say.

His next words, preposterous and bewildering though they were, revealed the direction of his thoughts. "Since you stayed late last night, as I myself know, and since you were alone for a long time after everyone else had gone, I'm afraid that all the circumstances point to one thing . . . that you are responsible for that radio's disappearance."

It was a direct accusation. Her cheeks drained of color. "That I was responsible? Are you now saying, on top of all the other insulting things you've called me in the past, that I'm a thief?"

The security officer's gaze, intent, assessing, never left her face. His arms were folded, his thick glasses magnified his staring eyes to a frightening size, and he had the look of a man who chose to believe the worst of anyone brought before him.

"My dear Miss Bourne," Drew's cool, patronizing tones were harder to bear than the security officer's incriminating regard, "what else are we to think? I'm merely saying that the situation is such that, try as we might, we cannot see how anyone else can possibly be blamed for the theft."

"But you went out with me, Mr. Major. If I'd had the radio you would have seen me holding it, wouldn't you?"

"You were carrying a shopping bag. How do I know what you had in that?"

She tried again. "But I wasn't the only one on the premises. There was the caretaker—"

"Mr. Robinson has been with us for many years. His character and his record are excellent. He's above suspicion."

So Drew Major had put himself out of reach of all reason. Her cheeks flamed. "And I'm not above suspicion. I'm a newcomer, an interloper, untried, therefore under no circumstances to be trusted." Sarcastically, "I must, therefore, be guilty." She flung at the security officer, who did not react by the flicker of an eyelid, "Hardly a considered and logical conclusion for a man to arrive at whose job it is to enforce the law fairly and without bias. If you're so sure I did it, why don't you march me along to the police station and have me arrested?"

Drew answered quietly, "In this firm, Miss Bourne, we don't do things that way. Out of the kindness of our hearts, we try to make it as easy as possible for the culprit. As I told you once before, staff pilfering is a hazard every firm has to cope with. We take it in our stride. We don't go running to the police every time it happens. We have our own method of punishing those members of staff found guilty of stealing the firm's goods—instant dismissal."

"And they get no chance to clear their names? You call that kind?" She cried passionately, "What is this, a court of law? If so, I demand to see my solicitor . . . at least," she corrected herself, "my father's solicitor. But it's not a court of law, is it? It's not even as fair as that. Instant dismissal, made as quickly and unthinkingly as instant coffee. You call this justice? Prove that I took it," she shouted, "Go on, prove it!"

"Prove that you didn't, Miss Bourne."

"You know very well I can't prove anything. You've made an accusation. I deny that accusation. I tell you," her voice was a mixture of outrage and appeal, "I didn't do it!"

"Miss Bourne," Drew persisted, "if you would produce the radio, return it to the department concerned, we might even, in your case, consider forgetting—"

"Produce it? Produce something I haven't got?"

"You haven't got it?" echoed the security officer sharply, speaking for the first time. "Then where is it? Have you passed it on to someone else?"

"Now what are you implying?" she shrieked at him. "That I'm a member of a gang dealing in stolen goods?"

"Don't be so stupid, Miss Bourne. He means have you made a present of it to someone, a friend, a relative, perhaps? I myself am aware, by means which we both know, of your financial circumstances at home—"

She would not let him finish. "Now you're telling me my family's so poor that they couldn't afford to pay for a transistor radio? Just how insulting can you get?"

"It was an expensive radio, Miss Bourne."

"I don't care," she cried, "if the thing cost 100 dollars. I wouldn't dirty my hands, let alone my conscience, by stealing anything from anyone, let alone . . . let alone . . ." She couldn't get out the word 'you.' It stuck in her throat and choked her to tears.

By the expression on their faces, she knew her hesitation had cost a high price. If her passionate denial of guilt had made any impression at all, its effect was now receding fast. "All right," she began, but realized in time that if she had continued the sentence, had said as she had intended, "I'll resign. There's no need for you to sack me," it would have underlined her guilt even more. They were waiting for her to speak again, waiting like dogs eyeing a meaty bone for the confession they were sure was coming.

The door opened and Warren came in. "Will someone kindly tell me what's going on in here? I heard her shouting and I'd like to know why."

Drew explained irritably, "A radio has been stolen from the electrical department."

"Well?"

"Miss Bourne stayed late last night. She was alone for some time." Warren froze as if he knew what was coming. "We've arrived at the unfortunate conclusion, and you have to agree that we have no alternative, that Miss Bourne now has that radio in her possession."

Warren said slowly, unbelievingly, "In other words, she stole it?" He jabbed a finger in her direction. "She stole it? You must be crazy," he looked disparagingly at Mr. Cunningham, "both of you."

She turned to Warren, crying, "It's all based on circumstancial evidence, Mr. Major. I was there, I was alone, therefore I'm guilty." She contracted the muscles of her throat. She was determined not to cry. "I'm new, I'm untried, therefore my morals are suspect, all the more so because I was once an art student, and as everyone knows," she flung her sarcasm at Drew, "art students' morals are unspeakable." She looked again at Warren. "I'm being sacrificed at the altar of the System, with a capital 'S.' I'm innocent, but I can't prove it, so I must suffer the punishment of the guilty . . . instant dismissal. I have no chance to defend myself. The System being what it is, it can only accuse, never excuse, never listen to reason. I have no redress. So I'm to be summarily dismissed." She turned on Drew. "You were right, so right, when you said you were ruthless. You're worse, much worse. You're cruel, you're merciless, you're unjust and you're . . . you're inhuman!" And because she realized she was abusing unforgivably the man she knew

deep in her heart she loved above all others, she started to
cry. She couldn't stop herself.

Warren's arm came around her and once again she
sought solace at the shoulder of the man who, in very
different circumstances, might have been her father.

He said over her head which was jerking with her
violent sobs, "Have a bit of compassion, son. Give her a
chance to prove her innocence."

"Thanks," her voice was muffled against him, "for
your belief in my integrity, Mr. Major, but I can't prove
I'm innocent, can I?"

There was a long silence, broken only by her intermittent sobbing. Then Warren said, "At least commute the
sentence into dismissal after a period of time. She's got to
get another job. You know that as well as I do. Dismissal
would prejudice her chances so much she might find it
impossible to get one. There's the question of references
for a start."

"She could resign."

"That wouldn't help, would it, son?" His voice was
quiet in its appeal for clemency. "Any future employer
would want to know why."

He was pleading with the man who, as he had once
claimed with pride, he had fashioned in his own image.
He was now entreating him to show a mercy, a kindliness of which he, by his own hand and by careful and
deliberate tuition, had 'gutted' him—his son's own
words—from adolescence onward. He now looked a little
sad, a little pathetic, as if he would have given everything
to undo the past and recreate this son of his in a more
forgiving, more compassionate mold.

His appeal must have touched the company manager,
whose eyes, although they did not lose their hardness,
assumed a filial forbearance. He said, "The dismissal

stands, but she may stay until she has obtained other employment. If her stay here is extended too long, I'll be forced to use my prerogative and dismiss her at any time I think fit."

Warren, without another word, led Juliet outside. He patted her shoulder. "Go to the rest room, my dear. Don't go back to your work until you feel ready." She nodded and thanked him. As she turned to go, Warren said, as if he could not hold back the question, "Your mother? She's well?"

"Yes, thank you. And my father, for the moment."

"Yes, yes, your father," as if mention of him was irrelevant. "With regard to this other business, Juliet," he motioned toward Drew's closed door, "you have an ally in me. Never forget it. I'll fight on your side."

She gave him a weak smile, thanked him again and walked slowly toward the elevator.

CHAPTER SIX

Girl Major was opened without announcement. No advertisement appeared in the press. Malcolm had said that even with the rather poor effort at a boutique which Curlews had made, they had at least announced it in the local paper. But because she was under notice, Juliet had not bothered to mention the matter of publicity. Her heart wasn't in the venture any more.

When she had told Malcolm the story of her dismissal, he had been furious. She had hardly been able to restrain him from picking up the phone and having a violent quarrel with Drew Major.

"Get a job at Curlews," he had urged her. "They want a new assistant in the boutique. I know it would be a bit of a comedown going from buyer to junior assistant, but it would be better than nothing."

But she told him she wanted to get away from the area, even if it meant moving. She had no quarrel with Warren Major, none at all, but his son . . . she couldn't tell Malcolm, of all people, how she felt about Warren's son.

She had not told her parents about the missing radio. She had spared them the indignity of knowing that their daughter had been accused of theft and given notice by the company manager himself, the son of the man her mother had once nearly married and the man her father resented so fiercely and tolerated only because he knew it would upset his wife if he did not.

One morning *Girl Major* was not open, the next it was. It was as straightforward as that. Consequently, business was slow. Juliet stood around listlessly waiting for the first customer, feeling that all her efforts, as well as the money spent on the fittings, the decor, and the models, had been in vain. A young girl, timid but inquiring, put her head around the entrance of the boutique, took a hasty look at Juliet's too-hopeful eyes and withdrew like a child afraid to go into a roomful of strangers.

An hour later, another young woman came in, wandered around, got the feel of the place, which somehow didn't seem to please her, and vanished as the other girl had done. Juliet began to fret.

The taped music, light pseudo-classical stuff drifting innocuously out of the public address system was putting out with sugary efficiency the high-class image which the store had so painstakingly built up over the years.

Curlews had consistently leveled their sights at a different class of clientèle. Although its standards were undoubtedly lower than those of Major's, it had obtained and retained the unwavering loyalty of those who would not have allowed even their shadows to venture into the superior air of the other store.

Perhaps that was what was wrong. The atmosphere, Juliet concluded, must be frightening away the shy young girls who were attracted to the boutique, but at the same time felt hopelessly out of place in such an exclusive establishment.

And all the time there was the music, that umbrella of pleasant, eminently orthodox sound which was 20 years behind the times. It was perhaps—although Juliet was reluctant to concede the point—the right kind of sound for the rest of the store, but it wouldn't do at all for the type of client Girl Major sought to attract.

The boutique, Juliet decided, should be provided with its own music. And, she thought with a delightful feeling of revenge, it should be loud enough to drown the insipid stuff which honeyed the air-conditioned atmosphere of the rest of the store. Should she bring her own transistor radio? But the very thought of the words made her wince. They reminded her of the scene in Drew's office when he had accused her of being a thief. No, music for the boutique would unfortunately have to wait.

Having nothing else to do, Juliet wandered out into the main store and saw with envy how busy her colleagues were, serving and smiling and wrapping customers' purchases. She felt bitter. Their jobs were secure. Hers was not. No threat of dismissal hung over their heads like Damocles's sword. She cursed her misplaced devotion to her cause when, over-zealous, she had stayed behind that unfortunate evening. She was the victim of her own enthusiasm and as a consequence was on her way out.

All those women in their high-necked black dresses were not rebels. They conformed, they worked set hours, went home and forgot about their jobs until next morning. She, with her burning desire to make the boutique succeed, had voluntarily worked overtime, and now she had been made the scapegoat for the real thief of that radio. It came to her with a shock that he or she was probably still working on the premises right now, undetected and uncaring.

She felt a resentment so strong it tasted bitter in her mouth. She put her hand to her throat and felt its bareness—she was still wearing the black dress—and another idea occurred to her. She was wrongly dressed for the part. That was something which could easily be remedied, so remedied it would be.

Her spirits revived. Her anarchistic tendencies, as Drew had disparagingly called them, came into their own. She searched through the clothes on the racks, selected tight-fitting scarlet pants, an equally tight-fitting multicolored long-sleeved top and an imitation fur waistcoat, as longhaired and shaggy as Highland cattle. She went into one of her own fitting rooms, put on the new clothes, bundled her black dress into her shopping bag and emerged looking like one of her own customers. She draped herself against the entrance to the boutique and registered with a fierce delight the gasps that came her way from other members of staff.

It took only ten minutes for her strategy to work. A young woman approached and pushed past Juliet as if willing to overcome all obstacles in order to get at the clothes Girl Major was displaying so enticingly. The colored lights moved and halted, moved and stopped again, changing the color of every object they settled on, even the girl raking feverishly through the racks. She selected three items and approached Juliet who was still leaning negligently against the entrance.

"Want to try them on?" Juliet asked, smiling encouragingly. The customer nodded. She went into a fitting room and Juliet resumed her place at the door. Another girl hovered outside, peering past Juliet, who moved slowly to let her in.

The first customer emerged and said, "I'll take all three," paid and went out smiling. The second customer chose a long-sleeved ribbed dress, paid for it without trying it on and went away, smiling just as brightly.

From that moment on, Girl Major didn't look back. The rest of the morning brought a constant stream of customers, all of them young, although some were certainly past their teens. Juliet didn't even have time for morning coffee. During the lunch break business became even brisker. Having no assistant, Juliet worked on, thinking longingly of her sandwiches, but finding no opportunity to slip away.

She did think of asking one of the assistants from the

main store to take over for ten minutes, but shrank from the thought. Heaven knew what damage might be done by one of those formally-dressed, tight-lipped women assistants.

It was during the afternoon that the general manager confronted her in a pause between customers.

"I've had complaints from other members of staff," Mr. Havering said, "that you are breaking one of the store rules by abandoning your uniform and wearing clothes totally unsuited to your position." So someone had told tales. He eyed her with distaste. "Kindly change back into your black dress at once!"

"But, Mr. Havering," she pleaded, "it would be disastrous if I did. I've proved by experience that it's absolutely essential for me to dress like this. It wasn't until I changed into these clothes that I started getting any customers at all. My black dress was frightening them away."

He was unmoved. "I'm sorry, Miss Bourne. Rules are made to be observed, not broken. If you don't agree I shall have to inform my superiors." His superiors! His military bearing was coming through. He talked like an officer in the army. Major and Son had chosen the right man here to enforce the company's rules, with his unquestioning acceptance and rigid application of the regulations.

But Miss Bourne, like a mutinous private, refused, even at the risk of being confined to barracks, to obey orders. "Then, Mr. Havering," she said quietly, spotting another customer wandering around, "you'll just have to inform your superiors, because I'm not changing back to my store uniform."

He made a short, sharp noise like the firing of a gun, turned on his heel and marched out.

Ten minutes later the extension telephone rang in her office. "Mr. Drew Major," the secretary announced, "wishes to see Miss Bourne immediately."

Juliet said, as slowly as if she were talking to a foreigner, "Miss Bourne is very sorry, but she is unable to comply with Mr. Major's request. If Miss Bourne did, there would be no one to serve all the customers who are lining up for her to wait on them." She slammed down the phone and ran out to serve the girls grouped around the shop, money and purchases in hand, waiting patiently for attention.

The phone rang again. She let it ring until she couldn't stand it. "Yes?" she asked into the receiver.

"Miss Bourne?" came the clipped, even tones of the company manager.

She didn't give him a chance to continue. "I'm sorry, Mr. Major, but it's absolutely impossible for me to leave the boutique. I can't possibly come and see you now." She hung up and ran back into the shop.

The phone rang again. She went into the office, removed the receiver and put it on the desk. Then she returned to her customers.

Three minutes later Drew Major strode in, looked bewildered at the crush, seached for the boutique buyer. It was difficult to distinguish anyone in that mass of highly colored femininity. When he found her, he stared as if he could not believe his eyes, turned on his heel as Mr. Havering had done and went out.

"Rounds one and two to me," Juliet thought, enjoying herself. "He can't sack me because I'm already under notice." The thought delighted her.

The shop closed its doors at five-thirty. At five-forty the last customer departed. Five minutes later, when everyone else was preparing to leave, Juliet sat down to eat her lunch. An announcement over the public address system caught everyone's attention. It said, clearly and distinctly, three times, "Will Miss Juliet Bourne go to the company manager's office at once."

Juliet munched on. She was going to finish her sandwiches if it choked her. A young man put his head around her office door.

"Can't you hear? You're wanted by the big white chief."

"I heard, thanks. I'll go in a minute."

He gazed at the sandwich that was disappearing fast into her mouth, murmured, "Everything stops for food," shrugged and went home.

When she did eventually make her way to the sixth floor, and stood with Drew's door only a few inches from her face, her courage started to melt like ice cream left standing too long.

It hit her like a giant wave hurling itself against rocks that she was guilty of disobedience of a high order, high enough, if she had not already been under notice, to get her fired on the spot.

But she had gone this far, and there was no turning back now. She knocked, received the summons to enter and went in. His look fixed her to the spot as surely as if he were pointing a revolver at her head. One false move on her part and he would fire.

"I want to know,' he said, each word hitting her as if she were an object being used for target practise by an expert marksman, "why, for the past hour and a half, you have resolutely and wilfully disobeyed my repeated instruction to come to my office. And," through his teeth, "since I feel at the moment as if I'd like to make mincemeat out of you, the explanation had better be good."

"The explanation," she said, her bravado forsaking her like a friend turned traitor, "is simply that I couldn't leave the boutique unattended. I tried to tell your secretary that, but she can't have got the message."

"The message was received all right, that Miss Juliet Bourne refused point blank to do what she was told and had no intention whatsoever of obeying my instructions."

"If you want me to be free to jump at your command, then I'll have to be allocated an assistant."

He swiveled sideways, letting his arm hang over the back of his chair. "Oh, will you? And where will the money come from to subsidize such a person?"

She shrugged. "Out of the firm's pocket, I suppose. I'm sure once the boutique becomes established, the earnings will justify an assistant for me. I haven't had time to calculate how much I've taken in today . . . I handed the cash over on my way here . . . but when the total is known even you will be staggered at the amount."

"After dealing with you, it would take a lot to stagger me." He eyed her outfit derisively.

She saw where his thoughts were leading him. "Mr. Major," her voice had a pleading quality that would have moved the company chairman to give her anything, but the company manager appeared as unmoved as a range of mountains, "I'm serious about the assistant. I've worked all day, apart from an hour or so this morning when there were no customers."

Despite the sandwiches she had swallowed before going to see him, hunger pangs caught her under her ribs. She looked around for a chair. "Do you mind if I sit down?"

He nodded. "Even if it is only a ruse to make me realize what a tired, harassed, hard-working girl you are."

"My tiredness is genuine." She sank down onto the chair opposite him. "I couldn't come and see you right away. You see, I had to eat my lunch."

"Lunch? Lunch? At," he looked at his watch, "five-forty-five?"

She nodded. "And that's why I'd like an assistant."

"I see no reason why you shouldn't have an assistant." She was about to express her gratitude at his sudden change of heart when he added, "We might as well start at once to train someone to take your place."

She should have known there would be a sting in the tail. "How can you be so cool," she cried, "about my leaving?"

"Have you forgotten the missing radio?"

"How could I forget? Anyone accused of doing something they didn't do and being punished for it could never forget the injustice being meted out to them. I promise you from the bottom of my heart that I'll never forget or forgive you for mistrusting me."

He frowned and studied the lines on the palms of his hands as if he were reading a map. He changed the subject, pointing. "Those clothes . . . there will be no more of that nonsense."

"This nonsense, as you call it," she pulled at the furry waistcoat she was wearing, "was the bait that brought the customers in. For two or three hours I was hanging around that boutique, very decent and nice in my black dress, and I didn't sell a single item. It wasn't until I changed into this outfit that the girls passing by . . . and I mean passing by . . . began to catch on. Then the real business of the day began."

"Very plausible, Miss Bourne, and I compliment you on your efforts to sell yourself to me." He smiled provocatively. "Don't misunderstand me, I mean in the purely business sense of the word." He seemed to enjoy the mutiny in her eyes. "But you're pouring out your sales talk to deaf ears. That outfit, when seen within the context of the rest of the store, is as out of place as a mountain in the heart of London. From tomorrow onward," he pointed his finger for emphasis, "and this is a directive from the top, from tomorrow onward you return to wearing your black dress while on duty. If you disobey, and my father can intervene on your behalf as much as he likes, it will make no difference, you're out. Out, you understand?"

"But, Mr. Major," she wailed, seeing her boutique, as she still thought of it, failing beyond resuscitation, "I must wear clothes like these. That horror of a black dress I was wearing was frightening customers away. Go into any boutique and you'll see the sales assistants wearing clothes like the ones they're selling."

His eyes darkened. "That 'horror of a black dress,' Miss Bourne, as you so rudely call it, is official store uniform. And what is more, you're no ordinary sales assistant, you're a buyer, a considerable step above the status of an assistant. Therefore, like all the other buyers, and despite the fact that you've maltreated it almost beyond recognition, you will wear that dress!"

This was war. She rose and confronted him. "I'm sorry, Mr. Major, but I will not wear that dress. If you try to force me to, job or no job, I'll walk out." Her fingers, as they clutched the edge of the desk, turned white with the pressure she was putting on them. "But before I go," her efforts to contain her anger were draining her face of color, "with my own hands," she held them up for him to see, "I'll tear the boutique apart."

He was standing now, breathing hard, lips compressed.

"I'll tear it apart," she went on, "as I tore up those

pictures you wouldn't let me put up in the marking-off room, and as I nearly tore up my black dress when you objected to it after I altered it."

"So you're challenging me, are you? By threatening violence you think you'll win." He moved slowly around the desk. "If you aren't the most unscrupulous, unprincipled, shameless little bitch I've ever come across. . . ." His fingers clenched in his pockets as if he were trying to restrain them from acting disastrously on their own. "You dare to challenge me?"

His eyes bore into hers, disregarding in his fury the whiteness of her face, and seeing only her stubbornness, her defiance, her unbreakable spirit. He raised his arms as though he could scarcely restrain himself from breaking that spirit with his own hands. She cowered instinctively.

"You'd better get out, Miss Bourne," his voice was dangerously controlled, "you'd better get out while I still have control of myself."

Still she defied him, making one last attempt to reason with him. "Will you let me wear these clothes?"

At her question, his control snapped. "Get out!" he shouted. He took her by the arms and forced her backward toward the door. She tripped and nearly fell. Without gentleness he righted her. She began to resist his pressure and his hands tightened, pressing into her flesh. She cried out with pain. He reached forward and opened the door, pushing her out into the corridor.

She was crying now with frustration and anger, misery and humiliation. Another door opened and Warren appeared. In her despair she turned to him. But he was staring at his son.

"What now, Drew?" It came out wearily, hopelessly.

But Juliet did not give the company manager a chance

to answer. "I hate your son, Mr. Major," she said, her voice low and intense, "I hate him as I've never hated any other human being in my whole life!"

Warren paled. "What goes on, son? What have you done to her now?"

Drew replied, his face almost as pale as his father's, "What have I done to her? My God, it's what she's done to me, not the other way around!"

Juliet ran away from them both.

Next morning she went to work in her black dress. She found on her desk an invitation in the form of a duplicated memorandum from the company manager. It was addressed to all Major employees, advising them that the annual garden party would be held at the Major residence in a week's time. Everyone was cordially invited to attend, and to bring their husbands, wives or other partners.

She flung it down contemptuously. That was one invitation she had no intention of accepting. From the office cupboard she took out the clothes she had worn the day before. Did she dare wear them? She returned the shaggy waistcoat to the racks, put into the till the money for the striped top and scarlet pants, then she went into a fitting room and put them on.

Stiff with defiance, she awaited her first customer, standing at the entrance as she had done the day before to give the first one enough confidence to enter. Across the store she saw a tall, familiar figure wending his way in her direction. She withdrew speedily into the sanctuary of the boutique, and had to struggle with the desire to run away while she still had the chance.

He stood in the entrance and saw her outfit, his eyes lingering on the striped jumper which revealed her shape as only a tight-fitting garment could, lowering his eyes to the equally tight pants hugging her hips and legs.

"I thought I told you," he said quietly, "not to wear those things."

"I know, Mr. Major, but," her eyes held his, pleading, moist, urging him to comprehend, "I've just got to, can't you understand? Please," she whispered, "please let me."

Her eyes were large with tiredness because she had slept badly and had left home without breakfast. Her hands, palms upward, in themselves pleaded her case, and she gazed at him willing him to relent. She didn't know what she would do if he did not.

He said, his voice hardly audible, "I wish, I only wish, I could up-end you and put you across my knee. My word, I'd give you something to remember me by!" He turned and went away. She sat on the nearest chair, her legs oddly weak.

A sales representative called and all the while she was talking to him, she had to dash out of the office to serve customers. Word seemed to have got around at last that there was a new boutique at Majors. The passers-by had stopped passing and were coming in thick and fast.

When the salesman had gone, Juliet rushed into her office and dialed Drew's extension, asking to speak to him. His secretary went away, came back and said, "I'm sorry, Miss Bourne, he's not available."

So they weren't on speaking terms now. "All right," she said, endeavouring to keep calm, "will you please give him a message? Will you tell him from me that I need the assistant he promised me right now, and if I'm not allocated one immediately, I shall either have to close the boutique or go out into the store and make someone help me."

The secretary went away, and in the distance through

the receiver Juliet could hear something that sounded like a loud expletive. She suppose it was Drew reacting and she smiled, a shaft of sunlight penetrating her gloom.

The secretary returned. "Mr. Major says that as long as you don't choose him, you can take your choice from every staff member in the building. He also says that if you asked his father to act as your assistant, he's sure he would be only too willing to oblige!"

Juliet made for the hardware department, keeping her fingers crossed. She knew the person she wanted. She had seen her often behind the cash desk and had been struck by her flair for clothes, her taste and her looks, all of which added up to excellent potential for a boutique sales assistant.

She approached the young woman who was puzzled when Juliet asked her name. "Selina Fawcett," she replied.

As gently as she could, Juliet explained why she wanted her. The woman's eyes lit up. "You'll have to get permission from the hardware manager."

"I'll fix that," said Juliet, and she did. The hardware manager was annoyed, but seeing Juliet's determination and hearing that she had the backing of the man in charge, gave in. He marched off to the staff manager in search of another assistant.

Selina proved a worthy choice. She had looked down at the regulation black dress she was wearing, then gazed enviously at Juliet's outfit. Juliet waved her arm toward the racks. "Take your pick, as long as it's not too outrageous, and as long as you pay for what you take, even if it's only in installments."

Eagerly Selina searched for what she wanted and found it. She disappeared into the fitting room and came out transformed. Life became easier for Juliet after that. She was able to take her coffee breaks at reasonable times and eat her sandwiches in peace while Selina served the customers.

It was while she was having her lunch that her mother put her head around the door. Juliet went to her, delighted. "Don't tell me you've come to patronize the boutique, Mom?"

Cynthia laughed. "No. I've been having a chat with Warren in his office. He phoned me this morning and invited me to have a look at some washing machines which have just arrived. They're not on sale yet. They're upstairs being priced in some special place—"

"The marking-off room?" Juliet suggested.

"That's it. Ridiculous price they're selling at, and they've only got one or two scratches on them. I said I didn't mind scratches as long as they worked satisfactorily. Warren told me the wholesaler had guaranteed that, but had to slash the price because they were seconds."

"Are you getting one?"

"If your father doesn't mind."

"But don't you think he might because of who's selling it to you?"

Cynthia sighed. "I hope not. It's so silly of him to be like that. It's not as though Warren means anything to me these days." Juliet felt a spurt of joy and a tremendous release from the anxiety that had worried her so much lately. Her mother didn't return Warren's love, might not even be aware of it. But her mother's next words had her worried again.

"Warren's invited me to lunch."

Juliet frowned. "Are you going?"

"Why not? It's only in the store restaurant. It'll be a nice change not to have to cook for myself." She bent down and kissed her daughter. "See you this evening, darling."

Cynthia went out, leaving a trace of perfume behind. It was something she rarely used, and the lingering scent disturbed Juliet, renewing her anxieties about her mother's relationship with her one-time fiancé.

When Malcolm called for her that evening, Juliet told him about the washing machine scoop which Majors had pulled off. She didn't bother to warn him to keep the fact to himself. She didn't care any more. She sensed his interest by the questions he asked.

"I couldn't tell you the name of the wholesaler. If you want to know, find out for yourself."

"I will, darling, I will. Be prepared to see me some time wandering about like an interested customer in Major's precious store. I know I'm not in the electrical department at Curlews, but I'd give a lot to get back at that nasty so-and-so for giving you the push for something you didn't do."

She shrugged. It was Malcolm's business what he did about the washing machines. "I'll have to get another job soon. I've been reading the ads in the local paper, but there's been nothing suitable for me yet. Everything I see that might be right for me carries a much lower salary than I'm getting at Majors. It'll be such a let-down for my parents if I have to take home less money. But it won't be long before Drew starts getting restless and asking me when I'm leaving. I can see the signs."

As Juliet walked past the front of the store one morning she decided it was time she was allocated some window space. As soon as she arrived she changed and asked Selina to take charge for a while.

"I'm going to the fourth floor to the art section. I'm

mixing with my own kind, as a certain acquaintance of mine would say." She didn't name the acquaintance.

When she tapped on the art room door, there was no reply, so she walked in. Seated on high stools at benches, or sprawling over long tables, were an assortment of oddly dressed young men and women. She watched for a while as they ruled, measured and painted. They were working on direction signs, making sketches of new goods for press advertisements and ruling out elaborate lettering for the forthcoming sales.

She was completely ignored. Feeling strangely at home despite the fact that she might have been a speck of dust as far as those dedicated artists were concerned, she crept around watching them work, experiencing a sharp stab of nostalgia for what she had left behind at the school of art. Her eyes wandered and she saw a small group working on some slogans. She caught her breath.

"Make Mine Majors", one of them said. "You get more for less at Majors", said another. "Major Reductions", announced a third. Her slogans, her ideas for bringing the store up to date! So her suggestions for giving the store a new image had not fallen on deaf ears. Drew had taken them to heart and soon a new store would be emerging from the old, one with greater popular appeal.

"What's all this?" she asked one of the artists.

He shrugged. "Directive from the top," he muttered, without removing his eyes from his work. "They dictate, we obey." Then he raised his head and stared. It wasn't a friendly stare, nor were his words, "What do you want?"

"To talk about being given some window space."

He gestured toward the door with his thumb. "Display, next door but two."

Display was different. The occupants of the room were gathered in a circle, leaning on the nearest available support and talking. They noticed her as soon as she went in. They too were slightly belligerent. Again she was asked what she wanted.

"Some window space."

Two of the young men roared with laughter. Another groaned.

"You're joking," someone said. "You have to take your place in line."

"What's your department?" a girl asked.

"Boutique."

"The one they've just opened? You haven't got a hope." The girl counted on her fingers. "There's about a dozen in front of you. Hardware for their special offer. Coats for their knock-down bargains of small sizes that wouldn't sell at the proper price. Underwear, shoes, furnishings. . . . Need I go on?"

"But," Juliet said, frowning, "I must have some publicity. How are people to know about the boutique if I'm not given any window space?"

"Oh, you'll get window space," one of the young men said. "In about three months' time." She'd be gone by then.

"But that's ridiculous!"

"Couldn't agree more, but that's how it is."

"I've got some good ideas I want to try out before . . . before. . . ." She couldn't tell them she was under notice to leave. "As soon as possible," she finished lamely.

"Who hasn't got good ideas?" The girl sighed. "Give up, dear." She took out a pad and pencil. "We'll put your name on the list. We'll look you up in, say, ten weeks and work out something between us. With any luck two or three weeks after that you might get your window space."

"Thanks," Juliet said shortly, going to the door. She nearly added, "For nothing."

She was sitting in the office at lunchtime finishing her sandwiches when Malcolm strolled into the boutique. She heard his voice and when she joined him he was eyeing Selina with as much dedicated interest as a judge eyes an entrant in a beauty contest.

"Hallo," said Juliet and he jumped guiltily. "I didn't know you had a roving eye, Malcolm."

"You'd be surprised what I have got, darling," he replied, addressing Juliet but keeping his eyes on her assistant.

Selina, obviously taken with him, smiled and said, "My name's Selina. What's yours?"

He looked at Juliet. "Shall I tell her? Or is it a dark secret?"

Juliet shrugged. "Tell her if you like. After all, we're just good friends, aren't we?"

Dipping his head in Juliet's direction, Malcolm said to Selina, "Don't take any notice of her. She's made it sound worse than it really is." He held out his hand. "The name's Malcolm. You new around here?"

"New to the boutique, not new to Majors. Miss Bourne got me moved from hardware to here."

Malcolm made a face. "Miss Bourne, is it? On our dignity, aren't we, darling?"

She frowned, showing her irritation. "I am supposed to be the buyer. Others show respect to buyers even if you don't."

"Temporary buyers included?" Malcolm sat himself on a chair and put his feet up on one of the circular display stands.

"What's the matter with you?" Juliet snapped. "Showing off?"

Malcolm merely smiled and offered her a cigarette. "You know I don't smoke," she said. "Nor does Selina, or any of Majors' staff while on duty."

"Implying that Curlews' staff do?" He shrugged, lighting his cigarette. "So what if we do? Only when the management's not around, though."

A girl came in trailing her boyfriend behind her. He hesitated at the door, saw Malcolm, and found the courage to go in with her. Malcolm stayed where he was, his feet still propped up, and watched the couple wandering around the racks. The young man took out a pair of trousers and held them against himself, asking his girlfriend what she thought of them.

Juliet was pleased. Was she going to have her first male customer? Apparently she was. The girl bought a long skirt, her young man the trousers. As they went out, Malcolm grinned.

"You owe me commission on that sale, Juliet. If I hadn't been here, her boyfriend would have been too scared to come in."

"Why have you come, anyway?" Juliet's good humor was only partially restored. "To snoop around the electrical department, as you said?"

"That and," he took her hand, "to tell you I love you." He winked broadly at Selina.

There were footsteps and Drew Major stood in the entrance. Malcolm didn't drop her hand, but put it to his lips instead.

Drew fixed her with his eyes. "Miss Bourne, if you choose to allow your boyfriend to make love to you in the privacy of your office, that is your affair. But if you let him do it here, in this boutique, with customers in and out all the time, I'll have no alternative but to remove you from your position as a buyer and put someone else in your place for the rest of your time with us."

Juliet tugged her hand from Malcolm's, started to apologize, but Malcolm cut in, "You're exaggerating just a little, sir." He lowered his feet to the floor and stubbed out his cigarette. "When I make love to Juliet," his eyes rose indolently to Drew's, "I . . . er . . . go a little farther than holding her hand. I do it properly."

His tone abrasive, Drew said, ignoring Malcolm as if he didn't exist, "When your visitor has gone, Miss Bourne, I wish to see you in your office."

Momentarily the loser, Malcolm turned, caught Juliet around the neck and kissed her full on the lips. " 'Bye, darling, see you later." He raised his hand to Selina. "See you some time." Selina nodded, smiling and not bothering to hide her admiration.

Malcolm turned at the door, knowing three pairs of eyes were watching him. He made the most of his exit. "By the way, darling," he said to Juliet, "I got the information I wanted." He saluted Drew insolently and left.

So now Malcolm knew the name of the wholesalers who had supplied those washing machines. Instead of the pleasure she had expected to feel at the prospect of getting even with Major and Son she felt afraid. Her standing in the eyes of Drew Major was bad enough. This could only make things worse.

She followed Drew into her office. She was on the defensive even before he could begin to speak. "I'm sorry, Mr. Major, but I didn't invite him. He just walked in." Drew sat on the only chair, leaving her standing. He crossed his legs and leaned back, his expression cynical.

"Anyway," she was belligerent now, "I don't see what harm he was doing."

Drew raised his eyebrows. "Just use your imagination, Miss Bourne. As an artist you're allegedly well endowed with it. What would happen if every girl on my staff allowed her boyfriend to visit her during store hours and sit as your boyfriend was doing, feet up, smoking and holding his lady love's hand?"

She frowned uncertainly. "But, Mr. Major, the fact that he was there actually had a good effect on sales. A young man came in with his girlfriend, and he bought something for himself."

"A young man?"

"Haven't you heard of unisex clothes? I've got plenty in stock. If Malcolm hadn't been there, the young man would have run a mile. I could see that by the way he hesitated at the door."

"Oh, good for you, Miss Bourne!" She could have hit him for his sarcasm. "Maybe you'd like Majors to adopt your boyfriend as a mascot and make him a permanent fixture in the boutique so as to encourage dozens of young men?" He rose. "My advice to you is to keep your boyfriend in his place, which is Curlews, not Majors."

She sighed. "Yes, Mr. Major. What did you want to see me about, Mr. Major?"

"The garden party. I take it you're coming?" She shook her head. He frowned. "Why not?"

"I just don't want to. You can't make me. It's outside office hours."

"But my father particularly wants you to go."

"I can't see what difference it makes if I don't. No one will miss me, least of all you. So I thought I'd relieve you of my presence by staying away."

"My feelings don't come into it. It's my father I'm

thinking of. For some reason he . . . er . . . seems to be fond of you. He's the one who'll be disappointed." He made for the door.

"Mr. Major?" He turned, eyebrows raised. "This morning I asked display for some window space. They said I couldn't have it for at least three months."

"Well?"

"In three months I'll be gone, won't I?"

"Perhaps. So why should you worry whether you get window space or not?"

"Even if I'm leaving, I've still got the interests of the boutique at heart. I . . . I want to see it succeed. After all, I've been in on it from the start."

"It's your baby, so you want to see it thrive, even if it is eventually taken from you and adopted by someone else?"

She dropped her eyes. "That's rather a brutal way of putting it, but yes, I'd like to see it do well before I go . . . if there's time."

There was a long silence. He said softly, "You're not under sentence of death, Miss Bourne."

"It seems like it to me, Mr. Major," she whispered.

"Juliet?" She raised her eyes, devoid of hope. "I. . . ." He checked himself and went to the door again, then stood still as though a thought had struck him. When he turned back he was smiling. "I'll make a deal with you. If I get you this window space, will you come to the garden party?"

Her spirits lifted like a released balloon. She smiled back. "Are you blackmailing me, Mr. Major?"

"Never!" he answered. "Let's say that one good turn deserves another. Agreed?"

She nodded. "Agreed."

She got her window space. Later in the afternoon she

had a phone call from display. A disgruntled male voice said, "Roy Hawkins here, display. We've received a directive from the company manager to let Miss Bourne have the window space she wants. So we've got to give Miss Bourne her darned window space in front of all the other deserving cases. We can't tell you how much we love you for going behind our backs to get what you want."

She ignored his ill temper, asking excitedly, "When?"

"Next week. What are you, dear? Teacher's pet? Have you got . . . er . . . connections with the company manager? I've never known him to put himself out like that for anyone else."

"No," she answered cheerfully, "no connections at all. Just the old feminine magnetism, you know. It never fails!" A snort from the other end closed the conversation.

As she put down the phone she realized that she was committed. Drew had kept his word, now she must keep hers. She would have to go to the garden party after all.

CHAPTER SEVEN

Juliet was determined not to go to the garden party alone, so she invited Malcolm to accompany her. He said he'd be delighted to oblige, that anything the Majors were giving away he'd accept with pleasure, whether it was food, drink or information.

She didn't bother to dress up. Selina, who had been to Major garden parties before, told her it was a very informal affair. "We usually lounge around the garden or, if the weather's fine, swim in the pool. If it rains, we gather in the large drawing room and eat and drink and talk."

The sun shone obligingly, rising to a crescendo of heat in the afternoon. Even the tar on the road surfaces showed signs of melting.

"Who could ask for more?" Malcolm demanded of no one in particular as they took the bus across the town to the Major residence. "The sun, a beautiful girl beside me and a garden party at Majors. Incidentally," he hooked his arm in hers, "watch the local paper on Monday for a splash advertisement by Curlews." He grinned. "Something about washing machines."

"You haven't told them?" Malcolm looked smug. "But, Malcolm, that's a breach of confidence."

"I don't see that it is." He seemed hurt as though she was deserting him. "You wanted to get back at your boss, didn't you, for firing you for something you didn't do?"

"All the same, it was a pretty mean trick to let things get as far as that."

He squeezed her arm. "Competition, dear. It's what

makes love and the business world go round. Life in either sphere would be dull without it."

Someone had put daisy chains round the necks of the lions. Someone else had tied large pieces of paper to their tails bearing the words "Going cheap". The inscrutable creatures looked a little more approachable as Juliet pulled Malcolm behind her and rang the doorbell.

It was answered by the housekeeper, Kate, but Mildred Major hovered in the background. She failed to recognize Juliet and said, "The garden party is in the gardens, not the house." She eyed Juliet with as much joy as she would have eyed a dead mouse the cat dropped on the mat. If Warren had not appeared behind his wife, Juliet would have been turned from the door like an unwelcome salesman.

Mildred and Kate melted away and Warren stretched out his hand, urging Juliet to come in. Because Malcolm's hand was still in her other one, he was pulled in behind her.

"My dear," Warren kissed her on both cheeks, pretending Malcolm didn't exist, "how nice of you to come." The inevitable question followed. "How's your mother?"

"Very well, thank you." She looked at Malcolm, wondering whether to introduce him, but Warren wasn't interested.

"Come in, my dear, and have a drink."

Feeling awkward and realizing that the invitation appeared to exclude her companion, she refused as gently as she could.

"I just had lunch, Mr. Major. It's very kind of you, but. . . ." She looked through the hall window, wishing she could smash the glass and dive out of it like a circus clown. It would at least get her out of her difficulties.

Warren, misinterpreting the glance said, "Of course, you're wanting to join the others. I won't keep you, then. Get out there and enjoy yourself. I'll see you later, perhaps."

"I like that!" Malcolm said as they walked away. "So I'm the invisible man now."

"He's got funny ways, Malcolm. He's like that about my father. He spends his time pretending I haven't got one and that my mother hasn't got a husband." How much should she tell him? "You see, a long time ago my mother was engaged to Warren Major."

"Good grief, she had a lucky escape, didn't she? What did he do, break it off?"

"No, my mother did."

Malcolm was muttering, "Good for her" when they turned the corner and found the garden party in full swing.

Girls in bikinis were sunbathing on the sacred Major lawns, couples were sitting on the benches in the rose garden, others, mostly men, were playing cricket. The tennis courts were in use and in the distance the swimming pool appeared to be highly popular.

Older members of the staff were strolling along the graveled paths dressed stiffly in their best. They looked quite out of place in both mood and manner among the scantily clothed, relaxed equality of the younger set. Miss Skimpton had on her best hat, which was made of swathed blue satin with rosebuds peeping from the folds. Mrs. Rouse of separates was self-consciously over-dressed in a bright pink trouser suit and was suffering from the heat.

As Juliet saw Drew, Malcolm saw Selina. Juliet's stomach muscles contracted with an odd sort of apprehension. Malcolm's facial muscles expanded into a grin and formed into an appreciative whistle.

He clutched Juliet's hand. "Keep a tight hold of me, darling," he murmured. "Did you say her name was Selina?"

Juliet tore her eyes from Drew's—he had seen Malcolm's movement—and looked at Selina. She was certainly stunning in her pink and white check bikini, her long fair hair partly covered by a matching sun hat. She saw Malcolm and took up an inviting pose.

Drew approached, his face as cold as his father's had been warm. Juliet wondered how soon she could slip away. She had done her duty, she had seen the man who had wanted her to come. Perhaps in half an hour or so she could say she had a headache. Malcolm would probably be delighted. It would leave him a clear field for making up to Selina, who certainly wouldn't repulse his approaches.

Drew said, "Nice of you to come, Miss Bourne." His eyes took in her clinging low-cut top tucked into skin-tight yellow pants. She could almost hear him thinking, "Major boutique stock?"

She answered his unspoken query defiantly. "Yes, it's from the Major racks, Mr. Major, but I haven't stolen it. I've paid the full price. I didn't even deduct my staff discount."

Malcolm sniggered, but Drew, like his father, pretended he wasn't there.

"I don't doubt you for one moment, Miss Bourne. And I'm sure it's far more effective on a figure like yours than suspended uninvitingly from a hanger in the boutique."

Malcolm's arm jerked up to her shoulders and pulled her close. *She's my girl*, the action said, *hands off*.

"Have you found the bar?" Drew's eyes shifted to Malcolm. "It's on the house."

Malcolm pulled Juliet toward it. "Somehow I could do with one, especially if it's free. Come on, darling."

Drew drifted away. Unreasonably disappointed, Juliet unhooked her arm from Malcolm's and told him, "You go. I'm not thirsty."

Malcolm shrugged and left her. She wandered among the roses, remembering the last time she had done so with Drew at her side. He had been interviewing her for the job and her expectations had been so high she had actually looked forward to being an employee of his. Now the wheel had turned full circle and through no fault of her own, her time with them had almost run out.

She passed the fountain and remembered how last time the wind had blown the spray all over her. Drew had stood and watched as she'd tried to dry herself. He hadn't offered to help and it had offended her, but she knew better now. Drew Major never helped anybody, unless it was to his advantage.

"Lost in thought?" She jumped as he appeared at her side. "And all alone?" He looked around. "Where's Romeo?"

"Drinking, probably."

"You looked a hundred miles away. What were you thinking, Miss Bourne?"

She smiled up at him, his nearness making her bold. "Bad thoughts about you."

"My word," he glanced down at her rear as if measuring it for size, "you're asking for trouble! Come on, out with it. What were these terrible thoughts about me?"

"I don't dare tell you. You might throw me in the pond."

He moved swiftly behind her and caught her under the

armpits, jerking her backward against him. "You're provoking me, Miss Bourne, and that's dangerous. The outfit you're wearing's provocative enough without your words goading me still more."

She struggled and he let her go. She faced him, her color high. "Your girlfriend might be looking, Mr. Major."

"My girlfriend isn't here, Miss Bourne."

"Why not? Wouldn't she deign to mix with the Major and Son rabble?"

"How did you guess?"

"So you're on the prowl for someone to take her place, purely on a temporary basis, of course."

He narrowed his eyes. "Do you really want to be thrown into that pond?" She shook her head violently. "Then behave yourself, Miss Bourne, if you can."

"Yes, Mr. Major. Sir."

He swung her around to face him, but after a few seconds controlled himself. "Listen to me, young Juliet. My father asked me to be nice to you today. For heaven's sake help me by being nice back. Otherwise, I hate to think what I'll do to you before the party's over."

"There's one way to be nice to me. Keep away from me."

His arm dropped from her shoulders. "Is that what you want me to do?"

Her heart was pounding, her pulses racing. She wanted him to pull her close again and. . . . "Yes," she said.

He walked away. Well, she'd asked for it, hadn't she? She wandered disconsolately back to the lawns, searching for Malcolm. No need to conjure up a headache now. She had one on top of her head as if one of those stone lions had made a new home for itself there.

She glanced up at the house and saw Mildred Major

through one of the windows arranging flowers in a pottery vase on the windowsill. She was as absorbed in her task as if she were alone in the world. With an infantile concentration, she was doing her best to forget that her gardens had been invaded by hundreds of strangers, all of whom, in her opinion, had no business to be there at all. She was pretending, as no doubt she pretended every night, that she had no husband, that everything was normal. As a family, Juliet reflected, they were very good at pretending.

She looked for Selina, feeling sure that if she found her, she would also find Malcolm, and she was right. Selina was stretched out on the grass and Malcolm was reclining on his elbow admiring her from head to toe. *If that's his loyalty to me*, Juliet thought, *then she's welcome to him*. She pushed her way to the drinks table and helped herself to a glass of lemonade. Seeing all the other couples laughing together and walking hand in hand forced her to acknowledge just how lonely she felt.

She had sent Drew away and Selina had taken possession of Malcolm. She wished she had never brought him, she wished she'd never come. Warren wouldn't really have missed her, whatever Drew had said.

She felt Drew watching her and, putting down her empty glass, pushed her way into a group of laughing people. She didn't know who they were, but she had to do something to hide from his accusing, unsympathetic gaze.

"Well, well," said one of the young men whom she identified as Roy Hawkins from display, "if it isn't the company manager's pet. All alone, dearie? Where's the boyfriend?" She knew he didn't mean Malcolm. Instinctively her eyes sought out Drew and Roy turned to follow her gaze. "Yes, he's over there, isn't he? Keeping his distance, in case the staff starts spreading rumors around about you and him?" He glanced at his friends. "Hey, you all, let's show this pretty little thing what we do to women who use their . . . er . . . influence," with his hands he fashioned the shape of a woman, "to get what they want from the man at the top."

Before she could utter a word of protest, he had scooped her up and run with her to the edge of the swimming pool. She screamed, "No, no, I can't swim!" but he didn't believe her.

"One," he said, swinging her tantalizingly over the edge, "two," he drew her back, "three!" He tossed her in. She screamed a second time, and the moment before she hit the water she screamed "No!" again.

She went under, her arms and legs flailing, trying to grab something to keep her afloat. She surfaced and gasped, then down she went again. As she came up once more she was aware of shouts and screams from all directions.

She lashed out madly with her limbs again, but it was useless. She knew it was nearly over. She gasped agonizingly and the waters closed over her head again. A splash and a shout above her penetrated her consciousness for a few seconds. Hands seized her under the armpits and dragged her up, turning her onto her back. "Drew, Drew," she gasped, then everything went blank.

She didn't come around again until she stirred to find herself flat on her face on the ground, fighting for breath while someone seemed to be grasping her ribs, pressing and releasing them alternately. Water was coming from her throat and nostrils and slowly her breathing became more normal.

She heard someone say, "I'm sorry, sir. I didn't realize she couldn't swim."

"But she told you, you half-witted idiot!"

"I thought she was fooling."

"Get away, all of you. Go on, enjoy yourselves. It's all

over, she's safe, so for heaven's sake, go away!" She heard Malcolm's voice, then Drew's. "I don't want you either, Watling. I'll deal with her. I don't need help."

Arms came around her and gathered her up and she flopped against a man's hard body, feeling the hairs of his chest soft against her cheek. "I've got you safely now, so hold on to me, Juliet," the man said, and she did with the little strength she had left. It couldn't be Drew, she decided, because the voice was so tender. Drew would never speak to her like that.

He carried her into a room and lowered her gently onto a couch. She opened her eyes and caught him unawares. Drew was gazing down at her with an odd mixture of compassion and anxiety. His look didn't make sense. He was wearing only his swimming trunks and his shoulders were glistening with water.

As soon as he saw her eyes open his expression changed to an awareness of the need for action. "What," he asked, "have you got on underneath that gear?" He didn't wait for her answer. He bent down, unhooked the waist band of her pants and undid the slide fastener.

When she realized what he was doing, she started struggling. "No," she cried, "no, no!" She gripped his hands and tried to stop him.

"Good grief, girl, what do you think I'm going to do, rape you? Nothing was farther from my mind. Come on, lift up, we've got to get these wet things off of you." He tugged off the trousers and saw the briefs of her bikini underneath. "Why, in heaven's name, aren't you running around in next to nothing like all the other girls? You're wearing a two piece swimsuit."

"I can't swim—"

"As well I know," he growled.

"So what was the use? I'd only be showing off if I did."

"And what do you think all the others are doing, if not showing off their figures? My word, you could beat the lot of them at it if you tried. Come on," his voice was brisk, "let's take off that soaking wet top."

She sat up and he helped her out of it. He disappeared into another room and emerged with a large soft bath towel. He threw it at her. "Dry yourself with that."

She looked down and said weakly, "My bikini top's wet."

"I'll give you one of my shirts to wear, then you can take that off, too."

She heard a drawer open and close and a shirt came flying through the door. "Put that on while I get changed."

When he returned he was wearing a pink open-necked shirt and fawn well-fitting trousers. He watched her drying her hair. The shirt he had lent her reached only to the lower edge of her briefs and he smiled at her efforts to pull it down.

"Where are we?" she asked.

"In my apartment. I had a wing of the house converted into a self-contained apartment, for my own exclusive use." He sat on the couch beside her. "I don't usually bring my employees here. You're an exception."

She rubbed at her briefs under the shirt in an attempt to dry them. She started shivering. Reaction was setting in and with it, disillusion. His reminder that she was only an employee had started it off, like the first boulder that precipitates a landslide. "I don't know why you bothered to save me."

"I appreciate your gratitude to me for having saved your life."

"I'm sorry, but it would have been so much easier for everyone if you'd have let me drown."

He gripped her shoulders and jerked her around. "What the hell are you talking about? Let you drown? How could I let you drown?"

She tried to pull away. "At least it would have got me out of your hair."

He leaned toward her and exerting his strength, pulled her against him. "How do you know I want to get you out of my hair?" His voice had softened and she guessed his intention. She began to struggle. She mustn't let him kiss her. He had done it once before and she had never forgotten the effect of his lips on hers. If he did it again, and in these circumstances. . . .

"No!" she cried. "You can't kiss me. You can't kiss a thief! That's what you call me, isn't it? To you I'm a thief," she was twisting her face right and left away from his mouth, "I steal transistor radios, I'm not to be trusted. You should have let me drown!"

Now his lips had nearly found their target. "You're at it again, aren't you? Trying to destroy yourself, to tear yourself apart. Well, my girl, destruction may be your second name but I swear you're not going to destroy me as your mother nearly destroyed my father."

His arms forced her to be still and accept his kisses. They were devastating and the effect shattering. When at last she was submitting because she had neither the strength nor the will to do otherwise, he threw her back onto the cushions and walked around the room. She was drained of life and totally subdued.

"You should have let me drown," she muttered again, her eyes closed, her lips stiff and painful, "it would at least have put me out of my misery."

He lifted his hand to his head. "Heaven preserve me from the artistic temperament! What misery?" He stood in front of her, legs apart, hands in pockets. "Come on, what misery? I want to know." His voice was sharp.

How could she tell him? The misery of loving a man she knew would never love her?

Receiving no answer, he asked, "You mean the loss of your job?" He wandered away and came back. "Juliet, I want to tell you—"

"How sorry you are? Oh, don't apologize. That would only be rubbing salt into the wound."

He caught her wrist and jerked her upright. "Will you listen to me for a change?" He released her and she flopped back, rubbing her wrist. He resumed walking. "I want to tell you that last night we caught the thief. I knew all along that it wasn't you, but the security officer was not so easy to convince. He insisted on positive proof of your innocence."

He sat beside her. "You might not know that the television scanners . . . the cameras . . . are left on when the store is shut. They remain on until midnight, when the store lights go out automatically."

He walked around again. "So every night, after the store closed, Mr. Cunningham, his assistant and I remained behind, watching the closed circuit television monitor and keeping track of every move the cleaners and caretakers made around the building. Because Mr. Robinson was the one who had 'found' you, as he said, hiding away, I suspected him most of all. You may not know we can tune in on the small monitor and watch any area of any floor and get the picture we most want to see on the larger screen. Last night we were watching each floor and Robinson did it again. He stole something else, quite unaware that three people upstairs could see what he was up to. We had parked our cars away from the store and he thought we had all gone home. He was caught red-handed. When Mr. Cunningham challenged him with the theft of the radio too, he admitted it. So tomorrow we advertise for a new caretaker."

He sat beside her again and smiled as relief transformed her face. "Well," he said invitingly, "do you want to fling your arms round my neck now and kiss me?"

She laughed. "So I keep my job?"

He nodded. "Why do you think I've let you stay on all this time? If I'd really suspected you, I'd have thrown you out long ago."

"It seems inadequate to say thank you."

"I don't expect your thanks. I'm the one who really should apologize for the agony and suspense you've been through. Did you ever tell your parents? No? Thank goodness for that."

He became restless again. "Where's Romeo?"

"Finding himself another Juliet."

"Do you mind?"

"It would be all the same if I did, wouldn't it? He's chasing Selina, who isn't running very hard the other way."

"You're letting her steal your boyfriend without putting up a fight? Surely that's out of character?"

"I only fight for what I really want."

"Do you, Juliet? Always?"

She raised her eyes and met his for a few seconds, wondering what he was implying. She frowned and looked away. "No, not always. For instance, you can't put up a fight, can you, when your two hands are tied behind your back?"

"What exactly do you mean by that?"

What did she mean? Make a man love her, fight for a man with a girlfriend like Camille, a man moreover who had vowed that if he ever married, the woman he chose. would have to be perfect . . . made to measure, as he had put it, in every respect?

"Those roses are beautiful." She rose and walked across to a vase in the center of a circular glass-topped table. She bent down to catch their scent.

"Don't change the subject."

"The perfume's marvelous."

He selected one from the vase and gave it to her. It was deep red. She took it, and twirled it between her fingers. "Now will you tell me what you mean?"

She continued to twist the rose around. "Oh, damn! I've pricked my finger." She put it to her lips to stop the bleeding. He pulled her into the bedroom, found a bandaid in a drawer and applied it to the wound.

She thanked him and shivered, looking at the bed, the luxurious furnishings, the thick carpet. She felt genuinely cold now and returned to the living room to look for her clothes.

He followed her. "They're still wet," he said.

The phone rang and Drew answered it. He looked at Juliet. "There's a young man making enquiries about you, name of Malcolm Watling. Interested?"

"No," she answered defiantly.

He said into the receiver, "Tell him politely to go away. Miss Bourne doesn't want to see him."

He looked her up and down and laughed. "You look a bit pathetic. But alluring at the same time." His gaze lowered. "Must be all that leg. Come on, I'll take you home. Unless you want to stay? The sun would dry your swimsuit."

"No, thanks. I'll go home." She picked up her wet clothes. "What about this?" She plucked at his shirt.

He waved it away. "Return it any time. Come through

the house. That way we'll miss the crowd." Still holding the rose, she followed him.

They met Warren in the hall. His eyes opened wide and he said, "What happened to you?"

"She . . . er . . . fell in the pool. I rescued her and she's been drying out ever since."

Warren was immediately concerned. "Come in, my dear, and have a drink."

"I don't think so, Father, thanks. She wants to get home." He felt her hair. "She's still a bit damp."

"Well, Juliet," Warren said, "did you enjoy the garden party, the part before you fell in the pool?"

"Yes, thanks." She wanted to say, "But I've enjoyed the other part more."

Warren looked at his son. "Have you told her about Robinson? And that her job with us is quite safe now? And was she pleased?"

"Delighted." Drew smiled. "So delighted, in fact, that I invited her to throw her arms around my neck and kiss me." Warren looked expectant. "Unfortunately, she declined the invitation." Warren looked disappointed.

"Have you been nice to her, son?"

"Yes, he has, Mr. Major. Nicer than I've been to him, I'm afraid."

Drew gave her a playful spank. "You should have heard her abusing me!" They smiled at each other.

Warren, his eyes watchful, shook his head. "Just like her mother again. Right below the belt, dead on target."

"Come on, woman," Drew put his arm across her shoulders. "Some day I'll hit her on target, then she'll know how it feels!"

He took her home. Outside the house she thanked him for saving her life. "And for being nice to me."

"My God, are relations between us normally so bad that you actually have to thank me for being nice to you?"

She put his rose against her mouth. "We agreed once that we were incompatible. Our temperaments, our natures, our ways of life are so different I don't think they could ever be reconciled."

"My dear Juliet," he took her hand and his voice was misleadingly soft, "you're talking as though I'd just proposed marriage. I haven't . . . yet. Is that what you want me to do, so that you can let me down and break my heart as your mother did my father's?"

She stared at him. Why the change of mood? What had she said to bring out the cynicism in him when all seemed good between them? Her lip trembled and she snatched her hand away and got out, slamming the door. His car moved on slowly, and she ran into the house.

Malcolm phoned that evening. "What do you mean," he demanded, "by saying you didn't want to see me? I was your partner, wasn't I?"

"Were you?" she asked innocently. "Selina's got something, hasn't she? Was she worth chasing?"

"Don't be an idiot, Juliet. You really think I'm serious about her? I was only having a bit of fun. After all, you left me high and dry."

"That was hardly my fault. If you'd been with me, Roy Hawkins wouldn't have dared to do what he did. If it hadn't been for Drew—"

"Drew, Drew! That's all you can talk about. What was he doing when you were in there so long, making love to you?" She colored and was glad Malcolm couldn't see her.

"Now you're being an idiot," she said, convincingly amused at the suggestion. "He had just saved me from drowning, remember? I was in a state of shock."

Malcolm was not fully convinced. "I wouldn't put anything past him. Don't forget he's throwing you out of your job for something you didn't do."

"No, he's not," she told him joyfully. "They've caught the man who did it. I've been reinstated."

"So you're not on your way out?"

"No. You sound disappointed! Perhaps you were hoping that with me out of the way, it would leave you free to chase Selina some more."

"If you're going to talk like that, I'm hanging up."

"I'll save you the trouble," she snapped. "I'll hang up first." She did. He didn't call back.

Cynthia washed and dried Drew's shirt and first thing next morning Juliet returned it to him. She took the elevator to the sixth floor and went into his secretary's office, asking if Mr. Major was free.

"No," the secretary said, "he's got Mr. Nolan, buyer of the electrical department, with him."

Of course, Curlews' advertisement! How could she have forgotten? The secretary was phoning him. "Miss Bourne is here, Mr. Major. Shall I tell her to wait or—"

"No, tell her to come in," was the terse command. "I was just going to send for her." The words sounded ominous, but in the circumstances how could she expect otherwise?

Mr. Nolan, a tall, thin man with a friendly face, nodded and smiled, still in ignorance of the part she had played in the washing machine intrigue. But as Drew started questioning her, Mr. Nolan's smile faded.

Juliet placed the shirt, which was in a paper bag, on Drew's desk. He didn't even notice it. "You know about this, Miss Bourne?" he asked, pointing to the newspaper opened in front of him. His voice was edged, like the blade of a knife. The look in his eyes showed that he had every intention of slicing through her.

"I . . . well, yes, I knew something of the sort was appearing."

"So you're at the bottom of it, you and your precious boyfriend? Have you seen it?" She shook her head. "Come here and look."

She went to his side. Curlews had taken a whole page advertisement in the local paper, saying in huge type that they had acquired a bargain purchase of washing machines (the word 'seconds' was in tiny print) and that their prices were undercutting all rivals and competitors. "Our sales representative has pulled off a mind-shattering deal and you, our loyal customers, will reap the benefit of his skill in talking the wholesalers into parting with these magnificent machines at throw-away prices."

"Our rivals," the advertisement concluded, "think they're offering you a bargain. Don't listen to them—we're giving the machines away!"

He closed the paper and looked up at her. "So, in spite of my warnings, you betrayed our secrets to that unscrupulous boyfriend of yours."

"It was an accident, Mr. Major. Your father offered my mother one of the washing machines at a very low price and when Malcolm came one evening I told him about it. He took it from there. Somehow he got the wholesaler's name from the electrical sales staff."

Mr. Nolan stirred uneasily.

"You call that accidental, Miss Bourne? I would call it outright disloyalty, deliberately passing on information with intent to damage Major's interests." He turned to Mr. Nolan. "Did you know about this?"

"Not a thing, sir. I've got one or two young assistants in my department who are still gullible enough to believe anyone who tells them a tale. That's probably how it happened. I'll have to investigate."

Drew turned back to Juliet. "I suppose you remember the penalty for passing on secret information to our rivals? I did warn you."

She flagged. "Yes, Mr. Major. Instant dismissal, Mr. Major." So they were back to square one. She was on her way out. She moved to the door. "I'll go now, Mr. Major. I couldn't stand hanging around again waiting for the axe to fall."

"Miss Bourne!" he shouted. She stopped in her tracks. More quietly he said, "I'll take over from here, Mr. Nolan. Thanks for drawing my attention to it."

"Yes, sir," Mr. Nolan said, lifting his finger in a salute and leaving the room.

"Sit down, Miss Bourne," the company manager said wearily. She sat down. "Tell me why you did this."

"So you're giving me a chance to clear myself? I don't know why. It's an ideal opportunity for you to get rid of me, Mr. Major. Why don't you take it?"

"You're at it again, Miss Bourne, intent on self-destruction. Yesterday I should have let you drown. Today I should throw you out of your job. Tomorrow you'll be suggesting I marry you and give you hell for the rest of your life. Come on, out with it. Why did you do it?"

"Because at the time, I didn't care a damn about Major and Son. I was under notice. I was so angry with you for dismissing me for a crime I didn't commit—"

"You don't have to go on. You were getting back at me. A perfectly normal reaction to be expected from anyone being unjustly punished. I'll forgive you . . . this time." She went to the door. "But, Juliet—" She turned and he smiled. "It mustn't happen again. Understand?"

She nodded and opened the door. On the other side stood Camille Wyngard, her hand raised to knock. Juliet stood aside to let her pass and she nodded condescendingly. Drew rose, not looking too pleased with his visitor.

"Darling," said Camille, "why the scowl? I haven't seen you for three whole days. Haven't you missed me?" She stared at Juliet, as if wondering why she was still there.

"Don't you have any work to do, Miss Bourne?" Drew asked sharply.

"Plenty, Mr. Major, sir," she answered, her tone insolent.

"Why don't you keep that girl in her place?" Camille's petulant voice drifted through the door.

Juliet's footsteps, quickening with jealousy, made tiny dents in the plastic floor tiles as she walked along the corridor to the stairs. She ran down the five flights without stopping, feeling the need to let off steam somehow.

Selina greeted her, her face all innocence, "Did you enjoy the garden party? I think your Malcolm's a dish. He wouldn't leave me. I had to persuade him to go and see how you were getting on after they threw you in the swimming pool."

"Oh, did you! Thanks for telling me."

Selina smiled smugly and got on with the job of tidying the racks. Dermot Edmond, the Fresco fashions sales representative, wandered in. Juliet's heart sank.

"I don't remember giving you an appointment," she said belligerently.

"You didn't, dearie. I took a chance on finding you free. Got some new stock I'd like you to have a look at."

"All right," she agreed reluctantly. "Bring it into my office."

He spread the clothes over her chair and desk. Juliet used the method she had adopted in the past, putting the clothes into separate categories of 'certainties,' 'possibles' and 'rejects.'

Then she argued over the price and having reached a certain figure, refused to budge from it. "You're getting hard," Dermot said, sitting in her chair and gazing into her face. "Don't get like all your colleagues, sweetie. I like 'em soft and inviting, like you are now."

"Miss Bourne?" Juliet turned swiftly. He was there again. It was almost as if he were spying on her, creeping up to her door and listening in on the conversation. It was plain by the look in his eyes that he had heard what Dermot Edmond had said.

Dermot rose lazily. "Free tonight?" he whispered in her ear. "You owe me a date. You let me down last time. I went . . . hungry all night."

She looked uncomfortably at Drew, knowing he had overheard. "Miss Bourne!" His tone held a warning.

"Sorry," she said to the sales representative. "I've got a date already with my boyfriend."

Dermot shrugged. "Better luck next time."

"Miss Bourne, if you would kindly tie up this transaction," Drew indicated the clothes spread around her room, "you have a customer waiting for you in the boutique. Miss Wyngard intends to patronize Girl Major. I want you to give her your personal attention."

And Juliet's personal attention Camille received. She went to disproportionate lengths to please her customer, waited patiently while each selected garment was tried on and rejected, suggested others which might be more suitable and almost ransacked the boutique in an effort to find just what her very difficult customer wanted. Juliet felt her sufferance dying a slow, painful death. *If the woman goes on much longer*, she told herself, *I'll be rude. I won't be able to stop myself.*

The turning point came when Camille tried on a particularly becoming and expensive pant suit, regarded herself in the mirror as though she was wearing a postman's delivery sack, took it off and threw it disdainfully on the floor. Juliet's patience uttered its last gasp and expired.

"If you don't want that, and you don't want this," she held up each rejected garment in turn, "and this doesn't please you, and that one you hate, then what the blazes *do* you want?"

Camille opened her mouth and forgot to close it. "I don't think," Juliet stormed, "you really know what you do want. I don't think you had any intention of buying anything from the moment you set foot in here. And I don't think," she threw caution to the winds, "I want you in this boutique ever again. You can take your money elsewhere."

Selina, who had been looking on, gasped. Camille snapped her mouth shut, seized her handbag and stalked out.

Juliet sank down on the customers' chair and surveyed the chaos of rejected garments. She also did a quick mental survey of her own position. She looked at her watch. "Three minutes to get up there," she said aloud, "another three to tell him what happened, five minutes to tell him what she thinks of me and," she calculated again, "two minutes for him to recover and call me up there. That gives me thirteen minutes to find another job." She looked at Selina. "Not enough, really, is it?"

"You think he'll fire you?" Selina sounded really afraid.

"No doubt about it." Juliet smiled. "But it was worth

it! She's been asking for it from the beginning. If I'm going to be shot at dawn, my goodness, it was a grand preliminary to the execution!"

She combed her hair and touched up her make-up. "I might as well look my best for the executioner."

On cue, the phone rang. Drew Major's secretary asked if Miss Bourne would kindly go to the company manager's office. Solemnly Juliet shook hands with Selina, who giggled, spoiling the dramatic effect. "I'll remember you in my will," Juliet promised, and obeyed the summons.

Camille was there, of course, her eyes large with wrath, her cheeks blotched with temper.

"I understand," Drew began at once, "that you've been unbelievably rude to Miss Wyngard. I also understand that you said some unforgivable things to her, making accusations and insinuations and telling her never to darken the boutique doors again."

Juliet looked at Drew. Was he being serious, or could she detect an underlying touch of amusement in his voice? His expression gave nothing away. "I'm sorry, Mr. Major," she said, "but there are times when one is goaded beyond control."

"You, Miss Bourne," he said through his teeth, "are telling me!"

"I'm only human, Mr. Major. I gave Miss Wyngard every possible attention, bringing out almost the entire contents of the boutique in order to please her only to have them all rejected as 'useless' and 'rubbish,' what am I expected to do? Grovel at her feet? Kiss the ground she walks on and tell her I'm always at her service?"

"Miss Bourne," his voice was dangerously soft, "may I remind you that in the circumstance, it would be advisable for you to become just a little more, shall we say, penitent and even submissive?"

She swallowed her defiance and tried to look docile. "I beg your pardon, Mr. Major." She had meant it to sound sincere, but it came out as sarcasm, and his eyebrows rose. "I'll have to cultivate the necessary subservience that customers who are always right seem to expect. I'll have to learn to pander to their every whim, and admit that my status is less than dust. I'll have to learn to be self-effacing, obsequious, servile. . . ."

"You'll have to learn when to shut up, Miss Bourne!"

Juliet recognized the extreme anger in his voice. Now she really had gone too far. She apologized to him, then she apologized to his girlfriend. "I'm sorry, Miss Wyngard, for being rude to you. I had no right to speak to you like that. I'll be glad to see you in the boutique any time you'd like to come." Had she prostrated herself enough?

Apparently she had. Camille Wyngard bowed her head graciously, and told Drew she would be going now.

"See Miss Wyngard to the elevator, then come back here."

He really was rubbing it in! She opened the door for Camille and walked by her side to the elevator, pressing the button and willing the elevator to appear quickly.

"My goodness," said Camille, her eyes gleaming, "Drew really does hate you, doesn't he?"

"The feeling, Miss Wyngard," Juliet lied defiantly, "is mutual."

"You know," Camille considered her, "that time you were at his house and he kissed you goodbye, I really thought he had you in mind as my successor, but—"

The elevator arrived and the doors opened. Camille stepped in.

"But," Juliet finished for her, "how wrong you were!" The doors closed and whisked Camille away. Juliet walked slowly back to Drew's office.

"Yes, Mr. Major?" she asked wearily.

"One more thing, Miss Bourne. I thought I told you not to fraternize with sales reps?"

"You did, Mr. Major. But I can't stop them if they pay me the compliment of fraternizing with me, can I?"

"You can at least put them in their place."

She was about to answer back and thought better of it. "Yes, Mr. Major."

"Don't let it happen again, Miss Bourne."

"No, Mr. Major."

He was around the desk and facing her. "And don't be so damned impudent!"

"I didn't intend to be, Mr. Major." Her tone was tearful. "Even when I'm polite you say I'm being rude. Whatever I do I can't seem to please you." In spite of herself, her eyes filled with tears.

He looked at her oddly, pushing his hands into his pockets. "I think you'd better go, Juliet."

"Yes, Mr. Major," she whispered and left.

CHAPTER EIGHT

Juliet spent the evening committing to paper her ideas for the window display. She decided on the stock she wanted to promote, which included some of the slower-selling lines, then selected the most eye-catching colors.

Next morning she left Selina in charge while she joined the two members of the display staff who had been allocated to her in the large shop window. She was glad Roy Hawkins was not one of them.

It took her a few minutes to get used to being stared at by passers-by, then she became so absorbed in directing the others that she forgot to feel like a goldfish in a bowl.

In the center of the display, which, she told them, was to be arranged like a room, she wanted several pairs of pants in assorted colors to be strung up like a giant lampshade. This they did, then at her suggestion borrowed a small coffee table from the furniture department. They searched the wine department for dummy bottles which they placed on the table and beside them they stood wine glasses from china and glass. Grouped around the table were four male and three female figures wearing party clothes.

Across the room was a record player borrowed from radio and electrical, and around it were a group of "dancers" wearing casuals and separates. As a backcloth they pinned up shaggy waistcoats, pull-on hats and matching scarves.

"Right," said Juliet, standing back and admiring the finished product, "I think everything is there except the kitchen sink!"

They laughed and complimented her on her idea.

"We've got another couple of windows to dress after this," one of them told her. "Then we've had instructions to smother the windows with Major's new slogans. Rumor has it it's part of the store's new policy. You know, 'Major Reductions', 'Money Means More at Majors , and so on, to make the place more approachable. They must have got some advertising firm working on it and they've come up with an 'appeal to the people' angle."

Juliet wanted to tell them, "I was the brain behind it," but modesty, or perhaps the feeling that they wouldn't have believed her anyway, held her back. But it didn't hold back her delight at the thought that Drew had taken her advice and put her suggestions into practice.

Someone tapped on the window and Juliet turned. Malcolm was outside grinning at her, his nose pressed against the window pane. He made a few faces, trying to get her to respond, but she maintained her disdainful expression. Good-humoredly he gave up, blew her two kisses, one with each hand, and passed on.

"Boyfriend?" asked the display girl.

"Ex," Juliet answered offhandedly. "He's got someone else in his sights."

"If you want him, fight for him."

"I don't particularly." And she meant it.

The window display increased sales. All day long young girls and their boyfriends came in, and left clutching their purchases.

"I'm tired," said Selina at the end of the afternoon, and sank down in the chair.

"For goodness' sake," Juliet looked at her anxiously, "don't go and get ill on me. Have an early night."

But next day Selina was away. Her mother telephoned. "Off color," she explained. "I'm keeping her in bed."

Juliet rang the staff manager and asked for a temporary assistant, but he said no one could be spared. She had to face it, she was on her own. The window display continued to bring in the public by the dozen. There was no time for a mid-morning break and she even had to eat her lunch in between serving customers. She was interrupted so often she gave up and put the rest away untouched. The coffee from the thermos grew cold in the cup, so she poured it back to take home and throw away. Unable to leave the boutique for the afternoon break, she worked on without a pause until closing time.

Then she sank down in the chair as Selina had done the evening before. Her face was flushed, her head was throbbing and her body ached with hunger. She thought of her sandwiches, but she had gone beyond wanting food. There was still the till to be emptied, the money counted and handed to the cashier.

Long after everyone had gone she sat at her desk making up the accounts. Then the boutique had to be tidied, discarded clothes returned to hangers and put back on the racks . . . work which was usually tackled by Selina as each customer left.

She was dragging on her coat when Drew came in. Her eyes opened wide. "How did you know I was still here?"

"Television monitor."

Fatigue soured her temper. "Checking up on me, making sure I'm not stealing anything?"

His eyes narrowed. "I could take offence at that, but something tells me you're tired out, so I'll overlook it."

She sat down and put a hand to her head. "Tired is hardly the right word. I've been on my own all day. Selina's ill." She held her middle. "I had hardly any lunch. I feel as though I've got an enormous empty cave inside me." She smiled weakly. "Big enough for a potholer to get into!"

He considered her drooping figure, glanced at his watch and said, "Come on, put on some make-up. I'm taking you out to dinner."

She recoiled from the thought. "Dinner? With you? Sorry. I've bowed and scraped to so many customers, I've got no small talk left. I'd bore you stiff. You once told me you never took out dull-witted women because they had nothing to say. But thanks for suggesting it." She hauled herself out of the chair and picked up her bag, but he took it from her.

"I'll ignore the speech of refusal to an invitation which was never given. It was a statement, not a question. You're coming out to dinner with me." He put his arm around her waist as if he sensed her need for physical support.

She went a few paces and made him stop. "What's the matter?" he asked. "Got a date with Romeo? You can forget him."

"No, but I have to let them know at home." He allowed her to do that and wandered around the racks while she explained to her mother that she was eating out. She hung up before the questions began.

She sat in his car and asked, "Where are we going?"

"Where I took you before. So you needn't bother about the make-up if you don't want to." He looked her over. "As far as I'm concerned you'll do as you are."

But she took out her compact and lipstick. "Would you object if I combed my hair?"

"Go ahead, as long as you don't comb it on me."

"Don't worry," she smiled, "if any of my hair lands on your jacket, I'll remove it. I'd hate to get into trouble with Camille."

He pulled out to pass a parked car and said under his breath, "At this point Camille can go to hell. She knows as well as I do there's no permanency about our relation-ship."

Juliet put away her comb and closed her bag. "I get the feeling she's dreading the end of your . . . relationship. She even said," she knew she was treading on dangerous ground, "she thought once that you had me in mind to take her place. You know, the next in line."

"Did she now?" His voice was soft. "And would Miss Juliet Bourne object if I made her my next girlfriend?"

She stared out of the window. "Strongly. In any close relationship I'd have with a man I'd go for permanency. So count me out of your calculations."

"That, as my father would say, is in character. You don't exactly pull your punches."

The restaurant was in semi-darkness. All around them couples were too absorbed in themselves to care who came and went. A powerful longing for the love of the man beside her stirred her emotions like a stick pushed into the glowing embers of a fire. A flame leapt and threatened to burn her. But tiredness took over and dampened it down.

She yawned, then apologized. "I did warn you."

"All right, no small talk. We can always converse in silence. Everyone else is doing it. They're just looking at each other." His fingers held her chin and brought her face around. "We can do that, too."

His eyes gazed into hers and she was too tired to hold anything back. But her eyelids drooped, cutting off the communication between them.

He laughed. "I wish I could decipher the message that was passing from you to me. Give me the key to the code and I'll unscramble it."

"No message. Too tired." She yawned again. "Sorry."

The food revived her temporarily. He watched her

brighten and said, "I'll take you to a movie. We might as well end the evening in style." She made no objection.

Back in the car Juliet closed her eyes. She hoped it was not far to the theater, because if it were, Drew would have to waken her.

"Sorry about the way I'm behaving," she murmured. "You must expect more of your women than this."

"So you admit it! You're one of my women."

She cursed herself for her slip, made only because of her exhausted state. "Of course I'm not." She felt herself drifting off. "Never will be."

It must have been hours later that she stirred. There was no movement of the car. No theater, no movie. Only arms around her and a comfortable shoulder under her head. She stirred, opened her eyes and looked up. Drew was gazing down at her and in the darkness she thought he was smiling.

"Had a good sleep?"

"I'm terribly sorry." She pulled herself out of his arms and smoothed her hair. She was horrified at what she had done. She looked at her watch. It wasn't as late as she had feared.

"What about the show? We've missed it, haven't we? And all my fault. I've ruined your evening."

"I wouldn't say that. I could see it coming. You went flat out on me, so I drove a short way out of town and parked on a side road." She saw the outline of hedges and trees. "I'll take you for a coffee."

He drove back into the town and they found a coffee bar still open. They sat side by side on high stools facing a mirror. "I look terrible," she said, touching her hair. "I always do after a sleep. You should see me first thing in the morning."

His reflection smiled mockingly. "Should I? Is that an invitation?"

"Yes," she grinned back. She could say things to his reflection that she couldn't say to him. He leaned closer. "Come around some weekend just before breakfast," she invited.

He drew away. "Pity, I really thought I was getting somewhere."

She yawned. "You know, I'm so tired that if you tried hard enough, you might even do that."

"There's encouragement for you! Should I take you to a night club?"

"You mean in order to soften me up?"

"If you like to put it that way, yes. Ever been to one?"

"No." She frowned deeply. "On second thoughts, I don't think I will. You should take your girlfriend there. She's sophisticated and would fit in. But me," she shook her head, drunk with tiredness, "I wouldn't want to risk the consequences."

He put his arm around her shoulders. "Tell me, what are they? And what do you know about them?"

"A lot," she grinned, fencing with him.

"Oh? From what sources? Personal experience? Romeo's teaching?"

"Malcolm? You must be joking! No, from movies, books, television."

He slipped from his stool, pulling her with him. "We'd better go. You're too tempting in your present mood. I'd better get you home before you start seducing me."

Outside the house he reached across and gathered her into his arms. She went without resistance. "I'm sorry," she whispered, "for passing out on you."

"Apology accepted. You must do it again some time. I enjoyed the sensation." His lips were tender at first, but as the seconds passed grew more demanding, seeking for a response she longed to give but did not dare.

At last he released her and she lay in her seat for a few

moments, lifeless and unwilling to move. His "Good-night, Juliet" was a little abrupt.

She left him with a final apology for spoiling his evening.

"I think it's high time," Cynthia said a few evenings later, "we returned Warren's hospitality and invited him to tea. And Mildred, of course. Drew, too, if he wants to come."

Cedric decided to be awkward. "I don't see why. With their money and position, it's a little like royalty—they ask you there, but you don't have to ask them back."

This annoyed his wife, as he knew it would. "Warren's not a bit like that. He's too human."

"Pity you didn't marry him, then," Cedric snapped, and left the room.

Cynthia said to Juliet, "I really don't know why your father always reacts so violently whenever I mention Warren. But don't you agree? We should ask them, shouldn't we? Warren's been so good in other ways, too."

Juliet laughed. "Dad's jealous. Yes, I agree, we should really. It would be bad manners not to, but," her throat tightened, "not Drew."

"We'd have to ask him, dear. After all, they included you in their invitation."

"That was different. I wanted a job. They had to ask me." Her imagination shrank from contemplating Drew as a visitor to their simple, and by comparison, rather poverty-stricken home. It would be bad enough having to entertain Warren and his wife, feeling apologetic all the time about their surroundings. But to have Drew there seeing for himself how stark their way of living was compared with the luxury he was used to she couldn't bear to think about.

But she needn't have worried. When Cynthia phoned

Warren the next day to issue the invitation, she was told that Drew would almost certainly be tied up with his own affairs. Warren had added, laughing, "And I don't mean 'business.'"

The night before Warren Major and his wife were due to visit them, Cedric was ill again. Cynthia sat up with him, listening in agony as he fought for breath. She insisted that, visitors or no visitors, he was not getting up. They argued, but he won, they had royalty to entertain. His wife said that if he hadn't been ill, she would have been really angry with him for his sarcasm.

Warren and Mildred arrived in their large yellow car, and all over the neighborhood net curtains were twitched aside and eyes watched as the Bourne's well-to-do guests made their way to the front door.

There were handshakes and smiles, Mildred's strained but Warren's broad and buoyant. His large, expansive personality seemed to increase and the house grow proportionately smaller as he stepped inside.

He thrust out his hand toward Cedric with a disarming gesture of friendliness and, as he eased himself onto the well-worn couch he seemed to be trying to scale down his opulence to fit in with the modest surroundings. But his affluence spilled out of him like an overfull bucket, and although he tried with his banter to mop up the spilled contents, he couldn't rid himself of his air of wealth.

Cedric, still pale from the aftereffects of his bad night, sat back and watched with the expectancy of a child watching a puppet show. Warren, with his joviality, was making a desperate attempt to show Cedric that he was not the only one who had a claim on Cynthia Bourne. Once she had nearly belonged to him, and now he was reaching out toward her like a baby making frantic attempts to grasp something just out of reach.

Cedric, perhaps moved by a forgiving pity, went to sit beside Warren. It was not long before they were deep in conversation about the affairs of the business world. Cedric had relented with the beneficence of the victor; after all, he had had the prize in his possession for years and nothing could take her away from him now.

Juliet had to admire her mother for the way she forced Mildred to talk. From the snatches of conversation Juliet heard as she drifted restlessly around the room, it seemed to be about flower arranging, "Clever Mother," Juliet thought, "to seem to be so interested in a subject which usually bores her to tears."

Cynthia left the room to get the food, motioning to Juliet to take her place beside Mildred. She did so with reluctance. The subject of flower arranging had apparently been exhausted and Juliet floundered, until Mildred, eyeing with distaste her tangerine-colored dress with its low neck and wrap-around skirt said, "I suppose that dress you're wearing came from this wonderful boutique I keep hearing about from Warren."

So Juliet talked about the boutique and Mildred listened, stiff and bored, until the trolley trundled and bumped along the hall and Cynthia pushed open the door. With immense relief Juliet got up to help her. Mildred's eyes seached behind Cynthia's back and seemed to be looking for a housekeeper or cook.

Warren remarked on the excellence of the food, and Mildred lukewarmly agreed with him. A car pulled up behind Warren's and he half rose from the couch and exclaimed, "I can't believe it! My son's arrived."

Juliet, unbelieving too, went to the window. Yes, it was Drew, locking his car and strolling to the front door. Why had he come? And how was she going to hide from him her delight at his sudden appearance, which was threatening to rob her of the ability to breathe?

Moving jerkily like a mechanical toy, she obeyed her mother's instruction to "Let Drew in, dear, while I get a cup for him."

"Hallo," said Drew breezily, "was I invited to the tea party?"

Cynthia, coming back from the kitchen, saved Juliet the necessity of answering. "You're always welcome, Drew," she said, joining the others.

"Am I, Juliet?" Drew asked.

Juliet, struggling to recover her poise, said, deliberately hesitant, "Er . . . depends on the circumstances. At work when I see your face, I want to run away. It usually means trouble."

"The impudence of it!" he said, as she showed him into the sitting room. "It's the other way around. When I see your face, I know it means trouble."

"You two at it again?" Warren asked. "They can't meet for more than a few minutes without being at each other's throats."

Drew, after being introduced to Cedric, accepted a plate and some sandwiches from Juliet. He smiled, answering Warren, "Not entirely true, Father. We're on good terms now and then, especially when she's giving me something. A sandwich, for instance." Their eyes met and she knew he was not really referring to that. "But I must admit it's a rare occurrence."

They laughed and Warren asked, "What happened to Camille?"

"I put her off until this evening. We're dining together."

That, thought Juliet, *puts me in my place*. Cedric had moved to his original seat and now Cynthia was beside Warren. His face was alight, his hands were restless as though he was having a struggle to keep them from touching her. There was a sparkle in her mother's eyes that was rare and Juliet wondered if Warren's nearness was affecting her, too.

She turned from them, refusing to acknowledge the unthinkable possibility that, after all these years, her mother still returned Warren's affection and was now regretting the impulse that had made her, so long ago, break off her engagement to him.

Drew had finished his tea and caught Juliet's eye. He seemed restless, like his father, and Warren, watching them, said, "Why don't you two go off and have a good fight? I can see Drew's spoiling for an argument. No doubt after a few minutes alone with Cynthia's daughter, a good subject for a quarrel will crop up!"

"Show him the garden," Cedric suggested. "If I didn't think my wife would throw something at me (she does the weeding) I'd say it was all my own work."

"We," said Mildred, with studied simplicity, "have three gardeners, full time."

Cynthia intercepted the disgusted look Warren threw at his wife. She hurriedly glossed over Mildred's childish boasting by saying she could well believe it.

Drew held the door open for Juliet, who said to him as they passed through the kitchen, "Shall I show you our estate?"

"No need for sarcasm, young woman. I get your not very subtle message."

"I'm sorry there weren't any inscrutable lions at the front door to greet you." She flashed a grin at him. "No pond, complete with fountain, no rose gardens, no—"

"No swimming pool to throw you into, unfortunately, which at this moment I would dearly love to do."

They walked around the garden and Juliet pointed to the vegetables and lettuce, saying that she thought Drew might admire them at least. He did.

"Shall I give you a lettuce to put in your buttonhole, just as you gave me a rose?" she asked mischievously.

His hands settled playfully around her throat and she did not attempt to remove them, putting her hands over his instead. They looked at each other. "What will the neighbors think?" she whispered.

"That I was about to throttle you." He looked at her hands. "And that you were helping me do it."

Confused by the emotions he could arouse simply by touching her, she pulled at his wrists and he removed his hands.

"Shall I," she asked, when her pulse rate had slowed down, "show you my apartment?" She smiled at him. "It's a little smaller than yours and more modest. One room."

"Lead the way, Miss Bourne."

She took him upstairs and with pride showed him the paintings—her own work, she explained—with which she had decorated the walls. "All part of my art training. Portraits, landscapes, still life. . . ."

He looked at each of them in detail and commented, "Pity you had to give it all up. You would have done well. If your . . . er . . . circumstances changed, would you ever consider going back to it?"

"Just give me the chance," she answered wistfully, "and I'd go back to art school tomorrow."

There was a short silence. "M'm," he said, "great pity you had to leave. A lot of talent there." He turned. "If I commissioned you to paint a portrait of me, would you do it?"

"Of course, but you would have to sit very still and not move a muscle even if I cursed loudly when I couldn't get the expression right. Now," she studied him, "what's your typical expression? A glower. Yes, you'd have to glower very nicely for me."

He laughed and stretched out on her bed. "What does Juliet Bourne see when she first wakes up in the morning?" He stared upward. "The ceiling."

"Wrong. I see your face frowning at me and telling me what a bad, bad employee I am and how I ought to be dismissed and thrown to the wolves."

He gripped her wrist and pulled her down until she was lying on top of him. "Don't mention wolves. I might devour you myself."

She struggled, trying to get up, but he held her still. "I suppose," she said, "if I called you 'darling' like Camille, you'd really feel at home."

"If that isn't provocation!" With a swift movement he had shifted off the bed and had her pinned face down, entirely at his mercy.

She glanced over her shoulder, saw his hand raised threateningly and shrieked, "No, no! I'm sorry, I'm sorry."

"I should think so." He let her go.

She stood up and smoothed her hair to give herself time to regain her dignity. "Now you've seen my living quarters," she said at last. "Hardly luxurious, but I call it my rabbit hole. I bolt into it when the world is too much for me." She lifted her comb and ran it through her hair. She regarded herself in the dressing table mirror. "Perhaps now that you've seen our house you understand what I mean by the difference between us . . . the sort of life you're used to versus the environment I live in."

"You know," he watched her reflection, arms folded, frowning, "I think there's a sadistic streak in you that delights in dwelling on how different we are. Why?"

Because, she cried inside herself, *I want you to refute it, that's why, but you never, never do.* She said aloud, "Can you think of any ways in which our thoughts and instincts do coincide?"

"Let me see." He rubbed his chin, watching her powder her nose. "Our thoughts, perhaps not. But our instincts—" His hand reached out for her, but she saw it coming in the mirror and evaded it, running from the room and down the stairs to the safety of the sitting room.

In the hall, as the visitors were leaving, there was the usual handshaking, thanks and good wishes. Warren watched his wife walk out to the car and, on an impulse he seemed unable to resist, said to Cedric, "Mind if I borrow your wife for a moment?" Without waiting for an answer he pulled Cynthia into his arms and kissed her.

Cedric grunted and said nothing.

Drew followed on with, "Mind if I borrow your daughter for a moment?" and pulled Juliet toward him, but she evaded him again.

"Now, now, son," came from Warren, "you're not making her one of your women. She's different."

"Don't I know it?" Drew muttered, walking down the path. He drove away without a smile or a lift of the hand.

Juliet did not see Drew for a few days. She missed him more than she dared to admit. Selina had soon returned to work and Juliet was able to attend to other things. The line up of salesmen with their wares was incessant and one or two invited her to visit their employers' factories and see the goods in the process of manufacture. One of them was a young man called Montague Weeks, "call me Monty," he had said and together they had fixed a date for her visit. He warned her that she would probably need most of the day for it, because she had to take a train to get there. He said he would be there and would take her out to lunch.

Another sales representative showed her a caseful of accessories, which included belts and handbags designed to meet the needs of the type of customer who patronized the boutique. She was impressed by the range of goods and, since it would be a new line, wondered if she should get permission to stock them.

She contacted Mr. Havering, the general manager, but he turned down the idea right away. "It would overlap with the accessories section of conventional fashion. The management wouldn't allow it, Miss Bourne."

But Miss Bourne refused to accept his ruling. She decided to ask Drew. "What's the use of having contacts at the top," she asked herself, "if I don't use them?" then she hated herself for adopting the "back door" methods she condemned in others.

But she did phone him. She asked if he could spare a few minutes. "And I promise you it will only be a few minutes, because I'm going out for the day."

He agreed to see her. Sitting at his desk, he seemed to be all executive. Could he, she wondered, be the same man who only a few days before had held her down on her bed and threatened to spank her?

He greeted her with a smile that was a mixture of mockery and cynicism. "I wondered how long it would be," he said, "before that bad, bad employee of mine would start pestering me again. It's been so peaceful these last few days. No irritant to drive me crazy." He pointed to a chair, which she occupied. "What do you want, Miss Bourne?"

"To start an accessories section in the boutique, Mr. Major."

"Just like that. What about the money?"

"I haven't spent all my allocation yet. It could come out of that."

"What sort of merchandise did you have in mind?"

"Belts, jewellery, handbags, the sort of accessories that many boutiques stock in addition to clothes."

His eyebrows rose. "Empire building, Miss Bourne?" She flushed angrily. "Because that's what the other members of staff would call it." He thought for a moment or two. "Sorry, can't be done. You would overlap with fashion accessories."

"That's what Mr. Havering said. And that's why I decided to appeal to you."

"Thinking you could use your influence with me and get me to override his decision?" She flushed at the truth his words contained. "Well for once, Miss Bourne, you aren't going to get your own way. The answer's no."

"But, Mr. Major, all I want to do is expand a little, and surely expansion is a healthy sign? The demand for such products is there, I'm sure."

"Have you been asked by any customers for these things?"

She had to be honest. "Well, no, not yet, but the goods the sales rep has shown me are marvelous and—"

"So that's it! You've fallen for the patter of the reps. You're an infant where buying is concerned, aren't you? You can still be taken in by sales talk."

"No, I wasn't taken in. You said once I had vision. Well, now I'm using that vision . . . I'm visualizing my boutique—"

"Your boutique?"

"Oh, I'm sorry, I suppose I should have said your boutique, providing an even better service to customers by giving them a greater variety of lines all under one roof."

"Now you're trying your sales talk on me, and I'm sorry, but I'm proof against it. I'm hardened, as a result of living with it over the years. I appreciate your enthusiasm and your devotion to your cause. But the answer is still 'no.' "

She rose angrily, looking at her watch. "If I had the

time," she said threateningly, "I'd stay until I did get my own way." He smiled as if he knew better. "But I've got to catch a train."

"Where are you going?"

"To town, to visit a clothing factory. One of the reps invited me to go."

"I've got a lunch appointment in town. I'll give you a ride."

"A ride? No, thanks. I'm going by train."

"You're going with me, Miss Bourne." His tone had the stamp of authority about it and so did his expression. She had no alternative but to go with him.

"I'll get my coat, Mr. Major."

"No, you won't. I don't trust you not to run out on me. You'll get your coat when I'm free to go with you, which will be in," he consulted his watch, "five minutes."

She fretted away the five minutes which stretched into 15. At last he put the phone down. He informed his secretary that he was leaving, gathered a pile of papers together, and pushed them into his briefcase, then said, "Right, we'll go."

Back in her office he looked on quizzically while she made up her face. She put on her coat and told him she was ready.

In the car he asked, "Where are you heading for?"

"A firm called Trendmaker Fashions." She gave him the address. "If it's out of your way, you don't need to bother. I've still got time to catch the train."

"It is out of my way, but I'm taking you there, all the same."

Juliet took a chance on his annoyance and asked, "Is it . . . is it Camille you're lunching with?"

"Camille? No, it is not. Camille belongs to my private affairs, not my business affairs."

She said with an irritation she immediately regretted, "There's no need to spell it out for me. I know exactly where Camille stands in your private life."

"Stands?" he mocked. "Camille stands?" She stared ahead, rigid with jealousy. He changed the subject. "How's Romeo?"

"I haven't seen much of him lately. He comes around some evenings, but—"

"Quarreled?"

"Not exactly. Since the garden party we've been . . . just friends."

"A sad end to a promising romance. I can't say I'm sorry. I never did fancy your liason with an employee of our rivals."

"It wasn't a liaison, as you call it. And I told you we're still friends."

There was a long silence. He broke it by saying, "You talked earlier of expansion." He gave her a quick glance. "How much can I trust you?"

"You should know by now."

"If I tell you something, will you swear not to breathe a word to anyone?"

She held up her right hand as if in a court of law. "I swear, on my honor."

"All right, I'll take a chance. You know we have another branch of Majors?" He named a town some distance away.

"Are you thinking of opening another?"

"Not exactly. We've been looking around locally for a suitable piece of land for building an extension. We think we've found it. Negotiations as to price and so on are proceeding now. The man I'm lunching with today is the firm's lawyer."

"It sounds exciting." A thought occurred to her. "You

wouldn't . . . no, I suppose you wouldn't." She found some courage and continued, "You wouldn't consider transferring the boutique and giving it more space?"

He threw back his head and laughed. "Opportunist to the core! We weren't thinking of that, no."

"What I really want, of course," she said cheekily, "is a shop of my own."

He laughed again. "Now, if I set you up in a shop of your own," she mistrusted his tone, "what would you be prepared to give in return?"

Her smile faded. "Sorry. Nothing doing. You heard what your father said. I'm different."

"All the same," he persisted, "you know what people would say about us if I did, don't you?"

"Don't worry," she muttered, "some of them are saying that already. Roy Hawkins said as much when you got me that window space. That's why he threw me into the swimming pool."

He frowned. "Was it? I never knew. I'd like to teach him a lesson for that." His good humor returned. "They're so wrong, aren't they? Isn't it a pity to disappoint them?"

"I think we're almost there," she said shortly.

He drove through a maze of side streets, stopping once or twice to ask the way, and turned off into a rocky, rough road. He pulled up outside a building that was little more than a series of shacks joined together and labeled in uneven hand-printed letters, Trendmaker Fashions.

"What do they call this?" he asked irritably. "A factory? I don't like the look of it at all."

"But, Drew," in her anxiety to persuade him to change his opinion she forgot to be formal, "some of their styles are fabulous."

"Well," he said reluctantly, "I'll be fair. We'll go in and have a look."

Inside he stared around disgustedly. Juliet pressed a bell on a desk marked "Inquiries", but nothing happened. In the distance there was the noise of machinery, but no one appeared in answer to the summons. The atmosphere was grim and dreary, the windows little more than skylights, and the air was stuffy and stale. After five minutes, Drew caught her arm. "Come on, we're not staying in this foul atmosphere a moment longer."

She resisted, pressing the bell again. "I promised, Drew. They're expecting me. We can't go now."

"Can't we?" He demonstrated that they were going and quickly. He almost carried her out and dumped her at the side of the car.

"How could you?" She was near to tears of frustration.

"We're not dealing with a firm like that. Look how they operate . . . in a squalid backyard with an unattended office. Shocking conditions of work. From the look of their premises, I wouldn't trust them an inch, any more than I'd trust their sales representative. If that's their method of manufacture, probably using cheap labor, and probably refusing to plough any of their profits back into the business to make improvements, then we're not dealing with them."

He drove off. "But," she wailed, "Monty Weeks, the sales rep, was going to take me out to lunch. He'll be waiting for me."

"So that was the attraction! Now it comes out. And I told you not to go out with any rep."

"I can't see anything wrong with going out with a man as pleasant as Monty Weeks." He gave a short, sardonic laugh.

"The trouble with you," she said after staring through the window for some time, "Is that you won't let me grow up as a buyer. You've tied me to your apron strings as though I were a baby who can't walk straight without support. Every time I try to break free, you haul me back. It's well known that buyers are treated like royalty because of their power and the money they have at their disposal. Yet you object even if I'm invited out to lunch. No wonder I'm rebelling against you all the time."

"I happen to have slightly more than a professional interest in you." She noted the word "slightly". "Because of the friendship of our parents, if anything . . . regrettable were to happen to you as a result of your work, I would feel answerable to your family."

"I don't see why. They haven't appointed you as guardian of my moral well-being. For some reason, you've set yourself up as a father figure where I'm concerned."

He laughed softly. "Father figure?"

Juliet said accusingly into the silence, "You don't treat other buyers in the firm as you treat me."

"The other buyers are all a good deal older than you, and a lot more experienced. They aren't young, attractive . . . and vulnerable."

"All the same, I don't need my hand held all the time."

Drew flicked her a smile. "Don't you?" He groped for her hand, his eyes on the road, but she clasped them together angrily.

"You see," she cried, "you still won't take me seriously. Anyway," she said, knowing she would be provoking him to anger, too, "not all men are like you with women. Not all men's morals are as questionable as yours."

His lips thinned. "You'd better take that statement back, my dear." He stopped at some traffic lights. "Otherwise on our return I'll take disciplinary action."

"What will you do?" she cried, "hold out the terrible

threat of dismissal? I'll save you the trouble." She had worked herself into an emotional state that was out of all proportion to the meaning of his words. She only knew that she could never talk on equal terms with this man, because it was within his power to slap her down whenever he felt like it. She knew, too, that with his taunts of so-called disciplinary action, history was repeating itself in a depressing, humiliating way. All she wanted to do at the moment was get away from the threat that was hanging over her like the roof of a partly demolished building. One day it would fall and trap her. And that, she knew, would be the end.

She gave way to an unmanageable impulse to get even with him. She wrenched open the car door and plunged into the road between the other vehicles which were just starting to move on as the lights changed.

"What are you doing?" he shouted. "Trying to kill yourself, you crazy little fool?"

She ran around in front of his car, weaved her way between the cars which were already inching forward and reached the pavement just in time. He shouted again, but over the noise of the traffic she couldn't hear what he said.

He had no alternative but to drive on, trying to edge the car toward the curb. But he was forced by the pressure of traffic behind him to turn left instead of going straight ahead as he intended. He found a suitable place to park and slammed his door behind him. The traffic lights were in his favor and he sprinted across the road, catching up with her as she stood impatiently at the curb in a crowd of people.

He took her completely by surprise. He came up behind her, and his technique was so subtle that she didn't realize what was happening until she found herself, arm linked in his, walking back with him to his car. "Hello, darling," he said softly and apologetically, but loudly enough for others to hear, "sorry I was late. Did you think I'd forgotten?"

When she realized what he had done she wrenched her arm away and turned to run, but he had been expecting an attempt to escape and caught her almost at once. She was back, arm linked in his, and he was saying, "If you make a scene, I'll lift you bodily and carry you, if necessary screaming and kicking, back to the car."

He did not let her go until he had forced her into her seat and fastened the seat belt across her to make escape more difficult. He drove on, and by a series of right turns, got himself back on his original route.

"This," she muttered, "is nothing less than abduction!"

"And what you did," he snapped, "was nothing less than a suicide attempt."

"I'd do it again to get away from you and the awful things you say to me." Tears of frustration splashed onto her handbag. She said thickly, "The only way you could make me stay with you is if you carried a pair of hand-cuffs around with you."

"Thanks for the hint," he said acidly. "One day I'll do that, and I'll use them, too. Good grief, there are times when you need to be physically restrained from doing yourself an injury!"

She stared dully out of the window. "Where are we going?"

"To keep my lunch date."

"I'm not going with you. You can't force me."

"But you are coming with me, my sweet. And if necessary, I could force you, very easily, simply by using my physical strength."

"Have you reserved a table for two?"

"I have."

She smiled triumphantly. "Then there won't be a place for me."

"I can change the reservation. It's a large hotel and I'm a fairly regular customer."

"But you'll be talking business. You won't want me in on that, will you? I might tell tales."

"You'll tell tales at your peril, my dear. I'm trusting you, and if you fail me in this, it will be the end, and I mean the irrevocable end between you and me, and you and the firm and you and your job. So you've been warned."

She could do nothing but sulk after that, but when eventually she was ushered into the smooth silence of the hotel, and was handled with the professional deference of the staff, she found she had been wooed, quite against her will, into a more amenable state of mind.

She was therefore able to greet Drew's guest, a sharp-eyed, quick-witted lawyer, with tolerable calmness and even a welcoming smile. The thought that she had been maneuvred into the postion of hostess did flit in and out of her mind, but she was so becalmed by the soft carpeting, subtle lighting and persuasive atmosphere of the hotel that she had by that time passed the point of caring.

Throughout the meal her thoughts wandered. She caught snatches of the discussion about the vendors, the price of the land and the legalities involved in buying it, but she took in very little of what the two men were saying.

"She's a friend of yours?" drifted into her consciousness and brought her mind back to her surroundings.

"Juliet?" Her eyes swiveled around to Drew's, catching his sardonic expression, "Mr. Finlay asks if we're friends. Are we?"

She smiled. "I think the best answer to that," she told

the lawyer, "is sometimes." She looked doubtfully at Drew. "I don't think we are at the moment."

Drew laughed, leaning back in his chair. "Oh, I wouldn't say that. To be honest, she and her parents are friends of the family. There are times when the two of us are . . . er . . ." he raised his eyebrows, "shall we say more than friendly?"

Juliet blushed as he had meant her to, and Mr. Finlay smiled knowingly. "It's not like that at all," Juliet blurted out, annoyed at what the lawyer must be thinking. "There are times when we hate each other."

"Don't all couples?" murmured Mr. Finlay.

Drew moved his hand from his glass to her hand and held it firmly. "We lead a cat and dog life, don't we, Juliet?"

"Yes, we do," she admitted grudgingly, "but that's not because of any personal relationship." To Mr. Finlay, "He's my employer, that's all."

Mr. Finlay's eyes dropped to their linked hands. "I must admit that it looks like it!" he laughed.

"It's true what she says. She is an employee of mine, but with a difference." Drew leaned forward and rested on his elbows, lifting her hand to imprison it between both of his. He parted her fingers and inspected them closely one by one. The action was almost a caress. "There are times, Mr. Finlay, when this girl almost drives me crazy. She's just about broken every rule in the book. She's been more trouble to me in the short time she's been working for me than the whole of my department store staff put together. I've threatened her with dismissal more times than I can remember, yet she's still with us. She comes bouncing back every time, like a ball thrown into a neighbor's garden." He touched her fingers with his lips, like a lover, and said, "I can't get this girl out of my hair, no matter what I do."

"It doesn't look," said Mr. Finlay, "as though you want to very much."

"Don't let appearances fool you, Mr. Finlay," Juliet said, tugging at her hand and managing to disengage it from Drew's. "The day I walk out of Major's store for the last time, Drew, I mean Mr. Major, will throw a celebration party."

"The day Juliet Bourne walks out on me," Drew smiled mockingly, "my heart will break."

"There's always the one way a man can prevent a woman from running away," said Mr. Finlay, pushing back his chair as the waiter presented Drew with the bill, "and that's to marry her."

"No good," murmured Drew, settling the account, "Juliet has a Romeo."

"And you," muttered Juliet, "have got a Camille."

"Ah, yes," Drew agreed, as they made their way to the door, "let us never forget Camille."

After a few more words of business, they left the lawyer with handshakes and a promise of action on his part.

On the way back in the car, Drew's provocative mood disappeared. He said a little sharply, "I rely on you implicitly not to breathe a word to anyone," he emphasized the word, "about what you've heard today. My discussion with the lawyer was completely confidential and you can consider yourself privileged to have been allowed to be present. It shows how much I trust you. I hope you'll fulfill that trust."

"Of course I will," she snapped. "In any case, I didn't take in a word of what you were saying."

"That I can't believe."

"If you can't believe what I'm saying now, then how on earth can you say you trust me?"

"Point taken, and I apologize. All right, so you didn't 'hear' what we were saying. Very diplomatic, very discreet, and I'm glad to know it."

"It also happens to be true. Legal matters bore me silly."

"So when you marry Malcolm, you'll either dispense with the legal side altogether," he paused for her reaction, but there was none, "or you'll leave it all to him."

"I'm not going to marry Malcolm," she answered calmly. "I told you, we're only friends. Not even that sometimes." She glared at him, daring him to dispute her statement. "So you needn't worry about my divulging any of your secrets about expansion to him."

"Glad to hear it. In any case, I've already warned you of the consequences if anything of the kind should occur."

Before they parted at the staff entrance she thanked him for the lunch. "And I'm sorry about running away from you."

He nodded. "Next time at your own suggestion it'll be handcuffs and no nonsense. So I'm warning you." He raised his hand and shut himself in the elevator.

CHAPTER NINE

When Juliet returned home one evening her mother told her, "Warren phoned. He's invited me to lunch again."

"Are you going?"

"Of course. Why not?"

"Just that . . . well, Dad might not like it. You know how he feels about Warren."

"My goodness," she was indignant, "will I never live that engagement down? First Cedric, now you. Don't either of you understand that was 30 years ago?"

"Sorry, Mom. You go out to lunch and have a nice time." Her tone was pacifying, but misleadingly so. She couldn't tell her mother about the niggling anxiety at the back of her mind that she might one day succumb to Warren's charm.

Malcolm called her at the boutique next day while Juliet was eating her sandwiches. He looked around ostentatiously and Juliet said, "Selina's gone to lunch. You're out of luck."

"It wasn't her I came to see. It's you I love."

Juliet laughed and offered him some of her coffee. He refused, taking out a cigarette instead. "You love me," she said, "as much as you love this thermos of mine."

"Darling, I can't kiss a thermos."

"Be honest and admit it was Selina you were after."

"No, truly, this time it was you. Business. Curlews need someone to run their boutique. Their buyer's walked out on them. How about it? To get you, now you've got more experience, they'd pay double the money you're getting here, if only to get back at Majors."

Juliet had to admit the idea was tempting, but . . . leave Majors? Leave Drew and never see him again? The thought appalled her. He could threaten to fire her every other day if he liked, but she knew she would never voluntarily walk out on him.

"Sorry, Malcolm. Good of you to think of me, but I couldn't do it."

He shrugged. "Let me know if you change your mind." He looked out into the boutique. "That girl has a long lunch hour, doesn't she?"

"I thought it wasn't true when you said you didn't want to see Selina. I can't blame you. She's got a lot to offer." She saw the appreciative gleam in his eyes. "I set you free to run after her."

"Thanks, darling. I'll kiss you for that." He did. "But I think running after her won't be necessary. She's the sort who stands still while you catch up." He lifted a hand. "I'll leave the offer with you. If you should change your mind contact personnel. They'll snap you up." He went out.

It was when she had finished serving a customer and was putting her thermos away that she first smelled smoke. It was faint at first, but grew stronger as the minutes passed. A fire? It couldn't be a fire! Not at Majors! Should she tell somebody? She looked out into the store. Others were getting worried, too. Someone was using the phone, saying, "Smoke, is the place on fire?"

Over the public address system came a voice calm but firm, "Will everyone leave the store, please? The store must be evacuated. There must be no panic. Will everyone leave the store in an orderly fashion?"

Over and over again the message came. Juliet thought, terrified, *Drew? What about Drew? He might not know.* She tried dialing his extension. No reply. She tried again, but still no answer. She had to get to him, to warn him. Someone must tell him the store was on fire.

The caretakers were showing the customers out. The fire bell began to ring. "Staff," the caretakers were shouting, "staff out, too. Everybody out! You heard the message."

Juliet went in the opposite direction, toward the stairs. She knew better than to use the elevator in a fire. A hand shot out and caught her. The caretaker said, "Wrong way, miss. That way to the exit."

But she shook herself free. "I'm just going upstairs for a minute. Forgotten something."

He dove after her, but she evaded him and was up the stairs before he could follow. She ignored his warnings. She must get to Drew. By the time she had reached the sixth floor, pushing against the tide of people coming down and resisting all efforts to stop her, she was gasping for breath and felt that her lungs had collapsed. She fell into Drew's office. He wasn't there. She looked along the corridor, now nearly empty, and he was striding toward her.

"What the hell are you doing up here? You heard the message. Get out with the others."

"Drew," she gasped, "I had to warn you. . . ."

"Warn me? I can hear the fire alarm as well as you can. Anyway, I was the first to know." They were in his office now. "Get out, girl!"

"You come, Drew, then I'll go."

"I've got to stay until the place is empty. Don't you understand?"

Like the captain of a ship, he wanted to go down with it? No, she couldn't let it happen. Now the corridors were silent and the smoke was beginning to choke her.

There was the sound of sirens. The fire brigade had arrived.

"Drew, you must come." she held onto his arms, pulling at him, using all her strength to make him move. But he shook himself free and half lifted her from his office. He put her outside. "Get out, Juliet! My God, you'll be overcome by smoke if nothing else. I order you to go."

She flung her arms around his neck. "If you're going to stay here, Drew, I'm staying with you." She whispered, "If you're going to die, I'll die with you."

He wrenched her arms from his neck. "Don't be a crazy, melodramatic fool! What is this? Another act? Another attempt at self-destruction?"

But her arms found him again and there was terror in her grasp, terror that she would lose him if she left him. "I'm not going," she said hoarsely, "I'm staying with you."

"You're demented. What do you mean you'd rather die with me than—" The phone rang. He took her hand and pulled her with him. "Yes?" into the phone. "False alarm?" He listened, relief making him sag. "What happened?" He listened again. "I see. Yes, yes. So he's been found now? All's well, then."

He put down the phone and his hand was shaking. He found his chair, using his hands as a blind man feels his way. He sank into it, holding his head. She put her arms around his neck, drooping with relief. He felt the pressure of her body against his and pulled her onto his knee.

His arms came around her and she lay against him shaking. "My sweet, crazy woman, what did you think you were doing?"

"I don't know, Drew, I don't know."

"I've heard of staff loyalty, but my word, I've never known an employee want to die with her boss before!"

She hid her face against him. "Don't make fun of me, Drew."

"My dearest girl, I wasn't making fun of you." He rested his cheek against her hair. "But this instinct for self-destruction you seem to have with such abundance terrifies me. Look at what you did the other day when you dove among the traffic. This is just another example, isn't it?" He said softly, "Juliet? Thank you for coming to find me."

She raised her head and his lips came down and rested tenderly against hers. Then their pressure increased and she clung to him giving kiss for kiss.

He pushed her away from him with a strange reluctance and she sat in the visitors' chair. "I think," he said at last, "we're both a little crazy. Suffering from reaction, I suppose."

"Drew?" He looked up. "Wasn't it a fire?"

"No. Apparently some passer-by threw a match into the rubbish cage we keep in the drive for scrap. The stuff caught fire and the smoke got drawn into the air conditioning system. The fan drove it around the building. The electrician was at lunch and no one else seemed to know where to switch off the fan. Hence the fire and the false alarm. Seems incredible when you look back on it, but not so funny if it had been real."

He came around to stand in front of her. "Feeling better, or would you like a drink?"

"No, thanks. I'll get back to work." He pulled her to her feet. "Sorry, Drew, to have been so stupid. You'd better forget it ever happened."

He held up her hands and inspected them like an archaeologist examining a rare find. "Artistic hands," he murmured, "and the temperament to go with them." He smiled. "I wish you weren't so impetuous. There are times when you have me really worried."

She shook her head. "I can't help it. It's just me." She tried to remove her hands from his. "Please, Drew. I must get back to work."

But he had not finished with her. "With your precipitate nature, a man who loved you would be afraid of letting you out of his sight. He might turn away, turn back and find you'd gone. Tell me, if you loved a man, would you do to him what your mother did to my father . . . walk out on him?"

She stiffened. "Let's face it, my mother did what she did because she didn't love your father. If she'd loved him, she would have. stuck to him come what may, as she's stuck to my father, come what may."

He let her go then. "I'm sorry. I had no right to talk about your mother like that." He sat down as though his legs were tired. "You'd better go."

She left him without another word.

At home, she found her mother alone and a little pale.

"Dad not back from work yet?" Juliet asked, washing her hands at the sink and drying them.

"No. Had a good day?"

There was something about her mother's voice that made her turn. It was brittle and determinedly bright. But she looked as calm as usual, so Juliet chatted with her about the false alarm and how the building had been evacuated. She said nothing about her interlude with Drew.

"So all in all you've had quite a day." Her mother's voice was still a little odd.

"Something wrong, Mom?" She expected a laughing denial, but to her horror her mother collapsed onto a chair and burst into tears. "Mother, what's happened? Is it . . . is it Dad?"

"No no, dear. Nothing like that." She dried her eyes. "Silly of me. It's just—" She looked up, her voice urgent. "Promise you won't tell your father?"

"Of course I promise."

"Well, I had lunch with Warren today. Juliet, he's . . . he's going away." So that was it. Her mother loved him after all! "He's going abroad somewhere. South America, I think. He said he's got to get away. He's at the end of his tether. It's his wife mostly. Things are terrible between them. Juliet," she looked up and there was a childish disbelief in her eyes, "he asked me to go away with him. He said he still loved me . . . more than ever, he said. He told me he was desperately unhappy. He had no interest in the business, no interest in anything. Without me, life had no meaning." She wiped her eyes again. "Darling, what could I say to him?"

"Mother," Juliet whispered, drawing up a chair and sitting beside her, "you're not going? Father, what about him?"

"Darling, how could you doubt me? Of course I'm not going. I told Warren, and it shattered him, that I loved my husband. I was tied to Cedric, I said, by the past, the present and all that was to come. He offered me money, position, whatever I wished for. But I said it wouldn't make any difference." She paused, as if trying to remember what had passed between them.

"I told him," she went on, "that I had a high regard for him, was fond of him even, and wished him well in every way. I wished he'd had a happier life, but he couldn't blame anyone else for his choice of wife. He said after I'd left him all those years ago, nothing mattered any more. He'd married the first woman who had come along. I said he couldn't really blame me, because that was life. He couldn't grumble, he'd had all that money could buy. Except, he said, the one woman he had ever really wanted . . . me."

"So now he's going away?"

"Yes. I told him to forget me, put me out of his mind. He said that would only happen on the day he died." She caught at her daughter's hand. "I was so sorry for him, Juliet. It was terrible sitting there watching his misery. But there was nothing I could do, nothing."

They sat, mother and daughter, silent and still, the one thinking of the man who loved her, the other thinking of his son, the man she loved. The irony of the situation struck Juliet, but she didn't want to laugh. She wanted to cry . . . for Warren and for herself.

The key turned in the lock. Her father had come home.

"Thank you for listening, darling," Cynthia whispered. "I feel better now I've shared it with you." They embraced.

Cedric came in and Cynthia greeted her husband with a smile and a kiss.

A few days later, Warren went away. Juliet heard it on the grapevine. "Business abroad," the rumor said.

It was almost the end of a particularly long and tiring day. Juliet was in her office, Selina was putting away the iron she had been using to freshen some of the customer-handled stock.

The phone rang. It was Drew Major's secretary. "Mr. Major," she said, "wishes to see Miss Bourne as soon as the store closes."

"Can't it wait?" Juliet asked. "I'll come as soon as I've cashed up and put things in order."

The mouthpiece was covered, a question asked. "Mr. Major says he'll give you ten minutes."

Juliet was puzzled. What was the mystery? She hadn't

seen Drew for days. She told herself it was better that way. What was the use of seeing him, talking to him but never being able to touch him? The kisses he had given her in the past he must have forgotten long ago. She wondered, as she counted the day's takings, if Camille was still in favor, or whether he had passed on to another woman.

When at the end of the stipulated ten minutes she went upstairs to Drew's office the store was almost deserted. The last customer had gone, the staff had drifted home and the doors had been bolted. Soon the cleaners would come with their mops and their chatter, but until then there was an uncanny peace hanging over the store, like the breath-holding stillness of trees before a storm.

The peace was shattered as soon as she saw Drew's face. The storm broke directly over her head. He was standing, his eyes were blazing and his mouth a taut and furious line.

"So you've done it again."

"Done what again?" She was stupefied.

"Don't turn on the Little Miss Innocent act. It doesn't work with me any more."

"I wish," she said faintly, "you'd tell me what I'm supposed to have done."

"Do I need to? Not content with betraying our scoop purchase of washing machines to Curlew's number one spy, your boyfriend Malcolm Watling, you had to go and blab to him about our negotiations for a site for our extension store. I knew I shouldn't have trusted you, although you touchingly swore on your honor to tell no one."

"And I kept that promise."

He smiled contemptuously. "You did, didn't you? And I believed you . . . of course. Especially when I hear from the real estate agents we were negotiating with that the deal has fallen through, that Curlews have beaten us to it by offering more money. Which leaves Majors right out in the cold."

"I'm . . . I'm sorry," was all she could find to say, but she knew that those two apologetic, innocuous words would condemn her in the eyes of this man as surely as if she had actually admitted to the crime of which he was accusing her.

He turned on her and she flinched at the violence in his face. "So you're sorry, are you, after the event, after giving away to that traitor of a boyfriend of yours the firm's most important secret?"

She had to make some attempt to defend herself. "But, Mr. Major, I swear I didn't breathe a word of it to anyone. You must believe me."

"Believe you? When this is simply a repeat performance of what has happened before? I'm sorry, but I'll never believe you again, never trust you again, do you hear?"

That she couldn't take. Her voice rose. "What evidence do you have that I passed the information on? How can you prove it? Her voice wavered. "After all that's happened, how can you doubt my loyalty?"

"Your loyalty? I don't give that," he snapped his fingers, "for your loyalty."

"No, you wouldn't." Now her anger equalled his. "How can you talk about loyalty? You don't know the meaning of the word. You and your legion of women, and your take-them-and-leave-them attitude. You wouldn't understand," she breathed deeply to steady her voice, "the sort of love and loyalty that someone could feel for another person that would endure for a lifetime."

"And what do you know about love that lasts a lifetime?"

"A lot," she cried, "more than you'll ever know. I have the example of my mother and father. I might be mad, in fact, in saying what I'm going to say, I know I'm mad, but . . . but," she was determined to get it out whatever the cost to herself, whatever the humiliation it would bring in its trail, "I wouldn't just die with you, as I said the other day, I'd die for you. That's how deep my loyalty is to you. Now do you believe me when I say I did not betray any secret of yours to anyone?"

He paled. "No," she rushed on, crying now. "I can see you don't. When I've gone . . . and I'm going for good this time . . . you can laugh and laugh at how you've enslaved another woman, made yet another conquest to add to your list." She ran to the door.

"Juliet!" He was after her and caught her arms, swinging her around. "Do you realize what you're saying?"

She tugged her arms away and ran, blinded by tears, down the six flights of stairs. He didn't follow. When she reached the boutique, she was quite alone.

"So that's that," she sobbed, "exit me, Juliet Bourne, from Major and Son. Curlews, here I come."

She glared at herself in the mirror. She had to stop crying. She scrubbed at her face with her handkerchief and with a shaking hand put on some make-up, but the tears kept coming and smudged it all and she had to rub it off and start again. The telephone rang.

Automatically she stretched out her hand and answered.

"Why are you crying, Juliet?"

"I'm n-not c-crying. You're imagining it."

"I'm not. I know you're crying."

"H-how do you know?"

"I can see you on the television monitor."

"That's all you can do, make f-fun of me. I'm going."

"You're not going. You're staying right there. I'm coming down."

"You're n-not. You'll be too late." But she was talking to herself. He had gone. She crashed down the receiver and started feverishly on her face again. It was no good, it would have to stay like that. She'd just have to hope no one looked at her. She grabbed her coat and her bag and flung herself at the entrance. He was there and her momentum made her hit him squarely on the chest. She was momentarily winded but recovered and tried to push past him. But his body, hard and unyielding, prevented her escape.

He edged her back into the boutique. She struggled. "It's no good trying to stop me. I'm leaving. I'm going to work for Curlews. Their boutique buyer's left and they're prepared to offer me twice the salary—"

He shook her to make her stop. "You, work for Curlews? Over my dead body! You think I'm going to let you go now, after what you told me upstairs?"

"You can't stop me!"

"Oh, but I can. Like this." His arms came out and secured her as surely as a rope tied around her. His mouth fastened on hers, pressing back her head and forcing her to respond.

But she struggled to get away. "It's no good. I'm not going to be one of your women. I'm not going to have an affair with you, so—"

"My darling," his voice was urgent, "I'm asking you to have an affair with me. A life-long affair, until death do us part."

She held back and looked at him, suspicious even now of his motives.

"I'm proposing to you, sweetheart. I'm asking you to marry me, Juliet."

"But . . . but if I accepted," she still could not bring herself to believe that what he was saying was sincere and genuine, "how would I know you wouldn't be unfaithful to me, like your father to your mother? You told me he taught you to be like him—"

"You've forgotten one vital fact. He chose the wrong woman to be his wife. I'm choosing the right woman from the start. And," he whispered, drawing her now acquiescent body to his, "I'm not going to make the terrible mistake he made. I'm not letting you run away from me, as he allowed your mother to do. We, my darling, are not even going to be engaged. We're going to be married. At once."

"But I haven't said," she whispered faintly, "that I'll marry you."

"You have no choice, my sweet. I know you love me. No woman would say to a man what you said to me in my office without loving him. Am I right?"

She nodded and this time there was no resistance to his kisses. Afterwards she rested against him, needing the support of his body to keep her upright.

"My darling," he said, lifting her face and cupping it with his hands, "my father's in South America."

"I know. My mother told me."

"I want us to do something. I want us to contact him now and tell him the news. I know the name of his hotel. He left it in case of emergencies." They walked, arms around each other, toward the elevator.

She smiled up at him. "And this is an emergency?"

"It most certainly is. If he doesn't come home at once, he'll miss our wedding!"

In the elevator he held her in his arms as if he was afraid to let her go. He told her, "I've discovered the answer to the mystery about the sale of the land. When you left me upstairs, I phoned Curlews's manager. I caught him just before he went home. He told me it was the estate agent's double dealing that was the cause of the trouble. Apparently, Curlews were contacted by the agents, who told them we wanted the land and if they were interested they could have it, provided they offered more money than we were offering. They did and they got the land. I told the man exactly what I thought of Curlews for such a miserable piece of deception, that we might even take them to court. He said that if Majors felt that strongly about it, we could have the land back and good luck to us."

They got out of the elevator and strolled to his room. "Will you ever forgive me for those accusations I made against you, saying you were to blame?"

She pulled his head down and whispered in his ear, "If you tell me you love me, which you haven't done yet, I'll forgive you anything."

He unlocked his door and took her inside and proceeded to convince her in a most satisfactory way of his love for her. So she forgave him.

He sat in his chair and pulled her onto his knee. She asked, touching his cheeks with her fingers, "How long have you loved me, Drew?"

His hands covered hers. "How long does it take for an avalanche to hit you after the first rock falls? The first one hit me the day I met you. The rest followed almost at once. That," he whispered, against her lips, "is how long I've loved you." They drew apart.

"But, darling, why didn't you tell me?"

"Why? Because when a woman tells a man she hates him more than she's ever hated anyone else in her whole life, what is that man to do, except what I did . . . keep silent?"

"I didn't tell you, I told your father. Anyway, I did

hate you, for being so horrible to me and for not loving me back when I loved you so desperately."

"What," he said, kissing her again, "a lot of time we've wasted."

It took Drew some minutes to contact his father's hotel and even more before they found him. But at last his voice came loud and clear over the thousands of miles and when he heard the news, the voice became even louder. The joy in it was unmistakable.

"He wants to speak to you," Drew said, handing her the receiver. "Don't worry about the cost. The call's on the firm."

"Juliet?" Warren said. "Words can't tell you how delighted I am. My dear, will you do something for me? Just once—" his voice cracked and recovered, "—will you call me Dad? After that you can call me Warren, or anything else you like, rude or otherwise. Go on, I'm listening."

She answered, shyly, smiling at Drew who had heard what his father had said, "Hallo, Dad. I'm . . . I'm glad you're pleased about us."

There was a brief silence. Then, "Thank you, my dear. Put my son back, will you?" Drew took the phone from her. "Drew? Marry her quick, son, don't let her get away like I let her mother."

"Don't worry, Father. A few days at the most. We're not even going to be engaged. Coming home for the wedding?"

"You just try to stop me! I'm on my way. But before I go, just tell your girl one thing, will you? Tell her thank God I'm going to be related to her mother in some way, even if it's only distantly. Tell her that, will you?" He hung up.

"You heard?" asked Drew.

There were tears in her eyes as she nodded.

"Come on," Drew said, "I'm taking you home to your parents. Then we're going to celebrate."

"I must get my things from the boutique. And do something to my face."

"Why bother? It's beautiful as it is."

In the boutique she combed her hair, but makeup was unnecessary. Her face was transformed. "You once told me," she said, as she gathered her things together, "that the woman you married would have to be perfect."

"I did not. I said 'made to measure,' which is a very different thing. You're certainly not perfect, my darling, and I wouldn't be marrying you if you were. Who wants a perfect woman? But, my word, as far as I'm concerned, you're certainly made to measure . . . my measure."

They kissed again, then made their way, his arm around her waist, to the parking lot, leaving the building by the rear entrance. The caretaker was standing beside it and as they approached he smiled and wished them every happiness.

Overwhelmed, they asked him, "How did you know?"

He laughed. "I saw you on the television monitor in the security room. My goodness, it was just like a movie!"

"Keep it to yourself," Drew urged him, "don't tell anyone yet, will you?"

"Not a soul, sir, I promise. Except my wife. She can't resist a happy ending!"

THE BRIDE OF ROMANO

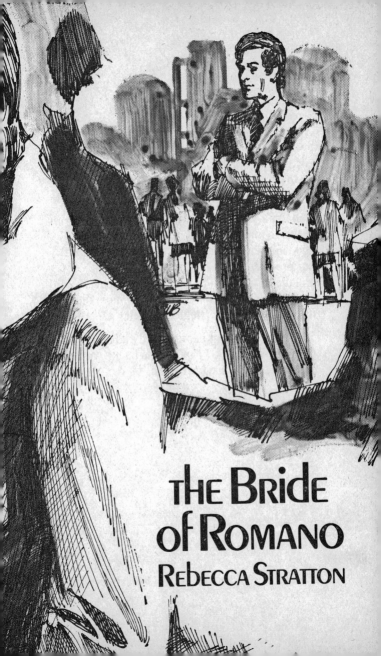

THE BRIDE
OF ROMANO
REBECCA STRATTON

Storm found it hard to visualize life without Alexei. It would be impossible to forget him, no matter how long they were apart.

Yet only a fool would continue living in Bellabaia—the place she had thought a paradise on earth only a few short months ago. For now that Alexei was convinced of her preference for Paolo, nothing would change his mind—he would never treat Storm as a proper wife. He would most likely have their brief marriage annulled.

Storm looked up at her husband and shook her head slowly. "I can't come back, Alexei," she said, "because I love you."

CHAPTER ONE

Dark men, Storm decided without hesitation, should always wear dazzlingly white shirts, especially when they were as tall, slim and attractive as the man on the quay. She had been watching him for several minutes now, ever since he had first caught her eye. Not openly, of course, but from behind the face-saving screen of a pair of sunglasses.

He was exactly what most English people think of as typically Italian. Olive-skinned, black-haired and with a kind of indolent self-confidence that amounted almost to arrogance. During the three days she had been in Bellabaia she had seen hundreds of people, men, women and children, all with that same coloring, smiling and good-natured people, but none as eye-catching as this man.

He was very good-looking—she could tell that much, even from her seat on a stone bench farther along the quay. Tall and slim-hipped, he wore that dazzlingly white shirt open at the neck with enough buttons undone to reveal the dark golden color of his throat and chest.

He had a little boy with him, a small, rather sad-faced little boy, although very much like the man, in a way, too. He appeared to be about five years old and was almost painfully thin, despite the healthy-looking tan he had.

At the moment, the child was engrossed in the activities of the local fishermen preparing their nets for the evening excursion after anchovies; he seemed prepared to stay there indefinitely. The man, however, bent his head after a minute or two and said something to him, urging him that it was time to go, if the boy's vehemently shaking head was anything to judge by. Again the man spoke to him, and Storm, wise to the ways of children, smiled to herself as she imagined the tussle of wills going on between the two of them.

The problem was solved a moment later, however, when the man lifted the boy and swung him up onto his shoulders, holding tight to the thin little arms while the child's legs dangled over his broad shoulders. There were no tears, only the sound of laughter as Storm watched them start along the quay toward her. She thought what a captivating pair they made, the man so tall and good-looking and the laughing child riding on his shoulders.

Although the boy was not really attractive, there was a certain wistful charm about him that was much more appealing than mere good looks, and she watched him with a faint smile as the pair came closer. The small bay, with its incredibly blue water glistening like gold with the sun on its barely rippling surface, the little fishing boats bobbing gently and peacefully on the tide, and the curving, dark stone quay hewn from the sheer rock that rose sharply at the far end, softened and bedecked with multihued foliage, made a perfect background.

They looked so right, somehow, the man and the boy, and the other brown, bright-faced people, so much a part of the scene that she felt a strange lilt of unexpected joy. During the past three days, there had been so much to see that gave her pleasure and somehow the man and the boy had contributed to her enjoyment.

Bellabaia was a beautiful, picture-postcard little place, with the rising cliffs soaring up from the quay and the dark volcanic sands—sheer cliffs that had been terraced by these industrious people into a pattern of fertile shelves on which crops of oranges, lemons and almonds, apples and pears grew. The scent of the lemon trees was every-where and had even invaded her bedroom, in a villa higher up the slope, where the soft wind carried all the scents and sounds.

It was a paradise she might never have found if a friend had not discovered it some years ago and recommended it. Storm had decided to take a holiday abroad before taking another job, and, as she had always liked the idea of Italy, the recommendation of Bellabaia had been fortuitous. She was staying in the same villa, with the same people her friend had known, and so far had enjoyed every minute of her stay.

Being a children's nurse, she had a certain rapport with most children, and the sight of the little boy riding high on the man's shoulders made her smile as they approached. Their laughter was infectious, and as they drew level with her, they both looked at her in a kind of friendly conspiracy, inviting her to join in their fun, the child's eyes showing the uninhibited curiosity of the very young, the man's an undisguised appreciation of her as a woman.

She was a woman that most men looked at more than once, even in England, and since she had been in Bellabaia she had grown accustomed to being openly ogled by the expressive dark eyes of the male population.

Her tawny gold hair, of course, made her more noticeable in a place where every other woman was dark-eyed and black-haired, for tourists were few in Bellabaia, and her small oval face was more than just pretty. Even with her big green eyes concealed behind dark glasses she was undoubtedly a very attractive woman, and the Latin temperament was not slow to appreciate the fact.

Accustomed as she was to admiration, however, something about this man's dark-eyed scrutiny gave her a swift and unexpected flutter of excitement in the region of her heart.

Her small neat figure showed to advantage in a bright

yellow dress, sleeveless and low-necked. The man must have noted everything about her, she thought, judging by the length and intensity of his scrutiny, which traveled from the top of her tawny head to the slim legs revealed to above the knee, where the yellow dress stopped short.

Under the circumstances, she felt almost bound to make some sort of greeting so she looked up at the child and smiled again. "Good afternoon," she said, but it was the man who answered her, and in excellent English.

His black head inclined politely, so that she felt sure he would have bowed if he had not had the child on his shoulder. With a warm glow of appreciation he gleamed boldly at her. "Good afternoon, *signorina!*" He had a pleasant deep voice, exactly the kind of voice she would have imagined him to have. "You are enjoying the sunshine?"

Storm nodded agreement. "Very much, thank you." She felt a quite inexplicable sense of excitement again as she met the boldness of those dark eyes, despite the protection of her sunglasses. As she took closer stock of him, she had a strange feeling of anticipation.

"You are staying in Bellabaia for a holiday?"

He seemed intent on furthering the acquaintance, and Storm's common sense was warning her of all the things she had heard about Latin men. Even the child was regarding her with boldly curious eyes, an expression strangely at odds with the waiflike features. Probably she was being rash speaking to them like this, but she could think of no reason for backing down now.

"For a little while," she said. "I'm between jobs, so I took the opportunity of seeing something of Italy." She looked around her and smiled. "It's very beautiful."

"Very beautiful!" The expression in his eyes attributed the description to herself rather than the scene around them. "You must allow me to show you some-

thing of the countryside while you are here, *signorina*."
One dark brow was raised discreetly. "You are here
alone?"

Wondering if she was doing the wise thing in admitting it, Storm nodded. "Yes, I'm staying up there, at the
Villa Lucia."

"Ah, but how fortunate!" A raised hand praised
heaven for such a fortuitous coincidence. "We are at the
Villa Romano, you know?" He looked as if he expected
her to recognize the name. "You could say we are
almost—how is it? Neighbors, *si*, neighbors. Permit me to
introduce us, *signorina*." He indicated the boy with a
brief glance. "This is Gino Targhese, and I am Paolo
Giovanni Oliviero Veronese."

He made the announcement with a flourish that almost
drew a smile from her. She had thought the boy was his
son, but obviously she was mistaken.

Her heart was tapping rapidly against her ribs. Such a
reaction was so unlike her usually cool and calm self that
it surprised her. Possibly the idyllic setting of Bellabaia
had something to do with it, but she found this man
affecting her in the most extraordinary way. He held her
hand for only as long as was courteous, but still managed
to give her fingers a brief squeeze as he bobbed his head in
a slight bow.

"I'm Storm Gavin." Her pulses were doing strange and
inexplicable things in response to that small but
meaningful gesture.

"Storm?" He pronounced it slowly, raising a questioning brow. "That is most unusual, is it not, *signorina*?"

"It's very unusual." Storm pulled a wry face for the
number of times she had been required to explain her odd
first name. "But you see I was born during a particularly
heavy thunderstorm."

"Ah, *si! Una tempesta!*" The dark eyes looked at her

in a way that set all sorts of wild ideas spinning around in her brain. "It is very beautiful," he decreed softly. "It is almost worthy of your own beauty, *signorina*!"

Storm was unsure whether or not she should respond to the outrageous glint in his eyes, but instead she merely smiled. Paolo Veronese, from the speed with which he became familiar, needed little encouragement from anyone. But he was quite the most devastating man she had ever met. She could quite easily make a complete fool of herself if she was not careful.

The boy, Gino, said something in Italian, and Paolo Veronese shook his head, smiling apologetically at her. "I am sorry, *signorina*, we should speak English."

"But why?" Storm asked with a smile. "I don't mind in the least!"

He made a wry face, his brows raised. "Ah, but Alexei *would* mind. When we are in the company of English people, he prefers that we speak English at all times, especially Gino. It is for his own good, you see, for when he is older. Alexei himself speaks it perfectly and he would have Gino as perfect."

Storm nodded, looking much wiser than indeed she was. Whoever Alexei was, obviously he was someone, whose word counted for much. "Oh, I see," was all she said.

It must have been fairly obvious that she had no idea what he was talking about, but Paolo Veronese had evidently meant her to be impressed. "Signor Alexei Romano is Gino's guardian, *signorina*!"

Somehow the name of Romano struck her as familiar, but it took her a minute ot two to wonder why. Then she remembered that she had heard her host at the villa mention the name in connection with an electronics firm in nearby Naples. She remembered also that there had been some comment on the fact that he must be one of the wealthiest men in Italy. Presumably Paolo Veronese was an employee of some sort, although possibly a privileged one if he was entrusted with the care of the boy.

"Well, I can understand the idea, of course," Storm said. "A second language is always an asset, but this little chap is rather small to be bilingual as yet."

Expressive Latin shoulders spoke volumes. "Alas," he replied, "Alexei does not always understand and Gino is sometimes. . . ." Another shrug. "He uses Italian words when he cannot think of the English one."

"But what is more natural?" Storm sympathized, as the warm, liquid brown eyes glowed darkly.

"You are so very *simpatica, signorina*, but. . . ." Again those expressive shoulders said a good deal more than words. "Unfortunately Alexei sometimes loses patience."

"Oh, but that's most unfair!" Storm protested without hesitation, seeing the child's side of it, as always. "He must be an awful bully!"

She had not thought before she spoke and realized suddenly that she was speaking to a complete stranger about his employer. However, Paolo Veronese looked no more than vaguely uneasy. "Please do not allow me to mislead you, *signorina*. They are very fond of one another, but Alexei is . . . firm, you understand?"

"I think so." Storm still thought that anyone who could lose patience with a wistful little waif like Gino Targhese merely because he occasionally lapsed into his own tongue must almost certainly be a bully, and she wished she could have five minutes alone with the man. She would tell him exactly what she thought of him.

Paolo Veronese's dark eyes were regarding her again with blatant admiration, and he smiled at her warmly. "How long are you to stay in Bellabaia, *signorina*?" he

asked softly, and Storm felt her heart turn somersaults
again at the effect of that voice. It was really quite
ridiculous for her to be blushing like a schoolgirl just
because a strange man looked at her with eyes that made
her think of all sorts of incredible things and spoke to her
in a voice that sent shivers of pleasure through her.

"Oh, only two weeks," she said, pulling a rueful face.
"Then I have to go back and find another post. I'm a
children's nurse," she added, anticipating the question.

"You are?" He seemed pleased about that for some
reason, and his dark eyes glowed. "But that is *molto
bene, signorina!*"

His enthusiasm puzzled her, but she smiled and
nodded.

"I think so," she said. "I enjoy it."

"*Bene!*" He glanced at his wristwatch and pulled a
face. "I think we must go, *signorina,* but if I may, I would
like to see you again. *Si?*"

"That would be very nice." She smiled at them both.
"Goodbye, Signor Veronese."

She gave an involuntary gasp when her left hand was
raised and his lips pressed warmly on her fingers. "*Addio,
signorina.* We will meet again!"

Storm sat there for some time after they had gone,
watching the activity on the quay. The fishermen worked
and chattered incessantly among themselves, their
laughter and lyrical Italian voices carrying on the warm,
sunny air.

Most of the houses were little cottages belonging to the
fishermen and their families or the workers from the
terraced fields above on the cliff face. There were also one
or two larger villas, like the one where Storm herself was
staying. The villas were perched higher up among the
fertile terraces. They were accessible only by steep,

narrow roads that rose to join the main road out to Naples itself, accessible from the quay only on foot up the even steeper paths with steps cut into them and protected by low walls.

She watched the man and the little boy again as they began to climb one of the paths. The boy held onto the man's hand as they went up the steep incline. A white villa stood fairly high, bright white against the tree-layered cliff side, like a child's toy. Bright yellow mimosa and scarlet geraniums, making splashes of vivid color where the gardens closed around the villa, as if to keep the more mundane crops at bay, caught her eye.

Another glance at her watch and Storm got to her feet. The warm, sea-cooled air made her feel incredibly lazy and she marveled at the boundless energy of the local people, who seemed to stop their frenetic round of activity only for the long midday *siesta*.

They always had a cheerful word for her too, and cries of *"Buon giorno, signorina!"* followed her along the quay.

Bright, friendly, but curious eyes noted her passing, and smiles appreciated the picture she made, but it struck her today that perhaps there was more than the usual mild curiosity in the looks she received. Although she tried to dismiss it as unlikely, she could not help wondering if her short conversation with Paolo Veronese had been the cause of speculation.

The climb up to the villa was hot and tiring, but it was well worth it for the view from the villa's garden. Away from the quay it was quieter and a little less hot, for the higher she went the more effective that breeze became, and the scent of the lemon trees titillated her nostrils as she climbed.

Below her the quay, with its bobbing boats and cluster

of little houses, looked like something on a picture postcard. As she paused part way up the steep path, from somewhere below a joyous, if less than perfect, tenor voice sang the strains of an Italian love song.

Anywhere else Storm would have felt the situation artificial and contrived, but here in Bellabaia it seemed a perfectly natural thing to happen. The sound of the voice singing, the sheer beauty of the scene above and below her, made her feel like laughing suddenly with uninhibited enjoyment. She ran a few feet up the steep path without even noticing the effort required to do so.

It was her host who answered the telephone the following morning while Storm was still having her breakfast. She frowned curiously when he called her into the hall to take the call. He, too, looked at her curiously as he handed her the receiver, one hand over the mouthpiece.

"Someone is speaking on behalf of Signor Alexei Romano, *signorina*," he told her. With a sudden flutter of apprehension, Storm took the instrument from him, wondering what on earth it could possibly mean.

"Hello," she said cautiously. "This is Storm Gavin."

The voice at the other end spoke excellent English, but it was less seductively low in pitch than she remembered Paolo Veronese's. "I am speaking for Signor Romano," the caller informed her and, as Paolo Veronese had done, sounded as if he expected her to be impressed by the name. "This is his secretary."

"Signor Romano?" It occurred to her suddenly that perhaps the great man himself had heard about her encounter with Paolo Veronese and his ward yesterday, and was going to put her firmly in her place.

Further inquiries of her host had produced the information that Alexei Romano not only owned the biggest electronics company in Italy, but was also the last of an ancient and very aristocratic family. There was also something else about the name that struck her as familiar, but she could not remember it now. But surely no man could be so autocratic as to object to a perfectly ordinary encounter, even if he was a business tycoon and an aristocrat.

"Signor Romano wishes to speak with you, Signorina Gavin," the smooth voice informed her. "Will you please call at the Villa Romano this morning at ten-thirty."

It was not a request, Storm recognized with sudden anger. It was more in the nature of a command, and she was very tempted to hang up there and then. But then she remembered how, yesterday, she had wished for five minutes alone with Signor Alexei Romano to tell him exactly what she thought of him. It seemed he not only bullied little children, but also issued orders to complete strangers, and expected to be obeyed.

"First I'd like to know why I'm expected to call and see Signor Romano," she told the secretary. She could visualize the shocked expression on his face from the silence that followed. "Why does he want to see me?"

"Signor Romano instructed me to make the call," she was informed stiffly. "No doubt the *signore's* reasons will be made plain when you arrive, *signorina*."

No doubt, Storm thought, her brain whirling busily, but she did not intend to allow herself to be bulldozed into obeying the summons without question. "I'm not at all sure that I understand," she told the man at the other end. "However, if I find that I have no other engagement for ten-thirty this morning, I'll call. If not, please offer Signor Romano my apologies. Good morning."

She hung up hastily and turned to face her host who had come into the hall again in time to catch her last words. His dark, friendly face looked quite stunned, and Storm wondered how on earth Alexei Romano, whoever he might be, could invoke such awe.

She was curious to see what kind of a man it was who bullied little boys and issued orders to complete strangers, via his secretary. He was probably some crabby old man with more money than he knew what to do with, and enjoyed making everyone jump every time he cracked the whip. Well, she would go, out of sheer curiosity, but she would go in her own good time.

Storm finished her breakfast and took her time dressing. Eventually she picked out a simple pale green jersey dress with long full sleeves and shirt-style neckline that offered a tantalizing glimpse of lightly tanned skin as far as the shadowy vee just above the top button.

She brushed her tawny hair until it shone like burnished bronze. She decided the total effect was cool and uncluttered enough to impress anyone with her complete disregard for Signor Alexei Romano's opinion.

As she started out, it occurred to her that to go alone would create something of a wrong impression on an autocratic and traditional Italian, but there was no one she could ask to go with her, and anyway, his opinion did not concern her in the least.

It was almost an hour later than the appointed time as she walked along the road and approached the Villa Romano from the front. It would have been much too informal to have come in from the path up from the quay. She wished she felt less nervous, but she was determined to hold her own, no matter what happened. Despite her vow, however, her hands were actually trembling when she turned into a tree-lined approach to the old villa.

The villa looked old and mellow and rather beautiful,

its white walls dappled with the shadows of trees that surrounded it and gave fragrance as well as welcome shade. The garden was a riot of color with the dark, stern straightness of cypress trees lending a background contrast to the scarlet and pink of geraniums, bright sun-yellow mimosa and roses of every hue.

A long porch ran the full width of the house, its tiled floor half covered with stone urns overrunning with flowers that scented the still, warm air. When she got closer, she saw the door was open. She hesitated briefly, her heart thumping heavily as she reached for the bell pull.

The man who answered her ring seemed to be expecting her, although his dark, rather dour face gave little away as he asked her to enter, and led the way across the hall.

The hall was a revelation to her, quite beautiful and quite unexpected. It was wide and cool and its walls were covered in the most beautiful frescoes in soft, light colors and exquisite workmanship. There were scenes of gods and goddesses amid scenery even more breathtaking than that outside. The slender nymphs and exquisitely beautiful young men reminded her uneasily of Paolo Veronese as they looked down at her from their painted paradise with limpid dark eyes.

The floor beneath her feet was tiled with soft colored mosaics, and to the right a beautiful marble staircase swept upwards to what looked like a gallery that disappeared on either side into shadowy coolness. She could, she thought, be forgiven for believing she had suddenly been transported back in time some two or three hundred years.

The manservant made his stately way across the hall and Storm was shown into a huge, high-ceilinged room, light and cool as the hall had been. On the walls hung portraits of dark, aristocratic-looking men and vaguely hostile-looking women, some of them quite beautiful, despite their discouraging expressions,

She was instructed to be seated, in much less perfect English than she had encountered so far, and the tall double doors were closed behind her. Left to her own devices with only the loud ticking of a clock to distract her, she looked around curiously.

The villa was much bigger than she had realized from seeing it from below on the quay, a good deal larger than the Villa Lucia, which was only to be expected. If she had not been so uneasy she would have walked around the room and admired the beautiful white marble mantel and the many expensive and beautiful *objets d'art*, but she found herself constantly listening for approaching foot-steps. She stayed where she was in a chair near the window.

There was no sound to be heard but the occasional hum of a car passing on the motorway above, and nearly ten minutes after her arrival Storm was still waiting. She was becoming more and more angry at the cavalier treatment she was receiving, but it did not take much intelligence to guess that Signor Alexei Romano intended teaching her a lesson in punctuality. She had kept him waiting, so now she was being made to wait in her turn, for him to put in an appearance.

Since it had been at his instigation that she was there at all, however, Storm saw no reason why she should be treated so, and she got to her feet at last. She picked up her handbag and clutched it tightly in both hands, her eyes bright and angrily green. If Signor Romano wanted to see her so badly, he could come and find her. She was not going to wait for him any longer.

CHAPTER TWO

Storm reached the double doors and her hands were already on the ornate brass knobs when they were suddenly twisted out of her grasp. She stepped back hastily to avoid colliding with the edges of the doors.

The man who confronted her, she supposed after one brief, startled glance, was the secretary she had spoken to on the telephone. She wondered vaguely if all Romano's staff were so devastatingly attractive.

This man was even taller than Paolo Veronese and less good-looking, but he had a fierce, almost animal magnetism that struck her like a blow. He was much less typically Italian, too.

His features looked as if they had been carved out of bronze. A square chin, deeply cleft, and high Slavonic cheekbones that added drama to a face at once discouraging and incredibly attractive. His mouth was wide and straight and at the moment set firm as if he were angry.

Hair that was not quite black grew thick and strong and quite low down in his neck, a heavy swathe of it lying across his broad brow. His bearing was proud and arrogant and he emanated self-confidence, but undoubtedly the most arresting thing about him was his eyes.

Whereas Paolo Veronese had the dark eyes that one expected of his race, this man's eyes were a light, almost icy blue. Such a contrast in the deeply tanned face drew immediate attention. Storm suspected that he was well aware of the effect they had, for one corner of that wide mouth tilted briefly and unexpectedly, as if he smiled to himself.

She would not have thought the terrain around

Bellabaia suitable for horseback riding, although there was a racecourse in Naples, but obviously this man had been riding, or at least he was dressed for it.

He wore fawn breeches and highly polished brown boots, with a fine white silk shirt whose texture was such that it was obvious he wore nothing under it. The crop he carried he flung away from him into a chair as he came into the room, and he looked at Storm with blatant and speculative curiosity.

"Miss Gavin?"

It was not the man on the telephone; she had already decided that. Apart from the unlikelihood of a secretary receiving her dressed as he was, his voice was deeper and more resonant, and he gave the impression that he would never serve anyone, in any capacity.

She nodded uncertainly, her heart suddenly in her throat when she began to suspect his identity. "I'm Storm Gavin," she admitted.

He cast a swift, exploratory glance round the big room. "You came alone?"

"Yes, *signore*, I did!"

The light eyes swept over her in a swift and icy appraisal, bringing color to her cheeks and the light of battle to her green eyes. She felt she had suffered quite enough indignity at this man's hands already, by being kept waiting, without being made to feel like some prize animal he was considering buying.

"You know my cousin, I believe."

So Paolo Veronese was his cousin, and she had no doubt at all now that this was the formidable Alexei Romano, the big man himself. Not the crabby old man she had visualized, but a much more formidable prospect altogether.

She remembered, ruefully, her wish to have five minutes alone with the guardian of little Gino, but five minutes alone with this man would certainly not have the effect she had envisaged. He was very unlikely to be crushed by any condemnation of him as a bully, nor would he care tuppence for her opinion of him, good or bad.

"If you refer to Signor Veronese," she said, striving to sound cool and aloof, "we met yesterday."

Her determination to remain cool and calm was rapidly losing ground to the strangely disturbing effect he was having on her senses. She could much more easily see now how he could command obedience and awe, not only from his staff and his family, but from strangers like her host as well. No wonder the secretary had been so shocked at her off-hand agreement to see him.

"I was sitting on the quay yesterday when Signor Veronese and the little boy came along," she informed him. "And we passed the time of day."

"Which was quite sufficient invitation for Paolo!" Again that cool, appraising glance swept over her. "You are a very beautiful young woman."

The words were without a hint of compliment or flattery, merely a statement of fact, and Storm resented them. It was obvious what he was implying about the meeting and it made her angry to be so misjudged.

"I believe I was the one who spoke first," she told him, stiffly resentful. "Not with any ulterior motive, but because the little boy was laughing, and it's an English custom to be polite and friendly." She made the last statement pointedly, and again that faint tilt at one corner of his mouth betrayed a hint of amusement.

"But my cousin was only too willing to further the

acquaintance, I have no doubt," he said quietly, in his precise English. "Do you intend to see Paolo again, Miss Gavin?"

Storm felt anger and resentment churning away inside her, but a strange kind of excitement too, as if he presented a challenge that she would not be able to resist. He had absolutely no right to question her about her meeting with Paolo Veronese, whether he was his cousin or not, and she had no intention of letting him get away with it.

"That," she told him firmly, "surely depends upon Signor Veronese and myself."

"Not quite!" The quiet voice had an edge of steel that matched the glittering eyes. "Paolo is not a complete fool!"

"You mean you'd. . . ." Storm stared at him, her green eyes kindling dangerously. "If your cousin chooses to let you threaten him, *signore*, I suppose that's his affair, but I for one take exception to your attitude, and if that's all you have to say to me, I'll. . . ."

"It is not," he interrupted brusquely. "I am simply seeking to establish that you are what you claimed to be when you spoke to my cousin, Miss Gavin, or if you are merely one of his *fantòcci*!"

The tone of his voice was enough to convey all too clearly what the word meant, and Storm clenched her hands tightly on the clasp of her handbag. She was trembling like a leaf and had never felt so angry and helpless in her life.

"I fail to see how it can possibly concern you," she said in a small tight voice, "but I'm a children's nurse, as I told Signor Veronese. And now, *signore*, I'm leaving. I refuse to stay here another minute and listen to your insults. You have absolutely no right to speak to me in this way, and I demand an apology!"

The air between them was taut as a drumskin, and the light blue eyes burned into her with a sensation like fire and ice, sending a shudder through her whole body. "You came here this morning quite alone, *signorina*, and you apparently spoke first to my cousin yesterday, also when you were alone. I was entitled to assume what I did. An Italian girl would have been much more careful of her reputation."

"I'm not an Italian girl!" Storm retorted swiftly. "And in the circumstances I can only thank heaven for it! I still think you owe me an apology for what you've said to me!"

For a moment the icy scrutiny continued, then the tight mouth seemed to ease slightly and he inclined his head, very briefly, as if reluctantly acknowledging her right to an apology. "Very well, *signorina*, it seems I have misjudged you, and I was perhaps too harsh. It would appear that your claim to be a children's nurse is true after all!"

"I can't imagine why you should have doubted it!" Storm told him. She felt horribly shaken by the events of the past few minutes, and wondered if anyone ever emerged unscathed from an encounter with this man.

He resented her temerity in answering him. That was evident from his expression, and for a moment she wondered if he would simply turn and walk out of the room, but then, once again, the tension eased. "I know my cousin, Miss Gavin," he told her quietly. "And you are obviously not only very attractive, but used to going around alone. It is a combination that Paolo would find irresistible."

"You took me for a . . . a pick-up?" she suggested, wondering if the colloquialism was beyond him. She was quiet-voiced herself despite the turmoil of her thoughts.

Remembering Paolo Veronese's well-practiced gallantry she was forced to admit that Alexei Romano's suspicions had probably been founded on experience, and she hastily lowered her eyes when she saw confirmation of it in his. "It was a natural assumption, *signorina*." He put a hand to the back of his head suddenly, brushing the thick dark hair absently as he stood in front of her, then with one hand he indicated that she should take one of the armchairs. After a brief hesitation she walked across and sat down again, sitting primly with her two feet on the floor and not crossing one leg over the other as she would more normally have done.

The pale green dress felt suddenly much flimsier than it really was, and she was inordinately conscious of the low fastening at the neckline, so that she put up a hand to it, her fingers surreptitiously pulling the two sides of the collar together.

He remained standing, and Storm guessed he intended keeping the upper hand. "You were on the point of leaving when I came in?" he asked quietly.

He took a cigarette from a box on the table and lit it, the flame of the lighter throwing the hard, clean lines of his features into relief for a second, so that he looked more than ever like a bronze sculpture. Exhaling the smoke slowly from his nostrils gave him a curiously primitive look that was infinitely disturbing and sent an involuntary shiver along her spine.

He did not, she noticed, offer her a cigarette, and she could well imagine that he was a man who disliked seeing women smoke and would therefore not even offer one out of politeness.

"I was leaving because I considered I'd waited quite

long enough," she told him, and one brow ascended swiftly while the light eyes narrowed behind the spiral of smoke from the cigarette.

"Even though you saw fit to be an hour late for your appointment?"

Storm felt herself flushing warmly again, and tilted her chin defiantly. "I'm no more accustomed to being ordered to keep appointments that are not of my seeking than I am to being kept waiting, Signor Romano." She looked at him steadily, her green eyes bright with defiance. "I assume you *are* Signor Romano?" The name was niggling at her memory again, as she tried to remember where she had heard the name before.

He inclined his head, seemingly unimpressed by her effort to put him in his place. "I do not usually have to identify myself, Miss Gavin. I am Alexei Romano."

His self-confidence, she realized, was virtually unshakable, but some small spark of determination made her affect a coolness she was far from feeling as he looked down at her with those ice-cool eyes. "I've been trying to think where I've heard the name before, Signor Romano," she told him in a light, slightly breathless voice.

For a moment he said nothing, but regarded her steadily through the haze of blue smoke, feet slightly apart, his dark, Slavonic features in shadow. A tall and rather menacing figure who looked as if he could have crushed her in one hand.

"So," he said at last, "you did not know my name, and yet you came here to see me, and alone."

"The fact that I came had nothing to do with you," Storm protested hurriedly, perhaps too hurriedly. "It was because you were the little boy's guardian. He looked so sad that I was ... touched."

"And you wished to see for yourself the brute who was

ill-treating him and making him look so sad, yes?" There was an icy glitter in his eyes again, and she felt sure he resented being accused of ill-treating the little boy more than he had anything else so far.

"I didn't say that," she objected mildly, too mildly, it seemed, for it was obvious he did not believe her.

It came to her then why the name had been familiar when she had heard her host mention it. Last year some time, in a British newspaper, she remembered reading something about a millionaire industrialist being killed in a car crash and a tiny boy being left heir to a vast fortune. The man's name had been Romano, she felt sure, but this little boy was called Targhese, according to Paolo Veronese.

"Gino is my late brother's child, Miss Gavin." Alexei Romano's voice recalled her, and she looked up hastily at the dark shadowed face with its light eyes. "I am his guardian, since his mother is also dead, and I do as well as I can for him."

"Oh, I'm sure you do, Signor Romano!"

She was very sure of it, suddenly. No matter what her opinion of him was in regard to herself and the way he seemed to rule everyone else with a rod of iron, she really felt that his affection for the little boy, Gino, was genuine. That difference in name could probably be accounted for by circumstances that a man like Alexei Romano would not dream of mentioning.

"Is there something wrong, Miss Gavin?"

His voice was edged with impatience and Storm dragged herself back from the realms of speculation, looking up to find him regarding her steadily, almost as if he followed her thoughts. He said nothing about it, however, but ran the fingers of one hand through the thick hair that covered half his forehead, and surprised her with a small, very brief smile that softened the sculptured lines of his face for only a second.

"You will find, Miss Gavin, that that large-eyed, soulful look is deceptive. Gino *does* miss his father, I cannot deny it, but twenty years ago if you had met my cousin Paolo, you would have seen a child very much like Gino is now."

"Oh, I see!"

She found it easy to accept the fact, but, while she was as concerned with Gino's welfare, as with all children's, she began to wonder when Alexei Romano was going to bring the conversation round to matters more pertinent to her visit. It startled her to discover that she was finding him so fascinating that she was reluctant to have things brought to a head, and perhaps never have the opportunity of speaking to him again.

"But he still touches your heart, yes?" He asked the question softly, and Storm brought herself back to earth, raising reproachful eyes to him.

"Well, it *was* his parents that were killed in that car crash," she told him. "And no amount of wealth is going to compensate for that."

Alexei Romano narrowed his eyes, nodding his head slowly. "So . . . you *did* know who I was!"

"I'd heard of you before," she allowed. "But I just couldn't think why the name was familiar. Now I've remembered."

"Thank you!"

There was sarcasm in the deep, quiet voice and she thought she detected a glimpse of ironic amusement in his eyes for a moment, but she guessed his pride had taken a blow, however small, from her admission.

"Oh, my host mentioned your business interests," she explained carefully. "But I was trying to remember about the car crash. I knew it was something about a child. That's all that interested me. Millionaire industrialists are of little interest to me, Signor Romano."

He stood silent and contemplative for a moment while Storm sat and waited, surprising herself with her willingness to do so. "Your being a children's nurse is the reason I sent for you." Storm looked at him in disbelief, her heart doing a sudden and quite alarming tattoo against her ribs when she realized the implication of the statement.

"It . . . it is?"

"Paolo tells me that you are seeking employment as a children's nurse."

Storm nodded, eyes hazy, her lips parted slightly as she gazed at him. "Yes, yes, I am, but—"

A long hand waved aside explanations. "You are fully qualified to cater for the needs of a small child?"

"Yes, I am."

She could scarcely believe that she was hearing him right. That he was actually suggesting that she should come and work for him and care for the little boy he set such store by. Once he had satisfied himself that she was not simply one of Paolo Veronese's more casual acquaintances, of course, and she could not blame him for that.

It was difficult to believe that she was not imagining the whole thing, that it was not real at all. But there was nothing unreal about Alexei Romano as he stood there in front of her. He was very much flesh and blood and very disturbingly masculine.

"But, Signor Romano," she ventured, bringing herself back to earth, "if it's for Gino, surely he needs to go to school, not have the services of a nurse."

Those icy eyes were regarding her again with disapproval, making it evident that he did not like having his decisions questioned. "Gino is not yet five years old," he told her. "And *I* will judge when he is ready for school, *signorina.*"

"Yes, yes, of course." It was not an ideal situation, with the little boy so near school age, but it would suit her well for the time being.

"I need someone to care for him until he is of school age, but there is no harm in him receiving some basic instruction in certain subjects."

"Basic instruction in—"

The expression on the dark, chiseled features cut her short. "Please allow me to finish, Miss Gavin." The autocratically assured air put her firmly in her place again, and he expelled a long plume of smoke from between tight lips before he spoke again. "My cousin tells me Gino appeared to like you during your brief meeting, and since you are looking for employment as a children's nurse, I think you will prove useful."

He leaned over and ground out the remains of the cigarette in an ashtray on the table beside her, long brown fingers crushing down relentlessly. The table was low and the movement brought him intimately close for the brief time it took the smouldering stub to die. As he drew back the back of his hand brushed lightly against her knee. The warm, almost sensual touch startled her so much that she instinctively drew back from it, fighting against the ever-increasing excitement that welled up inside her.

This man was a stranger, a wealthy, remote stranger who had offered her a job, nothing more and it was ridiculous for her to be so affected by him. It was, nevertheless, very difficult to remain unconscious of him as a man when he stood so close, his hands behind his back, like some tall, dark Nemesis looming over her.

"I must ask you for an immediate answer," he told her. "In the event of you refusing the post, I shall have to make other arrangements."

It was quite evident that he considered the likelihood of a refusal most improbable, and was possibly ready to conclude the interview there and then. Storm's head was spinning with a thousand and one reasons why she should not take the job he offered, not least the fact that she was not a qualified teacher and he had said he wanted some tutoring for the boy, however basic.

Heaven knew what academic qualifications he imagined she possessed, but obviously something more than she had. He might even be under the impression that she spoke Italian. There was the prospect of having him as her employer too. He was arrogant, confident to the point of being overbearing and the most disturbing man she had ever met. She must be quite crazy to even consider working for him, but the truth was she *did* want to.

After a long silence, during which time she felt those disturbing eyes watching her closely, she looked up and took a deep breath. Before she could say what she had to say, however, that cool, slightly impatient voice cut across her thoughts.

"I assume that you are attempting to make up your mind, Miss Gavin," he said. "I must remind you that I asked for an immediate answer."

"I was about to—" she began, but was again cut short by that impatient voice.

"It is surely not such a difficult decision to make!"

"But I'm not a schoolteacher, Signor Romano!" She was determined to be heard this time. "I'm not qualified to teach, even young children, like Gino. I'm a nurse, a nanny, if you like, but not a teacher."

Another impatient frown and she saw the likelihood of her getting the job slipping away if she raised any more obstacles. Alexei Romano was obviously not a patient man and what little patience he possessed was rapidly running out.

"You may call yourself what you wish," he informed her brusquely. "I am only concerned with your ability to care for Gino. If you are not capable of doing that then I shall conclude that you have been deceiving me after all, Miss Gavin."

There was a chilling threat in the cool voice, and Storm looked up at him indignantly. Her professional ability in question was something she would not stand for. "I've done nothing of the sort!" she denied.

"Then I take it you accept my offer. At five years old, Gino does not need a university professor!"

She was breathless and a little bewildered from being swept along at such a breakneck pace, bent and maneuvered to suit this man's purpose. She could only look at him, wide-eyed, for several moments and shake her head slowly.

"I . . . I could try," she said. "The little I've seen of Gino, I like him."

"It is more important that Gino likes *you*," Alexei Romano informed her shortly. "That is the reason I am employing you. Gino has met you, at least briefly, and you will not be completely strange to him."

Storm yielded gracefully; there was little else she could do, she felt. It would be fighting a losing battle to try and do anything else, for it was obvious that once Alexei Romano had decided on something, it had to be.

"I'll do my best," she promised, and he nodded, evidently considering the matter settled. "But, Signor

Romano, I. . . ." Another impatient frown condemned her persistence. "I don't know if you realize it, but I don't speak any Italian."

"Of course you do not, otherwise you would have used it, however badly." The cool eyes glittered briefly with derisive amusement. "Most people with a smattering of a foreign tongue insist on using it, no matter how unintelligible it may be to the natives."

Storm ignored the apparent slur on lesser mortals, and pressed home her point. "As long as you understand that anything I teach Gino will have to be in English."

"Of course. I wish him to speak English as fluently as he does Italian. You will suit admirably for a short time."

"Until he starts school?"

"And probably for a time after that," he informed her. "Until he settles down to the routine of school. It would distress him if he was suddenly deprived of someone he had become attached to."

Like a favorite teddy bear, Storm thought. She wondered how on earth she had got herself involved like this. She had merely passed the time of day with an attractive man and a small boy who happened to be passing, and there she was, only a day later, faced with the prospect of staying in Italy for an indefinite period, in charge of a child who was worth a fortune.

Her friends in England would not believe it. She scarcely believed it herself yet. "I hope I can come up to your expectations, *signore*," she said.

The ice blue eyes regarded her steadily. "I hope so too, Miss Gavin. You will start tomorrow morning and you will, of course, be paid your salary for the whole month. My secretary will go into the details with you. If you have any queries, please see him."

He seemed prepared to leave it there and half turned towards the door. "Oh, but, Signor Romano!" He looked down at her impatiently, and Storm had the feeling that only with difficulty did he refrain from telling her to forget the whole thing. But Gino liked her, and she suited his purpose at the moment.

His eyes were narrowed again and the sculptured bronze features had a hard, ruthless look that made her pulses flutter nervously. "Do you wish to work for me or not, Miss Gavin?" he asked and, almost without realizing it, Storm nodded. "Then you will do as I decide, *when* I decide. Good morning, Miss Gavin!"

He turned on his heel and strode across the room, his long muscular legs covering the distance in seconds, while Storm sat there staring after him. Then, as he bent to retrieve the riding crop he had thrown down on his way in, she got to her feet, her mouth set determinedly.

"Signor Romano!"

He turned swiftly, ice blue eyes glittering warningly, the crop tapping against one shiny boot. "*Signorina?*"

She hesitated to make the objection in the face of such obvious discouragement, and shook her head rather vaguely. "I . . . you didn't bother to ask if it was convenient for me to start tomorrow morning," she told him, much more mildly than she had intended, and she saw his lips tighten ominously.

The fascinating face with its high, Slavonic-looking cheekbones betrayed the beginnings of a formidable temper, and the crop, gripped hard in strong fingers, tapped threateningly against a polished leather boot as he stared at her.

"You told me that you were at present unemployed, Miss Gavin, and seeking another post. I have offered you employment, but if you wish to work for me there is one thing you should get clear from the beginning. I expect to have my wishes carried out without question and without delay. Do you understand?"

Her own temper was threatening to show itself and ruin the whole thing, so she swallowed hard on the word that rose to her lips, and nodded slowly. "Yes, Signor Romano."

"Good!"

He turned on his heel again and was gone. The double doors closed firmly behind him, while Storm subsided breathlessly into a chair. She shook her head in disbelief, both at her own compliance and at the events of the past few minutes.

She supposed she should feel honored to have been chosen for the job, and certainly staying on in Bellabaia would mean she could see more of Paolo Veronese, her employer permitting, of course. But of one thing she was quite certain. She was going to find it an uphill fight to keep her temper with an employer as insufferably arrogant as Alexei Romano.

CHAPTER THREE

Storm found herself nervous when she came to report to the Villa Romano next morning. As she walked down the shady approach to the villa, she realized it was because she feared Alexei Romano would have had second thoughts since yesterday and she would perhaps be summarily sent packing even before she had set foot in the place again.

She was admitted, however, by the same solemn manservant she had seen yesterday. This time he asked her to wait in the hall while he fetched Signor Romano's secretary, the young man she had spoken to on the telephone. When he came from the stairs behind her, he bowed over her hand and introduced himself as Rafael Caldorini.

He was very good-looking, something she had half expected, and he, too, reminded her of those voluptuous young men pictured on the frescoed wall behind him, a comparison borne out by the gleam of pleasure in his dark eyes when he bowed over her hand. He was shorter than either his employer or Paolo Veronese, and he had curly black hair and a smooth olive brown skin. He would, Storm thought, become very plump in a few years from now.

"I am to tell you of the financial arrangements made by Signor Romano, *signorina*," he informed her softly. Storm nodded, relieved that it was him and not his employer she was to see this morning.

"Yes, of course, Signor Caldorini."

Her smile seemed to encourage him and the dark eyes glowed warmly. "You will come with me, *per favore*, *signorina*?"

"Signorina Gavin!" The wide hall echoed to Paolo Veronese's deep, warm voice and Storm turned, smiling at him rather cautiously. Now that she was to work for his cousin, she was a little uncertain just how she should behave toward him. She need have had no such doubts, however, for he seemed to have the situation well in hand. "You are to work for us! Mmm!" He kissed the tips of his fingers extravagantly. "Oh, I am so ... *molto felice!*"

"Thank you, *signore.*"

She was very conscious of a knowing and slightly resentful gleam in the secretary's eyes as he watched them, and wished, at the moment anyway, that Paolo Veronese would be less Latin in his enthusiasm. It had been he, of course, who was responsible for her having the job, but she needed no second guess at what had prompted the generous gesture. It showed clearly enough in the warm dark eyes that looked down at her so meaningly.

"I must show you our gardens," he told her, and Storm saw the frown that marred Rafael Caldorini's good looks, forestalling her own objection.

"But, *signor,*" he interposed softly, "I was told. . . ."

"I will bring the *signorina* to the study when we are ready, Rafael," Paolo Veronese informed him loftily. "You need not wait."

"*Si, signore.*" A slight bob of the black head acknowledged defeat, and the secretary disappeared back up the stairs to the shadowed gallery behind them.

Paolo smiled down at her, well pleased with his minor triumph, but Storm was less happy about the secretary's dismissal. There was the question of what Alexei Romano would have to say about her disobeying his instructions on her very first day, and she was not happy about it.

"You do not mind that I sent him away, *signorina?*"

His confident smile dismissed the very idea of her objecting, and she was unable to resist a smile in the face of his bold, persuasive charm. He was almost as self-confident as his cousin but much less aggressive and arrogant.

She shook her head, pushing back the tawny hair from her forehead with one hand. "I'm flattered, Signor Veronese, but I really should have gone with Signor Caldorini. Signor Romano will probably be very angry with me for not doing as he instructed, and on my very first day here."

Paolo Veronese made a rueful face, his hands in resignation. "I suppose you are right," he admitted. "But first, *signorina. . . .*" He took her two hands in his own and lifted them to his lips, his mouth warmly pressed to her fingers. "First you will agree to call me Paolo, yes?"

"I . . . I don't know." She felt an insistent tapping at her ribs where her heart responded to that very Latin gesture, and the brown fingers that squeezed hers gently. "I'm not sure that Signor Romano would approve."

"Ah, *assùrdo!* Why should Alexei mind if you call me by my name?"

Storm could think of no good reason why he should object, but she had no doubt that he would because he would not like her being on too familiar terms with his cousin. "I don't really know," she confessed.

"Then you will call me Paolo, yes?"

The dark gaze and the deep, persuasive voice were irresistible, and she laughed softly, unconsciously provocative. "All right, I'll call you Paolo!"

"*Bene! Bellissima!*" He kissed her fingers again fervently. "Now we go and see the gardens, no?"

"I don't think so," Storm told him, and could not resist

a smile for the genuine disappointment in his eyes. "I'm sure there's a lot to see, and—"

"And I shall show it to you, hmm? Not just the garden, but everything! The countryside, Naples . . . ah, *bellissima Napoli*!" He kissed the tips of his fingers again, his dark eyes beaming at her persuasively so that she was bound to respond.

"I'd love to see everything there is to see," she said, "and I'd like you to show me, Paolo, but I'm not sure yet how much time I'll have."

For a moment he simply looked at her in silence, then he leaned forward suddenly and kissed her lightly but firmly on her mouth, startling her into a soft cry of surprise. "Storm, *cara mia*, you worry too much about Alexei, I think. I did not get you this post so that you could spend every minute of the day and night with Gino. *Comprende?*" He swept his gaze over her face and figure and smiled. "You are much too beautiful, *cara*, to waste on a *bambino*!"

Such words had a heady effect, even though she knew quite well their meaning was only superficial, and she could feel the rapid warning thud of her heart as she sought to remain sensible, and not be swept along by something that was almost irresistible.

"But I do *work* for Signor Romano," she reminded him, and he shrugged with Latin carelessness.

"Even Alexei does not expect you to spend every minute with Gino. He will not—how is it?—eat you if you spend some time with me. In fact he will expect it in the circumstances."

In the circumstances! He had inveigled his cousin into employing her to look after the boy, but, as he said, even Alexei Romano would not be in ignorance of the real reason behind the recommendation, and she wondered suddenly if it had happened before.

"Does your cousin often take people on your recommendation?" she asked, and he looked at her steadily for a moment before answering. Then he gently stroked her cheek with one caressing finger.

"No, *cara mia*, Alexei has never before approved of my taste. You are to be congratulated!" He smiled, the gentle finger moving hypnotically against her cheek. "As for the rest of the family, they will adore you."

"The rest of the family?" She looked startled, all sorts of new possibilities arising. "How many more of you are there, Paolo?"

"Only two." He shrugged carelessly. "You cannot count Rafael, although he lives here." He raised her fingers to his lips again. "Do not be timid, *graziosa mia*, no one will trouble you. There is only Lisetta and my mama that you have not met."

She did not ask who Lisetta was, but assumed she would be either an aunt or a sister. "Oh well," she sighed resignedly, "I expect I'll get used to you all."

"*Si*, of course you will!" He caught her unawares again and kissed her mouth. "Now, if you will not see the gardens with me, we will go and find Rafael before he has time to tell Alexei about me!" It was quite obvious, she thought, that there was quite a bit of competition between Paolo and his cousin's good-looking secretary.

He took her hand and drew her with him across the hall to that rather awe-inspiring marble staircase, taking the wide steps with long familiar strides so that she was hard put to keep up with him.

The floor up here was carpeted, with thick luxurious pile into which she sank, ankle deep. She barely had a chance to notice more than the fact that the walls were white and hung with protraits, before a door opened further along the hall and Rafael Caldorini appeared.

He looked at Paolo with what Storm recognized as a

malicious gleam in his dark eyes, and he bobbed his head briefly. "Signor Romano asks that you go to him *immediatamente, signore.*"

"*Si, si, ben intéso!*" Paolo frowned and sighed as he raised Storm's hand to his lips, kissing her fingers lightly. "I will see you again soon, *cara mia. Arrivederci!*"

"*Signorina!*" Rafael Caldorini's soft voice recalled her as she watched Paolo hurry along the gallery, and she smiled at him apologetically.

"I'm sorry, Signor Caldorini. I hope you didn't have too much difficulty explaining to Signor Romano—I mean about my not coming with you the first time."

"Ah no, *signorina.*" Eloquent shoulders accepted the inevitable. "Signor Romano understands." For a moment the bold black eyes met hers and she felt the color in her cheeks at the unmistakable implication she saw there. It was obvious that, at least as far as some of the Romano household was concerned, she was another of Paolo's affairs and quite casually accepted as such.

He led her along the hall to a room that served as a study—a long, cool room, less ornate than the room she had seen downstairs yesterday.

A flickering little pattern of lights played over the high carved ceiling, and it took her a moment or two to recognize it for what it was. The fluttering, ever-changing pattern was reflected off water. Possibly a pool or a fountain, for it was much to high for the reflection to be from the sea, and there was a garden below the window.

Rafael Caldorini seated himself behind a desk in the center of the room and indicated that she should take the chair facing him. Then he shuffled for a moment or two through some papers—a gesture meant to impress her, she felt.

"Ah! Now, *signorina!*" He beamed at her across the

desk, and began to explain the financial arrangements that his employer had made for her. They were generous in the extreme and she had no complaints, but he did not once ask if they suited her, or whether she had had second thoughts about taking the post. Such a thing was not to be considered, she guessed. No one would ever refuse to work for the Romanos.

Having disposed of the arrangements to his satisfaction, he got to his feet again, bowing briefly, a wide smile on his face as if he was rather pleased with his own efforts. "I shall now take you to see Gino," he informed her. "He is waiting for you, *signorina*."

Apparently she was to be plunged headlong into her work without delay, but Storm was not prepared to be rushed along at the pace that seemed to be taken as normal in the Romano household. Whoever it was that said the Latin races preferred the principle of *manana* had obviously never had contact with Alexei Romano and his staff.

She had been a little dubious about living in the same house as Paolo Veronese, and wondered if it would be possible for her to come daily to the villa instead of living in. "I wonder, Signor Caldorini," she said, as she followed him across the room, "if it would be possible for me to stay on at the Villa Lucia for the time being."

He turned swiftly, his dark eyes regarding her for a moment in puzzled silence. "You do not wish to work for Signor Romano, after all, *signorina?*" he asked, and Storm smiled, shaking her head at his misunderstanding.

"Oh no, not that at all," she denied. "But I thought perhaps, for the time being, until I get more used to . . . to everything, I could go on staying where I am and come along here each day."

Dark brows drew together in a frown of deep concentration. "I cannot answer that, *signorina*, but if you wish me to, I will speak of the matter to Signor Romano."

Storm was doubtful that any suggestion coming from her stood very much chance of being adopted, but she smiled her gratitude for his offer. "I'd be very grateful if you'd mention it," she told him. "I'm really quite happy where I am."

She realized that the dark eyes were speculating on the extent of her gratitude, but before she had time to do more than register the fact that Rafael Caldorini was another good reason for not staying there, he was bobbing his head briefly and politely.

"*Molto bene, signorina*," he said softly.

He held open the door for her, indicating another, immediately across the hall, and leaned over to knock on it lightly. Without waiting for an invitation he opened it and he signed to Storm to go in first.

The sun was as bright as it had been in the study, but a striped awning shaded out the worst of the dazzle and extended out over a small balcony beyond an open French window. Out there she could see Gino, the little boy, sitting curled up on a white-painted reclining chair piled high with striped cushions. He looked lonely and rather bored.

He looked up when the door opened and a second later came running across the room, his small thin face curious but smiling. His huge dark eyes looked from her to Rafael Caldorini.

"*Signorina*." He bobbed his head politely. "Welcome to Villa Romano!"

Storm smiled down at him, her heart touched again by that oddly pathetic little face and the grave, grown-up welcome. No matter what his uncle said about it, she still believed that it was because he was unhappy that he looked the way he did, and she found it difficult to believe that Paolo Veronese had ever looked quite so heart-rendingly soulful.

"Hello, Gino," she said. "Didn't your uncle tell you that I was coming to look after you?"

"Ah, *si, si eccètto*. . . ." He shrugged off whatever it was that concerned him, and took one of her hands, pulling her across the room and out on to the balcony to where he had been sitting. "Signorina Gavin, *desidero andare—*"

Storm placed a gentle finger over his mouth. "You have to speak English, Gino," she told him. "I don't speak Italian."

Once more the black head bobbed, "I am sorry, *signorina*."

Storm turned and saw the secretary still standing just inside the room, watching them, and she smiled. "Thank you, Signor Caldorini. You won't forget to mention that matter to Signor Romano, will you?"

"*Certamente, signorina!*"

She smiled again and immediately reminded herself that she must not be too encouraging, when she saw the quick, dark glow in the man's eyes. "Thank you."

The black head bobbed in the customary brief bow and white teeth showed briefly in a wide smile across the olive-skinned face. "*Grazie, signorina.*"

Gino offered her his seat with a flourish she felt would have been worthy of Paolo Veronese at his most gallant, and she accepted it with a slight inclination of her head, looking down at the garden below the balcony.

It was terraced to fit into the steepness of the cliff side, but it flourished on that dark fertile soil as the farmers' crops did. There were shading trees around a pool with white stone seats surrounding it, the water making the same shifting light patterns on this ceiling as they had in the study.

Geraniums and roses spilled in profusion everywhere, crowding the steps and the edge of the pool. Dark, plume-topped cypresses looking almost black in contrast to the bright sun and myriad colors around them. There were even one or two white marble figures, slender, rounded goddesses with heads bowed coyly, half-hidden behind the yellow, fluffy boughs of mimosa.

The whole thing stood above the blue Mediterranean like a floating paradise, and Storm thought she had never seen anything quite so beautiful in her life. It was cool and lovely and very inviting on such a hot day.

"Signorina Gavin!" Gino was tugging at her arm, reminding her that he was there, and she turned back to him with a smile. "You are going to stay?" he asked.

Storm put down her handbag beside the seat, and put an arm round his thin little body, drawing him close. "I hope so, Gino," she said. "If we get along together."

"And we will have—fun, no?"

"I hope so," Storm agreed, wondering just how much he was in the picture, and how much she was expected to tell him about his uncle's plans. "But we must work too."

He half leaned against her, looking up with those huge, persuasive dark eyes, then he smiled. "We will go sailing, *si, signorina*?" he said softly. "I have friend with a fishing boat and he say he will take me sailing one day."

It seemed a pity to have to disappoint him so soon, but she doubted if Alexei Romano would approve of his nephew going sailing in one of the fishing boats, and it seemed pretty obvious too that he expected her to amuse him rather than teach him.

"Perhaps," she allowed vaguely. "But for the moment there are other things to think about, Gino. Can you count, for instance?"

It was evident that this was the first obstacle, and Storm recognized it with a brief sigh. There was a definite suggestion of a sulk about that full lower lip and, sad little boy or not, she began to suspect that Gino had quite a lot in common with his autocratic uncle. He disliked not having things his own way.

"Why do I have to learn to count?" he demanded, and Storm smiled.

"Because everyone has to," she explained patiently. "You want to grow up and be able to run the business like your uncle does, don't you?"

Gino shrugged, rebellion in his eyes. "I would rather go sailing," he insisted firmly.

"I'm sure you would." She was tempted by the appeal of those huge eyes, but knew she had to be firm if they were to make any progress at all. "But we have work to do, Gino."

"And if I do not *wish* to work?" There was speculation and a look of challenge in his eyes that reminded her again of his uncle. There was altogether too much of Alexei Romano's implacable will in this seemingly frail little boy, which probably meant that he took after his father, and she sighed inwardly at the prospect before her.

"If you do that, your uncle will send me away," she told him quietly, and Gino considered that for a moment.

"*Si, molto bene*," he agreed gravely at last. "I work."

She had no time to express approval of the decision, before the door opened, and Gino was off in a moment, flying across the room in a flurry of arms and legs.

"Zio Alexei, Zio Alexei!" he cried as he flung himself at his uncle, and Storm got to her feet, annoyed to find herself feeling quite ridiculously nervous and wondering why Alexei Romano should have such an effect on her.

He was not dressed for riding this morning, but wearing a light gray suit and a white shirt that served to emphasize the dark bronze color of his skin. That irresistible magnetism she had experienced yesterday struck her again like a blow when he walked across the room.

"*Calmo, piccolo!*" One large hand ruffled the boy's hair and he spoke softly, gently in Italian. "Miss Gavin."

He stood in front of her, his hand still on the boy's head, his feet slightly apart, a stance that somehow made him look even more overpowering. The slim-fitting trousers emphasized lean hips and strong muscular legs and the jacket swung open showing a shirt of fine white silk, like the one he had worn yesterday, and which again showed the shadowy darkness of his body through its fine texture.

There was more speculation than coldness in the light eyes at the moment, although she thought he was here in response to her request to Rafael Caldorini. He made no secret of his inspection of her pale green sleeveless dress and the lacy white shoes that complemented it and once again she was made conscious of the fairly low neckline and put up a hand in a gesture that was almost defensive.

He looked at her steadily until her heart was rapping at her ribs as she waited for whatever he had to say. "You wish to alter the arrangements I have made, I understand," he said.

"No, not exactly," Storm denied, shaking her head. "Actually we made no arrangements about where I should stay, *signore*. At least nothing was said to me about them."

"You dislike your room here?"

She shook her head. "I haven't seen my room, Signor Romano."

She suspected that the way those dark brows drew together boded ill for Rafael Caldorini, and wondered if she had been a little unfair to him.

"Then you have not brought your luggage with you?" She shook her head. "I will send someone for it, *signorina*."

"But I thought it might be possible for me to stay on at the Villa Lucia for a while," she ventured.

"You are perhaps fearful for your reputation?" The question was put in a soft voice, steel-edged, so that she was left in no doubt of his opinion, or what the outcome of the request would be.

"No," she denied, and would have said more, but was given no chance.

"You need not be concerned," he told her. "There are two other ladies in the house as well as the servants."

"I know, but—"

"If it is not the moral aspect that troubles you," again he interrupted her, "then why do you wish to change the arrangements I have made? You are accustomed to living in the house of your employer, are you not?"

"Yes, yes, of course I am." She was annoyed to find herself so pliable, so unwilling to insist on her own opinions. "I didn't intend making a major issue of this, Signor Romano, I just thought—"

"Whatever you thought, Miss Gavin, it is out of the question." He pushed one hand into a trousers pocket, relaxed and yet fully confident that he was in full command of the situation. "I am employing you to take care of Gino at all times—day and night."

"Oh, but surely," Storm protested, "I get *some* time for myself!"

"Naturally," he agreed calmly. "Once Gino is in bed for the night, there will be little call upon your services and you may then do more or less as you please. But you will never stay away from the villa all night, no matter what your reason, is that quite clear?"

Somehow he made her possible reasons for staying

away at night sound far from the innocent one behind her request and she looked at him challengingly from beneath her long lashes. "I don't like what you're implying, *signore*," she told him. "I had no intention of living *here* and staying out all night, and I resent the suggestion that I would."

The ice blue eyes surveyed her coolly for a moment and she found her own gaze lingering on that strong, firm jaw and the deep cleft in the square chin. She found Alexei Romano fascinating to a degree that disturbed her intensely. "I assume you will be spending quite a lot of time with my cousin when you are not with Gino," he said quietly. "I have no doubt about his powers of persuasion, Miss Gavin. I am therefore insisting that you move into the Villa Romano and that you return here at a reasonable hour every night."

"Where you can keep an eye on me!"

The angry retort was almost involuntary, but she was fighting a chaos of emotions and hardly knew what to think. She was angry, partly because she objected to being treated in such cavalier fashion, but also because she knew she would comply with his demands, sooner or later.

He held her angry gaze for a second in silence, then raised a brow in acknowledgement. "Exactly!"

Her resentment showed plainly in her eyes as she faced him, her hands trembling so that she clenched them tight at her sides. "I dislike having my way of life dictated to me, Signor Romano," she told him, her voice shaking. "I understood that slavery had been abolished, but judging by your behavior, you still seem to be living in the Middle Ages, thinking you have the *droit du seigneur* over your employees!"

She felt a sudden shiver of panic as he stood there towering over her, and the look of savagery she had glimpsed on their first meeting was nothing to the expression that now showed taut and fierce on the hard, sculptured features. The ice blue eyes were narrowed above those high cheekbones, and hard as blue steel.

"You will apologize, *signorina*!" His voice too, was as cold as ice, but still did not rise above its normal quiet pitch and she marveled at his self-control. She would have refused, angrily, but something about this man filled her with emotions she had never experienced before, so that she was no longer sure of her own strength of will, and she stayed silent. "Very well!" His mouth was a tight straight line. "It is your own choice, Miss Gavin."

For one panicky moment she wondered if he was going to strike her, but then Gino chose to intervene. His small, thin face looked puzzled and more soulful than ever as he looked up at his uncle and tugged at the sleeve of his jacket.

"*Zio Alexei, che c'è?*" he asked, but the icy gaze did not shift from Storm.

"*Stia calmo*, Gino," he told the boy quietly.

Gino, however, was not prepared to keep quiet. He was curious as well as a little apprehensive, and he was enough of his uncle's nephew to want to know what he was going on. He tugged at the jacket sleeve again, raising his voice.

"*Zio, che cosa é successo?*" he demanded.

The man's stern features softened for a moment and he looked down at him. "*Niente affato, piccolo*," he said softly, and put a consoling hand on his head. "*Stia calmo, per favore.*"

"*Signorina?*"

Gino looked at her, frowning. He had probably never

seen anyone defy his formidable uncle before, and he knew well enough which one of them was going to have to back down. He was merely reminding her, trying to have the episode over and done with.

Storm still hesitated. She did not want to leave and admit defeat so soon, but she was not sure that she was ready to eat humble pie either, and she must do one or the other now. Alexei Romano was looking at her again, waiting, and she felt a shiver along her spine again.

"*Signorina?*"

He echoed Gino's one-word question and it left the decision squarely with her. Without quite knowing what to do or say next, she stood there without moving, sensitive to every breath he took, and amazed at her own reaction to him as a man.

It seemed quite incredible that she should even consider backing down, but she knew she was bound to and she took a deep breath. "I'm . . . I'm sorry, Signor Romano."

"*Bene!*" he breathed softly, and she could have sworn that a glint of relief showed briefly in his eyes.

As for Gino, he obviously approved of the outcome and for a moment Storm felt like laughing hysterically at the whole unbelievable episode. She would never have acted with such compliance last year at this time, in fact she would have immediately walked out and never come back. Her independence had always been dear to her, and yet here she was ready to swallow her pride so that she could remain in the employ of a man who behaved as if he had the power of life and death over her.

For a moment, as he leaned across to ruffle the boy's hair, his hand came in contact with her bare arm and she felt her pulses leap in response to his touch, drawing back instinctively. He looked at her steadily, closer now, and with a curious expression in his eyes. "I beg your pardon, *signorina*," he said softly.

Storm said nothing, but tried to steady her heartbeat as it thudded wildly at her ribs. There was so much more than his arrogance that she was going to have to cope with, if she stayed on at the Villa Romano, and she wondered if she was biting off more than she could chew.

CHAPTER FOUR

It was a relief to Storm to learn that both the ladies of the Romano household were away for the day, so she would not have to meet them, at least for a while. Signora Veronese, Paolo's mother, was away visiting her married daughter, and the mysterious Lisetta had an appointment with her dressmaker in Naples.

As both Paolo and Alexei Romano spent the rest of the day at the works in Naples, Storm lunched alone with Gino in their makeshift schoolroom overlooking the garden. Dinner with Paolo, Gino and her employer proved more of an ordeal in the grand surroundings of the villa's dining room. She was thankful that at least she was spared the addition of two ladies who would probably disapprove of her being there at all.

If they were as close-knit a family as Paolo claimed they were, the women of the family might well resent a stranger living with them, especially if she was a foreigner and taking charge of a child they were fond of.

Rafael Caldorini had informed her that she would be living as part of the family. Gino had never been relegated to a nursery, so there was nothing she could do about sharing her meals with the family. Feeling as she did at the moment, she decided she would have been more at home in the company of the domestic staff.

Her luggage was brought from the Villa Lucia during the morning and put in her room, as Alexei Romano had promised. She supposed she should have been perfectly happy, but the thought of living *en famille* in a household that included Alexei Romano was surely daunting enough for anybody.

462

She retired to her own room as soon as she had put Gino to bed, much to Paolo's disappointment, for he had had plans for them to spend the evening in Naples, dancing. She felt she simply had to have time to breathe, some time to herself, and Paolo was not the most placid of companions.

She could find no fault with the room she had been given. Indeed, she was delighted with it. Like every other room she had seen so far, it was luxurious. It was surprisingly feminine, so that she wondered who its last occupant had been.

The high ceiling was richly ornamented with scrolls and gilt curlicues and it made her feel, yet again, as if she had stepped back several hundred years in time. A high wide window opened above the garden and the pool. Soft rugs, deep piled, and, unbelievably, a lace-draped bed, all seemed to her to be slightly unreal, and she lay there in the morning cool the following day wondering how it all came to happen.

Who would have believed that three weeks ago when she left Mrs. Marley's in Surrey, she would so soon be living in a villa in Italy, *and* getting very generously paid for it? It was still a bit difficult for her to believe it all, and she only hoped she would not suddenly wake up and find it all a dream.

The thought that clouded her waking peace this morning was the idea of meeting the two women of the household. It would be too optimistic to hope that neither of them would be a female version of Alexei Romano, and Storm pulled a face in sympathy with herself as she got out of bed.

Gino declared himself not yet ready to get up when she looked in on him, and she decided that it could do no harm to leave him where he was for a while. He had already informed her that he never ate anything in the mornings. For herself, she was more than ready for rolls and coffee and she went downstairs.

The kitchens, she knew, were on the ground floor, and she started down the marble staircase, after a swift look around to make sure that there was no one else about. It might just be possible to appease her hunger without having to appear at the breakfast table.

She was no more than halfway down the stairs, however, when she heard the sound of a door closing somewhere, and a moment later someone called her from the gallery. "Miss Gavin!"

Turning swiftly, she looked up at the dark, inquiring face of Alexei Romano and half smiled, her fingers curling instinctively into her palms at the sight of him. "Good morning, Signor Romano!"

"Are you going out?"

She shook her head, unwilling to tell him that she had been bent on seeking food from the kitchen rather than sit at the breakfast table with him and his household. "No, *signore*, I was . . . I was. . . ."

"We always breakfast on the terrace. You do not know the way?"

Why did he never let her finish a sentence? It was no use trying to lie to him and she certainly had no intention of telling him the truth, so she merely shrugged—a Latin gesture that she was beginning to find increasingly useful.

In a moment he was beside her on the stairs, one hand under her arm, his palm warm on her bare flesh, which sent that inevitable tingling sensation through her as she walked beside him down the rest of the stairs.

"I will introduce you to the two ladies," he told her. "It is well I caught up with you. Paolo, I suppose, is not down yet."

"I don't think so. I haven't seen anything of him."

Her expression must have betrayed how she felt at the prospect of meeting the two women, for he looked down at her with a small frown of curiosity, but said nothing for the moment. It was when they stepped down on to the cool tiled floor of the hall that he curled his fingers around her arm and brought them both to a standstill. She looked up inquiringly to see a half smile softening the stern lines of his mouth.

"What is it that troubles you?" he asked, and Storm shook her head hastily.

"I . . . I just feel rather as if . . . as if I'm being led to the slaughter," she confessed, again visualizing a feminine form of him, and trembling at the prospect.

"So?" The strong fingers tightened their hold, digging into her soft flesh. "You are not being thrown to the lions, *signorina*. We no longer throw our slaves to the wild beasts to be torn to pieces for our amusement. Have no fear!"

It was a studied and deliberate reference to her rash accusation of yesterday. She looked up at him, her green eyes reproachful, trying to stop the alarming force with which her heart beat at her ribs. It was confusing how the touch of his hand could play such havoc with her emotions and at the same time reassure her.

"I'm nervous enough, Signor Romano," she told him, her mouth pursed softly. "There's no need for you to try and make me more so."

"I did not intend to." He looked down at her for a moment in silence, his hold on her easing, the fingers moving slowly and soothingly on her arm and playing havoc with her senses. Then the chiselled features softened into a smile again. "No one will eat you, I promise!"

"That's what Paolo promised about you!" Storm retorted without thinking. "And I'm not sure I believe either of you!"

Blue eyes regarded her steadily for a moment and the caressing movement of his fingers stilled again. "You may believe us both with confidence, Miss Gavin. But I do not relish the idea of being discussed by you with members of my family, especially in a derogatory manner."

"Oh, but we weren't—"

Her words were cut short when he suddenly put a hand under her chin and raised her face sharply. His fingers spread to hold her firmly while she bore the scrutiny of those blue eyes with a fluttering sensation of panic.

"Always you argue with me," he said softly, as if the fact both annoyed and intrigued him. "No one else argues with me, *signorina*, not if they are wise. Why do you persist in doing so?"

"Because I don't think any man has the right to absolute power over others!" She spoke far more bravely than she felt, and with one hand tried to release her chin from that iron grip. "Please don't hold me like that, you're hurting me!"

A small, tight smile touched his lips for a moment and deliberately the fingers tightened their hold briefly before releasing her. "I could hurt you much more," he said. "Remember that, *signorina*, hmm?"

Storm made no reply, but rubbed gently at the marks his fingers had left on her skin, her eyes wary and puzzled. "Signor—"

"You *will* have the last word, will you not?"

He gave her no time to retort to that one, but took her arm again and led her across the hall, under the gaze of those erotic creatures of fantasy that smiled down at them from the painted walls.

The double doors in front of them led into the big room she had seen on her first visit. He did not go straight in. Instead he stopped again, one hand on the ornate gold handle, looking down at her steadily. She gasped in audible surprise a second later when the soft, deep sound of laughter startled her into stillness.

"You look so much as if you expect to be devoured, Miss Gavin, and I assure you it is not so." For what seemed like an eternity he studied her in a way that set her pulses racing wildly, and she almost cried out when he reached out and touched her face gently where the grip of his fingers still tingled on her skin. "I suppose I may not call you Storm, as Paolo does?" he suggested softly, but gave her no time to reply before he shrugged and shook his head. "Come! Let us go in."

Storm was trembling as she walked across that big, beautiful room again. The carpet, richly woven in red and gold, contrasted with the white walls and that wonderful white marble fireplace she had so admired. The last time she had not noticed several paintings around the walls, dark and somber in contrast to their surroundings, looking down at her with bold dark eyes that reminded her more of Paolo Veronese than the man beside her.

With barely time to glance around her, she was led toward the wide open French windows and out on to a paved terrace, cool and shaded in the morning sun. The garden smelled fresh and lovely and she could see the glitter of the sea far below, that deep, deep blue as only the Mediterranean can be.

A white wrought-iron table was set for a continental breakfast with coffee, rolls and fine porcelain jars of jam. Two women were already seated at the table, and at the sight of them Storm swallowed hard.

One of them looked just as she had feared they both would. Stern and unbending, if her expression was anything to judge by, dressed in all-enveloping black, despite the warmth of the sun. It was to this unpromising prospect that Alexei Romano took her first.

"This is Miss Gavin, Aunt Sofia." Thank heaven he introduced her in English. "Miss Gavin, my aunt, Signora Veronese."

So this was Paolo's mama! Storm would never have attributed such an extrovert son to this stern, unfriendly woman, except that there was some facial likeness somewhere.

Her black hair was well streaked with gray and drawn back from a face that could never have laid claim to beauty, and yet bore a quite definite resemblance to Paolo's good looks. A tight-lipped mouth, Storm felt, disapproved of almost everyone, though there was nothing personal to her in its censure.

"*Signora.*" The hand Storm offered was pointedly ignored, and the unfriendly dark eyes openly suspected her of conniving her way into the villa simply to be near to Paolo. It would never occur to her to suspect that the opposite was the fact.

Storm turned from her with relief, for her companion looked quite another matter. She was already smiling, one long slim hand extended in greeting, when they turned to her, and shrewd but kindly dark eyes welcomed her.

Her hair was so red that it was impossible to suppose that it was other than artificial, but her face, despite some obvious signs of aging, was still lovely, and at least it was free of artifice.

"Lisetta!" Alexei Romano leaned over her, one arm lightly about her shoulders in a gesture of affection that surprised Storm. "This is Miss Gavin, Lisetta. Miss Gavin, the Contessa Luisa Berenitti."

"Oh, but, Alexei *caro*, how enchanting!" She winked an eye at Alexei before smiling again at Storm. "Welcome to our family, Signorina Gavin, we have heard so much about you. *Dio!* But you have caused such . . . *eccitamento* among our young men! Eh, Alexei?" She used expressive hands to enlarge her meaning and her eyes rolled as she laughed delightedly. Not for the Contessa the dullness of black; she wore a bright green summer dress that revealed plump bare arms to the shoulders. Her bright curious eyes smiled up at Storm encouragingly. "You will like being with us, *signorina?*"

Storm nodded, a little overwhelmed by the woman's bold, bright character. Storm liked her just the same, and was glad that she was such a complete contrast to Paolo's deterring mother. "I hope so, Contessa."

"And you are to take care of our *piccolo, si?*" The red head tilted to one side, the bright eyes inquiring. "He is a charming *bambino*, our Gino, no?"

"He's a dear little boy," Storm agreed willingly. "We get along very well together so far."

"*Bene!* He will adore you too." Again that uninhibited laugh shrilled out and she glanced at her sober neighbor with wickedly twinkling eyes. "Like his uncle, *si?*"

Quite forgetting for the moment that Gino also called Paolo his uncle, Storm turned and looked up at Alexei Romano with wide, startled eyes, and to her surprise and dismay saw that the usually icy blue eyes were warm with laughter.

"Gino also calls Paolo his uncle," he reminded her softly, and she felt the warm, bright color flood into her cheeks again. She had never felt such a complete fool in her life, and she supposed that it was inevitable that the one time she had seen Alexei Romano laugh, it had to be at her expense.

The Contessa's dark eyes had missed nothing of the byplay and they flicked from Alexei to Storm swiftly, then she pulled a wry face. "Oh, but of course I meant Paolo! *Mi spiace, signorina!*"

Sorry or not she was amused by the mistake, and Storm wondered how on earth she could have been so idiotic as to make it. "Oh, please don't think. . . ." She sought to explain, knowing she had attempted the wrong thing as soon as she spoke. "It was . . . I mean I. . . ."

A long finger was laid firmly across her lips and she raised startled eyes to see Alexei Romano shaking his head at her slowly, that warm glimpse of laughter still lingering in his eyes. "*Quieto, po'oca!*" he said softly, and the Contessa smiled.

"You are not yet used to us, *signorina*," she smiled kindly. "You will soon accept our ways and forget about being so. . . ." Expressive shoulders consigned her English reserve to the things best forgotten.

Storm liked the Contessa, although she was none the wiser, even now, as to who or what she was to the family, or even if she was one of them. Alexei had given her no other title than Contessa. Whoever she was, Storm decided, she would make a valuable ally in times of stress.

The next few days passed rather like a dream for Storm, although Gino kept her on her toes with his constant barrage of questions about England. He wanted to go there one day, he confided; his Uncle Alexei had been and he liked it.

The latter rather surprised her, for she could not see the English temperament appealing to Alexei Romano at all, unless she had misjudged him badly. Paolo, she knew, had never been to England, for he made much of the fact that he had never been to the country of her birth. Paolo

was given to making extravagant and emotional statements like that, and she was learning to take them in her
stride.

He had arranged to take her to see the famous Bay of
Naples, and she had breathed a sigh of relief when Gino
went to bed without too much fuss, giving her more time
to bath and change. She surveyed the result in a long
mirror and smiled at the sense of unreality the reflected
bedroom always gave her.

The reversed picture of the lace-draped bed and gilt-
scrolled ceiling, with the high, curved window, gave even
her own reflection a dreamlike quality. A sleeveless dress
in turquoise blue softly flattered her figure and made her
tawny hair look almost gold, and her green eyes almost
jade. It was a very pleasant picture altogether.

She swung her shoulder length hair back from her face
and smiled at her reflection. The Italian sun had already
given her a soft tan and she refused to disguise it with
makeup so that her skin had a natural glow.

Leaving her own room at last, she quietly opened
Gino's door and found him still looking at the picture
book she had left him with. He beamed a smile at her and
she opened the door wider and went across to him,
shaking her head at him.

"You are going out with Zio Paolo?" he asked, his
bright dark eyes approving of her dress and the burnished
softness of her hair. There was something disturbingly
adult about Gino sometimes that reminded her of Paolo.

"We're just going for a ride," she told him. "And I
think it's high time you went to sleep, young man."

He made no objection when she took the book from
him but sat curled up in his bed like a little black-eyed
gnome, his small gamin-like face bright with mischief and
not a bit sleepy. "Zio Paolo he is. . . ." His hands and

expressive rolling eyes conveyed his meaning all too clearly, and as only a Latin could, even one as young as Gino. "*Molto amoroso, si, signorina?*"

"Gino!"

Her voice held a warning note, but she struggled with the laughter that rose to her lips and Gino knew it. "You like Zio Paolo, *si*?" he insisted, and Storm pulled back the covers and pulled him down in the bed.

"Sleep!" she told him.

"*Si*, Signorina Gavin!" He lay back on his pillows, the light bedclothes up under his chin, and when she turned in the doorway to smile at him, he winked an eye expertly. "*Ciao!*" he said softly, and his black eyes danced wickedly above the edge of the sheet.

The ride along the coast road to Naples was wonderful. The beautiful Amalfi expressway provided breathtaking scenery all the way from Naples to Salerno, right round the Sorrento peninsula. It was well worth a long drive, but this evening they had to make do with the section of it from Bellabaia to Naples.

Storm had less time to appreciate it than she would have liked because Paolo drove so fast, careering along at a hair-raising speed. There was so much to look at that she was tempted to suggest that he drive a little more slowly, but she hesitated to say anything.

Acres of citrus groves, oranges, lemons and limes, sweetly scented; apples, pears and peaches too, all grew in this rich fertile soil. Storm had noticed, at intervals, what looked like little straw roofs over the tree tops and asked Paolo about them. He laughed, apparently only too pleased to air his knowledge.

"The *pagliarelle?*"

She cocked her head to one side, not attempting to repeat the name. "Is that what they are? What are they for?"

"To protect the fruit, *cara mia*, what else?" His smile teased her. "Even here we can have unexpected bad weather, you know. *Tempesta!* Like you, *bella mia*, only that sort of storm can ruin the harvest!"

Storm gazed up at the clear evening sky, finding it difficult to visualize the weather here as anything but perfect. "I find it hard to believe there could be storms here."

"Ah, but it is true, *cara!* How else would anything grow? We have to have rain sometimes."

She leaned her head back against the seat and sighed with sheer contentment, feeling more relaxed than she had for days.

The countryside was like one vast orchard, the rich, dark soil producing crop after crop of oranges and lemons, and almost every other fruit imaginable, with neat acres of tomatoes, cauliflowers and onions in between. It was, as she said, too good to be true, a veritable garden of Eden with the wide fast expressway leading to Naples and the markets of the world.

The road swept along the cliff tops, and gave breathtaking glimpses of the deep blue Mediterranean beyond the groves on the cliff face, and beyond those acres of trees on the other side. Hazy glimpses of hills included the promise of Vesuvius somewhere ahead of them. Storm felt she could have gone on for ever.

Before long, however, the fertile stretches began to give way before the first signs of industry. Fat, round tanks of oil refineries, and towering cranes in shipbuilding yards broke the skyline instead of trees. This was quite a different character from the picture of Italy as she had visualized it. There was even a cement works with its white dust falling over everything.

It was the new, more ruthless side of the country that she supposed gave Alexei Romano, and others, their immense wealth, but had little appeal for Storm. It was, however, interesting to discover that so much industry existed in a place she would never have expected it.

She was happier when they left the industrial belt behind them and ran down towards Naples itself. The view from the top of a hill was every bit as wonderful as she had been led to expect.

The famous bay looked huge and sparkling deep blue in the evening sunshine with terrace upon terrace of little houses. Many of them were multistoried and of varying shades of white, scattered in the hills behind the city, with Mount Vesuvius sitting menacingly in the background.

Hot, flamboyant and exciting, all those words came into her mind as she looked down at Naples through the trees, and her heart was suddenly beating even more rapidly as Paolo took the car plunging down toward it, creating a fresh cool breeze moist from the sea.

"It's . . . wonderful!"

Paolo turned his head briefly and looked at her, smiling and well pleased with her reaction. He took the car into the side of the road, a rather hazardous thing to do on such a road. He braked to a halt high above the city. "So," he said softly. "You like Napoli, yes?"

"It looks marvelous!"

"Shall we go down?" His dark eyes were warmly persuasive and she mentally hardened her heart to resist the inevitable plea. "We could go to a night club, *cara mia*. Dance a little, maybe a little *romanza, si?*"

"I don't think so, Paolo." She still had Alexei

Romano's warning in mind, about getting back at a reasonable hour and how Paolo would probably persuade her otherwise. But the hint of hesitation in her voice was her undoing.

Paolo leaned across and touched her cheek lightly with a caressing finger. "Why are you so afraid to come with me, *bellissima?*"

"I'm not afraid," Storm denied, smiling despite the flutter in her heart. Paolo might not have his cousin's forceful magnetism, but he was quite effective in his own right, and very hard to resist.

"Afraid of Alexei, then?"

His eyes challenged her to deny it and she lowered her gaze, unwilling to debate that point. "Not exactly afraid," she told him. "But I do have to mind my p's and q's, Paolo."

"Your. . . ." He dismissed the unfamiliar phrase with the inevitable shrug, intent on persuading her. "Forget about Alexei. Come and dance with me, *carissima*, hmm?"

It was inevitable, of course, and Storm sighed as she yielded. "All right, Paolo," she said. "I'll come and dance."

"*Bene!*" He leaned across and kissed her lightly on her mouth, content to have his way.

Down in the city itself, the life and bustle in the teeming streets was almost overwhelming, but Storm was carried along on the tide of excited and good-natured banter that followed their progress through the narrow streets from the waterfront.

It was the old Naples she was seeing, a city of rich, florid buildings, heavily and almost rakishly endowed with rich carvings and fluted columns, reaching up above the narrow streets to the clear blue sky. Some of them were shabby with age, some slowly decaying, but still impressive, beautiful and used.

Even the tall, once proud *palazzos*, which had housed the wealthy and influential of another age, now gave shelter to whole families in their vast basement rooms. Families who lived close and called vociferously and cheerfully to one another in friendly argument.

It was a noisy, bright and overcrowded maze of history and humanity, and Paolo seemed to know every inch of it. He drove the big car down small streets that Storm would never have dared venture along.

Soon, he took them to a much newer part, where the houses and shops were modern and much less impressive. The new Naples, Paolo told her, and she decided that they could have been in almost any city in the world. She had little time to lose interest, however, for he turned into a car park and smilingly helped her out of the car.

The night club was garish and noisy, and she was not altogether happy about being there. Paolo seemed to be known there and he was quite happy about it, so she made no comment. Whatever she felt about her surroundings, she had no complaint about her escort, for Paolo was, as always, attentive and flattering, very good for her ego and the target of a number of interested feminine eyes. The noise made her head ache, but with such an escort she had not the heart to ask him to take her home.

They were driving along the road on the way back before she fully realized how late they were, and she bit on her lip anxiously when she thought about Alexei Romano. "It's nearly two o'clock, Paolo," she said, and he shrugged carelessly.

"So, does it matter, *cara*?"

"It does," Storm told him. "I have orders to be in at a reasonable time, and I'm quite sure Signor Romano won't call two o'clock in the morning a reasonable hour."

"Orders?" He laughed shortly. "*Madre di Dio!* Alexei can be quite feudal!"

"I had noticed," Storm said. "I said as much to him once and almost lost my job."

"*Si?*" He flicked her a brief glance, his eyes almost luminous in the bright moonlight, then he shrugged. "It is his Russian mama, of course. I do not remember Aunt Natasha very well. She went off and left them when Alexei was still a little boy, but she was very Russian! Gloomy and stern, *comprende*?"

"Oh, I see, he's half Russian!" She nodded her head in understanding, her questions about his unusual features answered at last. "I wondered. There had to be something to account for those blue eyes and that wonderful bone structure."

She did wonder if she had been a little too effusive, and Paolo's next words confirmed it. "Which the ladies find irresistible," he declared with a surprising hint of envy, and Storm looked surprised.

"Do they?" Somehow she had not thought of Alexei Romano as a ladies' man despite his incredible attraction.

"He does not notice, or so he pretends!" He shrugged resignedly and Storm almost laughed aloud.

"Well, I don't think you have much to complain about in that direction, Paolo!"

"No, we have our share of good looks in the Romano family." He spoke without a trace of false modesty and she smiled to herself. Paolo was really quite refreshingly honest. "My mama was a Romano, of course. She and Alexei's father were brother and sister."

"Oh, I see." She pondered on that for a moment as they sped through the cool moonlit night, with the scents of the citrus groves heady and sweet around them.

"You're not very much alike, are you? You and Alexei?"

"No, no, I suppose not." He made the admission with a shrug. "Alexei thinks of nothing but the business—except for his precious racehorses, of course. He's so mad about them that he even helps to exercise them when he has time."

So that explained another mystery about Alexei Romano, she thought. Why he had been wearing riding clothes when she first met him. She was learning quite a bit about her employer tonight. It seemed there were any number of facets to that complicated character, and most of them intriguing.

CHAPTER FIVE

It was a quarter past two when Paolo let them into the villa, and Storm felt terribly guilty. Paolo assured her that it was not very late by his standards, and since Alexei knew she was out with him he would surely not expect her very early either.

It was very quiet in that big, ornate hall and the tiled floor whispered under Storm's light shoes as she crossed to the stairs. The lights were still on, but she was not sure that they did not stay on all night, so it did not surprise her too much. What did surprise her, however, and made her gasp audibly was to hear her name called as she prepared to follow Paolo up the stairs.

"*Signorina!*"

The one word in that harsh cold voice brought her to an abrupt halt, her eyes wide and wary as she turned. She had no doubt who called her even before she saw Alexei Romano's tall figure in the doorway of the sitting room. She wanted Paolo out of the way before he became involved in whatever his cousin had in mind for her.

"I'll see you in the morning," she whispered to him. "Goodnight, Paolo!"

"But, *cara*—"

"*Please,* Paolo!"

His instinctive gallantry made him want to stay and lend her his support, but the sight of his cousin's stern features, and with Storm's anxiety to send him away so obvious he at last made up his mind. The inevitable shrug both recognized her reasons and apologized for not staying, and he continued on up the stairs.

The tall figure in the light suit had stepped back into

the room. Storm sighed deeply as she turned from watching Paolo go, and she walked across the hall. He stood in front of the huge fireplace, dark and menacing, his hands behind his back, that square chin thrust out aggressively. When she came into the room he looked at his wristwatch.

"Is two-fifteen in the morning your idea of a reasonable hour, *signorina*?" His voice was as cold as the ice blue eyes that looked at her, daring her to offer a defence.

Storm felt a shiver run through her, suddenly cold after the long cool drive, and she put a hand to cover the top of her arm, shrugging her shoulders protectively. "I didn't realize how late it was, Signor Romano."

"No doubt in my cousin's company you lost all sense of time!"

The hint of sarcasm brought a glitter of resentment to her green eyes, but she managed to keep her voice steady. She was conscious as always of the churning sense of excitement he aroused in her. Her heart was thudding heavily and a pulse at her temple fluttered warningly.

"No, *signore*."

"Were you then delayed by an accident?"

"No, Signor Romano, I simply didn't notice the time." She looked at him as steadily as her chaotic emotions allowed. "I'm sorry if you think I've been remiss, but I did see Gino safely into bed before I left, and I was under the impression that I had done all that was required of me for the day."

"So?" The ice blue eyes condemned her without mercy. "I have to inform you, *signorina*, that less than an hour ago Gino was calling for you! He had a bad dream. He has them quite often since his parents were killed, and he was very distressed that you were not there."

"Oh, I'm so sorry!"

There seemed little else she could say in the circumstances, although she could see that he considered it no excuse for her absence. "If you had been here at a reasonable hour as I instructed you to be, you would have been able to deal with it."

"I'm—"

"Fortunately I heard him calling when I went up to my room, or he would have been even more distressed. No one else can hear him when he calls."

She knew that was true, for Gino's room was between her own and his uncle's and only the two of them were close enough to hear a cry. "I'm sorry. I really *am* sorry, *signore*. But. . . ." She hesitated to voice any criticism in the circumstances, but he could not deny the truth of what she had to say. "You could have warned me about Gino having nightmares, Signor Romano."

"It would have made a difference?"

The cold eyes dared her to confirm it, but she nodded vehemently. "Yes, of course it would!" He looked as if he was in two minds whether or not to believe her. "Now that I know," she went on, "I can arrange to always be back at a reasonable time."

"Good!" he snapped. "I am glad that at last I have managed to impress on you the importance of your duties. That you are here to care for Gino and not to amuse Paolo until the early hours of the morning."

Storm could feel her heart racing wildly as anger and frustration battled for precedence. Why would he always believe the worst of her? "You have no right to say that, Signor Romano!" She curled her hands tightly into fists at her sides. Her eyes shone like green jewels in her flushed face as she defied him.

To her surprise he did not immediately put her sharply in her place, but merely stood there looking down at her, tense and alert, a small nerve at the base of his throat throbbing rapidly. "Always you defy me, argue with me," he said softly, at last, "Will you never learn, *signorina?*"

"That you own me body and soul because I work for you, *signore?*" She stuck out her chin, angry enough to be uncaring. "You don't, Signor Romano! No one does!"

"Perhaps that is a pity!" The blue eyes, she noticed with a start, were no longer icy but full of emotion that was betrayed in the slight huskiness of his voice. The way he stood as usual with his feet slightly apart, his hands behind his back, the open neck of his shirt revealing the muscular brown throat. Every nerve in his body seemed tensed, and she felt a flicker of fear for a moment when he moved suddenly.

She stepped back instinctively, her left hand still covering the top of her right arm, hugging herself against the chill she had felt earlier, although she was glowingly warm now. He noted the instinctive move and for a moment his eyes blazed at her, as if it angered him further, then he smiled. A small, tight and quite humorless smile that did nothing to reassure her.

"Do you judge me by Paolo's standards, *signorina?*"

Storm shook her head, uncertain for a moment just what to do or say. Then she realized suddenly what he was implying and she shook her head more vehemently. "Oh no, Signor Romano, I know you have no other interests but your factory! I would not expect you to behave as Paolo would!"

She barely had time to notice the blaze of anger in his eyes before he reached for her suddenly and pulled her against him. His arms were hard and tight as steel bands, holding her so close she could feel the fast, steady beat of his heart. His mouth was hard, ruthless and passionately angry, and she would have cried out if she could.

He took no notice of her ineffective struggles, but pressed her against his lean hardness as if he wanted to hurt her. She stopped struggling at last, only pressing her hands against his chest, submitting to the chaos of emotions that filled her with both fear and elation.

When he released her at last, she did not stop to consider how she felt, nor what he would do next, but ran as fast as she could, out of the room and up the wide marble staircase without pausing. In the quiet of her own room, she stood for several seconds with her back against the door, her breathing noisy and erratic, one hand to her head, her legs feeling weak and trembling.

Why had she run? She sought an answer as she walked to the bed and sat down on it. She had never run from Paolo when he kissed her, but then she had always more or less expected it from Paolo. Alexei Romano was another matter.

She had told him that she would not expect such behavior from him, implied that he was not capable of it, and apparently he had resented it, more than she anticipated. She would not have run, she felt sure, if he had kissed her in the same spirit that Paolo did. But it had been anger that prompted him, not affection, or admiration, as it was with Paolo. Storm felt strangely bruised, in spirit as well as in body.

"You are finding us quite easy to live with, Signorina Gavin?" The Contessa's dark and mischievous eyes smiled at Storm across the dinner table, and Storm responded as she always did to the Contessa.

"I'm learning, Contessa." The brief glance she gave at Alexei Romano at the head of the table was instinctive rather than deliberate. "After three weeks, I think I'm beginning to fit into the routine now."

"*Bene!*" The Contessa too looked at Alexei, and one fine brow arched briefly. "You have chosen well for our Gino, *caro mio*. Signorina Gavin is no—how do you say, *signorina*?—country mouse, huh?"

Storm smiled. "There is such an expression, Contessa, but it's a misconception to apply it to all English girls."

"But of course," the Contessa agreed. "It is simply that a friend of mine had an English girl too, to take care of her *bambini*, and she was—oooh! *Madre di Dio!*" The expressive hands added meaning to her words. "She was such a *mouse*, that girl!"

The hard, sharp eyes of Signora Veronese expressed disagreement even before she spoke, and Storm could have guessed that she would be at variance with the Contessa's view.

"If you are referring to the nurse of the Baldonis'," she said, in her rather stilted English, "she was of excellent character, Lisetta, and not seeking to further her own cause as so many of her countrywomen are in such a position."

It was not the first time that Storm had been the target for the Signora's acid implications and she supposed it would not be the last. She caught Paolo's eyes on her and half smiled at the wry face he pulled, out of his mother's sight. The Contessa, however, was never prepared to let injustice pass without comment. She made some remark in Italian which Storm could not understand, but which brought a flush of anger to Signora Veronese's face.

For the moment her venom was redirected at the Contessa, and Storm took time to consider why the two women continued to live in the same house when they so obviously disliked one another. In the Signora's case, of course, it was as her son had quite blatantly admitted. They would be very poor without Alexei Romano's assistance, but it was more difficult to understand why the Contessa remained.

Even after three weeks at the villa, Storm had been unable to discover just where she fitted into the family tree, and she would not have dreamed of asking, no matter how curious she was. She liked the Contessa even more, now that she knew her better. She had the strangest feeling that it would embarrass her to have her status in the household defined too explicitly.

While Storm had been preoccupied with her own thoughts she was aware that a conversation was going on in Italian. It was one sharp, unmistakable word, spat out by Signora Veronese, that brought her back sharply to earth. The Signora's face was flushed and her black eyes glared viciously across the table at the Contessa, who was at the moment reaching across to put a soothing hand on Alexei's arm.

"No, Alexei *caro, per favor. Lei è molto gentile, ma, . . .*" The eloquent shoulders dismissed the insult as unimportant, although it was obvious that Alexei was less ready to allow it. His dark brows were drawn together as he looked at his aunt sternly.

"Zia Sofia!"

Storm knew that cold stern voice well enough, and she could almost find it in her heart to pity Signora Veronese, even though she had insulted the Contessa. Alexei in that angry mood was enough to deter anyone, even the Signora, for after a moment she lowered her sharp black eyes.

"*Mi spiace,* Lisetta." The apology was reluctant and made with bad grace, but it was made, and the Contessa was the first to recover her temper. She smiled at Storm and made a moue of apology.

"We are very rude to speak in Italian, Signorina

Gavin, please forgive us. But. . . ." She shrugged again. "It was perhaps as well, hmm?" The shrill but very infectious laughter warmed the chill atmosphere. "If one is to be insulted, it is as well to be so in one's own language, *si?*"

She was a really remarkable woman, Storm thought, and willingly enough joined the Contessa when she signed that she should do so, as they rose from the table. She gave a hasty glance at her charge, but saw that he was quite happy for the moment with his uncle and followed the Contessa to the cool of the garden.

The breeze from the sea was cool and refreshing. The scent of the lemons mingled with that of roses was sweet and heady, as they walked beneath the trees, in silence for a moment or two. Then the Contessa turned and looked at Storm, her red head tipped to one side, in an oddly birdlike pose.

"You do not speak any Italian at all, Signorina Gavin?"

Storm shook her head. "No, Contessa, I'd like to learn, but I don't have much time really."

"Ah, *si!*" Those expressive eyes rolled wickedly. "Paolo is busy teaching you other things, eh?" She laughed uninhibitedly, as always. "You should ask Alexei, *cara mia.* I am sure he would be very pleased to help you learn our language."

"I'm sure he wouldn't!" Storm laughed, without giving much thought to the impression she was giving, and the Contessa looked at her shrewdly for a moment.

"You do not think that Alexei has time for such things?" she asked, and Storm hesitated for a moment before replying.

"I doubt if he would consider teaching me Italian was very worthwhile, Contessa. Signor Romano does not—well, he doesn't altogether approve of me—most of the time."

"Ah! But the rest of the time, *piccola*!" She put a wealth of meaning into her eyes and Storm could feel the color in her cheeks, something that seemed to delight the Contessa, who smiled broadly.

"I work for Signor Romano, that's all," Storm said firmly. "That's *all*, Contessa!"

Her very vehemence seemed to convince the Contessa that there was something more than that, and she nodded her head. "You are a very beautiful young woman, Signorina Storm, *si?*" Storm nodded with a smile. "You misjudge my Alexei if you think he is any more the blind man than Sofia's Paolo!"

"But, Contessa—"

"Ah, no, no! I am right, you will see."

Storm could not help remembering that kiss, some two weeks ago when she had come home very late with Paolo, but that had been prompted by anger not whatever it was the Contessa had in mind, and she hoped no one else had similar thoughts on the same subject.

"You like Paolo?"

The questions sounded far more than merely idle curiosity and Storm looked at her for a moment, then nodded. "I like Paolo very much, Contessa, but there is nothing serious there, either." She smiled wryly. "With Paolo it would be foolish to expect there could be!"

A long slim hand was laid gently on her arm and the red head nodded approvingly. "I am glad you can see that, *cara*. Sofia would never allow it." She pulled a dismal face and shrugged those eloquent shoulders again. "When Paolo marries, it will be someone with much money."

It was a little embarrassing to be the receiver of such

confidences, but Storm supposed that the family took such matters in their stride. Paolo had admitted himself that he and his mother were very poor, or would be, without Alexei's help, and it would be accepted as quite logical for him to marry a wealthy girl, when one could be found who would turn a blind eye to Paolo's past record.

"I suppose marriages are still arranged sometimes?" she ventured, and the Contessa laughed shortly, the bitterest sound Storm had ever heard her make.

"Ah, *si, si, piccola mia*! They are more easily made than undone!"

"Of course." She remembered that divorce was not the easy matter in Italy that it was in most of the rest of the world.

They walked in silence for a while, then the Contessa smiled at her, one hand reaching out to touch her arm again. "I like you, Storm, *cara mia*, you—how is it? Listen well?"

"A good listener," Storm smiled, and the Contessa nodded. "*Si*, a good listener." She said nothing else for several minutes again, then spoke more slowly, as if she sought for the right words. "You wonder who it is that I am, is that not so, Storm?"

"Oh no, I—"

The red head was shaking vehemently. "It is so, *cara*, I know. You cannot think if I am an aunt or what I am to my Alexei, no?" She did not wait for confirmation, taking it for granted. "Did you know that his mama went away when he was a little boy?"

"Yes," Storm admitted. "Paolo did tell me that."

"But no more, eh?" She smiled gently. "He is much more the soft heart than his mama." Storm remembered that word spat out so viciously at the dinner table, but said nothing. "In some way it was my fault that Signora

Romano left her two little boys, *cara.* I was to blame, only partly, you will understand, but *si,* I was to blame."

"You were?" Storm stared at her uncertainly.

"She was a woman of no laughter, you understand? And I was. . . ." Those expressive shoulders described her own more youthful image as clearly as any words could have done. "I was the cause, but yet who can blame a man if he seeks laughter and a happy face? She went away, and the two little boys needed a mother. I adored them and they like me—my *bambini.* No!" She shook her head sharply, and her dark eyes suddenly misted as she remembered. "Now there is only Alexei!"

It was difficult to know just what to say after such confidences, but the dark eyes showed only sorrow for her fosterson, no resentment. She shrugged resignedly. "As you will know, *cara,* marriages are made to last in Italy, and the Signora is still alive."

"Of course, I'm sorry."

"Ah, *si piccola mia,* you too have the soft heart, more so even than Paolo, I think, but you must not feel sorry for me, *bimba.* I had some happy times with Luigi and my boys!" A long gentle hand lay on Storm's for a moment. "If one has love, there are many things one can face." That bright, rather shrill laughter shattered the stillness of the garden for a moment. "Even the scorn of Sofia!" She shook her head slowly, her eyes sad again, the expressive, mobile face uncharacteristically bitter. "Poor Gina, she was not so able."

"Gina?" The name told Storm most of what she wanted to know, and the Contessa's words confirmed it.

"Our little Gino's mama, *cara.* She was very beautiful, but Benito had less sense of what is right than Alexei. Alexei would have married her."

So Gino was not a Romano, Storm thought ruefully.

Poor Gino, as bereft of social standing as the Contessa, and yet safely housed under Alexei Romano's roof, as she was. It seemed as if every soul in the house owed Alexei Romano their love and gratitude, but only half of them really gave it.

"Gino's adorable," she said, more to try and lighten the sudden air of sadness that had descended on them than for any other reason.

The Contessa smiled. "He is *poco folletto, si?* And he is very lucky little boy too, I think. Alexei loves him like a son, he would adopt him one day, so that he can be a Romano."

"Oh, but that would be—"

"Signorina Gavin!"

The cool, familiar voice cut across her words, and she turned, a faint and disturbing sense of guilt making her flush when she looked into Alexei's light eyes. "Yes, Signor Romano?"

"Gino is waiting for you." He came across toward them, his footsteps deadened on the softness of grass, the stern lines of his face softened by the shadows thrown by the trees.

He had changed into a shirt that was almost the same ice blue as his eyes and open at the neck, showing a deep vee of strong brown throat and that soft, throbbing pulse at the base of it. As always when he came near her, Storm felt her fingers curl instinctively into her palms, and she was aware of the Contessa's dark eyes watching her shrewdly.

"I'll go to him," she said hastily, and moved off immediately, making a wide detour so as not to pass too close to him.

Quickly as she moved, it was not fast enough to avoid hearing the Contessa's rather carrying voice, scolding her fosterson gently. "Oh, Alexei, *caro mio!*" And she had no difficulty in imagining that vivid red head shaking reproachfully.

Storm lay in her bed, too hot to get to sleep. She was thinking about the lovely evening she had had with Paolo, and was glad she had managed this time to get him to come home at a reasonable hour.

She had been out with Paolo quite often since the night of four weeks ago when they had returned to the villa at two o'clock in the morning to find Alexei waiting for her. But each time it had been far later than she liked, and each time she had prayed that Gino would not have another disturbed night, and Alexei would find her wanting in her duties as nurse.

That night was firmly fixed in her mind, and she told herself that she had no wish to repeat any part of the experience, although if she was quite honest, she was not sure whether she entirely believed it.

She enjoyed going out and about with Paolo, partly because he was very good for her ego, and partly because he was such excellent company and made her laugh a lot. Also, for some perverse reason she could not quite explain, she liked to see that faint frown that sometimes appeared on Alexei's uncompromising features when Paolo chattered at the table about their outings. She felt neither Alexei nor the Signora Veronese approved of their outings.

Quite often she found herself wondering what Alexei Romano would say about some of the things they did and the places they went. He never passed comment, but she sometimes suspected he was tempted to.

She suddenly raised her head from the pillows when she thought she heard a faint cry from Gino's room. He had been safely asleep when she looked in on him before she came to bed, but he could have woken, and she must go to him if he called out.

Only once in the four weeks since that night had he had another nightmare and then, fortunately, she had been back and no one but her the wiser. Another cry confirmed her suspicions, and in a minute she was out of bed and reaching for her robe.

Another cry, this time louder and more urgent, and she opened the door of Gino's room, turning on the overhead light as she came in. "Gino!" He sat up in his bed, a tiny pathetic figure with tears rolling down his face and his huge eyes wide with some already half-forgotten fear, not really awake, nor asleep, but in a no-man's-land of fear, and seeking comfort.

He reached out his arms to her as she came near, and she sat on the edge of the bed, hugging him close, rocking gently and soothingly, a hand on his head. "It's all right, Gino, it's all right," she consoled him in a whisper. "Don't cry any more, *piccolo*. Sssh, *caro mio*!" The Italian words came instinctively to her tongue as she consoled him, and he clung to her tightly for a moment, his hands hot and anxious, his body shaken with sobs, until gradually he quietened.

"Gino?"

She had left the door open when she came into the room and she started nervously when someone spoke behind her. A tall, dark figure stood in the doorway, a deep red silk robe tied carelessly about his waist, revealing a bare muscular chest. Storm looked across him and immediately felt her heartbeat speed up rapidly as she met his anxious gaze.

"What is wrong?" he asked, and she shook her head, her face resting gently against Gino's black head.

"Gino had a bad dream," she explained, soft-voiced,

because Gino had not stirred, and she wondered if he was already half asleep again. "It's all right, Signor Romano."

"I heard him cry out."

His room was on the other side of Gino's, so it was quite feasible that he had been disturbed as easily as she had herself. She wondered too, if he had thought to check on her and make sure she was with Gino. "He was frightened." She rocked Gino gently in her arms, not daring to look at him when he came and stood beside them in a protective attitude.

"One feels so. . . ." The broad shoulders shrugged, but not carelessly; rather as if he wished he could take onto his own broad back whatever was troubling Gino and Storm felt a sudden exquisite agony of tenderness for both the man and the boy.

"He'll be all right now," she said softly, one hand still soothing Gino's hair. "I'm sorry he disturbed you, Signor Romano."

"How could you help it?"

The question was reasonable enough, she supposed, but yet she felt bound to apologize, because he held her responsible for Gino's welfare and she had once fallen short of what was expected of her. "I couldn't," she whispered back. "But I thought you were probably asleep."

She cradled the little figure gently in her arms still, and tried not to notice how the ice blue eyes of the man took note of her tousled hair and the flimsy softness of her robe and nightgown. "Were you not also asleep?" he asked, and she shook her head.

"It's too hot. I'm not used to it yet, and I closed the window earlier because it seemed cooler, now I can't open it again."

"It is never closed at this time of year," he told her, and

she smiled inwardly at the hint of criticism in his voice, even at a moment like this.

"Well, perhaps I shouldn't have touched it then, but I did feel a bit chill earlier."

"Is he asleep?" He looked down at his nephew, bending to peer at the dark little face close to her breast, and bringing his own face much too close for comfort so that she felt her pulses respond as they always did.

"I think so." She moved Gino gently back against her arm and looked down at the small face with his eyes fast closed, the remains of those fat rolling tears still on his cheeks. She gently brushed them away with a fingertip before laying him back onto his pillow. "It soon passes if there's someone to reassure him."

"And he trusts you."

She pulled the covers carefully over the sleeping boy, so as not to disturb him, and also to delay having to straighten up and find herself close beside Alexei Romano. Her pulses were thudding heavily at her ribs and her temple, and she could feel that taut sense of excitement that he always seemed to generate.

It was instinct, too, that made her bend and kiss the little boy's face before she left him, straightening up swiftly when she felt a hand on her arm. Turning away from the bed, the back of her fingers brushed the softness of silk and she shivered when the warmth of his body burned her through the thin material.

He walked just behind her to the door and he turned off the light, leaving them in the dim softness of the wall light. "Good night, *signore*." She would have turned and gone back to her own room, but he was still beside her when she reached her door and she looked up at him wide-eyed and startled.

"Your window must be opened if you are to sleep," he

told her, keeping his voice low, and she looked at him for a moment, scarcely able to believe that he was offering to do it himself.

"Oh, it doesn't matter really," she whispered. "I can manage if I stand on a chair or something; it's just the top of it that's stuck, that's all."

"I will not allow you to damage yourself or whatever it is you would choose to stand on," he informed her firmly. "I will open the window for you, then there will be no fear of broken legs, either yours or one of the chairs."

The ice blue eyes dared her to read any other reason into his offer to help and eventually she nodded, opening her door and holding the neck of her robe close up under her chin. "Thank you, *signore*," she said demurely.

He strode across the room with an air of familiarity that seemed to establish his claim to everything in it, and Storm watched as he reached the top of the obstinate window easily, without the aid of a chair or anything else. He hit it hard with the heel of his hand, then pushed it open as far as it would go, letting in the cool air from the garden.

In the short time it took him to do all that, she studied him. She noticed the way the silk robe clung to the lean, muscular length of his body, and the strong brown legs that showed from the knees down. Judging by what was revealed top and bottom of the robe, she thought it unlikely that he wore anything at all under it.

"Is that right for you?"

He swung around and looked at her so suddenly that she shook her head hastily to clear it, her lips parted in surprise, caught unawares. "Oh! Oh yes! Thank you, *signore!*"

"*Bene!* Now perhaps you will sleep."

"Thank you very much."

The blue eyes looked at her for a moment while he still stood by the window, and she would have sworn that she saw a glimpse of laughter in their depths. "That is the third time that you have thanked me, *signorina*," he said softly. "The service was really far too small to warrant such effusion!"

"I'm . . . I'm sorry."

She dared not look at him again, and she instinctively held her hands tightly together in front of her when she heard him walk across the room. He stopped in front of her and she could feel the increasing beat of her heart, alarmingly conscious of the way he was looking down at her.

Her soft tawny hair was tumbled from the pillows, and her lightly tanned skin softly flushed with pink. She stood there not knowing what to do or what to say, but increasingly aware of him as a man, and of the deep surge of excitement he aroused in her.

"Would it worry you as much if it was Paolo who was here with you?" he asked softly then, and Storm looked up at him wide-eyed and reproachful.

"Paolo would never come into my room!" she denied firmly.

"Indeed he would, if you allowed him to." The light eyes speculated as they looked down at her, and she suddenly felt herself growing angry when she suspected he was trying to trap her into an admission of some sort.

"I have no intention of allowing him to, Signor Romano!"

"Of course not."

She looked up at him suspiciously, her green eyes glowing. She had no reason to think he was being sarcastic, but her senses were alert to every hint, every word he said. She chose to read sarcasm into his denial whether he intended it or not.

"At least Paolo wouldn't come into my room without an invitation, *signore!* You wouldn't be here if you hadn't taken it upon yourself to come in. I didn't invite you!"

For a moment she had the wild idea that he might hit her, for the icy eyes blazed at her furiously. His reasons for coming to her room had been perfectly innocent, she felt sure, with only the intention of helping her, and by implying otherwise she had made him angry. The last thing she wanted to do.

"Very well, Miss Gavin!" He bowed his dark head briefly and managed to make it both dignified and autocratic, despite his unconventional garb. "Please forgive me for compromising you. Good night!"

"Oh!" Storm watched him as far as the door then, for some quite inexplicable reason, ran after him and put a hand on his arm, her heart fluttering wildly when she touched him. "Please, Signor Romano, I . . . I didn't mean, I mean I'm grateful to you for opening the window for me, but I. . . ."

He said nothing for a long moment, and Storm was shaking like a leaf while he stood there looking down at her, that irresistible excitement he generated reaching out to envelop her until she could have cried out. Then, without a word, he reached out his hands and pulled her into his arms, the unbelievable strength of him leaving her no will of her own as he crushed her against him.

His mouth was hard and demanding, angry and hurtful, as it had been last time, but she made no effort to break free for several moments, merely submitting to the wild and quite irresistible excitement that coursed through her. Then, suddenly, she became aware of some faint, almost indistinguishable sound from outside in the hall, and realized with a flick of panic that someone else was about, and that her bedroom door was wide open.

Alexei Romano too had heard whatever it was, and in a

moment he released her and strode to the doorway, looking along the dimly lit hall, but apparently he saw no one. He looked back at her suddenly, and the ice blue eyes were darkly shadowed, so that she instinctively shivered when she lowered her own eyes hastily.

"My apologies, Miss Gavin." He bobbed his head briefly again in dismissal. "Goodnight!"

Storm stood there for several seconds, her hands to her breast, her mind clear of sleep and whirling chaotically, and this time she did not call him back.

CHAPTER SIX

It was Paolo who made the first mention of Alexei's indiscretion after dinner the following day. Paolo and Alexei were seldom in at lunch time, but had their meal at the works; an idea that Paolo was not very enthusiastic about, but was wise enough not to say so within his cousin's hearing.

Storm noticed at lunch time that Signora Veronese looked rather smug, and the change of face rather troubled her, although she could not have said why. The Contessa had noticed the change, she thought, too, and would probably extract the reason for it when the opportunity arose. It was silly of Storm to bother, of course, but with Alexei Romano's visit to her room still so vivid in her mind, she supposed she felt a little guilty and more sensitive than usual.

After dinner Paolo asked her to join him in the garden. When she had seen Gino into bed, she went out to find Paolo. It was a bright golden evening with the sea below the garden a deep, deep blue and as calm as a mill pond. It was so clear that she could have sworn she could see the curve of the Sorrento peninsula in the distance.

The longer shadows of evening gave the sheltered garden a soft cool look that was enchanting, and Storm suggested that they sit beside the pool on one of those ornamental white seats.

"You look very beautiful, *cara mia*!" Storm knew that the pale blue dress she wore suited her well, and she put a tentative hand to her tawny hair and smiled. He took her hand in his, looking down at it as he lifted her fingers one by one.

"It's so much easier to *feel* beautiful here," she told him, but did not attempt to explain her meaning.

He still did not look at her, nor did he smile, and she frowned at his bowed head. She was reminded of Signora Veronese's smugness earlier, and a niggling suspicion began to rise as to the reason for both that and Paolo's reticence.

"You must look very beautiful and very sexy in your pretty pink *roba, carissima.*" He spoke softly, meaningly, and Storm's suspicions were confirmed, although she said nothing. His dark eyes looked up at last, deep and soulful, like Gino's. "Ah, *cara mia*, why Alexei? Why not me?"

She met his eyes for a moment, not wanting to believe what was in his mind, although his words made it plain enough. "You surely don't believe I asked. . . ." She shook her head vehemently. "You're wrong, Paolo, you're quite wrong!"

"Am I?" She did not really expect him to believe her and it was fairly obvious from his expression that he did not.

"Signor Romano came to my room only to open a window for me. I'd closed it earlier and it was jammed, I couldn't move it."

"I would have done it for you, *cara.*"

She shook her head. "No, you don't understand, Paolo."

"Why did you not ask me, *carissima*?" He kissed her fingers softly, his eyes dark and soulful.

Storm took a deep breath, determined to put things right. "Paolo, will you listen to me? Please? Alexei simply came and opened a window for me, there's absolutely nothing to make a fuss about."

"Storm! *Bellissima!*" He kissed her fingers again,

shaking his head slowly. "At one o'clock in the morning? But you do not have to explain to me, *cara*. I am not asking for excuses, you do not have to make them to me!" He put one hand on his heart and sighed. "That is what hurts, *carissima!*"

"Paolo! Will you stop it? You're wrong, I tell you, you're quite wrong! Now please stop making such accusations!"

She wanted to convince him, as much for Alexei's sake as her own, she realized, but no amount of persuasion would convince Paolo. It was plain that he had made up his mind, probably with the encouragement of his mother, that she had invited Alexei to her room last night for something much more serious than opening a window.

"I know you find Alexei attractive." He took her hands again and held them in his own. "It is that stern, cruel look, *si?* I told you the ladies find it attractive, did I not? But he is not for you, *bellissima*. He is not a woman's man. He will not make you happy, as I will. I could not believe it when Mama said she saw him leaving your room this morning! And yet I know she would not lie to me, not even to part me from you, *cara mia!*"

And that was exactly what the Signora had hoped to achieve, Storm thought bitterly. She had hoped to turn Paolo against her so that he would give his attention to someone more eligible. Paolo had merely expressed disappointment and was now trying to persuade her to invite him to her room instead of his cousin. Had it not been so serious it would have been laughable, and she supposed she should have been flattered by the turn of events, but instead she felt rather as if she was getting out of her depth.

"Signora Veronese misjudged whatever it was she saw, Paolo," she insisted. "Gino had a nightmare and I went in to him. His cries disturbed Alexei as well and he came in to see that Gino was all right. Then I mentioned that I was so hot because the window in my room had jammed and he came in to open it for me. It's as simple as that!''

"And he was kissing you good night?' Paolo suggested softly, and Storm bit on her lower lip. Apparently the Signora had left out nothing.

"He kissed me," she admitted reluctantly. "I don't know why exactly. He took me by surprise and, well, he just kissed me, that's all."

"You do not know why? He is a man, *bellissima*, and he means to have you for himself! That is not by any means all, *cara mia!*"

"Paolo!"

"Well, he shall not have you, you are mine!"

"Stop it!" She pulled her hands away from the tight clasp of his fingers and looked at him with bright, angry eyes, her breathing short and erratic as she sought for words to convince him. "I'm *not* yours, Paolo!"

"So!" Expressive shoulders shrugged reluctant resignation. "I have lost you to Alexei."

"No, you haven't!"

He seemed not to hear her, however, but was intent on bemoaning his plight. "I had never thought Alexei would take a mistress," he said, his dark eyes reproachful and a sulky look about his mouth. "And now he has to take *you* of all women! *Madre di Dio!* There is not justice in this world!"

"Paolo! Will you stop it!" She clenched her hands and jumped to her feet, her eyes hinting at desperation. "I have no intention of becoming Alexei's . . . you have no right to even suggest it!"

"But, *cara*," Paolo told her, his eyes sad and regretful, "he will not marry you. He is the last of the Romanos, it would not do."

"Ooh!" Too angry and frustrated for words, Storm turned swiftly and ran into the house, leaving him staring after her.

She started almost guiltily when she found Signora Veronese alone in the big drawing room. She stopped in her headlong flight, breathing shortly, her cheeks flushed with anger and exertion. For a moment she stood there in the open French doorway and looked at the grim-faced woman, noticing the gleam of satisfaction in her black eyes.

It was obvious that she was drawing her own conclusions about Storm's hasty departure from the garden and the company of her son, and was well satisfied. Storm, however, was not prepared to let her have it all her own way without making some attempt to put matters right. She had been maligned, her reputation torn to shreds by this woman and she meant her to know how wrong she had been.

Her heart was beating fast and she wondered how kindly Alexei Romano would take to a member of his family being put in her place, even if it was as much in his defence as her own.

"Signora Veronese." She swallowed hard. Meeting those unfriendly black eyes head on was not easy. "You made a mistake last night—this morning. About seeing Signor Romano, I mean—"

"I saw Signor Romano with my own eyes, *signorina*, leaving your room at one o'clock this morning." Her English was excellent, but Storm had never before heard her use it for so long, and her manner was cold, calm and implacable.

"And you told Paolo!"

"Of course! I was honor bound to inform my son that the woman he had been so generously entertaining was receiving her employer in her bedroom."

"No!" Storm's green eyes blazed furiously. "That isn't true, *signora*, and you have no right to say it!"

The tall, gaunt figure drew itself up to full height and the autocratic Romano features condemned her out of hand. "I saw for myself, *signorina*! I will not be called untruthful by a servant!"

"But you're wrong!"

A long hand dismissed her protestations scornfully. "I do not care if my nephew takes a dozen mistresses, but I will not have my son involved with such a woman, *signorina*! He now sees you for what you really are, and I trust he will be rid of his foolishness and seek a suitable match in his own station of life!"

Such arrogance, Storm thought, her brain spinning with anger and confusion. Such arrogance from a woman whose own son admitted that they lived on the generosity of the nephew she appeared to hold in such contempt was almost unbelievable. For a moment she said nothing, but stood with her hands clenched tightly at her sides, her eyes sparkling and angrily green.

"You may believe what you like, *signora*," she said at last, in a voice that sounded surprisingly calm in the circumstances. "But you are wrong in what you believe, and if you speak to Signor Romano himself about it, he will tell you so."

One dark brow rose, and the tight lips curled derisively. "You think I would be so indelicate, *signorina*? You are mistaken!"

It was useless, Storm realized when she looked at the hard, unrelenting features and the malicious gleam in the black eyes. No amount of talking would convince Signora Veronese, any more than it would her son and, after a moment, she shook her head and turned away, walking across the room with her back stiff and resentful, her head held high.

The double doors opened seconds before she got there and the Contessa came in, smiling when she saw her. Then the flushed cheeks and bright, angry eyes registered and she impulsively put out a hand to her. "Storm, *cara!*" The friendly dark eyes switched quickly from Storm to the *signora* and back again, "*Cara*, what has happened?"

It was more difficult, in the face of the Contessa's obvious friendliness, to remain calm, and Storm felt a choking sensation in her throat as she shook her head. "Oh, nothing really, Contessa, it's all right."

"*Piccola!*" Gentle hands squeezed hers sympathetically. "It is not all right when you look so distressed, as if you would cry. Tell me what is troubling you!"

From the look she sent across the room to Signora Veronese it was obvious that she knew where the blame lay for whatever it was. Storm was tempted to tell her about the conclusions that Paolo and his mother had drawn from Alexei's visit to her room. However, she was afraid she would cry if she went into too much detail at the moment, so she merely shook her head, and raised the ghost of a smile.

"It seems to be the popular conception, Contessa, that I am Alexei's mistress!" With that she turned and ran up the stairs to her room.

Storm decided that breakfast was one meal she could afford to miss, so the following morning she did not go down as usual, but spent the time with Gino in his room, and then went straight to the makeshift schoolroom. That way she could at least avoid seeing anyone but Gino until lunch time.

It was shortly before lunch, however, when the door opened, and she looked around with a blink of surprise. It was unusual for anyone to visit them, for Alexei had given instructions that they were not to be disturbed, and no one would dream of defying him, except possibly the Contessa, who had done so on a couple of occasions.

It was not the Contessa, however, but Alexei himself, and Storm's heart fluttered uneasily when she saw the dark, brooding look. Even Gino seemed to sense that this was no time to give his uncle his usual exuberant welcome, and he merely smiled at him curiously and stayed on his chair.

"Miss Gavin, will you come to the study, please?"

He gave no preliminary greeting, and hardly even seemed to notice Gino, which was unusual. Storm nodded and glanced at her watch as she slowly put down the book she had been reading.

So this was it, she thought breathlessly. This was the moment when he told her he could no longer keep her in his household, when he got rid of her as quickly as possible to prove to his aunt how wrong she was. It would have been the Contessa who told him, of course, although not with the intention of seeing her dismissed, she knew.

She managed a smile for Gino, and gave him a book of his own to look through while she was gone. "I don't expect I'll be very long," she told him, and wondered for the first time how Gino was going to take her going away. He had become very fond of her lately.

She followed Alexei across the few feet of hallway that separated the two rooms, her hands tightly curled into themselves. Her heart was heavy as lead and there was a slight sensation of sickness in her stomach as she followed him into the study.

He had apparently been in the study for some time and was without his jacket, for the big room was very warm. A pale blue shirt was open at the neck and showed a deep vee of bronze-colored throat, with that intriguing little throb of pulse at its base. The cool color of the shirt gave an even more icy look to his eyes and she could feel her heart racing wildly when he touched her arm and indicated a chair behind her.

He sat himself on the edge of the desk, one foot swinging slowly, light grey trousers fitting smoothly over long muscular legs. One hand clasped the opposite wrist and rested on a knee and the blue eyes regarded her steadily. It was a disconcerting experience that kept her own gaze downcast to the hands in her lap.

He was much too close for comfort and she could sense, as always, the indefinable feeling of excitement that he could always arouse in her, despite knowing what he was going to do and say.

He said nothing for several seconds, but took a cigarette and lit it. The smoke concealed the hard, sculptured lines of those high cheekbones and the tight, straight mouth.

"I have to commend you on the way you seem able to deal with Gino when he has those bad dreams."

It was not what she had expected to hear, and she looked at him warily, wondering if he was already unconsciously framing the words of a testimonial for her next employer.

"It only requires a little gentleness to console a frightened child, *signore*," she said softly, feeling a sudden and almost irresistible urge to cry.

"But you have such gentleness." One large hand gave meaning to the word. "Not everyone has that gift of comforting a child."

"Thank you." His delaying the moment gave her the strangest feeling, as if they were antagonists, circling one another, sounding each other out, and she wanted to shout at him to please dismiss her now and get it over with.

"You can see now why I did not want to send him to school until it was absolutely necessary?"

"Perhaps." She was not really thinking about Gino, but was anxious to hear her own future decided.

It was difficult to know exactly what went on behind that carved bronze mask of a face as he studied the fingers of one hand before speaking again. "You do not agree with me?"

She brought herself back to the subject in hand. "No, not entirely, Signor Romano."

The inevitable frown greeted even such an offhand admission, for he did not like criticism, as she should have remembered, and a dark brow flicked upward in question. "You have something more to say on the matter?"

Storm hesitated, then shook her head. "Not at this point, *signore.*" She refused to be drawn further on the matter because she felt sure he was merely delaying the moment when he had to tell her the worst.

"I see." He got up from the desk and walked restlessly across the room, pausing only briefly by the open window, then walking back again to stand looking down at her. "But you do not agree with the way I am dealing with Gino, *si, signorina?*"

It was so seldom that he sprinkled his English conversation with Italian words, as Paolo did, that she guessed he was more disturbed than he appeared on the surface. "I didn't say that," she denied quietly.

"But?" The probe was relentless, and she drew a deep breath, determined not to be drawn further.

"I don't want to say any more about my opinions, Signor Romano, please don't ask me."

He looked down at her steadily, holding her gaze. Her

hands, her whole body seemed to be trembling with some wild, uncontrollable emotion that was suddenly increased when he took a step nearer suddenly. Tall, almost menacing, he stood over her and much too close for comfort.

"You are stubborn, too," he said in a soft voice and Storm bit her lower lip anxiously.

It was unfair of him to wreak such havoc on her senses when he knew quite well what he had to do. "I'm sorry if you think so, *signore*." She was appalled at the way her voice shook, and wondered if he really knew what effect he was having on her.

He turned suddenly and walked back to the window, his broad shoulders and arrogant head silhouetted against the clear blue sky, and Storm, freed of that disconcerting gaze for a few seconds, studied him surreptitiously.

It was incredible the irresistible, almost sensual feeling of intimacy he aroused when he was near her, that blood-tingling sense of excitement that persisted no matter how she tried to quell it. She had lived in his house now for well over a month and she was still not immune to it.

He turned again, and for a moment their eyes met, then he moved back across the room and stood looking down at her again for several seconds. "It was not to talk about Gino that I asked you to come here, Miss Gavin."

"I know," she said, and her own quietness surprised her. She looked at him for a moment then hastily down again at the hands in her lap. "I guessed there was something else on your mind."

"Am I so easy to read?" The deep voice was curiously gentle.

"No, not really, but it isn't difficult to guess what's on your mind, *signore*."

He said nothing for a moment, but looked down at her

steadily, then sat himself on the edge of the desk again. "Of course you can guess," he said quietly. "I believe that my aunt has been. . . ." Broad shoulders gave meaning to the rest of the sentence. "For that I am sorry. I am afraid that I did rather more harm to your reputation than I realized, Miss Gavin."

"Oh, please don't. . . ." She knew what was going to happen next, and her heart was curled into a tight, cold little ball inside her as she sat there waiting to hear him say it. That he was sorry about her being compromised, but he was the last of a proud old family and he could not afford to have such gossip spread about him, etc. It was inevitable, she knew, and she faced the prospect bleakly.

"Unfortunately the incidence of my being in a woman's room at that hour of the night is sufficiently novel for it to have aroused more comment than if I had been. . . ." He did not complete the sentence, but it was obvious to anyone that he referred to Paolo.

Storm sat still for a moment, her head bowed, looking at the folded hands on her lap and feeling as if all the world had suddenly come to a standstill. The tawny thickness of her hair swung forward and hid her face, and she looked very small and rather defenceless sitting there on the ornate gilt chair in that big sunny room.

"You'd like me to leave, Signor Romano." It was a statement, not a question, for she told herself there could be no other answer. "Of course, I understand."

"Leave?"

She looked up hastily, something in his voice setting a new hop skipping through her heart, and she found the ice blue eyes watching her steadily and with a small frown between his brows. "I . . . I thought. . . ." The words refused to come, and instead she shook her head slowly, wondering what possible alternative he could offer.

"It was at my instigation that I came to your room, Miss Gavin." He sounded more businesslike suddenly, as if he had made up his mind about something and would not be persuaded otherwise. "You pointed out to me yourself, at the time, that you did not invite me, and therefore the onus is upon me to take the right steps to remedy the harm I have done."

"I don't understand." She got to her feet, for it was difficult to talk to him in this vein while she was sitting down, and so much out of touch with him.

"Since you said as much to the Contessa, you are fully aware that Paolo and my aunt have decided that you are my mistress, and since my aunt is not a woman to keep such gossip to herself, by tomorrow when she has visited her dressmaker again, half of Naples will know it."

Put so bluntly it sounded crude and far worse than she had feared and she felt the blood pounding wildly against her temple as she clenched her hands. "But it's ridiculous! You know it isn't true and so do I!"

"Have you tried to convince Paolo?" he asked softly, and Storm nodded, her eyes dark and unhappy.

"He didn't believe me."

"Of course not! Paolo, unfortunately, attributes more of the family traits to me than he should. He imagines that my mind travels along the same devious routes as his own."

The blue eyes had an icy look again, and she could imagine something of the beating his pride had taken at the hands of his cousin and his aunt. The accusation was not true, but the only evidence was that of Signora Veronese's malicious eyes and she would never consider giving him the benefit of the doubt, especially if she thought it would convince her son of Storm's promiscuity.

She could even imagine that Paolo would find it to his liking, in one way, to have his autocratic cousin at his mercy, trying to explain what he was doing in her room in the early hours of the morning. Paolo was charming and attractive, but he had been prepared to believe that she had invited Alexei to her room for one reason only, and had even expressed his jealousy.

"I don't know what to say, Signor Romano." She looked up at the dark, chiseled features appealingly, feeling completely at a loss. If he did not expect her to leave, what possible alternative could there be?

"It was unfortunate, to say the least, but you were completely blameless and in the circumstances I was forced to act as I thought best." He spoke in a cool, quiet voice while Storm looked at him from under her lashes, her heart uneasily tapping at her ribs as she waited. "There was very little point in denying that I was in your room at all and, since family history is very much against my visit being as innocent as it was, I have taken the only step possible."

"You have?"

She eyed him warily, green eyes anxious, one hand nervously pushing the tawny hair from her face, and he did not look at her when he spoke, but ground out the remains of the cigarette in an ashtray, with fingers that showed white with the force he used. "I said that I intended to marry you and it was therefore quite in order for me to visit you, briefly, in the privacy of your bedroom."

Storm held her breath, refusing to believe she had heard him right. Her heart was hammering so loudly that she felt sure it must be audible to him as he stood there, tall and so dismayingly composed, reaching for another cigarette and lighting it.

"You seriously mean to tell me that you—"

"I am not likely to jest about such a serious matter, Miss Gavin . . . Storm." He added her Christian name, as if it was part of his new role to use it and he meant to play it well.

"But you don't have to marry me," she whispered, a hand to her throat where a pulse throbbed uncontrollably.

"You expected me to dismiss you out of hand?" he demanded, and she realized for the first time how she had wronged him by thinking just that.

"I'm sorry. But you don't have to go that far to make things right for me, Signor Romano. It doesn't make sense!"

The arrogant bronze features, like some ancient carving, with ice blue eyes glittering above those high, Slav cheekbones, looked stern and harsh and she could feel the tension that held his temper in check. It struck her like a blow and she put her hands to her mouth as if to make sure no other words escaped.

"Do I understand that you find the idea of marriage to me so distasteful that you reject it out of hand?" She could have curled up and died at the scorn he put into his voice, and almost instinctively she shook her head.

"No, no, of course not, but—"

"Or perhaps you preferred being thought of as my mistress!"

"Oh, please, I. . . ."

Storm was horrified to discover that there were tears in her eyes and she hastily brushed them away with a trembling hand. Before she could recover herself completely, however, strong brown fingers reached out and touched her cheek gently, and again that familiar sensation of excitement swept through her at his touch.

"I have perhaps been too abrupt in telling you as I have," he said softly, and in such contrast to his earlier harshness that she scarcely believed it possible. "I have not, as you will have already discovered, Paolo's gift for acting the courtier."

Storm looked up at him hazily, unsure whether to respond to this more gentle mood, or to be on her guard in case he changed back again as quickly. "What did Paolo say to. . . ,"

"To the idea of my marrying you?" For a brief moment the wide, straight mouth tilted into a half smile. "I believe that he was too stunned at the time to say very much at all, but I have no doubt that he will remedy that when he has had time to get used to the idea." The blue eyes regarded her for a moment steadily. "And you, what have you to say, Storm?"

She turned and walked over to the window, looking down at the garden below, at the tall trees and the pool glinting in the bright July sunshine and making little dappled patterns on the ceiling. He must, she thought, have taken advantage of her absence from breakfast to make his pronouncement and she thanked heaven that she had stayed with Gino instead of going down as she usually did.

It required a lot of thinking about, the idea of marrying Alexei, in the prevailing circumstances, but she doubted if she would be given very much time. Alexei Romano was a man who made up his mind and acted without hesitation, expecting everyone else to do the same.

"I can't think straight at the moment," she said without turning to look at him.

"You find it very difficult to accept?"

Storm shook her head hastily. "Oh no, not really." She turned then and looked over her shoulder at him. "I've talked to the Contessa," she said softly, and the blue eyes showed understanding. "She said. . . ." She hesitated to go on, to be too frank with the Contessa's confidences, but he was watching her and she found his gaze very hard to resist. "She said you would have married Gino's mother if you had been in your brother's place."

For a brief second he frowned, as if he resented the criticism of his dead brother, and she feared she had gone too far, but then he shrugged, and the frown vanished. "Perhaps I would have done," he admitted, but Storm felt in her heart that he quite definitely would have done. If he was prepared to do so much for her, how much more would he have been prepared to do for the mother of his child?

"She is a wonderful woman, the Contessa," she ventured, and he nodded firm agreement this time.

"As I know her better than most," he said. "And knowing about the Contessa you will better understand my decision now. It is an invidious position for any woman, and I have vowed that no woman shall ever find herself in such a position because of any action of mine."

"I'm grateful for your consideration, Signor Romano."

"I do not know how grateful you should be," he told her. "That remains to be seen. It will of course make no difference to you, except that you will now have the protection of being my fiancée and later my wife."

"But surely," Storm interrupted swiftly, "if we become merely engaged it will be enough to solve the problem."

Again the blue eyes looked at her icily and the firm mouth tightened ominously. "You seem determined to avoid marrying me," he said brusquely. "I find your reluctance rather odd in the circumstances, *signorina*, and not very flattering!"

"Oh, but I didn't mean to sound either evasive or unflattering," she said. "I'm sorry, it's just that I don't want you to go through with anything you'll regret later, Signor Romano."

He made no move to join her by the window and she was glad because he disturbed her as no man had ever done before, and she needed time to think. "I do not anticipate having any regrets," he said quietly. "And I think it would be as well if you called me Alexei. Such formality from my future wife might fall oddly on other ears."

She was too shy to experiment with it at the moment, but moved across and stood beside him again. "Of course."

"Perhaps you think I am too concerned with matters that many people take for granted now," he suggested, and Storm shook her head.

"No, no, of course I don't."

He sat on the edge of the desk and she could see his strong brown hands gripping the polished wood, feeling an inexplicable urge to reach out and touch them. "My father, my brother, for generations the Romanos have taken what women they wanted and thought it their right." He sounded so harsh in his judgement that Storm felt a small cold shiver of apprehension trickle down her spine for a moment. Then he looked up and held her gaze. "So you see there was plenty of foundation for Aunt Sofia's suspicions."

He straightened up suddenly, standing over her tall and straight, his unusual features showing a strange hint of anxiety as he watched her face. "Now, Storm, will you give me your answer?"

Faced with an immediate decision, when she had thought the matter cut and dried, she almost panicked.

Her heart was thudding wildly at her ribs and she felt her legs so weak and trembling that she feared they might at any moment let her down.

Then she looked at the dark, strongly defined features and the ice blue eyes below dark brows, and knew what she would say even before the words formed on her lips. "I will marry you, Alexei," she said in a huskily sóft voice.

CHAPTER SEVEN

It was three weeks since they were married, a quiet ceremony in Naples, with the warm September sun lending a rather inappropriate air of sadness to the occasion. Storm was not yet used to being addressed as Signora Romano, but it gave her a strange feeling of panic each time she heard it, wondering if she had made a mistake in taking such an irrevocable step.

Not that her life had changed very much in any other way, for Alexei seemed to consider he had done as much as was required of him when he gave her his name. She still occupied her own room, with Gino's room between her and Alexei, an arrangement that Signora Veronese had viewed with much raising of the brows and pursing of her thin lips.

It was obvious that the Contessa thought it a disgraceful state of affairs, and Storm suspected that she had said as much, quite bluntly, to Alexei. Paolo, on the other hand, took it as a good sign for his own future activities, and had once or twice tried to tempt Storm to go out with him for an evening.

She had resisted his attempts so far, but the weather was so lovely and there was so much that she had not seen yet that she thought she would be bound to succumb before very long, if he persisted. Being Paolo, of course, he persisted, and at last she weakened.

It was a lovely day, the sun warm enough to be comfortable and without the sultry heat of summer, and Paolo had put his head around the door, smiling hopefully. It was only mid-morning and Storm glanced at her watch, frowning at him curiously and demanding to know what he was doing at home instead of being at the works.

"I am—how is it—playing truant," he told her with an irresistible smile, and Gino laughed, sharing his secret willingly.

"But, Paolo."

"*Quièto.*" He put a finger over her lips and silenced her, then turned to Gino with a sly wink. "*Vade via*, Gino, hah?"

Gino beamed knowingly, put down his book and went out on to the balcony while Paolo took his seat beside Storm. She tried not to smile, but Paolo reminded her so much of Gino and his mischief that she was hard put to keep a straight face as he took her hands in his and leaned towards her, his smile persuasive.

"Paolo!"

"Ssh!" Again that silencing finger lay across her mouth. "Where shall we go, *cara mia?*"

"Paolo, I can't go anywhere with you. You know that. I have to give Gino his lessons."

"Lessons, pah!" He dismissed the idea scornfully. "Does the Signora Romano give lessons like a *governante*? You are Signora Romano, *bellissima mia!* You should remember that!"

"I was wondering if *you* remembered it," Storm told him quietly. "It isn't quite the same now, Paolo, is it?"

"Ah, Storm, *bella mia!* I have taken this chance to be with you. Are you cruel enough to dismiss me? It is only for a little time, *carissima*, a little ride, hmm?"

It was inevitable, Storm recognized as she met those persuasive dark eyes, that she would surrender, but she did so with some misgivings. "All right," she said with a sigh. "I'll come with you, Paolo, but only for a while."

"*Bene!* Where shall we go, *cara mia?*"

She shook her head, laughing despite herself at his

pleasure in persuading her at last. "There are so many places I'd like to see," she told him. "For instance, I'd like to go to Pompeii. It isn't very far away, is it?"

"Pompeii?" He looked appalled at her choice, his dismayed expression making her laugh again. Paolo always made her laugh, he was very good for her morale, and truth to tell Alexei took very little more notice of her than he had before, and she found it somehow demoralizing.

"I'd like to see Pompeii," she insisted. "But if you don't want to take me, I can go alone and get myself a guide."

"And get yourself a lot of trouble from Alexei also, *cara mia*!" He rolled his eyes expressively. "Do you think he would allow you to go walking around with a guide, like a tourist, and alone? *Madre di Dio!*"

"Well, he never takes me anywhere himself, so I haven't much choice, have I?" She wished, as soon as the words had left her lips, that she had not said that, and Paolo's smile confirmed the rashness of it.

He leaned across and kissed her on her mouth, the first time he had even attempted to do so since her marriage, and his dark eyes glowed warmly. "Oh, *povera piccola*! I will take pity on you, *sì*?"

He seemed not to care that Gino was no further away than a chair on the balcony, and that they were quite audible to him. She dared not think, either, what Alexei would say if he knew he was there, and she wondered, yet again, why he *was* there.

"Paolo, how have you managed to come back here?" she asked. "Does Alexei know you're playing truant?"

He shrugged, very casual and offhand. "Maybe. I am supposed to be fetching some plans from the study. It was a good excuse to see you, *carissima*!"

Again he leaned across and kissed her mouth and she drew back, glancing out on to the balcony and Gino apparently engrossed in the vista below the window. "Paolo, please don't do that!" She had to chance that Gino would tell his uncle about this surreptitious visit, and she sincerely hoped he would not.

"Oh, *cara*!" His mouth sought hers again, but this time she managed to evade him, pushing at him with both hands when he attempted to get even closer. He looked down at her soft mouth and sighed deeply. "He does not kiss you either, does he?" he asked softly. "Such a pity, *cara mia*! If I had such a beautiful wife I would not spend all my time at the works!"

"If you had a wife I doubt if you'd spend much time with *her* either!" Storm retorted, and laughed when he looked at her reproachfully. "You're not the marrying kind, Paolo."

"Nor is Alexei, it seems," Paolo retaliated. "He has not made a very good husband so far, *carissima*, has he?"

Storm frowned, looking down at her hands and shaking her head. "Please don't say things like that, Paolo," she said. "There are things you don't understand, and Alexei *is* my husband; I don't like to hear him maligned."

"Then he should behave like a husband!" He took her hands in his and kissed the fingertips gently, his dark eyes persuasive. "But at least his not caring allows me to take you out, *bella mia, si*?" He shrugged resignedly and pulled a face. "If you want to go to Pompeii, then that is where we will go, but not with Gino, huh?

Storm glanced again at the little figure on the balcony, his black head turned away from them but probably fully aware of all that was going on. "I can't leave him, Paolo," she said, and he frowned impatiently.

"But of course you can, *cara*. Lisetta will take care of him for a few hours, if I ask her to!" He rolled his dark eyes wickedly, and Storm had no doubt that Lisetta would do as he asked. Whether Signora Veronese would be so co-operative was another matter. If anyone told Alexei about their outing it would be his aunt.

"I don't know."

"Oh, *cara mia*!" He leaned forward and kissed her unexpectedly, so that she had no time to draw back. "You get ready and I will go and beg Lisetta to be *bambinaia* for a little while, *si*?"

Storm sighed resignedly. Arguing with Paolo was almost as useless as arguing with Alexei about anything. It got one nowhere. "*Si*," she echoed, and he kissed her again lightly as he got to his feet.

Storm watched him go, already having second thoughts about the wisdom of going, especially as Paolo was taking absence without leave from the works. Then she sighed and went out to explain to Gino.

He was curled up on the seat and he turned and looked at her with that mischievous, knowing look. "Zio Paolo is very—ya, ya, ya!" His eyes rolled wickedly and Storm shook her head at him.

"Gino, please don't talk like that! Your Uncle Paolo and I are simply. . . ." She shrugged, acknowledging the futility of trying to explain. Explanations would probably involve her even more deeply than she was already, and she sighed again, resignedly. "You won't mind staying with Zia Lisetta for a while, will you darling, while I go out for a drive?"

"With Zio Paolo?" He reached up and put his hand in hers. "Where are you going, Zia Tempesta?" He had been told to address her as aunt, but the Italian version sounded so much prettier that she had encouraged him to use that instead.

"We're going to Pompeii. Have you ever been there?"

She half hoped he would ask to come too, for she would have been happier with Gino along, despite Paolo's dislike of the idea, but Gino shrugged his shoulders with Latin disregard for history. "It is only old stones," he told her scornfully. "The tourist goes there. I do not want to go."

She smiled at his scorn and bent to kiss the top of his head lightly. "Then you will not mind staying with Zia Lisetta while I go, will you?"

He shook his head, his huge dark eyes looking up at her as wisely as an old man. "And I will not tell Zio Alexei where you have gone," he promised gravely.

"Gino!" She looked at him appalled at the suggestion of intrigue, but Gino seemed quite unperturbed.

"You go," he urged her solemnly, but with a belying glint in his eyes. "I do not mind. You will have fun, no?"

Storm opened her mouth to protest again, but there seemed little point. In the face of that mischievous look, she was defeated before she began. Instead she bent and kissed him again on his forehead.

"You're far too much like your Uncle Paolo," she told him firmly. "*Ciao*, Gino!"

Storm made no secret of the fact that she enjoyed being with Paolo, and she told herself that Alexei had no real cause to complain in the circumstances. It was not as if theirs was an ordinary marriage, or that Alexei ever showed any inclination to take her out anywhere. He was not a man who enjoyed the social life, but preferred to give all his time and energy to the affairs of the companies he ran.

Paolo, on the other hand, gave only as much time as he was obliged to to the companies, and as much time as possible to enjoying himself. In the circumstances, Storm felt, Alexei was very lenient with him.

He obviously would have preferred to drive to one of the charming little resorts along the coast and swim, or just laze on the beach, but Storm had insisted on going to Pompeii, and he had yielded eventually with one of those shrugs. She somehow felt that a trip of that sort would appear less reprehensible to Alexei than merely lazing on a beach somewhere.

The drive out to the ruined city made the journey well worthwhile without any other inducement, and she enjoyed it immensely. It was the same expressway that passed the villa and along which they had traveled to Naples, but this time they had turned the other way and come further south, turning off when they got nearer their destination.

Paolo always drove as if there was some emergency at the other end of the journey, and this time Storm did not hesitate to ask him to drive more slowly, to give her time to appreciate the beautiful views that the journey offered.

"It's so beautiful," she told him. "I want to be able to appreciate it, Paolo."

Obligingly he reduced speed, and pulled a face at her over one shoulder. "*Si, signora!* Your word is my command! Is that not the phrase, *cara mia?*"

"It is," Storm agreed. "But I doubt very much if it's true in this case!"

"Oh, come, *bellissima*, have I not slowed down so much that I am almost standing still, so that you may see the countryside?"

"Don't you want to see it too?" she asked, laughing at his exaggerated claim. "It's very lovely, and I'm sure no one ever gets blasé about such scenery."

"It is very beautiful," Paolo agreed with a smile. "And

so are you, *carissima*. You go together, you and this beautiful country."

"I hope so." Somehow his words made her feel wistful suddenly, and she looked at the wonderful country around them, wishing Alexei could have found the time to show it to her.

At times they seemed almost to be hovering on the edge of the cliffs above the deep, sparkling blue Mediterranean, with a carpet of trees and vines between. On the other side were the inevitable acres and acres of citrus groves and the many other crops that this lush, fertile land produced.

The groves filled the air with their scent as well as providing a colorful picture under the paler blue sky of the dying year and Storm found it all endlessly enjoyable.

A woman, watching her man at work under the twisty gray trunks of olive trees, raised her head from the knitting that absorbed her and crinkled her weathered brown face into a toothless smile when Storm waved a hand at them. It was a refreshing, carefree ride and she felt grateful to Paolo for suggesting it, turning to smile at him and catching his eye.

"*Cara?*" He smiled inquiringly, and Storm shook her head.

"I'm just very happy," she told him, laughing softly. "Why should I be anything else?"

"Why should you, *po' gugina?*"

She looked at him curiously. "That's a new name for me," she said. "What does *that* one mean? Or shouldn't I ask?"

Paolo's shoulders shrugged carelessly. "Why should you not, *cara?* It is only little cousin."

"Oh, I see. Yes, I suppose I am your cousin now, aren't I?"

"Since Alexei married you, I suppose you are," he agreed. "Although I wish he had left you free, *cara mia*, or else would make a proper wife of you. This way you are a temptation just out of reach, and yet not fully appreciated by anyone."

"Paolo, please!"

She did not want to discuss her relationship with Alexei, especially at this moment, when she was feeling so delightfully lighthearted. The ride had brought color to her cheeks and a bright shine to her green eyes and she looked quite beautiful, especially to Paolo's appreciative eyes.

"It is such a waste, *carissima*!"

"It's *my* concern and Alexei's," she told him quietly. "Now please don't let's talk about anything, Paolo. I want to enjoy my ride."

"And talking about Alexei would spoil it for you?"

She looked at him for a moment, at the good-looking profile and the long lashes that swept down to half conceal his eyes, making shadows on the golden brown face. He was very attractive and she sometimes wondered if she could fall deeply in love with him, but then there was always Alexei. Alexei had married her and behaved as if he was still her employer. Paolo behaved as a newly acquired husband could be expected to behave, but would never have married her, she felt sure. It was a confusing situation, and she sometimes wondered how it would all eventually evolve.

Pompeii proved just as interesting as she had expected, and she was glad to find it fairly free of visitors, thanks to the lateness of the time of year. There were visitors, but not the endless crowds that swarmed through the ancient city during the height of summer.

There seemed such a sense of occasion about seeing a

place that had, until now, been no more than something she had read about at school. Tall fluted columns, the remnants of beautiful villas and temples, rose up into the clear sky, looking surprisingly new and giving some idea of how impressive the living city must have been.

Avenues, rediscovered from the dust of centuries, where wealthy families once lived, their well-worn routes now trodden by thousands of foreign feet and laid out in the sun.

She rediscovered the temple of the god Apollo and was immediately attracted by the huge bronze statue of him that stood on a stone block amid the steps and fluted colomns that had once been raised to his glory. It was a wonderful piece of work, with the god poised for flight, his hands extended as if they had once held the bow and golden arrow with which he slew the monster, Python.

There was such a sense of life about the statue, such perfection in its craftsmanship that she felt herself compelled to stand before it in admiration as one of those ancient worshippers might have done.

Paolo waited for her, none too patiently, leaning against some nearby steps and not nearly as enthralled as she was by his surroundings. "Storm!"

His voice recalled her, and she abandoned her daydream reluctantly. "Have I been here too long?" she asked, smiling at his impatience, and he laughed softly, coming across to put an arm round her shoulders.

"You have been admiring Apollo for long enough, *cara mia*, I shall be envious if you give him any more of your time."

"I'm sorry."

"That I shall be envious of him?"

She shook her head, pushing back the tawny hair from her flushed face and laughing. "No, that I kept you waiting. You've been very patient." She glanced at the small gold watch on her wrist and frowned anxiously. "The time's gone so quickly, I think we'd better go back, Paolo."

"You think your *hus*band will miss you?"

He sounded very scornful of the likelihood of that being so and Storm felt her cheeks color furiously. She did not know for certain whether or not Alexei would mind her being with Paolo, but she was quite sure he would be angry about Paolo taking leave from the works to take her out and she would have liked to be back before he returned and found them still missing. Also she did not like to hear Paolo make such obviously scathing remarks about his cousin.

"I think he probably will miss me," she said quietly.

"As he misses any of his property that is missing for a while," he declared, and Storm clenched her hands, her eyes sparkling angrily.

"Paolo, you have no right to talk like that!"

Paolo, however, was in no mood to be tactful and his dark face betrayed a jealousy she had never seen before, and which startled her in its vehemence. "I have no rights about anything," he said harshly. "I am the *povre cugino*, the poor relation! I have no rights, no property . . . Oh, *Madre di Dio*! Sometimes I could hate Alexei!"

"Paolo! Please don't say that!" Storm put a hand on his arm and looked up at him anxiously. She had never before seen him express such resentment, and she wondered what had suddenly given rise to such passion.

For a moment he said nothing, but gazed at her in silence with those warm, dark eyes that were so like Gino's, then he moved closer and put an arm right round her waist, hugging her close to him, his lips pressed to her neck. "I am sorry, *carissima*," he whispered, then drew back and looked at her with a comically rueful face. "I am anticipating what Alexei will say when I see him again," he told her. "I know I shall be—how is it you say?"

"For the high jump?" Storm suggested quietly, and laughed when he pulled another face.

"*Si, si!* Alexei will put me to the high jump as he does his horses, and I shall have to jump too, *bella mia*, or he will crack the whip as he does at them!"

She remembered her own first estimation of Alexei. How she had visualized him as a crabby old man who cracked the whip and expected everyone to jump. She had been wrong in the first part of her estimation, but not, it seemed, in the second.

"Poor Paolo!"

She could do nothing about the laughter that glinted in her eyes for his outrageous self-pity, and he tightened his hold on her suddenly, pulling her round into his arms. They were in a quiet corner, away from the scattered crowd of visitors, but she was not at all happy about the situation, and put her hands on his chest to try to ward him off, for his intention was obvious.

"You are cruel," he accused, in a softly husky voice that betrayed his intent as clearly as his actions did. "Like all beautiful women you are cruel, *carissima*. You laugh at my fate, you find it amusing that your husband will presently. . . ." A great sigh vibrated through her as well, and he drew her even closer, despite her attempt to stop him.

"Paolo!"

He kissed her softly and lingeringly. "*Carissima!*" he whispered, and Storm closed her eyes slowly.

It was something she should not allow. She knew that quite well, but there was something irresistible about

Paolo always, and she could feel a persistent little pulse tapping away at her temple, telling her she was enjoying being kissed by Paolo again, married woman or not.

"Please don't, Paolo!"

She regained breath enough at last to push him away, but he stayed close enough to be disturbing, his arms still holding her close. "Oh, *cara*, who is to know?" He kissed her again beside her left ear, moving aside the tawny hair, his fingers gently caressing against her skin.

"No, Paolo, please!"

She put her hands to his chest again and pushed hard against the strength of his arms. As she turned her head to avoid another kiss she stared, her lips parted, her eyes huge with surprise. Paolo, his eyes on her face, frowned curiously at her.

"Storm? What is it?"

Then he too turned his head and a second later stepped back hastily. There was no mistaking the tall striding figure in light gray trousers and a white shirt, his hands swinging loosely at his sides as he came towards them. There was an air of menace about Alexei Romano that gave grimness to those bronzed, chiseled features and sent a shiver of apprehension through Storm's body.

Even from yards away she could see that those ice blue eyes had never been icier, and she wondered which one of them was the target for most of his anger. Neither of them said a word, but waited for the striding figure to reach them and Storm could feel her heart thudding away heavily at her ribs.

It was the first time she had ever felt this strange, almost elated sense of anticipation, and she told herself it was fear for what would happen to Paolo. Somewhere in her brain something kept reminding her that this figure of vengeance striding towards them was her husband. It was a curiously exciting sensation to realize it so suddenly.

He came to a halt immediately in front of Paolo, ignoring Storm completely for the moment, so that she instinctively stepped back. His voice was steel-edged, and much more harsh than she had ever heard it before.

"You left to fetch some plans, I understand," he said, and Paolo nodded. There was a faint hint of defiance in his dark eyes.

"I forgot about them," he said, as sulkily as Gino might have done. "I am sorry, Alexei."

"You preferred to drive around the countryside with my wife, it seems, while Picerni waited for the plans."

The claim to her as his wife had a chilling sound, and offered no hint of jealousy, certainly not of affection, and Storm could feel herself almost literally shrinking. She wished the dusty ground beneath her feet would swallow her up into the same volcanic oblivion as the city it had once buried.

"*Ma,* Alexei, *lei si è sbagliato. . . .*"

"My wife does not speak Italian." The cold voice cut across his words. "Please speak in English."

He meant to humiliate Paolo as much as possible in front of her, that much was obvious, and Storm's senses rebelled at the harshness of it. She stuck out her chin defiantly, knowing that he would dislike her intervention, but determined on it just the same.

"There's no need to make quite so much fuss about it, surely," she said in a voice that she wished could have been more firm and less liable to shake and betray her feelings. "It was my fault as much as Paolo's that we came here, and I'm sorry if you've been inconvenienced, Alexei, but please don't take it out on Paolo."

For a second he did not move or speak, and she wondered if he was going to ignore her still, although she could feel the anger that emanated from him, and her hands were trembling as she held tightly on to her handbag. Then he turned slowly and looked down at her. his eyes as cold as ice, but at the same time blazing angrily.

"I do not need to be informed that you were in part to blame for this expedition," he said coldly. "But I also have no doubt whatever that Paolo was the instigator." He looked at his cousin again, his dark head held arrogantly so that the square chin thrust aggressively. "You will drive back to the works and take the plans to Picerni," he told him.

Instinctively Paolo glanced at Storm, and Alexei was on to the glance in a moment. "I will drive my wife back," he said.

"I'd rather drive back with Paolo!"

She had no idea what on earth prompted her to say such a thing, and for a moment both men stared at her in disbelief, then Paolo shook his head slowly, his dark eyes appealing with her to change her mind.

"You will drive with me!" Alexei said, and looked at his cousin. "*Andare immediatamente*, Paolo, *per favore!*"

Paolo, after one last glance of resignation at Storm, turned and walked off to where they had parked the car, and she watched him go with a certain feeling of guilt. It was true that he had persuaded her to come out with him, but if she had been more adamant in her refusal this whole incident would never have happened, and she fervently wished it hadn't.

She did not look directly at Alexei, but only glanced up through her lashes, not encouraged by his grim, angry look. Then, without a word, he suddenly took her arm in a grip of iron and took her along beside him as he too headed for the car. His long stride made it necessary for her to half run to keep pace with him, and she felt rather like a runaway child being brought back by an irate parent.

"Stop it!" She stood her ground suddenly, although he almost pulled her over as he went on. His fingers eased slightly on her arm, but he still held on to her and she knew it was useless to try and shake free. "I can't keep up with you, Alexei, and I refuse to be hauled through this place like a runaway slave!"

For a moment she could have sworn that a glint of amusement showed briefly in his eyes, but then he set his mouth firmly straight and looked down at her icily. "You have used that simile once before about our relationship," he told her quietly. "And I might tell you, *fanciulla mia*, that this is a time when I wish you *could* be bought and sold!"

"Oh, if you want to get rid of me," Storm told him rashly, "that's simple enough! You just send me packing!"

The dark, strong features did not change their expression, but something in his eyes did, and she shivered as she saw the change. He held her gaze, and she could feel the heavy thudding of her heart against her ribs, and that strange sense of elation again.

"Would you go?" he asked softly, but gave her no time to answer. He started walking again, taking her along with him, although at a much less hazardous pace. "You are required to be Signora Romano, officially, tonight," he told her brusquely, and for a moment Storm's heart fluttered wildly until she realized she had misunderstood him.

"How?" she asked breathlessly. "I mean where?"

The ice blue eyes looked down at her for a moment, a gleam of speculation in their depths so that she hastily lowered her own. "Oh, do not fear," he said quietly. "I simply require you to act as hostess to an important business acquaintance."

"Oh! Oh, I see."

"You have a suitable gown, I know," he went on, while Storm tried to still the sudden sense of panic that filled her at the idea. "You will have time when we get back to change and make yourself presentable in time for his arrival, although you would have been better prepared if you had been at home when I arrived."

"I'm sorry."

He opened the car door and helped her in, his dark, chiseled features coming close as he bent to tuck her skirt in over her knees. "I trust you will prove that by not doing such a thing again," he said quietly, and Storm flushed with resentment.

"I'm sorry I inconvenienced you by not being there when you arrived home," she told him, rashly uncaring. "I'm not sorry I went out with Paolo. I like going out and you. . . ." She bit on her lip hastily when she felt him slide into the driving seat alongside her, his bare arm brushing against hers, the vibrant warmth of him tingling against her skin.

He started the engine, then turned his head and looked at her steadily. "You find me very much lacking as a husband," he suggested, and she did not answer. "I imagined that you had your needs in that direction well taken care of by Paolo. You do not need anything from me, *amante*."

Storm would have argued, would have told him he was wrong about her feeling for Paolo, only he would have seen her being kissed in the ruins of Apollo's temple, and drawn his own conclusions. She must, she thought as an afterthought, ask Paolo what *amante* meant.

CHAPTER EIGHT

Paolo did not return to the villa until some time after Storm and Alexei got back. Storm was leaving her bathroom, half dressed, and on her way back to her bedroom when she saw him, and chanced Alexei making a sudden appearance to ask about the visitor they were expecting. Apart from saying that he was coming, Alexei had been annoyingly uncommunicative about him.

"Sir Gerald Gordon," Paolo informed her. "Very wealthy and very English, *carissima*."

"English?" She looked surprised at that. "Alexei didn't tell me he was English."

"Perhaps he was hoping to surprise you." Paolo's dark eyes swept over her slim figure covered by a pale blue robe that was flimsy enough to reveal the contours under it without it being transparent. "You look very beautiful, *carissima*. That robe is . . . mmm!" He kissed his fingertips extravagantly, and Storm shook her head, glancing along at Alexei's door as she spoke.

"I'd better go and dress," she said. "Before Alexei comes looking for me."

Paolo's dark eyes glowed wickedly. "If he sees you in that *roba, bella mia,* you will melt even his icy Russian heart. *Madre di Dio,* but he is no Romano, that one!"

"Paolo, please!"

"But he does not appreciate you, *bellissima*, and therefore he does not deserve you!"

"Please don't. . . ."

A faint sound from further along the hall made them both glance towards Alexei's bedroom door, but before his cousin appeared Paolo had slipped swiftly in the bath-

535

room that Storm had just vacated. Storm had some vain hope of hurrying along to her own room and slipping in without being seen while Alexei was closing his door, but it was a vain hope in the circumstances.

It was not customary for them to dress formally for dinner, but tonight was a special occasion, and it was the first time Storm had seen Alexei in a dinner jacket. The expensively tailored white mohair jacket fitted his lean frame perfectly and each movement he made revealed the smooth ripple of muscle in his arms and shoulders.

There was a hint of frilled shirt cuff showing at each wrist, saved from effeminacy by the strong brown hands. The whiteness of the shirt and jacket gave his dark head and bronzed features an almost primitive arrogance that set the blood tingling in her veins at the sight of him. And for the second time that day she reminded herself that this man was her husband.

It was evident from the way he looked at her that he appreciated the flimsy revelation of the blue robe, although whether it melted his icy Russian heart, as Paolo had said it would, was debatable. The blue eyes made a swift, calculated appraisal of her from head to foot, and then regarded her steadily for a moment. There was still a hint of that cold anger she had seen on their earlier encounter, but the worst of it had vanished, apparently, and she thanked heaven for it.

"You will have to hurry if you are to be ready in good time!"

Storm looked at him, feeling a little guilty, especially when she thought of Paolo disappearing into her bathroom, and she fervently hoped Alexei had not seen him go in. She nodded, but did not venture to smile. "I know I have to hurry." She hesitated, and her hesitation sent a dark brow upwards in query. "Alexei, I wondered if you'd mind my not wearing the green dress after all."

He had especially asked her to wear a particular gown, mostly, she suspected, because it was very grand and luxurious. It was a beautiful and very expensive gown of deep jade green slipper satin and it gave her a feeling of almost sensual pleasure to feel its smooth shiny folds around her. The problem was that it had a zip fastener the whole length of its back seam. It would be hopeless for her to try and struggle with it herself, and the one and only maid allocated to such duties was already busy with Signora Veronese and the Contessa, and likely to be so for some time yet.

"May I ask why you do not want to wear it?" he asked.

"It isn't that I don't want to wear it," Storm explained, hoping this wasn't a prelude to an argument. "But Clemente is busy with Signora Veronese and the Contessa, and I can't reach the zip at the back of the green dress to fasten it myself. I thought that if I wore—"

"I prefer that you wear the green one!"

So, Storm thought, he was going to be stubborn about it, and she looked at him reproachfully, disappointed that he would not unbend sufficiently to be reasonable. "Then you'll have to forgive me if I'm late," she told him. "I'll have to wait for Clemente to come and help me."

"There is no need. I will help you."

She stared at him for a moment unbelievingly, her pulses racing furiously at the prospect of having him do anything as personal and intimate as helping her to dress. "You . . . you will?"

A small frown of impatience drew his dark brows together. "I *am* your husband," he reminded her shortly.

"Oh yes, yes, of course!"

"You find it easy to forget that, hmm?"

Storm sighed inwardly, guessing that she would not be allowed to forget that visit to Pompeii in a hurry. Alexei would make sure of that. "No, I don't find it easy at all," she denied quietly, determined not to be provoked. "And if I'm to be ready in time, I *must* go and finish dressing. If you'll excuse me."

"I have said I will help you with your gown."

She hesitated, her cheeks flushed, uncertain just how she felt, except that she was surprised to find eager acceptance uppermost in her mind at the moment. "I don't . . . I mean, you don't have to bother, Alexei."

He regarded her steadily. "You would prefer that I get Paolo to help you, perhaps?" he asked softly, and Storm stared at him open-mouthed for a moment, then held the frilled neck of the robe close under her chin and swept past him into her room. She spun round swiftly a second later when she heard the door close and found him standing just inside, those glittering blue eyes challenging her to deny his right to be there.

"You must hurry," he told her quietly. "There is not very much time before our guest arrives."

"He's English."

She realized as she spoke that she made it sound like an accusation, and she thought she saw the corners of his wide mouth curl in ironic amusement. "You do not sound very pleased about meeting a fellow countryman."

"You didn't tell me he was English."

"No, I did not."

"Even though you must have known I would be glad to see someone from my own country."

The cool blue eyes regarded her steadily for a moment, and she could not have sworn just what was going on behind that Slavonic mask. "I did not think a business acquaintance of mine would interest you to that extent."

"Oh!"

He was obviously thinking deeply about something, and she watched him surreptitiously from the shadow of her lashes, wondering what was on his mind. "I want you to understand, Storm," he said at last, slowly and as if he considered every word before he said it. "As far as Sir Gerald Gordon is concerned it could be very useful that I have an English wife."

"Oh, I see." She met his eyes for a moment or two and hastily smothered the bitter feeling of resentment she felt at the idea of being used to further his business interests. "Well, I'm glad I'm useful for something in your estimation!"

She had not meant it to sound quite so bitter, and she saw a brief hint of surprise in his eyes before he frowned. "Please do not be sarcastic, Storm, it is not becoming, and quite uncalled for."

"I think I. . . ."

"I hope, for this evening at least, that you can remember you are married to me and not to Paolo. It will create a better impression if you do."

Storm felt the color flooding into her cheeks and she curled her hands into tight little fists at her sides. He had said very little on the way home about finding her with Paolo, but it looked as if he now intended to make up for it. Despite the unlikelihood of it, she had nurtured a little spark of hope that part of his annoyance was prompted by jealousy; now it seemed it was strictly fear for the impression it would make on a business acquaintance.

"You have no call to talk to me like that, Alexei," she told him shakily. "It's unfair and quite without foundation to suspect me as you do."

He looked down at her coolly, it seemed, although something in his manner set her own pulses pounding crazily, as if in anticipation. "In view of the situation in which I found you only a very short time ago, I think I have every right to talk to you like that," he told her shortly. "It was fortunate that my aunt was able to tell me where to find you, for it would have made a very unfortunate impression upon our guest had you arrived home late for dinner, looking as if you were returning from a rendezvous with a lover, and in the company of my cousin."

"Oh . . . oh, you . . . I don't *care* what impression I make on your precious guest! I don't care what *any*one thinks, you. . . ." Words tumbled over one another, but failed miserably to make any sort of sense, and her green eyes blazed at him furiously.

"Well, it matters to me!" The cold voice cut across her tirade. "And you will behave like a reasonable adult in front of my guest, no matter what childish tantrums you indulge in in your bedroom."

"You monster!"

Her breathing was wild and erratic and she stepped back hastily when he came across the room towards her. "As you please," he said quietly, and his hands reached out for the tie at the neck of her robe. "Now please do not waste any more time, Storm. It is getting late and I want you downstairs ready to meet Sir Gerald when he arrives."

Storm felt dismayingly close to tears, but she could see the futility of further argument with him. He was bound to be the victor, for she could not deny that she had been in a compromising enough position to anger any husband, and he had seen her with his own eyes. To have found her like that would have been a blow to his pride and he would not be quick to forgive.

"I can help myself, thank you!" She knocked away his hands, refusing to have him help her, at least at this stage. The robe parted and she had it halfway down her arms when she paused, suddenly conscious of the little she wore under it. "You—"

"*Si, abrighi!*" he ordered curtly, and the robe was pulled forcibly from her arms and thrown carelessly across the bed. "Stop seeking excuses, Storm, and get dressed, or I shall lose all patience with you!"

She would have argued that he had done so already, but the silk slip she wore clung closely to the contours of her body and exposed a smooth expanse of pale gold skin above the low-cut lacy top, and she felt suddenly very vulnerable with those icy blue eyes on her.

She turned hastily and reached for the jade green dress he wanted her to wear. It slipped easily over her head and she slid her arms into the brief sleeves, then reached behind her with both hands in an attempt to close that elusive zip. In a moment, however, Alexei was round behind her, brushing her hands impatiently aside.

"I am here to help you," he reminded her. "Must you be so difficult, Storm?"

"I'm not being difficult, I. . . ." She swung round, half way to facing him, but he gripped her upper arms roughly and turned her back again.

"I promise you that if I lose my temper you will be very, very sorry," he warned. "Now please make some attempt to co-operate. I am trying to help you!"

"Thank you!"

She sounded meek and very quiet, in direct contrast to the chaos that was going on inside her. She could feel the warmth from his body on the nakedness of her back as he stood close behind her, and his fingers touching her skin was like a touch of fire. Instinctively she closed her eyes on the wild, incredible longings that his touch aroused in her, banishing everything else from her mind.

"Keep still!"

Inadvertently she had swayed slightly, and the deep-voiced command made her stiffen hastily, reminding her that he was impatient with her, anxious for her to be ready to welcome his important guest. Nothing would be further from his mind than the effect he was having on her.

"I'm sorry, Alexei."

"You are a capricious and perplexing woman," he accused. "And I do not begin to understand you!"

"Have you tried?" Her voice had an oddly husky sound, and she felt him pause in his task.

"I have tried," he said quietly. His long brown fingers slid softly along the length of her spine as the zip closed together, and she shivered. "Are you cold?" he asked.

"No, no, of course not!"

Her hands were curled tightly and the pulse at her temple almost blinded her with its throbbing, but she did not move, only stood there, close to the strong warmth of him and almost praying aloud for him to put his arms around her. She wanted that to happen more than anything else in the world at the moment.

"You look very beautiful." He spoke softly and startlingly close to her ear, so that his breath stirred the tendrils of hair on her neck, and her heart responded so violently that her head swam with it. Then he bent his head and pressed his lips lightly to the soft skin of her neck, moving aside the tawny gold hair with caressing fingers, his dark head brushing softly against her face.

"Alexei!" She whispered his name, wanting him to know how she felt, but half afraid he would find her wild emotions a subject for scorn.

"*Si, amante?*" He too spoke softly, and his arms slid around her at last, turning her slowly within their circle until she looked up into the strong, carved bronze face with its light eyes. Eyes that no longer looked cold and icy but darker with some deep passion that made her shiver with anticipation. He had never spoken to her so often in Italian as he had today, and she told herself it was a good omen, a sign that he no longer considered her a stranger.

"I . . . I wish I. . . ."

She shook her head, too unsure of herself and afraid to tell him how she felt and how sorry she was that she had gone off with Paolo as she had, and he smiled. That rare and gentle smile that softened the stern lines of his face and made him look so much more approachable and less overpowering. She had seen him smile at Gino like that, and once or twice at Lisetta, but never before at her, and the effect of it was breathtaking.

He held her close and studied her for a long moment with those light blue eyes. "*Amante mia!*" he said softly. He pulled her closer, until her body was crushed against his own muscular strength and she could feel the tense, exciting warmth of him through her thin gown, and the steady, strong beat of his heart, faster than normal, under the spread of her fingers.

"Alexei!"

She whispered his name, with his mouth touching hers, his lips brushing lightly, teasingly against hers until she wanted to cry out to him. Her whole being ached for his lean, hard body to possess her completely, for the strong brown hands to caress her passionately, urgent with the same consuming desires that burned in her.

He made a sound that was almost a moan, a soft indescribable sound, and her head was forced back as his mouth became suddenly more hard and dominant, possessed of a fierce hunger that swept Storm along on a tide of elation and excitement she could not hope to control.

"Carissima! Po' amante mia!" Soft Italian words, whispered against her ear as he lifted her into his arms and carried her across to the bed, his voice deep and husky with a passion barely contained.

He turned swiftly, his eyes glittering, when a soft knocking sounded at the bedroom door, and he laid her gently down and looked at her curiously, bringing his mind back to immediate things with a shake of his dark head.

Storm sat there on the edge of the bed, her lips parted, hating whoever it was that had disturbed them with an intensity that frightened her. "It could be Clemente," she whispered, but Alexei was frowning, almost as if he suspected who was on the other side of the door.

"Storm! *Carissima!*"

The voice was scarcely above a whisper, obviously hoping to remain unheard except to her, but there was no mistaking to whom it belonged, and Storm closed her eyes on the agonizing irony of it. Paolo had never before ventured to come to her room, and he had to choose this moment to come knocking and whispering at her door. Who could help but suspect an intrigue, a prearranged meeting? Certainly not Alexei, not after the scene he had witnessed earlier at Pompeii, and her heart sank coldly into a void of hopelessness.

She knew, even before she looked at him, what she would see on Alexei's face, and she could have cried aloud at the harshness, the stark fury, she saw there. He looked down at her, and from the expression in those cold eyes, she knew he was despising himself for succumbing to a moment of weakness, as much her as for her deception, as he saw it.

"It seems I have been made a fool of," he said in a cold

hard voice. "I congratulate you, *signora*. It is not easy to make a fool of Alexei Romano."

"Alexei, I—"

But he was in no mood to listen and brushed aside her attempt to explain with one disdainful hand. The tenderness, the passion of a few moments before had been wiped out as if they had never existed. "I hope you do not find my presence in your bedroom too much of an embarrassment." He turned on his heel and strode to the door, flinging it wide.

"Alexei!" Her cry followed him and reached Paolo, who stood beyond in the hall, staring at his cousin in disbelief.

"*Madre di Dio!*" he breathed piously, realizing his blunder, but Storm ignored him, her eyes following Alexei, dark with unhappiness and bright with unshed tears.

He turned in the doorway, his arrogant dark head in deep contrast to the white wall behind him. "I hope you are as adept at playing charades when you meet our guest," he said coldly, ignoring Paolo as if he did not exist. "I would prefer to have Sir Gerald convinced that our marriage is at least normally tolerable. If that is not imposing too much upon you."

"Oh, Alexei, please don't!" She was almost in tears and her eyes looked huge and shinily green in the yellow light from the overhead lamps, but he remained unmoved.

"I shall expect you downstairs in the *salotto* in five minutes' time," he said shortly, and turned and strode off along the carpeted gallery.

There was a heavy, meaningful silence for several moments after he had gone, and Storm thought she had never in her life felt so utterly lost and helpless. No matter if Alexei had been prepared to forget her previous indiscretion in those few wonderful minutes just now, there was little likelihood of his ever doing so again, and she had only herself and Paolo to blame.

"Oh, *cara mia,* I am so sorry!" Paolo's dark eyes looked unbelievably contrite, and it was very difficult to become really angry with him, especially when her own eyes were brimming with tears.

"How could you, Paolo? How could you come to my room like that? You've never, ever done it before, why now?"

"*Cara,* I did not know, how *could* I know, that Alexei was with you? He too has never been to your bedroom before, has he? Not since your marriage?"

Storm shook her head miserably. "It was the first time, and—oh, Paolo, what am I going to do?"

His shrug was instinctive rather than uncaring, and he reached out and brushed away a tear from her cheek with one gentle finger. "There is no time for you to do anything at the moment, *piccola,*" he reminded her softly. "You have to hide your tears and be downstairs in less than three minutes. We will straighten it all out when our important visitor is gone, no?"

Storm looked at her wristwatch through a blur of tears and nodded. "I suppose so," she said. "I don't know if I can, Paolo."

"Oh, Storm! *Graziosa mia,* you look so sad!" He leaned across and kissed her lightly on her forehead. "Does Alexei's anger mean so much to you?" It was quite the wrong thing to have said in the circumstances and the tears flowed anew down her face, tears she was unable to check, and Paolo pulled her to him, her face against his shoulder, rubbing one hand soothingly over her bowed head. "Oh, *cara mia*, please don't cry so! Shall I tell them that you have a bad headache and cannot come down to dinner?"

"Oh, no, no!" She pushed away from him, brushing a hand across her eyes. "I must go down! Alexei will never forgive me if I don't!"

Sir Gerald Gordon proved to be both charming and garrulous, and in this instance Storm was very glad not to have to make much effort to entertain him. For one thing he seemed quite delighted with the company of the Contessa, and also he was something of a story-teller and seemed to have an endless repertoire of anecdotes. Her own rather unhappy silence, she thought, went unnoticed, except by Alexei.

From time to time she tried to catch his eye down the length of the table, but each time he avoided looking at her, and she found it increasingly difficult to maintain her appearance of calm when he was so persistently cool and hostile. Dinner seemed to go on endlessly and all the time she was afraid she would cry, sooner or later, and stand even less chance of seeing Alexei relent.

It was toward the end of the meal that Sir Gerald looked at Storm with a smile of polite inquiry. "Will you be visiting the old country with your husband when he comes to see us next month, Signora Romano?" he asked, and Storm blinked for a moment in confusion.

Alexei had said nothing to her about going to England and she was very uncertain how she should answer, but the very idea of visiting her old home again in the near future gave her spirits a sudden lift, and she looked down the length of the table at Alexei with wide, hopeful eyes.

"I'm not sure, Sir Gerald," she said.

"I think not, Sir Gerald." Alexei's deep, quiet voice

cut across her question. "My wife has to stay and look after my young nephew. He is my ward, you will remember, and not really old enough to be taken on what is after all purely a business trip. I shall be in England no more than two days at most, and it is scarcely worth all the disturbance it would cause."

Storm felt as if he had dealt her a physical blow, and she could only stare at him in blank dismay for several seconds before hastily looking down again. There was no limit, it seemed, to Alexei's thirst for revenge, and she fought wildly with the sudden aching desire to get up from the table and run out of the room, regardless of the impression it made on their guest.

"Ah yes, of course," Sir Gerald murmured politely, obviously impressed by his host's single-mindedness. "Pleasure and business don't mix, eh, Romano? And a wife is happiest in her own home! Well, the old ways have a lot to recommend them. I regret the passing of some of those old ideals, I can tell you, my dear chap!"

Storm could feel the curious eyes of the Contessa on her, but she dared not look up at her or she knew she would have weakened beyond control. Later, she knew, the Contessa would ask her all about it. Why Alexei had been so deliberately callous, and she would have to try and find the words to explain.

"Old-fashioned standards have very little meaning now," Alexei said. "Even to wives." He looked directly down the table at Storm, an icy glint in his eyes telling her that the jibe was intended for her. She had never before seen him so deliberately cruel and she found it incredibly hard to bear.

Sir Gerald shook his gray head in regret. "Well, I'm very glad to see such a complete and happy family circle in your home, my dear Romano. I'm always impressed by a happy family atmosphere; it tells me a lot about a man if his home life is in good order."

Such a glaring misconception was almost too much for Storm, and she held her two hands tightly together for a moment, trying to still their trembling. Somehow, soon, she must get away from this coolly polite atmosphere and give way to her own feelings, or she would burst.

But it was only when they got up from the table that her chance came. Alexei and Paolo apparently had some business to discuss with their guest, and they went off to the study together, leaving the three women alone. The Contessa and Signora Veronese went downstairs to the big drawing-room with Storm, but she was in no mood for small-talk, and she saw Alexei's absence as her chance to escape at last.

"If you'll excuse me," she said, "I'll just go and see if Gino's settled down to sleep."

Signora Veronese might possibly have been fooled by her excuse, but the Contessa certainly was not, and she turned anxious eyes on her, gently concerned for her obvious unhappiness. "Storm, *cara*, what is wrong?"

Had they been alone, Storm would not have hesitated to confide in her, but the cold, malicious presence of Signora Veronese deterred her, and she merely shook her head, feeling the threat of tears again, prickling at the back of her eyes and choking her throat. She had never, she felt certain, ever been so abjectly miserable in her life.

"Is it not obvious what is wrong, Lisetta?" Signora Veronese asked in her harsh voice, before Storm could find the words to answer. "To be discovered by one's husband in the act of seducing another man must surely be disturbing to even the most brazen, although I for one can find little pity in my heart for such a woman!"

"*Nome di Dio,* Sofia! You would not find it in your

hard heart to pity a starving child!" The Contessa's defence was swift and fierce, and Storm felt grateful to her for her unflinching support, but she still desired nothing more than the chance to flee to her own room.

Lisetta Berenetti, however, having taken up cudgels on her behalf, was not yet ready to relinquish the fight, and her dark eyes blazed below the brightness of her red hair. "As for your *prezioso*—your *bambino*—huh! He is the seducer, Sofia Veronese, and well you know it! He has the eye of the Romanos, that one!"

"*Silenzio!*" Signora Veronese's harsh features were twisted into a caricature of themselves with the violent emotions that tore at her, and her voice was barely above a whisper. "You dare to speak so of my Paolo when you are not better than a—"

"*Basta,* Sofia, *per favore,*" the Contessa told her quietly, although her dark eyes shone with anger. "Do not say something you will be sorry for!"

"Oh, please," Storm begged, her voice choking in her throat as she listened to the bitterness between the two women. "Don't quarrel because of me! Please don't!"

Signora Veronese's black eyes switched to her, sharp with malice, narrowed and burning with a hatred that Storm could not fully understand. "Alexei should never have married a foreign woman, a *domestica!*" The harsh voice spat scorn at Storm's original position in the household as she saw it.

"Signora Veronese, I know you dislike me—" Storm began, but was given no chance to complete the sentence before that harsh voice cut her short again, thick with venom.

"I despise you, *signora*! You are no fit wife for a Romano and Alexei, I think, is at last beginning to see what a fool he has been. Now perhaps he will annul this ridiculous mockery of a marriage and send you away before the name of Romano is further disgraced by having English blood passed on to its descendants!"

"So!" The Contessa's tight little smile understood at last, and Storm too saw a glimmer of light. The reason why Signora Veronese hated her so much. "You hated poor gloomy Natasha, did you not, Sofia? Because she brought Russian blood to your precious Romanos, and now you fear that Alexei's sons will shame you further by being partly English!"

Signora Veronese's sharp chin angled defiantly, her eyes glittering as much hatred for the woman who faced her as for the absent Natasha Romano. "The Romanos," she declared coldly, "were a proud old Italian family, and will be so again!"

"When you have your Paolo safely installed, *si*, Sofia?" the Contessa asked softly. "Oh, I can see so clearly now what it is you want. Benito did not marry, so his poor little Gino is not a Romano, and while Alexei had no wife Paolo was safe as the heir to all that Luigi and Alexei have built here!"

It was obvious that the Contessa's estimate of the situation was an accurate one, and also that the Signora resented it bitterly, for her black eyes looked from Storm to the Contessa with a chilling, virulent hatred that made Storm shiver.

"Paolo has a right to it all," she said coldly, and fiercely. "He is the only *real* Romano left! He has no foreign blood, nor will he marry beneath his station for the sake of some stupid servant girl's honor!" Her gaze raked scornfully over Storm from top to toe. "But I have faith in the sense of duty of the Romanos, even in Alexei. He may have married a *domestica*, but he will not disgrace his name by letting her bear his sons, I would swear to it!"

"Oh, please, please!" Storm put her hands to her ears,

her face flushed and crumpled with threatening tears, shaking her head violently from side to side. "Paolo can *have* it all! I don't care! You're right, *signora,* there'll be no sons, not mine and Alexei's, not now. Paolo made sure of that!" She held her hands together in front of her in a tight ball, her body shaken with sobs. "I . . . I'm going away, as far as I can get, from you, from Paolo, from Alexei! I never want to see any of you again. Never, never, never!"

She did not stop to heed the Contessa's entreating hands, outstretched to her, nor to see the gloating satisfaction in Signora Veronese's black eyes, but ran from the room and on up the marble stairs to the long hall above, seeking the sanctuary of her own room. She felt abused and humiliated, obliged to face the fact that what the Signora said was probably true.

Alexei would never treat her as a proper wife, not even for the sake of carrying on his ancient name. He could do that by adopting Gino, as the Contessa had said he meant to do, and Gino, at least, was all Italian. Even Signora Veronese could not contest that.

It was instinctive that she went into Gino's room first when she got upstairs, and she found him peacefully asleep. Smoothing back the black hair gently from his forehead as he slept, she cried softly to herself while she decided her own future.

She would miss Gino, she would miss her life at the Villa, no matter how unsettled it had been at times, but most of all she knew she would miss Alexei. She had known in the first few moments of their meeting that he was a man she would not easily forget, but she had not for a moment anticipated becoming so closely involved with him.

Now she found it hard to visualize a life without him,

but she knew that if she stayed on here she would be living in a fool's paradise if she hoped ever to see him as warm and passionate again as he had been for those few minutes tonight. Now that he was convinced of her preference for Paolo, nothing would change his mind. That facet of his character had been one of the first things she recognized in him.

She went into her own room and, without turning on the light, walked across to the window and pressed her forehead to the cool window glass. He would most likely have their brief marriage annulled; there was certainly no legal impediment to his doing so.

She pressed her face harder to the shiny coolness of the window and wept for something she had never really had. Outside the bright moonlight shimmered on the smooth bay, and down in the garden the shading trees stood darkly wavering in the soft wind that blew in from the sea.

Bellabaia—beautiful bay, the place she had thought a paradise on earth only a few short months ago, and which she had expected to see for only two short weeks, during a holiday. If only she had not spoken to a good-looking stranger and a little boy!

CHAPTER NINE

It took Storm quite a few moments to persuade the Contessa to ring for a taxi for her, to take her to the airport. She begged her not to tell Alexei that she had gone until there was no way of keeping it from him. That way she had the idea that she could perhaps be well on the way to England before he knew. Of course it was most likely, after his treatment of her tonight, that he would not care where she was, but he might just feel sufficiently slighted at the idea of being deserted to follow and make her come back.

The Contessa had not pleaded with her, as she had half expected she would. She had asked her, quietly, what had upset her so much before dinner, and she explained as best she could, how that fateful afternoon and evening had evolved. The Contessa shook her head, but said little, and Storm had the feeling that probably she had seen this parting as inevitable sooner or later.

She had kissed her gently on both cheeks and given the taxi driver instructions to take her to the airport, and then gone back into the villa with scarcely a backward glance, leaving Storm feeling finally and utterly deserted.

The drive in the taxi, along the moonlit road to Naples, reminded her of when she had driven along there with Paolo, and she felt the hot, salty sting of tears again. The citrus groves, so sweetly scented, and with their little straw roofs to protect them from inclement weather. The dark glow of the sea below the terraced cliffs, it was all so familiar, and she knew she could not stop herself from crying again.

She would arrive at the airport looking forlorn, and

very much like what she was—a runaway wife. Desperately, as they ran into the airport approach, she sought in her handbag for make-up to disguise the ravages wrought by tears, using the dim interior light of the taxi to do the repairs.

Her reflection in the purse mirror appalled her. Her eyes looked huge, and dismayingly redrimmed, and her face was as pale as death. There was no trace of the hurriedly applied lipstick left on her mouth. It was hard to imagine that the ghostlike creature who stared at her from the mirror was the same girl who only hours before had been delirious with delight when her husband made love to her.

She had left the jade green dress on the bed, a memento of her brief happiness that she had had no room to bring with her. Her packing had been done in haste and she would not have crumpled and spoiled the gown for anything.

She faced the fact now, that she had so far avoided admitting, even to herself. She loved Alexei in a way she had never dreamed was possible, and far too much to stay and be a make-believe wife only. She had loved him even before she agreed to marry him, for surely no enlightened modern girl would have accepted such a marriage on such flimsy grounds if she had not been blinded by her own feelings.

It would have been enough to save her own reputation if she had simply left the villa, there and then, and gone back to England. She could see that quite clearly now. But she had wanted to stay and she had taken any opportunity offered, no matter what the conditions. Alexei had probably meant to dispense with her in time, anyway, when it suited his book.

She took a last look at herself and a great shuddering

sigh escaped her as she closed the clasp of her purse and looked out at the bright, busy bustle of the airport. The taxi driver was probably already curious about her and the sound of her sigh prompted him to turn briefly and look at her over one shoulder.

"*Signora?*"

Storm shook her head. "Nothing, I'm sorry."

"*Si, signora!*"

She thought he was more than curious about her, having had that brief glimpse of her tear-stained face, and she wondered if she would have the nerve to mingle with the others in the crowded terminal. At least in a crowd she would be less conspicuous.

The man accepted the generous tip she gave him and touched his cap, his dark eyes surreptitiously studying her while he took her suitcases from his taxi. He knew who she was, for she had heard her own name among the Italian instructions that the Contessa had given him, and she was suspicious that his mind was working along obvious lines.

"Thank you, I can manage now."

He looked down at her two suitcases, the same ones she had brought from England with her. "*Due scatole, signora? Con permesso—*"

"No, no, please, I can manage! Thank you." She was anxious to be on her way. To disappear into the faceless crowd in the terminal; out here she felt somehow vulnerable, and she picked up her cases, while the driver shrugged resignedly and watched her disappear into the crowded and brightly lit building.

It must have been her pale face and red-rimmed eyes, Storm told herself, that made the ticket clerk look at her so oddly, and she wished she could have done a better job of disguising the signs of her distress. She did not mind how she got to England, she told him, as long as it was on a plane that left very soon, but the clerk was shaking his sleek black head regretfully.

"*Mi spiace*, Signora Romano," he said. "There is nothing for two hours."

"Two hours?" Storm stared at him in dismay, her heart racing in panic, her anxiety to be away even more urgent when she thought of Alexei knowing she was gone long before two hours from now.

"*Mi spiace, signora!*"

"But isn't there one to . . . oh, somewhere!"

She could feel those persistent tears about to start again and dreaded making a fool of herself in a place as public as Naples airport, and the clerk was already looking at her as if he too feared an exhibition he would have to cope with.

"*Signora*, it seems you are distressed." He used his hands to convey a good deal more than he said. "I will call a young lady to help you. Perhaps the *signora* would care to rest a while, in private, *si?*"

He was kind, but anxious to have her transferred to some other responsibility, and she nodded wearily. "I really don't feel very well, *signor*, if I could—"

"*Si, si, certo, signora!*"

She was shown into a small, quiet room furnished with two armchairs and a small desk and chair which, she felt sure, was not normally available to passengers, and she looked inquiringly at her guide when she opened the door.

"Is . . . is it all right for me to be here?" she asked, and the girl nodded, smiling understandingly.

"Oh *si, certo*, Signora Romano!"

The use of her full name gave her the clue as to why she was privileged and she hesitated only briefly before nodding her thanks. She might as well make the most of being Alexei Romano's wife, just this once. "Thank you," she said, and the girl smiled briefly.

"*Prego, non ne parli, signora.*"

With a bob of her head the girl was gone and Storm was alone in the quiet little room. It was then that she realized that she had not booked herself a seat on that plane that left in two hours from now. The armchair she sat in was comfortable and suddenly she felt very, very tired, so she leaned back her head and told herself that it could do no harm to rest for a moment or two before going to book her seat. Such an emotional upheaval as she had just gone through could be incredibly exhausting and she needed time to gather herself together again.

She had not meant to go to sleep, but she realized as she opened her eyes that she must have done just that. The little room felt stuffy and she stretched her arms above her head to restore the circulation, glancing at her wristwatch as she did so. Thirty minutes of one of those two hours had passed already and she felt much less distressed.

A glance into her purse mirror confirmed that she looked better too. True, her eyes were still red from crying, but it looked much less obvious and her cheeks had more color. There was still a dark, sad look about her green eyes and she wondered how she would face up to life as a working girl again.

She would, of course, revert to her maiden name and so save Alexei any embarrassment when he came to England, but she looked down at the heavy gold ring on her marriage finger with regret. She would return the ring to him after she got back.

In a reverie between sleepiness and nostalgia, she could have started crying again, but she pulled herself up sharply and got to her feet, determined to be practical. A light, tentative tap at the door made her spin around swiftly and she almost breathed a sigh of relief when the dark pretty face of the airport stewardess smiled at her warily.

"*Signora . . .*" she began, then stepped back hastily when someone brushed past her, striding purposefully into the little room as if he owned it, and sweeping all before him, as always.

"*Vade via, per favore, signorina!*" he told the stewardess, and the girl, after one brief uncertain glance at Storm, nodded her head and hastily withdrew.

"*Si, signore!*"

For a long moment after the door closed after her Alexei stood there, just inside the door, looking at her, and Storm kept her back to him. Those tears would surely get the better of her now again. "May I ask why you saw fit to walk out of a dinner that you knew was very important to me?" he asked then, and she did not answer.

Apparently it did not matter that she was unhappy, too unhappy to go on living in the same house with him. He was only concerned with his own affairs. He waited for several seconds and when she did not answer he spoke again to her unfriendly back.

"I think I am entitled to an answer," he said quietly.

"I'm sorry."

Her voice was husky and not much more than a whisper, and she heard him move closer, presumably to enable him to hear what she said. "You realize that your running away like this has probably cost me a great deal of money, and an important business contract in England?"

Money and business, Storm thought wildly, the only things he ever cared about, according to Paolo, and it looked as if Paolo was right. Anger suddenly rose uppermost in her tangled emotions and her hands were clenched tightly as she turned to face him, her green eyes blazing, her cheeks flushed.

"Is it so important to you?" she asked, her voice shaking with both anger and those pent-up tears. "Do you want to buy England as well as most of Italy? Does nothing else matter to you?"

He said nothing for a second, but those icy blue eyes were far from being as cold and chilling as she expected, and the firm, straight mouth was not set like an angry line as she had often seen it. "I would not be here if that were so," he said quietly, and Storm looked at him warily.

Her lips were parted and her eyes huge and green as she tried to decide just what he meant. "I don't understand," she said.

The immaculate white jacket, she noticed for the first time, was open and there was an unusually untidy look about his dark hair where it fell across his forehead. "I am assured by Lisetta that Paolo has never been to your room before."

"No, no, he hasn't," she said, in a small quiet voice, not daring to hope that he was going to admit he had been wrong.

"It seems that I owe you an apology for that."

She waved her hands to dismiss it as unimportant, but she knew what it would have cost him to apologize. "Oh, it doesn't matter," she said, and realized, suddenly, how incredibly weary she sounded. Then she looked up at him briefly. "I'm sorry about your business deal, but you shouldn't have come for me, not when it was so important to you."

"You do not think that having my wife desert me is important?"

She felt her heart leap suddenly. Even the faintest hint that he cared was enough to set her pulses racing and she told herself she was a gullible fool. "I didn't mean you to follow me. I hoped I'd be gone by the time you realized."

"Lisetta knew there was no flight for England for over two hours, she made sure of that before she rang for your taxi." His wide, straight mouth tipped briefly at one corner in a hint of a smile. "The name of Romano carries some weight around here. I drove as fast as I could, and I'm afraid Sir Gerald is rather puzzled by my behavior."

Storm shook her head, her eyes wide and uncertain. "You left him? To come and find me?"

He nodded. "Of course. It is a matter of pride when a man's wife deserts him."

"I see." She looked down at her hands again. "I'm sorry, but I was upset."

"The quarrel with my aunt?" he asked, and she nodded.

"I'm afraid Signora Veronese doesn't like me," she said. "She despises me for a *domestica*, and I don't have to have that translated!" She smiled ruefully, but failed to find a response on that serious face. "I suppose my pride was hurt."

"I can understand that. Pride is not the sole prerogative of the wealthy or the aristocratic. You have as much right to yours as anyone else."

It was unexpected to hear him being so agreeable, and she laughed uneasily. "I'm afraid your aunt doesn't share your view, and as I'm married to you she was afraid. . . ." She stopped there, unwilling to go into the intimate details of Signora Veronese's tirade.

The unfailing sense of excitement that he had always aroused in her was coursing through her body now, like an irresistible fire, and she wished he would either go and leave her, or make some move to satisfy her longing for him. It would be impossible, she thought, for her ever to forget Alexei, no matter how long she was away from him.

The blue eyes held hers for a brief moment before she hastily lowered her own gaze. "If my aunt and Paolo were to go away," he said quietly, "would you come back, Storm?"

She did not answer, she could not, for several moments; her heart was hammering so insistently at her ribs that she had a strange breathless feeling. Then she shook her head, slowly and with such obvious reluctance that he must have realized it. "I couldn't, Alexei."

At once the blue eyes took on the cold, icy look she had hoped never to see again, and there was a faint flush on the high Slavonic cheeks. "Because I speak of sending Paolo away?" he asked, and Storm looked up hastily, anxious to deny that at least.

"Oh no! How could you still think Paolo means anything to me?"

"Then why will you not come back?"

She simply stood there for several moments with her head bowed. How did she tell a man she could not come back and live with him because she loved him too much? It must surely be the most ironic situation any woman ever found herself in.

"Storm?" He spoke her name softly, and its gentleness, the hint of anxiety she thought she detected in his voice was her undoing. Great rolling tears coursed down her cheeks and she brushed them away impatiently with a clenched hand.

"I can't come back, Alexei, because I love you."

There, it was said, and he could now realize how she felt, why she could not go on as she had been. He must surely understand now, but he neither spoke nor moved for a full minute.

"Then come home, *carissima*," he said softly.

"Alexei!" She looked up at him, wide-eyed, not daring to believe that she really saw that warm, exciting glow in those light eyes as they looked at her.

He moved then, reaching out his arms for her and drawing her close to the lean hardness of his body as if he would crush her until she was part of him, and she could feel the warmth of his flesh and the throbbing beat of his heart through the white frilled shirt. She leaned her face against his heart, but he pulled back her head by the length of her tawny hair, and found her mouth.

Even in those few unforgettable moments in her bedroom he had not kissed her like that, and she felt as if every fiber in her body was responding to his touch. A fierce, erotic sensation that made her moan softly as he caressed her, his mouth drawing the very breath from her, until her head spun with a kind of wonderful delirium.

"Storm! *Bella Tempesta mia! Carissima!*" His voice, deep and soft, breathed warmly against her mouth, her neck and the soft vulnerable base of her throat, the strong brown hands unbelievably gentle as they caressed her. "You will come back, *mia bella*, will you not?"

Storm looked up at him with bright, shining green eyes, her tawny head tipped back as she smiled at him. "You know I will," she told him. "I don't really know if I could have gone when it came to the point. I love you, my darling Alexei. I think I always have."

"Always?" He looked down at her with a small doubting frown between his brows. "You were never—that way about Paolo?"

"Never," she denied firmly. "I knew Paolo wasn't serious about me either, but he was good company, especially when my husband seemed determined to ignore me." She kissed that firm, square chin and laughed softly in her new-found confidence. "He said you didn't deserve me."

"Perhaps I did not," Alexei admitted with uncharacteristic modesty. "But I loved you and I would never have let Paolo take you from me. If you had loved him enough—" He stopped, and his reticence surprised Storm so much that she looked at him anxiously for a moment.

"*Caro?*" she prompted him gently, the Italian endearment coming easily to her lips, and he drew her close again, holding her so tightly that she could not have moved even had she wanted to. His mouth was urgent with the fierce hunger that thrilled her so.

"If you had loved him enough, *carissima*," he said quietly, "I think perhaps I might have let you go, if it would have made you happy, and if you had begged me to."

"Oh no, my love!" She pressed her lips to that small throbbing pulse on his throat that she had always noticed when he was moved or aroused, even to anger. "There was never any question of that, and Paolo could never have married me, anyway. Signora Veronese has plans for Paolo to provide the Romano line with the Italian sons she thinks it should have."

For a moment he was silent, then that fascinating, bronze carved face looked down at her earnestly. "She has said all these things to you, *carissima?*"

Storm nodded. "The Contessa was there too."

"And you ran away because you loved me and you thought. . . ."

She traced the shape of that firm mouth with one finger. "I thought your aunt might possibly be right," she said softly. "That you had married me because both our reputations were at stake, but that you would never allow me. . . ."

"*Si, cara mia?*" he prompted gently, and the blue eyes looked down at her with an expression that robbed her of any false modesty.

"She was quite sure you would never allow me to bear your sons and disgrace the Romano name with English blood."

"*Cagna!*" The venom in the one word startled her and she looked up at him curious and wide-eyed. To her surprise he laughed, only the second time she had ever heard him do so. "I am being very uncomplimentary to my Aunt Sofia, *carissima mia!*" His fingers undid the buttons of her coat and the two at the neck of her dress and slid the soft material from her shoulder, then he bent his head and put his lips to the soft warmth of her flesh. "We will show Aunt Sofia whether or not you will bear my sons," he whispered softly. "We will go home now, *amante mia*, and soon Paolo will have no hope of being the provider of the Romano line, hmm?"

"Even if I'm not Italian?" Storm asked, her shining eyes showing that she knew the answer to that well enough.

"*Silenzio!*" Alexei said firmly, and Storm was content with that.

Lodge in Vietnam

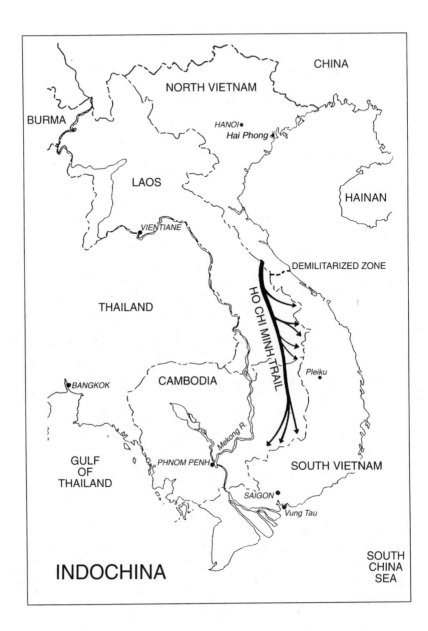

Frontispiece. Map of Indochina, 1963–1964, showing Ho Chi Minh Trail through Laos and political divisions. Courtesy of U.S. Army Center of Military History.

Lodge in Vietnam

A Patriot Abroad

Anne E. Blair

Yale University Press

New Haven and London

Published with assistance from the Louis Stern Memorial Fund.

Designed by James J. Johnson and set in Century Book Condensed type by Rainsford Type.
Printed in the United States of America by Vail-Ballou Press, Binghamton, New York.

Library of Congress Cataloging-in-Publication Data

Blair, Anne E., 1946–
    Lodge in Vietnam : a patriot abroad / Anne E. Blair.
        p.   cm.
    Includes bibliographical references and index.
    ISBN 0-300-06226-5
    1. United States—Foreign relations—Vietnam.   2. Vietnam—Foreign
relations—United States.   3. United States—Foreign relations—1963–1969.   4. Vietnam—
Politics and government—1945–1975.   5. Lodge, Henry Cabot, 1902–1985.   I. Title.
E183.8.V5B47   1995
327.730597—dc20   94–38192

A catalogue record for this book is available from the British Library.

The paper in this book meets the guidelines for permanence and durability of the Committee on
Production Guidelines for Book Longevity of the Council on Library Resources.

10   9   8   7   6   5   4   3   2   1

For Jim Blair

The United States can get along with corrupt dictators who manage to stay out of the newspapers. But an inefficient Hitlerism, the leaders of which make fantastic statements to the press, is the hardest thing on earth for the U.S. Government to support.

—Henry Cabot Lodge II of Madame Nhu in August 1963, from his unpublished book "Vietnam Memoir"

For Jim Blair

The United States can get along with corrupt dictators who manage to stay out of the newspapers. But an inefficient Hitlerism, the leaders of which make fantastic statements to the press, is the hardest thing on earth for the U.S. Government to support.

—Henry Cabot Lodge II of Madame Nhu in August 1963, from his unpublished book "Vietnam Memoir"

Contents

Introduction

This is the first book to deal with the initial ambassadorship of Henry Cabot Lodge II to Vietnam as a period in its own right. It seeks to explain what happened in the months immediately before the decision to commit American ground troops to the war.

I was surprised to find that a large section of the American side of the story of the Buddhist suicides by fire in Saigon in 1963 had not been brought together. As I moved through the drawn-out and complex negotiations of President Ngo Dinh Diem and the Buddhist leaders on the one hand, and of John F. Kennedy and his advisors on the other, I came across two odd gaps in a literature and documentary record that was of staggering bulk in other respects. The first was the absence of an informative account by Lodge himself of his two embassies to South Vietnam. His memoir *The Storm Has Many Eyes: A Personal Narrative* (New York, 1973) glossed over that part of his life in a short chapter entitled "In the Sixties." His *As It Was: An Inside View of Politics in the 50s and 60s* (New York, 1976) was even less helpful. Moreover, there existed no detailed study of Lodge's performance as U.S. ambassador in Saigon. The second gap was in the record of cables between the American embassy and the U.S. Department of State. After the death of Diem on November 1, 1963, and the U.S. recognition of the successor government of Duong Van Minh six days later, the traffic almost ceased until March 1964, when it increased again in volume as President Johnson began to turn his attention to Vietnam.

President Kennedy was assassinated exactly three weeks after the murder of Diem in Vietnam. The months that encompassed the change-over of administrations in Washington and a transition from a civilian to a military regime in Saigon, followed by a further coup in January 1964, must surely have been important to the shaping of U.S. policy in Vietnam, I thought, especially as they fell in the period before America was engaged in the shooting war. Yet apart from George McT. Kahin's groundbreaking *Intervention: How America Became Involved in Vietnam* (New York, 1986), very little had been written on this time span.

One reason for this gap suddenly became clear to me. Many American writers had asked: How did we get into Vietnam? Accordingly, they had moved quickly from the question of the U.S. role in the coup against Diem to events surrounding Johnson's July 1965 decision to commit troops. The rather messy period after the Diem coup had been neglected. I am from Australia, a country that also sent soldiers to Vietnam. I was interested in why the U.S. and my own country had ignored the opportunities to disengage that must have arisen from time to time, and the period between the two deaths and the two coups seemed a fruitful place to start.

Lodge's first ambassadorship to South Vietnam framed the mystery period. Requests under the U.S. Freedom of Information Act eventually yielded all the numbered sequence of cables from the Saigon embassy to Washington, and much else besides. The clue through this maze of reports proved to be Lodge's personal account of his dealings in Vietnam. This, the hitherto missing link, was in manuscript form and entitled "Vietnam Memoir." Lodge had prepared the five-part, 238-page typewritten piece in 1967—not for publication but "in the belief that knowledge of the secret events in which Lodge took part and of which he had uniquely intimate knowledge should not be lost. It is, hopefully, source material for history; not the finished product."

The circumstances surrounding Kennedy's appointment of Lodge and Lodge's motives in accepting the Saigon ambassadorship, a second-rate position, were now much clearer. But the problem of the paucity of the cable traffic for several seemingly critical months remained. A fresh approach to the whole period began to suggest itself. Perhaps the key to the processes of decision making in the American mission in South Vietnam between the two coups lay in the personality and modus operandi of Ambassador Lodge himself and in his relations with his staff. The biographical approach to history had been an unfashionable one during most of my lifetime, but here it proved the means of giving shape to a cumbersome body of evidence from many sources.

This is not a full-scale biography of Henry Cabot Lodge, and certainly not a Freudian psychological profile. But as I continued my research, I increasingly found that coincidence, personal style, individual ambitions, and the clash of strong wills shaped events more than explicit policy goals or the functioning of systems. Lodge emerged as a man of immense authority and charm, motivated by personal loyalties and his conception of duty, impatient of detail, and inclined to move on once a solution to a problem appeared to have been found. He was in some ways a nineteenth-century figure functioning in modern professional structures of whose workings he remained splendidly unconscious.

Perhaps the distance of thirty years from an event is an appropriate time for reflection, when the security question is no longer compelling and much of the story has worked itself out. In the course of my investigation I received generous cooperation from many who had served with Lodge in Saigon and Washington. Among those I interviewed were William and McGeorge Bundy, presidential consultants on Vietnam; William Colby, chief of the Far Eastern Division of the CIA in 1963–1964; and Lucien Conein, the legendary agent who had operated in Vietnam since 1945. Frederick Flott and John Michael Dunn, special assistants to Lodge during his first ambassadorship in Vietnam, and Barry Zorthian and the late Philip Habib, his minister-counselors, gave me privileged insights into the politics and culture of the U.S. mission and its agencies. In 1964, President Johnson had taken the radical step of sending Foreign Service officer David Nes to Saigon to act as Lodge's chief of staff, that is, to take over the ambassadorial functions of management and coordination that Lodge disdained to perform. Twenty-five years after those events, Nes spoke at length of his efforts in conjunction with Gen. William Westmoreland to bring some order to the runaway independence of the agencies of the mission, whose resources he saw as devoted more to the creation of American career paths than to the prosecution of the war.

Among the Vietnamese witnesses, I spoke to Gen. Nguyen Khanh, South Vietnamese head of state in 1964; Gen. Tran Van Don, the leading conspirator in the overthrow of Diem; Bui Diem, South Vietnam's ambassador to the United States; and the late Nguyen Ngoc Huy, who served on the cabinet of the post-Diem Minh government. All these men gave me valuable assistance and insights in the complex world of South Vietnamese political culture.

Lodge's first embassy in Saigon occurred at a time in the development of U.S. policies in Vietnam when several alternatives to an American takeover of the war remained open. During the eight months of his presence as U.S. chief of mission, these options were gradually closed off. Lodge played a central role in this process because of his approach to his diplomatic assignment, the choices he made, and the openings he failed to see at the time. Indeed, after the November coup he was often disengaged from the work of the mission. At the beginning of the first Lodge ambassadorship, civilians and the Department of State were in charge of U.S. Vietnam policy; at the end, the armed forces and the Pentagon were firmly in control.

When Lodge accepted the Saigon mission from Kennedy, he did so as an American patriot who believed in his country's goal of containing the spread of communism in Asia. He brought the acuity of the politician and the authority of the statesman to the embassy rather than the skills of management that any ambassador needed to apply to the challenge of coordinating American activities in South Vietnam. Lodge was the man on the spot at the critical time. Ironically, it was to be Lodge's dogged interpretation of his duty as a patriot that prevented him from pressing Washington to adopt his insights into the nature of the war, so different from the received wisdom of the time, and his understanding of the difficulties that American soldiers would face in fighting in Vietnam.

A Note on the Terms "Viet Cong" and "NLF"

Readers may be puzzled by the use of the term *Viet Cong* throughout the text, when some reference to the NLF, or National Liberation Front, of South Vietnam might be expected. The official U.S. position was that American advisors were present in Vietnam to help the Saigon government resist an outside-directed insurgency. The possibility of an indigenous Communist force in South Vietnam was therefore an embarrassment, if not a logical impossibility. Some United States planners of the 1960s used the pejorative Viet Cong to refer, rather vaguely, to the NLF. Ambassador Lodge took an uncompromising position. Noticing shortly after his arrival in Saigon that American embassy documents referred to the enemy's forces as "The Peoples Army of Vietnam," he issued a firm directive: the term *Peoples Army* was to be dropped; the enemy was "the Communists" or, alternatively, the "Viet Cong." Viet Cong, of course, was a shortened version of Vietnamese Communist, but in American popular culture of the time, the term gained an alien and sinister ring.

Lodge did not refer to the three arms of the government of North Vietnam by their full titles. He made no distinction between the Vietnamese Workers Party (VWP), the Peoples Army of Vietnam (PAVN), and the Democratic Republic of Vietnam (DRVN), preferring the terms "North Vietnam," "Hanoi," and "the Communists," the last a general term which implied that the North Vietnamese were backed by Beijing. The various governments in Saigon, none of which ever had complete control over the whole territory known as South Vietnam, represented the Republic of Vietnam (RVN). These regimes were referred to by the U.S. Department of State, for obvious reasons, as the Government of Vietnam (GVN).

Lodge's title during his first embassy in South Vietnam was United States ambassador to Vietnam.

The NLF is generally agreed to have been established in 1960, but the circumstances of its foundation and direction—by southerners or by Hanoi—have been the subject of impassioned debate. Interested readers are referred to Carlyle A. Thayer, *War by Other Means: National Liberation and Revolution in Vietnam, 1954–60* (Sydney: Allen and Unwin, 1989) and Gabriel Kolko, *Anatomy of a War: Vietnam, the United States, and the Modern Historical Experience* (New York: Pantheon, 1985).

Acknowledgments

Many people have helped in the preparation of this book, and it is a pleasure to acknowledge them here. My greatest intellectual debts are to David Chandler, director of research at the Centre of Southeast Asian Studies at Monash University, who introduced me to Indochina studies and supervised the doctoral dissertation which formed the basis of the research. David and Susan Chandler have encouraged the manuscript along over the last two years with much advice and good humor. Helen Soemardjo of the Monash Main Library provided imaginative assistance, as she always has done, and I must acknowledge the staff at Victoria University for urging me to make time for the book.

I am grateful to Michael Godley and Anthony Wood of the Monash History Department, who both read many drafts of my writing. Val Campbell and Karin Von Strokirch gave excellent administrative support. The community of the Centre of Southeast Asian Studies at Monash University assisted with exchange of views and information, and in particular, my colleague Pham Van Luu gave me access to his extensive research in the Vietnamese, French, and English sources on Ngo Dinh Diem and his Buddhist opponents. Carlyle A. Thayer made useful suggestions when he examined the dissertation. The great George McT. Kahin suggested the present form of the work.

In the United States, David C. Humphrey, as archivist at the Lyndon Baines Johnson Library, gave me leads through masses of documentation and cumbersome declassification procedures, while the staff of the Massachusetts Historical Society provided unfailing assistance. I am indebted to the late Emily Sears Lodge, who graciously gave me permission to quote from her letters from Saigon, and to Henry Sears Lodge, who kindly lifted the many restrictions surrounding quotation from "Vietnam Memoir." My gratitude also goes to Otto Bohlmann and Harry Haskell at Yale University Press, who oversaw the completion of the whole.

I wish to express my gratitude to the many people who answered letters, granted interviews, and gave their their time in recalling the details missing from the written record. In addition to those mentioned in the bibliography of this work, I wish to thank Philippe Devillers, Arthur J. Dommen, Thich Giac Duc, William J. Duiker, Mrs. Jane Floweree, William C. Gibbons, Ted Gittinger, Mrs. Swarna L. Gunawardene, Edward C. Keefer, Fredrik Logevall, Alfred W. Mc Coy, Nguyen Van Canh, Douglas Pike, Quang Luu, the late Dean Rusk, Peter Tarnoff, Denis Warner, Morris West, and Gareth Woodard.

Brian Caddell and Trevor Cooke helped with sound technical advice and Gordon Reid, drawing on his Aircraft Industry Archive at Tullamarine, Victoria, solved several otherwise impenetrable mysteries. My husband and best friend, Jim Blair, a man of broad interests and talents, gave me much wise advice and encouraged the project at all times.

Glossary of Acronyms

ARVN   Army, Republic of Vietnam (South Vietnam)
CIA   Central Intelligence Agency
DRV   Democratic Republic of Vietnam (North Vietnam)
GOP   Grand Old Party (Republican party)
GVN   Government of Vietnam (South Vietnam)
MAAG   Military Assistance Advisory Group
MACV   Military Assistance Command, Vietnam
MRC   Military Revolutionary Council (Minh government; term retained also by Khanh regime)
NATO   North Atlantic Treaty Organization
NLF   National Liberation Front (South Vietnam)
SVN   South Vietnam
USIS   United States Information Service
USOM   United States Operations Mission (Saigon U.S. mission name for office of Agency for International Development)

Chapter One

A Presidential Mission

When Henry Cabot Lodge II was United States ambassador to the United Nations in 1953, a question arose during debates over the Korean conflict on which the vote promised to be closely divided. After much discussion, the U.S. Department of State advised Lodge to vote yes. But the next morning Robert Murphy, head of the U.N. section of the Department of State, read in the newspapers that Lodge had voted no. He put through an urgent call to Lodge in New York. "Apparently our instructions failed to reach you?" he asked. "Instructions?" queried Lodge. "I am not bound by instructions from the State Department. I am a member of the President's cabinet, and accept instructions only from him." Murphy protested, "But you are also the head of an Embassy, and our ambassadors accept instructions from the Secretary of State." After a pause, Lodge replied, "I take note of the Department's opinions."

Murphy took the problem to Secretary of State John Foster Dulles, who listened without comment, then slowly replied, "This is one of those awkward situations which require special consideration." Subsequently, the Department of State did not instruct Lodge, or even make strong suggestions, although, Murphy recorded, Lodge would accept with good grace a call from the secretary of state or a private word from the president.[1] Ten years later, Lodge had not changed, although the American leader in the White House had. This, then, was the man President John F. Kennedy chose to be his ambassador to Vietnam.

Dwight D. Eisenhower had appointed Lodge to the United Nations post in 1953 at the height of the Cold War precisely because of his haughtiness and independence, seeing in him the qualities needed to confront the Russians on the Security Council floor. Lodge, who knew himself to be photogenic, quickly realized the possibilities of television as the new popular medium for information. Bearing the chiseled features of his Massachusetts ancestors, he set out to project himself as the very image of free America. On a daily basis he defeated the Soviet representative in the nation's living rooms, meeting every Communist charge with an immediate and flourishing rejoinder. Theater was the means by which Lodge sold the United Nations to the American public and to the country's government: U.N. interpreters, in response to his praise, hung copies of the sections of his speeches they had translated above their desks, and diplomats noted that the USSR's Andrei Vishinsky came to relish his role as television's Bolshevist villain.[2]

Stalin's death and Sen. Joseph McCarthy's fall from power, both in 1954, allowed the administration some relaxation on the anti-Communist front. Lodge now came to focus on the growing influence of newly independent states in the Security Council. He made friendly contacts with their leaders, urging Eisenhower to travel in the third world and to distance American policy from that of the colonizing powers Britain and France.[3] As the Eisenhower administration drew to a close in 1960, it was indisputable that Lodge's high profile as United Nations ambassador had contributed to widespread acceptance of the value of American membership of the international body, although he himself, as the grandson of Republican senator Henry Cabot Lodge, the leading opponent of the Wilsonian League of Nations in 1919–1920, had started his life in politics as an isolationist.

U.S. foreign policy and the nation's military preparedness had been the dominant concerns of Lodge's long career in public life. He had been elected in 1932, at the age of thirty, to the lower chamber of the Massachusetts State Legislature, and had gained a seat in the U.S. Senate four years later. By that time he was already establishing a place for himself in the dialogue on U.S. foreign policy; in 1932 he published a collection of essays on America's military deficiencies under the severe title *The Cult of Weakness*. In this work, which was greeted with favorable reviews, he had set out the classic Republican stance that government should be small, save for ensuring a strong navy to defend the coastline. No doubt the views of his grandfather, who had died six years earlier, were the chief influence on his thinking at that time. All his life he would retain his central belief that individual initiative flourished best in conditions of liberty. In response to his experiences in the Second World War, however, he departed from his grandfather's position on defense and became convinced of the value of collective security. On his return to the U.S., he used his considerable range of contacts in Washington and the Congress to advocate American membership of the

United Nations as a forum on global issues. He regarded this changed posture as an evolution in GOP thinking and not as a reversal of family tradition.[4]

After his graduation from Harvard in 1924, he trained every summer with the Army Reserves. During 1941, before Pearl Harbor, he took leave from the Senate to take up active duty with the First American Tank Detachment, then with the British Eighth Army in Libya. In February 1944 he resigned his seat in order to join the regular Army, the only senator to do so since the Civil War. He served in France as senior liaison officer and translator for General Jean de Lattre de Tassigny of the First French Army, and later with Generals Patton and Eisenhower in the final liberation of Europe. After his reelection to the Senate in 1946, he worked with Sen. Arthur Vandenberg to push through the Marshall Plan for European recovery and recruited Republican support for the North Atlantic Treaty Organization (NATO). Much decorated, he remained active in the Reserves and rose to the rank of major general, the title by which Nikita Khrushchev addressed him when Lodge escorted the Russian chairman on a tour of the United States in 1959.[5]

Lodge was descended from several of America's most prominent families. George Cabot, founding member of the Federalist party and elected senator from Massachusetts in 1791, the year of the Bill of Rights, had entertained Washington at his home in Beverly and acted as advisor to Alexander Hamilton. Cabot's adventures as a privateer in the American Revolution entranced the young Lodge. Lodge's paternal grandfather had married a cousin, Anna Cabot Davis, a descendant of Cabot and the daughter of Rear Adm. Charles H. Davis, Lincoln's commander on the upper Mississippi in the first year of the Civil War. Davis established a naval tradition in the family, honored by Lodge's own father in service under Capt. Charles H. Davis, an uncle, off Cuba during the Spanish-American War. Lodge's mother, Elizabeth, had been a Freylinghuysen Davis; his sister Helena married Edouard de Streel, court secretary to the queen of the Belgians; and his wife, Emily Sears Lodge, was descended from Richard Sears of Yarmouth, one of the earliest of the Plymouth settlers.

Why would a man of such prestige accept, let alone seek, an ambassadorship in Saigon at the age of sixty-one? There are several possible answers. In the early 1960s, not only Americans but diplomats of other countries represented there saw South Vietnam as a second-rate appointment. The careers of many China experts in the Department of State had been destroyed during the McCarthy period; the dampening effect had flowed into the department's Vietnam and Indochina sections.[6] Apart from his wedding trip through Indochina in 1926, Lodge had no knowledge of the area. His training, experience, acquaintance, and contacts pointed to the European capitals or the NATO Council as his natural focus, should he be interested in further government service. During his early adolescence, from 1912 to 1914, Lodge had attended a French-language school in Paris, where his mother had taken her children after their father's death in 1909. He had majored in Romance languages at Harvard. His family and their acquaintances regularly sojourned in Paris and Rome, where they mixed with the European aristocracy and expatriate artistic communities. Lodge had served with the French Army in World War II, and it was largely in the medium of French, the common language of many of its members, that he had made his wide range of contacts during his tenure at the United Nations.

In 1963, in spite of well-publicized disclaimers to the contrary, Lodge wished to make a late bid for the presidency.[7] His own strengths were in foreign affairs, and he believed that historically the American public looked to the GOP for leadership in foreign policy. Indeed, in 1960, when Lodge himself was not a contender in the primaries and the party asked him to serve as Vice President Richard Nixon's running mate, he replied that he could serve the Republican cause more effectively by remaining at his post in the United Nations rather than by resigning to campaign at Nixon's side. He could do more good, Lodge explained to Nixon, by addressing nonpartisan groups on foreign policy issues than by "campaigning in the usual sense," meaning, as he expressed it, "hammer and tongs Republican meetings and attacks on the Democrats."[8] This patrician attitude to statesmanship also informed his view of the road to the presidency. In seeking the Vietnam appointment in 1963, he was thinking in terms of an election-year draft into the White House, such as he had helped organize for Eisenhower in 1952. A whistle-stop campaign was abhorrent to his temperament; he had had enough of tramping through the New England snow gathering votes for the March primary in New Hampshire. He enjoyed good press relations: Vietnam offered him the high media coverage as the United States ambassador fighting communism in the field that would increase his chances of gaining the Republican nomination in 1964 or 1968.

That Lodge should have at some stage aspired to the highest office in the land was only to be expected, given his family, ambitions, and background. The surprise to many might be that he did not pursue the goal more vigorously, more consistently, and from his earliest days. His career, so glittering in many ways, had lacked clear direction. He was a U.S. senator at thirty-four but found the deliberations in the Senate tedious.[9] He had been so absorbed in engineering the draft of Eisenhower for the presidency in 1952 that he had lost his own seat to the much younger John F. Kennedy. His 1960 campaign for Nixon—apart from the bombshell he delivered in Norfolk, Virginia, by declaring that a Republican administration should include an African-American in the cabinet—struck the voting public as tepid. Kennedy's victory was all the more remarkable in that he was a Catholic, a descendant of Irish immigrants who, even one year earlier, might have appeared to face more obstacles in succeeding to the Oval Office than a candidate long famous in public life and bearing the names of both Cabot and Lodge.

Even Lodge's influence on the GOP's direction was less than might have been expected from his life-long membership. It is not clear that Lodge's efforts as U.N. ambassador to convey the importance to America of the new African and Asian nations did in fact affect administration policy. Eisenhower in 1954 had recruited his assistance in forming a new centrist or "Whig" party, to be based on the middle ground of the existing Republican and Democratic parties, but this had come to nothing. In 1961, Lodge found himself with no public position at all and accepted an offer from his friend Henry Luce, the owner of *Time,* to act as a consultant on international affairs. In comparison to his checkered history in politics, Lodge's military interests show a striking consistency. His enthusiastic service in the Army Reserves, his correspondence with General de Lattre until the Frenchman's death in 1952, and his continuing friendships with American generals such as Crittenberger and Patton suggest that he might have enjoyed a life of more personal satisfaction had he switched in 1945 to an alternative career in the professional army. There is no indication that he seriously considered making such a change.[10]

Lodge's personal maxim, which became a weapon in the hands of his opponents during the lackluster campaign of 1960, was that physical health and a good appearance were more important in politics and diplomacy than intellectual agility. His practice of preparing himself for public appearances with exercise in the morning and the occasional nap in the afternoon might suggest an attitude of noblesse oblige, even dilettantism, out of place in the professional world of the later twentieth century. Yet in his service in Vietnam he was seen by turns and by different observers as a leader to inspire love and loyalty, an implacable opponent, and an authoritative, even ruthless chief of mission. His first embassy in Saigon was to set in place the direction of American policy in Indochina for a decade.

The absence of a close and driving focus in Lodge's public life before Vietnam requires some comment. Prejudice might explain it as due to a nonchalance engendered by privilege, but the circumstances appear to have been more complicated. As a young man, Lodge clearly found it a less than straightforward proposition to forge an individual course for himself against the powerful influence of his grandfather, his "beloved counselor and friend," on the one hand, and the omnipresent reminders of his father's short but brilliant career in letters on the other. The grandfather was Henry Cabot Lodge, Republican leader in the Senate, advocate of America's Manifest Destiny, sponsor of the Spanish-American War, Woodrow Wilson's great adversary in the fight over the Treaty of Versailles and the League of Nations. This man of towering personality had doted on his own eldest son, George, or "Bay," Lodge. He appears to have transferred all his ambitions for Bay to his grandson, his namesake, on Bay's sudden death in 1909.[11]

Bay Lodge, much more interested in poetry than politics, had become the protégé of his father's intellectual friends in Boston and Paris. The childless Henry Adams treated him as an adopted son and discussed with him the problems of writing in a philistine society; Bay later entertained Adams on tours of the nightclubs of Paris. William Sturgis Bigelow taught him the mysteries of Japanese Buddhism; Edith Wharton and the diplomat Cecil Spring Rice presided over his literary development. Even Theodore Roosevelt was charmed by Bay and took him hunting in the American West. Lodge and his wife, Nannie, carefully smoothed Bay's path to greatness through Harvard and the Sorbonne; Lodge and Roosevelt badgered publishers with his manuscripts. "Nothing so good had been written in English since Shakespeare," friends of the family declared. Lodge never understood the burden his own success and will to promote Bay's talents placed upon him, although Wharton would later observe that the father had kept the son "in a state of brilliant immaturity."[12]

Alas, "Adonais cannot live to be old," Nannie Lodge's friend Margaret Winthrop Chanler lamented. Bay the poet, described by Chanler as "himself the poem," died in 1909, when his own eldest son was only seven. He died at the summer home of Sturgis Bigelow on Tuckanuck Island, north of Boston, of a heart attack brought on by acute spasms of indigestion which followed a meal of spoiled shellfish. The consensus of concerned family and friends over many preceding years had been that Bay overstressed an already weak heart by working too hard and too long with insufficient holidays.[13]

The circumstances of his father's death help explain Lodge's precautions regarding his own health, his dietary restrictions, and his exercise and rest regimes. Always wary of a recurrence of the ulcers he had developed at a young age, by the time of his appointment to Vietnam he had quit smoking, took little alcohol, and made bland soups a staple of his food intake.[14] Earlier he may have enjoyed his summer maneuvers with the Army Reserves and in the company of physically flamboyant men like Gen. George Patton, his Massachusetts neighbor, in part because of a driving urge to cultivate a strong constitution.

After Bay's death, Cabot—now styled Henry Cabot Lodge, Jr.—his brother, John Davis Lodge, and his sister, Helena Lodge, on their return from Paris at the outbreak of war in 1914, grew up in their grandfather's circles in Boston and Washington. It was to be a nineteenth-century upbringing for the Lodge children in their formative years.

Surrounded by the intellectuals who had admired their father, they were also in constant contact with America's ruling elite, including several presidents and members of their administrations. Henry Adams, a strong influence in the young Cabot's life, had written a memoir of Bay's life, published by the Lodges in conjunction with Bay's poems and dramas, a collection that Roosevelt introduced.[15] Cabot in fact flirted more than briefly with a writing career in journalism. Having spent one summer working for the *Boston Transcript* during college, he sought a more serious position with the *New York Herald Tribune*, where he worked variously as editorial writer and political reporter, and on the overseas desk. He was employed intermittently by *Time* from 1924 to 1932. In later life, Lodge explained away this period as mere preparation for public service. His grandfather, however, was deeply concerned about his ambitions at age twenty-two. Shortly before his death in 1924, the elder Lodge summoned the proprietor of the *Transcript*, Theodore J. Joslin, to his office. He explained that he himself could take Cabot to the forthcoming Republican convention, but that he felt it good for discipline that Cabot should attend as a working newspaperman. He wished "to confide" in Joslin that although Cabot might dream of one day owning a newspaper, his own fondest hope was that his grandson would follow in his footsteps and be Republican leader in the Senate.[16] Six years later, Cabot did indeed enter Congress, as did his brother John, who eventually became governor of Connecticut.

Although evidence is scanty—for in regard to personal matters Lodge adopted his grandfather's habit of editing his papers—it appears that at each of the crossroads in his life Lodge adopted the touchstone of patriotic duty in deciding his future. He had gone on active duty during World War II, and he seems to have regarded his service in Europe as the high point of his life. Yet the war over, he returned to the Senate, where he felt less than fulfilled. He accepted the U.N. ambassadorship on the basis of duty, at presidential request, although he had hoped to be named secretary of state. He blamed Dulles, not the president, for his failure to win the secretaryship.[17] Lodge consistently resolved personal setbacks by making a renewed commitment to public duty. After his defeat in the 1960 election, when he might have retired honorably to Beverly, his mind once again turned to service of the nation.

At some point in 1961 or 1962 he visited Secretary of State Dean Rusk and told him, informally, that "he felt that he had one more tour of public duty in his system.. . .He did not want an easy job, but if there was a challenging job which came up," he would be interested. He was to use exactly the same words to Kennedy when approached at presidential level in 1963.[18] It is probable that he was already thinking of Vietnam. The ambassadorial post there promised him a last chance in the presidential race; in addition, it brought together the roles of statesman and warrior to a degree no other of his many positions had or could.

In mid-1963, America had only a limited representation in Vietnam. Less than fifty American lives had been lost. Eleven thousand U.S. troops acted as advisors to the South Vietnamese Army of President Ngo Dinh Diem, but for the United States the war had not begun. The state of South Vietnam had existed since 1954, perpetuated by the Geneva Accords that had ended the French colonial presence in Indochina. Saigon was a gracious city renowned for its food and its tree-lined boulevards; the rare bombing incidents did not disrupt the leisurely pace of life. The United States embassy building operated on such a relaxed schedule that it habitually locked up for the night at six o'clock.[19]

This is not to say, however, that Vietnam was unimportant to American global thinking. As early as 1950, the small Asian country had become a key issue in U.S. domestic politics. After China became the People's Republic, the further "loss of Vietnam" to communism, successive presidents thought, might bring condemnation from the American right and, in a loss of votes, endanger liberal freedoms and liberal programs at home. Three U.S. administrations deepened America's engagement in Vietnam, seeing Indochina through the prism of the Cold War, accepting that local "wars of liberation" were always orchestrated by the monolithic Communist movement centered in Peking and Moscow. Truman was concerned that, as Eisenhower's later formulation put it, if any Southeast Asian "domino" fell to communism, the rest would swiftly follow. By 1961, America had chosen South Vietnam as the place to take a stand against the spread of communism in Asia. Eisenhower made South Vietnam an American responsibility, giving military and propaganda assistance to Ngo Dinh Diem. Kennedy extended Eisenhower's commitment to Vietnam by pledging to guarantee the neutrality of Laos. In this global view, communism was a monolithic movement and local wars of national liberation were always directed from Moscow and Peking. As we shall see, although many American planners involved with Vietnam with Lodge were aware of the Sino-Soviet split of 1961, they did not take this information into account to any marked degree.[20]

In South Vietnam, President Diem had held power for nine years. He had been the U.S.-sponsored candidate for leadership because he had been connected with neither the French nor the Japanese colonizers and was not associated with any of the Vietnamese political parties whose checkered histories might easily prove a diplomatic embarrassment. His family had a long and distinguished record as mandarins in Hue. Diem was a bachelor and a Roman Catholic. His natural constituency was among the Catholics who had moved south at the partition of Vietnam and among the Catholics already there. He trusted only his immediate family. His brother Ngo Dinh Thuc was Roman Catholic archbishop of Hue; Ngo Dinh Can ruled as his unofficial vice regent in central Vietnam; Ngo Dinh Luyen served as his ambassador in London; Ngo Dinh Nhu was his political counselor and Nhu's beautiful wife his palace hostess.

The Virginian Frederick Nolting had served as U.S. ambassador to Vietnam since April 1961. Following Department of State instructions, Nolting had made Diem his personal friend. His brief was to counteract the coldness and strained relations that had developed between the Ngo brothers and his predecessor, Ambassador Elbridge Durbrow, after Durbrow had attempted by forceful demarche to have Nhu dismissed from Saigon. The arrangements that had cushioned Diem from criticism during 1961 and 1962, however, were about to come to an end. By early 1963 Kennedy's chief advisors in the State Department were confiding to each other that Nolting was "too indulgent" of Diem's stubbornness. They determined to recall him to Washington.

Since 1960, if not before, various United States policymakers had contemplated replacing Diem as the leader of South Vietnam. Maintaining a pro-American regime in Saigon was an important consideration, since all U.S. operations in Vietnam must be seen to be conducted south of the seventeenth parallel, in accordance with the Geneva Accords. Diem's American critics had consistently argued that he was too close to Ngo Dinh Nhu, that he did nothing to draw his opponents into the political process, and that he was insufficiently responsive to American policies disguised as requests and advice. While these doubts brewed in Washington, Diem and Nhu had begun to ask themselves whether admitting American advisors into the country was the unmitigated blessing it had previously seemed. Diem confided his fears to Roger Lalouette, the French ambassador to South Vietnam, early in 1963. The Frenchman warned him that the advisors might prove to be the first step toward an eventual U.S.

takeover of the country. Lalouette encouraged Diem to open a dialogue with Hanoi and offered French assistance in effecting a rapprochement between North and South Vietnam.[21] Ngo Dinh Nhu privately resolved that he would leak stories of his contacts with Hanoi to Western journalists as the diplomatic moment arose: America might feel compelled to give greater support to the family regime if he hinted at impending capitulation to the enemy.

Lodge's interest in the ambassadorship was consolidated in January 1963, when he spent a three-week tour of duty at the Pentagon as a general in the Reserves. There he was briefed on Vietnam and counterinsurgency. He began to voice his interest in the problems of the war and produced a paper giving his own views on counterinsurgency theory.[22] One young officer, who saw war service as advantageous to his own career, realized that Lodge might be interested in going to Vietnam. He was Lt. Col. John Michael Dunn, whom Lodge subsequently chose as his right-hand man in Saigon. Dunn had been initially attached to Lodge by Pentagon officials "to keep him out of the way" since, understandably, Army professionals resented the intrusion of high-summer Reserve officers into their domain. As we shall see, in Saigon Dunn was to keep unwelcome visitors and others out of the ambassador's way.[23]

It was probably during that tour of duty that Lodge began to float his name as a possibility for Vietnam. What cannot be doubted is that during his Pentagon briefings, a meeting between Lodge and the president was arranged by or through Gen. Chester Clifton, the president's military aide. At that time, Kennedy made generalized offers to his old political rival of a NATO posting or an ambassadorship in an area such as Portugal or Pakistan, or, as Kennedy said, somewhere the future of U.S. bases in the region was a concern.[24]

The aristocratic Lodge was not in any way disdainful of the glitter of the Kennedy presidency. Utterly self-confident, conscious that he and his acquaintances represented individualism in a society he saw as becoming increasingly constrained and bureaucratic, Lodge, as Michael Dunn recalled many years later, found the style, the originality, and the ability of Kennedy and the men with whom he surrounded himself attractive.

Kennedy's advisors, his court, were known as the "New Frontiersmen." They valued Kennedy's "vigor" in decision making. Serving in foreign affairs positions in 1963 were William Bundy as deputy assistant secretary of defense, his brother McGeorge Bundy as special assistant to the president for national security affairs, and Michael V. Forrestal, Jr., as Far Eastern advisor to the National Security Council. Robert McNamara, who had left a managerial position with the Ford

Motor Company to join the administration, was secretary of defense. Roger Hilsman, late of an American guerilla unit in Burma, was initially the director of the Bureau of Intelligence and Research and in May would become assistant secretary of state for Far Eastern affairs. W. Averell Harriman, under secretary of state for political affairs, would become the leader of the State Department campaign against South Vietnam's Ngo Dinh Diem in the second half of the year.

Many of these men had known wealth and privilege all their lives: William and McGeorge Bundy hailed from a well-to-do old Bostonian family; John Mc-Cone, then director of the CIA, had made his fortune building ships in World War II; Harriman's family had controlled money and power since the heyday of railroad building in the 1870s and 1880s. Lodge had met them all through his own circles, as well as in the course of government service.

Both Kenneth O'Donnell, a close Kennedy associate, and Roger Hilsman have repeatedly asserted that Kennedy intended to withdraw from Vietnam after the 1964 presidential election gave him a stronger base in Congress. The evidence they adduce for this assertion, however, suggests a different interpretation: that Kennedy was postponing a major policy review on Vietnam until after he had made the electoral gains in 1964 which would make his congressional position safe. The Joint Chiefs of Staff did indeed have a plan for withdrawal of American advisors in 1963, but this was one among many, and, as Kennedy explained to Sen. Mike Mansfield at the time, if he showed an unwillingness to prosecute the war in Asia to stem the spread of communism, he would invite severe criticism from the American right. He therefore had to hold the line in Vietnam and prevent a public debate on U.S. involvement there until, as he hoped, he had gained a stronger popular mandate in November 1964.[25]

Kennedy was well aware of the ideological advantages of a war against communism in a far-off place. As his biographer Herbert Parmet has suggested, he may also have consistently sought to display strength in the foreign affairs field—in the Asian case, in an actual shooting war—given the complexities of the civil rights problem at home and poor Democratic party discipline in Congress.[26] But suddenly, in May 1963, Vietnam started to take up too much of his time. Indeed, as Rusk told Lodge in June, "the question of Vietnam" had come to take up "more of the President's time than any other single subject."[27] Kennedy wanted the war, but he wanted it to drop back to its old, steady, low priority among his concerns. The way to achieve this end, Kennedy thought, was to appoint a strong U.S. ambassador to Saigon, who could manage his press relations from there.

In the back of Kennedy's mind may have been Major General Lodge's reply to his query the preceding January, when Lodge had said that he "would always be glad to serve the President." He was "really not interested in a job, for a job's sake, or in a quiet post," but was "available to take anything that was challenging." The name and the position would soon click.[28]

Discussions in the State Department regarding a successor to Nolting as U.S. ambassador in Saigon were conducted with some reference to a report on the situation in South Vietnam that had been prepared in January 1963 by Roger Hilsman and Michael Forrestal. The report was critical of the dictatorial tendencies of Diem and Nhu on the one hand, and on the other of Madame Nhu's habit of making outspoken statements in the Western media. In particular, it targeted Diem's lack of responsiveness to suggestions from the U.S. ambassador and his poor relations with the American press.

In a secret annex, which had an even higher security classification than the general report, Hilsman and Forrestal went on to criticize the American government's organization in Vietnam. This is so important to the subsequent unfolding of events that it deserves extensive quotation. Of the management of the U.S. mission in South Vietnam, Hilsman and Forrestal wrote:

> There is no overall planning effort that effectively ties together the civilian and the military efforts. There is little or no long-range thinking about the kind of country that should come out of victory and about what we do now to contribute to this longer-range goal. . . . The real trouble, however, is that the rather large U.S. effort in South Vietnam is managed by a multitude of independent U.S. agencies and people with little or no overall direction. No one man is in charge. . . . What is needed, ideally, is to give authority to a single, strong executive, a man perhaps with a military background but who understands that this war is essentially a struggle to build a nation out of the chaos of revolution. One possibility would be to appoint the right kind of general as Ambassador. *An alternative would be to appoint a civilian public figure whose character and reputation would permit him to dominate the representatives of all the other departments and agencies* [emphasis added].[29]

This analysis, while it identified the problem of coordination between the U.S. mission's agencies and departments, skirted the need for any review of America's Vietnam policy, a need to which its findings so clearly pointed.

Although speculation in Washington ran high that Edmund Gullion, a career diplomat who had recently served as U.S. ambassador in the Congo, would be chosen for Saigon, Rusk wanted a representative of even higher rank. He put forward Lodge's name, on the grounds that his personal stature as a distinguished

Republican would "reflect the bipartisan support which Kennedy had for his Vietnam policy." Lodge, he argued, would serve to deflect the appeal of Barry Goldwater, representing the Republican right, who was demanding a more bellicose American posture in Vietnam.

Kennedy welcomed Rusk's nomination of Lodge. Lodge, he thought, would serve admirably as Republican asbestos against the heat of possible future criticism of his foreign policy. But Kennedy had an additional private motive for sending Lodge to Vietnam. Kenneth O'Donnell remembered that "the President told us that when Rusk suggested sending Lodge to Saigon, he decided to approve the appointment because the idea of getting Lodge mixed up in such a hopeless mess as Vietnam was irresistible."[30] He was amused, O'Donnell went on, at the thought of deflating what he saw as Lodge's pomposity. Perhaps he wished also to destroy, once and for all, his old political rival and remembered the grandfather's slighting of his own father.

As history was to show, the Lodge appointment did achieve the goal of deflecting criticism from Kennedy's involvement in Vietnam, although ultimately with great cost to America's reputation in the foreign relations field. As William Safire wrote in 1977, Kennedy's appointment of Lodge to Saigon "foreclosed . . . Republican opposition to the way the war was conducted until 1967."[31] But in mid-1963, America's policies in Asia—which amounted to the containment of communism—had widespread domestic support. These policies were not expected to involve the loss of American lives. While the war in Vietnam remained popular, Congress could be counted on to supply funds.

For several months, however, a small group of young American newspapermen in Saigon, led by David Halberstam of the *New York Times* and Neil Sheehan of United Press International, had been very critical of the Diem regime's ability and will to fight. By their own admission, they had taken up the story of a developing dispute between Diem and various Buddhist groups as a vehicle for writing about the political situation in South Vietnam with the quite conscious motive of promoting a coup against Diem.[32] The Halberstam-Sheehan group made the "Buddhist Crisis" story their own; their copy was the basis for almost all the reports that appeared in major American daily newspapers and weekly magazines such as *Time* and *Newsweek*. The group's promotion of the story put Vietnam on front pages for several weeks, prompting many editorials and readers' letters abhorring U.S. support of Diem. This development threatened to open up public debate on the conduct of the war that Kennedy wished to avoid.

To Kennedy's dismay, on June 11 an event occurred that could not be ignored: an aging Buddhist monk committed suicide by gasoline-fueled fire at a

Saigon intersection as a protest against the Diem regime's alleged persecution of Buddhism; his clerical colleagues had carefully alerted the American reporters to attend the event.[33] Malcolm Browne's photograph of the fiery sacrifice went around the world and profoundly shocked many Americans who were in a position to protest to the U.S. government.

On the very next day Lodge met Kennedy by appointment at the White House. Lodge knew, of course, of Rusk's memo recommending him for Saigon, although the purpose of his visit was to present the president with a report he had prepared on the activities of a Paris-based international forum, the Atlantic Institute, of which he was director general. After he had made a brief statement, Kennedy cut him off and shifted with some intensity to Vietnam. Turning to a copy of Malcolm Browne's picture of the fiery suicide, the president said, "I suppose these are the worst press relations to be found in the world today." According to Lodge, the president went on to say that "the situation in Vietnam was extremely serious. I had undoubtedly seen the news dispatch about the Buddhist monk who burned himself alive. The United States Army was present to an important degree. He said the bad situation in Vietnam endangered our position in all the surrounding countries and that an American reverse in Vietnam might have far-reaching repercussions." He would like, he said, to persuade Lodge to go to Vietnam as his ambassador. Kennedy then spoke again of the bad relations between the U.S. embassy in Saigon and the press, saying, "I wish you, personally, would take charge of press relations." The Diem government was "entering its terminal phase," Kennedy stated.[34]

Lodge said gravely that he would need time to discuss the transfer to an overseas posting with his wife. Lodge had every intention of accepting, as Kennedy was probably well aware, and he was back in Washington for briefings five days later.

It is difficult to establish what instructions, if any, Kennedy gave to Lodge regarding the future of U.S. relations with Diem. Lodge's confidential journal seems to indicate that he was not apprised of any new policy; Averell Harriman merely advised that he should get to Vietnam in August. "Diem is the best man," Harriman told him. Madame Nhu's outspokenness was a problem and the Buddhist situation had been handled "stupidly," but "who would succeed if Diem dropped dead?"

Rusk described the Saigon assignment to Lodge as "the toughest post in our service, and we are all very grateful to you for taking it on." The secretary of state added that real progress was being made in the war, "but the press wander

around and pick up small gripes of the junior Americans and, of course, there is real incompetence in other quarters." Lodge listened most attentively to Rusk's next comment that "we need an ambassador out there who is tough; who can act as a catalyst; who will take responsibility and make decisions and not refer many detailed questions to Washington. We want to make the political side of things go as well as the military side has been going." Apparently, Rusk was not at that time contemplating a radical change in U.S. policy for Vietnam, such as encouraging a change in the government. He spoke instead of a possible widening of the war, for he went on to confide that "if Laos should go, then the question would get onto a new level."[35]

John Michael Dunn and Frederick Flott, whom Lodge chose to be his personal aides during his first ambassadorship in Saigon, have both said recently that Kennedy gave his new ambassador no specific instructions for Diem's overthrow. Dunn argued that Kennedy was extremely concerned about the adverse publicity the South Vietnamese president was receiving in the dispatches of the Halberstam-Sheehan group of journalists. The newspapermen were in effect acting as an additional agency of the U.S. mission, although they had no responsibility to the Department of State, he said. It was this situation, as Dunn understood it, that Kennedy wished Lodge to address as a first priority. Although the Department of State's instructions to Nolting in the cable traffic of June–August 1963 were that the U.S. ambassador should urge Diem to reform his treatment of the Buddhist majority, Dunn stressed that his perception was that Kennedy was less interested in democratizing Vietnam than in dealing with his own domestic problem of clamorous demands that Diem be made to reform. Lodge, Dunn continued, conceived his role as that of a special emissary of the president whose mission was to resolve the impasse between Diem and the U.S. Department of State.[36]

The Kennedy administration's disposition to campaigns and crusades on many fronts helps to explain the hasty and uncoordinated decisions on Vietnam that were to be taken in the coming months. Southeast Asia was the only area in the world where America was involved in a shooting war, but many other issues divided the attention of the president, his advisors in the White House, and members of the Department of State. At home, the civil rights movement and recent revelations of the serious nature of poverty in America presented these men with seemingly intractable problems. In foreign relations, the Berlin question and the projected nuclear disarmament treaty with the Soviet Union consumed Kennedy's interest.

In September 1963 Kennedy was to realize that the members of his administration were deeply divided as to maintaining U.S. support for Diem. That this was so was not entirely clear in June. Kennedy's preferred approach to decision making was to form ad hoc groups to deal with pressing policy issues. The small group he would choose as his consultants on Vietnam naturally contained many men who also served on the National Security Council. But the wider membership of the council, a body that had been designed precisely to prevent the kind of improvisation in foreign policy in which Kennedy was about to indulge, had been aligning into diametrically opposed groups regarding Diem and the conduct of the war since the beginning of the year.

Secretary of Defense Robert McNamara and Gen. Maxwell Taylor, chairman of the Joint Chiefs of Staff, were less concerned with the political situation in Saigon than with the war in the field, which they believed on the basis of military reports to be going well. The U.S. intelligence community tended to share that view. But as Vietnam's Buddhist Crisis developed and American public opinion turned against Diem, officials of the Department of State began to prevail with the argument that the political situation in South Vietnam was the crucial factor in the conduct of the war, and that victory would not be possible unless Diem reformed or quit.

From South Vietnam, Gen. Paul Harkins and John Richardson, head of the CIA station in Saigon, advocated continued support of Diem. Many junior officers in the agencies of the U.S. mission there, however, were critical of him, perhaps because their duties put them into close contact with the Vietnamese opposition. By mid-June the voices most often raised in criticism of Diem were those of Averell Harriman, Roger Hilsman, and Michael Forrestal. Rusk offered a moderating voice to put criticisms of the Asian leader in context.[37]

During the summer of 1963, Kennedy seems to have conceptualized Vietnam as a political and public relations issue rather than a war. He consulted only with a select few from State, especially Harriman and Hilsman. Representatives of the Defense Department, the Joint Chiefs of Staff, and the CIA were not included in these discussions. As a result, William Bundy recorded, these principals did not know the thinking of Harriman, Hilsman, Kennedy, and Lodge on the political situation in Saigon.[38]

If Kennedy's bypassing key representatives of the National Security Council on Vietnam policy seems grave enough, there was yet another twist. In effect, the Department of State team had also cut themselves off from those officials most in a position to advise them on how to deal with Diem and his family. Two of these men were John Richardson of the CIA, whose special job it was to liaise with Ngo Dinh Nhu, and William Colby, then chief of the Far Eastern Division of the CIA in Washington and formerly head of the agency in Saigon. Colby believed that he understood Nhu better than any other American.[39] As for the incumbent U.S. ambassador, Nolting was not informed of the adverse Hilsman-Forrestal report of January on Diem and the U.S. mission. He learned that he was to be replaced by Lodge only weeks before the event, when he picked up a newscast on ship's radio while touring on vacation in the Mediterranean.[40] Nolting remained bitter until his death in 1990 that he had been prevented from counseling Diem when the Vietnamese leader most needed his advice. Lodge himself preserved no record of his thoughts on Nolting's removal from the Saigon post, or of the discussions in Washington he attended in July.

Not only were decisions in this period taken in an atmosphere of secrecy and acrimony, they were often taken precipitously and without due consideration for the possible and indeed likely outcomes. Two days after the first Buddhist suicide by fire and four days before he advised Lodge that U.S. policy toward Diem remained constant, Dean Rusk had contacted the deputy chief of mission in Saigon, William Trueheart, instructing him to approach the South Vietnamese vice president, Nguyen Ngoc Tho. Trueheart was to explain that the U.S. would support Tho as "constitutional successor" to Diem if the internal political situation in South Vietnam deteriorated. Rusk offered Tho military assistance, "should this become necessary."[41] Such an action may have seemed like a reasonable diplomatic precaution. Rather predictably, however, given media interest in Diem's Buddhist Crisis, the instruction leaked, and on June 14, 1963, the *New York Times* published its contents on page 1.

At a meeting in the White House on July 4, after discussing the possible outcomes of a "spontaneous coup" in South Vietnam, the president instructed Nolting to go back to Vietnam to use his "remaining good will" with Diem in urging him to conciliate the Buddhists, while Lodge, now publicly known to be the new American ambassador, would journey there after briefings.[42] Nolting duly returned to his office in the U.S. embassy and stayed for a galling month. He reported on his departure on August 14 that he had failed to move Diem, in spite of his best efforts.[43] Since Diem was expecting Nolting to return to Saigon on a continuing basis after his vacation, Department of State shifts in policy could only serve to make him feel besieged and betrayed by his American patrons, while doing nothing to advance the war effort.

Was Lodge the right man for the Saigon job? In asking his Republican opposite to take control of his press relations in South Vietnam, and to get Vietnam out of the American newspapers, Kennedy no doubt had in mind Lodge's public relations successes as U.S. ambassador to the United Nations. But although skilled in press management and with the insider's knowledge of a newspaperman, Lodge was a poor choice as the official to coordinate the U.S. mission in South Vietnam—the primary responsibility, after all, of the ambassador there. Lodge had not trained himself to operate as a member of a team. He had no experience as an administrator, admiration for the bureaucrat's art having no place in his vision of public service. If he seemed to have several excellent qualifications for the Vietnam position, these did not address the problems outlined in Hilsman's January report on the American mission. Lodge's military experience, for example, seemed to promise that he would be able to work with the U.S. Army in Vietnam. He knew General Harkins, the head of the Military Assistance Command, Vietnam (MACV), having been attached during 1945 to the military headquarters in France of which Harkins was commander. Indeed, this connection had struck Kennedy as fortuitous when he had met Lodge during the latter's tour of duty at the Pentagon in January.[44] Long acquaintance, however, was no guarantee that the commander and the ambassador would agree on what type of war was being fought in Vietnam or how to direct it to achieve specific objectives, let alone work together to formulate a blueprint for a "free nation," as Hilsman had recommended in his January report.

Again, Lodge's fluency in French seemed to many at State to be an important asset for an ambassador to a former colony of France. But Lodge's very confidence in conducting international negotiations in French implied a traditional view of the diplomat's role which did not include the complex managerial skills needed to organize the resources and personnel of a modern American mission. This distinction was not immediately clear to observers at the time. Hilsman, whom Kennedy had made assistant secretary of state for Far Eastern affairs at the outbreak of the Buddhist Crisis in May, for example, recorded in his memoir of his own involvement with U.S. policy making on Vietnam that he was pleased with the Lodge appointment because the Republican met his and Forrestal's suggestion of "a civilian public figure whose reputation and character would permit him to dominate the representatives of all other departments and agencies." The reasoning in the rest of the relevant passage, however, suggests that by June 1963 he may have been more concerned with Lodge's potential to dominate and so to reform Diem himself.[45]

The coordination of the activities of the U.S. agencies in South Vietnam was not the uppermost concern in Lodge's mind as he prepared for his Saigon assignment. His disposition to see himself as responsible only to the president was reinforced by remarks made to him by Rusk during their first consultation on Vietnam, which he recorded in this way: "I (HCL) will have the last word on personnel—who I want to have and who I do not want to have. I will have priority on people, money and everything else, just as though this were a war theatre."

Presumably the secretary of state did not intend to give the new ambassador to South Vietnam quite the powers his choice of words, or Lodge's interpretation of them, appeared to promise. There can be no doubt, however, that Rusk did permit Lodge to choose his own staff. He did not appoint a trained administrator as his second in command, the usual practice with a non–Foreign Service ambassador. In particular, Rusk later acquiesced in Colonel Dunn's assumption of a preeminent position in the Saigon chancery. Lodge's creation of a position for Dunn in the embassy with powers above even those of the deputy chief of mission was to be the cause of strife in the mission during the critical first months of 1964.

Rusk's reference to Vietnam as a "war theatre," whatever his exact intention in using the term to Lodge, might have alerted attention to a point needing clarification in Kennedy's circular of May 29, 1961, on the authority of chiefs of mission. Both Elbridge Durbrow and later Nolting had pointed out the problem. While the 1961 order, like Eisenhower's earlier directives, put the ambassador in complete charge of all U.S. missions, in the case of Vietnam, the military commander enjoyed a quite separate chain of command.

The relationship between the "area military commander" and the ambassador outlined in Kennedy's letter to ambassadors is important to an understanding of Lodge's later conflicts with General Harkins. While the ambassador was in charge of "the entire United States Diplomatic Mission," not only "the personnel of the Department of State and the Foreign Service" but also "the representatives of all other United States agencies," including those attached to Military Assistance Advisory Groups, Kennedy had affirmed, the ambassador's authority did not extend to the military commander of troops in the field.

Where U.S. forces were engaged in fighting, "the line of authority to these forces runs from me, to the Secretary of Defense, to the Joint Chiefs of Staff in Washington and to the area commander in the field," Kennedy's directive stated. That is, the area military commander was to report directly to the president, and not through any ambassador. Kennedy's May 1961 circular, however, was a general one. It did not address the vexed case of Vietnam.[46]

In his period as U.S. ambassador to South Vietnam from 1957 to 1961, Durbrow had repeatedly asked Washington for a ruling on his authority in relation to Gen. Samuel Williams, then head of the Military Assistance Advisory Group in Vietnam, who had been in the habit of countermanding programs initiated by the embassy. Nolting during his ambassadorship faced an even more delicate problem. He was technically in charge of the operations commanded by Gen. Lionel McGarr and then Gen. Charles Timmes, but when four-star general Paul Harkins arrived in 1961 to take charge of the recently created Military Assistance Command, Vietnam, this new high-ranking military commander was clearly in a position to claim absolute primacy in the U.S. mission on matters relating to the war.

Technically, the "area commander" in Vietnam was the commander in the Pacific, Adm. Henry Felt, based in Honolulu, and not General Harkins in South Vietnam. But although the Department of State strained credibility to the limit in avoiding mention of a key reality in the correspondence on the matter, Harkins and later Westmoreland were in practice operationally in charge of troops in the field. This was the problem Kennedy's 1961 directive did not resolve.

Nolting, foreseeing potential for disputes, had applied to State for clarification of the relationship between the ambassador and the head of the Military Assistance Command, Vietnam. Nolting confided in Secretary of Defense McNamara. McNamara warned him that the Joint Chiefs could not be expected to consent to a ruling that put four-star generals under ambassadors. Nolting, a career diplomat, then let the matter rest.[47]

During his briefings on his duties as U.S. ambassador to South Vietnam, Lodge received a copy of the Kennedy circular, with the country of reference left blank. The word "Vietnam" had been merely penciled in. There is no documentary record of Lodge making any request for clarification of the authority chain in the U.S. mission before he left for Saigon. It is probable, however, that he did not pursue the matter because Harriman, as Rusk had done in June, advised him he was in "absolute charge," as William Bundy later related.[48]

Lodge, like Diem in Vietnam, was inclined to believe that government was largely a matter of good understanding between men at the top. But given the history, and the possibilities for conflict between a civilian ambassador and the head of the Military Assistance Command, Vietnam, it is remarkable that the problem was not thought through at the time. Harriman, who had asserted that civilians must have primacy in the U.S. missions; William Bundy, who had negotiated for Defense when the Kennedy order was drafted in 1961; McNamara; and Kennedy himself—any one or all of these men should have anticipated that Lodge would refuse to accept parallel chains of command in Vietnam. Such an acceptance went against Lodge's disposition and all his previous experience, while the increasing importance of the military in the balance of mission activities dictated that the ambassador, whoever he was, must eventually take a stand on his own ultimate responsibility for coordination of projects.

Although he appears to have taken little interest in any State briefings he may have had in making his assessment of the political situation in Saigon, Lodge began to develop his own sources of information before he left Washington. One of his earliest requests of Rusk, immediately after his first meeting with the secretary of state, was for permission to discuss his assignment with Henry Luce, the proprietor of *Time*. Luce and Lodge were long-time friends. An old newspaperman himself, Lodge asked Luce for leads. Luce gave him access to his magazine's Vietnam files, especially those of Charles Mohr, who at that time worked for *Time*. Lodge was particularly impressed by one article, to the point where he retained an abstract in his own files.[49] The piece, dated May 2, 1963, was entitled "Vietnam—Where We Stand and Why."

In the article, Mohr argued that the U.S. military and the Vietnamese government had been too optimistic regarding progress in the war, while the U.S. press and American junior officers in Saigon, predicting from a different standpoint, had been too pessimistic. Mohr went on to say that Diem was nepotistic, corrupt, and tyrannical but the only available leader for South Vietnam. The essential problem, he said, was that Ambassador Nolting had been "too weak" in pressing Diem to set his own house in order and to respond to American directives. Mohr concluded that the U.S. and the Diem government were like "two teenagers playing head-on collision chicken in souped-up hot rods. . . . The trouble is, the U.S. chickens out before Diem does." The phrase "game of chicken" was to remain in the new ambassador's mind as a metaphor for his dealings with Diem.

Fresh from reading these files, Lodge prepared a speech whose text he subsequently used in total during his first interview with Diem. In an air-conditioned American office, long before he had encountered the world of intrigue that surrounded the court in Saigon, he wrote, "I want you to be successful. I want to be useful to you." He went on, apparently without a blush, "I don't expect you to be a 'yes man.' I realize that you must never appear—let alone be—a puppet of the United States." Opening pleasantries aside, he came to the core of the matter: "The American President, unlike some Chiefs of State, does not have unrestricted power. While his word is absolutely good and can never be questioned, the American President, nevertheless, cannot undertake future commitments which would not be supported by public opinion, as this public opinion is influenced by the press and is expressed in the Congress, notably in the Senate." Without American public opinion on your side, he would say to Diem, you cannot get funds for the war.

Immediately before their departure for Saigon, Lodge and his wife accepted an invitation to dinner from a person he named in "Vietnam Memoir" as "a very prominent Vietnamese in Washington." This was none other than Madame Tran Van Chuong, South Vietnam's observer at the United Nations, the wife of South Vietnam's ambassador to Washington and the mother of Diem's official hostess, the vociferous Madame Nhu. Madame Chuong urged Lodge that oppressive acts of the Nhu regime comprising "arrests, imprisonments and executions, a reign of terror," meant that "unless they leave the country, there is no power on earth that can prevent the assassination of Madame Nhu, her husband Mr. Nhu and his brother Mr. Diem."[50]

From Saigon, Madame Nhu had embarked on a campaign against the activist Buddhists monks shortly after the first suicide by fire. A member in her own right of the South Vietnamese National Assembly and president of several women's organizations, including an all-female paramilitary group, she used the English-language *Times of Vietnam* to publicize her own and the government point of view. In a television interview broadcast in the United States on August 1, she had asked: "What have these so-called 'Buddhist leaders' done? They have neither program or man to propose in place of program. All they have done is barbecue a bonze, and that not even with self-sufficient means, since they had to use imported gasoline." The solution to the Buddhist problem, she said, was to ignore the monks; "if they burn thirty women we will go ahead and clap our hands."[51]

Her position deeply offended readers of such papers as the *New York Times* and the *Christian Science Monitor*, who saw in the Buddhist cause their own concerns for religious freedom and representative government. Yet she also presented a compelling visual image wearing the exotic *ao dai*, the Vietnamese national dress, or in army fatigues, with her female troops. She had adopted the title "Madame" Nhu after Madame Chiang Kai Shek, the wife of the Chinese Nationalist leader, the darling of U.S. media in the 1930s. The American reading public, however, quickly identified her with the cartoon strip *Dragon Lady*, and editors eagerly took up variations on the theme of Lucrezia Borgia and the decline of the state when women wield excessive power.

From a U.S. government point of view, Madame Nhu lost all sympathy for the cause of defending her family when she jeered at the appointment of Lodge as U.S. ambassador to Vietnam, editorializing in the *Times of Vietnam*, "They are sending us a proconsul!"[52] Lodge was adept at turning the forms of verbal onslaught in which Madame Nhu specialized to his country's advantage. In Saigon, she would play into his hands.

As Lodge embarked for Saigon on August 17, 1963, he was undoubtedly acting from motives that sprang from his conception of duty, as he believed his country to be engaged in Southeast Asia in order to stem the spread of communism. He was also aware that the Indochina position could do him no harm in Republican political circles. The office of U.S. president was untarnished by Vietnam, the American defeat of 1975 then inconceivable. Lodge, tall, authoritative, one of the most famous of America's sons, and accompanied by his gracious wife, Emily, departed from Boston as a representative of a free people bringing their bounty to the South Vietnamese. He was convinced that he could reform the tyrant in the Gia Long palace by persuading him that American public opinion was the most important factor in the survival of his country.

Chapter Two

The First Eight Days

On the night of August 22, 1963, forty journalists waited at Saigon's Tan Son Nhut Airport to greet the new American ambassador. Rain drizzled into the oppressively hot night. The city had been under curfew for twenty-four hours, the airport closed. Expectations rose as a Pan Am jet began to circle in; it was met by fire from the ground but not hit. Kenneth Rogers, staff aide first to Nolting and now to Lodge, suspected that the explosions were from firecrackers, but he checked the Luger in his shoulder strap. He had come from the tense city prepared for all contingencies. A rumor started up. The Viet Cong firing on the American ambassador? No, ran the counter rumor, the blast was from the anti-aircraft guns of the Diemist authorities themselves! But the Pan Am was not carrying Lodge. Another two-hour wait ensued. Eventually, a U.S. Air Force jet landed and approached the VIP terminal.

Lodge had radioed ahead from his plane that he did not want to conduct a press conference on his arrival. However, when he saw the assembled newspapermen, he spoke to them for five minutes on the vital role of the press in American democracy: he said that he would assist them as best he could to do their jobs. He regretted that he could make no declaration of policy at the time, but assured them that their long wait had not been in vain. The journalists' feelings of warmth toward the new ambassador could only increase when they found that he had allowed four of their colleagues, Keyes Beech among them, to travel with him. Lodge had said exactly what the newspapermen wanted to hear but had told them nothing substantive. John Mecklin, then head of the United States Information Service in Saigon, wrote subsequently that the U.S. embassy problem with the press finished "then and there."[1]

On the eve of Lodge's arrival in Saigon, the U.S. mission in South Vietnam appears to have been suffering from a syndrome that the diplomat William Macomber later described with the phrase "first-rate people, third-rate system." The various agencies of the mission were pursuing their own projects, protecting their budgets, but not pooling the information on the local scene that each collected. Moreover, the embassy had been without an ambassador since May, when Nolting had departed on leave, and Washington had left his second in command, William Trueheart, to perform as acting chief of mission. It seems clear that Trueheart was not receiving summaries of all outgoing reports, as would have been the case in a well-organized mission.[2]

Kennedy's instructions to Lodge regarding his official cables indicate that he may have been aware, intuitively, that there was a problem with information from his Saigon representatives, although he was not prepared to think through the implications of this for policymaking on Vietnam. The president instructed his new ambassador to prepare a major telegram once a week, in response to a list of questions that he himself would supply. Lodge described his understanding of Kennedy's idea in 1965: "Those telegrams were due to his impatience, I think, with the fact that he was being required to read telegrams from a wide variety of government agencies, all coming in on different days, and none of them focussed on exactly the same things although being rather close to the same things. It put an impossible burden."[3]

In 1963 the agencies of the mission in South Vietnam were the United States Operations Mission, the agency in charge of economic aid; an office of the United States Information Service (USIS); the CIA station; and the two military agencies, the Military Assistance Advisory Group (MAAG) and the Military Assistance Command, Vietnam (MACV). Hilsman and Forrestal had touched on the difficulties produced by this multiplicity of government agencies, autonomous in practice if not in conception, in their January report. Lodge continued with his explanation of the Kennedy approach, saying that as he understood the matter, Kennedy had said, "Look we've got to get some one man to pull all this stuff together and give me one telegram and the best man placed to do that is Lodge."

Lodge went on to describe his own procedure in Saigon: "I would take the CIA reports, the military, the State Department, USOM, USIA [USIS], everything we had, and I would pull it all together. It was one man's telegram, written by one man, which I think is the only way anything can be written anyway." In Lodge's view, that way Kennedy "was getting the distillation of the very best material in the governmental agencies, but it was all pulled together by one person. It seems to me that he was absolutely right; the president should depend on the ambassador to do that job and have it done out there not have it done in Washington."

The more usual procedure, of course, was to have the analysis of the source material done in offices of the Department of State. Kennedy's reliance on Lodge "to pull it all together" was something of a gamble, but characteristic of his style.

The personal exchange with Kennedy fitted Lodge's conception of himself as the president's man on the spot making his own observations and suggesting initiatives. He was fond of saying to Frederick Flott that "I am in Saigon for my political insights and knowledge of the U.S. Congress and not to be one more FSO [Foreign Service Officer, career diplomat]." But Lodge's political insights had been developed in Paris and the capitals of Europe, not in Southeast Asia: it also remained to be seen how the heads of the agencies would react to his high-handed approach.

Kennedy had asked Lodge to go to Vietnam as his ambassador in response to the first Buddhist self-immolation in Saigon. We have seen that Kennedy was concerned primarily with U.S. press reports on Diem's Buddhist Crisis, but the religious situation in South Vietnam, like all other political matters in that country, had a complex history. The event that had precipitated the Buddhist confrontation with the South Vietnamese government was an incident during the Buddha birthday celebrations on May 8, 1963, in Hue, when nine people were killed, eight of them children. The immediate cause of trouble was an official ban on the flying of Buddhist flags, despite the regime-approved use of the Vatican flag at the jubilee of Archbishop Ngo Dinh Thuc, Diem's brother, only days before. The long-term cause of religious friction stemmed from Diem's patronage of both the Roman Catholics who had migrated from Communist North Vietnam into South Vietnam at the time of the division of the country in 1954, and those Catholics already there. The actual sequence of events on May 8 was difficult to establish at the time, and the situation has not been clarified since, as Vietnamese religious and political groups have continued to hold to irreconcilable versions. Diem's officials testified that the deaths had been caused by Communist grenades thrown into the crowd, although other witnesses, among them Erich Wulff, a German medical professor then assisting at the University of Hue who publicized his case in the American press, claimed that bodies he saw, at the morgue in Hue, had been decapitated by artillery fire. Diem had Maj. Dang Sy, the Catholic officer who had been in charge of crowd control on the night of the incident, placed under arrest but refused at the time, and later, to admit government responsibility for the deaths.[4]

The Buddhist lay and clerical leaders in Hue subsequently mounted such a well-organized civil disobedience campaign, culminating in the suicide by fire of Thich Quang Duc in Saigon on June 11, that many U.S. officials assumed that the protest movement was Communist-led. Some, such as General Harkins, continued for years after the events of 1963 to hold to the position that the Buddhists were Viet Cong–controlled. None of the evidence that subsequently emerged from official U.S. sources or independent research, however, points to Communist inspiration in the movement, although Hanoi subsequently made effective political capital from the organized protest movement in South Vietnam.[5]

The Buddhist activists' skills had arisen from quite a different source, outside Vietnam. The activist monks were adherents of the "New Buddhism" that had found textual authority for a socially engaged role for bonzes (monks) and political teachings in the words of the Buddha. The founding of the World Buddhist Fellowship in 1950 brought Buddhists from many countries into contact and gave a forum for discussion of new approaches to the role of Buddhists in the world. The Vietnamese umbrella group formed under the inspiration of the New Buddhism was the General Association of Buddhism in Vietnam, established in South Vietnam in 1952 with its headquarters in Hue. The Xa Loi pagoda in Saigon, which became the focal point for the religious crisis of 1963, was the center of the Buddhist revival in Southern Vietnam.[6]

The Halberstam-Sheehan group of reporters, whose writings had so disturbed Kennedy and his advisors, however, knew nothing of this history. Their interest was in the potential of Diem's dispute with the Buddhists to bring his government down. From the first, the Buddhist leaders had turned to the American reporters to publicize their case: after Quang Duc's suicide, the U.S. newspapermen assembled regularly outside the Xa Loi pagoda, where there were English-speaking monks, and the banners hung out were in English as well as Vietnamese.[7]

During August, the Buddhist Crisis developed to a tense climax. This was fueled in part by the publicity given to it by the American newspapermen, television being a minor factor in American perceptions of the war before the advent of satellite cable. The Halberstam-Sheehan reports were not only the basis for concern on the part of the *New York Times* reading public and officials at the Department of State but also the source of information for the Saigonese, when they were relayed back to Vietnam by the Voice of America (voa). The regime used the American-owned and English-language *Times of Vietnam* as its mouthpiece; all independent Saigon newspapers, of course, were censored. The Western reports were also of great interest to Hanoi. The Communists turned Diem's allies' criticisms of his religious policies into propaganda against him, which they broadcast in North Vietnam and back into South Vietnam through their channel there, the Liberation Broadcasting Station.[8]

Buddhist suicides by fire occurred on three consecutive days, from August 14 to 16. On August 18, crowds gathered outside the Xa Loi pagoda, where the body of Quang Duc had been carried on June 11. Quang Duc's heart was on display there; it was said to have survived the flames intact and had become an object of veneration. The laymen in attendance outside the pagoda fasted throughout the day and night, while leading monks took turns in addressing them, ostensibly on the history of Buddhism in Vietnam.

These demonstrations were clearly linked to the impending arrival of Henry Cabot Lodge. The American newspapermen, who anticipated Lodge's arrival date as August 26, contributed to the sense of an imminent confrontation between Buddhists and the South Vietnamese government with a constant stream of copy, alleging cries from the crowd of "Down with Thuc! Down with the Nhus!" and, at times, even calls for the removal of Diem himself.

Yet in spite of comprehensive reports being compiled in the U.S. embassy Political Section and by the CIA, the embassy had very little accurate information on Diem's Buddhist opponents. Neither Ambassador Nolting nor Deputy Chief of Mission Trueheart knew as much about the structure of the Buddhist groups opposing Diem as they could have done from materials that had been collected by the U.S. agencies and were therefore directly available to State. Nolting tended to side with Diem's view that the Buddhist campaign was being run from Hanoi, and while he did recognize in contemporary cables that the Buddhists might have legitimate grievances, he feared above all that the dispute would play into the hands of the Communists. Moreover, in view of his brief, he was more inclined to speak to members of the government regarding their reactions than to confer with the Buddhist leaders. Trueheart recalled that "nobody guessed the Buddhists had such an important role to play. We had zero knowledge of Buddhism. Nobody ever thought it important to look at their organization." He thought that the monks involved in the opposition to Diem were a rebel group and not part of the Buddhist "hierarchy."[9]

But reports were available giving extensive details of the history and structure of the General Buddhist Association and its credentials as a legitimate Buddhist sectarian organization. CIA dossiers, based on material gathered in July and August, contained data on the leaders of the association, their complaints of discrimination by Diem against them in favor of Catholics, and, moreover, consistent notations regarding the lack of evidence for Communist infiltration of the movement at the dates of writing. One report compiled by the U.S. embassy Political Section showed that the activist bonzes had held important positions in multiple Buddhist structures over prolonged periods and detailed their connection with the international New Buddhism movement; a major Bureau of Intelligence and Research memorandum making the same points and others, and based on information from all the agencies, was distributed at State on August 21.[10]

In fact, nothing in these reports was not available elsewhere, since the *Far Eastern Economic Review* had reported on the proceedings of the World Buddhist Fellowship since its inception and State had an expert on Buddhism at its disposal. Indeed, Lodge had been briefed in the department's newly created Office of Buddhist Affairs by Richard Gard, a scholar of Buddhism who had previously worked as an Asian specialist with the United States Information Service, shortly before his departure for Saigon. Gard had been surprised at the interest Lodge had taken in what he, Gard, had to say, whereupon Lodge had explained that his family had been long connected with Buddhism, through his "cousin" William Sturgis Bigelow, who had introduced Buddhism to Americans and given public lectures on the religion at Harvard in 1908, and who had been a formative influence on his father. Gard urged him, as a first for an American ambassador, to meet with Buddhist leaders in Asia.[11]

But at the American Embassy in Saigon, leading officials had not, apparently, thought the Buddhist issue important enough to warrant extensive reading or research requests. The U.S. Mission in Saigon was not firmly geared to respond effectively to the situation which confronted it in mid 1963. Saigon was still a diplomatic backwater. John Mecklin, speaking for United States Information Service, subsequently admitted before U.S. Senate Hearings that prior to the Buddhist-led confrontation with the South Vietnamese government, his men had not been sufficiently astute in gauging the sympathies of the population. "There was little effective effort to keep tabs on the political attitudes of the Vietnamese people, despite the known fact that our adversary gave first priority to this" he first wrote in 1965. Further, in addition to a customary free-wheeling independence, each agency had its own lines to Washington. General Harkins maintained his own private channel over and above the usual communications systems of the armed forces in Vietnam, for consultation with Gen. Maxwell Taylor, chairman of the Joint Chiefs of Staff.[12]

An even more disturbing trend, which Michael Dunn isolated as a key concern of Kennedy's, was that discontented members of the U.S. embassy staff and the military groups took their grievances to the American journalists in Saigon.

As Halberstam later wrote, in a remarkable revelation of a breach in military discipline, since 1962 American advisors had complained to the newspapermen that the war in the countryside was going badly, to counterbalance the optimistic reports that reached Washington through official channels. Again, after Diem's arrest of Buddhist leaders in the dawn of August 21, the Halberstam-Sheehan group were quite open in their revelation that they had been approached with accurate information predicting the pagoda raids by lower-echelon workers in the U.S. mission. These U.S. government employees, the journalists claimed, had turned to them because their analysis had been ignored by high-ranking Americans in Saigon.[13]

Lodge would act to cut off the agencies' back-channel communications with Washington within days of his arrival in Vietnam. As for the thorough overhaul of procedures and discipline in the mission which was so clearly needed, the incoming ambassador believed that he was in Vietnam on a shorter-term and more specific assignment: to correct the impasse between the American president and the Diem regime.

Ambassador Nolting had departed from Saigon on August 15, leaving Diem feeling isolated in the palace without his American friend. It was U.S. diplomatic custom that the departing ambassador never briefed his successor at the post. However, no protocol or practical difficulty existed to explain the two-week gap between Nolting's departure from Saigon and Lodge's projected arrival on August 26. Indeed, in the discussion at the White House when Nolting's tour of duty had been formally terminated, Lodge had been scheduled to leave Washington "as soon as possible after 14 August," thus minimizing the transition period. Lodge may have journeyed to Saigon in easy stages in order to avoid "jet-lag" and thus approach his new position refreshed and alert, as his aide Frederick Flott and Douglas Pike, then with United States Information Service, have argued. But the evidence also suggests that even before he reached Saigon, Lodge was implementing the policy of "silence and correctness" that he described in his major "wrap-up" cable to Kennedy on November 6, after Diem had been replaced with a military government. The policy of silence and correctness he explained, was designed to show Diem and Nhu that "the U.S. was not hooked" to them.[14]

Kennedy had appointed Lodge as a consultant on Far Eastern affairs, as well as U.S. ambassador to South Vietnam; he therefore anticipated stopovers in Tokyo and later at the U.S. military base in Manila and in Hong Kong, the major China-watching post. But the planned delay in arriving in Saigon seems best explained in tactical terms. As Fletcher L. Prouty, a military officer responsible for support of CIA operations with the Joint Chiefs of Staff in 1963 later explained, a hint dropped or a diplomatic slight often accomplished more in giving heart to the opposition in American-supported dictatorships than resort to the cloak-and-dagger methods the popular imagination attributed to the agency.[15]

The gap between ambassadors, then, may have been intended to give a signal to possible alternative leaders of South Vietnam that a move to takeover the Vietnamese government might be viewed favorably by the U.S. Lodge undoubtedly intended to show Diem that he could not manipulate the new ambassador as he had the former. And although an editorial in the *New York Times* on August 22 complained that "Mr. Lodge has been curiously nonchalant—in a period when tension was nearing the explosion point—about getting to a post vacated by a former envoy who was far too admiring and indulgent toward Mr. Diem," the wait certainly had the effect of creating dramatic tension and widespread expectation of a climax.

Lodge spent Monday, August 19, at Pacific Command headquarters in Honolulu receiving a final briefing at meetings attended by Adm. Harry Felt, U.S. commander in the Pacific; Paul Kattenburg, the new chairman of the Vietnam Task Force in the Department of State; William Colby of the CIA; and Roger Hilsman. Nolting was at the Honolulu meeting, deeply concerned as to what the South Vietnamese president would do in his absence. In his last conversation with Diem on August 14, Diem had refused to bend to U.S. requests that he conciliate the Buddhists, but he had appeared deeply depressed, attributing his troubled state of mind to American newspaper stories against him.[16]

The public stance of the officials attending the Pearl Harbor meeting, the one Lodge explained to Nolting and subsequently held to in interviews and his own writings, was that there had been no change in U.S. policy toward the Diem regime. This, however, was disingenuous, because all involved parties believed that the Lodge appointment marked a watershed and were acting on that expectation.[17]

Nolting's worst fears were dramatically fulfilled within hours of his meeting with Lodge. On August 20, 1963, the president of South Vietnam declared a state of martial law, to take effect the next day. Under the martial law provisions, Gen. Tran Van Don became acting chief of the Army General Staff, while Gen. Ton That Dinh, commander of 3 Corps, became military governor of Saigon. By declaring martial law, Diem gave nearly all internal powers over to the generals of the regular Army. However, as all secret police and Special Forces units were under the control of Col. Le Quang Tung, a fellow Roman Catholic and native of central Vietnam, a man who had the absolute trust of Diem and Nhu, Diem retained the capacity to continue with the divide-and-rule tactics that he had used to maintain power for the previous nine years.

Just as Lodge was distancing himself from Diem, Diem may well have wished to place distance between himself and Lodge. Apparently suspecting this, the Communist party newspaper *Nhan Dan* in Hanoi asserted that martial law had been declared to prevent anti-Diem, pro-U.S. elements from contacting Lodge. Such commentary, when broadcast into South Vietnam, could only increase the expectation of a showdown on Lodge's arrival.[18]

The news of the declaration of martial law in Saigon did in fact reach Pacific Command headquarters in Honolulu before Lodge's scheduled departure. He continued on to Tokyo. Shortly after midnight on August 21, units of the Army of the Republic of South Vietnam (ARVN) led attacks on the main pagodas in Saigon and Hue and arrested dissident monks. The Saigon Domestic Service immediately began broadcasting as "The Voice of the Armed Forces of the Republic of Vietnam."[19]

Among the first reports on the pagoda raids to reach the Department of State was copy from the Halberstam-Sheehan group of newspapermen, who, having anticipated this development in the Buddhist Crisis story for some days, had been on the spot to witness the assault on the Xa Loi pagoda. In view of the collapse of commercial facilities during the emergency, the journalists approached Trueheart, who opened a special line for them from the chancery building. One of Halberstam's earliest accounts, transmitted from the U.S. embassy, began with the breathless news that "hundreds of heavily armed combat police and soldiers stormed this city's main pagodas and arrested hundreds of monks" in the early hours. He continued that his sources named Ngo Dinh Nhu as the instigator of the attacks.[20]

Astute as they were, however, the newspapermen's information was incomplete, for they were interested mainly in what had happened in Saigon, and most especially at the Xa Loi pagoda. There were no American reporters in Hue, the old capital of Vietnam, which had been and still was the Buddhist religious and cultural center. There the pagoda invasions had been met with spirited resistance from the local population. The Vietnamese regular Army (ARVN) quite openly admitted the involvement of its forces in the raids on pagodas throughout South Vietnam in their "Voice of the Armed Forces" broadcasts. As for Counselor Nhu, while he was undoubtedly manipulating the ARVN generals for his own ends and forces under his command were certainly involved in some Saigon attacks, the evidence is quite conclusive that ARVN troops acting alone conducted the assaults in Hue. These distinctions, which were not immediately clear, and the extra complicating factor of a twelve-hour time difference between Washington and Saigon, would allow Lodge to interpret the evidence available to him in the light that most suited the purposes of the dominant group at the Department of State.[21]

The emerging picture of what had happened was indeed confusing. Over two days, scores of different accounts passed through the U.S. chancery, the sprawling U.S. mission having many different reporting bodies both military and civilian, each with its own sources and institutional interests in the Vietnamese upheaval. Initially, Trueheart's informants gave conflicting reports as to whether the main striking force at the Xa Loi had been composed of police or ARVN troops. Gradually, however, confirmation emerged that Colonel Tung's 31st group of Special Forces, units specially trained and funded by the CIA to be South Vietnam's vanguard in fighting the Communists, were implicated. No mention of Ngo Dinh Nhu was made in the earliest cables from Saigon. Trueheart also reported that two monks had taken refuge in the USOM building and that he had refused to surrender them, in spite of requests from the Saigon police chief. The Department of State replied that no further action could be taken on the question of monks who had, in effect, sought asylum on U.S. property, until the arrival of the American ambassador.[22]

Lodge's plane left Honolulu on August 20. He arrived in Tokyo on the afternoon of August 21. He had therefore left Hawaii before news of the pagoda raids could reach Pearl Harbor. Hilsman's account in *To Move a Nation* has Lodge, himself, and Nolting receiving the news of the attacks on the Buddhists while together in Honolulu, and later accounts have followed the same chronology. It may be, of course, that Hilsman remembered the news of Diem's declaration of martial law for South Vietnam.[23] Lodge's records and those of his closest aides, in contrast to the received version, show that the new U.S. ambassador received his instructions on how to proceed after the crackdown on the Buddhists in Saigon from Kennedy himself, and that Kennedy was probably acting on information gathered by the Halberstam-Sheehan group of journalists, as transmitted through embassy channels.

At his Tokyo hotel, Lodge retired early. He told Flott that he was not trying to prove himself by working around the clock; apparently he did not call for the cable traffic from Saigon. At about 8 P.M., Flott was called to the U.S. embassy building to receive a "most urgent message from the President." Kennedy said that Ngo Dinh Nhu's Special Forces had raided the Buddhist pagodas; Lodge was to cancel his additional consultations along the way and get to Saigon the next day, but not before he had met with Buddhist petitioners who had asked to meet him in the Japanese capital.[24]

Washington's first statement on the pagoda raids was issued at 9:30 A.M. on August 21, deploring the action as a "direct violation by the Vietnamese Government of assurances that it was pursuing a policy of reconciliation with the Buddhists." Lodge had seen a copy of this cable by the time he met with the Buddhist delegation, some of them from Vietnam, on the morning of August 22. In the course of the audience, he accepted mementoes of William Sturgis Bigelow, who, as an initiate of a Japanese sect, had requested that his ashes be returned to his Asian monastery on his death. A Japanese monk in attendance at the meeting, Riri Nakayama, could therefore dissuade a young Buddhist nun from her resolve to fast to death unless the bonzes who had been taken into custody in Saigon were released, by reminding her of the Lodge family's sympathies toward Buddhism. The American ambassador to Japan subsequently reported that Lodge had established excellent relations with the local Buddhists. In fact, Lodge had only a sketchy knowledge of Buddhism and little information on the South Vietnamese culture to which he was heading, but he had polished political instincts, and in Japan he gave the Diem regime due warning of his stance on its religious policies and of a new firm line in U.S.-South Vietnam relations.[25]

The nine-hour journey from Tokyo to Saigon on August 22 was a productive one for Lodge. Prior to his departure from Japan, he received two high-priority cables from Washington urging him to assist American journalists as much as possible in order to "put relations with press corps on better footing."[26] Lodge allowed four newspapermen, who had made contact with his aides during the night, a passage on his plane to South Vietnam. He therefore had an excellent chance to gain information from them and to establish a working relationship. As the ambassador, he also had copies of the cables from Saigon that gave the U.S. embassy information on developments there, the dated text of Diem's declaration of martial law, reports from Hue, and transcripts in English of the "Voice of the Armed Forces" broadcasts on Saigon radio.[27] He must certainly have known that the evidence contained in this material made the Department of State's later cover-story that Ngo Dinh Nhu had acted to crush the Buddhists without the knowledge of the ARVN a diplomatic fiction.

It would not have done, of course, to have the ARVN implicated in an event as shocking to American public opinion as the violation of religious freedom, especially since many at State saw a South Vietnamese military government as the only possible alternative to Diem. But the population of Saigon, still awaiting Lodge's arrival, could have had no doubt that the ARVN had perpetrated the attacks on the temples. "Voice of the Armed Forces" bulletins on the radio announced that ARVN troops had searched pagodas in all the main coastal cities, explaining that this had been necessary because "Viet Cong dressed in monks' robes" had penetrated the sanctuaries. There could be no doubt that these were official military broadcasts, for the various South Vietnamese generals now in charge and the regional corps commanders identified themselves by name as they gave directives to implement martial law.[28]

At the time of their first statement on the pagoda raids, officials in Washington accepted that the ARVN had been responsible. The later position was that Ngo Dinh Nhu alone had planned and executed the raids, using Colonel Tung's Special Forces group as well as "combat police," and that "to further implicate the army, some of the combat police wore paratroop uniforms." The ARVN was thus exonerated, not only in the American official records but also in a public apology requested by General Don and authorized by State, as broadcast on Voice of America on August 25.[29]

The accepted story flew in the face of the evidence. Brig. Francis Philip Serong, commander of Australian forces in Vietnam from 1962 to 1965 and later senior adviser of the National Police Field Force (SVN), recalled the details some twenty-six years after the event in response to Neil Sheehan's account in *A Bright and Shining Lie: John Paul Vann and America in Vietnam* (1988). The "combat police" group, more properly known as the National Police Field Force, had not been formed until 1965, at then Colonel Serong's instigation. Serong asserted that the Special Forces official uniform *was* paratroop gear, and so the story of disguises was a fabrication. Sheehan's informants, apparently, had misled him. Moreover, no less a person than General Harkins knew that the ARVN had conducted the raids, having his information from Gen. Tran Van Don himself, while the CIA, the agency most in touch with the intricacies of political life in Saigon, named Nhu as the real force behind Diem's martial-law decision and the ARVN planning for the raids.[30]

Catching up on what exactly had happened on the night of August 21 would have been a demanding task, even given unlimited time. Lodge had no time. He took a shortcut and drew speedy conclusions on the basis of preconceived notions. These were to remain unshakable and, reflecting a year later, he strengthened the evidence that the Diem government was "entering its terminal phase" before his own arrival in Saigon by backdating the Hue incident and placing innocent bystanders in the temples on the night of the raids. He recorded: "There wasn't any doubt that the Pagoda incident marked the beginning of the end of the Diem regime. They had ceased to exercise the effective powers of government since April of that year, but when the troops went in *and fired at people who were worshipping* [emphasis added], it was just a matter of time before they would be through." But, he continued, it was the Vietnamese themselves who were overthrowing the regime "and didn't need any outside help."[31]

While it was true that all the coup plots forming in and around Saigon, as far as can be ascertained from CIA reports of the period, were Vietnamese in their origins and participants, any aspirants to power would most certainly seek to ascertain probable U.S. reactions to a change in the South Vietnamese government before they acted. And if casuistry were cast aside, Lodge had already given a number of signals, even before he took up duty in Saigon, that America was no longer prepared to support Diem unconditionally and might not rebuff overtures from enemies of the regime.

After his arrival at the Saigon airport, Lodge drove to the U.S. chancery building. Awaiting him was a cable from Hilsman, assistant secretary of state for Far Eastern affairs since May, giving him carte blanche in deciding what actions to take. Crucial to the events of the next two or three days would be the absence of Dean Rusk in Moscow to sign the Nuclear Test Ban Treaty, for Rusk typically acted as a moderating voice in U.S. foreign affairs policy decisions.

Washington had been surprised by the rapid developments in South Vietnam; the only official statement had been that of twenty-four hours before. Therefore, for three days Lodge was to be in sole charge of both tactics and formation of U.S. government policy in regard to the Diem regime. The Hilsman cable instructed Lodge to ascertain who was in charge in South Vietnam and to establish the various power alignments. He was authorized to take whatever actions he saw as necessary, "bearing in mind the importance of international opinion for U.S. foreign policy."[32]

These were the lines along which Lodge's thinking was already running. He had decided before leaving Washington that the influence of Nhu on Diem must be removed. His opinion was reinforced within hours of his arrival in Saigon by reports from his own sources that Nhu was taking drugs. This was a favorite rumor at State, since a drug-addicted Nhu could be dismissed as irrational and unpredictable. An alternative interpretation—that Nhu was not himself a user but the man in charge of the Laos-to-Marseilles opium trade—was not current in U.S. reports. Neither story has been adequately documented: what is clear is that allegations of Nhu's drug habit to U.S. officials came consistently from Vietnamese who had a vested interest in his fall from power. This is not to say that Nhu was an innocent. There is abundant testimony to his violent methods, including an attempt in 1959 to assassinate Prince Norodom Sihanouk of Cambodia with a parcel bomb, which instead killed the Cambodian chief of protocol.[33]

Lodge wrote of Madame Nhu in several places in his notes—"She deliberately creates impossible publicity. U.S. can get along with dictators (see Thailand) but not this kind"—and at more length in 1967, in "Vietnam Memoir": "Madame Nhu, while giving a superficial appearance of brilliance, was apparently unaware that she was creating the bad publicity which is the one thing which a government like that of the United States—so strong in many other ways—cannot stand." He continued: "The United States can get along with corrupt dictators who manage to stay out of the newspapers. But an inefficient Hitlerism, the leaders of which make fantastic statements to the press, is the hardest thing on earth for the U.S. Government to support."[34]

Lodge did not immediately gauge the violence of politics in the country to which he was accredited. His initial actions in Saigon were calculated to underline a new U.S. policy of distance from the regime. Fortuitously, the ceremony in which he was to present his credentials as American ambassador could be delayed, due to the resignation of the Vietnamese minister for foreign affairs, Vu Van Mau, in protest against the regime's raids on the pagodas.

The new ambassador began his first morning in South Vietnam with a slight to the Diem government. He visited the bonzes who had taken refuge in the USOM building, instructing that they should be supplied with vegetarian meals for the duration of their stay. He noted, significantly, in his report on the visit to State that "if need be, we can hold them [the Buddhist monks] for some time." As always, his actions had been technically within the bounds of protocol, but the message must have been clear to Diem. It certainly struck a chord in American public opinion; the following day, the *New York Times* reported with strong approval on Lodge's visit to the monks who had taken refuge on U.S. property.[35]

A major part of Lodge's assignment, of course, was to improve Kennedy's press relations on Vietnam. Accordingly, that very day, on August 23, Lodge and his wife began a program of entertaining the members of the Halberstam-Sheehan group of journalists and others to lunches at the residence. During that first week, Mrs. Lodge recorded, they were visited by Halberstam, Sheehan, and Malcolm Browne. As a result of his own luncheon at the residence, Sheehan, at first skeptical of the influence that a young reporter might have on ambassadorial thinking, came to believe that Lodge had based much of his subsequent analysis of the ills of the Diem regime on what he, Sheehan, and his group had told him, based on the testimony of Col. John Paul Vann, then American advisor with 4 Corps of the ARVN. Although there is no evidence in Lodge's writings to suggest that this was so, the incident attests to Lodge's considerable personal charm.[36] Lodge's initial diplomacy regarding the U.S. newspapermen was to bear fruit in the days and weeks to come.

The logic of the position in which Lodge now found himself dictated that he must quickly establish a strong United States position in relation to the regime. Kennedy wanted it; American personnel in Vietnam expected it; editors in the United States demanded it; groups and individuals in South Vietnam, both military and civilian, were poised to act in response to a signal from the new U.S. ambassador.

Lodge was to record in "Vietnam Memoir" that he found the U.S. embassy and the CIA less well informed than he thought they should have been. The available evidence suggests that the pagoda raids had taken most departments of the mission by surprise. Lodge did not, however, as might have been expected, call an immediate meeting of the "Country Team," that is, of the heads of all the U.S. agencies and departments with programs in Vietnam. For the ambassador to meet with the heads of the agencies, often on a daily basis, was standard U.S. diplomatic procedure, and indeed the assembling of the Country Team was the only means which existed for the coordination of the activities of the agencies. Lodge did not use that approach to communicate his criticisms. In particular, he did not inform John Richardson, the CIA station chief, of his negative assessment of the agency's performance.[37]

Instead, in nineteenth-century diplomat-as-lone-wolf fashion, Lodge drew upon his own sources. He immediately sought the advice of Monsignor Salvatore Asta, the apostolic delegate to Indochina. He knew Asta from his days in Europe, but there was another compelling reason for the connection. Kennedy, the first Catholic president of the United States, had planned ahead to avoid a Catholic electoral backlash at home in the event of the U.S. dissociating its policies from Diem. He had therefore instructed Lodge to maintain close contact with the apostolic delegate and other Vatican representatives in Vietnam. The intention, apparently, as Lodge recorded in "Vietnam Memoir," was to make sure that "every action Kennedy took in relation to the Diem regime had the approval of Asta, and therefore of the Vatican."[38]

Lodge also developed a close relationship with Giovanni d'Orlandi, the Italian ambassador, whose European urbanity matched his own and in whose company he and his wife felt more at ease than in that of most of the Americans in Vietnam, who were, after all, at least twenty years their juniors. A third private source, from whom Lodge obtained initial reports, was P. J. Honey, a British scholar of Vietnamese culture from the School of Oriental and African Studies in London, and possibly a consultant to the British government, who was in Saigon from August to October 1963.[39]

It was his personal style to prefer to work with a limited circle of men well known to him or with strong recommendations from his own contacts. In addition to his distaste for team work, he was initially wary of placing too much trust in members of the U.S. embassy staff who might have Democratic party affiliations, according to John Burke, then in the Political Section. The two staff members whom he did take into his confidence were Rufus Phillips and Lucien Conein. Phillips was the principal American advisor to the South Vietnamese government on the Strategic Hamlets program, the Diem government strategy for protecting peasant farmers from Viet Cong infiltration through networks of villages fortified at their perimeters, and was attached to the AID agency in Saigon. Formerly of the CIA, he had been a close associate of agency operative Edward Lansdale, who had advised Diem in his early days as president. Lansdale was well known to Lodge, and in September Lodge would request Lansdale's services to build a CIA staff loyal to himself in South Vietnam. According to William Colby, Phillips was not at that time in the pay of the CIA, but, nevertheless, his connections to the agency remained strong.[40]

Lucien Conein was a French-speaking American who, although a creator of myths about himself, is known to have trained with the British Office of Strategic Services (OSS), to have commanded a partisan group in France in the last year of the Second World War, and to have been on American service in Vietnam since 1945. In 1963 he took orders from the CIA. State instructed Conein that he was to operate in strict obedience to Ambassador Lodge's commands, in response to public criticisms of the free-wheeling role the agency had taken in the Bay of Pigs affair in Cuba two years before.[41]

Apparently relying on his political instincts as much as on information from his informants and from the CIA reports he called for, Lodge arrived quickly at his assessment of the local scene, and in spite of the complexity of the situation, he made firm recommendations. In one of his first cables, which he sent directly to the White House, Lodge warned that resentment building up in Saigon against the government of South Vietnam for its handling of the Buddhists might well be turned against the U.S. Indeed, one rumor enjoying widespread circulation held that the Americans had planned the pagoda raids, since the U.S.-supported Special Forces were involved. Lodge's sources had informed him, he reported, that some Saigonese were openly expressing the feeling that they might fare better under communism than under the present regime. His first instinct was that the Nhus must go, he continued, concluding: "In our opinion conditions are rapidly developing to a point of open demonstrating leading to violence and bloodshed."[42]

He had experienced the first assassination threat against himself before noon, when he had been compelled to return to the residence to warn his wife of a suspected bomb.[43] The young newspapermen were as impressed with the courage of the ambassadorial couple as with the copy they supplied.

Lodge had delivered a clear message to Diem in the course of his first morning. Over the next three days he would establish his position in relation to the heads of the agencies. Following consistently from his preparations for the Saigon post and from the answers he had gained to his questions at State, he set out to establish that he, as the ambassador, had the ultimate authority in the U.S. mission.

The two major concentrations of power which threatened his primacy lay with the U.S. military groups, the MACV in particular, and the CIA station in Saigon, whose offices at the time were in the embassy building. The ambiguity in Kennedy's executive order of 1961 regarding the authority of the ambassador in relation to the area military commander was compounded by the presence of eleven thousand U.S. advisors in South Vietnam. Of Lodge's attitude to the pervasive activities of the CIA in South Vietnam and elsewhere, his sentiments are clear. In an aide-memoir dated October 1, 1963, he wrote: "CAS [Controlled American Services: the term used in CIA documents] has more money; bigger houses than diplomats; bigger salaries; more weapons; more modern equipment. A Joint Congressional Committee on CIA?" The date is significant, for four days later the CIA station chief was recalled to Washington.[44]

After initial consultations with General Harkins, during which the American military commander appears to have told him that "there has been no effective government in Vietnam since May 1963," the ambassador sought an independent assessment of Harkins's direction of the war effort. Establishing the practice of using his own nonembassy sources, Lodge consulted Colonel Serong. The Australian could speak frankly, as he was not a part of the U.S. military structure and had a far less cumbersome bureaucracy with which to deal. Serong strongly criticized Harkins's understanding of the nature of the war. Lodge then asked for the notes from which the Australian commander had spoken, and curtly presented these to Harkins, in front of Serong.[45]

Lodge had won an initial tactical round with General Harkins. The snub, however, was achieved at the expense of Harkins's good will, and although Lodge cannot have appreciated it at the time, he had cut himself off from the possibility of a free and collegial exchange of views with the military commander and from friendly access to MACV's resources of information on the Vietnamese generals. This would prove a costly mistake.

The opportunity to limit the power of the CIA in Saigon arose almost immediately. It came on August 26, when Harkins received a private communication through military channels from General Taylor commenting on a radical directive—discussed in detail below—which Harriman and Hilsman had sent from State to Lodge two days earlier. Lucien Conein carried a copy of this from MACV headquarters to John Richardson at his office in the U.S. embassy building. Lodge entered the CIA office while Conein was still there: he demanded surrender of the cable, asserting that he would brook no private channels of communication in the embassy while he was ambassador. From then on, Conein recalled, Lodge refused to allow Richardson access to copies of any cables from Washington to the ambassador.[46] Richardson would be returned to Washington within six weeks.

At the U.S. embassy, reports of plots against the Vietnamese government came in on a daily basis. Conspiracy, after all, had characterized the political life of South Vietnam since its inception. A disaffected group of senior Vietnamese generals, however, had attracted attention at State in July. These men, by virtue of their profession, were of more interest to key U.S. planners than other Vietnamese dissidents. They were led by Gen. Tran Van Don, who was nominally commander of the Army, though under the Diem system of divided chains of authority, his powers were in practice limited, and by Gen. Duong Van Minh, who held the title of military advisor to the president but without command of troops. Conein, long a roistering buddy of the Vietnamese generals, had gained the confidence of the key members of this group. According to Conein, on the evening of July 4, immediately after the Independence Day celebrations at the U.S. ambassador's residence, he and the Don-Minh group of generals went on to an underground nightclub bar on Tu Do Street. Here, on the premises of the Caravelle Hotel, the favorite meeting place of journalists and dissidents, Tran Van Don informed Conein of his intention to overthrow Diem.[47] Conein, who assessed this as a serious plan with extensive ARVN backing, awaited further developments.

Within a day of his arrival in Saigon, Lodge had received the text of three confidential interviews that were to prove decisive in the formulation of a new

U.S. policy toward the Diem regime. General Don, now acting chief of the Joint General Staff of the Armed Forces of South Vietnam under the martial law provisions, met with Conein on August 23. Don hinted that the ARVN might be contemplating a coup but would give no further details. Conein concluded that Don himself did not have the power or the influence over the other generals to overthrow the government.[48]

On the basis of U.S. journalists' as well as embassy information, Lodge had already begun to suspect that Ngo Dinh Nhu could manipulate and dominate Don. His analysis seemed to be confirmed by a report of a further conversation, this time between Rufus Phillips and Gen. Le Van Kim, Don's brother-in-law and special assistant. Kim said that he and seven other officers of the General Staff had been forced on August 22 to take an oath of loyalty to Diem which compelled them to assume responsibility for the Nhu-instigated raids on the pagodas, but he added that they had signed under duress and in fear of Nhu's secret police. The Army would unite against Ngo Dinh Nhu, Kim confided, if the United States gave an appropriate signal. Phillips also spoke to Nguyen Dinh Thuan, Diem's minister of defense and secretary of state. Thuan reiterated Kim's words, urging that the United States must act to curtail Nhu's dangerous influence over Diem. Thuan, however, stressed that Diem must be preserved as the only possible leader acceptable to the Vietnamese people.[49]

In spite of the contradictions in these reports, by August 24 Lodge's information led him to believe that the ARVN offered the only possible alternative source of authority to the Diem regime. There is no evidence that Lodge sounded out Diem's civilian opponents at this stage, although the CIA was forwarding copious details of nonmilitary coup cabals that had emerged in the encouraging atmosphere. One CIA report entitled "Plans and Activities of Tran Kim Tuyen's Coup Group" dealt with the activities of Diem's intelligence chief, or "Chief of Spies," as the agency called him.[50] Such reports appear to have been of little interest to Lodge and to the leading group at State.

Lodge was aware, however, of factions in the Army which, according to his best information, gathered around General Don, Gen. Ton That Dinh, now military governor of Saigon, and Col. Le Quang Tung, in charge of the Special Forces and known to be loyal to Diem and Nhu. Therefore, in spite of the evidence available to him that Nhu had not acted alone in attacking the Buddhist sanctuaries, his keen sense of the importance of American public opinion in legitimizing U.S. foreign policy decisions and thus securing congressional authorization for funds prompted him to recommend to State a Voice of America broadcast exonerating the ARVN from responsibility for the pagoda raids. But, he continued, the time was not ripe for the decisive signal to the ARVN that the United States would support a military coup. At this stage, given the unclear leadership of the Vietnamese generals, action would be "a shot in the dark," he said.[51]

One cautionary note from Saigon, however, was not enough to put a brake on the eagerness of the anti-Diem forces in Washington, energized by recent developments, when Lodge himself had contributed to the impression that a major coup was brewing. Officers of the Bureau of Public Affairs had paid close attention to editorials in the major American newspapers since the pagoda raids. The summaries of this opinion furnished by the bureau indicated a general mood that the U.S. had been "insufficiently firm" in its dealings with Diem.[52]

On Saturday, August 24, Harriman, Hilsman, and Forrestal decided that strong action on the Diem issue could no longer be delayed. Hilsman, with the support of these two colleagues, drafted a message to Lodge in Saigon indicating a radical policy change toward the Diem family regime. Conveniently, because it was a summer weekend, the trio encountered "difficulties" in gaining authorization for their demarche from the secretary of defense, the Joint Chiefs, and the CIA principals. But it seems likely that, in spite of Kennedy's later vacillation on the question of the advisability of a U.S.-backed coup in South Vietnam, the president had known of his staff's intention to initiate an action, as Forrestal had included a memo giving an outline of Hilsman's proposed cable in the president's "Weekend Reading File."[53]

The Saturday cable, which Hilsman later described as "a cable along the lines that were usually done in such circumstances," instructed that "it is now clear that whether military proposed martial law or whether Nhu tricked them into it, Nhu took advantage of its imposition to smash pagodas with police and Tung's Special Forces loyal to him, thus placing onus on military in eyes of world and Vietnamese people." Lodge was to impress upon members of the Vietnamese government that the U.S. could not accept the actions of Nhu against the Buddhists, and thus prompt measures of redress must be taken. The text continued: "We must at the same time also tell key military leaders that US would find it impossible to continue to support the Vietnamese government militarily and economically unless above steps are taken immediately which we recognize requires removal of the Nhus from the scene. We wish to give Diem reasonable opportunity to remove Nhus, but if he remains obdurate, then we are prepared to accept the obvious implication that we can no longer support Diem."

Then came a later controversial instruction: "You may also tell appropriate military commanders we will give them direct support in any interim period of breakdown central government mechanism." A Voice of America broadcast was to make the new U.S. attitude to the Vietnamese generals clear, while the ambassador, with the Country Team, was to make "detailed plans as to how we might bring about Diem's replacement if this should become necessary."[54]

This precipitous directive had the power to change the course of U.S.-Vietnam relations, but such was the ad hoc nature of policymaking for Vietnam at the time that although many of the principals thought that someone else had authorized the text, there had been no high-level discussion on its advisability or wording. Indeed, it contained a contradiction, for how could Lodge offer Diem a chance to reform if he was simultaneously promising support to the generals in the event of a coup?

Lodge did not ask for clarification on this point, or on the intention of the instruction as a whole. As General Taylor, Lodge's successor as chief of the U.S. mission in South Vietnam, noted in his memoir of this period, he himself in the same position would have done so. Instead, the American ambassador offered his own suggestion, which in effect preempted the policy toward Diem. He notified Rusk: "Believe that chances of Diem's meeting our demands are virtually nil. At same time, by making them we give Nhu chance to forestall or block action by military. Risk, we believe, is not worth taking with Nhu in control combat forces in Saigon. Therefore propose to go straight to generals with our demands, without informing Diem." With this cable, Lodge made it quite clear that he was firmly in favor of a coup, although he had little to go on as to what exactly the Vietnamese generals offered the U.S. in terms of improved performance in the war, more amicable relations with the U.S. mission in South Vietnam, or improved domestic harmony.[55]

An absence of top-level guidance from Washington had put Lodge in the driver's seat on Vietnam. He directly instructed CIA operatives to seek out their Vietnamese military contacts to develop an immediate plan. Richardson was not in a position to question this order, although he and other officers of the CIA continued to support Diem, for Colby had enjoined upon him absolute obedience to the U.S. ambassador in Saigon, again as a policy response to the Bay of Pigs scandal. In any case, Lodge was in no mood to accept unsolicited advice from the heads of the agencies. He informed Deputy Chief Trueheart, General Harkins, and Lt. Gen. Richard Weede, chief of staff at MACV, of State's instructions. But although he had been instructed by Harriman and Hilsman to do so, Lodge did not call a meeting of the Vietnam Country Team to discuss the new policy toward the Vietnamese government.[56]

By Monday morning, several key officials in Washington, among them McNa-

mara, Taylor, and John McCone (as director of Central Intelligence), were deeply disturbed by what had happened over the weekend, as much by the manner of authorization as by the contents of the Hilsman-Harriman cable. They gathered to attend a meeting of the National Security Council. At this meeting Kennedy did something that Roger Hilsman had never seen him do before: he went around the room and asked those present whether they wished to back away from the directives in cable 243 of August 24, and if not, if they would agree to an alteration allowing Lodge to avoid addressing Diem. Each member of the council in turn expressed support for the directive and agreed to the change for Lodge. This unanimity may have been deceptive. As Colby later wrote, "It is difficult indeed to tell a President to his face that something he has approved is wrong and to do so without anything positive to offer in its place."[57]

Since there was no real consensus in Washington that a Vietnamese coup was necessary, uncertainty as to the form the U.S. role should take led to an intense exchange of cables between State and the Saigon embassy over the next six days. The U.S. mission in South Vietnam was also divided. Although Lodge had acted on the Hilsman instruction as a direct order to prepare for a coup, General Harkins warned Taylor via his private channel that such a move would be inadvisable, arguing that the turmoil in Saigon was not affecting the conduct of the war. Whereas he would unhesitatingly obey orders from the Pacific commander in Honolulu, Harkins said, his support for a coup as it had been expressed in embassy cables to the Department of State had been "volunteered," he continued, by which he appears to have meant that Lodge had either not consulted him or had ignored his advice.[58]

But there can be no doubt, in spite of the alleged lack of consultation with MACV, that the Department of State had ordered preparations consistent with possible American assistance in a Vietnamese coup, and that these measures went beyond provision for the evacuation of U.S. personnel, amounting to the alert of a stand-by force of some seven thousand American troops.[59] So on August 28, when Kennedy sent separate cables to Lodge and Harkins requesting their independent assessments of the likelihood of a successful coup and Rusk cabled separately to ask how long the U.S. could delay giving unequivocal signals to the Vietnamese generals, Lodge responded firmly, "We are launched on a course from which there is no *respectable* turning back: the overthrow of the Diem government. There is no turning back in part because U.S. prestige is already publicly committed to this end in large measure and will become more so as facts leak out."[60]

The next day, however, produced a public relations embarrassment. As Conein, undoubtedly Lodge's informant, later explained, the various Vietnamese cabals had overlapping memberships, which made consolidation difficult. Moreover, a leak from Saigon military headquarters had reached the ears of General Harkins, who was known to be firmly pro-Diem. Lodge found himself obliged to report that the Vietnamese generals had made little progress in their conspiracy. He wrote to Rusk, "My single greatest difficulty in carrying out the instructions of last Sunday is inertia. The days come and go and nothing happens....I am sure that the best way to handle this matter is by a truly Vietnamese movement even if it puts me rather in the position of pushing a piece of spaghetti."[61]

A few hours later, Kennedy cabled his reservations about a coup privately to Lodge: "Until the very moment of the go signal for the operation by the generals, I must reserve a contingent right to change course and reverse previous instructions. While fully aware of your assessment of the consequences of such a reversal, I know from experience that failure is more destructive than an appearance of indecision." No doubt he was recalling the Bay of Pigs.

Lodge may have felt a certain exasperation at Kennedy's indecisiveness, which possibly explains the extreme politeness of his reply: "I fully understand that you have the right and responsibility to change course at any time. Of course I shall always respect that right. To be successful, this operation must be essentially a Vietnamese affair with a momentum of its own. Should this happen you may not be able to control it, that is, the 'go signal' may be given by the generals." The Vietnamese generals' coup plot was a dead letter by August 31.[62]

Of the relationship between Lodge and Kennedy in this period, William Colby later wrote of his attendance at National Security Council meetings in the week beginning August 26: "I had the impression that Kennedy was quite content to give Lodge his head in deciding how far to go against Diem, because Lodge's involvement and Republican credentials would protect him [Kennedy] from recriminations whatever developed."[63] In addition to asking his old rival to manage his press relations on Vietnam, Kennedy had appointed Lodge as Republican hostage to Democratic policies in South Vietnam. An American power game ran parallel to that which was to be played out between Lodge and Diem in Saigon. In the home game, Lodge always held the winning card, in that he could resign his post as U.S. ambassador at any time, a gambit whose use was only restrained by his sense of patriotic duty. As far as Lodge's own reputation was concerned, the ouster of the Diem regime would be a popular move in the United States, and would bring no opprobrium to his wing of the Republican party.

Within two days of Lodge's arrival in Saigon, he had made judgments with far-reaching implications on the basis of testimony from informants with vested interests of which he could know little. At the end of six days, he had taken a major role in activating a coup. It was now properly Kennedy's responsibility to reclaim the initiative in policymaking on Vietnam.

Chapter Three

The Days of Silence
and Correctness

Lodge and the Department of State had miscalculated in
the timing of their signal to the ARVN generals that a coup
might be favorably regarded. It was clear by August 31 in
both Saigon and Washington that the South Vietnamese
generals had been unable to unite to overthrow the Vietnam government. Gen.
Le Van Kim told Rufus Phillips of his distrust of Duong Van Minh and of his own
lack of faith in U.S. blessing for the overthrow of Diem. Generals Tran Thien
Khiem, chief of staff of the Joint General Staff, and Nguyen Khanh, commander
of 2 Corps, failed to muster sufficient troops for an action. Tran Van Don, moreover, confided to Conein that the other generals did not respond to his orders,
even though he had been promoted to the position of acting chief of the Armed
Forces under the martial law provisions of August 21. Duong Van Minh, the
South Vietnamese general with the greatest local popularity because of his earlier role in fighting the French, had been unwilling to act without watertight assurances of U.S. support for a coup, and had asked accordingly that economic aid
to the Diem regime be cut off as a demonstration of the new American resolve.[1]

The Vietnamese generals, then, were disunited, unsure of each other's loyalties, and utterly dependent on patronage. Diem's policy of divide and rule under
which he had provided himself with his own praetorian guard was only the short-
term cause of their weakness. The wider problem was that there was little basis
for the development of consensus or polity in South Vietnam, and the state, dogged by conspiracies since its inception, was held together largely by American
dollars. The established U.S. policy of making a stand in South Vietnam against
the expansion of communism in Asia demanded the justification that the "Viet
Cong" represented an invasive force against an anti-Communist population living

in a sovereign nation. This was a simplistic picture at best, since clearly many of the population sympathized with the local Communists.[2] But Lodge himself, in common with his colleagues in the Department of State, was not about to question the underpinning of the doctrine of containment which he held as an article of faith. He did not stop to analyze the reasons for the Vietnamese generals' hesitation or its implications: he did not pause to consider that if they could not rise to a clear American signal, they could hardly be expected to form a forceful government; if they distrusted the U.S., they might prove unreliable allies; if they were suspicious of each other, they would not perform better in fighting the war than had Diem.

Instead, Lodge went ahead to prepare a disclaimer of U.S., and particularly his own, involvement in the August debacle. His most blatant denial of any American interference whatsoever in Vietnamese affairs would come after his return to the U.S. and on the eve of the Republican Convention. His position on the unsuccessful August coup, however, turned on a feigned reading of a cable he had received on August 30. This communication he treated in all his personal notes as an instruction overturning the directives of the Saturday cable, although the text clearly urged caution in moves to encourage a coup rather than its abandonment. In any case, the Saigon security operatives had been vigorously in action from the morning of August 25 and the damage against Diem had been done, whatever the cultivated mechanisms of the ambassador's memory. The coup was dead, but that did not mean it had never existed or been encouraged.[3]

Lodge in Saigon was in step with the prevailing mood in Washington. At the National Security Council meeting on August 31, the consensus among Rusk, McNamara, Taylor, Nolting, and Vice President Lyndon Johnson was that the U.S. should not promote a coup but should address all its resources to winning the war and should reaffirm that there would be no American withdrawal. Paul Kattenburg, chairman of State's Vietnam Task Force, who had just returned from Saigon, listened with growing concern. At last he felt compelled to break with convention and interrupt the meeting. Diem, he pointed out, had no intention of changing his policies or dismissing his brother Nhu. Therefore, he urged, since the situation in South Vietnam must inevitably deteriorate, "it would be better for the U.S. to withdraw honorably."

Kattenburg was summarily silenced at the time and was to be removed from Vietnam responsibilities in January 1964. Commenting on the August 1963 meeting in 1979, he recalled his despair: "There was not a single person there that knew what he was talking about. . . . They didn't know Vietnam. They didn't know

the past. They had forgotten the history. They simply didn't understand the iden-
tification of nationalism and Communism. . . . I thought, 'God we're walking into
a major disaster.' "[4]

On the afternoon of August 26, Ambassador Lodge had met with President
Diem. What ensued was the only exchange between them during nine bitter
weeks. Although he had had no contact with Diem during the four days since his
arrival in Saigon, Lodge was well informed of Diem's mood. Under Secretary of
State Ball had transmitted a report of a meeting between the British ambassador
and the Vietnamese president, and so Lodge knew that Diem continued to blame
the Communists for the Buddhist demonstrations against his government.[5] The
ambassador presented his credentials at a formal ceremony in the morning and
then prepared for a long and difficult confrontation in the afternoon.

Lodge arrived at the palace accompanied by twelve aides and wearing the
white shark-skin suit which protocol demanded. Diem was similarly attired.
Lodge opened forcefully, stating his entire case before Diem could settle into a
monologue, his well-practiced style in interviews, which had thwarted many earlier American efforts at conversation. Lodge reported his own delivery in a cable
sent that evening as follows: "I said that the United States Government, as the
term is used in foreign affairs, does not include Congress and that in the broad
sense it is impossible to hook the United States of America because public opinion is essential to any long range policy and without the support of public opinion you cannot get the support of Congress and without the support of Congress
you cannot get funds."

Diem regarded him calmly. Lodge urged him to conciliate the Buddhists and
to caution Madame Nhu, whom, he said, many people he knew in America mis-
takenly regarded as the head of state in Vietnam, so often was her picture on the
covers of U.S. magazines. Diem made a joke that he had more than once threatened her that he would take a wife himself. Suddenly changing mood, he explained that his Buddhist opponents represented only a small minority of the
population, and produced a publication of the Xa Loi pagoda in which the figures
given for clerical adherents and lay supporters of the General Buddhist Association amounted to less than one million, or 15 percent of Buddhists in South Vietnam. Diem's figures in fact corresponded with independent findings regarding
the General Buddhist Association, in spite of the desire of some American officials and others to find in Buddhist protesters a "third force" in Vietnam with
greater following and credentials as an indigenous movement than either international communism or French Catholicism.

But Lodge was not interested in third-force arguments or the structure of Vietnamese Buddhism. He pocketed the Xa Loi publication and allowed it to fall from history by neither pouching it to State nor retaining it in his personal collection. He waited with growing irritation for a further chance to speak, which did not come.

Diem was absorbed in an intense discourse regarding his own and his family's role in the development of Vietnam. After two hours, during which he had chain-smoked two packs of cigarettes, he drew to a close on a warning note. He hoped, he said, that Lodge would bring discipline to the activities of U.S. personnel in Saigon. Diem wished to hear no further reports of interference "by various United States agencies" in Vietnamese affairs. Lodge replied disingenuously that he knew nothing of such rumors, as he had only just arrived; he promised to look into the matter. He was keenly aware that he had been able to engage Diem's attention for just ten minutes.[6] Diem had, in fact, won the first round.

After the audience, Lodge determined to refuse any further contact with Diem. He would use silence in much the same way as Diem used speech to avoid discussing U.S. requests for domestic reform. He was not, however, without intermediaries through whom he could make contact with the palace. On August 31, he met with the apostolic delegate, apparently with a view to using Asta to intercede with the Catholic president. He confided to his wife that the talk had been "very valuable," and the next day, apparently operating on Lodge's suggestions, Monsignor Asta paid a call on Diem and members of his family. Asta must have been impressive. He gained an undertaking from Ngo Dinh Nhu that he would withdraw from public life, persuaded Madame Nhu to leave the country for a time, and arranged for Ngo Dinh Thuc to make an extended clerical visit to Rome.[7]

On September 2, Lodge followed up on the initial visit by calling on Ngo Dinh Nhu in the company of Monsignor Asta and Ambassador d'Orlandi. Nhu played a new card. He was prepared to leave politics, he said, but this decision was to please American opinion only. His absence must inevitably weaken Vietnam, he added, because he was the only intermediary accepted by the North who could start a dialogue toward a peace settlement. Of course, a peace settlement was the last thing on Lodge's mind at this time, in keeping with the prevailing mood in Washington, but Nhu's revelation could serve a different purpose. Lodge would use it to further darken U.S. perceptions of the Diem regime.

Ngo Dinh Nhu reneged on his promise to withdraw from politics five days later. In Washington opinion hardened against him: the one point on which there was consensus at the National Security Council meetings in early September was that Diem must be separated from his brother.[8]

Lodge regarded the judicious leaking of information to the press as part of his function in Vietnam, and saw contact with the newspapermen as his exclusive domain, in spite of the claims of the U.S. Information Service this area. John Mecklin recalled him saying, "The leak is the prerogative of the ambassador. It is one of my weapons for doing this job." Indeed, Lodge brushed aside criticisms of his embassy that surfaced at the beginning of the Johnson administration on the grounds that "President Kennedy specifically wanted me to leak and to cultivate good relations with the press in Saigon."[9]

Accordingly, when the veteran Republican journalist Joseph Alsop, an old friend and colleague, arrived in Saigon, Lodge invited him to a private supper at the residence on September 14. Four days later Alsop published one of the most influential stories against Ngo Dinh Nhu ever to appear in the American press in his column for the *Washington Post*. In this report, entitled "Very Ugly Stuff," he referred to Nhu's meetings with representatives of Hanoi, allegedly with the purpose of negotiating a cease-fire.[10]

The next day the Alsop piece was the subject of a CIA Research Report.[11] And although the agency found corroboration for Alsop's claims, it did not pinpoint the journalist's source as the U.S. ambassador nor trace Lodge's information to Lalouette, the French ambassador, d'Orlandi, and Monsignor Asta. If, on the other hand, any newsman suspected that Lodge was the source for the Alsop story, blowing a reputation for confidentiality must have seemed too high a price to pay for the scoop. The Alsop story clearly did its work in preparing *Post* readers, in company with those of the *New York Times*, to accept a coup in South Vietnam as inevitable and to be desired.

Three useful allies in Lodge's campaign to isolate Diem burst through the doors of the U.S. embassy on the first day of September, claiming that they were fleeing from Diem's police. They were Vietnamese bonzes. One of them was Thich Tri Quang, a leading activist who had escaped imprisonment on the night of the pagoda raids. The American ambassador granted the three monks asylum in the chancery building. Lodge went on to cultivate Tri Quang as one of his extra-mission contacts, noting after several conversations with him that he was "a highly intelligent and able individual." William Bundy later described Lodge's action in keeping the three Buddhists at the U.S. embassy as "arguably a case of political interference." Lodge's act of mercy toward the Buddhists, however, and his subsequent refusal to surrender them to the South Vietnamese authorities were enormously popular with American newsmen in Saigon. His gesture stirred the public imagination to such an extent that eleven days later it was mentioned by Sen. Frank Church in his resolution to cut American aid to the Diem regime; Kennedy himself had highlighted the event immediately, in an interview televised on September 2. Lodge subsequently recorded that, in his opinion, the granting of asylum to Tri Quang was one of his key steps in establishing that U.S. government policy was not irretrievably "hooked" to Diem.[12]

Lodge was waiting for Diem to come to him, but the Vietnamese was even more imperious than the American ambassador. Diem refused to ask anything of the U.S. government, and so Lodge could not bargain with him to reform in exchange for favors. He refused to listen to any more advice on his domestic affairs, in spite of Lodge's warning that congressional funds were tied to American public opinion. Four weeks passed in stalemate. Diem was in fact refusing to play the role of a client, and so the usual forms of diplomatic "leverage" were not available, either to him or to Ambassador Lodge.

It was still necessary, however, for the U.S. embassy to know what the Ngo brothers were thinking. On hearing that an Italian correspondent, Giuseppi Gambino, had gained an interview with Nhu, Lodge had Trueheart sound him out and urged State to check what Gambino had filed in Rome. An even more promising conduit to the palace was on his way to Vietnam. In mid-October the Australian Catholic author Morris West arrived in Saigon to investigate the religious situation. By this time, Diem's vigilance had extended to vetting applications for entry visas, but, according to West, Diem allowed him into the country because, on the suggestion of his mentor, the philosopher Jaques Maritain, Diem had read West's novel *The Devil's Advocate,* which deals with a controversial beatification. West would go on to write a further novel entitled *The Ambassador,* about the assassination of Diem himself.[13]

As the Australian embassy retained good relations with Diem, U.S. officers approached its staff to negotiate an interview for West at the Gia Long palace. West had an interview with Ngo Dinh Nhu, who told him that he was in contact with a group within the Communist party of North Vietnam who were aligned neither with Moscow nor with China but had become Communists after Dien Bien Phu. However, the real matter of concern for American policymakers when the Australian embassy had duly passed along West's information was not so much Nhu's contact with the North but his attitude to the U.S.-funded war. Nhu remarked, West reported, that Diem had decided that he wanted to limit the scale of the war. The Vietnamese government needed American money, armaments, and equipment, Nhu declared, but wanted no further American soldiers or officials in South Vietnam.[14] Since forces at State, not to mention the chiefs at the Pentagon, were anxious to extend and intensify the belligerence, this was serious news indeed.

Roger Hilsman defended a proposal for new tactics toward Diem at a National Security Council meeting on September 17. These were to consist of two "tracks": reconciliation with Diem, if possible, and then graduated pressures upon him until he consented to U.S. demands. Kennedy's advisors agreed to adopt a policy of "pressures and persuasion." This appeared to represent a compromise that held out hope both to those who opposed a coup and to those who advocated one. In fact, the ambassador had already preempted the issue when he had refused to meet with Diem: the official temporizing policy was cowardly in that its likely outcome was the death of Diem. To be fair, Lodge may have been interested only in persuading Diem to dismiss Nhu and to reform his domestic policies, as he later claimed. The effect in practice, however, was predictable. Lodge's tactics toward Diem met with the approval of the Halberstam-Sheehan group of journalists, who continued to campaign vigorously against the Ngo family. Their attacks became so vehement that at last Joseph Alsop felt compelled to point out that their crusade was driving the brothers into a "galloping persecution mania which sees plots around every corner" and predictably "right round the bend."[15]

Finally dismissing any misapprehension that U.S. aid came with no strings attached, Lodge said of his policies toward the Diem government during a 1965 interview: "I think we have an absolute right, frankly, to use legitimate pressure and influence as part of a bargain with another government . . . talk about 'no strings' aid is a rather artful bit of propaganda."[16]

The key economic lever was the U.S.-paid Commodity Import Program Subsidy (CIP) on which the finances and power of the Diem regime largely depended. Initially Lodge was loath to axe the CIP. He had advised Rusk against the U.S. aid cuts General Minh had asked for on August 29, arguing not that reactivating the coup plotters was unwise or improper but that American interference in Vietnamese affairs should not be publicly demonstrated. The next day he returned to the possibility he had suggested to Diem: that the American people and not the administration might cut off his U.S. aid monies. Long experienced in the ways of pushing bills through the Senate, Lodge asked Rusk if the House Foreign Affairs Committee might be induced to deny funds to the Vietnamese government. This would allow him as U.S. ambassador in Saigon, he explained, to argue that his own hands were tied but that the money might be restored if Diem reformed. Hilsman and McGeorge Bundy worked with Senator Church, who was sympathetic to their views, to negotiate the wording for a congressional resolution.[17] When the speech introducing the resolution came on September 12, it emphasized Diem's "religious persecutions" as its motivation.

The problem of how to implement aid sanctions was a complex one, given their effects on the Vietnamese economy and the jealousies among the agencies of the U.S. mission in South Vietnam. Lodge was aware that the Diem family had been able to stockpile large amounts of money and equipment and could survive without U.S. dollar assistance for a considerable time, as Nhu had often told journalists and others. Lodge had little understanding of economics, but he knew how American politics worked. Cuts had to be made, he warned, in such a way as to put pressure on the Diem family without harming the war effort or the living standard of the population. Then, possibly having taken embassy advice on the matter, he continued that cuts might lead to inflation, shortages in industry, or layoffs of workers. Finally, there was the problem, of which Nhu himself had repeatedly warned, that U.S. actions might push Diem and Nhu to seek an accommodation with Hanoi.[18]

When Lodge addressed a different front, American programs in Vietnam, he found even fewer openings, and in relation to the CIA and U.S. military command, he confronted a blank wall. Lodge had come up against the bureaucratic rivalries of the agencies and departments of the U.S. mission itself. The agencies refused to accept cuts in their budgets. When he asked the chiefs of the CIA and the MAAG to let him know of programs in their domains that could be held up without harm to the war effort, they each advised him that there were no such programs. The chief of USOM, on the other hand, suggested that funding for the CIP could easily be cut. Lodge cabled Rusk that he did not want to "burn his bridges" by dropping the commercial imports subsidy, thus risking an appropriations bill that strangled finances for the whole coming year, with no guarantee of a coup.[19] The ambassador, like his heads of agencies, appears to have been well aware of the need to establish high claims for funds in the one year in order to ensure the supply in the next.

Although without a firm idea of what he wished to do in Vietnam throughout September, Kennedy decided to defer approval for the projected CIP for South Vietnam, valued at 18.5 million dollars. On October 5, when the president first concluded that Diem would have to go, he authorized the withdrawal of U.S. financial support for the Vietnamese Special Forces, which his advisors informed him had become Ngo Dinh Nhu's de facto private army, as well as the suspension of the imports subsidy.[20]

Lodge was to record triumphantly after the coup that the effects of U.S. aid sanctions had offered most leverage in his campaign to alter the behavior of Diem and Nhu. On September 19 he observed to Kennedy that if withholding payments worked in Vietnam, "it would be one of the greatest discoveries since the enactment of the Marshall Plan in 1947 because, so far as I know, the U.S. has never been able to control any of the very unsatisfactory governments through which we have had to work in our many successful attempts to make these countries strong enough to stand alone."[21]

Lodge did not name the countries the U.S. had strengthened for continued struggle against the Communists, in spite of the incumbent government. His service in World War II had been the high point of his career, and so the mention of the Marshall Plan, which he had selflessly promoted in the GOP and against his family's traditional stance in foreign affairs, came naturally enough. But even four years after his September 1963 observation to Kennedy, when he transcribed the Marshall Plan analogy for "Vietnam Memoir," he does not appear to have paused to reflect on the difference between supplying aid for reconstruction and withdrawing it to bring down a government.

If the Lodge-Diem impasse had slowed developments in Saigon, Washington policymaking was also stagnating. As George Ball later noted wryly of events in September 1963: "In Washington tradition, a fact-finding mission can serve as a substitute for policy, and so the President sent his advisors to Vietnam." Kennedy sent two successive missions to South Vietnam in September 1963. The first, led by Joseph Mendenhall representing the administration's State Department planners, and Marine general Victor "Brute" Krulak speaking for the Pentagon, left for Vietnam on September 6 and reported back four days later. In the two frantic days the team had spent on the ground, its military and civilian heads had come to diametrically opposed conclusions. This was not surprising, since Mendenhall, director of the Far East Planning Office, believing that the problem in the Vietnamese government's direction of the war effort was political, had spoken to U.S. officials in Saigon and so decided against Diem, while General Krulak, who maintained that the war would be won in the countryside, spoke to U.S. military advisors in the field and so reported ongoing progress in the rural zones in spite of the turmoil in the cities. Their conflicting statements led to Kennedy's memorable query: "You two did visit the same country, didn't you?"[22]

Kennedy was faced with three choices: to persevere with current military strategies, to send U.S. ground soldiers to Vietnam (John Mecklin, head of the Saigon USIS, had sounded an ominous note at the National Security Council meeting of September 10 by proposing that South Vietnam could only be saved by an unlimited commitment of American troops), or to promote a coup in the hopes that new leadership would improve the war effort. Kattenburg's suggestion that disengagement was advisable had been dismissed, but Kennedy did not have the numbers or the discipline in Congress to contemplate asking the House for a resolution to permit the dispatch of troops.[23]

Once again Lodge was in the driver's seat. Kennedy's relief must have been great when, just a few hours after the bewildering National Security Council meeting of September 10, his ambassador explained away the contradictions in the Krulak-Mendenhall team's reports and provided a solution that steered a middle course between withdrawal and military intervention. Every argument in Lodge's cabled analysis proceeded toward a blunt summation: "The time has arrived for the US to use what effective sanctions it has to bring about the fall of the existing government and the installation of another. . . .

"Renewed efforts should be made to activate by whatever positive inducements we can offer the man who would take over the government—Big Minh or whoever he might suggest." He warned, "We do not want to substitute a Castro for a Batista . . . by a wait-and-see approach, we insure that when and if we decide that we cannot win with the present regime, we shall have even less to work with in terms of opposition than we have now." Delay might play into the hands of the Communists, Lodge continued, alluding pointedly to America's failure to prevent the Marxist Castro from coming to power in the Cuban revolution of 1959. Lodge reconciled conflicting reports of the mood in the cities and countryside of South Vietnam. American officers seldom gave less than optimistic reports to their seniors, he said, referring to his own background as a military man, but morale in the ARVN must be affected by political turmoil in the cities because the Vietnamese officer class, as everywhere else, he claimed, came from urban families.[24]

Suspension of U.S. aid, Lodge argued, was the key to the overthrow of the Diem regime. Characteristically, he suggested a series of leaks to the press as the means of creating the right impressions. The South Vietnamese population should believe that the American dollars had been cut off because of Diem's refusal to dismiss Nhu; soup kitchens or other assistance could be provided to the Saigon poor for the sake of American public opinion; the evacuation of U.S. dependents would serve as a decisive signal to Diem and the ARVN generals, he advised. He concluded with the pregnant suggestion that a way might be found for the U.S. to supply the ARVN directly, thus "totally bypassing the government of Viet Nam."[25]

Kennedy congratulated Lodge on his helpful cable with a private note: "Your

478 is a major cable." The next day the National Security Council notified the U.S. mission of its agreement to evacuate dependents, urge Congress to suspend aid to Diem, and finance programs in the provinces without reference to the government of South Vietnam. The ostensible aim of these measures was still "to remove Nhus from the scene"; Lodge was instructed, somewhat hopefully, "to continue frequent conversations with Diem."[26]

General Harkins reacted angrily to this anti-Diem directive. The American commander in Vietnam sent urgent cables to Admiral Felt, the Joint Chiefs of Staff, and the key policymakers at State asserting that the war was being won under Diem's leadership. He further revealed that the monks in asylum in the U.S. chancery building, in particular Tri Quang, had admitted to CIA officers the details of their participation in a long-term conspiracy to overthrow the government. He urged rethinking, but his cable was ignored.[27] In hindsight, Harkins's suggestions, if heeded, might have helped to soften some features of the coup that was to open up a catastrophic period in U.S.-Vietnam relations. But it is clear that Kennedy had sided with Lodge's analysis: he may already have realized the capacity of the commander of MACV, in conjunction with the Joint Chiefs of Staff, to subvert the authority of the president himself, as supreme commander of the Armed Forces.

At this time in Saigon, the Lodges' leisure reading of books on Vietnam led Emily Sears Lodge to remark in a letter to a friend, "The more you read the more confusing it becomes. It's just frightful what the French army went through—class after class of Saint Cyr wiped out." She was referring to a passage from Graham Greene's *The Quiet American,* which in fact warns against the consequences of U.S. intervention in Vietnam, its leading character based on Gen. Edward Lansdale, whose services Lodge was about to request as his chief of the CIA station in Saigon.[28]

Within three weeks of his arrival, Lodge was moving toward the position he held in 1965, when he commenced his second ambassadorship in Saigon, namely, that South Vietnam was not a sovereign state but simply the geographic area from which the U.S. had chosen to repel the spread of communism in Asia. This is not to say that the idea of America supporting the ARVN without dealing through a central government, which he returned to in his Marshall Plan cable of September 19, was exclusively Lodge's own, for the possibility had been touched upon in the controversial cable of August 24 and again in a feasibility study accompanying Hilsman's action plans for South Vietnam presented to the National Security Council on September 17.[29]

In his suggestions on logistics, Lodge was completely in step with the Hilsman-Harriman group at State, although Hilsman has consistently denied that the line offering independent assistance to the ARVN was in the original draft of the August 24 cable. Hilsman attributed the offer of direct supply to Rusk, who in his 1990 autobiography implicated Ball. Rusk thus had the final word in demonstrating that the responsibility for the Saturday cable was collective, although he spared Kennedy, whether from lack of knowledge of the contents of the president's Weekend Reading File or from loyalty to the office of chief of state.[30]

The tension between U.S. rhetoric and practice in Vietnam is clear in Lodge's policy suggestions and personal notations at this time, although he seems to have been unaware of some obvious contradictions. In a set of notes regarding his own possible responses to the Church motion, he observed that "the U.S. had been aiding foreign governments economically since 1947, but had never been able to control such governments' behavior, because the U.S. was not a colonial or an imperialist power."[31]

Again, in addressing the problem of how to change the Saigon government without "substituting a Castro for a Batista," the thoughts of the ambassador and other consultants to the National Security Council turned quickly from lofty sentiments to money. Rufus Phillips, whom Michael Forrestal named to McGeorge Bundy about this time as one of America's best authorities on Vietnam, recommended that in order to give the Vietnamese "a government worth fighting for," Ngo Dinh Nhu could be neutralized by cutting off dollar support for the military units under his control while ensuring "the necessary funds to go around Saigon" to secure support for a coup.[32]

Lodge was in accord. In a long cable to Rusk on September 27, he wrote, "If we should ever get ourselves in the unfortunate position of fighting a war on the side of rebellious generals while the Ngo family still retains power in Saigon, we could pump in dollars or military scrip and make that acceptable currency in the regions we control."[33] It is hard to understand how Lodge could suggest such measures while denying their colonialist and imperialistic intent.

But in 1963 the logic of supplying the ARVN without a South Vietnamese state was not, apparently, pushed to its conclusion, certainly not in any recorded discussions of the time. American planners continued to think in terms of a central government in Saigon. Lodge still accepted the need for a Saigon-based Vietnamese government when he smoothed the path to power for General Khanh as the new chief of state during early 1964, after it had become clear that the first post-Diem government had failed to meet U.S. expectations.

William Colby was later to record in his memoir of this period his frustration with the lack of analysis in Washington as to who could replace the Diem regime's leadership. In vague references to "the generals," he recalled, little consideration was given to what these unknown men could offer the U.S. or South Vietnam.[34]

The crucial problem in September and October 1963 was that Kennedy and his advisors continued to put out fires one by one when what was needed was a major policy review. There were other contributing considerations, however. The U.S. was in Vietnam to fight a war against communism; generals who had or could be presented as having nationalist and anti-Communist credentials were attractive as an alternative source of authority to Diem. The successor government must be led by men who were fluent in French, as this was the lingua franca for U.S.-Vietnamese relations. The "generals" the National Security Council members referred to in 1963 had all been trained in France, in patterns of military thinking familiar to members of the American elite. Although Tri Quang, for example, had impressed Lodge as intelligent and politically acute, the monk's refusal to speak any language except Vietnamese, had he come to power, would have created enormous difficulties for the embassy and the Department of State. Again, Buddhist leaders, an unknown quantity, seemed mysterious and alien compared to the comparatively Westernized military officers.

Lodge himself habitually started his notes for speeches on Vietnam with the entry "Confucian, tropical rice-growing society."[35] Nowhere in his writings did he reveal any appreciation that professional soldiers had always commanded little esteem in a Confucian society.

In spite of Lodge's advice that a "wait and see" approach to the political scene in Saigon might play into the hands of the Communists, Kennedy was still unsure as to his Vietnam policy. The president stalled by sending a second "fact-finding mission" to South Vietnam, this time under the leadership of Robert McNamara and the chairman of the Joint Chiefs of Staff, Gen. Maxwell Taylor. Lodge protested at once: "It is inconceivable to me that direct questions asked on a whirlwind tour of the countryside can elicit any new and deep insights into the situation which you do not already possess."[36]

Kennedy insisted, and so Lodge determined to put his own interpretation of the situation in South Vietnam as persuasively as possible before anyone else could do so. He invited McNamara to stay at the residence. When the American official party arrived at the airport, the ambassador moved quickly to greet McNamara, while Harkins found himself trapped behind two of Lodge's staff members. According to David Halberstam, who observed the event, Harkins was initially stranded, protesting, "Please, gentlemen, please let me through to the Secretary."[37]

The itinerary of the mission was controlled by the military. McNamara, formerly a corporate executive with the Ford Motor Company, was well known as one who was impressed by neat columns of figures and reams of statistics. American officers in the provinces—talented, ambitious, but underemployed in the war effort because their role so far was solely advisory—were well equipped to present just such material. They gave the secretary statistical "proofs" that the war was being won in the countryside and would progress all the more quickly as more U.S. advisors became available.

Mrs. Lodge wrote of the six-day visit: "What a week and what a man is Sec. McNamara!! Really a super super man—Breakfast at 6:15 A.M. then goes catapulting himself all over the country until 11 P.M.... The group are never ready to dine before nine."[38] Lodge was well aware that he would have his work cut out in persuading the Washington mission that the war was not going well and that fighting could not improve under the leadership of Diem.

When McNamara and Taylor met with the Vietnam Country Team on September 25, they found the U.S. mission divided. Harkins and his staff spoke first, presenting an optimistic picture of the war and stressing that rapid and measurable progress had been made in the Strategic Hamlets program. Lodge then embarked on his own presentation. He opened with an indictment: "Truth in Vietnam was not obtained by asking direct questions, as MACV appeared to do." He continued, as with a rubric, "The current government is probably beginning its terminal phase.... We must get ready for some really tough weather because it is at least theoretically possible that this thing will disintegrate to a point where the Vietnamese army cannot cope with it and a Communist take over of the government here in Saigon will become a possibility.... Our interest in the land and our interest in the people is such that it transcends the question of who happens to be in control of the government at any particular time."[39]

Five days later, Lodge threw down his trump card. On their last day in Vietnam, Lodge orchestrated a meeting between McNamara and Taylor and South Vietnamese vice president Tho. Tho told the two visitors that the U.S.-sponsored Strategic Hamlets program was not working. It was not working, he said, because the peasantry were dissatisfied with the government. In fact, he continued, there were not more than twenty or thirty properly defended hamlets in the whole country, while the Viet Cong had increased its strength during the previous two years, in spite of the government killing over a thousand Communists a month.[40] Lodge rested his case.

McNamara's report was prepared during the fact-finding team's journey back to Washington. William Bundy, who served as McNamara's chief of staff on the tour, recorded his impressions of its compilation several years later in the following words: "In the twenty-seven-hour flight across the Pacific from Saigon, McNamara had slept no more than six hours, and I only two. . . . The report of the group was worked and re-worked, on the express understanding that it should reflect the views of all the members except as specifically noted. The intensive drafting process was an unforgettable experience—in hindsight it was also a very poor way to conduct the top business of the U.S. Government. Neither draftsmanship nor judgement is likely to be at its best under such working conditions."

Bundy went on to explain that "the haste reflected the almost desperate urgency with which the President sought to resolve the policy issues and the differences in his Administration." But, Bundy noted, he and the original readers of the report in Washington did not notice that it contained a clear internal inconsistency: the military sections of the paper assumed that continued improvement depended on reform in the government, but its political sections clearly stated that no such reform was likely.[41]

McNamara met with Kennedy on October 2. He reported so optimistically on progress in the war that Kennedy approved an announcement to the press that one thousand U.S. advisors would be withdrawn from Vietnam by the end of the year. This was a controversial decision. Phased withdrawal of forces had been one of the Pentagon's contingency plans for some time, but Kennedy's October announcement, coming as it did so soon before his death, has led to speculation that had he lived, Kennedy would have withdrawn from Vietnam. This is probably wishful thinking, colored by the later outcome of America's involvement in Vietnam. According to his aide Kenneth O'Donnell, Kennedy was firmly resolved to withdraw the thousand men and had given the appropriate orders before he left for his fatal tour of Texas in November. However, the fact remains that troops withdrawn for public relations purposes at home, at one period, could always be rotated back in at another.[42]

Kennedy's counselors, such as William Colby, chief of the Far East Division of the CIA, then on duty in Washington, were hesitant to tell him when he was wrong, as had become clear during the August coup preparations, and there appear to have been no adequate procedures in the capital for distilling the gist of the masses of reports that came in from the U.S. mission. That was why the president had taken the gamble of asking Lodge to perform this service in Saigon. The fact-finding missions, however, were a symptom of Kennedy's impatience with Vietnam, combined with his desire to delay a major policy review of Amer-

ica's aims there. Such tours were extraordinarily wasteful of resources: after all, McNamara could have read all the reports he received in Vietnam without leaving Washington.

The way in which the secretary of defense drew his conclusions seems to have been even more irregular than his "catapulting himself all over the country" for sixteen hours a day. William Bundy's perception was that McNamara made his final decision on the political situation in South Vietnam on the basis of two secret communications from informants whose names he withheld in writing his memoir of the period. The first of these was from Nguyen Dinh Thuan, secretary of state to the Vietnamese president and minister of defense, the Vietnamese official whom many Americans found the most congenial member of the Diem regime cabinet. Lodge himself hoped that Thuan would succeed Diem and had even chosen for him a revealing title—that of prime minister, not president. The other was P. J. Honey, the British scholar and possible London government consultant on Vietnam. Both these men argued strongly that Diem had lost his capacity to lead: in less hectic times, Thuan's report might well have been regarded as treachery and self-seeking, while Honey had no responsibility for the outcome of his criticisms.[43]

On October 5, Kennedy edged toward a decision regarding the Diem regime. This was the stage of relations with the South Vietnamese government that Lodge subsequently described as one in which he was told "not to thwart" a coup. In "Vietnam Memoir," he recorded that Kennedy's instruction was, "Do not thwart, do not stimulate, do not deny economic or military aid, do not give advice"—the position to which he held in all future statements on the matter. In fact, the president directed him actively to seek out and build contacts with anyone who might serve to form an alternative leadership to the Diem regime. This message was conveyed to Lodge through CIA channels: he was instructed that the effort was to be "totally secure and fully deniable."[44]

Lodge was also directed to continue suspension of the Commodity Import Program Subsidy and to suspend funding for the Vietnamese Special Forces. On the same day, McGeorge Bundy cabled Lodge: "The President thinks it of the greatest importance that, to the very limit of our abilities, we should not open this next stage in the press. The decisions and instructions in following telegram are being held most tightly here, and we are making every possible effort to limit public knowledge and to let the Vietnamese Government itself learn from what we do and not what the papers say, so that your negotiations with Diem may be run on your terms."[45]

Lodge's solution for keeping the new policy a secret was to provide the American reporters with sensational alternative copy. Lodge also felt it was his responsibility to conceal the new phase in relations with Diem from a visiting party of Congressmen. This eight-man group, led by Clement J. Zablocki, chairman of the Foreign Affairs Far East Subcommittee of the House Foreign Affairs Committee, planned to arrive in Saigon on October 6 for a three-day tour. Zablocki had wired ahead asking the embassy to arrange meetings for him with President Diem, Ngo Dinh Nhu, and Secretary Thuan. Such consultations would not fit in with Lodge's determination to run his negotiations with Diem on his own terms. He resolved to prevent the Congressmen from meeting Diem, and to keep the newspapermen off the trail by occupying them with his own actions.

On the fateful day of October 5, David Halberstam and NBC reporters John Sharkey and Grant Wolfkill were in the central marketplace to record another Buddhist suicide by fire. Lodge himself had predicted that such events would be timed for the congressional visit. Saigon police forced the young newspapermen back, and John Sharkey was injured in the melee. He was admitted to the American dispensary, where Lodge visited him, recording a formal protest to the South Vietnamese Foreign Office immediately afterwards. When the Congressmen arrived at the airport, the ambassador presented Sharkey to them, saying, "Here's John Sharkey of NBC who was beaten up by the South Vietnamese police. They had a perfect right to be there and they were beaten up by the police." Lodge had broken his silence toward the Diem regime only once before, in reply to Madame Nhu's statement from Rome that U.S. junior officers in South Vietnam "behaved like little soldiers of fortune." To this charge he had made a short but scathing public response on September 26.[46]

As Lodge had intended, the *New York Times* made much of the attacks on the reporters and the ambassador's defense of them, and so was slow to follow up the story of cuts in U.S. aid to the Vietnamese government. Further, and this time fortuitously, the attentions of the newspapermen in Saigon were absorbed over the next few days by Diem government charges made through the *Times of Vietnam* that they themselves had "stage-managed" the latest Buddhist suicide.

And although Lodge might successfully tie up the attention of the American pressmen, he could not control the *Times of Vietnam* itself. On Monday, October 7, the paper's banner headline stated that the U.S. had suspended economic aid in order to bring pressure to bear on the South Vietnamese government. The Congressmen protested to embassy officials both against the suspensions and against State's attempt to conceal the truth from the Foreign Affairs Subcommittee. Lodge, alerted to the problem on Monday night, called a meeting the next morning, when he equivocated as to whether a new policy was in place, using the truthful statement that Diem had not mentioned the matter to him. The delegation insisted that they would interrogate Diem. According to his own account, the ambassador had to draw "on all his diplomatic skills" to deflect them from this course.

Lodge's outline for a cable to Rusk, which he subsequently decided not to send, throws new light on his view of his own role in relation to the Kennedy administration during his first tour of duty in Vietnam: "I have no criticism whatever to make of the ["Zablocki" scratched out] Subcommittee and I do not in the least begrudge the fact that distinguished visitors take up practically all of my time when they are here, meaning that the regular work must be squeezed in late at night or early in the morning. I have a responsibility to the home front which I shall always try to discharge. But I do fear that it can be dangerous to bring high-ranking official United States people who are not in the executive branch into conferences with the Chief of State at the same time that the Executive Branch is planning elaborate diplomatic maneuvers. . . . We were, for a while, skating on very thin ice last night."[47]

The meeting between the Vietnamese president and the Congressmen in fact passed without incident, although Lodge noted that the visitors had been "very impressed" by Diem. On Zablocki's return to Washington, a nervous Kennedy asked him in writing his official report on the visit "not to build up Diem too much." Zablocki replied robustly that he saw no alternative to Diem as leader of the Vietnamese government. American reporters had exaggerated the case against him, he said; he added that he was concerned that "forces" in Washington and Saigon seemed intent on deposing the South Vietnamese president.[48]

By mid-October, coup rumors abounded in Saigon. Speculation ran high that fighting would break out on National Independence Day, October 26, but the celebration passed without incident. CIA reports of the period give details of plots by various Vietnamese groups, both in the military and in the government. Widely circulated anecdotes, significantly, placed Americans as the initiating agents.

As the month drew to an end and Diem against all the odds remained in power, the U.S. ambassador and Mrs. Lodge planned to visit Dalat to attend the inauguration of an internationally funded Atomic Energy Center there on Monday, October 28. Diem, hearing of their intentions, invited Lodge and his wife to stay with him at one of his villas in Dalat, his favorite hill retreat from Saigon. At State, Ball responded to the news of the invitation with enthusiasm. He drew up instructions on the various matters that Lodge should raise during the visit, concluding, "We realize of course that Diem may keep conversation on plane of interest only to him." The Lodges accepted Diem's invitation. They agreed to accompany him to Dalat in the presidential plane: the entire party was to leave Saigon early in the morning of the following Sunday.[49]

On that morning, both the American ambassador and Gen. Tran Van Don arrived at the Saigon airport ahead of schedule. They had important business to transact. Don had asked Lucien Conein, his CIA go-between with the embassy, to arrange for him to meet the ambassador, since some days before General Harkins, speaking as the U.S. military commander, had firmly informed him that he would not condone a coup. Confronted with this evidence of division in the U.S. mission, Don had decided upon the extraordinary step of asking Lodge if Conein in encouraging a takeover did in fact speak with Washington's voice. Don had resolved that if Lodge said Conein spoke for him, the ARVN would take this as the official U.S. signal for a coup. Lodge, for his part, had made no previous contact with Don and so needed his assurance that the Don-Minh group of generals favored a continuing American presence in Vietnam, the key question for the U.S.[50]

In the brief 7 A.M. encounter at the airport on October 27, before Diem arrived fifteen minutes later, Lodge gave Don the signal to commence his moves to overthrow the South Vietnamese government—he told Don that Conein in encouraging a military coup did indeed speak for him. In the course of further exchanges, in answer to a direct question from the ambassador, Don refused to give exact dates or times. This was accepted without protest. Although Don did not realize it then or later, he had played into Lodge's hands, for a degree of American ignorance of the exact details of the Vietnamese plot was highly desirable in the cause of future "plausible denial" of U.S. involvement. Don answered the much more important, indeed the really critical, question, in volunteering that he did not think the war could be won without American assistance, as Lodge conclusively demonstrated by recording in his "Vietnam Memoir" this part of the morning's transaction as "Don's secret statement to Lodge."[51]

The compilers of both *The Pentagon Papers* and *U.S.-Vietnam Relations, 1945–1967*, working on U.S. government documents and the cable traffic between Lodge and the Department of State, concluded that Lodge had met General Don at the Saigon airport on the morning of Monday, October 28, in the course of embarkation for the Dalat opening ceremony, after a day-long confrontation with Diem on Sunday during which the Vietnamese had once again refused to concede on any point of U.S. requests.[52] This reconstruction was incorrect. Lodge had in fact made a deal with General Don *before* his projected conversation with Diem.

On October 27, the official party did not arrive in Dalat until 3 P.M., as Diem had first led it on an inspection tour of a strategic hamlet preceded by a seven-course lunch high in the mountains, served on antique settings from the palace in Saigon. No day-long struggle to establish a dialogue occurred, although Lodge did speak privately with Diem during the late afternoon, when Diem, far from maintaining the reported pose of stubborn and unresponsive silence, confided that he could not continue to govern without U.S. financial assistance. In the evening, Diem entertained the Lodges to another sumptuous meal at which six people only were present. The Lodges stayed overnight in the president's guest house on beds covered with purple silk quilts, for Diem had kept them too late for a return to Saigon. "He talked constantly till 1:30," Mrs. Lodge recorded the next day, when Lodge had departed for the atomic center opening at 10 A.M. and she took up her pen to record a description of the events of the Sunday in the welcome 64 degree temperature of the hills.[53]

At a luncheon in Dalat after the opening ceremony, Lodge spoke openly with Secretary of State Thuan, giving him the impression that his attempts at negotiations with Diem the previous day had been fruitless. Back in Saigon that evening, he made sure that it was the detailed text of this conversation, and not of that with Diem, which arrived in Washington first. He then filed his account of the earlier meeting with Gen. Tran Van Don as if it were a Monday cable, at 7 P.M. from the embassy and via the secure CIA channel, although he had departed from Dalat just two hours earlier after the overnight stay in the hills, which made a Monday morning meeting with the Vietnamese general in Saigon an impossibility.[54]

Contrary to the received version of Diem's stubbornness during the October 27 meeting, Lodge recorded in his own personal notes and in a later cable to Kennedy that Diem had raised the subject of the restoration of U.S. aid, confiding that without it he could not continue to govern. Of this overture, Lodge later commented, "I had written a letter to publish in the press as to why I was resuming commercial imports. And we were like two boys on bicycles playing 'chicken' and he gave way first."[55]

In Washington, the imminence of a coup, its desirability, and U.S. determination to support it were now fully established. The National Security Council meetings of October 29 were all devoted to preparations for the fall of the Vietnamese government. The Pacific Command in Hawaii alerted a naval and air task force to stand off the coast of South Vietnam, to evacuate American dependents and civilians if necessary.[56]

In Saigon, Lodge waited tensely. On October 30 he reminded McGeorge Bundy that the ARVN generals "may well have need of funds at the last moment with which to buy off potential opposition";[57] as a further precaution, he canceled arrangements for his scheduled departure for Washington the next day. It was now the morning of November 1. Early that day, unannounced, and much to the irritation of the ambassador, Admiral Felt, the U.S. commander in the Pacific and therefore the commander in the field in Vietnam, had arrived from Honolulu. A pricking in his thumbs had stirred the Admiral Felt to find out what was going on in Saigon behind his back. His presence necessitated a courtesy call on Diem, and at the very least desirable time.

Taking advantage of the protocol visit, Diem made contact with Lodge. The palace notified the U.S. ambassador that the president wished to speak with him alone for fifteen minutes after the interview with Admiral Felt, scheduled for 10 A.M. Lodge hoped that Diem could be cut off quickly, for it was no secret to U.S. officials that ARVN units were massing in and around the city, and journalists were already watching the movement of troops from the roof garden of the Caravelle Hotel. The American supreme commander remained unaware of these developments: he later remarked to Lodge in some puzzlement that he had never seen General Don, who accompanied them on the visit to the palace, so edgy or indeed chewing gum.[58]

After Admiral Felt had left the palace, Lodge listened impassively to Diem's private confidences to him. He thanked him for his kindness at Dalat and assured him that rumors of death threats against himself in his position as U.S. ambassador had not affected his "feelings of admiration and personal friendship" for Diem. He got up to leave. Diem restrained him. He took President Kennedy's suggestions very seriously, Diem said, and wished to carry them out. It was all a matter of timing, he tried to impress upon his American ally.

Lodge filed his report of the morning conversation with Diem at 3 P.M. He designated it "Priority," the lowest category possible for an ambassadorial cable. The category "Critical Flash," reserved in most U.S. embassies for the outbreak of war but in the Saigon case used for coup information, would have ensured instantaneous reception in Washington; indeed, the CIA was already filing cables under this designation, as Lodge was no doubt well aware. Again, Lodge would normally have put the conclusion in the opening paragraph of a policy suggestion paper, but in this case, the key point lay buried. Toward the end of the long telegram, which read as an account of a typical Diem monologue, appeared the remark: "If U.S. wants to make a package deal, I would think we were in a position to do it. In effect he [Diem] said: tell us what you want and we'll do it."[59]

As Lodge's cable telling of Diem's capitulation made its slow passage to Washington, general after Vietnamese general gave notice of allegiance to the

Don-Minh-Kim coup group by contributing forces to the operation to capture the key points of the city. Nguyen Van Thieu, commander of the Fifth Division of the critical 3 Corps zone around Saigon, contributed the artillery; from Pleiku in 2 Corps, the promising young Gen. Nguyen Khanh signaled his support. Diem's praetorian guard at the palace mounted an already doomed defense.

Hours before Lodge's 3 P.M. cable was received at State, page after page of CIA reports describing the coup had arrived, and at least twenty other communications from Lodge himself. At 4:30 in the afternoon, the beleaguered president of South Vietnam contacted the American ambassador at the embassy. When the *New York Times* published the official transcript of the exchange in 1969, many Americans were disturbed by its tone. The summary of the call read in part:

> Diem: Some units have made a rebellion and I want to know what is the attitude of the U.S.?
> Lodge: I do not feel well enough informed to tell you. I have heard the shooting, but I am not well enough acquainted with all the facts. Also it is 4:30 A.M. in Washington and the US government cannot possibly have a view.

Lodge's own records and several witnesses, however, attest to a longer exchange than that published, in which Lodge offered Diem transport to the airport in a car under the American flag and a safe passage from South Vietnam to the U.S. base in the Philippines. It seems that Lodge included only the substantive content of his comments in his cable to State, knowing full well that Diem would not accept rescue on American terms.[60]

There can be no doubt that Lodge silenced some of Diem's rejoinder, supremely confident as he was in his ability to control not only the American press but the official government records as well. Time may well have embellished the memories of bodyguard Coa Xuan Vy when he recalled Diem as replying to Lodge's statement regarding the Washington time: "Mr. Ambassador, do you realize who you are talking to? I would like you to know that you are talking to a president of an independent and sovereign nation. I will only leave this country if it is the wish of my people. I will never leave according to the request of a group of rebellious generals or of an American Ambassador. The U.S. government must take full responsibility before the world in this miserable matter." The drift here, however, seems consistent with other testimony, and with other speeches of Diem.[61]

The "game of chicken" was almost at an end. Lodge retired to bed early on November 1, his customary practice as Vietnamese political crises unfolded. Artillery fire continued through the night. The relatives of Vietnamese servants crept into the residence compound for refuge. At 5 A.M. Lodge mounted a balcony to observe the city and stayed there until the fighting stopped at seven o'clock.[62] He nowhere recorded his thoughts during those hours.

Embassy staff assumed that Diem and Nhu were still in the palace on the morning of November 2. In fact, they had left by a back gate the afternoon before and had taken refuge in the house of Ma Tuyen, the head of the five associations that controlled the Chinese population of Saigon-Cholon and possibly Nhu's chief contact with the Chinese syndicates in the opium trade. There, chain-smoking and drinking tea, they tried to make telephone contact with ARVN unit commanders they had reason to believe might still be loyal. They had no success: commander after commander reported that there was no transport across the Mekong River. In the morning they were carried in Ma Tuyen's car to St. Francis Xavier Church in Cholon, the Chinese district of the city, where they took communion. A former palace servant recognized the president as military vehicles pulled up in front of the shrine and troops seized the brothers. Diem and Nhu went in silence. During their journey under arrest to the Joint General Staff headquarters of the Vietnamese Armed Forces, they were killed, by most accounts on the orders of Duong Van Minh.[63]

1. During the liberation of Europe in 1945, Lodge served in France as senior liaison officer to Gen. Jean de Lattre de Tassigny. Gesturing at center left is Major Lodge, with General de Lattre in foreground. To the right of Lodge are Gen. Dwight D. Eisenhower, Gen. Omar Bradley (face hidden), and staff officers. Courtesy Massachusetts Historical Society.

2. Lodge was United States ambassador to the United Nations from 1953 to 1960, during the Eisenhower administration. His experience in World War II had convinced him of the value of collective security. Here he is shown addressing a convention of newspaper editors and publishers in New York in 1954. UPI/Bettmann Newsphotos.

3. Ambassador Lodge and President Ngo Dinh Diem of South Vietnam. Lodge had only one other conversation with President Diem, after the accreditation ceremony at the presidential palace in Saigon on August 26, 1963, seen here. UPI/Bettmann Newsphotos.

4. A Buddhist monk commits ritual suicide in a Saigon street, October 5, 1963. President Kennedy had a similar newspaper photograph on his desk when he asked Lodge to go to South Vietnam as his ambassador. UPI/Bettmann Newsphotos.

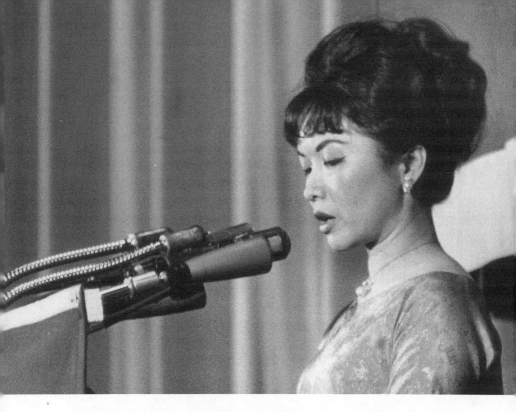

5. Madame Ngo Dinh Nhu, the sister-in-law of Catholic President Diem, profoundly shocked American public opinion by referring to the Buddhist suicides as "barbecues." She is seen here on a public-speaking tour of the United States in September 1963. UPI/Bettmann Newsphotos.

6. Gen. Duong Van Minh replaced Diem as head of state in South Vietnam in November 1963. Rumors quickly arose that Minh was negotiating with Communist North Vietnam to end the war. Courtesy Massachusetts Historical Society.

7. Lodge making a Voice of America address in support of Gen. Nguyen Khanh from Saigon during the 1964 U.S. presidential campaign. Lodge had such popular appeal as an American ambassador fighting communism in South Vietnam that he won in the first Republican primary in March 1964. Dunn Collection.

8. Lodge had severe reservations about the conduct of the war under the leadership of the American commander, Gen. Paul D. Harkins. Gen. William C. Westmoreland, who arrived as Harkins's deputy in January 1964, is to the right of the reception line with Mrs. Lodge. The other figures, from left to right, are Gen. Nguyen Khanh, Mrs. Westmoreland, and Mrs. Nguyen Khanh. Dunn Collection.

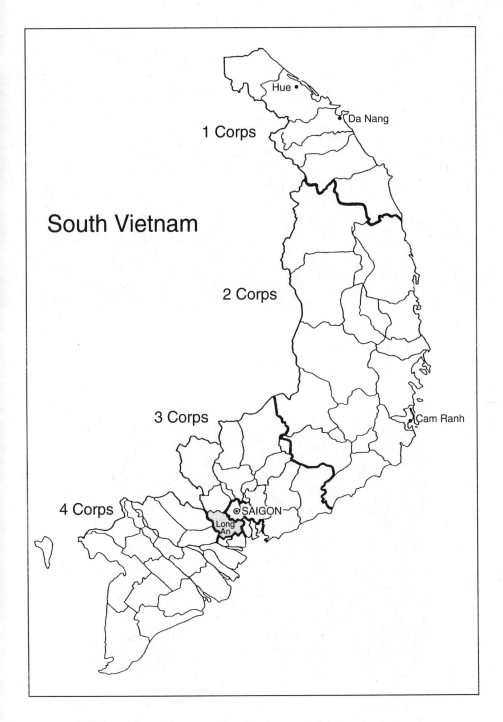

Hue •

• Da Nang

1 Corps

South Vietnam

2 Corps

3 Corps

Cam Ranh

4 Corps

SAIGON

Long
An

9. South Vietnam in 1963 and 1964. Military commands around Saigon were more
popular than those on the border with North Vietnam. Map courtesy of U.S. Army Center
of Military History.

10. Renewed religious conflict broke out in Saigon in the closing days of Lodge's first embassy to South Vietnam. In June 1964, Catholics demonstrated to protest alleged discrimination by the Buddhist government Lodge had brought to power in November 1963. The banner in the center reads, "Go Home, Cabot Lodge." Dunn Collection.

11. Ambassador Lodge presents the 1966 constitution of South Vietnam to Minister for Foreign Affairs Tran Van Do. The irony of the transaction was apparently lost at the time. Courtesy Massachusetts Historical Society.

Chapter Four

Calm Before the Storm

In his evaluation for Kennedy of the November coup, Lodge summed up: "All this may be a useful lesson in the use of U.S. power for those who face similar situations in the future. Perhaps the U.S. government has here evolved a way of not being everywhere saddled with responsibility for autocratic governments, simply because they are anti-Communist. . .a course which can eventually lead many people to believe that the foreign Communist autocracy which they don't know is preferable to the local autocracy which they do know." He went on: "Nothing could put the cause of freedom into a stronger position than for those on the side of freedom to be able to clean their own house and not be so often in a situation in which we have to put up with autocrats at the very worst or at the best with Colonel Blimps in order to avoid being taken over by Communism."[1]

All this had been achieved, he continued, without the United States having "to act like a colonial power." For Lodge, as for other former U.S. cold warriors, by definition American intentions were never colonialist. However, the above rationale of the ends justifying the means, with its denial of self-determination to small states everywhere, cannot be seen in any other light than as a statement of an ideology-driven neocolonialism. It is exactly the logic that Lodge had imputed to the Communist bloc powers for the preceding twenty years. Unmindful of the irony, he moved on.

The dominant note in his assessment of his own role in events was pride in a presidential mission accomplished, and in the contributions he had made to the statesman's craft. He emphasized the effectiveness of his policy of "silence and simple correctness" in relation to Diem, and its fulfillment in the withholding of funds for the CIP, which had forced the Vietnamese president to offer to negotiate. He noted only in passing that had Diem and Nhu listened to the advice he had conveyed to them, they would have remained alive.

The coup had been Vietnamese, and Americans could neither have managed nor stopped it after it was in progress, Lodge asserted, although it had been U.S. actions that had "made the people who could do something about it start thinking hard about how to get a change of government." This formulation is remarkably close to that revealed by CIA operatives such as L. Fletcher Prouty in later testimony as to the established procedures of the agency in destabilizing American-funded third world governments: drop hints of U.S. displeasure; allow the palace guard to desert; stand by as the coup plotters coalesce. Assassinations then "just happened," Prouty explained, specifically in relation to Diem.[2]

Lodge's sense of propriety in the conduct of government business would not have permitted him to reveal conventions of this sort. Instead, he rehearsed a formula as to what had taken place and used it in all his subsequent statements on the matter. Even in his own ostensibly private notations and memoirs, he used the same phrasings: "the Diem government had been in its terminal phase"; "if it had gone on another month, a Communist takeover would have been inevitable"; "a prominent Vietnamese told me they were heading for assassination before I left Washington." He understandably refused to admit to any hand in planning the details of the coup. What is more remarkable is that he appears to have erased from his mind all recall of the details of his own duplicitous role at Dalat and later.[3]

With the removal of Diem, Lodge appears to have thought that his mission for Kennedy in Asia was over. He was complacent as to his achievement in installing a new government in Saigon, optimistic regarding progress in the war under a regime of Vietnamese generals led by Gen. Duong Van Minh, Diem's former chief military advisor. He composed his report on the coup five days after its occurrence, when he felt that the new Minh government had achieved a smooth transition to power. "Now that the revolution has occurred," he opened, "I assume you will not want my weekly reports to continue, although I will, of course, gladly continue them if you desire." It seems to have been with some relief that he wrote, "Herewith my 'wrap-up' report for the week ending 6 November."

As Dunn, Lodge's closest assistant at the time, recalled some thirty years later, Lodge had understood his assignment in terms of Kennedy's problem with Diem; after the coup he quickly wearied of the politics of South Vietnam and of the U.S. mission there.[4] The cable record bears out this interpretation, as does the internal evidence of the Lodge Papers. Fewer than two hundred cables were sent from the U.S. embassy in Saigon in the first five weeks of the Minh regime, compared with the thousands during the same time span before the coup of November 1 and the week thereafter.

Another ambassador might have viewed the immediate post-coup period, bound to be fluid, as no less important to U.S. foreign policy interests, if not more so, than the pre-coup period. But as evidence of Lodge's detachment at this time, "Vietnam Memoir" contains only forty lines on the Minh period, of the five chapters devoted to the first tour of duty in Vietnam. Most of the other seventy pages of this section, Part Two, are devoted to Kennedy's appointment of Lodge as his ambassador to Saigon and the subsequent contest of wills with Diem. Significant also is the complete absence from the whole Lodge Papers collection of any material relating to procedures for coordinating the activities of the agencies and departments of the U.S. mission or solving the problems Hilsman had identified in his report of January 1963. If anyone had been so brave as to attempt to brief Lodge on these matters, the advice had not impinged sufficiently for him to keep a record; all the material he chose to request before his departure from Washington and subsequently preserved, all the records of conversations, deal with press reporting of the war and Kennedy's problems with Diem and his family.

In early November, Lodge seems to have reasoned as follows: he had accomplished the mission on which he had been sent to Vietnam; as the desired change of government had occurred, his only remaining duty as U.S. ambassador must be to advise the incoming leadership on establishing good relations with the American government and the American public. Lodge was now gracefully preparing to disengage. Little did he realize that rather than resolving the problems of winning the war, the period of the Minh regime would be only the beginning of America's involvement in Vietnam.

Writing to his sons on November 5, he commented, "The Generals conducting the coup did a masterful job.... There had been absolutely no leaks. I understand that there was no paperwork at all, everything having been committed to memory. Perhaps in other places, some lessons might be learned about not having leaks and not drowning in paper." In his mention of paperwork and leaks, he was touching upon a vexed problem in the cable traffic between Saigon and Washington; he seems, moreover, to have been admitting to his own growing impatience with the difficulties of running the embassy. And, in an attitude ominous for the future, he appears not to have noticed that when he praised the generals for their efficiency, they were conducting a conspiracy and not a government.[5]

In their anxiety to rid themselves of Diem, the dominant forces in the U.S. Department of State had not paused to evaluate what the Vietnamese generals whom they were encouraging to seize power had to offer. There was a new government in Saigon now, but the U.S. ambassador had no coherent policy guidance to extend to it. In part this state of affairs was due to the preceding weeks of hectic, uncoordinated instructions from State to the U.S. embassy. Unfortunately, however, in the succeeding critical period, when searching questions should have been asked regarding America's aims and future in Vietnam, the ambassador in the field had lost interest in his job.

During the whole course of the coup, State had been aware of the need to monitor the announcements of the rebels themselves, in order to construct a cover story to legitimize to Americans the violent change of leadership in Vietnam. Rusk had initially instructed Lodge that "if the coup succeeds, acceptance and understanding of its purpose here will be greatly increased if generals and their civilian associates continue to develop strongly and publicly the conclusion reported in one of their broadcasts that Nhu was dickering with the Communists to betray the anti-Communist cause. High value of this argument should be emphasized to them at the earliest opportunity."[6]

The first problem to be confronted was the embarrassing dilemma of the deaths of Diem and Nhu. Lodge had suggested two days before the coup that the brothers could be flown if necessary to a destination far from the Asian mainland, to Saipan (capital of the Marianas), "where the absence of press, communications, etc. would allow us some leeway to make a further decision as to their ultimate disposition."[7] This had not worked out. The American newspapermen in Saigon were on Lodge's side on the change of government, but they also wanted copy. Pictures of Diem's and Nhu's bodies began to appear in the U.S. press on November 2. These pictures threatened to cast doubt on the conduct of the men the U.S. had brought to power in Vietnam and to give Diem martyr status, for the brothers' hands appeared to be bound behind their backs and the fatal wounds were in the backs of their necks.

Lodge initially suggested that the Vietnamese generals could explain the deaths as the "kind of thing that will happen in a coup d'etat."[8] McGeorge Bundy was appalled. He had seen the pictures of the bodies and he faced the ongoing task of dealing with domestic U.S. sentiments. He instructed Lodge that the new leadership of South Vietnam must remove the taint of the deaths from themselves and, moreover, remedy the impression they had given to the world that political assassination was acceptable to the United States.

When Conein first learned of the deaths, Duong Van Minh claimed that Diem and Nhu had committed suicide. Conein, a Catholic himself, warned Minh that if they had committed suicide in a Catholic church and any priest then said a mass for them that night, "the story would not hold water." McGeorge Bundy was emphatic that the next explanation tendered, that of "accidental suicide," must be quashed. Rusk urged Lodge to persuade the generals to make a statement that they had plans to ensure the brothers' safety; underlining the gravity of this matter, he warned that U.S. aid could not be restored until this was done.[9]

The South Vietnamese generals themselves were acutely aware of the need for good relations with the U.S. government. They seem, however, to have had less understanding of the connection between American public opinion and congressional funding for the war, the point that which Lodge had tried so strongly to impress upon Diem. Of the sophisticated world of image creation in which Lodge was an adept, they appear to have known nothing at all.

Washington was ready to recognize the new regime in Saigon immediately, using the formula that the U.S. "deplored forcible changes of free and democratically elected governments" but could understand that the Vietnamese generals had acted to save their country from communism and wished only to improve the prosecution of the war under a constitutional leadership. On the day of the coup, Generals Minh and Don repeatedly asked Conein, who was present for most of the afternoon at Vietnamese Joint General Staff headquarters, when and under what conditions the United States would recognize their government. In the face of the new South Vietnamese leaders' eagerness, Rusk judiciously warned that they should avoid the appearance of "reporting in" to the U.S. ambassador. In the same vein of giving credence to the official story that the U.S. had not been involved in the coup, when Lodge advised that the Commodity Import Program Subsidy should be restored, he added that this information should be kept out of the newspapers. The White House quickly promised extra funds for the war effort and development projects, including an additional twenty million dollars for the CIP.[10]

Lodge met with the generals on November 3. A dominant theme in his advice to them was in regard to press relations and American public opinion; the day before, General Kim had made the helpful statement that no foreigners had been involved in the coup.[11] Lodge asked Don and Kim if they planned a press release clearing themselves of the deaths of Diem and Nhu. When they replied in the negative, he told them that the Department of State required a public statement and suggested liberal reforms that could be announced at the same time, to create the right impression.

He continued with the matter of the three children of Ngo Dinh Nhu, who had remained in Vietnam while the eldest daughter, Le Thuy, had accompanied Madame Nhu on her speaking tour of America. Madame Nhu, he was aware, had contacted journalist Marguerite Higgins in Los Angeles seeking news of her younger children and of Ngo Dinh Can. He advised Don and Kim that they should arrange a well-publicized reunion between the children and their mother, noting in his report to Washington that this struck them as a good idea, "although they evidently had not thought about it at all."

Lodge then asked about the form of government the generals envisaged. They said that they had debated whether to have an entirely military structure, to involve some civilians, or, as they had finally decided, a government in which the ARVN would play only a small role. Although they had suspended the Diem regime constitution, a provisional government would devise a new constitution within a few months. Until then, General Minh was to be president of a Military Committee, with Nguyen Ngoc Tho, Diem's former vice president, as prime minister for the sake of continuity, and below him a cabinet of mainly nonmilitary men. Although this answer was vague, Lodge was enthusiastic. He summed up his impression of the meeting, saying, "We did more business in fifteen minutes than we used to be able to do at the palace in four hours."[12]

Lodge was also sanguine about the military prospects of the men whom he had assisted to power. Once again bypassing General Harkins in favor of a non–U.S. mission source, he asked Robert G. Thompson, the head of the British advisory team in South Vietnam, for his opinion. Thompson told him that if the Vietnamese generals could stay together, the coup should help in shortening the war. Lodge recorded this observation without comment on the stipulation that the generals must remain united to be successful, or on the difficulties that might arise in a military leadership based on a committee structure. He further noted that "Harkins concurred," although, even if this were so, the American commander's reaction to the high-handed procedure of consulting a foreigner first can only be imagined.[13]

The issue of the rescue of the Nhu children was predictably popular with the American press. When they were collected from Dalat, where a French priest had taken them into hiding for fear that the local population might harm them, Lodge, with cloak-and-dagger flourish, had the Italian embassy authenticate fake travel documents for them. They were then escorted by Lodge's aide, Frederick Flott, to Rome, where they were surrendered into the care of their uncle, Ngo Dinh Thuc. According to Flott, Lodge had calculated that the presence of the children in Rome would draw Madame Nhu out of Los Angeles, where her accusations against the American ambassador to South Vietnam were proving an embarrassment to the Kennedy administration. Madame Nhu, however, refused to leave the U.S.[14]

If the case of the children was straightforward, the question of the disposition of Ngo Dinh Can was more complicated. As Lodge pointed out, the crowds demonstrating against Can in Hue had justification for their anger at his past tyrannies. Yet a lynching would produce bad publicity, as would tearing him away from his ailing mother, since he was the last representative of the family in South Vietnam. Can applied to the U.S. consulate in Hue for asylum, but this did not present Lodge with an insurmountable obstacle, since a consulate did not have the same powers to offer asylum as an embassy. Finally, on November 5, Lodge resolved the matter by handing Can over to the South Vietnamese authorities, on the assurance that he would be given "a fair trial."[15]

Lodge had been much less punctilious regarding the diplomacy of asylum when he had given sanctuary to Buddhist bonzes in August, on quite flimsy evidence of persecution, as John Helble, the U.S. consul in Hue, was very much aware. On Helble's return to Washington, he was given the doleful task of answering letters protesting against his surrender of Can to the ARVN. Lodge, by contrast, escaped opprobrium. He also received many letters on the subject of Can as successive South Vietnamese governments failed to bring him to trial. These he fielded using a duplicated statement explaining the protocol of Can's application for asylum and his offer of asylum and safe passage to Diem and Nhu on November 1.[16]

The children of the former Vietnamese ruling family must now be allowed to bring a note of humanity into the whole affair. They made their passage into exile with heads held high. As Flott recalled, the eldest, Ngo Dinh Trac, accidentally glimpsed a headline in an Indian newspaper during their transit through Delhi. This described Nhu's body as having had the skull "crushed in." The boy covered his dawning realization of what had happened by asking for his crucifix. He revealed nothing more of his feelings on the long journey to Rome.

Washington passed its note of official recognition to the Minh government on November 7, 1963, two days after Lodge's "wrap-up" report. Lodge was informed that U.S. aid payments to the GVN would recommence when the interim government had formed.[17]

Later, Lodge quietly quashed a forthcoming debate in the General Assembly of the United Nations on the report of a U.N. fact-finding team that had visited South Vietnam in October and November to investigate Buddhist complaints of human rights abuses. U.S. officials in New York advised State that an airing of the findings of the U.N. mission would reflect badly on members of the new Saigon regime who had served under Diem. Moreover, a public debate might show the new regime to be not much different from the old in terms of tyrannical practices, and invite renewed charges of U.S. involvement in the coup from Hanoi and Beijing.[18] Lodge understood the difference in impact between denunciations in the international forum, which would be publicized by the press of the world, and fragmentary evidence in a written report few would read. During a December visit to Washington, he simply asked Sir Senerat Gunawardene of Ceylon, the leader of the U.N. group that had gathered depositions on the Buddhist affair, to desist from pressing for a debate based on his findings. Gunawardene agreed to do so as a personal favor to Lodge, whom he had known during the Bostonian's period as U.S. ambassador to the United Nations. Like so many others who came into contact with Lodge on government business, Gunawardene had fallen under his charm and regarded him as a personal friend.[19]

Lodge would do almost nothing as head of the U.S. mission in South Vietnam to tutor the Minh government in solving its internal problems. He was willing to advise the new Vietnamese leader on "image" and to arrange protection from criticism using his considerable contacts in the United Nations and the American administration, but he had little continuing interest in South Vietnamese internal affairs after the November coup.

Lodge had recorded shortly before the change of government that he did not think that South Vietnam was ready for a democratic election. Although the attitude was cynical given the rhetoric, it is understandable that Washington was more interested in a stable government for South Vietnam than in a representative one, since changing the leadership had been to help the war effort. But with hindsight it is most regrettable that Lodge took so little interest in the formation of the interim government and its proposal for a representative council. Never again in the short history of the state of South Vietnam would there occur such a propitious moment to harness the energies of its divided elite and diverse constituencies to the construction of popularly accepted institutions of government. The challenge was monumental and experience was lacking, but so was constructive advice from the American ambassador, who might at the very least have pointed out the usefulness of his own maxim that "political solutions include people while military solutions exclude people."[20]

When the Vietnamese generals, calling themselves the Military Revolutionary Council (MRC), announced the composition of their provisional government on

November 6, the American ambassador reported briefly that it contained no politicians but was "largely made up of technicians," while the "military clearly have the upper hand." He did not remark upon the possibilities for confusion inherent in the new power structure: "The Revolutionary Military Council [sic] holds legislative and executive powers 'pending amendment of the constitution' and President of Council, 'Big' Minh, is Chief of State. Council 'entrusts' executive power to Provisional Government, whose members are chosen by Premier Tho but subject to Council's approval," Lodge continued without comment. "Moreover, Chief of State Minh, Minister of Defense Don and Minister of Security Dinh, in addition to being members of Revolutionary Council, are Chairman and Deputy Chairman respectively of Council's Executive Committee." His description appears to have been based on the text of the Provisional Constitutional Charter as announced on Saigon radio without further commentary. He concluded his report on the provisional constitution by remarking only that the coup had been welcome and that the ARVN had wide popular support.[21]

Nguyen Ngoc Huy, then assistant to Prime Minister Tho, who had had to try to work with the above arrangements, did have an analysis and an overview. Huy, a long-time member of the Dai Viet party, had been in self-imposed exile during the Diem period but had returned from Paris after the November 1 coup. Many years later, and once again a refugee, in Boston, he described the problems that arose. "Generals Don, Dinh. . .were both in the Council [MRC] and in the Government. As members of the Council, they were superior to Tho, and as members of the Government, they were under Tho. So when Tho gave an order, they refused. They went into the Council and gave a counter order. This was chaos."[22] It seems, however, that Lodge did not discuss the structure of the provisional government with Minh. Lodge's failure to offer the Vietnamese generals his own considerable understanding of workable relationships between the executive and legislative powers could not have been a product of diplomatic tact alone. As we have seen, he believed that acceptance of U.S. aid implied acceptance of U.S. stipulations, and he later took a leading, and public, role in writing the 1966 constitution for South Vietnam. He knew the importance of the Vietnamese generals forming a workable government, and it was he who argued that they must be given time without undue demands for "performance" when he attended the post-coup meeting of the Vietnam team in Honolulu on November 20. His laissez-faire attitude seems therefore to have stemmed from disengagement from Vietnam and too few hours spent on U.S. embassy business at this period.[23]

Again, Lodge was distinctly unenthusiastic in his response to the MRC's proposal to establish a council through which representatives of the various leadership groups in South Vietnam could express their views or give advice to the provisional government. This body was to be advisory in function, its membership decided by recommendation of the new government. It was to be known as the Council of Notables, a reference to French political tradition, from which the French-speaking elites of South Vietnam drew their inspiration. Lodge was not interested in this point. He indiscriminately referred to the proposed council as the Council of Sages and Council of Wise Men. Indeed, he specifically noted in his first cable on the subject that his information had been drawn from the Saigon newspapers: there is no evidence that he discussed the proposed council with the MRC leadership at any time in November.[24]

Although the American ambassador thought that the Vietnamese were not ready for democracy, a forum through which representatives of the South Vietnamese populace could channel their views to the government was surely something to be encouraged. Even for the sake of American public opinion, U.S. patronage of such a body should have recommended itself. But within three months Lodge would advise the successor to the Minh regime that the Council of Notables could be disbanded, and he did not attempt to defend its possible role in South Vietnamese political life.

When the composition of the representative council was decided on December 28, Lodge merely remarked: "For better or for worse, MRC, Minh government, has created organism which, despite assigned function as 'advisory' body and lack of any electoral mandate, will probably attempt to act like a legislative body." He regarded it as a talking shop for "intellectuals and educated classes pending development of more solid political groupings." Yet this was surely a shortsighted view: at the very least, the Council of Notables could have served as a bridge to the MRC to maintain the goodwill of the South Vietnamese nonmilitary elites during a difficult transitional period. Among those nominated for membership of the Council of Notables were many who had declined positions in the government and therefore might be expected to cause dissension were they not drawn into the political process. Also serving on it were many of South Vietnam's most able minds.[25]

It was not the fault of the Council of Notables that it was disbanded before it could present suggestions for legislation; it did in fact devise many of the by-laws for the city of Saigon and made some trenchant suggestions concerning the black market and corrupt practices on the part of members of the government.[26] It must stand as one of the lost opportunities of the war that the American ambassador neglected to sponsor the only representative body that South Vietnam was ever to have. For although periodic elections were held under the 1966 constitution, in whose devising Lodge had a large hand during his second tour of duty in South Vietnam, the document was designed to keep the Ky-Thieu military government in power and did not permit "neutralists" or antiwar candidates to run.

It is difficult to assess whether the November coup was popular among the rural populations of South Vietnam, where stability and security may have been more important values than liberal reform, as Lodge himself wrote when describing his 1964 plans for civil defense in the countryside. In the city, however, and so confirming his fixed position on the unpopularity of Diem, the U.S. ambassador received a rousing welcome during a November 5 visit to the Xa Loi pagoda. Mrs. Lodge described her impressions in a letter to a friend. "The atmosphere here is extraordinary. I had not realized how feared and hated the government was. All the pagodas are open again with their priests out of jail. The people in them are delirious with joy—terribly moving—crowds mill around them in there—all their flags are hung out." She went on: "We have just had a marvelous experience—as Cabot was early for lunch we walked two blocks to the Xa Loi Pagoda—Cabot was recognized—great smiles—bows—some cries of Vive Capa Lodge and out came a bonze who hurried us into the pagoda with the crowd following—they were so excited seeing Cabot they nearly squashed us. It was incredibly moving."[27]

When Duong Van Minh came to power, there can be little doubt that many had high expectations of the new regime and that the urban population strongly desired political reforms. In schools and universities, students demonstrated for the removal of the Diem government's surveillance structures. On November 8 crowds greeted the return of opponents of Diem who had been imprisoned on Poulo Condore, the former French prison island. Political activist Dr. Phan Quan Dan was covered in garlands and carried on the shoulders of students to the Vietnamese Joint General Staff headquarters. Two days later, the Confucian scholar and long time Vietnamese nationalist Phan Khac Suu, who was to be head of state for a short time in 1964, was welcomed by a large crowd at the city hall after his release from another prison.[28]

Whether through enthusiasm for the new government, or in an age-old maneuver to ensure survival, leaders of the major groupings in South Vietnam quickly presented pledges of loyalty to the Minh regime. Representatives of the Chinese community met with General Minh on November 15 to express support of the MRC and the provisional government. The Cao Dai military chief, Gen. Le Van Tat, returned from self-imposed exile in Cambodia, where he had retreated with the Caodaist pope in 1955. Presenting himself to Minh, he volunteered to put himself at the disposal of the MRC and negotiate for the return to South Vietnam of the several hundred soldiers of his religion who had followed him across the border eight years before. A delegation from the Hoa Hao sect of the Western provinces made their representations on November 20 and promised more effective support for the war against communism.[29] This cautious goodwill, however, quickly dissipated: factional and sectarian fighting was renewed and erupted in unprecedented violence within months.

In spite of the mood of expectation and tentative goodwill in Saigon in November 1963, Lodge did little to promote the participation of civilians in Minh's government or to advise upon the desirability of their inclusion or even nominal representation. He was strangely inattentive to the political ferment among the urban South Vietnamese, while at the same time urging Washington that no demands could be made of the new regime until it could consolidate its leadership and administration.

American recognition of the Minh government had depended on the MRC making professions that it would move quickly to adopt a constitution and include civilians in its councils. Indeed, the MRC generals' early intentions to include nonmilitary men in their cabinet had strongly recommended them to the U.S. administration.[30] However, for Lodge in Saigon, civilian representation and civil rights issues were not important considerations in their own right. When Lodge expressed pleasure that after the long period of press control under the Diem regime, many new newspapers were starting up and had applied for licenses, he was apparently thinking of the popularity of the issue of freedom of the press with the American public, and not of the opportunities the new journals offered for political debate or for a diversity of viewpoints in the formation of new legislation. For example, he made representations to the new government over the arrests of labor leader Tran Quoc Buu and of Assemblyman Nguyen Phuong Thiep during the coup because Washington was concerned over the welfare of these two men: they were both well known in U.S. congressional circles and questions might therefore arise in the House about their fate.[31] After Tran Quoc Buu's release from custody on November 5, Lodge—who had earlier recommended him for a position in a post-coup government—commissioned him to prepare a paper on reform of labor conditions in South Vietnam. He appears, however, to have subsequently lost interest in the project, for although Buu's report was highly praised by the U.S. embassy labor attaché, Lodge did not send it on to Washington.[32]

Within days of the Minh government taking power, many civilian politicians had found reasons to distance themselves from it. Buu threatened to file charges for illegal arrest and declined to serve in the Minh government but kept his options open by offering to act as an advisor. Bui Diem, a long-time member of the Dai Viet party and Saigon newspaper proprietor, who was invited to accept a position by Gen. Le Van Kim on the evening of November 1, took umbrage over the appointment of Nguyen Ngoc Tho as prime minister because Tho had been so closely associated with Diem. Dr. Phan Huy Quat, Bui Diem's patron and later head of state of South Vietnam, who had held office under Bao Dai, declined a post in the interim government when offered the Ministry of Health, saying, "It was the physician, not the politician who was approached." Quat resolved to form a new Nationalist party.[33]

Although initially declining appointments to the MRC's cabinet, these men kept their stakes in the political arena. They all accepted positions on the Council of Notables, where they were joined by the powerful Buddhist layman Mai Tho Truyen. Arguably, the patronage of the American ambassador might have encouraged the development of solutions to the organizational problems that confronted this body at its outset.

The quiescence of the activist Buddhists at this period is another mystery that failed to interest Lodge. In fact, for the final two months of 1963 the members of the General Buddhist Association were occupied with a reorganization of their institutional structures. Minh would attend the opening ceremonies of the Unified Buddhist Church on January 1 of the new year, but he did not otherwise consult with the Buddhists, apparently regarding them as an unreliable and potentially revolutionary force. Thich Tri Quang, having left the shelter of the chancery building on November 5, sought a conversation with an embassy official four days later. He confided that he would advise Buddhists to remain aloof from direct involvement in politics but to cooperate with the new government. Tri Quang also made clear his reservations regarding the appointment of Tho as prime minister.[34]

Here indeed was potential for political strife. Yet Lodge did not comment on the defections of the civilians from the Minh government either in his official cables or in his memoirs. Nor did he seek to encourage Minh to recruit Buddhist laymen to his inner circle or to court the Buddhist clergy, although he himself would later see "nation building" potential in these men and their organizations.

As for the "revolutionary" intentions of the MRC, it seems clear that whatever other attributes Generals Minh and Don may have had, they had few new ideas on fighting the war or social reform. Lodge was slow to grasp this and continued for several weeks to report enthusiastically on their progress and prospects. In an extended interview with Rufus Phillips on November 18, Minh emphasized the value of small-unit operations and civil defense. He said he supported the Strategic Hamlets program but blamed its previous failures on Ngo Dinh Nhu, who had "exploited it for personal gain," extending it too fast. He suggested an alternative approach of arming the members of the Cao Dai and Hoa Hao to defend the areas in which they were strongly represented. There was nothing new in this, however, since it was the old French strategy. And that experience had demonstrated, over many years, that alliances with the Vietnamese sects were chronically unstable.[35]

In regard to social and economic reforms, Tran Van Don told me in 1989 that Gen. Le Van Kim was in charge of working out a new program for the conduct of the war and social reform but had not completed his task by the time of the coup in January 1964 that overthrew the Minh government. Don recorded in his memoirs that "toward the end of January, after a series of contacts with many political, religious and military leaders, I had been able to plan out the main orientation of our *revolutionary program* [emphasis added]." In fact, in November and December they had no program, although Lodge thought they did. When Don told him at a social function that he wished to eliminate forced labor in the strategic hamlets and to control the "Chinese racketeers and extortionists" whose power had recently increased because Diem "had fallen under their influence," Lodge reported this to Washington. He apparently did not notice the appeal to an old Southeast Asian scapegoat on the one hand and to his own prejudice on the other, noting to Rusk: "Altogether a sound program convincingly started."[36]

It seems that the MRC generals may have been grasping at straws in their answers to the questions of U.S. embassy officials regarding their policies. Journalists noticed the "wait and see" nature of the deals which various groups of Cao Dai and Hoa Hao struck with Minh in this period, and it was well known that Duong Van Minh and Nguyen Ngoc Tho had trapped and executed the Hoa Hao leader Ba Cut in 1956, as the culmination of a long campaign they had led for Diem against the sects. Indeed, Don seemed surprised in my discussions with him to hear that Minh had told Phillips he was planning to use alliances with the sects. Although these groups may have supported the MRC in the final months of 1963, Don said, the Cao Dai in the delta and Hue and the Hoa Hao in the western provinces were not unified for military action, and the support of the sects could not be relied on in the long term.[37]

The MRC's lack of a coherent program was particularly evident in military matters. Minh would quickly fall afoul of U.S. policy planners in his protestations that the war should not be expanded and that American advisors should not penetrate Vietnamese society below the province level. As for Lodge, even regarding the civil defense program, a topic in which he was ostensibly interested, the U.S. ambassador did not notice in the first five weeks of the new government that the MRC generals' ideas were, in the words of Earl Young, USOM advisor in the critical Long An province, essentially "the same re-heated French tactics of 1954 beefed up with more helicopters and tanks."[38]

Observers at the time agree that Lodge's main advice to Minh was on how to improve his relations with the Vietnamese public by using techniques that Lodge had learned during his own electioneering in New England. He advised Minh to take his hat off, so people could see his face. In fact, so important was the question of Minh's "image" to Lodge that he sent a cutting from a South Vietnamese newspaper to Averell Harriman when Minh finally removed his cap, with the notation, "You would be impressed with Gen. Minh's progress towards becoming a *true popular figure* ... yesterday he took his hat off for the first time and was almost overwhelmed!"[39] Lodge's political instincts usually served him well. On other occasions, he could gauge what would impress the Vietnamese, although in reality he knew little of their culture. But his advice to Minh regarding public relations, which echoes CIA operative Edward Lansdale's earlier efforts with Diem, was almost a caricature of an easily caricatured American approach.

On November 17, Lodge instructed State from Saigon, "Tell press I see President Monday." But as he stopped over in San Francisco on November 22, he heard the news that Kennedy had been assassinated in Dallas.[40]

The political forces operating in Washington suddenly changed. Lodge always regarded the presidency as naturally open to him, or at least in his gift; he now shifted his focus from 1968 or 1972 to 1964. Not that he contemplated his goal with the ruthless ambition of a Lyndon Baines Johnson. He did not and never had. The tone was set, rather, by a leak that appeared in Roscoe Drummond's column in the *Washington Post* on November 9 to the effect that friends had sought Lodge's permission to organize a write-in campaign for his candidacy in the March 1964 New Hampshire primaries.

Perhaps Lodge, after a dignified pause for the obsequies, might have found himself more keenly engaged by the possibility of playing his old role of kingmaker at the now critical GOP convention in July. But events moved quickly. His own appeal as the Republican who could gain most votes in the northern states suddenly increased, for Johnson, now president, would undoubtedly carry the South for the Democrats. The GOP needed to field a liberal internationalist in the North in order to balance Johnson's strength on the issues of war, peace, and civil rights: the *New York Times* went so far as to speculate on December 8 that Barry Goldwater, formerly tipped as the most likely contender against Kennedy, might decline to run against Johnson, as Goldwater's own support, strongest in the southern states, might not match that of the new president there.

The point had not been lost on General Eisenhower at his office in Gettysburg. He telephoned Lodge during his sojourn in the United States, the purpose of which was now consultations with Johnson rather than a "wrap-up" with Kennedy, and urged him to seek the Republican nomination. First Eisenhower had to ascertain from Lodge himself that he had had nothing to do with the assassinations of Diem and Nhu, or "the King and his brother," as he termed them. Lodge duly delivered his account of the offer of asylum in the embassy. Eisenhower then urged him to return from Vietnam and run for the presidency.[41]

Both men, of course, were forced to deny any correspondence regarding an Eisenhower imprimatur for a Lodge candidacy during the mourning period for Kennedy. Moreover, Lodge was still a diplomat on government service. The story hit the front page of the *New York Times* via an Eisenhower leak on December 8: if Lodge was aware that Eisenhower had made the same seeming promise of support to Gov. William Scranton of Pennsylvania a week later, he left no evidence in his writings or memoirs. He maintained his silence, revealing only that in October he had rejected the offer of a write-in campaign.

Within days of the ambassador's return to Saigon, however, his wife noted in a letter to a friend that "people telephone Cabot from home about running for P. constantly."[42]

What, then, was Lodge doing as the American ambassador in Saigon at this period? When Lodge attended the post-coup meeting of the Vietnam team in Honolulu on November 20, he reported that the immediate prospects for South Vietnam under the leadership of the Minh government were good. What was needed was more U.S. aid, he argued. He continued in a simplistic vein that the aim of America's policies must be to convince the average Viet Cong that "he will surely be killed if the war goes on" and that "if he stops being a Viet Cong a good life beckons for him." This last statement he recorded in "Vietnam Memoir" as the gist of his report to the Vietnam team in Hawaii after the overthrow of Diem.[43]

This optimism was very different from the prognosis in the Earl Young report regarding conditions in Long An, dated December 7, which arrived in Washington two weeks later. Indeed, the Long An report so disturbed President Johnson that he recorded part of its first paragraph in his memoirs. The Earl Young cable began: "The only progress made in Long An Province during month of November 1963 has been by the Communist Viet Cong. The past thirty days have produced a day-by-day elimination of U.S.-Vietnamese sponsored strategic hamlets and the marked increase of Viet Cong influence."[44]

The ambassador's response to the USOM report, which he himself had transmitted with the comment that Long An was the province closest to Saigon and so its loss could cut off the city's food supply, was to accept assurances from General Don that immediate action would be taken. He then sent his personal assistant, Colonel Dunn, to Long An for "follow through." Having put Dunn in charge of this problem, he seldom returned to it.[45]

Dunn quickly located a Vietnamese report on the Strategic Hamlets program in Long An that had been submitted to Diem in September. In it, a high-ranking local official argued that the Vietnamese government controlled only 10 percent of the two hundred strategic hamlets in the area, while the Communists controlled the other 90 percent. Dunn noted that "attached is of the greatest value to us here since it proves beyond a doubt that the terrible security situation now existing in Long An does *not* have its origin in the coup—and that the previous government had information at its disposal which indicated this but which apparently it did not see fit to communicate to us." As late as March 1964, Lodge was still blaming Diem for poor security in the provinces.[46] His habit of dismissing all reports of inefficiency under the MRC administration as indicative of the continuing effects of corruption under Diem would have far-reaching consequences.

The cause of the discrepancies in Lodge's opinion of the MRC leadership and the assessment of USOM, in this case, stemmed from an aspect of his ambassadorial style that had been at work since his arrival in August. Lodge had quickly lost personal and collegial contact with the heads of the agencies, especially Harkins as leader of MACV, the chief of the CIA station in Saigon, and, to a lesser extent, the top officials at USIS. This meant that in what was to be a critical period of U.S.-Vietnam relations, he had less free and informal access to the information available to these men than he needed.

When, on October 5, John Richardson was recalled from Saigon to Washington, speculation was rife as to Lodge's role in his removal. Had his effectiveness been compromised when the *Times of Vietnam* had revealed his identity? This was the theory most popular in the international diplomatic community. Had

Lodge had him recalled because he had been used to too much autonomy, complete with secret lines of communication, in his relationship with Nhu? So thought the CIA. Was there a general directive from Washington to limit the independence of the agency in the wake of the Bay of Pigs fiasco? U.S. investigative journalists had worked for this and now publicized the evidence, along with the claim that the Saigon station had been less than obedient to the ambassador in recent events. It seems that all of these factors had played a part in Richardson's withdrawal from South Vietnam. But Peer de Silva, Richardson's replacement, had no doubt that Lodge had had the last word in the matter.[47]

Lodge had shown himself as committed to limiting the power of the CIA station since his arrival in Saigon, if not before. On September 13, in the middle of his struggle with Diem, he had requested that "Edward Lansdale be sent out to be a sort of 'Lawrence of Arabia' " to take charge *under my supervision* [emphasis added] of all U.S. relationships with the change of government here." He also recorded in "Vietnam Memoir" that "I asked that Lansdale be put in charge of the CAS station in the Embassy so that I would have a staff. This was turned down."[48]

Although there is no indication that Lodge knew why Lansdale was not sent to Vietnam in 1963, his request was turned down on the practical grounds that Lansdale was at that time in charge of "Operation Mongoose," the CIA program in Cuba to overthrow Castro, and Kennedy wanted him to continue to pursue that goal. In the area of political judgment, according to Paul Kattenburg, Harriman and Hilsman at State were against Lansdale's return to South Vietnam, although Lodge expressed admiration for his public relations work with Magsaysay in the Philippines and his former close relationship with Diem. As for General Taylor, the head of the Joint Chiefs "flatly refused to have Lansdale" in Indochina.[49]

Richardson felt that Lodge had no quarrel with his own expertise, and Lodge had at no time expressed dissatisfaction with the flow of information from the Saigon station. Lodge's personal notes on his intentions to circumscribe the activities of Richardson's replacement are therefore revealing. On October 1 he wrote: "CAS Station should be out of Chancery building. . . . Head of Station *not* to be Special Assistant to the Ambassador . . . should end the backgrounding of press by CAS people of high and low degree. CAS *should not* continue efforts to build up a Vietnamese counterpart."[50] Lodge would accordingly be in charge and the CIA agents would, as far as possible, be under his control. There would be no relationship of first among equals between the ambassador and the heads of the agencies.

There was no CIA station chief in Saigon from October until late December 1963. When Peer de Silva was dispatched from Hong Kong to fill the position at the urging of William Colby, Lodge told him at their first meeting that he did not need or want a new CIA station chief, being quite happy with the services of a more junior officer, David Smith. The next day, the Ambassador told de Silva to remove the plaque on his office door bearing the title "Special Assistant to the Ambassador."[51]

Lodge's relationship with the directors of the USIS in South Vietnam, while less acrimonious than those with the chief of the CIA and the military commander, had the same general tendency. John Mecklin, head of USIS in Saigon when Lodge arrived there, believed that he himself had been recalled to Washington in December 1963 because he had taken too much responsibility in briefing the press, particularly the American newspapermen, a job that Lodge considered his own preserve. Mecklin's reading seemed to be borne out by the ambassador's response to the appointment of Barry Zorthian to the USIS position, when Lodge cabled Washington that Zorthian would have no contact with the press, "as I do this work myself." Zorthian's rank in Saigon was minister-counselor for public information, but, a man of extraordinary presence and personal power himself, he was well aware that Lodge wanted only the services of a press officer.[52]

In his confrontation with General Harkins to establish the primacy of the ambassador in the mission, Lodge had stopped showing cables from State to the U.S. commander as early as August 1963 and had continued in this policy in spite of protest from Washington. Harkins, for his part, was aware and annoyed that Lodge had kept pertinent details from him, as the head of MACV, regarding the development of the November coup. He was not speaking to Lodge. Harkins, of course, had been close to Diem, whom he even claimed had regularly spoken to him in English. He had reported to Admiral Felt in September that he had never seen General Minh contribute anything to the war effort, and that although this was in part because of Diem's suspicions of him, Minh was an unknown quantity militarily and far too given to political intrigue.[53]

In analyzing the effects of the reshuffle in commands and government positions that understandably followed the November coup, Harkins was more prescient than Lodge, although he communicated his thoughts to the chairman of the Joint Chiefs of Staff in Washington rather than to the ambassador in Saigon. On the day after the coup, Harkins confided to Taylor his concern that the MRC would make wholesale dismissals of chiefs of provinces who had served under Diem, when U.S. advisors regarded most of these men as able and efficient. But for a month and a half personnel changes continued. For example, thirty-one heads of government departments, chiefs of province and district military commanders were given "leave without pay for an indefinite period" on November 22. These men were all ARVN officers, a legacy of Diem's militarization of the state at all levels. Indeed, shifting positions in the ARVN consumed a great deal of the provisional government's energy. There was much jockeying for the command of the 3 Corps zone around Saigon, which was the richest territory for the farming of licenses and levies, and also the key to control of the city.[54]

Although as a military man Harkins kept his generalizations optimistic, and it is doubtful that he knew the political motives behind the disputes between the Vietnamese generals, the details of Harkins's reports to the Joint Chiefs of Staff reveal his growing concern over divisions among the Vietnamese commanders, and particularly with the volatility of Gen. Ton That Dinh, whom no one seemed able to control. In spite of Harkins's advice, Dinh refused to relinquish his command of 3 Corps, although he was also minister for the interior. If Lodge was aware of Harkins's concern over the performance of the MRC generals, and it seems that he was not, the knowledge did not change his own assessment that they were making good progress. Even when he heard reports that the South Vietnamese generals were divided and plotting against each other, he did not investigate, in spite of an earlier CIA cable giving details, transmitted under his name to Washington. Instead, he accepted Don's assurance that the rumor of dissension had arisen when low-ranking soldiers, overhearing the proceedings of the MRC meetings, had mistaken healthy debate, rare in Vietnam, for factional infighting![55]

Undoubtedly, the new provisional government needed time to consolidate itself, and some loss of efficiency might be expected in the transitional period when necessary changes in the ARVN commands were made. Political Counselor Melvin Manfull and John Burke of the embassy's Political Section both attempted to impress this point upon Lodge, warning that the strategically crucial province of Long An might be lost in a campaign for too fast results. But U.S. political realities, as Kennedy had pointed out in his reply to Lodge's "wrap-up" cable, did demand fast results. The president had not needed to remind his ambassador that the leaders of public opinion on Vietnam were American journalists, whose careers depended on producing dramatic stories and, in this case, accounts of measurable progress in the war.[56]

The "honeymoon period" between the MRC and the American press, which had gone on for five weeks, suddenly ended. On December 3, the *Washington*

Post published a syndicated article in which Sanche de Gramont, reporting from Saigon, gave details of renewed political arrests, alleging that the MRC was settling back into the "pattern of arbitrary justice, surveillance and secret police methods that besmirched the regime the generals overthrew." These charges immediately registered in the House, where Speaker John McCormack reopened questions on the safety of Ngo Dinh Can, which Rusk was forced to refer to Lodge. The *Post* reported new Buddhist suicides by fire, and now government persecutions of Catholics. The *Times* weighed in with daily reports of Viet Cong gains and government losses. By December 14 the paper was claiming that U.S. officials believed the new regime had "failed to live up to the expectations it had aroused and had failed to provide leadership in the prosecution of the war."[57]

The first hints that major U.S. intervention into South Vietnamese affairs was being considered in sections of the State Department arose within days of the adverse press reports. On December 10, Col. F. P. Serong, commander of Australian forces in Vietnam, called upon Lodge and argued that "in its five weeks of existence, GVN has shown itself incapable. Meanwhile the war and the nation is disintegrating—*You* must take control of the GVN. Force it to accept policy and executive direction at all levels." He urged Lodge to "tell Minh that the government of Vietnam should accept an American commander for their Army as no-one in Vietnam is up to it."

Lodge transmitted the text of Serong's memorandum to him verbatim. On receiving his copy of this cable, Forrestal marked it for McGeorge Bundy's attention with the following pregnant words: "Mac: The diagnosis is alarmist and the cure too drastic; but the direction is right." By the end of 1963 the idea that greater American control in South Vietnam was the only course open to improving the conduct of the war seems to have been gaining acceptance at the highest level of the presidential advisory staff.[58]

It may be that there was no avoiding a U.S. commitment of troops to Vietnam, so strong, as we shall see, were the forces at the Pentagon who wanted and needed a war. Where Lodge missed his opportunity for diplomacy in December 1963 and January 1964 was in spreading responsibility for the outcome in South Vietnam more widely across the international community. This he failed to do through a combination of patriotism, prejudice, and a less than flexible imaginative response.

President de Gaulle of France offered to help in finding a settlement to the conflict between the two governments of Vietnam shortly after the pagoda raids in August 1963. In fact, what he said was rather vague: "France's knowledge of the valor of the Vietnamese people permits her to discern the role they could play in Asia's present situation, for their own progress and to the benefit of international understanding; as soon as they could deploy their activity in independence vis-à-vis the outside, in peace and unity at home, and in concord with their neighbors." The French foreign minister, Couve de Murville, alerted Rusk to a forthcoming statement, adding pointedly that to him the situation in Vietnam seemed insoluble, and that removing Diem would achieve nothing, as there was no one to succeed him.[59]

This first French offer came when Lodge was least prepared to listen to advice regarding Diem, and at the height of his confidence in his tactic of "silence and correctness" in bending Diem's will to U.S. demands. Lodge's view in general terms that Vietnam was solely a U.S. responsibility was in accord with that of most of America's contemporary internationalists, and was spelled out specifically by Kennedy in his September 2 reply to de Gaulle's remarks on CBS television news.[60]

Moreover, Lodge had a longstanding personal antipathy to de Gaulle. He had seen him as something of an unreliable renegade during the last year of World War II, when Lodge had served as liaison officer with General de Lattre of the First French Army during the liberation of Western Europe. Lodge therefore chose to interpret de Gaulle's August statement as a direct criticism of America's presence in South Vietnam, and the French president's reference to Vietnam's "neighbors" as an indication of France's desire to interfere in U.S.-Cambodian relations.[61]

General de Gaulle repeated his offer to help resolve the differences between the two Vietnams on January 18, 1964, when the situation in South Vietnam was far more unstable than before and the time should have been ripe for considering the wisdom of a deepening unilateral U.S. involvement there. De Gaulle now suggested that the Geneva Accords of 1954 might still provide a basis for a solution.[62]

But de Gaulle's January announcement was tied to his impending recognition of China. For Lodge, as for other members of the Cold War generation of American leaders, recognition of China, and most especially its admission to the United Nations, were anathema. Lodge wanted to preserve the existing balances of power: France back in Asia meant France treating with Communist China, and change in the existing balance. Lodge had fought long and hard to exclude mainland China from the United Nations. Even as Nixon's running mate in the presidential election of 1960, he had taken the position that rather than campaign in the usual sense, he would do more good for America and the Republican cause by remaining at his post in the U.N. and "defeating the Communist candidate for President of the General Assembly, and so keeping out the Red Chinese."[63]

Moreover, Lodge viewed France as an unreconstructed colonialist power, and he had reason to distrust the French plantation owners in South Vietnam, some of whom he knew were willing to pay protection money to the Viet Cong as well as the Saigon government.[64] Lodge not only refused to consider the French offer: he began to attribute blame to de Gaulle for all the plots in South Vietnamese politics. This feature of his thinking was to become a liability in early 1964. Any constructive ideas de Gaulle had to offer he left unexplored.

Undoubtedly, de Gaulle had his own agenda in making his proposals. He wanted France to regain her status as a world power, and France retained a strong interest in Vietnam. In 1963, for example, there remained seventeen hundred French citizens in South Vietnam, the French controlled the rubber industry which accounted for 89.6 percent of South Vietnam's exports, and French teaching staff in the secondary schools served about thirty thousand students. Yet de Gaulle also was genuinely concerned with the fate of the postcolonial peoples.[65] And French advice regarding America's attempts at coup making had proved demonstrably sound at least by mid-January 1964. It is an indictment of American policy planners' lack of flexibility that de Gaulle's offer of a way to spread responsibility for the fate of South Vietnam was never seriously considered in Washington.[66] Lodge as the U.S. ambassador in the field must bear a large part of the blame for this oversight.

Chapter Five

Two Coups: Saigon and New Hampshire

President Johnson was on the telephone to William Fulbright, chairman of the Senate Foreign Relations Committee. It was December 2 and Johnson had been in the White House for ten days. He proceeded from Cuba— "I'm not getting into any Bay of Pigs deal"—to Vietnam. "Now what about Vietnam?" he asked. "Why did you send Lodge out there for God's sake? I think he's got things screwed up good, that's what I think. . . . What would happen if I moved Lodge? Who does he satisfy?" Fulbright replied that he thought that Lodge satisfied some elements in the Republican party, and a few moments later Johnson rang off.

Eight days later Johnson phoned Dean Rusk: "What about the story in the morning paper that these generals out there are fussing among themselves, and they can't have a government by committee in Viet Nam?" Rusk replied: "Well, there's some truth to that, unfortunately, and we've sent Lodge some rockets to get on with that job, because that's his big job. His big job is getting these generals working together."

Johnson was impatient "He's got to decide—either he's got to interview the press about Eisenhower's suggestion—which Ike said he didn't make. He's too busy on that, I imagine, to take care of Viet Nam very much. . . . We're fighting a war out there now and we don't want to get into one here at home." With that, he thanked Rusk and said goodbye.[1]

Lodge would have been shocked to learn that the president thought he had been slacking on Vietnam. After all, as we have seen, he did not share Dean Rusk's view of Lodge's main duty in Saigon at this time. As for Johnson's suspicions, a letter from Peter Kalischer of CBS News regarding a December conversation sheds light on an interest, perhaps only a dabble, that he shared with his intimates. Kalischer wrote to him from Tokyo in April 1964:

> Speaking of insight for which you give me credit, please recall an off the record conversation we held in the Caravelle last year after you recorded a statement regarding General Eisenhower's apocryphal letter. You said, if I remember correctly, that there was no chance of getting the Republican nomination unless a candidate wanted it and fought for it at home and you weren't going to. And I said, if you remember, that there was one way the lightning might strike: if, at convention time, Barry Goldwater was considered too far out in right field, Rockefeller's wife was an albatross around his neck, Scranton and Romney were too little known and Dick Nixon still had "loser" written on his forehead, then the image of an ambassador out there in the rice paddies fighting Communists would be well-nigh irresistible.[2]

If Johnson had his doubts about Lodge, American reporters in Saigon did not. On November 13, Halberstam had written an article for the *New York Times* alleging that Harkins might well be withdrawn from South Vietnam because of his poor relations with the Minh regime. In highlighting dissensions in the U.S. mission, Halberstam, of course, had focused his criticisms on Harkins and spared Lodge. When Forrestal protested on behalf of the White House that Halberstam had been motivated by a personal grudge against Harkins, he found an alarming drift in the thinking of the members of the *Times* editorial board: the more publicity the paper gave to the problems of the organization of the U.S. war effort, the more convinced its editors became that the only solution lay in reconvening the Geneva Conference on Vietnam.[3] Moreover, this is what Sen. Mike Mansfield had been suggesting to Kennedy and now to Johnson for months, and what Fulbright had recommended in the last minutes of his December 2 phone conversation with the president. It is what most officials at the Department of State wished to avoid, and what the Pentagon and U.S. military advisors in South Vietnam wanted least of all.

In the wake of the assassination of the president of South Vietnam and that of Kennedy in the United States three weeks later, the last months of 1963 and the first half of 1964 were to prove a time of political intrigue in both countries.

As Lodge journeyed to Washington after the November 20 meeting of the Vietnam team in Honolulu, he had no idea that his own performance as the American ambassador to Vietnam was under scrutiny. But two days after the Pearl

Harbor conference, at the daily White House staff meeting, McGeorge Bundy summed up his impressions of the operations of the U.S. team in Vietnam: "Lodge is clearly the dominant personality, but it is not at all evident that he can handle the job he is now faced with. He is a strong-willed close operator who keeps only his personal staff involved. This was just the type needed during his first months in Saigon when he was supposed to create a posture which would indicate to any would-be revolutionist that the U.S. would not automatically side with Diem. Now, however, what is needed is a good manager, who can develop a team to do a very complex job."[4] This first indication of some real soul-searching on the implications of the coup against Diem stopped short of the needed major policy review.

Before Lodge reached the U.S. capital, Johnson had been sworn in as president of the United States. More interested in domestic reforms than in foreign affairs, the former vice president nevertheless had some firm views on America's role in Asia. After an official tour of Southeast Asia and the Indian subcontinent in May 1961, he had reported that Asian leaders, due to their recent colonial experiences, did not want American troops involved in the area other than for the purposes of training local forces. He concluded, "American combat troop involvement is not only not required, it is not desirable."[5]

Lodge himself had recently come to the conclusion that what was needed in Vietnam was not ground troops but a very limited number of highly trained civil and political advisors assigned to the central government and the provincial administrations. Further, he had briefly considered the possibility that since the U.S. mission did not, apparently, speak with one voice, its efficiency might be increased by having fewer, not more, American officials in South Vietnam. He had therefore given the embassy administration officer instructions aimed at the rationalizing of staff numbers.[6] Since both Johnson and the ambassador in Saigon distrusted the notion of increased U.S. intervention in Vietnam at the beginning of the new administration, it was to be doubly tragic that with the objective of ending the war Johnson felt compelled to expand it first.

Although Lodge and Johnson had known each other in public life over many years, they were not close. Indeed, as McGeorge Bundy remarked to Harriman after Johnson's first meeting with Lodge, "The President never thought much of him."[7] Johnson was not part of the Eastern establishment or the internationalist foreign policy grouping to which Lodge and Kennedy belonged. On the contrary, Johnson believed that great presidents made their mark in domestic affairs. He had been appalled at the public divisions in Kennedy's administration caused by the coup question, but he would pledge to honor Kennedy's foreign policy commitments. The arrival of the U.S. ambassador from Saigon for discussions obliged Johnson to consider Vietnam sooner than he might have wished. At dinner one night shortly after Lodge's arrival in Washington, he confided to his press secretary, Bill Moyers, "I have this terrible feeling of something that's grabbed me around the ankles and won't let go."[8]

The ambassador and the new president met on November 24. Present also at the meeting were Rusk, McNamara, Ball, and McGeorge Bundy. Lodge opened by saying that with a new government in South Vietnam, he expected a speed-up of the war and marked progress by February or March. "The tone of Ambassador Lodge's statements was optimistic, hopeful, and left the President with the impression that we are on the road to victory," recorded John McCone, director of Central Intelligence, in his notes of the meeting. Johnson responded that he approached the Vietnam situation with misgivings: a great many people throughout America questioned the wisdom of the U.S. role in the overthrow of Diem, while strong voices in the Congress urged disengagement from Vietnam, he said. McCone interpolated into his notes at this point his inference that had Johnson been in power, he would not have supported the coup. McCone then stated that CIA estimates of the situation in Vietnam were much less optimistic than those of the ambassador; Viet Cong activity had stepped up and the MRC generals were having trouble organizing their government. They were receiving no help from competent civilians, who continued to pursue their "traditional role" as critics, McCone added. Perhaps trying to bring the meeting to a close, Johnson said it was a mistake to try to reform every Asian in America's image. He "was anxious to get along, win the war," he said, but he "didn't want as much effort placed on so-called social reforms."[9]

Three days after this meeting, Johnson telephoned his old friend Don Cook, head of the American Electric Power Service Corporation. He needed good men, he said. Specifically, he had no one to run the war in Vietnam: "Lodge is just as much an administrator as he is a utility maintenance man . . . he never had to do it and he doesn't know one damn thing about it . . . just leaks to the press and keeps everybody fighting each other . . . we need a damn tough cookie, with enough judgment to realize that he can't turn Vietnam into an America overnight."

The obvious solution would have been to recall Lodge to Washington. That Johnson did not do so, when clearly many of his advisors thought he should, was due to his own political agenda.[10] Kennedy had needed a Republican ambassador in Saigon to maximize American public support for a war he wished to continue. Johnson quickly realized that he needed to humor Lodge to stay on in Vietnam as a symbol of a bipartisan anti-Communist stance on a far-off struggle upon which he had no desire to disperse his energies.

Johnson was aware of Lodge's presidential ambitions, just as he was aware of Eisenhower's November overture to him. He kept a special file on Lodge's activities. He kept files on everyone and had scoured the newspapers for information since the beginning of his political career. Moreover, on December 9, McGeorge Bundy informed him: "Mike Forrestal is just back from Saigon and reports that Cabot has indeed begun to think in terms of political possibilities. Mike's guess is that Lodge would very much like to be honorably free of his responsibilities in Saigon and is hoping to be able to report to you in about two months that the situation is so much better that he can now fairly ask for relief."[11]

It was not that Johnson feared competition for the presidency from Lodge, whom he considered a dilettante, nor was he afraid at this stage that Vietnam would become a campaign issue in 1964. Rather, he was aware that if Lodge resigned from his ambassadorial post, let alone was withdrawn, and publicly criticized the conduct of the war, the ensuing debate would detract from his domestic agenda.[12] To have Vietnam consume precious time in the early months of his administration would be disastrous: his pressing concern was to have passed a backlog of bills on civil rights and other social and economic issues that Kennedy had been unable to push through Congress. Vietnam would have to wait until he had gained a popular electoral mandate in his own right.

Later, suspicious that Lodge might make political capital by charging that the president had ignored his policy suggestions and recalling MacArthur's bid for the Republican nomination from the front in Korea in the spring of 1951, Johnson instructed first Michael Forrestal and then William Bundy, who did not know that Forrestal had had the brief before him, to keep a close watch on Lodge's requests from Saigon. He wished to make sure that each was met promptly.[13] Johnson did not want to be the first American president to lose a war; nor would he give Lodge the chance to accuse him of neglecting the struggle against communism.

Toward the end of his life, Kennedy appears to have had similar forebodings regarding Lodge. On receiving the news of Diem's death, General Taylor observed that "Kennedy leaped to his feet and rushed from the room with a look of shock and dismay on his face which I had never seen before." Richard Helms, then deputy director of the CIA, who also witnessed the scene, saw matters with a colder eye. He concluded that in authorizing Lodge to use his judgment in Saigon, Kennedy had not been able or willing to think through the probable consequences. After Diem's overthrow, the president asked Robert Kennedy to help him find a way to remove Lodge from responsibilities in Saigon. He also sent William Colby to South Vietnam in November to make a post-coup report, apparently no longer trusting his ambassador there.[14] The evidence of Lodge's memoirs, and the testimony of his aide, Frederick Flott, is that Lodge had no inkling of either Kennedy's or Johnson's doubts about him.

In Massachusetts, the American ambassador to South Vietnam's elder son, George Lodge, was quietly sponsoring the endeavors of a group of young Bostonians to "draft Lodge" into the presidency. On the afternoon of December 23, to coincide with the expiry of the thirty-day moratorium on electioneering that had been observed after the Kennedy assassination, Lodge supporters distributed thirty-three thousand postcard ballots on commuter trains bound from New York to New Haven. The majority of the 12 percent of the cards returned predictably put Lodge's name first. These cards were sent to Lodge in Saigon.[15]

The "Draft Lodge" team comprised four elegant amateurs: Paul Grindle, at forty-three, was a successful New England businessman with experience in journalism and public relations; David Goldberg, a Boston lawyer, thirty-four, had acted as campaign manager for George Lodge in his unsuccessful run for the Senate against Edward Kennedy in 1962; a very young Sally Saltonstall, daughter of the Massachusetts senator, had left the Peace Corps to join the group; Caroline Williams, a former Boston schoolmate of Saltonstall's, had campaigned for the younger Lodge in 1962. In late December this group opened a storefront headquarters in Boston. In fact, the Massachusetts secretary of state refused to register the organization because their endeavors lacked the official authorization of their candidate. They were undaunted. After all, the point had been to gain national publicity for the name of Lodge as a possible GOP candidate and to float the suggestion that the ambassador in the field had a stronger record in foreign affairs than had Johnson.[16]

For their movement to continue and gain momentum, it was necessary to have the ambassador give a sign that although he could not endorse a "write-in" campaign to place his name on the ballot for the first primary, he would accede to a movement of the national will. It seems probable that George Lodge contacted old family connections within the GOP in order to find someone to liaise with his father during the Lodges' projected New Year break away from Saigon in Hong Kong. Meade Alcorn, a prominent Republican, met the American ambassador on the neutral ground of the British colony. As a consequence of the discussions between Alcorn and Lodge, Goldberg and Grindle opened an office in

Concord, the capital of New Hampshire, under the banner "Draft Lodge for President."[17]

Since the Lodge supporters had little money and few staff, they devised an original method of campaigning. Using imagination rather than the massive spending of Goldwater and Rockefeller, they organized a mail-out package. This was subsidized by Richard Jackman, the first delegate to file for Lodge, who owned a large printing firm. Their brochure, which was accompanied by a pledge card and a return envelope, did not address any political issue. Instead, it reflected on Lodge's history as an American patriot: his resignation from the U.S. Senate to serve in World War II; his service as U.S. ambassador to the United Nations; and the personal hardship he had endured as the American ambassador in Vietnam. To take advantage of Lodge's appeal on television, Goldberg purchased an old newsreel clip of Eisenhower endorsing Lodge as the Republican vice presidential candidate in 1960. The image of Eisenhower with his arm around Lodge inevitably gave the impression that the ambassador was the general's choice in 1964.[18]

From South Vietnam, Lodge continued to present a dignified appearance as the beleaguered U.S. ambassador in a war zone. His position recalled Eisenhower's own role as the 1952 Republican nominee while he served as supreme commander of NATO forces in Europe; the press did not highlight the fact that Eisenhower had also given his blessing to Governor Scranton of Pennsylvania. Lodge made the occasional good-humored reference to the campaign, but in public he treated the whole matter light-heartedly.[19]

As the new year approached, Johnson set out his instructions regarding the future performance of the South Vietnamese government. Under the guise of a public New Year's greeting to Minh, Lodge was to make a secret oral presentation. He was to warn the Vietnamese head of state that "it is vitally important to act rapidly to reverse the trend of the war within the next sixty to ninety days." The demand was for fast results in the lead-up to the 1964 U.S. electoral race. Johnson also told Lodge to assure Minh "that he has the complete support of the United States Government as *the* leader of South Vietnam." This last was less than convincing in view of the comparisons recommended; Minh should strive to become like "Magsaysay in the Philippines, Sukarno in Indonesia, even Sihanouk in Cambodia." He should strive to "magnetically rally the Vietnamese people."[20] It would seem that in the closing days of 1963, Minh had anything but the whole-hearted support of the U.S. administration.

By mid-December, many American officials had decided that Gen. Duong Van

Minh was a poor administrator who had failed even to impose discipline on the members of his government. The first meeting of the Military Revolutionary Council on November 13 produced no legislation. There were divisions between the MRC and the provisional government: a falling-out between Minh and Prime Minister Tho became public at a press conference on December 11, after which U.S. reporters expressed to embassy officials their dissatisfaction with Minh's "pedestrian" performance. The CIA continued to report disputes between the MRC generals and on-going changes in commands which, the agency warned, threatened the Strategic Hamlets program. As the breach between Tho and Minh widened, it seemed to diplomats and reporters alike that Minh would dismiss his prime minister, and the old endemic rumors of plots to take over the Saigon government arose once again.[21]

Although Johnson was wary of Kennedy's East Coast and Harvard-educated advisors on foreign affairs, information on the Minh government in Saigon became a pressing necessity for him as U.S. newspaper editors came out more and more firmly against the new regime in South Vietnam. Secretary of Defense Robert McNamara appears to have been Johnson's closest advisor on Vietnam in the first months of the new presidency. He drew severely critical conclusions on the Minh regime after a two-day visit to South Vietnam on December 19 and 20. His main working session with the key members of the government, Generals Minh, Don, and Kim and Prime Minister Tho, took place on the second day.

According to Lodge's report of the proceedings, McNamara began characteristically "by asking Gen. Minh how he proposed to organize the command in Vietnam so as to accelerate the war effort." There was concern in the U.S., McNamara said, about the speed and intensity of the war. The secretary was clearly disturbed that no one in the MRC appeared to have the powers of supreme commander of the ARVN. He criticized the arrangement by which General Don was both minister of defense and chairman of the Joint General Staff and General Dinh both commander of 3 Corps and minister for security. When he asked bluntly who was chief of state, General Minh, defending the committee structure of his government, answered that he was in charge, but that when he was away, General Don took charge, and when Don was absent, Kim took over, and so on, proceeding through the entire list of the twelve generals of the Military Revolutionary Council!

Minh appears to have been aware that U.S. officials thought of his government in terms of analogy. In response to McNamara's criticisms, he tackled a comparison of himself to General Neguib of Egypt (who had nominally led the 1953 revolt against King Farouk, only to be overthrown by Gamal Abdel Nasser in

1954). Minh said that "if a stronger or abler man could be found," he would "step aside in his favor." He was "not Neguib and there was no Nasser." The Neguib-Nasser metaphor was a favorite of Roger Hilsman, who later revealed that he had always relied on Minh's overthrow and replacement by a more forceful Vietnamese leader "because he was Neguib." Indeed, Minh's December 20 statement had hardly been in the "magnetic" style of a Magsaysay or a Sukarno. McNamara's exasperation must have reached its climax when, after he had exploded that the MRC appeared to have no policy for fighting the war, General Don assured him that there was a new plan but failed to present him with detailed evidence of what it was.[22]

The meeting concluded after advice on "General Minh's acting like a Chief of State," given by both McNamara and John McCone, met with a wall of resistance. When McCone suggested that Minh should emulate the example of President Johnson and gain popular support by giving more speeches, Minh, Don, and Kim all responded that the Vietnamese people would become "extremely difficult" if many speeches were made. Talking would make them appear as dictators, they said, whereas quiet accomplishment would make them appreciated for their works. Lodge cabled the English translation of what they had said without comment.[23]

McCone began his report of the visit with the succinct verdict, "There is no organized government in South Vietnam at this time." He commented on the lack of an outstanding leader as an ominous sign, and concluded that the war effort probably could not succeed "under present programs and with moderate extensions to existing programs."[24] McNamara recommended major increases in U.S. military and USOM staff to solve the problem. Lodge did not append his usual interpretative paragraph to his long, apparently verbatim report; perhaps he was taken by surprise at the severity of the verdict of the secretary of defense and the CIA chief on the performance of the Vietnamese leaders he had brought to power.

The first indications of critical differences between the Minh government and the Johnson administration arose over U.S. plans for expansion of the war. The new administration's post-Honolulu strategy was outlined in National Security Action Memorandum (NSAM) 273, issued on November 26, 1963.[25] It initiated planning for selective bombing of North Vietnam, which, as we shall see, Lodge supported enthusiastically. It also demanded stepped-up action against the Viet Cong in South Vietnam, which implied more American intervention into Vietnamese affairs at the local level, although this was not immediately spelled out.

U.S. advisors had previously worked with the ARVN commanders at the province level of Vietnamese government and not below.

In response to the new action plan, Lodge wrote a paper outlining his own ideas for a counterinsurgency strategy, which he sent to Johnson on January 6, 1964. His formulation was that a military strategy could not work without political organization at the grass-roots level. He stressed the need for "a proper political atmosphere" to win in Indochina, quoting Gen. Bedell Smith, Eisenhower's former chief of staff. His own thinking stemmed from American police precinct organization: he argued that "the war cannot be won without there being the rough equivalent of a nation-wide precinct organization so that ultimately every family in Vietnam will be known to a precinct worker and the government will become favorably known to every family."[26]

He continued that political workers, in addition to the existing activities of ARVN commanders and province chiefs, must operate and sleep in the villages if this plan was to be effective. He wished to start, or in his own words to "showcase," his program in Long An province. He translated the paper into French, and on January 10 he went through its main points with Generals Minh, Don, and Kim, Prime Minister Tho, and the South Vietnamese minister for foreign affairs, Pham Dang Lam.

The leaders of the South Vietnamese government said that there was much to be praised in the ambassador's paper, but they proved unimpressed by Lodge's idea that they could in this manner develop an "ideology which would match the appeal of Communism." Minh, as before, objected to the advice that he should make more speeches, saying that the Vietnamese people were not much moved to action "by having a clear picture of a program." To the idea of dividing the country into precincts, he replied, "If I were to go into California and divide it up into three-acre lots and give it away, the people to whom I gave it would be pleased, but this was not a question of ideology so much as a question of banditry."[27]

Then the U.S. ambassador and the Vietnamese head of state reached the sticking point. General Minh, supported by Kim, spoke of "the extreme undesirability" of U.S. advisors being assigned to the district and village levels of the Vietnamese administration. Such a change in policy would seem "more imperialistic than the French" and give substance to North Vietnamese charges that the government of South Vietnam was a U.S. lackey. Don complained that U.S. advisory support to the Cao Dai and Hoa Hao served only to allow the sects to play off the United States against the Saigon government.[28]

Perhaps Lodge already had his doubts about these men, for he had written in his police precinct paper of January 6, "Without passing on the question of whether the Vietnamese generals are second rate generals or second rate politicians it is obvious that they are all we have got and that we must try as hard to make them into successful politicians as we are trying to make them into successful military men." It was utterly essential, he continued, to develop a new corps of political workers "if Vietnam is to be dragged into the twentieth century."

Ten days later, on January 16, General Taylor attended a meeting of the Special Group for Counterinsurgency in Washington. After hearing that the South Vietnamese government had made no clear statement of policy on the new Strategic Hamlets program the group had devised, he announced that "no problem exists in placing U.S. military advisors down to the necessary levels in the Vietnamese military establishment." Advisors would also make contact with the Vietnamese religious sects.[29] General Taylor was a step ahead of Lodge and about to make a ruling on the MRC generals: they were not only second-rate but also an obstacle to U.S. plans.

If there was ample evidence that Vietnamese and Americans did things differently and did not communicate their differences well, this was nowhere more apparent than on the vexed question of "neutralism." For Lodge, Vietnamese neutralism meant support for de Gaulle's proposal that the war could be settled on the basis of the 1954 Geneva Accords.[30] For him this was anathema.

The extent of support in South Vietnam for a neutralist solution of some sort to the war and the political problems of Indochina after the overthrow of Diem and in early 1964 is difficult to gauge. Au Ngoc Ho, secretary general of the University of Hue, explained the linguistic problems involved to Robert Miller, first secretary of the U.S. embassy, in March. American usage, he said, distinguished, say, among Switzerland's independent "neutrality" in foreign affairs, the "neutralization" of Laos by international agreement, and "neutralism" in the sense of nonacceptance of foreign military aid. This last was the policy Prince Sihanouk of Cambodia had adopted immediately after the November coup in South Vietnam. Vietnamese usage in the French language did not distinguish these different concepts, Ho said. Clearly, differing shades of meaning complicated discussions with American officials, for whom the whole subject had connotations of anti-American sentiments and ingratitude.[31] Moreover, under Diem and later, antiwar statements were treasonable.

Undoubtedly, many South Vietnamese civilians yearned for an end to the war and saw some form of neutralism as a solution. Au Ngoc Ho told Miller that he himself saw a neutral united Vietnam as the only possibility for peace in Southeast Asia given the might of China. He tactfully reserved the solution for the long term. On the other hand, it seems implausible that senior military men, whose advancement depended on the war, would suddenly convert en masse to pacifism. However, so concerned were U.S. officials that the ARVN commanders might harbor neutralist sentiments and so endanger the continuation of America's crusade against communism in Vietnam that a rumor floated with the correct timing could promote a career or destroy a rival.

Gen. Ton That Dinh, who insisted on keeping the command of 3 Corps as well as acting as minister for security, appears to have used this ploy in his struggle against the advice of Harkins and McNamara. He had everything to gain from the continuation of the U.S.-funded war and had his personal promoters among the American newspapermen. He claimed to have masterminded the coup against Diem on the very grounds of the Ngo brothers' intent to negotiate with Hanoi. Yet in December he confided to embassy officials that he was preparing to "accommodate himself to a neutralist solution for Vietnam." State reacted with concern; Dinh got his way in retaining both 3 Corps and the security ministry for a little while longer.[32] Gen. Nguyen Khanh, six weeks later, would use the unsubstantiated charge that the leading MRC generals were neutralist to clinch American support for his January 1964 coup.

Lodge in Saigon was concerned that any talk of neutralization proposals or reconvening of the Geneva Conference would undermine the will to fight of members of the South Vietnamese government. In December he had had to reassure a worried Foreign Minister Pham Dang Lam that the U.S. was *not* contemplating a negotiated settlement when Sihanouk proposed that Cambodia and South Vietnam form a neutralist federation, and called for an international conference on the matter. He urged Rusk to give him reassurances that Sihanouk's proposals would be rebuffed in the strongest terms, in order to relay the message to the south Vietnamese government. Armed with the requested statement from Washington at his meeting with Lam and Minh on December 11, he had still to go to great lengths to explain that whatever Walter Lippmann or the editors of the *New York Times* wrote about the desirability of an international conference on Indochina or the wisdom of de Gaulle's proposals, they did not speak for the U.S. government, which was consistent, Lodge said, in its "win the war policy."[33]

When de Gaulle announced his offer to bring about a cease-fire in Vietnam in an Agence France Presse dispatch on January 18, pending France's recognition of China, Lodge decided that stern measures were required. He alerted Rusk that he was concerned as to Minh's possible reactions. So strongly did he feel that he used the odd phrasing that he intended to summon General Minh the next day "to repudiate French plans to recognize Peking" and "the whole line of thought contained in the AFP article, which equates U.S. actions in SVN with those of North Vietnam and Viet Cong." In order to strengthen Minh's trust in American might and technology, he wrote, he intended to reveal ahead of schedule the new U.S. plans to put heavy pressure on North Vietnam.[34]

The U.S. plans Lodge had in mind to describe "in broad outline" to Minh as a morale-boosting exercise were those related to bombing raids against targets in North Vietnam as envisioned under Natinal Security Action Memorandum 273. The detailed program, code-named OPLAN 34-A, had been in preparation under the direction of Maj. Gen. Victor Krulak for some weeks. Only three days before, Lodge had received a cable informing him of Johnson's creation of an interdepartmental committee of State and Defense representatives to oversee the operations of OPLAN 34-A. He would reply to this enthusiastically through CIA channels on January 20.[35] Lodge had advocated bombing of North Vietnam since the beginning of the Johnson administration: he was well aware that bombing would be popular with the American public, whereas an early commitment of troops would not.

The meeting which appears to have convinced Lodge that the U.S. could not work with the MRC took place on January 21. Accompanied by General Harkins and CIA operatives, Lodge met with Generals Minh and Kim, Prime Minister Tho, and Foreign Minister Lam. The U.S. ambassador began by saying that the proposed operation had the full backing of the American president and was scheduled to commence on February 1. The focus would be on the enemy's petroleum reserves and ports such as the harbor at Hai Phong; the goal was to convince the Communists that they would face military and economic devastation if they did not withdraw the Viet Cong from the South.

The reaction of Minh and the key members of his government to the proposals was negative in the extreme. They questioned in particular the underlying conception that the bombing would demoralize the leadership of North Vietnam. Tho and Minh said that the South Vietnamese government was better organized to act on the Communists' infiltration routes through Laos and Cambodia, and they would prefer help with equipping themselves to act against the Viet Cong in the South. Moreover, they continued, Hanoi would not be deterred by bombing but would most probably react by sending regular units of the People's Army of North Vietnam into the South.

His American advisors assured Minh that the bombing would be "plausibly denied" by Washington at all stages and at all levels, and the South Vietnamese government could reserve judgment on whether to use their knowledge of it, say, in negotiations. But Minh was adamant. He moved ahead to the central question. War against China was the logical consequence of the proposed program, he said. Was the American public prepared to accept open war against China?

Lodge knew that the American public was not prepared to accept war against China. He replied that what was sought was a "unilateral cease fire" by the Viet Cong on the orders of Hanoi, and that "once VC had stopped fighting, GVN and U.S. would decide what to do next."[36] On the question of the likelihood of the North sending regular units of the Peoples Army of Vietnam into South Vietnam, Pham Dang Lam recalled later, "Lodge had no answer."[37]

The objections of the Minh government to the bombing of North Vietnam were overridden. It seems clear that the ambassador had not contemplated that the bombing might fail to demoralize Hanoi. Further, no contingency planning related to the Krulak program appears to have been available at the Department of State. Lodge's report of his January 21 meeting with the South Vietnamese government, sent via CIA channels and styled "CAS Saigon 3943," was the subject of a joint State-Defense-CAS message relayed immediately to Admiral Felt in Honolulu and to the White House on January 22. Later the same day, the Joint Chiefs dispatched a memorandum to Secretary of Defense McNamara. It recommended that the U.S. put aside "self-imposed restrictions" to its actions in South Vietnam and induce the Saigon government to surrender responsibility for the conduct of the war to the American commander. MACV's contingent of advisors should be enlarged, the Joint Chiefs suggested, supported if necessary with increased U.S. forces.[38] The Minh regime had de facto signed its own death warrant.

Lodge's role in the coup that toppled the MRC was to be largely a passive one. He gave no "green light" to the conspirators, nor did he liaise with them. Washington wanted the ground war in South Vietnam against the Viet Cong and the secret war against North Vietnam to go ahead under the unilateral direction of the American commander. What was needed was clear. But this time, when U.S. planners sowed the coup seed in Vietnam, they were careful to ensure that the evidence did not appear in the *New York Times* on a daily basis.

Gen. Nguyen Khanh was regarded highly by many U.S. officials, both civilian and military. As the commander of 2 Corps during the August 1963 coup plot, he had contacted the CIA's Lucien Conein offering to pass on the evidence Washington needed as to Diem's and Nhu's negotiations with the Communists and asking for a statement of the U.S. position. Under Secretary of State Ball had at that time recommended him to Lodge, saying: "Our impression is that Khanh is one of the best of the generals, both courageous and sophisticated." General Harkins thought him the most capable of the Vietnamese generals, as did General Taylor, and even high-ranking North Vietnamese were aware of this.[39]

Khanh was on record as having told U.S. officials that South Vietnam "must rely on American support." He had received his early training in France, but he had also attended Fort Leavenworth Command and General Staff College in Kansas. This was important, as no senior officer in the U.S. Army at this stage spoke fluent Vietnamese and General Harkins, in particular, could not carry on a technical conversation in French. As Lodge's aide Colonel Dunn recalled, Khanh did not merely speak English well, "he spoke American; American Army in fact."[40]

When the Joint Chiefs of Staff decided definitively against the Minh regime on January 22, no doubt having dropped hints before that date, there were no shortage of would-be coup makers in South Vietnam. Many of the ARVN generals were disgruntled with the commands and positions they had received after the November coup. Gen. Tran Thien Khiem, formerly commander of the armed forces but displaced from that position after the coup against Diem, had long been making preparations for his own coup. His launching position was improved when he was given control of 3 Corps after Dinh's final removal from that position in early January. He soon received the support of several younger generals, members of the Dai Viet party, and most importantly of Nguyen Van Thieu, later president of South Vietnam from 1965 to 1975, who at that time commanded the Fifth Division of 3 Corps. Both these men were Catholics and were wary lest the organized Buddhists, let alone the U.S. government, failed to support their coup. General Khanh, a frequent guest at the American colonels' billet in Saigon, which the advisors had nicknamed "The White House," was advantaged by the troop maneuver of the Catholic conspirators in staging his own bid for power.[41] Indeed, so common and so frequent were rumors of conspiracies, and so inadequate were the procedures for evaluating them, that when in mid-December Conein alerted the embassy to General Khanh's statement to him that he intended to take over the South Vietnamese government, officials there ignored this intelligence.[42]

One key American, however, did take Khanh seriously. General Harkins had made no secret of his low opinion of Minh's abilities and of the MRC's committee structure for the command of the ARVN. Above all, Harkins held in contempt what he called "political generals." He liked the young, nominally Buddhist Khanh, who had stood aside from the Diem coup until the final hours, who had accepted no position in the Minh government, and who had brought order to the population of Hue as commander of 1 Corps in the troubled days there after the Buddhist Crisis of Diem's Catholic rule.[43] This Vietnamese acted like a soldier; he was happy to accept remote commands in Military Region 1 on the border and at Pleiku, in Military Region 2. In Khanh, Harkins saw an American-style professional. His patronage of the young Vietnamese general extended to provision of quarters adjoining his own for the use of the 2 Corps commander on his visits to Saigon.

General Khanh has recently attested that at no stage in the first weeks of 1964 did he and General Harkins discuss South Vietnamese government politics. It may be added that no direct conversations were necessary. In the event, at least five days before he staged his own bid for power, Khanh told the American commander of his intentions. Harkins did not inform Lodge of this development but he notified his chief, General Taylor, using his own channels. Significantly, he thought, he received no return instructions;[44] the Pentagon would welcome a coup against Minh. In the days and weeks before the end of January, U.S. military advisors had turned a blind eye to the significance of ARVN troop maneuvers as alliances formed and fell apart, while Khanh's advisor, Col. Jasper Wilson, for one, was actively promoting his own Vietnamese candidate for power.

Khanh made his penultimate move from his headquarters in Pleiku on January 28. Through Colonel Wilson, he informed the CIA station in Saigon that within three days he expected a pro-French neutralist coup. This would be initiated by Vietnamese returnees from Paris such as Lt. Col. Vuong Van Dong and Col. Tran Dinh Lam, who were in league with Generals Don, Kim, and Xuan of the MRC, he said. He did not reveal his sources. The station passed the information on to Ambassador Lodge and General Harkins but found Khanh's claims difficult to evaluate.[45] It was therefore necessary for Khanh and Wilson to address the American ambassador himself, for without his attention, they apparently reasoned, the change of government might not be recognized in Washington.

On the afternoon of January 29, General Khanh finally spoke with Lodge at the embassy. The Vietnamese, whom Lodge had met only once before when Ngo Dinh Diem had introduced them at Dalat in 1963, seems to have chosen his arguments with great shrewdness. He informed Lodge that the MRC generals would make a move toward neutralism in the course of the coming two days. When Lodge urged Colonel Wilson to press Khanh for details, the young Vietnamese general alleged that Generals Don, Kim, and Xuan publicly opposed neutralism but were in fact secretly dealing with the French: he claimed to be in possession of documents that established this. Khanh hinted that he was prepared to stage a preemptive coup.

Lodge quickly assessed the situation. Khanh had said the bid for a French settlement "might succeed because of war weariness among the Vietnamese, including the junior ARVN officers." He decided to speak against the advisability of a coup but silently to back Khanh; he agreed that Colonel Wilson should be Khanh's exclusive contact with the U.S. mission. In his assessment, he wrote that Khanh was "considered to be the most capable general in Vietnam, that he controls the 1 and 2 Corps, which is the most orderly part of Vietnam, and that in addition to being a capable soldier, he has the reputation of being politically perspicacious. . .*even though I hardly know him at all* [emphasis added]."[46]

Lodge then, as before with Diem and Nhu, allowed events to take their own course. After his meeting with Khanh, he contrived to have several hours elapse while cables on other matters were transmitted to Washington: one of these was a long report on village administration, filed at 5 P.M.;[47] six other documents went out before his report of his conversation with Khanh. This was sent at 8 P.M. under the category "No Distribution," which he himself had presumably assigned to it before he left the chancery building at 5 P.M. The cable did not bear the designation "Critical Flash," the standard usage for coup information, which would have sped its progress had it indeed been filed with the intention of its reaching Washington before a transfer of power had been accomplished in Saigon.

It had been the custom of the U.S. mission to pass on coup rumors to the South Vietnamese government, although Lodge had omitted this courtesy in the period immediately before the Diem coup. He chose to start his report on his meeting with Khanh by advising Rusk to warn de Gaulle that he must cease his machinations via a "secret agreement between him and the ChiComs [Chinese Communists]" to bring about a neutralist state in South Vietnam. Since Ball had told him on January 28 that U.S. relations with France were so poor that any approach to de Gaulle regarding Vietnam would be fruitless, it seems that Lodge was indulging his longstanding suspicions of the French leader's interference in Vietnamese politics. To make matters worse, France had given formal recognition to China on January 27. Lodge may also have thought it expedient to create a smoke screen around America's complicity in Khanh's coup. What Saigon-Washington cables make clear is that Khanh did not confront Minh as head of state with his accusations against the key members of his government as French-inspired plotters, nor did he warn of his own intentions lest they desist, and the

Department of State did not instruct Lodge to pass on the rumors and information of which he was in possession to General Minh.[48]

At about 5 P.M. on January 29, Lodge left the chancery building, having given his deputy chief of mission "strict instructions that coup or no coup, he wasn't to be disturbed until the next morning." Between January 28 and the early morning of January 30, key officials of the American embassy in Saigon knew that preparations for a coup were in progress. They wrote nothing. But two Americans independently decided that the U.S. should be more responsive. Late on January 29, Col. Jasper Wilson called on Lodge's aide, Dunn, at his apartment, informing him that there would be an uprising that night. According to Tran Van Don, after the meeting with Lodge, Wilson had informed rival coup maker Tran Thien Khiem that the embassy had agreed to support Khanh as leader of South Vietnam. Presumably, Wilson's motive now was to steer U.S. government support for Khanh's coup.[49]

At the residence, Dunn—one of the few who would dare to attempt such a feat—tried to rouse Lodge. The ambassador was determined to stick to the policy he had followed on other similar occasions and to sleep through the change of government. He nevertheless gave Dunn permission to do as he saw fit. Thus Dunn opened the chancery building and set up a communications channel from the embassy to Washington. Wilson, from the Vietnamese Joint General Staff headquarters, relayed messages on the progress of the coup by this means.[50] Lodge did not record in personal records or memoirs his feelings about this initiative on the part of his aide.

In the early morning of January 30, General Khanh's agents arrested four of the MRC generals, including Don, Kim, and Xuan. They surrendered without a struggle, having been caught without bodyguards or troops to defend them.[51] The men were placed under house arrest in Dalat, where they subsequently became known to the American press as the "Dalat Generals."

On the day when General Khanh was welcomed to power by the American government's representative in South Vietnam, key MRC figures had been taken completely by surprise in a city notorious for its rumors and its irregular information networks. As Bui Diem, later South Vietnam's ambassador to Washington, shrewdly noted, a coup of which so many Americans and Vietnamese had prior knowledge could have been prevented by a U.S. diplomatic initiative. But clearly that was not Washington's wish, although, as Bui Diem continued, the Khanh coup "was a messy sort of thing."[52]

As Khanh's star rose in South Vietnam, so did that of Lodge in the lead-up to the GOP primary in New Hampshire. His name topped the list in opinion polls published on January 25. As Kalischer had predicted, of Lodge's two main rivals, initially Barry Goldwater appeared to be "too far out in right field," advocating to a group of students in the first week of March that North Vietnam could have been defoliated by a low-yield atom bomb ten years before. Nelson Rockefeller, who had divorced his first wife to marry a mother of four, plummeted in the voting stakes when he commenced campaigning with the new Mrs. Rockefeller. Journalist Theodore White described a scene in Hollis, New Hampshire, in the last week of the campaign. Mrs. Rockefeller, heavily pregnant, was the only person seated in the high school gymnasium where Rockefeller was to make a speech to a group of flinty New Englanders. The citizens of Hollis made their judgment on the Rockefellers at the polls: on March 11 they would vote Lodge, 238; Rockefeller, 120; Goldwater, 85.[53] The Draft Lodge campaign received an unexpected fillip when Rockefeller managed in late February to place a call to the ambassador in Saigon, challenging him to declare his intentions to stand as a candidate or step down; Lodge had pledged in August, before leaving Boston, that he would support Rockefeller as GOP nominee in 1964. Grindle and Goldberg met the challenge with press releases portraying Lodge as the hard-working servant of his country, abused at home by the playboy Rockefeller. As the deadline for the New Hampshire primaries approached, organizer Robert Mullen orchestrated a renewed burst of publicity for Lodge by titillating jaded journalists with the question of whether Lodge would take part in the next primary, in Oregon, and so confirm that he was a serious contender in the presidential race.[54]

On March 11, as Lodge returned to the embassy from an exhausting field trip to Hue with McNamara and Taylor, his shirt covered in red dust, he received the news of his write-in victory in the initial Republican primary. He had won by a comparative landslide, with 33,007 votes, 36 percent of the GOP total. In the six-person field, Goldwater had gained 20,692 (22 percent), Rockefeller 19,504 (21 percent), and Nixon 15,587 (17 percent). His public stance on that day was that he was honored by the result, laughing it off as "unexpected radio activity in New Hampshire." A campaign biography, however, was swiftly assembled. Entitled *The Remarkable Henry Cabot Lodge,* the work commences with a pen-portrait of Lodge dismounting from a DC-6 accompanied by the chairman of the Joint Chiefs of Staff and the secretary of defense. In the introduction, ordinary Americans are quoted as saying, "Lodge is cut out of the same cloth as Kennedy."[55]

The New Hampshire campaign seems to have been on Lodge's mind when he reflected on the significance of the Khanh coup in South Vietnam. Two days after Khanh's accession to power, Lodge cabled Washington. "At first blush," he said, the coup had been "extremely disconcerting." On second thought, he continued, Don and Kim were still French citizens and "one realized that Generals Don and Kim had never at any time foresworn the possibility of a neutral solution at what might seem to them to be the proper time." Making a coup seemed the normal way to change a government in South Vietnam, he said, and General Khanh's action did not appear to have shocked Vietnamese sentiments.

"The forward steps of history are often not made by one man or group of men. In U.S., for instance, the men who manage a successful campaign for the party nominations are often not the same as those who manage the election campaigns and they, in turn, are not the same who occupy the big posts after the election is won. Similarly, the group that ended the Diem regime and cleaned out much of its dry rot has rendered a service and now a new man has the job of winning the war. Our side knows how to do it; we have the means with which to do it; we simply need to do it. This requires a tough and ruthless commander. Perhaps Khanh is it."[56] Thus, with an inappropriate analogy, Lodge vested in Khanh American hopes for improvement in the war.

Part of the problem of U.S. perceptions of Vietnam was almost certainly that most Americans saw that country's problems through the prism of American concerns. Lodge's analogy between a U.S. election and the Khanh coup exemplified this tendency. Lodge acknowledged the differences between the two societies at some levels, or when it was convenient to do so, as when he argued that coup making was a means of changing a government acceptable to the Vietnamese. But he was impressed by Khanh exactly because he appeared to be an American-style professional soldier with modern administrative skills. As we shall see, Khanh also had the attributes of a more traditional military figure—the war lord of old China. In common with planners in the Department of State, Lodge seems to have had little knowledge of the realities of the Vietnamese administration. The Khanh regime did not start with a group of officials cleansed of the "dry rot" of the Diem period: the disintegration in the provinces continued and was in large part due to the reassignments of positions that followed each successive change of government. In fact, the Khanh coup did not produce strong leadership but ushered in a period of extreme instability. The process by which preferment in the South Vietnamese Army was linked to coup making was no longer an option for adventurers; coup making had become a U.S.-funded institution.

Lodge was aware of none of this on January 30, 1964. At 6 A.M. he dismounted from an unmarked car and entered Dunn's apartment by means of the service elevator. He had arrived incognito for a secret meeting with the new leader of South Vietnam. Khanh requested the meeting through Colonel Wilson; Lodge agreed but could not use U.S. premises until Washington had clarified the American position on the change of leadership in Saigon. The ambassador's key consideration on that morning was to prevent the U.S. media from implicating the American government in the coup.

Dunn suddenly noticed that his usual household staff had been augmented by unfamiliar servants in white formal dress. When he whispered enquiries, he was informed smartly that preparations had been set in train "for the big meeting." While Dunn's servants hastily laid out delicacies, fruit, and flowers, he and Lodge walked to the balcony. From below, they were greeted by a huge Vietnamese crowd, as Khanh arrived accompanied by seven jeeploads of aides and supporters. Khanh, apparently feeling totally in control of the situation, strolled into the salon and embraced Lodge. Speaking a mixture of English, French, and Vietnamese, he asserted that he would prosecute the war more vigorously, make democratic reforms, and be guided in all matters by American advice. He even suggested the installation of direct telephone lines between the Vietnamese Joint General Staff headquarters and the U.S. embassy. "So much for secrecy in the Orient," Lodge murmured.[57]

Of his first conversation with Khanh as Vietnamese head of state, Lodge reported: "Although he didn't say so at any time, underlying many of the things that Gen. Khanh said was the belief that a big deal was underway between Gen. De Gaulle and Mao Tse Tung in which neutralization of Viet-Nam and restoration of French influence was a big consideration and that Gen. De Gaulle had quite artfully penetrated the Vietnamese government and been rather effectively moving the country towards neutralism."[58] It is clear that, for Lodge, Vietnam was a part of NATO, not of Asia.

Lodge may have been inclined to believe in the rather far-fetched idea that Don, Kim, Dinh, and other MRC generals were instruments in a French neutralist plot because Ambassador d'Orlandi had suggested this to him a few days earlier. As far as the available evidence allows for the construction of a case, it seems that Tran Thien Khiem, Nguyen Van Thieu, and Nguyen Khanh orchestrated a rumor campaign against Don, Kim, and Xuan to justify a coup, using the MRC generals' contacts with the returnees from Paris to add plausibility to the charge that they themselves were neutralists. Under Secretary of State Harriman was advised as much by Department of State officers on January 30 but found Khanh's story a convenient justification for his takeover of the South Vietnamese government. Flott, whom Lodge placed in charge of American-French liaison in South Vietnam, found no evidence of French involvement in the Khanh coup, although he was well aware that individual French businessmen and plantation owners had preferences as to which Vietnamese they might like to see in power. Indeed, French officials despaired at the lack of influence de Gaulle's suggestions had had with the American-supported South Vietnamese generals. Kim may have favored a negotiated settlement of the war, but Don's and Minh's position was that the war should not be expanded. Younger generals, American-trained, favored intensification of the war, of course, and portrayed themselves as "bitter enders" on the question of negotiations, as the French newspaper *Le Figaro* found.[59] What seems clear is that this coup in South Vietnam was not ordered by the president of the United States and that Johnson had no inside knowledge of its preparation and mechanics.

As for the documents allegedly proving the neutralist conspiracy of the MRC inner circle, Khanh did not present them either to the embassy or at the ensuing trial, and they have never been located. In fact, the "Dalat Generals" were not charged with neutralism or treason when they were tried in Dalat on May 28, 1964; they were merely found guilty of "lax morality, insufficient qualifications for command, and a lack of a clear political concept."[60]

Khanh could play Lodge like a musical instrument when it came to justification for his overthrow of the Minh regime. The day after his accession to power, moving on from the end-the-war charges against the older Vietnamese generals, he suggested grounds for an even graver concern. He said: "General Don still had the briefing papers on the subject [bombing the North under OPLAN 34-A]." He, Khanh, "feared that these papers would get into the hands of neutralists and then into the hands of Communists, and he was trying to recover the documents." Lodge immediately transmitted this information to the White House for McGeorge Bundy and to the Pentagon for General Krulak and the Joint Chiefs of Staff, using the CIA channel to preserve secrecy.[61]

For this was the heart of the matter. On January 31, Lodge satisfied himself as to the new Vietnamese leader's enthusiasm for U.S. plans for bombing the North and "intensified activity against the Viet Cong," presumably meaning acceptance of U.S. advisors at the village level. To this radical change in policy, Khanh would speedily and openly agree.

On the same day the U.S. ambassador and the new Vietnamese head of state cleared up the details of U.S. recognition and statements to the press. To avoid the appearance of chaos in Vietnam, the formula agreed upon was that there had been a change in the chairmanship and composition of the Military Revolutionary Council. This meant that there was no need for the U.S. to acknowledge the overthrow of a government or extend formal recognition to the new regime, since normal relations would simply continue. Khanh agreed to retain Minh as nominal head of state as a symbol of continuity and because of his popularity, something Ball had suggested as his first response to the news from Saigon, but, adopting the title for himself of premier, Khanh dropped Tho as prime minister. Lodge then gave the new Vietnamese premier some pertinent advice: "I told him . . . that he would rise and fall, as far as American opinion was concerned, on the results which he obtained in the effort against the Viet Cong. Nothing could be more fatal as far as U.S. confidence was concerned than another six weeks interregnum, or a period of any length devoted to fumbling around and so-called 'reorganization.' "[62]

Johnson, waking in Washington on February 1, was disturbed by news of the coup in Saigon. But he took the advice of his aide, Bill Moyers, who pointed out that if Lodge and Harkins could get Khanh to make some fast gains in the struggle against communism, the president could maintain the support of Congress for both his domestic reforms and the war. In his first note to Khanh, Johnson pledged every assistance for the war effort.[63] He then dispatched McNamara to South Vietnam with the message that there were to be no more coups.

The editors of most of the key U.S. newspapers welcomed the Khanh coup. The words "strong man" appeared in almost every article about him. Americans demanded battlefield feats and fast results; Khanh was happy to present the desired image. For *Time* photographers, the young general donned a paratrooper's camouflage uniform, presumably to symbolize his commitment to action, and vowed that he would "fight Communism to the final victory."[64] Adverse reports by American journalists had been a factor in nurturing impatience with the performance of the MRC in the Department of State. But at the time, few if any editorials criticized the role of story-hungry newspapermen in Minh's demise, or reflected that the MRC generals had hardly had time to prove what they could accomplish.

In March the U.S. secretary of defense toured the countryside with the new Vietnamese head of state. The American's towering height, compared to Khanh's, gave the inevitable impression of puppet and puppeteer. The picture rasped on Vietnamese nationalist and postcolonial sensibilities. "Vietnam *muon nam* [Vietnam for a thousand years]," McNamara exhorted, "Long live Vietnam!"[65] He did not realize that in giving the Vietnamese words a rising tone and then a falling tone, the natural rhythms of hustings electioneering, he had changed the phrase to mean, "Vietnam wants to lie down" or "Vietnam wishes to sleep."

Lodge's attitude to the coup that had deposed Minh resembled the position he had adopted on the overthrow of Diem. For Lodge, when something was done it was done, and he cleared his mind of all but the cover-story. Just as he always claimed that he had been unable to gain firm information on who had been responsible for the deaths of Diem and Nhu, he chose to remain officially uninformed regarding the details of the Khanh coup, recording only that "the best information was that the coup was planned and carried out by General [Nguyen Van] Thieu with the aim of getting rid of the Minh administration and putting General Nguyen Khanh in as Prime Minister."[66]

Khanh had gained U.S. endorsement as head of state in South Vietnam because of his image as a soldier ready to take on the Communists at the front. But Lodge's image as the American ambassador fighting communism in far-off Southeast Asia could not match the active campaigning and massive spending of Rockefeller and Goldwater at home. His appeal in the presidential race steadily declined when he could not speak regarding his policies. He was defeated in the Oregon primary, held on May 14, and gave his delegates to Rockefeller, thus concluding his candidacy in the 1964 elections.

Chapter Six

The Descending Curtain

In response to Johnson's reservations as to Lodge's performance as U.S. ambassador in Saigon, as early as November McNamara had urged that Lodge should be provided with a deputy to act as his chief of staff. McNamara argued that this measure could help solve the problem of teamwork in the U.S. mission, but in effect he was advocating that Deputy Chief of Mission Trueheart's replacement be a man who could take over the ambassadorial duties of direction and coordination. After his December visit to South Vietnam, the secretary of defense reported that he, Rusk, and McCone had tried to show Lodge how better to coordinate the operations of the different agencies of the Country Team, but that "he has just operated as a loner all his life and cannot readily change now."[1]

Lodge's reaction to this criticism suggests that he did not grasp its meaning; in his 1973 autobiography he explained the comment as a misunderstanding that had arisen because of Kennedy's secret instruction that he was not to disclose the exchange of cables between himself and the president during the Diem crisis of 1963.[2] Since the diplomatic style that came naturally to Lodge was that of the nonprofessional in the nineteenth-century manner, operating on political instinct and hunches, he did not understand, or wish to learn about, the managerial skills necessary to a modern ambassador in charge of a large overseas team. This antiquated approach would no longer do in a period when stepped-up operations under National Security Action Memorandum 273 and OPLAN 34-A (1964) were envisioned.

Not wishing to withdraw Lodge from Vietnam, Johnson initiated a search at the highest levels for a suitable Foreign Service officer to act as Lodge's administrator. Trueheart was recalled to Washington in what was ostensibly a routine change. According to David Halberstam, however, it was because McNamara objected to Trueheart's criticisms of U.S. military estimates of progress in the war: personnel changes were easier to deal with than the much-needed full-scale policy review of Johnson's options in Indochina, which he wished to delay until after the November elections. The name of David Nes, who had served as deputy chief of mission in Libya and most recently as counselor of the U.S. embassy in Morocco, consistently emerged in discussions. Nes was nominated for the position by Rusk, Ball, Harriman, and Hilsman, and after his confirmation for the position, he accompanied McNamara to Saigon on his December visit, bearing the title deputy chief of mission.[3]

Perhaps McGeorge Bundy and Forrestal would have preferred a clean break and the recall of Ambassador Lodge. On February 4 they started memorandums on the subject of Vietnam staff changes with the words, "If Lodge must remain" and "If Lodge must stay." If Lodge was to stay, they concluded, the other option open was to replace Harkins with an able and "modern-minded general." For both of them, Gen. William Westmoreland fitted the bill, and although he had only three stars, they reasoned that the very fact of his more junior rank might end the bickering that had occurred between Harkins and Lodge in their respective positions as military commander and ambassador. Westmoreland had arrived in Vietnam as deputy to General Harkins in January. He took over from Harkins as commander of MACV in June.[4]

Lodge had met Nes in Libya on a visit to Africa under the Kennedy administration and had been favorably impressed by him; Harriman confided to McGeorge Bundy that it was a good sign for future harmony in the embassy in Saigon that Lodge, as he thought, had chosen Nes himself. Johnson had the final say on the choice of Nes for the U.S. mission in Vietnam. So much hinged on the appointment that Johnson asked Nes to write his own job description, instructing Rusk, "I want him to sit down and write his ideas of what authority he needs and what kind of a set-up it ought to be." Rusk agreed, saying, "I think if we build a new job that he [Nes] ought to take part in building it."[5]

Nes, then, carried with him to Saigon an enormous responsibility for the direction of the American mission in South Vietnam. Johnson embraced him powerfully on his departure. "People might say that Truman lost China," said the president, but "Lyndon Johnson is not going to go down as the President who lost Vietnam."[6]

The principal instruction Nes was given "from the President on down was to go out to Saigon and effect the overall coordination of the U.S. effort in Vietnam since the normal Country Team approach was not being used." Although he had served in Burma during World War II, Nes, as he himself was well aware, had little experience in insurgency situations. The American government, however, gave him no briefing on the war or the history of Communist movements in Indochina; this information he gleaned from British and French sources. The prospects of him succeeding in his assignment, even with the ambassador's cooperation, were a great deal less than rosy.

Nes had been advised in Washington that Lodge might not offer his "active participation" in pulling together the operations of the Country Team, since the ambassador had made it clear that he had no intention of meeting with the heads of the agencies on a regular basis.[7] But the situation that Nes encountered after his arrival in Saigon rendered him unable to perform the duties of deputy chief of mission at all.

Lodge continued to assert the primacy of the ambassador in the U.S. mission and would not delegate his authority even within the chancery building. He refused to give Nes access to the official cables from State. Colonel Dunn, controlling the outer office of the ambassador, created a barrier between the ambassador and the deputy chief of mission, preventing Nes from consulting with Lodge. Further, as suited Lodge, Dunn himself had been performing many of the duties of deputy chief of mission since the departure of Trueheart, whose withdrawal he had welcomed, and he continued to do so after the arrival of the new appointee.[8] Nes had arrived too late to change Lodge's habit of relying only on his personal staff.

Lodge prevented Nes from acting as deputy chief of mission. Nor was Nes permitted to enter the inner circles of embassy society, let alone that of Lodge's confidants. Barry Zorthian described Nes as "but a laborer in the vineyard." Nes accordingly addressed himself to making his own overview of America's policy options in Vietnam. Because he was neither an agent in a process nor part of a bureaucracy that generated its own rationale, he was in a good position to do this. Moreover, possessing an income of his own, he could risk the displeasure of the Department of State, even to the point of having to resign his post.

Nes wrote to Roger Hilsman in biting terms: "My most disillusioning experience has been with the MACV-MAAG operation which seems to be tailored largely towards providing the U.S. military establishment, within the framework of World War II conventional doctrine, organization and weapons, a fertile field for the utilization and promotion of its senior officers rather than as an instrument to deal with guerrilla war." Mindful of his sworn obligation not to disclose secrets of state, he continued, "I will have a great deal more to say about our Vietnamese adventure as time goes on but you may rest assured that I will say it only through channels," specifically, "to you and to Ambassador Lodge."[9]

In February, he presented his assessment to Lodge in the form of a paper "Where We Stand in Vietnam." Starting from the basic premise that the American objective in Vietnam was to contain the spread of communism in Asia, he argued that General de Gaulle was possibly correct in his contention that the choices open to the U.S. were a negotiated political settlement to the war or escalation to direct military confrontation with North Vietnam and China. The South Vietnamese peasant was exhausted by war, he continued, but the South Vietnamese government had little to offer in terms of either orderly administration or social justice. American advisors of whatever quality or numbers would not change the attitudes and thinking of the South Vietnamese military or officialdom within any reasonable period of time. The Communists, by contrast, he considered, were disciplined and could identify themselves with the people's needs. Their strongest asset was that they clearly had the backing of China and so could present themselves as the inevitable winners. Against this background, Nes argued, counterinsurgency efforts would not work.

The ARVN, designed as a World War II military establishment, was not suited to deal with Viet Cong tactics but provided a perfect spawning ground for coups, Nes continued. Therefore, America must accept the possibility of war with China, as neutralism was fueled by perceived U.S. lack of will. As deputy chief of mission, he recommended that Lodge impress on Washington the need to make a firm announcement that the U.S. was prepared to face conflict with China to maintain a position in Southeast Asia, to inform de Gaulle of this resolve, and to press for the "acceleration and expansion of OPS Plan 34A-64 [OPLAN 34-A (1964)]."

These were the issues that should have been addressed at an American policy summit on Vietnam. Lodge himself, shortly after his arrival, had noted the military tendency to overly optimistic reporting on progress in the war. Indeed, much of what Nes wrote contained the conclusions to be drawn, had Lodge so wished, from his own shrewd but largely scattered observations. But Lodge did not allow this good advice to influence his recommendations. He did not preserve a record of any response he may have made to his deputy chief of mission's analysis; he did not mention Nes in "Vietnam Memoir," and the deputy chief's name does not appear in the index to Lodge's papers.

The ambassador's reasoning became clear after Nes had resigned from his position. Nes was to return to Washington in July, after a clash with General Harkins in May, when he had put to the American commander his criticisms of MACV tactics in the war. Lodge refused to make an efficiency report on his period of service. Speaking of him in 1966 at a Chiefs of Mission Conference at the U.S. base at Baguio in the Philippines, he remarked: "I work for the President, I work for the Secretary of State, and I work for Bill Bundy, but I will not have my deputy chief of mission telling me what areas of the work he will take care of and what areas I should be concerned with."[10]

The war had not stopped during the extended period of political upheaval in the U.S. and in Saigon. Indeed, some critical developments were taking place. On February 7, 1964, the CIA reported that North Vietnam had undertaken a major policy review in January, and as a result, Viet Cong activity in South Vietnam had been steadily rising in intensity. Some four months later, Hanoi would begin to mobilize its forces in anticipation of bringing regular units of the Peoples Army of Vietnam into the war and to strengthen the Ho Chi Minh network of supply lines to the South. The North Vietnamese review had undoubtedly been in response to the expansion of American advisory programs in South Vietnam.[11] The deposed Minh and his cabinet had anticipated this development, but their warnings had fallen on deaf ears.

Washington was about to authorize massive funding increases to give support to the newly installed Khanh government. All the agencies would be granted more generous budgets, and hundreds of U.S. officials were about to arrive in South Vietnam to supervise the implementation of counterinsurgency plans, as McNamara had recommended in November. Yet this unprecedented wash of dollars and projected intrusion of Americans at all levels of the South Vietnamese government coincided with an extraordinary low in the organization of the U.S. administrative apparatus.

The difficulties of coordinating the work of the various organizations of the U.S. mission had reached herculean proportions by the beginning of February 1964. The heads of the agencies, in Dunn's words, acted as "barons." There was no lateral communication in the embassy. Functions were compartmentalized to such a degree that people in one section in the chancery building itself had very little idea of what went on in another. Most important, no instrument for coordinating the activities of personnel working with the various U.S. agencies in the provinces had existed during the previous three months. Trueheart had chaired weekly meetings of a Committee on Province Rehabilitation, through which members of all agencies and groups concerned with counterinsurgency programs could meet. But these gatherings had ceased in early December, shortly before

Trueheart's departure, because of the confusion caused in the Vietnamese provincial offices by the dismissals and relocations which had followed the November coup.[12]

After seven weeks of wrestling with the problem of how to coordinate the activities of the agencies, Nes accepted General Westmoreland's invitation to act as vice chairman of a body known as the Pacification Committee, of which he, as deputy chief of mission, had previously been the chair.[13] The Pacification Committee, which after its restructuring the ambitious young general tactfully called the "Nes Committee," was designed to overview implementation of the South Vietnamese government's counterinsurgency programs. It also acted in effect as a parallel Vietnam Country Team.

The Pacification Committee's new charter specified that the heads of the agencies, Joseph Brent for USOM, Barry Zorthian for USIS, Peer de Silva for CIA, and Melvin Manfull for the embassy, would attend its meetings, as well as representatives of MACV and MAAG, Gen. Charles Timmes for MAAG and Westmoreland as deputy commander of MACV. Nes was to coordinate the presentation of reports by the civilians, Westmoreland the reports of the military.[14] In fact, this arrangement gave Westmoreland the upper hand on the duplicate Country Team, since the U.S. military organizations in Vietnam were more united than the civilian agencies.

U.S. officials such as William Colby and Michael Forrestal—who, within weeks of Westmoreland's arrival in Vietnam, had noticed the deputy commander's ambition "to take over the complete direction of the war from the ambassador"—had been aware of the capacity of MACV to absorb all counterinsurgency operations since its creation in 1961.[15] And Nes, of course, could have no influence over the military chain of command, with its separate communications channels to Washington. So although Nes's intentions were to improve the organization of the U.S. mission in general, he had inadvertently accelerated a trend in militarization of the war effort. Lodge would be unable subsequently, if indeed he had ever stood a chance of doing so, to put this into reverse.

The Nes Committee met over a period of four weeks. Its members liaised on a broad cross-section of the U.S. mission's concerns. William Sullivan, director of the newly created Interdepartmental Vietnam Coordinating Committee in Washington, praised the activities of the Pacification Committee as "the only truly executive operation we have had in Viet Nam for many months," continuing that he had read, and distributed, Nes's minutes of its meetings as "the best source of information about U.S. action in Viet Nam."

Dunn, who like Lodge received copies of all the Pacification Committee's proceedings, eventually grasped the reality: the deputy chief of mission and the deputy military commander were running the U.S. mission to the exclusion of the ambassador and General Harkins. He alerted Lodge. During a session in the U.S. chancery building in early April, Lodge interrupted the discussion. He called Nes out of the room, telling him to cancel the meeting and disband the group. Nes wrote to Sullivan: "If Ambassador Lodge has the executive skill and is able and willing to give the time and effort which Westmoreland and I put into the Pacification Committee, we will have achieved the result desired by Washington, and in a far preferable and more normal way. If not, the operations of the Mission will revert to the chaotic and unco-ordinated state in which I found them on my arrival in January. We shall see."[16]

Johnson should have recalled Lodge at this stage, if not sooner, when he first became aware of the deputy chief of mission's dilemma. To recall the ambassador was the normal presidential procedure when his overseas representative rejected the services of an administrator appointed precisely because of the head of mission's lack of skills in one or another area—in this case, coordination and resource management. The Nes appointment could not be salvaged by sending someone else to act as Lodge's "chief of staff," as Michael Forrestal was to suggest on March 30, for Lodge did not want such an officer.

The problem was not so much that Lodge was a nonprofessional and had no training as a Foreign Service officer. Kennedy, in particular, had looked to quite other qualities in Lodge in sending him to Vietnam, and the appointment of nonprofessional ambassadors to overseas posts was not uncommon in U.S. diplomatic tradition. The problem was that he would not delegate. As even David Nes attested, had the ambassador been prepared to delegate responsibility, some much-needed coordination might have been brought to the contribution of the various U.S. agencies and departments to the war effort. But Lodge refused to devolve any ambassadorial function, although, as his deputy chief of mission later observed, he spent not more than four to five hours a day on desk work in Saigon.

Lodge's reliance on Colonel Dunn was inappropriate and tactless; Dunn could not possibly perform at the same time the roles of special assistant to the ambassador, deputy chief of mission, and Lodge's special envoy in the Vietnamese provinces. Indeed, Dunn's appointment as executive secretary of the U.S. mission shortly before Lodge's departure from Saigon in June came close to a major breech of discipline, although the ambassador seems to have been unaware of this. Lodge was to reflect in writing "Vietnam Memoir" in 1967, "While recognizing the importance of organization, I believed that I did not perhaps attach quite as much importance to it as was attached in Washington. *I believed that able men with a real understanding of a subject can make a thing go* [emphasis added]."[17] But in a period when organization was to prove vital, Lodge had lost contact with the heads of agencies and, as we shall see, his extra-mission sources did not serve him well.

Johnson's motivations for keeping Lodge in Saigon were peculiarly his own: he wanted to temporize on Vietnam until he could achieve electoral victory as president in his own right in November. He therefore had to negotiate the demands of the Joint Chiefs of Staff for escalation, while keeping the question of how the war was being run from becoming an issue in the press. Barry Goldwater's very extremism, Johnson apparently reasoned, could play into his hands as he held back from an open commitment to war on North Vietnam. There was also the problem of liberals such as Senators Fulbright and Mansfield, who opposed America's increasing involvement in Vietnam. To neutralize them he would instruct William Bundy, assistant secretary of state for Far Eastern affairs since Roger Hilsman had resigned from the post in March, to prepare a resolution intended to gain congressional support for the president's actions in Vietnam without a declaration of war. Johnson would carry this document in his pocket from May until August.

In August, a suitable demonstration of alleged North Vietnamese aggression against U.S. personnel and property would be located in the Gulf of Tonkin, although Halberstam and others have persuasively argued that the North Vietnamese government attacks on American vessels had followed extended CIA harassment of North Vietnamese boats. The subsequent Gulf of Tonkin Resolution achieved Johnson's aims for a holding operation on Vietnam. The resolution did not declare America at war. It did not specifically authorize the dispatch of troops; Johnson already had the power to use U.S. forces for combat duty in his capacity as commander in chief. Rather, as Johnson had intended, the Gulf of Tonkin Resolution recorded a common U.S. approval and support for the actions of the president.[18]

In the light of these considerations, in March 1964 Johnson set aside his earlier criticisms of Lodge and resolved to have him continue in Saigon. What could Lodge be offered to make him stay? What was his price? The answer was not long in coming: Lodge was a patriot and a veteran public official; Johnson would wrap him in the flag. As McNamara prepared to leave for his March inspection tour, the president instructed him: "One of the most important things you can do for me in South Vietnam is to talk privately on my behalf with Cabot Lodge. I have the highest regard for him as a patriot and a public servant, and I want him to know at first-hand of my determination that we in Washington must do everything we can to back him up as the top American in Vietnam." He then went on, apparently without a qualm: "He is an old friend of mine from the Senate, and the simplest way of emphasizing my high opinion of him is to say that I recommended him for your job after the election of 1952." Johnson then consulted White House aide Forrestal regarding his record of State's responses to Lodge's suggestions from Saigon. According to Forrestal, only two major policy requests had been less than fully met. These were, first, the old Lodge perennial of having de Gaulle make a statement clarifying the terms of his call for the neutralization of Vietnam, and second, urgings for "more pressure" to be brought on North Vietnam. Johnson instructed McNamara to tell Lodge that Washington was doing everything possible to give his ambassador support in both areas, and further that Lodge must unhesitatingly advise him of anything else he might need.[19]

Johnson achieved what he had set out to do. The cable traffic from Saigon increased markedly in volume, particularly on the two subjects of de Gaulle and pressures on North Vietnam. Indeed, General Khanh quickly responded to the U.S. ambassador's new tone and promoted his own ideas for a general South Vietnamese mobilization and belligerence against the North.

But Johnson had read Lodge incorrectly. Lodge had no intention of leaking to the press to open a debate on the conduct of the war, although this was an option open to an ambassador. To go public while on government service would have been utterly against his sense of the need for discipline in the conduct of foreign relations.

Lodge was, however, concerned with one issue in particular. This was the increasing role of the U.S. military in Vietnam programs. He stressed repeatedly to American planners, as he had to Minh on January 10, the need to create "the proper political atmosphere" in which people would trust the South Vietnamese government. He argued that the U.S. had paid more attention to the military side of the war than to the civil "ideological" and security side: writing to McNamara on May 20, he asked that he, McNamara, and Maxwell Taylor put out a joint internal directive to the effect that the military saw the advantage of political programs, that they were complementary to the fighting activities of MACV, and that the responsibility for all such work lay with the ambassador. He had urged much the same ideas upon Rusk four weeks earlier, stressing that it was not in the interests of MACV that the ambassador be a soldier. On both these occasions, he used the personal letter form he regarded as the only legitimate vehicle through which men at the top could express policy criticisms.[20]

As he wrote in "Vietnam Memoir," when he felt in 1967 that he should resign his position as U.S. ambassador over the same issue—the increasing militarization of the war—he did not do so for three reasons. He agreed with the basic aims of the American effort in Vietnam, he felt he could best achieve policy change by face-to-face discussions with the president, and "he felt a public disagreement would have led to him revealing official secrets, which he felt bound not to do."[21]

William Bundy told Johnson as much in June. Johnson asked Bundy in April "to keep a close check on Lodge's recommendations on belligerence, and to ensure that each was met with a response." Two months later, the then assistant secretary of state for Far Eastern affairs reported orally to Johnson. Lodge would not leak to the press, Bundy said, because his sense of patriotism would prevent him from doing so.

But the mission coordination problem remained. According to Robert Miller, the former first secretary of the U.S. embassy in Saigon, "Washington's concept of counterinsurgency for South Vietnam was devised to be a bureaucratic nightmare." Components of the program grew to serve the needs of the various American organizations at home: the Pentagon required a large military representation; CIA demanded intelligence assignments; the Department of State needed a political section; AID wanted economic programs to administer; and so on. All of these initiatives were imposed from above, from the White House, and not as a response to local needs in Vietnam, Miller said.

The minutes of the Pacification Committee's meetings illustrate the problem.[22] When a Charter for Psychological Operations was discussed on April 7, the following advisory monster saw the light: MACV would advise the South Vietnamese government on military psychological operations, USOM on civilian technical assistance, and CIA on covert operations; the embassy would give political guidance and USIS would supply overall coordination. This committee would be subordinate to the Pacification Committee, which would coordinate liaison with the government of Vietnam.

One of the Pacification Committee's main functions in its short life was to generate other committees. As Nes had warned in his "Where We Stand in Vietnam," a vital policy decision had to be made on whether or not the U.S. was prepared to enter a military confrontation with North Vietnam and, ultimately, with China. Otherwise, the American presence in South Vietnam would simply expand of its own momentum without providing effective assistance to the South Vietnamese government in fighting the war. For growth in the American organizations in South Vietnam had another stimulus; Vietnam had become a posting of opportunity and a destination for opportunists. Service in Vietnam guaranteed speedy promotions in the U.S. Armed Forces. Colonel Dunn, for instance, did not hide the fact that he had sought a Saigon assignment to increase his chances of rising to the rank of general, an ambition that he did indeed fulfill. Reports proliferated in part because generating them was the way to preferment in both the military and civil administrations. In conjunction with the March McNamara visit to South Vietnam, Chester Cooper, formerly a CIA analyst but at that time chairman of the Reporting and Intelligence Subcommittee of the Interdepartmental Vietnam Coordinating Committee, prepared a set of recommendations for the improvement of reports interpreting progress in the war. He wrote that although he had tried to streamline their compilation, there was a "substantial amount of reporting from all elements of the U.S. Mission that appears to be of marginal use, duplicatory or otherwise unnecessary." His recommendation, however, was that *more* U.S. officials were needed at South Vietnamese province level to process the data.[23]

Lodge, predictably enough, did nothing to address the issue of excessive paperwork. Whatever else his failings in this period, he did, however, maintain a keen sense of the role of press reporting on Vietnam in influencing congressional funding for the war.

Nes, the administrator, was impatient with requests from Washington for comments on newspaper stories, an insensitivity for which Sullivan mildly admonished him, saying, "Vietnam appears too much in the news and is followed so closely by our highest officials." Lodge understood. Thirteen provinces of the Mekong Delta had been targeted as the focus of intensified pacification programs since the Honolulu conference of November 20. In March, MACV suggested that two more provinces, Gia Dinh and Bien Hoa, be added to the U.S. mission's critical list; MACV's concern was based on evidence of Communist bases in the area and the proximity of the provinces to the capital. Lodge, however, refused permission.[24] The newspapermen, after all, were based in Saigon. If the provinces closest to the city received a rating that could be interpreted as indicating a downturn in the progress of the war, the headlines could be disastrous.

At the end of March, Forrestal reported on the state of the U.S. mission in South Vietnam in much the same terms as he and Hilsman had used in January 1963. There was no overall concept for running the war, Forrestal wrote, since Harkins was wedded to use of the battle tactics of a conventional war, but Westmoreland, who understood counterinsurgency, was not working with the ambassador. It was difficult to find leaders for the agencies who were also team players; Nes could not perform all the coordination functions he had been appointed to handle; it might be necessary to find Lodge another officer to serve as his chief of staff; to make matters worse, Lodge might resign and the search would have to begin again for an ambassador who could control both civilian and military superiors and staff. Forrestal ended on a note of despair: "Chet Cooper is completely right. This is a Greek tragedy, and the curtain is slowly descending."[25]

Nguyen Ngoc Huy, under Premier Khanh assistant to Vice Premier Nguyen Ton Hoan, described the situation in South Vietnam in 1964: "In a nutshell, the Diem regime was more authoritarian, but less corrupt, the generals' regime was more corrupt but more liberal . . . everyone exploited his position as the Americans poured more money into Vietnam."[26]

In an effort to boost the morale of the Vietnamese troops, and so to strengthen the war effort, Lodge requested on February 20 that the U.S. fund an increase in ARVN pay and in aid monies in general. Johnson had promised him two days before that he should have whatever he felt was necessary: such hope was invested in Khanh's ability to lead South Vietnam that Washington's new grant carried no conditions regarding better performance.[27]

Khanh was therefore able to announce a 20 percent increase in pay for all privates and corporals at Vietnamese New Year. Khanh then moved to ensure loyalty to himself among the young colonels who had supported his coup by giving them promotions and creating new ranks in the hierarchy to accommodate them. The increase in U.S. aid was quickly absorbed by the members of the new Military Revolutionary Council, each one of whom had a large entourage in addition to the usual Vietnamese extended family. Temptation must have been hard to withstand, for as much as Ambassador Lodge denied it, the U.S. was in search of clients in a colonialist situation, and so cynicism among the Vietnamese officers was to be expected. As Lucien Conein remembered, "Hell, all of them had refrigerators and air conditioners . . . you might only get one chance at the trough."[28]

Patronage in all its forms was traditional in Vietnamese society. Hence the charge against the commander of 2 Corps who was accused of corruption in September 1964 was that of "inordinate dishonesty." He was not charged with extortion as such: the point was that his greed had exceeded customary expectations. But with the influx of American money the acceptable demands and rake-offs increased. Members of the government and the bureaucracy cornered monopolies on the distribution of licenses such as permits to build and to sell commodities, and services such as the connection of electrical power. Given the complicated funding arrangements for the American counterinsurgency advisory programs, payrolls could easily be faked. Again, the South Vietnamese military controlled the roads and so could charge for safe passage. By March the situation was grave. Although America was funding the war at the level of two million dollars a day, some civil servants and army officers were being paid late or not at all, and peasants in various areas received no U.S.-funded subsidies when they were asked to relocate as part of pacification programs.[29]

If Lodge was aware of corruption and graft in South Vietnam, he cannot have appreciated its extent and relation to the increase in U.S. aid. He may have accepted, as did other officers of the mission such as Nes and Pike, that a certain leaching of funds was to be expected in any underdeveloped country and that disorganization was difficult to overcome once it had set in. He notified Rusk at the end of May that he had heard rumors concerning the distribution of USOM supplies in the provinces, recommending that "some incisive and incorruptible inspection out of Washington is needed." But rather casually, given the actuality of millions of U.S. dollars disappearing per week, he washed his hands of the problem with the phrase, "Of course, I have not the facilities to investigate."[30]

Lodge was notoriously bewildered by economics and budgeting procedures. Philip Habib, his political counselor during Lodge's second tour of duty in Vietnam, recalled that Lodge was inclined to ask, "What was that all about?" after he had listened to the simplest excursion into economics. When the ambassador queried the Vietnamese generals in April regarding the funding situation, he accepted their explanation that the bookkeeping system they had inherited from the French had "immobilized" their best efforts. In his cables he subsequently described the problem as due to "lack of piaster support" for programs and to "slow release of piasters."[31]

The key meeting occurred on April 30. State had inquired why dollars and supplies had not reached projects in the provinces for which they were intended, and why the ARVN had been unable to increase its manpower and expand its paramilitary units. Westmoreland and Brent were present with Lodge when Khanh's new minister for national economy, the Harvard-trained Nguyen Xuan Oanh, representing the South Vietnamese government, once again tendered the explanation of the French-inherited bureaucratic problem. No one denounced the lie. The deputy military commander, the director of USOM, and the secretary of state all accepted the cover-story, along with the ambassador. The continuation of the war was more important than the truth.[32]

It would seem then that Lodge, with his reliance on his own sources and political instincts, did not have the range of contacts in this period to inform himself of what was common knowledge. Nguyen Ngoc Huy, as a member of the

South Vietnamese government, knew of the growing corruption, as did Lucien Conein, the American confidant of the Vietnamese generals. It was evident to observers from countries other than America, such as Dennis J. Duncanson, the British observer, and a byword among the newspapermen.[33]

The promotion system tended to sift bad news from official reports. Therefore, Lodge's own failure to provide Washington with accurate information was a lapse of the gravest import, no matter what considerations he may have had of the continuing need to mollify Congress. The evidence seems to be that he simply did not know what was happening: on May 16 he cabled that the solution to the dispersal-of-funds problem was for the president to send more money, in order to give "evidence of U.S. faith" in the efforts the Vietnamese were making.[34]

Although by May 1964 there had been no major policy review on America's options in Vietnam, one tendency was firmly in place: when the Vietnamese were perceived to be inefficient, more Americans were sent in. Rusk's comments on the situation in South Vietnam a week after Lodge's "need to prove U.S. faith" cable exemplified this process. Rusk began, "I can't see why we are just now able to approve a January budget. I can't see why materials in warehouses and pipelines cannot be moved promptly to the countryside to achieve the purpose for which such materials are being supplied." He recognized the problems of making haste in "the East," but "surely administration can go on a war footing and French techniques of triple entry bureaucracy can be set aside in order to get prompt action? *Somehow we must change the pace at which these people move and I suspect that this can only be done with a pervasive intrusion of Americans into their affairs* [emphasis added]."[35]

At first Khanh appeared to promise much. On February 21 he agreed to accept U.S. military advisors at the district levels, the point on which Minh had demurred six weeks before. He also welcomed American civilian advisors at the ministerial level of his government. On May 4 he accepted American bombing of North Vietnam as policy and began to enthusiastically support the idea. Khanh also requested an Army Corps of ten thousand Special Forces, saying, "One American can make soldiers out of ten Orientals." Lodge transmitted the sycophantic remark without comment.[36]

The skills for which Lodge had been sent to Vietnam were in public relations, and so in March he devised a program for Khanh. The Vietnamese leader in the tropics should give "fireside chats," over the radio, in the manner of President Roosevelt. By this means, the American said, the South Vietnamese government could "appropriate the social revolution." Lodge was enthusiastic about the broadcasts, which an informant told him "were getting to be like a holy hour," with people traveling miles to hear them. Rusk duly congratulated him on the improvement of U.S. press reporting on Khanh's performance. Lodge apparently did not realize, however, that Khanh had taken over a Sunday series of addresses from his vice premier, Nguyen Ton Hoan. Subsequently, Hoan's name was increasingly linked with coup plots to overthrow the regime.[37]

Lodge welcomed Khanh's May resolution to put the country under martial law. There is no indication in the major cables Lodge transmitted on this matter, or in his personal papers, that he suspected that Khanh had taken this decision because he feared for his own position, although rumors of plots against the premier were rife in this period. In answer to Rusk's query as to Khanh's motive in declaring martial law, he replied simply that Khanh was thinking "as any professional soldier" who wanted victory.[38]

When Khanh promulgated a decree dissolving the Council of Notables, the representative body that had been established by the Minh regime, promising elections within four to six months, Lodge's optimism continued undaunted. He cabled, "The details of intended steps towards a constitution are as yet unknown, but one point is crystal clear: Constituent Assembly when it materializes will have something both government and Military Revolutionary Council lack, i.e., a popular mandate." At his first press conference, Khanh had announced his intention to establish the basis for a popularly elected parliament within one year. However, this was something of a ritual promise and one that General Minh had made after his own coup; elections could always be postponed by an appeal to the exigencies of the war.[39]

With hindsight, the collapse of the Council of Notables in April 1964 stands out as one of the great missed opportunities for America to spread responsibility for the fate of South Vietnam. In summing up the gist of reports from embassy officials two weeks after the Khanh coup, Nes noted that many Vietnamese had come to the conclusion that early elections were not possible under the prevailing security conditions. If politically aware Vietnamese had at first criticized the Council of Notables as an appointed and not an elected body, Nes reported, these criticisms had subsided, because the council did at least have broad geographical, religious, and factional representation.[40] The council may have been better suited to South Vietnam's complicated and overlapping constituencies than the two-party system of government that American planners always envisioned. If some of its members were neutralist, this very circumstance may eventually have offered America a way to spread responsibility for the fate of the region. There is no evidence, however, that Lodge ever considered this possibility.

In "Vietnam Memoir," Lodge recorded that he had thought in May 1964 that Khanh "was really taking hold. I never could understand what happened to Khanh during the summer of 1964 and how the whole situation blew up so that there was a succession of changes of government."[41]

Lodge was certainly aware of continual coup plotting among the generals on Khanh's Military Revolutionary Council because this was a matter of priority in his cables to State.[42] But he was not in touch with what was happening at the province level. Khanh himself proved to be no administrator; many competent officials had been lost in the reorganization after the November coup, but almost all experienced people disappeared after the Khanh coup.

In the first half of 1964, U.S. military reporters strove to be optimistic, but the evidence was bleak. If in some places the attitude of the ARVN had improved as a response to pay rises, everywhere the morale of the militia and youth units, necessarily the backbone of counterinsurgency, was poor. In several provinces the paramilitary forces were reported to be, at best, only marginally effective. Training programs were stalemated, often due to lack of funds from the central government but also as a result of inexperienced leadership. Almost everywhere the story was the same: frequent changes in province chiefs and officials led to inefficiency and distrust on the part of the population. The province of Phuoc Thanh, for example, had four different chiefs between January and May. Where the people expressed a preference for the South Vietnamese government rather than the Communists, this seemed to be related to the government's inefficiency at collecting taxes, as against the Communists' outstanding abilities in this respect.[43]

U.S. embassy officials reported much the same picture. They also elaborated on extremely complex factional deals and maneuvering for power between Buddhists and Catholics, Cao Dai and Hoa Hao, Communists and South Vietnamese government officials, and between French plantation owners and all these local groups. Regarding Tay Ninh province on the border of Cambodia, one American official reported that the area was ready for pacification, although 80 percent of its territory remained outside government control! Land reform was minimal, since landlords and their agents moved in to gather back taxes once an area was wrested from the enemy and was back under South Vietnamese government control.[44]

USOM officials in the provinces complained that they could only implement effective controls at the "spigot" end of the U.S. aid channels where security and stability already existed.[45] But this denied the reality. By May 1964, in some areas of South Vietnam USOM and MACV structures provided the only administrative organization there was, apart from that of the Viet Cong.

Lodge was also unaware of his own role in demonstrating that coup making was a lucrative way to advancement. The consequences of the two precedents were not long in coming, admittedly after Lodge's return to Washington. An abortive coup against Khanh occurred on September 13, 1964; on October 27, a civilian government was formed with Phan Khac Suu as president and Tran Van Huong as premier; on December 20 a group of younger military officers known to the American embassy as the "Young Turks" wrested power from the civilians; a further civilian government under the leadership of Pham Huy Quat was formed on February 16, 1965; real power, however, remained with the "Young Turks," who included Nguyen Cao Ky and Nguyen Van Thieu. On February 24, 1965, Nguyen Khanh left the country at Ambassador Taylor's urging, to become "ambassador-at-large" for South Vietnam. There was a further coup attempt on May 20. On June 12, 1965, a new military government was formed. Nguyen Van Thieu, who had participated in the Diem and Khanh coups as a divisional commander, gained the position of commander in chief of the Armed Forces, while Nguyen Cao Ky, a vice marshal in the well-equipped South Vietnamese Air Force, became prime minister. These two men retained the reins of power until the fall of South Vietnam in 1975. This, then, was the political culture in South Vietnam with which American planners had to work in saving the country.

As an open answer to letters he received in Saigon regarding the U.S. role in Vietnam, Lodge forwarded an essay of his own composition to Under Secretary of State Harriman in March 1964, suggesting Harriman arrange to have it published in *Foreign Affairs*. Pursuing his usual concerns, he wrote: "Foreign Affairs is widely commented on by columnists, editors and so-called 'opinion makers' generally—Undoubtedly the most important single factor in the whole Vietnam problem is support from the American home front." The article, which Lodge had originally titled "Persistence in Viet-Nam," was published eventually in a modified form in *Life* Magazine under the title "How the World's Hottest Spot Looks to Me."[46] Since Lodge had intended publication in *Foreign Affairs*, the piece must be taken as a serious statement of his views on the war in the first quarter of 1964, and of the group at State with whose thinking he kept in step.

Lodge opened with a restatement of the domino theory. "Vietnam is the keystone for all Southeast Asia. The conquest of South Vietnam would immediately disturb Cambodia and Laos, and bring strong repercussions farther west in Thailand and Burma. It would shake Malaysia to the south. It would surely threaten Indonesia. Then, if Indonesia were unable or unwilling to resist, the Chinese

Communists would be on the doorstep of Australia. Finally, eastward, the repercussions for the Philippines and Formosa would be severe." The American investment in the war had by 1964 raised the stakes considerably. Lodge now called Vietnam the test case in stemming the spread of Chinese-backed "wars of liberation" everywhere. Further, America's reputation for strength and willingness to honor commitments to allies and be the policeman of "the free world" were now on trial in Indochina.

Since the enemy did not confine its efforts to borders and treated the Mekong basin as one strategic area, Lodge went on, so should the U.S. Talk of neutralization of South Vietnam was a trick, for how could a weak, neutral South Vietnam negotiate at the conference table with a strong North Vietnam present as a member of the Communist bloc? Any conversations with Hanoi must depend on the North immediately ceasing its aggression in South Vietnam. Meanwhile, America should fight on the grounds in which it was superior to the Communists, Lodge argued, for U.S. troops could probably not match young "Oriental" guerrillas who were used to heat and deprivation. The Communists' main advantage was "a molelike patience"; Americans must develop a similar persistence and the will to use the technological force at their command.

Here is the tragedy: Lodge in common with American planners, in a seemingly barely conscious shift, had made U.S. honor and the fate of the free world the stakes in Vietnam, without a commitment to total war, and in full knowledge of the weakness of both the South Vietnamese government and the American popular will to persist year after year.

As we have seen, U.S. officials of the State Department were not prepared to push for a full-scale review of policy options, let alone disengagement. And it is now clear that the Joint Chiefs and others at the Pentagon were determined to enlarge the war.

One of the possibilities left largely unexplored in the period of policy-stalling in mid-1964 was to spread responsibility for the fate of South Vietnam to a larger world community. And although Lodge was no mission coordinator, he did have the skills to draw other nations' leaders into commitments to U.S. ends. He had his European contacts and those from his United Nations days. Indeed, he had contemplated his former appointment at the Atlantic Institute in exactly such political and diplomatic terms. In May 1962 he presented a working paper to Secretary of State Rusk, proposing that the institute could serve as a "free world" forum—including France and Japan—to "make it easier for the U.S. when it felt obliged to act unilaterally" to induce another member nation to act as "initiator . . . for the action which the U.S. desires."[47]

But Johnson was not thinking along lines such as these: he was thinking of undeclared bombing raids on the North accompanied by feelers to Hanoi for surrender. In mid-March the president adopted a policy of "tit-for-tat" air strikes on targets in North Vietnam, in addition to covert actions across the borders of Laos and Cambodia on the enemy's supply lines under OPLAN 34-A. The formula Lodge and Johnson agreed upon was that the U.S. would bomb only in retaliation for Communist attacks on American property; the U.S. ambassador was instructed to search for a key incident.[48] Lodge had earlier suggested that d'Orlandi, the Italian ambassador in Saigon, could facilitate contact with the leadership in Hanoi through the Polish representative on the International Control Commission, the inspection body supervising the 1954 Geneva Accords. In March, Johnson accepted Lodge's further suggestion that the Canadian diplomat J. Blair Seaborn, a more recent appointee to the commission, be used as the emissary to North Vietnam. Seaborn had the advantage over the Pole, Meiczyslaw Maneli, in that Lodge knew him well from the days when they had both served at the United Nations.[49]

Seaborn opened a year-long dialogue with the North Vietnamese premier, Pham Van Dong, in June 1964. The bombing raids, enthusiastically endorsed by Lodge, served as a "Goldilocks" option in the election year: not too hot, as troop commitment would have been, and not too cool, as doing nothing would have appeared.

In spite of his public stance on the war effort, in Saigon Lodge felt increasingly disillusioned as to the possibility of Americans working through the Vietnamese. The projects in which he took an interest foundered one after another. In May he wrote in a rare letter to a friend that "the obstacles succeed one another, many of them delicate and complex to the last degree. Just when I heave a sigh of relief because one thing is settled, something else looms over the horizon. But I really do think that we are laying the ground for something very good and that we will really be on our way in a year if General Khanh is not murdered."[50]

In the middle of April 1964, Khanh's radio talks petered out. Sporadic efforts made to recruit Buddhist energies to the service of American foreign policy came to nothing. The fragmented groups that established themselves as welfare organizations tended to turn into political parties, which the embassy then could not fund. Lodge received so many rumors of splits in the Buddhist leadership and feuding between Buddhist factions that he suggested to Rusk that the Dalai Lama should be invited to South Vietnam to explain what life was like for religious believers under communism![51]

In spite of concern in the Department of State over mounting public sympathy in America for Diem's brother Ngo Dinh Can, who had not been brought to trial by either Minh or Khanh, Lodge could do little to speed matters up. It seems that both Minh, as chief of state, and Khanh, as chairman of the MRC, had the authority to grant a pardon to Can, but neither would give way to the other. The labyrinthine complexities of South Vietnamese political life allowed no simple solution, although Lodge spoke to Khanh repeatedly and took the extraordinary step of traveling to the religious center of Hue in an attempt to persuade Tri Quang, the monk he had saved from Diem's police in August, to intercede for Can's life.[52]

On the related question of the trial of Maj. Dang Sy, held in custody since May 1963 in connection with the Buddha birthday deaths, Lodge received an urgent message from Monsignor Asta, the papal delegate, almost exactly a year after the initial event. Asta warned that the South Vietnamese government's choice of date for the trial would coincide with the lunar calendar anniversary of the Hue affair and thus might precipitate a religious war. A letter the South Vietnamese bishops delivered to Khanh a day later charging that the Khanh government attack on Dang Sy was an attack on the church itself appeared to make the possibility all the more likely.

In response to the bishops' letter, Lodge summoned Khanh to a secret meeting at the residence. It was vital to avoid religious strife, he urged in the gravest terms. He advised, "If public opinion in the world thought that Christians were being discriminated against and persecuted in Vietnam, then many people would see no, I repeat, *no* reason to support this government against the Communists, and bloodshed would make the efforts of thoughtful people well nigh useless."[53] His frustration must have been great; these were almost the same phrases he had used to Diem regarding his relations with the Buddhists eight months before.

Lodge's exasperation with Vietnamese internal politics reached a climax when he found that Khanh was unable to make appointments of ambassadors abroad in order to attract contributions for South Vietnam's struggle against communism because of factional rivalries within his government. The issue was critical. Rusk wanted a representative of South Vietnam at the United Nations

Security Council meeting scheduled to take place on May 21 to deny U.S.–South Vietnamese government cross-border raids into Cambodian territory and so avert a U.N. investigation. But by the time Saigon could supply an observer, the Cambodians had had several days to publicize their case.[54]

Lodge tartly observed that it might be more efficient for Americans to assume complete responsibility for representing the South Vietnamese. "You can find many Vietnamese around town who will tell you frankly that they would like the Americans to run the country for ten years," he continued. Dean Rusk was equally impatient. "Is there any way we can shake the main body of the Vietnamese leadership by the scruff of the neck?" the secretary demanded on May 21.[55]

The U.S. ambassador finally felt compelled to address himself to the idea that American officials might have to be put in control at all levels of the South Vietnamese government. On May 22 he wrote, "This unhappy country emerged from colonialism ten years ago and has been trying to get along since then with help from us that is, in all truth, advisory and not at all colonial. The question clearly arises as to whether this 'advisory' phase is not about to be played out and whether the United States will not have to move into a position of actual control. This time has clearly not arrived yet, but it may be approaching. Whether it means that we will have a High Commissioner or a Commissioner General, or a man who really gives the orders under the title of Ambassador will have to be determined in the light of circumstances as they develop."[56] As Lalouette had warned Diem and Nhu the year before, the U.S. had come with advice at first, but eventually the advisors would take over because they thought they alone had the expertise to run the country.

On June 18, 1964, Lodge wrote to Rusk, telling him that he was leaving Saigon in order to influence the Republican convention, to be held in July. It seems this was a respectable way to for him to resign from a post that was becoming increasingly onerous and frustrating. His letter of resignation to Johnson, dated June 19 and effective from the end of the month, stated that he was resigning his position as U.S. ambassador to Vietnam "entirely for personal reasons." His official explanation that his wife's health had deteriorated in the tropical climate was an acceptable way out.[57]

The expedient time for Lodge to return to America would have been March or April. That he did not do so immediately after the New Hampshire victory was undoubtedly due to his sense of duty. His scruples in not going to the press regarding his criticisms of the conduct of the war may have deprived him of his last chance to take a stand against the militarization of the American effort in Vietnam and MACV's increasing control of pacification programs. Again, he did not recruit support in Washington for his view that it would be counterproductive to commit U.S. ground forces to South Vietnam. Organizing the numbers for debate was not his way. Instead, he communicated his views in an urgent, personal letter to the president, notifying Johnson that this would arrive via special courier. His prescient words deserve extensive quotation. Lodge wrote in June 1964: "I still have faith that naval and air power, with clearly limited and very specific actions on the ground can give us what we need. If the Chinese communists attack on the ground in a place of their own choosing, I cannot see why we must oblige them and why we cannot retaliate in a place and a way of our own choosing. It is dangerous for us to put the *manpower* of a nation of 190 million against the *manpower* of a nation of 900 million and thus put us on the short end of the stick. A largely U.S. venture of unlimited possibilities could put us onto a slope along which we slide into a bottomless pit." He urged Johnson to conduct a top-level secret meeting with his advisors and the Joint Chiefs of Staff to review the strategic options open to America in Vietnam. Johnson did not reply: no doubt he mentally consigned the letter to the trashcan. Lodge was yesterday's man.[58]

The 1964 GOP convention in July spelled the end of Lodge's presidential aspirations and the sunset of his own internationalist grouping in the Republican party. He returned to America too late to influence the outcome of the proceedings. He made a last-minute bid to support Governor Scranton's candidacy against that of Goldwater, but he found to his considerable bewilderment that the center of gravity of the GOP was now in the southern states and was drifting to the right. He complained that he knew hardly anyone at the convention. Goldwater's policy on Vietnam was to "tell the military commanders it was their problem and to get on with solving it."[59] Lodge could expect little sympathy from that quarter for his reservations as to how the war was being fought.

Given the man he was, Lodge's only option henceforth was to support presidential policy. He left Vietnam with feelings of greater pessimism for the direction of the war than he was prepared to say after his single bid to express his criticisms to Johnson.

Lodge's public stance throughout 1964 remained constant: the U.S. was winning in Vietnam. Accordingly, he reported to the Senate Committee on Foreign Relations on June 30: "I believe we ought to determine to stay with it. We have an American team and a Vietnamese team now that are aggressive with a really sharp focus. You might get the provinces around Saigon cleaned up in two years. That doesn't mean that there still isn't a lot of work to do, but it is mopping up work. As you know, mopping up work is just a much more cheerful occupation. So I would put it that way, that you might clean up these provinces right around Saigon in two years."[60]

Epilogue

In early February 1965, McGeorge Bundy placed a confidential telephone call to Lodge in New York. "The Boss wants to have a chance to catch up with you," he said. The president's special assistant for national security affairs went on to explain that the appointment of General Taylor as ambassador to Vietnam had not worked out on the political side. There were "real problems of communication between Max Taylor, Ky and the Buddhists." "More U.S. pressure was needed for police programs," and especially "more follow up." Could Lodge get to Washington before the end of the month?

By late February so many coups had occurred in South Vietnam that Barry Zorthian coined the term "revolving-door government." A second civilian government, formed that month under the nominal leadership of Dr. Phan Huy Quat, the medical man and politician who had stood aside from the Minh regime in November 1963, promised no greater stability since real power remained, if somewhat shakily, with air Vice Marshal Nguyen Cao Ky and Gen. Nguyen Van Thieu. By this time Nguyen Khanh was in New York. Lodge would entertain Khanh to a consolation dinner there on March 16 and sound him out on what position in the U.S. would keep him from further conspiracies, an initiative Lodge had suggested to Johnson in his capacity as informal special consultant to the president, which he had accepted on his return from Saigon.

Lodge was flattered to be summoned to the Oval Office on Vietnam policy, noting in his record of the first meeting on January 26 that Johnson had called upon him and not the other way around. He set to writing a lengthy paper entitled "Recommendations Regarding Vietnam," detailing his ideas for civil defense and political work, which he presented on March 8. Johnson responded to the paper, saying, "I marvel at your ability to do so much in so short a time. You

141

must have worked like hell." Johnson's praise struck the right note. Lodge had found himself unexpectedly bored in Beverly and was ready once again for the challenge of public service.[1]

At Johnson's request, Lodge had already made representations of U.S. policies in Vietnam in eight European capitals and also at the Vatican and in Japan during August and September 1964. *Newsweek* had run a special issue on the success of this NATO tour. He made a further circuit through the Pacific and Asian members of the Southeast Asia Treaty Organization in April and May 1965. On both tours he argued the American internationalist case that the spread of communism could be stopped by a strong stand against it in South Vietnam, and reported that in each country he visited commitments were undertaken to make some form of contribution to "Vietnam's struggle to remain free from Communism." He appears to have enjoyed the assignment enormously; his memorandums on his travels as the president's special representative read in marked contrast to the frustrated tone of many of his cables during his final weeks in Saigon in 1964.[2]

This mission as roving ambassador fulfilled the criteria Lodge had outlined to Kennedy in 1963 for a final public appointment: "not an easy job but something challenging." Johnson, with his usual political perspicacity, would appoint him as his ambassador-at-large after the conclusion of his second tour of duty in Vietnam, in March 1967.

As his influence in the U.S. political arena dimmed, Lodge found his satisfaction in the service of the presidency and loyalty to the incumbent. He was criticized by other Republicans, including his own brother, John Davis Lodge, for accepting Vietnam assignments under two successive Democratic administrations. But he strongly defended his commitment, arguing that there was no contradiction in a Republican serving the Democrats' Vietnam policy, as Republicans supported that policy in Congress. As he wrote to a critic, "I work for the President of the United States and not for any partisan administration."[3]

Lodge had a conventional point of view regarding the aims of the American presence in Vietnam. His occasional heretical suggestions were sporadic and lacked follow-through. He quickly returned to the modes of thinking prevailing in the Department of State and he did not pursue his instincts where they conflicted with the received wisdom or political exigencies in the U.S. But his difficulties in dealing with the dilemma of U.S. ends and means in Vietnam, during his first tour of duty in particular, can serve as a lens on the wider problems of the American engagement there.

On the same day as his first meeting with Johnson in November 1963, Lodge suggested to Harriman an interpretation of the vital interests of North Vietnam that ran contrary to a key assumption in the rhetoric of containment. Optimistic that there would be a speedy improvement in the war under the Minh regime, he said that "when SVN had made sufficient progress and clearly had the upper hand," word should be transmitted to the government of North Vietnam that the U.S. planned an air strike on targets in the North unless Hanoi desisted from support of the Viet Cong. He believed that North Vietnam feared an American air attack and that the Communists in North Vietnam were wary of the possibility of having to call on China for support, as they felt that once Chinese soldiers were on their territory, "they would never be able to get Red China out."[4]

Lodge, as we have seen, put his faith in American technology as the means of fighting the shooting war; as he wrote to Johnson in June 1964, China would always have the overwhelming advantage if the war were fought in terms of matching manpower. What was original about his November proposal was that it took cognizance of the possibility that there might be splits and differences in the Communist camp, regarded in the domino model as monolithic. China, of course, was U.S. planners' concern rather than Russia, North Vietnam's real patron, due to Truman's alleged "loss of China" in 1949–1950, and this concern clouded analysis in 1963 and 1964.

It is possible that Lodge grasped the significance of the historical enmity between Vietnam and China under the influence of P. J. Honey, the British scholar and possible London government consultant who was present in South Vietnam in August and September of 1963. Honey had many conversations with Lodge about Vietnam, he recalled. However, Lodge did not press this perception upon American officials during the period of plans for increased pressure on North Vietnam, which lasted throughout 1964. He quickly returned to the conventional view that North Vietnam was a dependent of China and that China might well enter the war on Hanoi's behalf: he had reverted to regarding Hanoi as aligned with Beijing as early as December 4, just ten days after his suggestion on North Vietnamese fear of China.[5] Indeed, in common with other members of the administration who had seen active service during World War II, he failed to remember that bombing designed to make the British sue for surrender had strengthened their morale, and that the same had been true when German cities had in turn been bombed with the same end in view.

Lodge's policy suggestions on U.S. relations with North Vietnam invariably contained a central misconception. To be fair to Lodge, he was not alone in this miscalculation, which was his consistent underestimation of the North Vietnamese Communists' powers of endurance and will to win, and the stalwartness of their supporters in the South. And so he welcomed plans for strategic bombing under National Security Action Memorandum 273 and the later memorandum 288 of March 17, 1964. He reasoned that such pressure would force Hanoi to negotiate, thus "bringing about a ceasefire by VC"—"and the neutralizing of North Vietnam, turning it into an oriental Yugoslavia." He later explained to Roger Hilsman that his plan for the neutralization of North Vietnam was *not* the same as that of de Gaulle, for what he envisioned was not a reunited Vietnam but a neutral North Vietnamese Communist state.[6] As history was to show, and as lone voices such as Kattenburg's at the National Security Council meeting after the failed August coup urged throughout the war, this was the most unlikely of scenarios. However, from the point of view of American public opinion in 1963 and 1964, Lodge was correct, as he usually was, for the bombing of North Vietnam then held more appeal than the options of either U.S. withdrawal from Vietnam or the commitment of ground troops.

Lodge did not want American infantry in South Vietnam. On this point he was consistent during his first ambassadorship, although later he accommodated to each step in the commitment of troops to the war. He believed that "Oriental" soldiers could fight better in the jungles of Indochina than Americans, and he foresaw some of the problems of morale that U.S. ground troops would face. As he explained to Premier Khanh on May 4, he "had been brought up on the idea, so often voiced by General MacArthur, that in Asia the United States could have great influence with its air power and its Navy and in working in support of Asiatic armies but that it was out of the question for the United States to commit a large land army to the mainland of Asia." He argued instead that a U.S. naval presence at Cam Ranh Bay could show the strength of American will and technology, without the risk of American military personnel swamping the efforts and independence of the ARVN.[7]

His instinct was to abhor the idea of large numbers of U.S. personnel overwhelming the country. He advocated instead that the South Vietnamese president be assigned four expert civilian consultants, to discreetly advise in matters of civil administration, foreign policy, press relations, and economics: he was delighted when Khanh suggested this idea back to him as his own request on in April 1964.[8] Yet in May 1964, only three weeks later, Lodge felt compelled to recommended that the U.S. might need to assume total responsibility for the administration of South Vietnamese affairs, and in the policy debates of July 1965 shortly before he returned for his second tour of duty in Saigon, he said little in the face of McNamara's arguments for the commitment of American ground troops to Vietnam.

Lodge's consistent perception that policing and political work might be as important as soldiering reached its clearest articulation in his police precinct civil defense program for Long An province. But even in his various papers and letters on this, there was more repetition of the necessity for "a proper political atmosphere" (Gen. Walter Bedell Smith's phrase) than clear conceptualization. He did not work out the details of his program and visited Long An province only once, in January 1964, reporting that the new political strategy he had recommended to the MRC was going well. His tour must have been superficial at best, for it subsequently turned out that Generals Don and Kim had not had the organization to achieve very much at all. He should have known that land reform would be a critical component of his program if it were to gain peasant support, and he did include the issue in his lists of objectives, but it appears that he never visited the land reform office in Saigon and possibly did not know of its existence.[9]

Indeed, in devising his countersubversion vision, Lodge seems to have succumbed to the rivalries among the U.S. agencies. He argued that his own plan "was not the old civic action program," that is, not the old CIA program. Yet the Agency did have the officers who had the longest experience in the political work Lodge advocated. When the Department of Defense took control of CIA's extensive paramilitary operations in Vietnam on November 1, 1963, in a post–Bay of Pigs disciplinary action, Lodge did not take advantage of Colby's subsequent offer to second his Vietnam men to MACV to supervise civil defense projects.

Lodge was out of his depth when it came to civil defense and the creation of ideologies for the energizing of the South Vietnamese. His ideas that Long An could be used as a "showcase" from which a "manual for defeating Communism" could be written, were superficial responses to complex situations.[10] But perhaps the real problem was in the concept of an American-led counterinsurgency program itself. The inappropriateness of Lodge's metaphor of U.S. metropolitan police precinct organization for a rural civil defense program, politely dismissed by Minh in January 1964, was only slightly more obvious than the later U.S. formulation of "Revolutionary Development" programs, when the Vietnamese revolution had clearly been appropriated by the Communists.

Lodge's true skill was in press management. This undoubtedly influenced his policy suggestions to Washington: bombing raids could be documented by U.S. journalists more dramatically than village security schemes.

Ambassador Lodge's attitude to American participation in international conferences dealing with Indochina issues illuminates one blind spot that drew the U.S. ever more deeply into the war. Lodge opposed all such meetings on the grounds that attendance would imply de facto American recognition of China. Second, he did not wish to give France a voice in Southeast Asian affairs. Accordingly, he advised against any U.S. response to Sihanouk's December 1963 proposal for a conference on Cambodian neutrality on the grounds that China and France would be entitled to attend; for the same reasons, six months later he opposed American attendance at a projected conference on Laos.[11] His usual arguments against neutralism, in these two cases, were secondary to his wariness of Paris and Beijing.

By 1964, of course, there were further pressing reasons for all U.S. planners to reject international investigations of American actions in Indochina, for the 1964 version of OPLAN 34-A had secretly endorsed illegal "overflights" of Laos using American planes and equipment but "non-U.S. crews." As a subject of even greater political delicacy, the Joint Chiefs of Staff lifted the original tight restrictions on cross-border operations on May 31, at which time a second phase of the plan came into operation. Therefore, when the Cambodians called in March for discussions at Geneva on suspected U.S. bombing of Khmer villages, Lodge cabled his objections in the strongest terms. He wrote: "Such a conference would certainly be used by France, the Chinese Communists, and the Soviets to torpedo our work against aggression in Viet-Nam. We must not treat France like an ally in Southeast Asia when she never acts like one nor wants to be considered as one."[12]

Lodge specifically did not wish to involve the United Nations in U.S. relations with Vietnam. Like other members of the Kennedy and then the Johnson administrations, he argued that the situation in Vietnam was one of direct military confrontation between the United States and the Communist bloc, and as such it was a problem for America to solve and not the U.N. As he said in an early 1964 letter to then Assistant Secretary of State Harlan Cleveland, any U.N. role in Vietnam would have to wait on "military stabilization." In reply to a query after an address at the Newport Naval War College in December of the same year, he wrote that the United Nations was not merely weak in its contemporary structure but was unlikely to serve U.S. interests in Indochina. Lodge said on that occasion, "I do not think the United Nations offers the solution to U.S. problems in South Vietnam. As at present constituted, it has neither the tools nor the will to do the job."[13]

Not long after his return from his first tour of duty in South Vietnam, Lodge set out his position on elections in that country. In writing to his old friend and Senate colleague Leverett Saltonstall in August 1964, he took an optimistic view of progress in the war. "Certainly we are not taken for granted; no one thinks today that the United States is hooked," he wrote, referring to his old problem with the Diem regime. "Nor does it seem to me very significant that it will probably not be possible to hold democratic elections and to introduce more of a civilian note in the conduct of the government. Vietnam has still not had the time to develop an elaborate democratic system such as exists in the West, and it must, in the immediate future, concentrate on military government which is efficient, just and humane."[14]

In his March 1965 "Recommendations Regarding Vietnam" paper for Johnson, he went much further: "The Vietnamese have no tradition of national government. They do not do it well. We should not hamper ourselves with the classic, diplomatic idea that for us to deal with anything below the national level is interference in internal affairs." He continued on to the logical conclusion from this analysis: a neutralist coup group that might topple the weak central government and invite the United States to leave should be ignored, as it would not represent the "true interests or desires of the Vietnamese people."

Shortly before accepting a second ambassadorship to Vietnam, Lodge in fact differed profoundly from Johnson in his view of the war. Johnson appeared to believe that a sovereign state called South Vietnam, to which the U.S. had treaty obligations, did in fact exist. Lodge was more inclined to see the geographic region called South Vietnam as the central part of the area in which the U.S. had chosen to demonstrate that it would not tolerate the spread of Communist-directed "wars of national liberation."[15] However, at the behest of State and against his own judgment, in 1966 he would assist air Vice Marshal Ky to develop a constitution and to hold elections. He would not oppose the president's interpretation that American honor demanded perseverance with troops in Vietnam. His own presidential ambitions laid to rest, Lodge at last became a team player.

By the beginning of 1965, the options for U.S. policymaking on Vietnam had narrowed to a choice between the "collapse" of the South and insertion of American troops. Bombing of North Vietnamese targets had commenced in early 1965. As America bombed North Vietnam to shore up South Vietnam, General Westmoreland, who had previously been against the introduction of U.S. ground troops, called for the dispatch of American soldiers, ostensibly to protect the

American airbase at Danang but in reality to assist the demoralized ARVN. Johnson agreed slowly to each demand from the Joint General Staff, whose bellicose suggestions were supported by many of his own civilian advisors. In 1965 he apparently had no real wish to negotiate while the South was weak, and after the success of his Tonkin Gulf maneuver he felt he could manage Congress without provoking a backlash. So began the escalation of the war. On March 8, 1965, two divisions of Marines landed at Danang; on May 4, Congress granted $700 million to support U.S. military operations in Vietnam; in July Johnson publicly approved the Joint Chiefs' plan for fifty thousand more troops.

The Tonkin Gulf Resolution, like so many other American initiatives in Vietnam, served to weaken further the already weakened South Vietnamese government. Khanh apparently read it as evidence that America was committed to preserving him in government. He granted himself near-dictatorial powers under his own legislation, the Vung Tau charter, and so triggered the first and ultimately successful coup attempts against his regime.[16]

Although McGeorge Bundy, Rusk, McNamara, and Robert Kennedy had all volunteered to replace Lodge as U.S. ambassador in Vietnam, Johnson appointed Gen. Maxwell Taylor as Lodge's successor in Saigon. Ignoring Lodge's earlier advice that the new appointee should be a civilian, Johnson chose his then chairman of the Joint Chiefs of Staff, apparently with the consideration of heading off the possibility of his military chiefs forming a lobby to criticize his Vietnam policy in an election year.[17] He may also have hoped that a soldier-to-soldier advisory relationship between the American chief of mission and the Vietnamese military government would produce efficient management and progress in the war.

The latter did not prove to be the case. Lodge could work with Khanh and Khanh was fulsome in his displays of affection for Lodge: when Lodge departed from Saigon in June 1964, Khanh presented him with a Vietnamese scholar's robe, which the tall, fair American wore clumsily but with good humor. Taylor, on the other hand, could not abide the Vietnamese general, whom he blamed for the endemic instability of South Vietnamese politics. On December 20, when Ky and Thieu staged a coup and Khanh arrested the members of the then civilian government, Taylor exploded to John Burke of the embassy Political Section: "If you took Khanh apart, you would not find one shred of principle." In Burke's words, when it came to South Vietnamese politics, Taylor simply "could not stand the mess."[18]

After Khanh left the country on Taylor's advice in January 1965 and Lodge met the ex-premier for dinner in New York, Khanh confided to him, "All my troubles date from your departure. You were like my older brother. You always gave me such good advice about politics. I don't know why Ambassador Taylor was so obviously hostile—The U.S. Ambassador to Vietnam should not be a soldier and he should not be a diplomat, but a politician—who's interested in the other man's point of view, which is the way a politician is."[19] Whatever else President Johnson may have felt about Khanh, he agreed with him on one thing: for his next ambassador to South Vietnam, he wanted a politician.

On March 24, 1965, Johnson asked Lodge who could replace Taylor in Vietnam. On the basis that there were few men available who could assume seniority to Taylor's deputy, U. Alexis Johnson, Lodge put forward his own name the next day. The appointment, a well-kept secret by Washington standards, was not announced publicly until July 9.

Johnson, like Kennedy before him, wanted a representative who would improve his press relations on Vietnam. The situation, of course, was grimmer than it had been in June 1963. American soldiers were about to be killed in combat, and in the universities the teach-ins had begun. Vietnam was on the front pages to stay. In briefing his new ambassador, Johnson complained to Lodge: "It seems impossible to get anything into the papers except having to do with bombs. I want so much to stress the non-military side, the political side." Lodge added, "He hoped that when I was there I would visit hospitals, orphanages, schools, agricultural projects and take all the press along with me."[20]

On July 22, Johnson finally decided to send U.S. troops to Vietnam, and in a closed meeting with the Joint Chiefs on the same afternoon, he agreed to what amounted to a secret, open-ended commitment of military forces. He refused to make a full public disclosure of what might ultimately be envisioned, not wishing to reveal either the whole financial cost of the war to Americans or the extent of U.S. engagement in Vietnam. Such revelations, he reasoned, could wait until 1966, after he had pushed his "Great Society" legislation through Congress.

Lodge attended the July 22 meeting as ambassador-designate. As the discussion between Johnson and his advisors progressed—Ball taking a stand against the dispatch of troops, Rusk saying that the decision was necessary to show the Communist world that the U.S. would pursue its commitments to the end, McNamara willing to go as far as calling up the Reserves for service in Asia—Lodge intervened with his own view of the proper nature of an American war effort in Indochina. He said, "We have great seaports in Vietnam. We don't need to fight on the roads. We have the sea. Visualize our meeting the Viet Cong on our own terms!—We don't have to spend all our time in the jungles".

But what Lodge had said was hardly heard, let alone taken up in debate.[21] The approach of preparing his numbers beforehand was alien to his temperament, and besides, as ambassador-designate he could hardly be expected to argue for a great deviation from the direction in which he sensed Johnson's mind to be moving.

After the swearing-in ceremony in the Rose Garden on August 12, Johnson presented Lodge with a photograph of the event inscribed "To Cabot, Statesman, Patriot, Friend." Whatever might be said of Johnson's sincerity, the description of Lodge at the beginning of his second tour of duty in Vietnam was accurate.

Saigon in August 1965 was much less charming than it had been two years earlier. Bombings and Communist-inspired acts of terror were more frequent, while riots in the coastal cities had increasingly anti-American overtones. U.S. officials' families had been evacuated from May onward; even before this, Barry Zorthian had sent his children to Delhi when they had been stoned in the street on their way to school. Lodge strongly urged Johnson that his wife Emily's presence in Saigon was essential to his own diplomatic function there, but he would now see his wife and closest companion only when security allowed for a journey into the war zone from Bangkok. Vietnam at this time was a hardship post. Asked why Lodge had returned to Vietnam for a second tour, Philip Habib answered briefly, "Why? Because the President asked him!"[22]

Lodge returned to Vietnam willing to perform as a team player. He was undoubtedly aware that his old independent style had lost much of its point, and his notes of his preparatory discussions in his Confidential Journal are full of references to coordination of the work of the agencies and the value of the Country Team approach.[23] The U.S. embassy in Saigon had become the largest America had abroad. Men such as William J. Porter, Lodge's deputy ambassador (U. Alexis Johnson having returned with Taylor to Washington), and Habib, his political counselor, were among the most experienced officers serving anywhere. There were greater numbers of staff at all levels and a score of Vietnamese linguists in the Political Section. The Mission Council, established by Ambassador Taylor, now met on a regular basis. Gone were the days when the chancery building locked up at 5:30 P.M., as it had done on the night when Gen. Nguyen Khanh had taken power.

If in Washington Lodge had thought that political programs in the villages of

Vietnam could turn the tide of the war, on reaching Saigon he privately recorded his first impression that the prospects for the survival of South Vietnam were bleak. He wrote: "The unending governmental instability, with ministries succeeding each other at intervals of a few months, had created a well-nigh hopeless situation. No officials had time to learn to do their jobs; what little time they had in government was spent in thinking of their own survival." Although, as Habib explained, an optimistic tone was obligatory in the cables they prepared together for Johnson, Lodge's thinking as reflected in his "Vietnam Memoir" was often closer to the summation of his then special assistant, Peter Tarnoff, twenty-five years later. Tarnoff said of Lodge's second ambassadorship in Vietnam: "Could anyone have made much of a difference at that time? The enemy was stronger; the enemy was more popular; the South Vietnamese government was weak. The U.S. embassy could never tackle these three problems at the same time."[24]

Since at the same time as Johnson had decided to send American troops into the war, he had also resolved to keep out feelers for negotiations using his diplomats, Lodge spent a great deal of his time during 1966 on a complex maneuver code-named "Marigold." In 1964 Lodge had recommended that the Canadian J. Blair Seaborn be used as the conduit to the North Vietnamese leadership. Seaborn had made five visits to Hanoi over the course of a year, before his offers of terms for a settlement were finally rebuffed by Pham Van Dong, the North Vietnamese premier, in June 1965.

In close touch with the foreign diplomatic community, his former U.N. contacts, and the members of the International Control Commission, Lodge was not particularly surprised when the Polish member of the commission, Januscz Lewandowski, met with him at Italian ambassador d'Orlandi's apartment on June 6, 1966, revealing that he felt Hanoi wished to parley with the United States. The Canadian commission member, Victor Moore, told him the same thing two days later. Lodge subsequently had six meetings with the Pole, each in d'Orlandi's apartment. The contact petered out in December, after the Christmas bombing pause.

Lodge later noted that "he sensed that the bombing had been conducted without regard to the diplomatic aspects and with inadequate control at the top." That is, while the U.S. ambassador was engaged in discussions with emissaries to Hanoi, he was not consulted on the timing and orchestration of the bombing of North Vietnam! Moreover, it appears that Westmoreland, as commander of MACV, had not been advised of the *diplomatic* initiative in train. Although Lodge had no knowledge of a secret Pentagon exercise carried out in late 1964, this had in fact demonstrated the futility of the air-strike strategy well before the bombing began in early 1965. War games conducted from September 10 to 15 had shown that even after all the listed North Vietnamese targets had been obliterated, Hanoi's capacity to increase the supply of weapons down its lines to South Vietnam would in no way be diminished. It therefore seems possible, as Franz Schurmann and others have argued, that in 1966 and 1967 the Department of State did not want a settlement, and further that it widened the war each time negotiations seemed likely.[25] Characteristically for Lodge at this point in his Vietnam association, he did not protest over these strangely secretive and seemingly self-defeating policy planning procedures.

Lodge's second major concern during his second embassy in Vietnam was, again, the increasing militarization of the war at the expense of civil defense. The developing domination of MACV over the other agencies we saw earlier in the relations between deputy commander Westmoreland and Deputy Chief of Mission Nes on the duplicate Country Team of early 1964. The theme reached its fulfillment in May 1967, when MACV gained control of all pacification programs. Westmoreland's defense of his campaign to gain control of the coordination of interagency projects, it must be said, was Lodge's lack of interest in the task, and the ambassador certainly gave up the fight midway by returning to the United States for a year in 1964 and 1965. Lodge's own surmise, as he recorded in "Vietnam Memoir" in 1967, was that, although he was never able to find out the exact terms of Westmoreland's mission assignment in Vietnam, "I came to the conclusion that the President wanted General Westmoreland to win a military victory by November 1968, by using conventional methods: war of attrition, seek and destroy, with American troops carrying the load of combat. As soon as I became aware of this, I objected to it orally and in writing."[26]

The connection of a win-the-war strategy with an American presidential election seems familiar enough, but Lodge's notation appears to be evidence for a lack of coordination in U.S. planning rather than for secret orders for an all-out attack on North Vietnam. The U.S. did not, after all, fortify the 17th parallel right across Laos and fight conventional battles against the Peoples Army of North Vietnam from there, the logical extension of the suspected directive and an approach Lodge himself had touched upon in his *Life* article "How the World's Hottest Spot Looks to Me."

In "Vietnam Memoir," Lodge devoted several impassioned pages and an appendix to the increasing power of the U.S. military in Vietnam; it was to be the incoming ambassador, Ellsworth Bunker, not he, who authorized Westmoreland's takeover of control of all counterinsurgency programs. But by March 1967 Lodge may simply, in Habib's words, have "had enough" of the beleaguered post in which he had served for thirty months in all. His second resignation from Saigon took effect on April 25, 1967.

In the second half of 1967, Lodge was to be found serving as a member of Johnson's assembly of senior consultants on foreign affairs, known to journalists as "The Wise Old Men," or WOM. On November 1, exactly four years after the death of Ngo Dinh Diem, Gen. Earle Wheeler, now chairman of the Joint Chiefs of Staff, was addressing the group. Wheeler gave a glowing report from the field: the military statistics, the body counts, the captured Communist documents—everything demonstrated that the U.S. was winning the war. The problem lay, as Johnson explained, in U.S. public opinion and negative reporting in the press. Lodge said nothing. Dean Acheson recommended citizen's committees in every city to talk up victory. McGeorge Bundy agreed. What was needed was a public relations campaign. What the administration should emphasize, Bundy said, was "the light at the end of the tunnel".[27]

Lodge died on February 27, 1985. He had served as U.S. chief negotiator at the Paris peace talks on Vietnam for eleven months in 1969 under the Nixon administration. His last private assignment, as Nixon's personal observer at the Vatican, the U.S. not officially recognizing the Holy See, may have been the position that gave him the most personal enjoyment since his service in World War II, moving then as he did in the European settings in which he and his wife Emily felt most at home. Of Vietnam, he wrote in 1977 in an unpublished essay: "Perhaps the most salient lesson to be learned from the Vietnam war is that, before undertaking a task of such size, it is vital to count the cost and be sure of one's aims. If we do not make a reasonably accurate count—if we indulge in wishful thinking—we pay a tragic price in life, in money and in spiritual distress."[28] The late date of this reflection is important, of course, but equally so is the fact that for Lodge such doubts would have been untenable on active service.

Conclusion

On his first Saturday in Saigon in August 1963, Lodge braved all his military aides' reports of demonstrations in the streets and threats of an attack on the residence to cooperate with a *Life* magazine team filming a photo-essay on the new American ambassador to Vietnam. He and Mrs. Lodge rode in an open jeep through intermittent showers to the zoo, where they were led to the prize exhibit, a large male tiger. Lodge stood by, relaxed, as the photographers prepared. Then he grasped that a persistent spray was not the rain: he turned to catch the tiger pumping a urine stream toward him. He sidestepped to protect his wife, who was already spattered, and shook his head, laughing, to clear a splash directly into his mouth. Flustered Vietnamese officials assured him that the event was most auspicious, the very best of luck! He put them at their ease and firmly repositioned himself in front of the tiger. "Altogether a unique experience, the like of which has never happened to me before," he wrote to his sons. "What can it mean?"

It had taken decades spent in public life, perhaps generations of gentlemanly breeding, to produce that reaction to personal inconvenience. For Lodge, sharing with U.S. planners on Vietnam, under both Kennedy and Johnson, the lessons of appeasement in Europe, and the Cold War view of the need to stand up to the Communists, came essentially from a much older tradition in the conduct of American foreign affairs. His own college education had not been his formative influence, as it had been for Harriman, Rusk, and the Bundy brothers, and he had not capped his Harvard years with training for the law or Wall Street. It had been his self-conscious membership of a distinguished family that was the main factor in the molding of his character and aspirations. Lodge had grown to adulthood surrounded by presidential advisors, originals and scholars, memories of aristocratic warriors, and above all an ethic that public service was expected as the due of privilege.

In his youth he had been imbued with the example of Theodore Roosevelt in national politics, in contrast to the professionals of Tammany Hall, and had formed a keen sense of his own obligation to contribute to the life of his country. He was the namesake of the Henry Cabot Lodge who had dominated the Republican party for thirty years and led America into empire with the seizure of the Philippines from Spain. The early death of his father had placed him as the eldest male in his immediate family, and in the resulting skipping of a generation, his upbringing had been in the mold of the Victorian certainties of his grandparents. He knew that public affairs was his vocation; even the short early divergence from the path to the Senate into newspaper work was in the field of national politics.

It is perhaps difficult from the vantage point of the 1990s, knowing the cost of the U.S. Vietnam adventure in terms of blighted lives and national prestige and the seemingly endless suffering of the peoples of Indochina, to recreate the spirit in which members of the American ruling elite of the early 1960s approached service in Vietnam. On learning of Kennedy's request to his fellow Republican, Eisenhower told Lodge it was his constitutional duty to support the president in his conduct of foreign affairs, although he added that he profoundly distrusted Kennedy himself and his capacity to "find leading people to do the evils of this Administration and give them these nasty, mean jobs to do." Dean Rusk described Lodge as a gallant member of "a rare breed" prepared to "drop what they are doing, make the sacrifices necessary for public service". McGeorge Bundy recalled, "He was a brave and honest man who liked to serve his country," and of his service in Saigon, "He did it twice, which was a lot—there were other people who were only willing to do it once."[1] In short, whatever criticisms Bundy and Rusk made of Lodge's limitations, they admired his attitude.

Lodge's acceptance of his Vietnam appointments was in the tradition of American patriots from John Quincy Adams to George C. Marshall. His conviction of America's power to improve the world and protect the weak formed by his service in World War II was implicit, his opposition to communism an article of faith. Undoubtedly, a draft into the presidency would have met with his cooperation, but it now appears that the 1964 campaign for the GOP nomination was an amateur affair, a tribute to him organized by his eldest son and associates. The motivation impelling him to Saigon in his sixty-first year was an unreflective need to be in harness at the front: the private life of retirement at Beverly held attraction only as a dream and he responded, like Washington's Cincinnatus, to a call to serve the Republic.

To continue to have faith in an American victory in Vietnam under the battle lines decided in July 1965 required from Lodge the application of considerable force of will, if not the active suspension of disbelief that seems evident in his June 1964 report to the Senate Foreign Affairs Committee that security was largely achieved in the key provinces of the Mekong Delta. He returned nevertheless to Saigon. Indeed, he continued to accept Vietnam positions until the end of his life.

Patriotism was the power that drove him. Following the November coup of 1963, with the discipline of a trained agent mindful of the possibility of capture by the enemy, he rehearsed an account of events in the preceding days and held steadfastly to this under all subsequent questioning. Having made his unheeded warning to Johnson in mid-1964 that an open-ended commitment of ground troops to the war could put the U.S. "onto a slope along which we slide into a bottomless pit," he pledged himself unquestioningly to each new step in escalation. In private life he did not reminisce about Vietnam; his published memoirs contain no revelations on government business there. Instead, Lodge set down a confidential record of the events in which he had taken part, committed it to the archives, and cleared his mind of doubt.

The first Lodge ambassadorship in South Vietnam came at a critical time in the development of U.S. Vietnam policy. In 1963 American colonels were present in an advisory capacity to the ARVN at the province level, but the United States had not yet tied its reputation for steadfastness as an ally, as the defender of the free world, as the bulwark against the spread of communism in Asia, to success in propping up governments in Saigon which, as Lodge came quickly to realize, had limited powers of control in the territory they claimed to rule. Disengagement was never an option during the eight months of the first Lodge embassy: it is now clear that the dominant forces in the Department of State, as well as even more powerful voices in the Pentagon, wanted the continuation of America's only current war, to the pursuit of which so many careers and interests were tied.

But America had fought in other foreign wars, and perhaps for some of the same reasons. The uniqueness of the Vietnam engagement was the way in which it later came to undermine the credibility of the presidency and to consume resources and energies at the expense of other foreign policy issues for twelve long years.

That this should have been so seems due to a massive political failure. In 1963 and 1964, U.S. options to control the terms of the American engagement in Indochina narrowed rapidly until a harrowed President Johnson could see only one course ahead, and that the path he least desired to take. The options to spread the responsibility for the outcome in South Vietnam—say, by having an ally of the U.S. re-present de Gaulle's cease-fire plan at a suitable time or by having nonaligned states "initiate" proposals through the United Nations at sticky junctures—were cut off without serious consideration. The opportunity to cultivate a forum of Vietnamese elders, such as the Council of Notables, who might conveniently issue America with an invitation to quit was lost. Short-term thinking suggested the encouragement of Khanh's disastrous coup in January and, above all, the enemy's stakes in victory, publicized from Hanoi several times a day, year in and year out, were underestimated whenever major decisions were about to be taken.

The difficulty Kennedy and then Johnson suffered in gaining a focus on the war stemmed largely from their tendency to treat containment of communism in Asia as a domestic policy issue. Decisions on Vietnam had to wait on electoral victories at home. Kennedy's instruction to Lodge to "personally take charge of my press relations" on Vietnam was a symptom of his ad hoc policymaking on Indochina; Kennedy must have known that Lodge could not perform the larger task awaiting him in South Vietnam as U.S. mission coordinator. The president and his advisors accepted Lodge's quite explicit indications that he had no intention of chairing meetings of the Country Team or liaising with the heads of agencies. Yet they did not attempt to provide Lodge with a right-hand man to act as his administrative advisor at the outset, the only time when a division of labor could have been successfully negotiated. Indeed, in deciding that the new ambassador should be a man of character rather than professional training, no one appears to have reflected that Lodge was too much a VIP to be subject to control.

Johnson fell into the same trap of putting short-term domestic considerations before a review of his policy options in the war. His tendency to set his advisors one against another prevented him from recalling Lodge at the time when Lodge himself considered his Vietnam assignment fulfilled, apparently on the sole ground of keeping him silent on the conduct of the war—a consideration that turned on a grave misjudgment of his ambassador's loyalty. Johnson then stopped his ears to the advice Lodge had to give on the conditions in South Vietnam which, he believed, made a war fought with American technology, from the air and the sea, preferable to one fought with U.S. soldiers on the ground. In

1964 and the first half of 1965, Johnson desperately needed more cards to play against his military chiefs' demand for troops: it was most unfortunate that in his reading of Lodge he saw a dupe and not an ally.

This said, it is also clear that Lodge was out of his depth in Vietnam. He quickly became exasperated with the sophistication and multilayered loyalties of the Vietnamese with whom he was called upon to work. Drawing swift rather than well-substantiated conclusions, he oversimplified the political picture in South Vietnam and came to throw up his hands at the difficulty of getting anything done in "the orient." His cables by early 1964 take on the color of the colonizer's attitude to "the natives"; the Vietnamese become lazy, unpredictable, insensible to good advice, and require to be addressed slowly, and with much repetition.

Yet Lodge himself was no racist. In 1960, when the idea was almost unthinkable, he had suggested that a GOP administration include a black, and the cosmopolitan composition of his staff bore witness to his lack of ethnic prejudice. The independence of the Vietnamese was the problem: it is noteworthy that Lodge's enthusiasm for a U.S. campaign to save South Vietnam from communism was at its height when he was absent from the country.

For the American enterprise in Vietnam was indeed colonialist. Lodge may have been right in believing that elections must wait upon security, but self-determination was denied the South Vietnamese under U.S. patronage, and each attempt at local expression was extinguished. Diem was overthrown because he would not be a puppet, Minh toppled when he advised against the bombing of North Vietnam. Khanh with U.S. approval dismissed the post-Diem representative Council of Notables; the 1966 constitution forbade the expression of neutralist and antiwar ideas. How could an "advisory phase" play itself out and the United States be compelled to "move into a position of actual control" if American assistance was only that?

And South Vietnam was not the only U.S. client third world state whose governments were treated as expendable in American foreign policy practices of the 1960s. In this respect, Vietnam was not unique, a tragic mistake, and therefore outside history. When Lodge requested that Edward Lansdale be transfered to Saigon to head the CIA station there in September 1963, Lansdale could not be spared because he was, with Kennedy's explicit authorization, chief of operations in the "Mongoose" program to depose Castro, the Marxist prime minister of Cuba. In 1975 a specially convened Senate committee found in its report *Alleged Assassination Plots Involving Foreign Leaders* abundant evidence that Eisenhower and his advisors were deeply implicated in the 1960 death of Prime Minister Patrice Lumumba in the Congo (now Zaire), and that Eisenhower and then Kennedy had sought the overthrow of President Leonidas Trujillo of the Dominican Republic, an end achieved by Trujillo's murder in 1961. Plotting for the assassination of Castro, the committee found, was a constant theme from Eisenhower to Johnson.[2]

Lodge's reactions to the war in Vietnam encapsulated a response held by many American planners. Himself motivated by patriotism and an internationalist viewpoint that had reached its most generous expression in his support of the Marshall Plan for the reconstruction of Europe, he did not grasp the elements of patriotism and internationalism in the motivations of the Vietnamese. For him, Communist-led wars of national liberation remained fraudulent, despite the evidence of the tenacity of the enemy, and he appears never to have considered the possibility that the "Viet Cong" had indigenous roots in the South, its cadres supported by family members there. He believed that members of the Viet Cong could be persuaded to desist by the promise of an affluent life funded by U.S. dollars, and he could draw no analogy between his own pride in the history of the free American Republic and the Communists' possible nationalist aspirations.

In his Vietnam assignments, Lodge was a figure of immense authority and prestige. It is a pity, then, that this authority and the noble aspirations on which it was based did not represent more coherent and better-judged policies. The full irony inherent in American efforts of the 1960s to contain the spread of communism is expressed in Lodge's "wrap-up" cable to Kennedy on the successful coup against Ngo Dinh Diem. Commenting on the effect of withholding U.S. funds to bring about reforms, the ambassador said: "Perhaps the U.S. government has here evolved a way of not being everywhere saddled with responsibility for autocratic governments simply because they are anti-Communist. The prospects now are for a shorter war, thanks to the fact that there is this new government."

Notes

Abbreviations of Archives and Other Sources

FBIS   Foreign Broadcast Information Service (U.S. government international monitoring service)

FOIA   U.S. Freedom of Information Act

FRUS   *Foreign Relations of the United States* (U.S. government periodical publication of declassified materials)

JFKL   John Fitzgerald Kennedy Library

LBJL   Lyndon Baines Johnson Library

Lodge Papers   Papers of Henry Cabot Lodge II. The six sections of the papers cited here are:

1. General Correspondence
2. Confidential Journal
5. Vietnam Papers
6. Emily Sears Lodge Saigon Papers (ESL Papers)
8. "Vietnam Memoir" (VNM)
11. Lodge-Eisenhower Correspondence

Unless otherwise indicated, all citations to the Lodge Papers refer to the Vietnam Papers, the most commonly used section.

MHS   Massachusetts Historical Society

NSF   National Security File. The CIA reports and MACV cables cited appear in the NSF, Country Vietnam, unless otherwise stated. The Department of State to Saigon and Saigon to State cables cited are from the NSF unless otherwise stated. The more important of these can be found in the relevant *FRUS*, Vietnam; those or parts and numbers which do not so appear are still classified at some level; information obtained under the FOIA.

NYT   *The New York Times*

OH   Oral history, as taped for the JFK or LBJ libraries

PP   *The Pentagon Papers*, Senator Gravel Edition (Boston: Beacon Press, 1971), 5 vols.

Post	*The Washington Post*
RLP	Rusk/Lodge/President Messages, vol. 1, box 198 (NSF, Country Vietnam), LBJL
SWB	BBC Survey of World Broadcasts
USVR	*United States Vietnam Relations, 1945–1967* (Washington: U.S. Government Printing Office, 1971), 12 vols. (U.S. Department of Defense version of Pentagon Papers).
WJC	William Joiner Center, University of Massachusetts, Harbor Campus, Boston. Holds complete collection of transcripts of recordings made by Stanley Karnow for *Vietnam: A Television History*.

Chapter 1

1. Fragment, Robert P. Murphy, *Diplomat Among Warriors* (Garden City, N.Y.: Doubleday, 1964), Lodge Papers, Lodge-Eisenhower Correspondence (part 11), MHS.

2. Translator's anecdote, entry for April 7, 1953, Lodge Papers, Confidential Journal (part 2); observation on Vishinsky in Murphy, *Diplomat Among Warriors*, 366; Eisenhower on choice of Lodge for U.N., Dwight D. Eisenhower, *The White House Years*, vol. 1: *Mandate for Change, 1953–1956* (London: Heinemann, 1963), 89.

3. Lodge to Eisenhower, June 26, 1956, and March 28, 1956, Lodge Papers, 11.

4. Henry Cabot Lodge, Jr., *The Cult of Weakness* (Boston: Houghton Mifflin, 1932); Lodge on evolution in GOP thinking in Henry Cabot Lodge, *The Storm Has Many Eyes: A Personal Narrative* (New York: W. W. Norton, 1973), 27, and Elliot L. Richardson, "Memoirs: Henry Cabot Lodge," *Proceedings of the Massachusetts Historical Society* 97 (1985): 149–52.

5. Lodge-approved entry in Charles Van Doren, ed., *Webster's American Biographies* (Springfield, Mass.: Merriam, 1974) and Lodge entry in *Who's Who in America*, 42d ed., 1982–1983, vol. 2 (Chicago: Marquis Who's Who, 1983); Khrushchev to Lodge, Lodge, *Storm*, 181.

6. James C. Thomson, Jr., "How Could Vietnam Happen? An Autopsy," *Atlantic Monthly*, April 1968: 47–53.

7. Lodge's presidential ambitions are particularly strongly expressed in his Confidential Journal, a collection of notes of conversations and memoranda on secret negotiations in government and GOP business. Many who served with Lodge in Saigon believed that he had accepted the South Vietnam post to increase his chances of gaining the Republican nomination (author's interviews with John Michael Dunn, Lodge's special assistant during his first ambassadorship to South Vietnam, Washington D. C., April 25, 1991; with David Nes, deputy chief of mission in Saigon, 1963–1964, Owings Mills, Md., July 2, 1989; with Brig. Francis Philip Serong, commander of the Australian forces in Vietnam, 1962–1965, Melbourne, March 5, 1990; with Barry Zorthian, minister counselor for public information and head of USIS in South Viet-

nam in 1964, Washington, D.C., July 3, 1989). See also John Mecklin, *Mission in Torment: An Intimate Account of the U.S. Role in Vietnam* (New York: Doubleday, 1965), 221.

8. "Conversation with Nixon," March 9, 1960, Lodge Papers, 2; and, on appeal of the GOP in foreign affairs, "Conversation with Nixon," entry for Jan. 23, 1960.

9. Lodge OH, JFKL, August 1965, 23.

10. Lodge and administration policy formation in H. W. Brands, Jr., *Cold Warriors: Eisenhower's Generation and American Foreign Policy* (New York: Columbia University Press, 1988), 181; discussion with Eisenhower regarding "Whig" party, entry for Jan. 21, 1954, Lodge Papers, 2; assignment for Luce on *Time*, William J. Miller, *Henry Cabot Lodge* (New York: Heinemann, 1967), 333.

11. John A. Garraty, *Henry Cabot Lodge: A Biography* (New York: Alfred A. Knopf, 1968), 422; Lodge reference to his grandfather as his "beloved counselor and friend" in Lodge, *Storm*, 27.

12. Bay Lodge literary discussions, *The Selected Letters of Henry Adams*, ed. Newton Arvin (New York: Farrar, Straus and Young, 1951), 255; for Paris nightclubs, *Henry Adams and His Friends: A Collection of His Unpublished Letters*, ed. Harold D. Carter (Boston: Houghton Mifflin, 1947), 411; Roosevelt hunting trips, Garraty, *Henry Cabot Lodge*, 192, and 193 for Wharton quote and "nothing so good in English."

13. Quotes about Bay, Mrs. Winthrop Chanler, *Roman Spring: Memoirs* (Boston: Little, Brown, 1934), 293; Bay's overwork and death, Garraty, *Henry Cabot Lodge*, 270–71.

14. Preference for bland soups, Miller, *Henry Cabot Lodge*, 381; minimal alcohol, Frederick Flott (Lodge's special assistant in Saigon, 1963–1964), letter to the author, October 1989.

15. Roosevelt's introduction to the collected poems and dramas of George Cabot Lodge (Boston: Houghton Mifflin, 1911) is in *Selections from the Correspondence of Theodore Roosevelt and Henry Cabot Lodge, 1884–1918* (New York: Scribner's, 1925), 2:399–402.

16. Lodge had described journalism as an early "career" for his entry in Van Doren, *Webster's American Biographies*; for grandfather's instructions to Joslin, Garraty, *Henry Cabot Lodge*, 422–23.

17. "Memo of Conversation with Joseph Sisco, Department of State," Feb. 19, 1963, Lodge Papers, 2.

18. Rusk letter to the author, August 1990; Lodge notes of discussions with Kennedy aides, entries for Jan. 18 and Feb. 14, 1963, Lodge Papers, 2.

19. Dunn interview, April 1991.

20. Nes interview, July 1989.

21. Sullivan interview with Roger Lalouette, Versailles, July 1972, Marianna P. Sullivan, *France's Vietnam Policy: A Study in French American Relations* (Westport, Conn.: Greenwood, 1978), 67.

22. Roger Hilsman, *To Move a Nation: The Politics of Foreign Policy in the Administration of John F. Kennedy* (New York: Doubleday, 1967), 478.

23. Dunn interview; Miller, *Henry Cabot Lodge*, 333.

24. Entry for Jan. 18, 1963, Lodge Papers, 2.

25. Kenneth P. O'Donnell et al., *"Johnny, We Hardly Knew Ye": Memoirs of John Fitzgerald Kennedy* (Boston: Little, Brown, 1970), 382; O'Donnell letter in *Life*, Aug. 7, 1970; Hilsman letter in *NYT*, Aug. 8, 1970, and again in January 1992. Kennedy conversation with Mansfield in Herbert S. Parmet, *JFK: The Presidency of John F. Kennedy* (Harmondsworth: Penguin, 1984), 329; and see Marcus Ruskin, "JFK and the Culture of Violence," *American Historical Review* 97, no. 2 (April 1992): 487–99.

26. Parmet, *JFK*, 309.

27. "Notes of Conversation, Rusk and Lodge," June 17, 1963, Lodge Papers, 2.

28. Entry for Jan. 18, 1963, Lodge Papers, 2.

29. "Hilsman-Forrestal Report, January 1963," and secret annex; *FRUS* 1961–63: 3:Vietnam:49–59 and 60–62.

30. O'Donnell, *"Johnny, We Hardly Knew Ye,"* 16.

31. Warren Cohen, *Dean Rusk* (Totowa, N.J.: Cooper Square, 1980), 189; Arthur M. Schlesinger, Jr., *A Thousand Days: John F. Kennedy in the White House* (London: Andre Deutsch, 1965), 842; Rusk quote from letter to the author, August 1990; Safire quote from Feb. 29, 1985, *NYT* obituary for Lodge.

32. David Halberstam, *The Making of a Quagmire* (New York: Random House, 1964), 194.

33. Malcolm W. Browne, *The New Face of War: A Report on a Communist Guerrilla Campaign* (London: Cassell, 1965), 178.

34. Quotes and account of Kennedy interview are from Lodge Papers, 2, entry for Jun. 12, 1963 and Lodge OH, JFKL, 6.

35. Meetings with JFK advisors and quotes from Lodge Papers, 2, entries for June 17, 1963.

36. Dunn and Flott interviews.

37. "The Overthrow of Ngo Dinh Diem, May–November, 1963," *USVR* 3, 4.B.5, 2; Hilsman, *To Move a Nation*, 460–61; William Colby, *Honorable Men: My Life in the CIA* (New York: Simon and Schuster, 1978), 206–7; interview with Ted Gittinger (historian coordinating Vietnam interviews for LBJL Oral History Program), Austin, July 26, 1989.

38. William P. Bundy, unpublished manuscript on U.S. decisions on Vietnam under Kennedy and Johnson, Papers of William P. Bundy, LBJL, Nine:8.

39. William Colby interview, Washington, D.C., April 1991, and Colby, *Honorable Men*, 206 (for Richardson and Nhu).

40. Frederick Nolting, *From Trust to Tragedy: The Political Memoirs of Frederick Nolting, Kennedy's Ambassador to Diem's Vietnam* (New York: Praeger, 1988), 95–96 and 111–13.

41. State to Saigon 1219, June 13, 1963.

42. Memo of Conversation, July 4, 1963, "Situation in South Vietnam," *USVR* 12: 526–28.

43. Saigon's 226, Aug. 14, 1963.

44. Entries for Jan. 18 and Feb. 14, 1963, Lodge Papers, 2.

45. Hilsman, *To Move a Nation,* 478.

46. Copy of Kennedy letter on the authority of chiefs of mission, dated May 29, 1961, Lodge Papers.

47. Durbrow OH, LBJL, June 1981, 1, 11–14. Nolting OH, LBJL, November 1982, 24–26.

48. W. Bundy interview, Princeton, N.J., April 1991.

49. Mohr abstract and "Talking Points for Conversation Between Ambassador Lodge and President Diem," Lodge Papers.

50. Quotes from Lodge visit with Chuongs, VNM Two, 1:14.

51. Recorded in Saigon's 190, Aug. 8, 1963; *NYT,* Aug. 8, 1963.

52. *Post,* Aug. 9, 1963.

Chapter 2

1. Details of suspected gunfire on Pan Am plane from "An American in Viet-Nam: Ambassador Henry Cabot Lodge," U.S. embassy translation of Vietnamese newspaper report on Lodge arrival, Lodge Papers; Kenneth Rogers interview, Washington, D.C., May 1991; John Mecklin, *Mission in Torment: An Intimate Account of the U.S. Role in Vietnam* (New York: Doubleday, 1965), 190.

2. "First-rate people, third-rate system" from William Macomber, *The Angel's Game: A Handbook of Modern Diplomacy* (New York: Stein and Day, 1975), 190.

3. Lodge quotes on cables to Kennedy, Lodge OH, JFKL, 25–26; "not just one more FSO," Flott letter, November 1989.

4. On the Buddha birthday deaths in Hue, Wulff interview, *Post,* July 27, and Wulff letter, *NYT,* Aug. 2, 1963.

5. Buddhists as "Communist-led" in Gen. Paul Harkins OH, LBJL, 1981, 26.

6. Joseph M. Kitagawa, "Buddhism and Asian Politics," *Asian Survey* 2, no. 5 (July 1962): 1–11.

7. "Bring the government down," Halberstam, *Making of a Quagmire,* 194; pictures of Buddhist banners in English, Browne, *New Face of War,* 180, and *NYT,* Aug. 22, 1963.

8. For the Saigonese and the news, Mecklin, *Mission in Torment,* 156–76; for Hanoi's Vietnamese News Agency (VNA) service and text from "Liberation Broadcasting Station," FBIS and SWB entries for North Vietnam and for South Vietnam; *NYT* for the Halberstam-Sheehan team reports.

9. For Nolting on Buddhist dispute, Saigon's 1044, May 19, 1963, and Saigon's 1065, May 25, 1963; Saigon's 173, Aug. 3, 1963, and Saigon's 190, Aug. 8, 1963; see

also *Trust to Tragedy,* 116. William Trueheart interview, Washington, D.C., July 1989, and Trueheart OH, LBJL, 1982, 32–33.

10. "The Buddhists in South Vietnam," Special Report, Office of Current Intelligence, June 28, 1963; CIA Current Intelligence Memo, "The Buddhist Issue in South Vietnam," Aug. 23, 1963. Saigon's Airgram A-162 (from embassy Political Section), "Transmittal of Biographic Information on Buddhist Bonzes," Aug. 22, 1963. The "major report" was Thomas L. Hughes, Bureau of Intelligence and Research), Research Memorandum RFE-75, "Diem Versus the Buddhists: The Issue Joined," Aug. 21, 1963.

11. Gard interview, Rick Fields, *How the Swans Came to the Lake: A Narrative History of Buddhism in America* (Boston: Shambhala, 1986), 254.

12. Mecklin quote, *Mission in Torment,* 102; Harkins's private line to Taylor, William Colby, *Lost Victory: A Firsthand Account of America's Sixteen-Year Involvement in Vietnam* (Chicago: Contemporary Books, 1989), 115.

13. David Halberstam, *The Best and Brightest* (New York: Random House, 1969), 205; *NYT,* Aug. 24, 1963.

14. The projected dates for Lodge's arrival in Saigon are from Memo of Conversation, *USVR* 12, 526–28, and *NYT,* Aug. 19, 1963. Pike and Flott comments are from Flott letter, November 1989, and Douglas Pike interview, Berkeley, Calif., April 1991; the "wrap-up" cable is Saigon's 949, Nov. 6, 1963.

15. Details of Lodge's appointment, Lodge Papers; projected route to Saigon, Flott letters to author; CIA destabilizing methods, L. Fletcher Prouty, "The Anatomy of Assassination," in *Uncloaking the CIA,* ed. Howard Frazier (New York: Free Press, 1975), 196–209.

16. Nolting cable on final meeting with Diem is Saigon's 226, Aug. 14, 1963.

17. The White House position was one of "no change" (State to Saigon 1280, June 27, 1963); Lodge himself later recorded, in a set of notes on Hilsman's 1967 book *To Move a Nation,* that there had been no discussion between himself and Hilsman at Honolulu on the matter, Lodge Papers; and that was what he replied to Nolting's questioning in Honolulu, Nolting, *Trust to Tragedy,* 120.

18. Saigon Domestic Service, Aug. 20, 1963, in FBIS for SVN, Aug. 21, 1963; *Nhan Dan* comments on Lodge's arrival, VNA, Aug. 22, 1963, SWB for NVN.

19. Saigon Domestic Service, "Voice of the Armed Forces of the Republic of Vietnam," Aug. 21, FBIS for SVN, Aug. 22, 1963.

20. Reported in Saigon's 268F, Aug. 20, 1963 (in fact, Aug. 21); "268" was a special number assigned to embassy transmissions of journalists' copy.

21. Saigon's 269, Aug. 21, 1963 (information from Hue in American Consulate Hue's 3, Aug. 21, 1963) and interview with John Helble (former U.S. consul in Hue), Washington D. C., April 1991; Radio Saigon's "Voice of the Armed Forces of the Republic of Vietnam," Aug. 21, 1963 in FBIS for SVN, Aug. 22, 1963.

22. Colonel Tung's role confirmed in Saigon's 267, Aug. 21, 1963. Saigon's (unnumbered) Aug. 20, 1963 (Aug. 21) for the monks in USOM building; State to Saigon 274, n.d., for the reply.

23. The *NYT* (Aug. 21, 1963) noted that Lodge had left Honolulu on Aug. 20; Hilsman's account of news of pagoda raids in *To Move a Nation,* 481, gives the date as Aug. 21; account echoed in Colby, *Honorable Men,* 208, giving no date; Nolting followed Hilsman version, *From Trust to Tragedy,* 120, giving the date of the raids as Aug. 21.

24. Flott to the author, November 1989; Lodge OH, JFKL, 7; JFK call to Lodge in Tokyo noted in *NYT,* Aug. 22, 1963.

25. Washington's statement on pagoda raids, State to Saigon 266, Aug. 21, 1963; U.S. ambassador to Japan on Lodge and the Buddhists in Tokyo's 581, Aug. 22, 1963; remarks on Lodge's political instincts, Kenneth Rogers interview.

26. State to Saigon 228, Aug. 22, 1963; State to Saigon 230, Aug. 21, 1963 (copies of both to Tokyo for Lodge).

27. Saigon's 267–299 sequence, Aug. 21, 1963.

28. Saigon Domestic Service, broadcasting as the "Voice of the Armed Forces," Aug. 21, in FBIS for SVN, Aug. 22, 1963.

29. "The Overthrow of Ngo Dinh Diem May to November, 1963," *USVR* 3, 4.B.5, 12–16.

30. For the "combat police" details of the Halberstam-Sheehan account, see UPI story in *NYT,* Aug. 22, 1963, and Halberstam, "Plan Said to Be Nhu's," *NYT,* Aug. 23, 1963; for the Serong corrections, see Ted Serong, "The Lesson of Ap Bac," *Conflict* 9 (1989): 325–40. Harkins's views on ARVN responsibility for pagoda raids in COMUSMACV to State, 6935, Aug. 21, 1963; for CIA, CIA Information Report 05574, Aug. 23, 1963.

31. "Coup of Nov. 1, 1963: My Recollection of What Happened in Vietnam up to Coup of Nov. 1," n.d. (June 1964), Lodge Papers, and Lodge OH, JFKL, 8.

32. State to Saigon 235, Aug. 22, 1963.

33. Lodge's note "Nhu drugging" in "My Recollection" and in VNM Two, 2:1; see also INR memo "The Problem of Nhu," Sept. 15, 1963; Nhu's possible control of Laos-Marseilles drug traffic in Alfred McCoy, *The Politics of Heroin in Southeast Asia* (New York: Harper and Row, 1972), 160–61; Nhu's attempt to kill Sihanouk in David P. Chandler, *The Tragedy of Cambodian History: Politics, War, and Revolution since 1945* (New Haven: Yale University Press, 1991), 106–7.

34. "My Recollection" and VNM Two, 2:1.

35. Saigon's 306, Aug. 23, 1963, for quote; American public response, *NYT,* Aug. 23, 1963.

36. Mrs. Lodge letter to a friend, Aug. 23, 1963, ESL papers; Neil Sheehan, *A Bright and Shining Lie: John Paul Vann and America in Vietnam* (New York: Random House, 1988), 360.

37. The agencies were taken by surprise at the pagoda raids: on the embassy, Trueheart interview; on the CIA, William Colby OH, LBJL, June 1981, 1:35; for other agencies and General Harkins's headquarters, Mecklin, *Mission in Torment,* 182. Lodge's opinion that embassy and CIA "were not well informed" from VNM Two, 1:15.

For history of the "Country Team" concept, W. Wendell Blancke, *The Foreign Service of the United States* (New York: Praeger, 1969), 137–39, and for Lodge approach to Richardson, Richardson letter to author, November 1990.

38. Kennedy and the Vatican in relation to Diem, VNM Two, 1:15.

39. "My Recollection." Honey "possibly a consultant," John Playford, "A Taste of Honey," *Outlook*, February 1967: 21–3.

40. John Burke interview, Washington, D.C., April 1991; Phillips allegiances in 1963 from William Colby letter to author, September 1990.

41. "State instructed Conein," author's communication with Roger Hilsman, April 1991.

42. CIA Information Report, "Frustration and Discouragement Among Vietnamese Army Officers," Aug. 23, 1963, and Lodge to White House, Aug. 23, 1963.

43. Assassination threat in Mecklin, *Mission in Torment*, 190.

44. "Notes on CAS Station," Oct. 1, 1963, Lodge Papers.

45. Lodge on Harkins about situation in SVN, VNM Two, 2:1; Serong anecdote from Serong interview, Melbourne, March 1990.

46. Conein interview, McLean, Va., April 1991. Conein's accounts of his activities in South Vietnam are known to have been self-serving at times, and often deliberately misleading, but William Colby in Colby interview, April 1991, confirmed the probability of this sequence of events.

47. Conein interview for Stanley Karnow, *Vietnam: A Television History*, May 1981, WJC.

48. CIA Research Report (TDCS DB 3/656, 252), Aug. 24, 1963, "Major General Tran Van Don Details the Present Situation in South Vietnam; The Plans to Establish Martial Law; and, His Views on South Vietnam's Future."

49. Saigon's 308, Aug. 23, 1963, for Lodge on Nhu and Don; Saigon's 320, Aug. 24, 1963, for Phillips-Kim conversation; Saigon's 324, Aug. 24, 1963, for Phillips-Thuan conversation.

50. See CIA Information Report, Aug. 21, 1963, "Plans and Activities of Tran Kim Tuyen's Coup Group," and CIA Information Report, Aug. 22, 1963, "Indication of an August 25 Coup d'Etat."

51. Saigon's 314, Aug. 23, 1963, for Lodge assessment of SVN military factions, and Saigon's 329, Aug. 24, 1963, for cautionary note.

52. Department of State American Opinion Summary, Aug. 22, 1963, copy marked to be sent to McBundy and Forrestal, NSF.

53. There are many accounts of the authorization problem surrounding the Aug. 24 cable from Washington to Saigon and the resultant NSC meeting on Aug. 26. Among the more dispassionate is that in William Conrad Gibbons, *The United States and the Vietnam War: Executive and Legislative Roles and Relationships*, vol. 2, *1961–1964* (Princeton, N.J.: Princeton University Press, 1986), 148–54. Accounts by those involved include Hilsman, *To Move a Nation*, 483–89; Colby, *Honorable Men*, 210; and Maxwell D. Taylor, *Swords and Ploughshares* (New York: W. W. Norton,

1972), 292. For memo in the presidential reading file, Gibbons, *United States and the Vietnam War,* 149–50.

54. Hilsman quote on Saturday cable, Hilsman letter to author, August 1990. The cable is State to Saigon 243, Aug. 24, 1963, *FRUS* 1961–1963:3:Vietnam:628–29.

55. Taylor's comments on Lodge and cable 243 in *Swords and Ploughshares,* 292; Lodge quote from Lodge to Rusk and Hilsman, Aug. 25, 1963, *PP* 2:735.

56. Colby to Richardson on obedience to Lodge, *Honorable Men,* 210–11; instructions to Lodge to call Country Team meeting in State to Saigon 243; "no Country Team meeting" John Richardson letter to the author, November 1990. Details of small group briefing, U.S. Congress, Senate, *Alleged Assassination Plots Involving Foreign Leaders,* An Interim Report of the Select Committee to Study Governmental Operations with Respect to Intelligence Activities, Nov. 20, 1975, S. Rept., 94–465, 94th Cong., 1st Sess., 1975 (Washington, 1975), 219.

57. "Kennedy did something that Roger Hilsman had never seen him do before," Hilsman letter, August 1990; Colby quote from *Lost Victory,* 138.

58. Accounts of the week Aug. 24–31 in U. S.-Vietnam relations are in Geoffrey Warner, "The United States and the Fall of Diem 1: The Coup That Never Was," *Australian Outlook* 28, no. 3 (December 1974): 245–58; George McT. Kahin, *Intervention: How America Became Involved in Vietnam* (New York: Alfred A. Knopf, 1968), 158–64 and Ellen J. Hammer, *A Death in November* (New York: Dutton, 1978), 178–96. A selection of the State-Saigon cables appears in *PP* 2:734–740. For Harkins's objections to Lodge initiatives, see Taylor, *Swords and Ploughshares,* 291 and "The Overthrow of Diem," *USVR* 3, 4.B.5:19.

59. See State to Saigon 249, Aug. 26, 1963, plans for "repositioning U.S. forces in case they required in Vietnam" and Joint Chiefs of Staff, Memo for the President (DJSM-1463–63), Aug. 30, 1963, "Availability of U. S. Forces for Deployment to Saigon," NSF (copy marked "taken from Pres. weekend reading dated 8/31").

60. "No turning back," Saigon's 375, Aug. 29, 1963; *PP* 2:738–39.

61. Vietnamese leaks, Conein interview. "Pushing spaghetti," Saigon's 383, Aug. 30, 1963; *PP* 2:739–40.

62. Kennedy's reservations in "Personal for the Ambassador from the President," Aug. 29, 1963; Lodge's reply, VNM Two, 2:4–5.

63. Colby observation, *Lost Victory,* 139.

Chapter 3

1. CIA Report, "(Conein) Contacts with Vietnamese Generals, Aug. 23 through Oct. 23, 1963," Declassified and Sanitized Documents in Unprocessed Files, Vietnam, Box 2, LBJL.

2. See Charles A. Joiner, *The Politics of Massacre: Political Processes in South Vietnam* (Philadelphia: Temple University Press, 1974), 63–76 and Jeffrey Race, *War*

Comes to Long An: Revolutionary Conflict in a Vietnamese Province (Berkeley: University of California Press, 1972).

3. The cable was State to Saigon 284, Aug. 30, 1963. Lodge recorded several times in his papers that he had received a communication on Aug. 30 telling him not to proceed with the coup; see in particular VNM Two, 2:3 and "My Recollections." Published accounts making the same claim include Lodge, *Storm,* 209, and Lodge interview for *Many Reasons Why: The American Involvement in Vietnam,* Program 4, "The New Frontiersmen Hold the Line," first transmitted Oct. 11, 1977, transcript in Michael Charlton and Anthony Moncrieff, *Many Reasons Why: The American Involvement in Vietnam* (London: Scolar, 1978), 95.

4. Reports of the NSC meeting of Aug. 31, are in *PP* 2:240–41 and 741–43; Kattenburg quote from Gibbons, *U.S. Government and the Vietnam War,* 161.

5. State to Saigon 239, Aug. 23, 1963.

6. Lodge reported on the first meeting between himself and Diem in Saigon's 340, Aug. 26, 1963; independent estimates of membership of the GBA in Robert Scigliano, "Vietnam: Politics and Religion," *Asian Survey* 4 (January 1964): 666–73 and Pham Van Luu, "The Buddhist Crisis in Vietnam 1963–1966," unpublished Ph.D. thesis, Monash University (Clayton, Victoria 3168, Australia), 1991. See Roger Hilsman's interview for "The New Frontiersmen Hold the Line" in Charlton and Moncrieff, *Many Reasons Why* and G. A. Carver, Jr., "The Real Revolution in South Vietnam," *Foreign Affairs,* April 1965: 388–407 for "third-force" argument.

7. Mrs. Lodge noted the Lodge-Asta conversation and Lodge's comments in a letter to a friend dated Aug. 31, ESL papers; the Asta and Asta-Lodge-d'Orlandi meetings with Diem and his family are discussed in *PP* 2:240–42 and in G. Warner, "The United States and the Fall of Diem, Part II: The Death of Diem," *Australian Outlook* 29, no. 1 (April 1975): 3–17, the source for which was Ambassador d'Orlandi's diaries.

8. "Nhu must go," *PP* 2:242.

9. Mecklin quote from *Mission in Torment,* 223; Lodge quote from his notes on *To Move a Nation,* 514, Lodge Papers.

10. Alsop arrival and contacts with Lodge, entries Sept. 8–14, 1963, ESL papers; Alsop's "Very Ugly Stuff," *Post,* Sept. 18, 1963.

11. The agency report on the article was "Possible Rapprochement Between North and South Vietnam," Sept. 19, 1963, CIA Research Reports, *Vietnam and Southeast Asia, 1946–1976* (Frederick, Md.: University Publications, 1985), microfilm.

12. The cables on asylum for the monks and Lodge's conversation with Tri Quang are Saigon's 396, Sept. 1, and Saigon's 408, Sept. 3, 1963. Bundy's comment on political interference from W. Bundy MS Nine:10; Senator Church allusion in "Revised Introductory Statement by Senator Frank Church, D-Idaho, to Accompany Introduction of His Resolution to Discontinue Aid to the Diem Regime of South Vietnam," Sept. 12, 1963. Kennedy on Buddhists in Sept. 2 broadcast, *PP* 2:241–42. Lodge on effects of granting asylum, VNM Two, 2:13 and Saigon's 949, Nov. 6, 1963.

13. Gambino interview with Nhu, Saigon's 640, Oct. 5, 1963; West communications with author, January 1990; and see Morris West, *The Ambassador* (London: Heinemann, 1965).

14. Bruce Woodberry (then second secretary of the Australian embassy in Saigon) communications with author, March 1991; Morris West transcript of interview with Ngo Dinh Diem.

15. The "two-track" tactic about Diem in "South Vietnam, An Action Plan: Vietnam Action Plans" (Sept. 16–21), 1963; Kennedy advisors' reactions, *PP* 2:246–47. Lodge's claim of intent to remove Nhu only, OH, JFKL, 11. Alsop's comment on Halberstam-Sheehan campaign against Diem regime in *Post*, Sept. 23, 1963.

16. Lodge OH, JFKL, 10; Mecklin, *Mission in Torment*, 220.

17. Lodge rebuffed Minh's request for aid cuts as a signal in Saigon's 383, Aug. 30, 1963. Lodge suggestion that Congress might be induced to implement aid cuts, Saigon's 391, Aug. 31, 1963; *FRUS* 1961–1963:4:Vietnam:68. Lodge-Hilsman-McGeorge Bundy negotiations on wording of Church motion, Gibbons, *U.S. Government and the Vietnam War*, 166–69.

18. Lodge's considerations of the problems involved in cutting aid to the Diem regime are detailed in Saigon's 279, Aug. 29, 1963 (*PP* 2:738), Saigon's 544, Sept. 19, 1963, and Saigon's 608, Sept. 29, 1963.

19. Saigon's 555, Sept. 20, 1963.

20. CIP suspended in State to Saigon 534, Oct. 5, 1963.

21. Lodge's Marshall Plan comparison in Saigon's 544, Sept. 19, 1963 (*PP* 2:746–48); specific quote appears in VNM Two, 2:6.

22. Ball quote, George Ball, *The Past Has Another Pattern* (New York: W. W. Norton, 1982), 373. Analysis of Krulak-Mendenhall visit to Vietnam from Colby, *Lost Victory*, 142, and W. Bundy MS Nine:12. JFK quote, *USVR* 3, 4.B.5:26.

23. Report on Sept. 10 NSC meeting, *PP* 2:243–44, and Memo, Mecklin to Murrow, "A Policy for Viet-Nam," Sept. 10, 1963, NSF. Carroll Kilpatrick, "The Kennedy Style in Congress," in *John F. Kennedy and the New Frontier*, ed. Aida Di Pace Donald (New York: Hill and Wang, 1966), 52.

24. Saigon's 478, Sept. 11, 1963, in *FRUS* 1961–1963:4:Vietnam:171–75.

25. Saigon's 478 (Section Two).

26. JFK private message to Lodge is State to Saigon 396, Sept. 12, 1963, recorded VNM Two, 2:5; information to U. S. mission about aid cuts is State to Saigon 391, Sept. 12, 1963.

27. COMUS MAC 1675 to Admiral Felt, General Krulak (and others of the Joint Chiefs of Staff); to CIA for McCone; to the White House for McGeorge Bundy; to State for Rusk, Ball, Harriman, and Hilsman, Sept. 12, 1963. For Tri Quang's admissions, see CIA Special Report, "The Nature of the Buddhist Conflict in South Vietnam," Sept. 12, 1963.

28. Mrs. Lodge's letter to a friend, Oct. 13, 1963, ESL papers.

29. Possibility referred to in Saigon's 544, Sept. 19 (*PP* 2:747), and "Feasibility of

Supply RVN Forces Without Use of the Port of Saigon," Tab. F, South Vietnam, "An Action Plan," Sept. 16, as well as earlier Aug. 24 Saturday cable.

30. See discussion of controversy surrounding Saturday cable in Charlton and Moncrieff, *Many Reasons Why,* 90–92, in conjunction with Dean Rusk, *As I Saw It: By Dean Rusk as told to Richard Rusk* (New York: W. W. Norton, 1990), 438.

31. "U. S. not a colonial power" from outline for a cable dated Sept. 16, 1963, Lodge Papers, and again in notes for a speech to McNamara scheduled for Sept. 25, VNM Two, 2:7.

32. Suggested use of U.S. funds to promote a coup, Phillips Memo, "Comments on the Necessity for an Advance Decision to Introduce U.S. Forces in Viet-Nam," Sept. 17, 1963.

33. Quote from Saigon's 608, Sept. 27, 1963.

34. Colby, *Lost Victory,* 147.

35. "Lessons of Vietnam," sets of notes dated 1970 and 1973, Lodge Papers.

36. Lodge's protest over the new fact-finding mission in Saigon's 577, Sept. 22, 1963; Kennedy's insistence, *PP* 2:247.

37. Halberstam, *Best and Brightest,* 283.

38. Mrs. Lodge's letter to a friend, Sept. 29, 1963, ESL papers.

39. *PP* 2:248 for Harkins's Sept. 25 presentation to the McNamara team, and VNM Two, 2:7 for Lodge's own and quote.

40. *PP* 2:249 for meeting; VNM Two, 2:8 for Tho's figures.

41. W. Bundy MS Nine:23–26.

42. For the 1,000-man withdrawal announcement, *PP* 2:251, and, for the broader contingency plans, *PP* 2:Part Three, the section's subject. O'Donnell's assertions regarding Kennedy's intentions, *"Johnny, We Hardly Knew Ye,"* 18.

43. W. Bundy interview, April 1991, referring to W. Bundy MS Nine:19; Lodge on Thuan, Lodge interview for *Vietnam: A Television History,* n.d., WJC.

44. CAP 63560 to Lodge, Oct. 5, 1963, *PP* 2:766–67; Lodge's cover story version from VNM Two, 2:8. Key works giving greater details than here of Lodge's subsequent contacts with the Vietnamese generals through Conein are Karnow, *Vietnam,* 270–312; G. Warner, "The United States and the Fall of Diem, Part II: The Death of Diem"; Hammer, *A Death in November.*

45. Instruction to suspend aid to Vietnam Special Forces in State to Saigon 534, Oct. 5, 1963; cable counseling secrecy is "For Ambassador Lodge from Bundy, the White House," Oct. 5, 1963.

46. Saigon police attacks on the reporters in *NYT,* Oct. 6 and 7, 1963; Lodge formal protest in Saigon's 639 and predictions of further suicides in Saigon's 637, both Oct. 5, 1963. Lodge response to "little soldiers of fortune," *Post,* Sept. 27, 1963.

47. Outline for a cable annotated by Lodge as "never sent," n.d., Lodge Papers (filed under "Congressmen").

48. Clement J. Zablocki OH, JFKL, 1965, 47–48. Zablocki would subsequently press for a congressional investigation into the death of Diem, but to no avail.

49. Diem's invitation from Saigon's 776, Oct. 24, 1963, and Ball's instructions to Lodge, State to Saigon 647, Oct. 25, 1963.

50. Details of the Don-Lodge meeting of Oct. 27, from Tran Van Don interview for *Vietnam: A Television History,* n.d., WJC, and VNM Two, 2:11, and from Tran Van Don interview, Washington, D.C., July 1989, and subsequent communications.

51. VNM Two, 2:11. "Don would not reveal dates," Don interview.

52. *PP* 2:219 and 257; *USVR* 3, 4.B.5:45.

53. Timing of events of Sunday Oct. 27, from Mrs. Lodge's letter to a friend, dated "Monday, Oct. (28), 9:00 A.M.," ESL papers.

54. The key testimonies are those of the Emily Sears Lodge letters and the sometimes self-serving Tran Van Don, whose correct dating of the coup-signal meeting with Lodge as Sunday, Oct. 27, was not picked up from the transcript of interview in the making of *Vietnam: A Television History.* The relevant U.S. government documents were not available until 1991. Lodge's report of his conversation with Thuan is in Saigon's 804, Oct. 28, 1963, *FRUS* 1961–1963:4:Vietnam:441–42; his report of his Sunday exchange with Diem is in Saigon's 805, Oct. 28, 1963, *FRUS* 1961–1963:4:Vietnam:442–46. The cable on the meeting with Don is Ambassador to State, Oct. 28, *FRUS* 1961–1963:4:Vietnam:449.

55. Substance of meeting with Diem in VNM Two, 2:11, and Lodge's "wrap-up" cable to JFK (Saigon's 949, Nov. 6, 1963). Quote from Lodge interview for *Vietnam: A Television History.*

56. *PP* 2:219.

57. CAS 2063, Lodge to State, Oct. 30, 1963, *PP* 2: quote from 791.

58. Diem's request for interview with Lodge is Saigon's 841, Nov. 1, 1963, which also gives Lodge account of the Diem-Lodge meeting (see below); Admiral Felt's visit and remarks from Hilsman letter, August 1990.

59. Quote from the 3 P.M. cable, Saigon's 841, Nov. 1, 1963; cable 841 was received in Washington at 9:18 A.M. local time (about 12 hours behind Saigon time) on Nov. 1, but the tide of CIA reports that swamped it had begun to arrive at 2 A.M. the same day.

60. The cable giving the summary of the afternoon exchange between Lodge and Diem is Saigon's 860, Nov. 1, 1963, as it appears in Sheehan et al., *The Pentagon Papers: As Published by the New York Times* (New York: Bantam, 1971), 232. Witnesses who have given accounts of Lodge's safe-passage offer to Diem are Kenneth Rogers (author interview, May 1991), Dunn (OH, LBJL, 27), and Flott (OH, LBJL, 41–45). Lodge recorded his offer of asylum to Diem and a passage out of the country in VNM Two, 1:30.

61. Pham Van Luu interview with Cao Xuan Vy, San Francisco, June 1986 (text kindly shown to author); several phrases of the account are similar to that set down by Flott (OH, LBJL, 43).

62. Mrs. Lodge's letter to a friend, Nov. 2, 1963, ESL papers.

63. "Assumed they were in the palace," Trueheart interview, July 1989; Ma

ma tuyen

Tuyen account of Diem's refuge in Cholon, Fox Butterfield, "Man Who Sheltered Diem Recounts '63 Episode," *NYT,* Nov. 4, 1971, and alleged drug links with Nhu, Mc-Coy, *Politics of Heroin,* 408n17. See also account of Diem's last hours in Hammer, *A Death in November,* 281–300.

Chapter 4

1. Saigon's 949, Nov. 6, 1963, *FRUS* 1961–1963:4:Vietnam:575–78.

2. L. Fletcher Prouty, "The Anatomy of Assassination," 205; Lodge quotes from Saigon's 949.

3. Lodge OH, JFKL, 25–26 (this and following quotes). For public statements, see *NYT,* June 30, 1963 (following similar statement to U.S. Senate Committee on Foreign Relations, same day) and Lodge, *Storm,* 210; for "off-the-record" notes, see VNM Three, Accomplishments-Vietnam, and Lodge OH, JFKL, 12.

4. Dunn interview, April 1991.

5. Lodge to his sons, Nov. 5, 1963, ESL papers; he made the same points in Saigon's 900, Nov. 3, and Saigon's 917, Nov. 4, 1963.

6. State to Saigon 674, Nov. 1, 1963.

7. Lodge to State, CAS 2063, Oct. 30, 1963, *PP* 2:791.

8. Saigon's 900, Nov. 3, 1963; same phrase in Lodge letter, Nov. 5.

9. "Accidental suicide," *Alleged Assassinations,* 223; Conein interview for *Vietnam: A Television History,* May 1981, WJC. McBundy's instructions to Vietnam generals about the deaths in CAP 63602 n.d.; Rusk's in State to Saigon 704, Nov. 3, 1963.

10. Outline for a cable, "U.S. Position Towards Events in Saigon," Nov. 1, 1963, NSF; Conein interview, WJC; "Should not appear to be reporting in" and Lodge advice, *USVR* 3, 4.B.5:59. Figures for proposed aid, Joint State and Aid cable to Saigon, authorized by Hilsman, n.d., NSF.

11. Kim's Nov. 2 statement from FBIS for SVN, Nov. 4, 1963.

12. The report of the meeting between Lodge and new GVN is Saigon's 900, Nov. 3, 1963; *FRUS* 1961–1963:4:Vietnam:546–49.

13. Saigon's 898, Nov. 3, 1963; "Harkins concurred" from VNM Two, 2:13.

14. Lodge, *Storm,* 210; Flott interviews; Flott OH LBJL, 51–57.

15. The problem of Can, Saigon's 917, Nov. 4, 1963, and Hue's 12–14, Nov. 2 and 3; resolution, Saigon's 930, Nov. 5, 1963.

16. Helble interview, April 1991; Lodge's duplicated statement on Can, the coup, and death of Diem appears in VNM Appendix 3.

17. Minh GVN to be recognized, State to Saigon 718, Nov. 4, 1963.

18. U.S. U.N. Office's 2380, Dec. 5, 1963.

19. Mrs. Swarna L. Gunawardene (Sir Senerat's daughter) letter to author, November 1989; Gunawardene's killing of the debate in State to Saigon 2444, Dec. 11, 1963.

20. Regarding elections in Vietnam, Lodge to McGeorge Bundy, Oct. 25, 1963, *PP* 2:781; Lodge maxim from Flott interviews.

21. For Provisional Constitution, SWB for SVN, Nov. 6, 1963; Lodge comments in Saigon's 951, Nov. 6, 1963, *FRUS,* 1961–1963:4:Vietnam: 578–79.

22. Nguyen Ngoc Huy interview, Boston, July 1989; the British diplomat, Dennis J. Duncanson, observed the same problems, *Government and Revolution in Vietnam* (New York: Oxford University Press, 1968), 346.

23. Memo of Meeting, Nov. 20, 1963, *FRUS* 1961–1963:4:Vietnam:609–10.

24. Saigon's 960, Nov. 7, 1963.

25. Comments on Council of Notables, problems and membership, in CIA Information Report TDCCDB-3/658,058, Nov. 30, 1963; see also Bui Diem with David Chanoff, *In the Jaws of History* (Boston: Houghton Mifflin, 1987), 108. Lodge quote "intellectuals and educated classes," Saigon's 1226, Dec. 28, 1963, which also details the forty-strong membership.

26. For achievements of the council, Saigon's Airgram 547, March 24, 1963; opinion on its potential from John Burke (main U.S. liaison officer, embassy-council) interview, April 1991.

27. Mrs. Lodge letter to a friend dated Nov. 5, 1963, ESL papers.

28. FBIS for SVN, Nov. 9, 12, and 18, 1963.

29. FBIS for SVN, Nov. 18, 20, and 22, 1963.

30. The CIA monitored the early lists of suggested candidates for the provisional government for inclusion of civilians. See CIA Saigon's 1135 to the White House, Nov. 1, 1963, for an example of this concern.

31. State to Saigon 704, Nov. 3, 1963.

32. Lodge's favorable comments on applications for newspaper licenses are in Saigon's 923, Nov. 5 and Saigon's 1066, Nov. 23, 1963. Lodge recommended Buu for the post-coup government in Lodge to McGeorge Bundy, *PP* 2:781; Buu's report, "CVTC (Vietnamese Confederation of Christian Workers) Recommendations for Labor Reform," Dec. 10, 1963, remains in the Lodge Papers.

33. For Buu declining to serve, Saigon's 941 Nov. 6, 1963; for Quat and Bui Diem, Bui Diem, *In the Jaws of History,* 106.

34. On the Buddhist reorganizations and Minh's attitude, interview with Thich Giac Duc (monk who led the rally outside the Xa Loi pagoda on Aug. 19, 1963), Boston, July 1989, and Pham Van Luu letter to author, December 1989; Tri Quang meeting with U.S. official, Saigon's 989, Nov. 11, 1963.

35. Record of Conversation, Phillips-Minh, Nov. 18, *FRUS* 1961–1963:4:Vietnam: 603–07; for alliances with the sects under the French, see Carlyle A. Thayer, *The Origins of the National Front for the Liberation of South Vietnam* (Ann Arbor, Mich.: University Microfilms, 1978), 171 and 181.

36. Don interview; Tran Van Don, *Our Endless War: Inside Vietnam* (San Rafael, Calif.: Presidio, 1978), 116; Lodge report to Rusk on MRC program, Saigon's 991, Nov. 11, 1963, *FRUS* 1961–1963:4:Vietnam:590–91.

37. For reporters' views of alliances of the sects with Minh, see *Post* for Nov. 16, 21, and 27, 1963. Ba Cut's death, Edward Geary Lansdale, *In the Midst of Wars: An American's Mission to Southeast Asia* (New York: Harper and Row, 1972), 321.

38. Saigon's 1122, Dec. 7, 1963, *FRUS* 1961–1963:4:Vietnam:687–89.

39. "Take your hat off," interviews with Flott and Charles C. Flowerree (second secretary of the U.S. embassy in Saigon, 1962–1964), Washington, D.C., April 1991. Newspaper cutting, Lodge to Harriman, Jan. 23, 1964, Papers of W. Averell Harriman, Box 484, Library of Congress.

40. Press instruction in Saigon's 1027, Nov. 17, 1963; Lodge received news of Kennedy's death, Lodge OH, JFKL, 27.

41. Details of November 1963 telephone call from Theodore H. White, *The Making of the President 1964* (London: Jonathan Cape, 1965), 84.

42. Mrs. Lodge letter to a friend dated Dec. 19, 1963, ESL papers.

43. Memo of Meeting, Nov. 20, 1963, *FRUS* 1961–1963:4:Vietnam:609–24; "if he stops being a Viet Cong," 610, and VNM Two, 3:1.

44. Lyndon B. Johnson, *The Vantage Point: Perspectives of the Presidency, 1963–1969* (London: Weidenfeld and Nicholson, 1972), 62–63 (commenting on Saigon's 1122, Dec. 7, 1963).

45. Lodge conveyed Don's reassurances on Long An in Saigon's 1121 and Saigon's 1122, Dec. 7, 1963; Dunn sent to Long An, Saigon's 1129, Dec. 9, 1963; Lodge's attitude to problem solving, interview with Robert Miller (first secretary of the U.S. embassy in Saigon, 1963–64), Washington, D.C., April 1991.

46. Memo, Dunn to Lodge, with the report attached, Dec. 27, 1963, Lodge Papers; Lodge still blaming Diem in March, see Saigon's 1755, March 15, 1964, RLP.

47. For general speculation, *NYT Magazine,* May 10, 1964; for explanation that Richardson had lost his cover, Meiczyslaw Maneli, *War of the Vanquished,* translated from the Polish by Mariade Gorgey (New York: Harper and Row, 1972), 143 and *PP* 2: 217; for Richardson's role vis-à-vis Nhu, Colby, *Honorable Men,* 206 and 212. For speculations on curbs of CIA powers after Bay of Pigs, see piece by Richard Starnes of the Scripps-Howard group reprinted in *Washington Daily News,* Oct. 1, 1963 (copy in NSF). "Lodge had final say," Peer de Silva, *Sub Rosa: The CIA and the Uses of Intelligence* (New York: Times Books, 1978), 303 and 209.

48. Lodge quotes from VNM Two, 2:5–6; the (secret) request is Lodge to State, Sept. 13, 1963, *FRUS* 1961:1963:4:Vietnam:205–6.

49. Reasons for withholding of Lansdale from Vietnam from Paul Kattenburg audiotape to author, September 1990.

50. Richardson letter, November 1990; "Notes on CAS Station," Oct. 1, 1963, Lodge Papers.

51. De Silva, *Sub Rosa,* 210–12.

52. Mecklin's opinion, *NYT Magazine,* May 10, 1964; "I do this work myself," Saigon's 1285, Jan. 10, 1964; Zorthian perception, OH, LBJL, May 1969, 3.

53. Lodge withheld cables from Harkins, Mecklin, *Mission in Torment,* 223; for

Harkins's protests over withheld information during November coup, Harkins to Taylor, Oct. 30, 1963, in *FRUS* 1961–1963:4:Vietnam:496–98 and 499–500, and on Nov. 1, 1963, 522–23. On Diem's English, Harkins OH, LBJL, 14, and on Minh, Harkins to Felt, *FRUS* 1961–1963:4:Vietnam:274–75.

54. Initial concern, Harkins to Taylor, Nov. 2, 1963, *FRUS* 1961–1963:4:Vietnam: 534–35; "leave without pay," SWB for SVN, Nov. 28, 1963; for popularity of 3 Corps postings, Duncanson, *Government and Revolution in Vietnam*, 345. CINCPAC's concern, Felt to JCS and White House, Dec. 10, 1963, Papers of LBJ, Box 1, LBJL (cable a response to Lodge's sanguine analysis in Saigon's 1121 and 1123, Dec. 7, 1963).

55. The problem of Dinh: Harkins to Felt and Taylor (MAC JOO 9144), Nov. 29, 1963, Papers of LBJ, Box 1, LBJL, and Harkins to Taylor, Dec. 4, 1963, *FRUS* 1961–1963:4:Vietnam:659–61. Lodge accepted Don's explanation in Saigon's 1121, Dec. 7, 1963; the CIA report on dissensions among Vietnam generals is Lodge to State, Nov. 4, 1963, *FRUS* 1961–1963:4:Vietnam:557–58.

56. John Burke interview, Washington, D.C., April 1991; Melvin Manfull in Saigon's Airgram A-407, Jan. 9, 1964; Kennedy's advice in President to Lodge, State's 746, Nov. 6, 1963, *FRUS* 1961–1963:4:Vietnam:579–80.

57. Newspaper reports on MRC, *Post*, Dec. 3 and 8, 1963, and *NYT*, Nov. 21–Dec. 14, 1963; Rusk to Lodge about McCormack on Can, State to Saigon 895, Dec. 4, 1963.

58. Saigon's 1141, Dec. 11, 1963; Serong letter to author, May 1990. The Forrestal to McGeorge Bundy notation appears on the NSF copy of the cable, which is from Forrestal's files.

59. De Gaulle text in Bernard Fall, "What de Gaulle Actually Said About Vietnam," *Reporter*, Oct. 24, 1963: 39–41; de Murville in Paris's 937, Aug. 29, 1963.

60. "Past Presidential Statements of U.S. Government Commitments in Southeast Asia," in *Vietnam, the Media, and Public Support for the War: Selections from the Holdings of the Lyndon Baines Johnson Library, Austin, Texas* (Frederick, Md.: University Publications, 1986), 1, 35.

61. Lodge attitude to de Gaulle in eulogy of de Lattre, circa January 1953, Lodge Papers. Lodge on de Gaulle and Vietnam's "neighbors" in Saigon's 388, Aug. 30, 1963.

62. Agence France Presse dispatch, Jan. 18, 1964 (see *Far Eastern Economic Review*, Feb. 6, 1964).

63. "Conversation with Vice-president Nixon," March 9, 1960, Lodge Papers, 2.

64. Trueheart interview, July 1989.

65. Philippe Devillers interview, Paris, October 1988; statistics from Sullivan, *France's Vietnam Policy*, 70, and passim for de Gaulle's postcolonialist concerns.

66. Paul M. Kattenburg, "Vietnam and U.S. Diplomacy, 1940–1970," *Orbis* 15, no. 3 (Fall 1971): 818–41.

Chapter 5

1. LBJ to Fulbright, Dec. 2, 1963, and LBJ to Rusk, Dec. 10, 1963, Transcripts of Telephone Conversations, 1, LBJL.

2. Kalischer to Lodge, April 15, 1964, Lodge Papers.

3. For concern over publicity of dissension in the mission, Memo of Discussion, Nov. 13, 1963, *FRUS* 1961–1963:4:Vietnam:593–94, and Forrestal memo of talk with *NYT* editor, 594–95. For Mansfield memos on a truce in Vietnam, *FRUS* 1961–1963:4:Vietnam:691–92 and *FRUS* 1964–1968:1:Vietnam:2–3.

4. Memo of Meeting, Nov. 22, 1963, *FRUS* 1961–1963:4:Vietnam:652.

5. Report to the President, May 23, 1961, "Southeast Asia Memos, vol. 1, Dec. 1963–April 1964," in *The Lyndon B. Johnson National Security Files: Vietnam, Special Subjects, 1963–1969* (Frederick, Md.: University Publications, 1987).

6. "Limited number of highly trained advisors" from VNM Two, 3:7–8 (March 1964); less, not more, advisors in Saigon's 577, Sept. 22, 1963, and instructions to rationalize staff in Saigon's 603, Sept. 27, 1963.

7. Memo of Conversation, Dec. 4, 1963, *FRUS* 1961–1963:4:Vietnam:665–66.

8. LBJ and divisions, Bundy MS Twelve:3; Bill Moyers interview for *Vietnam: A Television History*, WJC, and Karnow, *Vietnam*, 324–25.

9. McCone's notes of the meeting are Memo, Vietnam Situation, Nov. 24, 1963, *FRUS* 1961–1963:4:Vietnam:635–37. On LBJ attitude to coup against Diem, see also Johnson, *Vantage Point*, 61.

10. LBJ to Cook, Nov. 30, 1963, Telephone Conversations, 1, and in *Economist*, Oct. 2–8, 39. For advisors on withdrawal of Lodge: Harriman and McGeorge Bundy, memo of phone conversation, Dec. 4, 1963, *FRUS* 1961–1963:4:Vietnam:665–66; Forrestal to McGeorge Bundy, memo, and memo, McGeorge Bundy to President, Feb. 4, 1964, *FRUS* 1964–1968:1:Vietnam:59–61.

11. A Dec. 15 cutting confirming that Lodge was in the New Hampshire primaries is the first entry in the Henry Cabot Lodge Name File, Dec. 1, 1963–Jul. 24, 1964, Box 246, LBJL. Bundy to President, "Re Ike and Cabot Lodge," Dec. 9, 1963, *FRUS* 1961–1963:4:Vietnam:692–93.

12. Colby interview, April 1991.

13. W. Bundy interview, April 1991. Some material from the Forrestal period of the "Lodge Watch" appears as Memo to the President, Responses to Ambassador Lodge, March 11, 1964, in *Memos of the Special Assistant for National Security Affairs: McGeorge Bundy to President Johnson, 1963–1966* (Frederick, Md.: University Publications, 1985).

14. Taylor, *Swords and Ploughshares*, 301; Thomas Powers, *The Man Who Kept the Secrets: Richard Helms and the CIA* (New York: Alfred A. Knopf, 1979), 165; Arthur M. Schlesinger, Jr., *Robert Kennedy and His Times* (Boston: Houghton Mifflin, 1978), 714–15. Colby dispatch to Vietnam in State to Saigon 694, Nov. 2, 1963; Colby, *Lost Victory*, 157.

15. Eugene Vasilew, "The New Style in Political Campaigns: Lodge in New Hampshire, 1964," *Review of Politics* 30 (April 1968): 131–52; Miller, *Henry Cabot Lodge*, 355 and Lodge, *Storm*, 192.

16. The "Draft Lodge" team from White, *Making of the President 1964*, 108–9; procedures from Charles Brereton, "A Yankee Surprise," *Historical New Hampshire* 43, no. 3 (1987): 253–82 (from a chapter in Brereton, *First in the Nation: New Hampshire and the Presidential Primary* [Portsmouth: Peter Randall, 1987]).

17. Meade Alcorn meeting from Kenneth Rogers interview, May 1991; White, *Making of the President 1964*, 109.

18. Vasilew, "New Style in Political Campaigns," 137.

19. Flott and Miller interviews, April 1991.

20. "Within 60 to 90 days" is from the Dec. 26 version of the message as transmitted to Lodge, in General Minh, Head of State Correspondence, Vietnam, Box 12, LBJL. See also State to Saigon 1000, Dec. 31, 1963, *FRUS* 1961–1963:4:Vietnam:745–47.

21. First meeting of MRC in Saigon's 1002, Nov. 13, 1963; reporters' dissatisfaction in Saigon's 1140, Dec. 11, 1963; renewed plotting rumored in Saigon's 1172, Dec. 17, 1963. The CIA report on danger to Strategic Hamlets program is "Situation Appraisal as of Dec. 14, 1963," Dec. 16, 1963.

22. "Minh proceeded through the whole list," John Burke interview, April 1991. The Neguib-Nasser metaphor apparently had wide currency: see Roger Hilsman OH, JFKL, 1970, 35.

23. Memo of Conversation, Saigon, Dec. 20, 1963, Saigon's 1192; *FRUS* 1961–1963:4:Vietnam:716–19.

24. McCone's report is "Highlights of Discussions in Saigon, Dec. 18–20," *FRUS* 1961–1963:4:Vietnam:736–38 and McNamara's recommendations are in Memo to President on Vietnam Situation, Dec. 21, 1963, 732–35.

25. NSAM 273, *FRUS* 1961–1963:4:Vietnam:637–40.

26. Saigon's 1257, Jan. 6, 1964.

27. Lodge to State, Jan. 10, 1964 (Saigon's 1290), *FRUS* 1964–1968:1:Vietnam: 16–22.

28. Saigon's 1287 and 1288, Jan. 10, 1964, reporting on same meeting as in Saigon's 1290, contents summarized in *FRUS* 1964–1968:1:Vietnam:16 and *PP* 2:307.

29. Memo of meeting of Special Group for Counterinsurgency, *FRUS* 1964–1968: 1:Vietnam:25–6.

30. W. Bundy MS Twelve:12.

31. Ho-Miller conversation, March 29, 1964, in Saigon's Airgram A-573, April 6, 1964.

32. Dinh quote, and concerned reaction, in State to Saigon 949, Dec. 16, 1963 (*FRUS* 1961–1963:4:Vietnam:710); Dinh's anti-Diem story in *Post*, Nov. 7, 1963, and Dinh appeared as reporters' favorite, *Post*, Dec. 8, 1963.

33. Lodge asked for statement on Sihanouk proposals in Saigon's 1135, n.d.; re-

quested statement in State to Saigon 922, Dec. 10, 1963, and GVN reaction in Saigon's 1142, Dec. 11, 1963, both in *FRUS* 1961–1963:4:Vietnam:695 and 697. The *NYT* articles were Walter Lippmann column, Dec. 8, and editorials, Dec. 8 and 10, 1963.

34. Saigon's 1337, Jan. 19, 1964, to State and White House; the text of de Gaulle's announcement is in *NYT*, Jan. 19, 1964.

35. An account of the foundation of OPLAN 34-A is in Gibbons, *U.S. Government and the Vietnam War*, 212–13. Lodge replied to the State/Defense/CIA cable of Jan. 16 on Jan. 20, 1964, in (CAS 3902 ref. 94963), *FRUS* 1964–1968:4:Vietnam:27–28. The code reference does not appear in the *FRUS* version but is found on the copies of the document and related sequence in *Memos of the Special Assistant, 1963–1966*.

36. Saigon's 3943, ref. 94963, Jan. 21, 1964; *FRUS* 1964–1968:1:Vietnam:28–31.

37. Arthur J. Dommen letter to the author, January 1993. Pham Dang Lam had discussed the Jan. 21, 1964 meeting between Lodge and the GVN with Dommen when both men were at the Paris peace negotiations in 1968, where Lam was present with the SVN delegation.

38. Joint State-Defense-CAS message ref. CAS Saigon 3943 (refers also to CAS Washington 94963: "we have no approvals beyond the actions listed in CAS Washington 94963") Jan. 22, 1964, Vietnam Special Category Messages, 1, Nov. 1, 1963–July 1964, Boxes 52–53, LBJL. Joint Chiefs memo to McNamara, Jan. 22, 1964, summarized in *FRUS* 1964–1968:1:Vietnam:35 and text McNamara to Rusk, Jan. 28, 1964, in *PP* 3:496–99.

39. Conein entry for Aug. 25, 1963, in "Contacts with the Vietnamese Generals"; Ball recommended Khanh to Lodge in State to Saigon, n.d. (Aug. 25, 1963). For Taylor on Khanh, Colby, *Lost Victory*, 71, and for North Vietnamese, Truong Nhu Tang with David Chanoff and Doan Van Toai, *A Vietcong Memoir* (New York: Vintage, 1986), 55.

40. CIA Memo, "Appraisal of General Nguyen Khanh," OCI No .0698/64, March 20, 1964. Harkins OH, LBJL, 22, and Dunn OH, LBJL, 44.

41. Account of Vietnamese military politics preceding Khanh coup based on Bui Diem and Tran Van Don interviews, June 1989, Nguyen Ngoc Huy interview, July 1989, and Manfull/Burke/Bui Diem record of conversation in Saigon's Airgram A-627, April 27, 1964. "Khanh at White House" in Keyes Beech OH, LBJL, 1983, 2, 60.

42. Khanh to Conein, Dec. 1963, Conein interview, April 1991; Karnow, *Vietnam*, 337.

43. Harkins OH, LBJL, 15–18.

44. General Nguyen Khanh communication to author, February 1994; Harkins secretly notified Taylor, Harkins OH LBJL, 44–5. See Kahin, *Intervention*, 195–202 for a detailed argument that the critical factor in the coup was the role of the U. S. military in Vietnam, with direction from the principals in the Pentagon.

45. CIA Saigon to Agency, Jan. 28, 1964, *FRUS* 1964–1968:1:Vietnam:36–7.

46. Saigon's 1431, Jan. 29, *FRUS* 1964–1968:1:Vietnam:37–9; Diem had introduced Khanh to Lodge, Khanh communication.

47. The cable on village administration was Saigon's 1424, Jan. 29, 1964; the critical report was Saigon's 1431.

48. Saigon's 949, Nov. 6, 1963, notes usual practice of passing on coup information to GVN but not to Diem; Lodge had cabled State accusing de Gaulle in Saigon's 1413, Jan. 28, 1964, and Ball replied in State to Saigon 1138, Jan. 28, 1964. Jan. 28–29 coup information not passed onto Minh, *PP* 2:309.

49. Nes OH, LBJL, 9, and Nes interview, July 1989. Dunn OH, LBJL, 31, and Don interview, July 1989.

50. Dunn OH, LBJL, 31–36.

51. Don, *Our Endless War,* 118.

52. Bui Diem interview, April 1991.

53. Lodge led the polls, *Post,* Jan. 25, 1964; for Goldwater and Rockefeller in March and votes cast in Hollis, White, *Making of the President 1964,* 106 and 108.

54. Rockefeller call to Lodge, *NYT,* Feb. 23, 1964; Brereton, "A Yankee Surprise," 275.

55. New Hampshire figures from Brereton, "A Yankee Surprise," 278; "unexpected radio activity," Miller interview, April 1991. The biography is Henry A. Zeiger, *The Remarkable Henry Cabot Lodge* (New York: Popular Library, 1964).

56. Saigon's 1467, Feb. 1, 1964; *FRUS* 1964–1968:1:Vietnam:54–55.

57. Dunn interview, April 1991; Lodge quote from Dunn letter to the author, June 1991.

58. Saigon's 1443, Jan. 30, 1964.

59. Lodge and d'Orlandi, *PP* 3:37 and 39. On Khanh's rumor campaign, Nguyen Ngoc Huy interview and Pham Van Luu letter to author, December 1990. Harriman alerted to probable falsity of neutralism charges in Memo from the Acting Assistant Secretary for Far Eastern Affairs to State, Jan. 30, 1964, *FRUS* 1964–1968:1:Vietnam: 43–45. For the French, Flott letter to author, October 1989, and Sullivan, *France's Vietnam Policy,* 70; groupings of the South Vietnamese generals, editorial and Max Clos article in *Figaro,* Jan. 31, 1964 (English-language summary in *Post,* Feb. 1, 1964).

60. Documents not presented, CIA Memo, "Appraisal of General Nguyen Khanh," March 20, 1964, 1; details of trial, Don, *Our Endless War,* 128.

61. Khanh quote and Lodge concern, Khanh's agreement to "intensified activity in North Vietnam . . . intensified activity against the Viet Cong in South Vietnam," all in CAS Saigon 4174, Jan. 31, 1964; *FRUS* 1964–1968:1:Vietnam:49.

62. Ball's suggestion about Minh, State to Saigon 1149, Jan. 29, 1964; U.S. formula on changes in GVN, *FRUS* 1964–1968:1:Vietnam:42 and Lodge quotes from Saigon's 1451, Jan. 31, 1964, 45–47.

63. "From the President's Bedroom," Feb. 1, 1964, CO 312, LBJL; State to Saigon 1170, Feb. 1, 1964, and see *NYT,* Feb. 2, 1964.

64. *NYT* and *Post,* Jan. 31–Feb. 2, 1964, *Time,* Feb. 14, 1964.

65. Halberstam, *Best and Brightest,* 352.

66. Lodge on deaths of Diem and Nhu, *Storm,* 210 and Lodge interview for *Vi-*

etnam: A Television History, WJC. On Khanh coup, WJC interview and VNM Two, 3: 6–7.

Chapter 6

1. Memos, McNamara to President, Nov. 23 and Dec. 21, 1963, *FRUS* 1961–1963:4:Vietnam:627–28 and 732–33.

2. Lodge, *Storm,* 213.

3. Halberstam, *Best and Brightest,* 273, and Memo, Bundy to President, Dec. 10, 1963, *FRUS* 1961–1963:4:Vietnam:693–94.

4. Memos, Forrestal to Bundy and Bundy to President, both Feb. 4, 1964, *FRUS* 1964–1968:1:Vietnam:59–61.

5. Lodge and Nes in Halberstam, *Best and Brightest,* 272, and Memo of Conversation, Harriman and Bundy, Dec. 4, 1963, *FRUS* 1961–1963:4:Vietnam:665–66. LBJ to Rusk, Dec. 10, 1963, Telephone Conversations, 1.

6. Nes interview.

7. Instructions from Nes letter to William Sullivan, Bureau of Far Eastern Affairs, April 7, 1964, Papers of David Nes, LBJL and Nes OH, LBJL, 2.

8. Nes and Dunn interviews and Nes to Sullivan, April 7, 1964.

9. Zorthian quote from interview, April 1991; Nes financial independence in Nes OH, LBJL, 12. Nes letter to Hilsman, Feb. 19, 1964, with enclosure "Where We Stand in Viet-Nam," *FRUS* 1964–1968:1:Vietnam:89–92.

10. Nes exposition of U.S. options in Vietnam from "Where We Stand in Vietnam." Nes resigned, Nes interview and Halberstam, *Best and Brightest,* 273. Lodge memo on Nes, June 14, 1967, Lodge Name File, Jan. 1, 1966–July 31, 1967, Box 247, LBJL.

11. "Situation in South Vietnam," Feb. 7, 1964, Southeast Asia: Special Intelligence Material, 1, CIA Research Reports: *Vietnam and Southeast Asia, 1946–1976*; for later NVN mobilization, George C. Herring, *America's Longest War: The United States and Vietnam, 1950–1975,* 2d ed. (Philadelphia: Temple University Press, 1979), 117–18.

12. Agency heads acted as barons, Dunn interview, April 1991; no communication between agencies and sections, Pike, Flott, and Rogers interviews, April and May 1991. Status of COPROR, Joseph Brent (USOM) letter to Nes, March 30, 1964, Papers of William Westmoreland, Box 1, 3, History Backup, 1, Feb. 17–April 30, 1964, LBJL (hereafter Westmoreland Papers, 1).

13. Office Memo, Nes to Westmoreland, Feb. 29, 1964, Westmoreland Papers, 1. All the following Pacification Committee materials are from this source.

14. Pacification Committee Charter, March 3, 1964.

15. Colby interview, April 1991, and Forrestal memo to McGeorge Bundy, March 30, 1964, *FRUS* 1964–1968:1:Vietnam:199–201.

16. "Best source of information," Sullivan letter to Nes, April 14, 1964. Lodge interrupted the meeting, Zorthian interview, July 1989; Dunn's role, Nes interview; final quote from Nes letter to Sullivan, April 7, 1964, Nes Papers.

17. Nes on Lodge refusal to delegate, Nes OH, LBJL, 10; on hours, Nes interview. Dunn appointment as executive secretary of mission, VNM Four, 5:3, and quote, Four, 5:1.

18. Halberstam, *Best and Brightest,* 402–4; details of the wording of the Gulf of Tonkin Resolution from Gibbons, *U.S. Government and the Vietnam War,* 306.

19. President, letter to McNamara, March 5, 1964, *FRUS* 1964–1968:1:Vietnam: 132–33, and for details of Forrestal, "Responses to Ambassador Lodge," 132n2.

20. Lodge letter to Rusk, April 30, 1964, NSF Intelligence File, Rusk/Lodge/W. Bundy Correspondence, 9, LBJL, and in *FRUS* 1964–1968:1:Vietnam 279–80. Lodge letter to McNamara, May 20, 1964, Lodge Papers.

21. Lodge quote from VNM One, 4. Bundy quote and details of W. Bundy's watch on Lodge from W. Bundy interview.

22. Miller interview, April 1991; Pacification committee meeting agenda, April 7, 1964, for "Draft Charter of the Psychological Operations Committee."

23. Ambition to be a general, Dunn interview. Chester Cooper memo to McNamara, "Recommendations on Intelligence Reporting," March 12, 1964, Westmoreland Papers, 1.

24. Quote from Sullivan letter to Nes, April 14, 1964; MACV's request for change in critical list, Pacification Committee minutes, March 24, 1964; ambassador's refusal, Pacification Committee minutes, March 31, 1964.

25. Forrestal memo to McGeorge Bundy, March 30, 1964.

26. Huy interview, July 1989.

27. Johnson offered more aid in State to Saigon 1256, Feb. 18, 1964; Lodge requests granted in State to Saigon CAP 14047, Feb. 20, 1964, RLP. No conditions on aid grant, *PP* 1:280.

28. Khanh created new ranks to ensure loyalty, CIA's March 20, 1964 "Appraisal of General Nguyen Khanh;" Kahin, *Intervention,* 204. Quote from Conein interview, April 1991.

29. "Inordinate dishonesty," Duncanson, *Government and Revolution in Vietnam,* 356–57; nonpayments from Karnow, *Vietnam,* 343.

30. On corruption, Nes and Pike interviews. Confidential letter, Lodge to Rusk, May 29, 1964, Lodge Papers, 1.

31. Habib interview, April 1991; "lack of piasters," Saigon's 2084, April 19, 1964, and Saigon's 2091, April 30, 1964.

32. Report of April 30, 1964 meeting, *PP* 2:317.

33. Dennis Warner interview, Melbourne, June 1989.

34. Saigon's 2232, May 16, 1964.

35. State to Saigon 2027, May 21, 1964; *FRUS* 1964–1968:1:Vietnam:344–46.

36. Khanh accepted advisors, *PP* 2:283 and 309. Accepted, then advocated,

bombing NVN in Saigon's 2108, May 4, Saigon's 2125, May 6, and Saigon's 2203, May 14, 1964, all in *FRUS* 1964–1968:1:Vietnam:284–87, 293–94, and 315–21 (quote from Saigon's 2108).

37. Broadcasts started, Saigon's 1836, March 26; "holy hour" quote from Saigon's 2115, May 5, 1964; Hoan's disaffection from Khanh, Saigon's Airgram A-658, May 18, 1964.

38. Khanh discussed martial law in Saigon's 2108, May 4. "Like any professional soldier," Saigon's 2125, May 6, *FRUS* 1964–1968:1:Vietnam:293–94.

39. Lodge quote from Saigon's 2070, April 28, 1964.

40. Nes from Saigon's 1555, Feb. 14, 1964.

41. Lodge quote, VNM Two, 3:9.

42. See Saigon's 2205, May 14 through Saigon's 2284, May 22, *FRUS* 1964–1968: 1:Vietnam:322–48.

43. Details from reports for the MACV designated "critical provinces," May 6 to May 30, 1964, Westmoreland Papers, 2.

44. Saigon's Airgrams A-512, A-565, A-600, A-616, A-651, March–May 1964. Tay Ninh situation in Saigon's Airgram A-684, June 3, 1964.

45. See *PP* 2:463.

46. Quote from Lodge letter to Harriman, March 3, 1964, and copy of "Persistence in Vietnam," *Memos of the Special Assistant, 1963–1966*; Lodge, "How the World's Hottest Spot Looks to Me," *Life* 56, no. 16 (April 17, 1964): 38D–38F.

47. Lodge (director general, Atlantic Institute) to Rusk, (marked "not sent"), Lodge Papers, 1.

48. White House to Saigon Ref. CAP 64079, March 15, 1964; Saigon to White House 1753–1757, March 15–17, 1964; State's 1454, March 17, 1964, for Lodge from the President, RLP.

49. Lodge suggested d'Orlandi and Maneli, Lodge letter to Harriman, Dec. 3, 1963, *FRUS* 1961–1963:4:Vietnam:656. Lodge suggested Seaborn, George C. Herring, ed., *The Secret Diplomacy of the Vietnam War: The Negotiating Volumes of the Pentagon Papers* (Austin: University of Texas Press, 1983), 4, and W. Bundy OH, LBJL, 39–40.

50. Lodge letter to friends, May 2, 1964, ESL papers.

51. U.S. projects with Buddhists, Saigon's Airgram A-678, June 1; Lodge interest in subject and conference with Buddhist leaders, Saigon's 1810, March 23, and VNM Two, 3:12; Dalai Lama idea, Saigon's 2185, May 13, 1964.

52. Story on Can, *Time*, Feb. 14, 1964; "neither Minh nor Can would give way," Tran Van Don interview, July 1989; Lodge traveled to Hue to see Tri Quang, Lodge to Monsignor Francesco de Nittis, May 26, 1964, Lodge Papers.

53. Asta message, Delegatio Apostolica Indosinensis to Ambassador, May 12, 1964, Lodge Papers; bishops' letter and Lodge to Khanh, Saigon's 2204, May 14, 1964.

54. Saigon's 2203, May 14, 1964.

55. SVN could not supply observers, Saigon's 2203, May 14; "shake the GVN lead-

ership," State to Saigon 2027, May 21; Saigon's 2284, May 22, 1964, all in *FRUS* 1964–1968:1:Vietnam:315–21;344–46;346–48.

56. Lodge quote from Saigon's 2284, May 22, 1964.

57. Lodge to Rusk, June 18, 1964, Lodge Papers, 1; Ambassador Lodge to the President, June 19, 1964; Lodge, *Storm*, 214.

58. Lodge to LBJ, VNM Four, 1:4 and *FRUS* 1964–1968:1:Vietnam:459–61 ("slide into a bottomless pit" from version in VNM).

59. Lodge at the GOP convention, Miller, *Henry Cabot Lodge*, 367; Goldwater's dispatch, *NYT* July 9, 1964.

60. U.S. Congress, Senate, Committee on Foreign Relations, *The Situation in Vietnam*, 88 Cong., 2d sess., 1964, 16.

Epilogue

1. Memo of Bundy call to Lodge, Feb. 15, 1965; memo of Feb. 26 meeting with LBJ; Lodge memo, "Recommendations Regarding Vietnam," March 8, 1965, and Johnson comment, all from VNM Three, "Consultant" (hereafter VNM Three). "Revolving-door government," Zorthian interview, July 1989; Lodge bored at Beverly, interview with Henry Sears Lodge (Lodge's son), Boston, April 1991.

2. Lodge to President, Sept. 9, 1964, "Visit to Western European Capitals as Your Special Representative" and "Visit to Pacific and Asian Countries, April 19–May 1, 1965," VNM Three. *Newsweek* report on NATO tour, Sept. 14, 1964.

3. Brother's objection to service of Democrats, interview with Thomas A. De Long (biographer of John Davis Lodge), Stanford, Calif., April 1991. Quote from Lodge letter to Charles W. Ferguson, March 12, 1965, Lodge Papers.

4. Memo of discussion, Lodge and Harriman, Nov. 24, *FRUS* 1961–1963:4:Vietnam:634.

5. Honey letter to author, June 1990; Hanoi as a dependent of Beijing in Saigon's 1107, Dec. 4, 1963, *FRUS* 1961–1963:4:Vietnam:661–63.

6. "Neutralizing of North Vietnam" in CAS Saigon to Washington Ref. 94963, Jan. 20, 1964; "this was not de Gaulle's plan," memo of discussion, Hilsman and Lodge, Nov. 24, 1963, *FRUS* 1961–1963:4:Vietnam:633–34.

7. Lodge did not want U.S. ground troops in Vietnam, "How the World's Hottest Spot Looks to Me," and explanation to Khanh of his position on U.S. troops, Saigon's 2108, May 4, 1964; Cam Ranh Bay concept described in VNM Two, 3:11, and Saigon's 2101, May 2, 1964, *FRUS* 1964–1968:1:Vietnam:283–84 (Saigon's 2108, 286–89).

8. "Khanh needed four experts," VNM Two, 3:7, and Saigon's 1899, April 3, 1964. On Khanh accepting his idea, Lodge to President, April 30, 1964, *FRUS* 1964–1968:1:Vietnam:277.

9. Tour of Long An province, Saigon's 1307, Jan. 15, 1964. Lodge and land reform office, Nes interview.

10. "Not the old civic action program" and "manual for defeating Communism," both from Saigon's 1257, Jan. 6, 1964; Colby's offer to second CIA men to MACV from Gibbons, *U.S. Government and the Vietnam War,* 213.

11. Saigon's 1103, Dec. 3, 1963; Saigon's 2325, May 27, 1964.

12. Joint Chiefs of Staff directive, JCS memo to McNamara, May 19, 1964, *FRUS* 1964–1968:1:Vietnam:338–39. Lodge on France, VNM Two, 3:10, and Saigon's 1826, March 26, 1964.

13. Lodge letter to Cleveland, Jan. 28, 1964, and Lodge letter to Commander Henry Walker, Jan. 15, 1965, Lodge Papers.

14. Lodge to Saltonstall, Aug. 4, 1964, Lodge Papers, 1.

15. Quotes about Vietnam sovereignty from Lodge, "Recommendations Regarding Vietnam," March 8, 1964, and same in "Note" (record of conversation, Lodge and LBJ), March 8, 1964, VNM Three. Lodge reservations about a constitution for SVN, VNM Four, 2:6.

16. Details of escalation from Herring, *America's Longest War,* 130–39; Khanh and Vung Tau Charter from Bui Diem, *In the Jaws of History,* 119–20.

17. Speculation on LBJ motives for appointing Taylor to Vietnam, Kahin, *Intervention,* 214 and 494n30.

18. Quotes from John Burke interview, April 1991.

19. Memo of Conversation, Khanh-Lodge, March 16, 1965, Lodge Papers.

20. Lodge notes for March 24 and March 25 discussions, and quotes, "Memo" (Lodge meeting with Johnson), May 27, 1965, VNM Three.

21. Account of July debates based on Brian VanDeMark, *Into the Quagmire: Lyndon Johnson and the Escalation of the Vietnam War* (New York: Oxford University Press, 1991), 185–209, Lodge quote, 191.

22. For the inscription on the Rose Garden picture, Lodge Name File, July 25–Dec. 31, 1965, Box 247, LBJL; LBJ refused permission for Mrs. Lodge, "Memo," May 27, 1965, VNM Three; quote from Habib interview.

23. Entries July 28–Aug. 3, 1965, Lodge Papers, 2.

24. Lodge quote from VNM Four, 2:1A; Tarnoff quote from Tarnoff interview, New York, April 1991.

25. Details of Lewandowski and Moore visits from VNM Four, 7:1–2, and 16, for Lodge quote on bombing (Chapter 7, Part Four of VNM is devoted to the "Marigold" diplomatic maneuver). Westmoreland not informed of diplomatic initiatives, Herring, *Secret Diplomacy of the Vietnam War,* 339; September 1964 Pentagon war games, Gibbons, *U.S. Government and the Vietnam War,* 353. Escalation argument, Franz Schurmann et al., *The Politics of Escalation in Vietnam* (Greenwich, Conn.: Fawcett World Library, 1966).

26. Comusmacv on taking control of CI from Lodge, Gen. William Westmoreland, *A Soldier Reports* (New York: Doubleday, 1976), 68; Westmoreland's 1967 takeover of all pacification programs, *PP* 2:615–16. Lodge quote, VNM Five, 20.

27. Report of the WOM meeting of Nov. 1, 1967, based on Walter Isaacson and

Evan Thomas, *The Wise Men: Six Friends and the World They Made* (New York: Simon and Schuster, 1986), 678–80, quote from 680.

28. Unpublished essay, "Lessons of Vietnam," February 1977, Lodge Papers.

Conclusion

1. Lodge record of conversation with Eisenhower, entry for June 12, 1963, Lodge Papers, 2; Rusk quote from *As I Saw It*, 524; Bundy from McGeorge Bundy interview, New York, April 1991.

2. *Alleged Assassination Plots*, 262–63; the final Lodge quote below is from Saigon's 949, Nov. 6, 1963.

Bibliographic Essay

The most important resource for a study of Lodge's attitude to his service in Vietnam is the Papers of Henry Cabot Lodge II collection, housed at the Massachusetts Historical Society in Boston. The papers were opened to research in 1989. In some ways, the most intriguing contribution to scholarship is Lodge's manuscript for a book never published, entitled "Vietnam Memoir." This is illuminating on the Kennedy period, but much less so on the Johnson period. It does, however, contain a twenty-eight-page chapter on Lodge's views of the proper conduct of the war, and other material scattered throughout deals with U.S. military-civilian conflicts regarding America's role in Indochina. The copious General Correspondence section of the papers contains much on Vietnam, in addition to the specific Vietnam Papers collection, which includes Lodge's own notes, speech materials, and outlines for telegrams from Saigon, some never sent. The Confidential Journal is not a daily record but a set of typewritten notes of significant conversations. Several of the entries deal with briefing discussions on Vietnam, including one with Kennedy.

No study of the American embassy in Saigon can be conducted without reference to the masses of documentation on U.S.-Vietnam relations now available. My own requests under the U.S. Freedom of Information Act resulted in the release of sixty-six airgrams, notes of interviews, and voluminous reports from the Political Section of the U.S. embassy, dated May 1963 to June 1964, as well as the full texts of all the numbered Saigon-Washington cables for the period. The most current published source for such newly released material is the U.S. Department of State serial collection *Foreign Relations of the United States, Vietnam* (Washington, D.C.: Government Printing Office). William C. Gibbons, *The U.S. Government and the Vietnam War: Executive and Legislative Decisions*, vol. 2, *1961–1964* (Princeton, N.J.: Princeton University Press, 1986) proved a useful exegesis. Volumes 3 and 4 of the Gibbons study are now available, covering the years 1965 to 1968.

For the culture of the U.S. mission in South Vietnam and relations between its various agencies, the oral histories recorded by the Kennedy and Johnson presidential libraries, used according to the customary rules of evidence, are a rich source. Among the most useful of these for a study of the first Lodge ambassadorship were those of William Colby, chief of the Far East Division of the CIA in 1963 and 1964, recorded in 1981; of John Michael Dunn and Frederick Flott, special assistants to Ambassador Lodge, taped in 1984; of Gen. Paul D. Harkins, commanding officer of the U.S. military in Vietnam in 1963 and 1964, recorded in 1981; and of David Nes, deputy chief of the U.S. mission in South Vietnam in 1964, taped in 1982. All these records were made under the Johnson Library Oral History Program. Lodge himself, in August 1965, recorded a description of his relations with Kennedy during the Diem crisis of 1963 for the Kennedy Library Oral History Program.

My own interviews with officers who served in the Saigon embassy during Lodge's first tour of duty, those who worked with him in South Vietnam, and former members of the U.S. Department of State, include:

Bui Diem, former South Vietnamese ambassador to the U.S. and member of the Minh government "Council of Notables"

McGeorge Bundy, special assistant to the president for national security affairs, 1963–1966

William P. Bundy, U.S. assistant secretary of state for East Asian and Pacific affairs, March 1964–1969

John Burke, second secretary of the U.S. embassy in Saigon during Lodge's first ambassadorship

William Colby

Lucien Conein, U.S. embassy CIA contact with the South Vietnamese generals in 1963

John Michael Dunn

Frederick W. Flott

Charles C. Flowerree, second secretary of the U.S. embassy in Saigon, 1962–1964

Philip Habib, political counselor to Ambassador Lodge in Saigon, 1965–1967

John J. Helble, American consul, American Consulate Hue, South Vietnam, 1961–1964

Roger Hilsman, U.S. assistant secretary of state for Far Eastern affairs, 1963–1964

Paul Kattenburg, director of the Vietnam Task Force in 1963

Robert H. Miller, first secretary of the U.S. embassy in Saigon, 1963–1964

David Nes

Nguyen Ngoc Huy, director of cabinet for Deputy Premier Nguyen Ton Hoan, 1963–1964 (Minh and Khanh regimes)

Kenneth Rogers, staff aide to Ambassador Lodge in Saigon, 1963–1964

Brig. F. P. Serong, commander of the Australian forces in Vietnam, 1962–1965, and senior adviser of Police Field Force for South Vietnam, 1965–1967

Tran Van Don, South Vietnamese military leader of the anti-Diem coup and minister of defense in the Minh government

William Trueheart, deputy chief of U.S. mission in South Vietnam, 1961–1963

Bruce Woodberry, second secretary of the Australian embassy in Saigon, 1963–1964

Barry Zorthian, head of joint United States public affairs office (JUSPAO), U.S. embassy in Saigon, 1964

Among the historical works central to a discussion of the first Lodge embassy, two articles stand out: Paul M. Kattenburg, "Vietnam and U.S. Diplomacy, 1940–1970," *Orbis* 15, no. 3 (Fall 1971): 818–841, and James C. Thomson, Jr., "How Could Vietnam Happen? An Autopsy," *Atlantic Monthly*, April 1968: 47–53. Stanley Karnow, *Vietnam: A History* (New York: Viking, 1983), combined with the transcripts of interviews made for *Vietnam: A Television History*, held at the William Joiner Center for the Study of War and Peace, University of Massachusetts, Boston Harbor Campus, remains one of the more comprehensive accounts of the November 1963 coup against Ngo Dinh Diem. George McT. Kahin, *Intervention: How America Became Involved in Vietnam* (New York: Alfred A. Knopf, 1986) is the definitive work on the 1963 and 1964 period in U.S.-Vietnam relations.

Some especially helpful memoirs of the period are William Colby, *Honorable Men: My Life in the CIA* (New York: Simon and Schuster, 1978), John Mecklin, *Mission in Torment: An Intimate Account of the U. S. Role in Vietnam* (New York: Doubleday, 1965), and Frederick Nolting, *From Trust to Tragedy: The Political Memoirs of Frederick Nolting, Kennedy's Ambassador to Diem's Vietnam* (New York: Praeger, 1988). Gen. William C. Westmoreland, *A Soldier Reports* (New York: Doubleday, 1976) gives brief but interesting insights into Ambassador Lodge's modus operandi in Vietnam. For accounts of the U.S. newspapermen's story in Vietnam, see Malcolm W. Browne, *The New Face of War: A Report on a Communist Guerrilla Campaign* (London: Cassell, 1965), introduced by Henry Cabot Lodge, and Neil Sheehan, *A Bright and Shining Lie: John Paul Vann and America in Vietnam* (New York: Random House, 1988).

An accessible discussion of the military aspects of the war can be found in Harry G. Summers, Jr., *On Strategy: A Critical Analysis of the Vietnam War* (New York: Dell, 1982).

Index